Fifty modern stories

FIFTY MODERN

Edited by Thomas M. H. Blair

Kent State University

Warren Beck
Thomas Beer
Stephen Vincent Benét
Arnold Bennett
Elizabeth Bowen
Clifford R. Bragdon
Pearl S. Buck
Morley Callaghan
Nancy G. Chaikin
G. K. Chesterton
Joseph Conrad
Peter De Vries
William Faulkner
Dorothy Canfield Fisher
F. Scott Fitzgerald
E. M. Forster
Pamela Frankau
John Galsworthy
Edmund Gilligan
Elizabeth Hardwick
Ernest Hemingway
Cyril Hume
Aldous Huxley
Henry James
James Joyce
D. H. Lawrence
Victoria Lincoln
Haniel Long
Katherine Mansfield
W. Somerset Maugham
James A. Michener
George Milburn
Frank O'Connor
Edwards Park
Frances Gray Patton
Katherine Anne Porter
Calvin Sallow
Mark Schorer
Irwin Shaw
Wallace Stegner
Ruth Suckow
Peter Taylor
James Thurber
Lionel Trilling
Edmund Ware
Eudora Welty
Edith Wharton
P. G. Wodehouse
Alexander Woollcott
Samuel Yellen

STORIES

Harper & Row, Publishers

New York, Evanston, and London

PREFACE

$F_{ifty\ modern\ stories}$ is designed especially for courses in literature and for advanced courses in writing. A larger number of short stories is offered in this book than can be found in most other anthologies. Consequently, the instructor may choose readings to his taste, while the student, going beyond the instructor's selections, may well choose to read the entire collection. I know that some students will do so; I hope that most of them will. For this is a book that should find its way to personal library shelves to be kept for many years in the service of those who read for enjoyment.

The book will introduce student readers to writers whom they will wish to know better. It will also serve another high purpose: that of sending its readers on to further exploration of good books and good magazines, to the discovery of other worthy writers.

A considerable number of these stories were written by authors who are well established among the important and influential writers of the present century: John Galsworthy, Joseph Conrad, D. H. Lawrence, James Joyce, and Katherine Mansfield; Edith Wharton, F. Scott Fitzgerald, and Stephen Vincent Benét. Most of the remaining stories were chosen to provide the widest possible variety in theme and form. Seven or eight stories have been included as personal choices. They are, I believe, good stories deserving to be more widely known than they are. I hope that the reader will agree that they conform to the quality of the book as a whole.

Of the fifty authors listed in the Contents, all, with the single exception of Henry James, belong to the twentieth century, and at least thirty are still writing. Eleven are British, one is Canadian, and three are Irish; thirty-five are American. A balance has been maintained between the memorable stories of the first thirty years of this century and those of the current period.

The stories are grouped under five headings, but the categories thus indicated are to be interpreted only in a general way. Each story is introduced by a brief headnote. Short biographies of the authors, arranged alphabetically, have been placed at the back of the book.

* *

For their work on the biographies and bibliographies, I am indebted to William Hildebrand of the Department of English and to Dean Keller of the Library of Kent State University. They are responsible for assembling most of the information relating to the writers of the fifty stories.

For sharing the work of reading proof and for much valuable assistance besides, I am further indebted to Dean Keller and to my wife, Louise Colebrook Blair.

Others, including several of the writers included in this anthology, have been generous with their time and helpful with their suggestions. I am grateful to them. Of these I should particularly name Mrs. Dorothy Mills, the late Mrs. Robert E. Eiche, and the late Mrs. Dorothy Canfield Fisher—to whom special acknowledgment is made in my introduction to her story.

March 1960   Thomas M. H. Blair

ACKNOWLEDGMENTS

Grateful acknowledgment is made to the publishers and authors who granted permission to reprint the following stories.

"Fantasy in the First Person" by Cyril Hume from *Harper's Magazine*, September, 1926. Copyright 1926, 1954 by Harper & Brothers. Reprinted by permission of A. Watkins, Inc.

"Remold It Nearer" from *The Finer Things of Life* by Frances Gray Patton. Copyright 1951 by Frances Gray Patton.

Reprinted by permission of Dodd, Mead and Company.

"The Glass Wall" from *Celia Amberley* by Victoria Lincoln. Copyright 1949 by Victoria Lincoln Lowe. Reprinted by permission of Rinehart & Company, Inc., New York, Publishers.

"The Duchess and the Smugs" from

CONTENTS

x

Part 1

Growing up | Youth | College

FANTASY IN THE FIRST PERSON

The stories of Part I have something in common: growing up,
discovery—of oneself, among other things—and learning,
which may take place in school or out. Their themes
are to be found in the experiences of youth. These stories need
not be read in sequence; they are brought together here—
as are the stories in the other parts of the book—
simply for the editor's convenience in introducing them.
    The first story is a series of reminiscences told in the first
person by Cyril Hume. He calls it a sad little story.
It is sad enough, certainly, as all youth in the past tense must be,
but it has (for the reader at least) its lighter moments.
The author does not say, but we may well wonder how much
of his story is pure autobiography. He writes of the difficult
transition from boyhood to that period when a boy moves
"alone through the world, sullen and shy with adolescence."
    "I wonder sometimes," Hume says, "what magic must enter
a man who has kissed his first love. Or is it the greater magic
never to have kissed her?" Separated from this magic by
the years that bring the philosophic mind, what
middle-aged writer is qualified to give the answer?

I think this will be a sad little story, for it is of my boyhood and
my first love. Writing of those two things is always a sad task if one dare
be truthful, because both of them were very happy once, and now both
are gone. Of course, it is easy to strain after realism and to say that, if
we could remember rightly, boyhood held for us as much loneliness
and sorrow and disillusion as does maturity, and our first love was more
unhappy than any other love which since has troubled our man's heart.
This may or may not be true. I think no one can remember so exactly
and unimaginatively as to be able to say for certain. And I cannot see
either what difference the question makes once a man has begun,
rather impatiently, to combat a sedentary plumpness, when the thirties
are at hand and the forties not far off. For it is always sad to look back
on anything whatever that once was even partly happy and to have to
say, "Well, that is gone now. It can never come again." And of boyhood
and first love every man on earth must say this. Both are always lost.

Now that I have begun, I feel almost ashamed of setting down the actions and betraying the thoughts of the three children which are to be my characters, a little girl and a pair of little boys. Granted that the little boy I intend exposing most shamelessly was once myself, and so I have a kind of right over him. Yet the other boy long ago was my best friend, and the little girl once seemed to me to possess all beauty and all perfection—my first love. Or, if I come to that, what right have I even to reveal the inadvertent confidences of the boy I used to be? He was a shy, sensitive boy with a passion for reticence, and he would suffer damnably if he knew. If he knew he might ask me, "What right have you, with your dull sneering assumption of grown-up omniscience, to bare my heart so clumsily? Are you my superior by so much?" And I am afraid I should be too confused to answer him. But that boy is long since dead (as, I suppose, are those two other children) and he can speak for himself only in my morbid conscience now. So I excuse myself by saying that all writers are of necessity sneaks and spies upon humanity, and by promising the uncomfortably reproachful child to do my best by him.

I must ask forgiveness also of those two other children and of the man and the woman they have become. The boy is, I know, happily married now, and if he chances to read this story and looks back for a moment thoughtfully over the wall of years and adolescence, he will say, "The fellow is writing of another person, not of me." So he will forgive me. But what of that very lovely little girl who once held our two hearts' devotion? Well, of her I shall betray least, young Lilith, because naturally I know least about her. But in any case I think she too would forgive me, for surely by now she has forgotten her old self, just as her boy adorers have so nearly forgotten. Perhaps even, if she sees this bit of writing and it causes her to recollect a little, she will smile, not without complacency, and show it to her husband.

The name of the other boy was Alonzo, although I believe his people were Scotch; and I think it is a tribute to his likeableness and strength of character that the rest of the boys in the school never called him anything but Steve. Steve was a few days older than I (we were eleven at the time) though several inches shorter, a dark spry little fellow with an impish face. I remember he had extraordinarily large and pointed eye teeth which looked as though they must puncture his under-lip whenever he grinned—which he did conspicuously and often. He was a fast runner and played a fine game at one of the wings on the Junior soccer team.

For the three years we knew each other Steve and I were closer, if not better friends than, I imagine, has been possible for either of us to become with other people since. The time we could devote to it! It seems to me we must have been together twenty-four hours of the day.

3

We were in the same form to begin with and had desks next each other. We shared our bedroom with two other boys, but even here our cots were side by side. Not content with this, we arranged to have adjoining places in the study-hall and in the dining room, and our free time was passed entirely in each other's company. In the winter we walked to the ice pond or to the sliding hill together. In autumn our cleats made a double track across the black cold-steaming earth to the football field. And in the spring our metal spikes clattered in unison over the sun-yellow stony path to the baseball diamond. In order to accomplish this co-existence it was often necessary for one of us to wait in boring idleness while the other completed some school task, but I cannot recall that either of us ever failed to wait, or that afterward we thought the sacrifice worth mentioning.

Naturally, our thoughts and inclinations ran parallel much as our bodies did. We developed similar tastes and antipathies. The same things excited us. For a time we had a passion for circus acrobatics and used to strip down to our long underwear in lieu of tights and perform remarkably pointless stunts. Sometimes we talked vaguely of getting permission to equip our bedroom with trapeze and flying rings. And one unfortunate Saturday morning we practically wrecked the school drying-yard trying to walk tight rope on the clotheslines. In winter we had a common igloo and a dually discovered cave on rocky little Mount Tom. We smoked flaring newspaper-and-oakleaf cigarettes in the autumn woods; and sometimes on precious spring holidays we risked dreadful punishment by going off together and swimming in the Sound.

Steve and I attended dancing class together and were identically smitten and disorganized by this phenomenon. . . . Mr. Warren's dancing school met every Friday afternoon in the assembly hall of the Parish House. This was a large gloomy room with many alcoves where shy or indolent dancers used to secrete themselves until an almost insanely exasperated Mr. Warren snatched them out again upon the polished publicity of the dance floor. Mr. Warren coincided exactly with my childish conception of the devil. He was a graying middle-aged gentleman who always seemed upon the point of peevishly regretting better days. He wore a sharp vandyke beard and black silk knee-breeches, and had no calves to his legs. And if Mr. Warren was the devil, then certainly that assembly hall was a convincing replica of hell —we children being the damned souls. Mr. Warren would draw us up in two lines, the girls facing the boys. Then he would strut briskly on his toes up and down the lane he had formed, clapping his hands and making unkind remarks, while a spinster in the corner tormented a hateful and unvarying tune out of a consumptive piano. When this degrading line work was over with its slidings and pointings, things became rapidly worse. It was not enough that some of the boys had already been sufficiently humiliated by being forced into Eton suits. But now Mr. Warren leered evilly and called out, "Take partners!" This meant walking up to some pleated and ruffled and loathsomely willing little girl, putting your hand on your stomach, bowing, and saying, "May I have the pleasure of this dance, if you please?" Then the little girl smirked and bobbed and replied, "Delighted, I'm sure." Then you'd have to put your arm around her and take her cotton glove in your own cotton glove even though the feel of it put your teeth on edge. And you'd have to dance round and round as long as the music played, with Mr. Warren clapping and complaining, and all the mothers along the wall whispering sentimentally. Mr. Warren had no tail, but there were little curled horns of gray hair at his temples.

I think no one—we least of all—ever doubted that our hatred of dancing school was genuine. But when it was over, and Friday night's dinner and study-hall were ended, how wonderfully it was transmuted in our memories! Then dancing school became for us something glamorous and very beautiful, a fountain-head of romance, the single link between reality and the ethereal world of our imaginations. We would draw upon it for characters which we wove into that year-long epic we used to whisper at night when it was dark in our little dormitory.

The two other boys in the room told stories too. However, Steve and I were always a little impatient of any story but that one heart-shaking epic we had built together. We dragged our beds close and turned our backs upon the other boys, and whispered—whispered sometimes until a remote clock far off in the quiet house had struck eleven. We would enter our huge cruising triplane which could be transformed, merely by pulling a little lever, into an automobile or a submarine. We would soar and speed impatiently until we came again to that lovely country our fancy had invented. To reach that country we always had to fly up out of sight of earth beyond the clouds. Presently a sweet vertigo would come over us. Our plane would plunge down through the clouds again and we would wake to find ourselves spiraling lower and lower toward a certain dear lake. So you see, we never knew exactly how we had entered that country. It must have been our hearts that guided us so unerringly above the clouds. Our plane would light on the wide lake shore, and the Lady of the Lake, the Queen of that country, would come up to greet us with her nymphs and nereids. Friendly bears lurched down out of the woods, and docile antelope, and merry dogs. Great tame fish basked like carp in the clear lake water, and we boys swam among them with the nereids. The Lady of the Lake floated white beside us in the sunny ripples, laughing with us, loving us. Here and there in the woods around the lake vast ruined palaces of marble lay in the midst of wild parks. We used to loiter along their terrace and down their corridors, laden with fruits and flowers bright as metal, until suddenly into the

5

classic repose of those palaces fear would well up suddenly from passages underground. Then we would cast our fruits and flowers away, and run back to our lake shore again, ready like otters to take to the safe water. As we fled through the woods, one of us had glimpsed a member of that gorilla band which hated us. Always below the sunlit beauty of our country this peril lurked, ready to spring upon us and slay us and steal away our nereids and our lovely Queen. But the warrior bears were friends, and all the shy antelope stood sentinel for us. We were alert besides, and agile and brave and cool-headed. So we always managed to take to the water in time, or to soar up above the savage gorilla faces in our plane as though on Pegasus. But sometimes we would come back to our lake to discover that in our daytime absences the Gorilla Band had managed by foul stealth to carry our playmate friends away. Then we and the bears made stern war and delivered them back into their happy lake. . . . Sometimes we grew weary of frolicking in the shallows or diving into the deep cool where no weeds grew, and we would bring the Lady of the Lake with her attendants up with us in our aëroplane. But they might not stay with us. We must always take them back to their golden beach, and kiss them all good-by, and return to school alone.

But what have such dreams as these to do with dancing school, with Mr. Warren like Satan making existence a burden? This: Many a night when dancing school was over many a primly sleeping little maiden was snatched from her slumbers by the faun fantasies of two whispering schoolboys. Then the great plane was hung and trailed with garlands, crowded with grave children which the tale endowed with an unearthly beauty and a kind of innocent projection of maturity. Loud propellers beat the perfumed air. There came a run, a lift, a rush of wind. The clouds dropped close. A pearl mist shut us in, and through the mist followed a wake of petals.

Of course, our voyages were not made all of happiness and color. Child cruelty, child humor, and child burlesque had places there. For instance there was a little brown plump girl in dancing school whom Steve and I called "The Juicy Pear," because we loathed that unfortunate little girl out of all reason. Why then did we ravish her from her slumbers in her starchy nightdress and lure her with us on our voyages? Simple enough. Once or twice when we were long lost above the clouds, and ravenous, her tender succulence proved welcome to us. Very often when the engine became dry and hot so that we were imperilled or delayed upon our impatient journey, we fed her to the engine as to a mincing machine. And she proved excellent lubrication indeed.

All of us little boys went to dancing school for the first time that following year on the street car as usual, with our pumps in our pockets.

Steve and I sat side by side, saying nothing because grown people were within earshot. But each of us was conscious that the other was speculating which of the little girls we knew would be back this year. Of course the first of the lot to board the car was the Juicy Pear, browner and juicier than ever. She greeted us so brightly that we mumbled and blushed, and all the mothers craned their grins at us. Our souls shuddered. We said nothing, but a wordless promise flashed between us that to-night our engines should not lack for lubrication. Then . . .

The wonder of our lives entered the car and sat down beside her mother across the way. And in that instant we loved her finally, completely. I think her mother suspected at once. A wise short lady, twinkling through her glasses at the small boys who tried not to look at her daughter but still looked, who tried to seem indifferent but still obviously adored. The little girl herself— Well, the fact is I cannot recall exactly what she looked like, except that she had brown eyes and very beautiful brown hair and a sweet mouth. If I were to see her now as I saw her then, I suppose I should say, "What a fine healthy-looking little girl to be sure!" But then her beauty hurt me and frightened me and made me weak.

I felt Steve trembling beside me, and I knew that he was thinking just as I was thinking, "Is she on her way to dancing school?" Obviously she was, as were all the rest of the children in the car. As a token of her intention she was carrying her slippers in a little silk bag with a drawstring. But even this was no reassurance for our anxiety, and we hardly dared breathe until at last we saw her sedately join the huddle of little girls at the far end of the Assembly Hall. Steve and I grinned at each other with clenched teeth, and fumbled at our stomachs. Involuntarily I made a small noise in my throat. . . .

It irritates me now to remember such a fact, it irks my masculine pride to have to set it down, but Steve was the first to summon sufficient courage to speak to her. When at last Mr. Warren ogreishly called, "Take partners!" Steve hurried unhesitatingly to the new adorable little girl. I saw him pause and bow stiffly before her. I saw his seat—I record this detail with conscious malice—jut out sharply below his ridiculous Eton jacket. I saw the little girl bob with half mature grace. Then they danced off together. Later in an intermission Steve walked stiffly past me. His face was flushed, his eyes moist. He was grinning so broadly for exultant nervousness that his sharp eye teeth seemed at last actually to have punctured his under lip. When we were abreast he hissed without turning his head, "Name's Helen!" And he had passed me. As I say, I am conscious of a slight jealous humiliation as I record this fact. In retrospect I resent Steve's audacity. But at the time I had no such thought. Because of the circumstance of our age Steve and I were yet in that state of innocence (an innocence, quite frankly, more physiological than intellectual) which put anything like genuine sexual jealousy quite out of the question. Hence it seemed in no way incongruous to us then that we, while loving her, should still be friends, or even that each of us should make the other sole confidant and adviser in the matter. Of course, it would be untruthful to pretend that there was no emulation between us. When February the 14th came, with valentines for both of us addressed in her round cheerful-looking writing, we debated for hours over the slight difference in these favors, and hence the possibility of an implied preference. I maintained then, as I do now, that mine was the gaudier fabrication. Again, when Mr. Warren announced the coming of a cotillion with favors and formal partners, and Steve obtained Helen's promise for the occasion before I was even half-done communing with my emotions in an alcove, we argued that also. Steve's arguments in this case amounted simply to *"Now!* Do you *see?"* while I (always, I am afraid, a hesitant and a lurking lover) urged, with what I still consider sound logic, that he had been successful merely because of his agility and lack of common reticence. Similarly, when I emerged from my alcove, primed with emotion and nervous apprehension enough to beard the devil (my way again), when I had not ineloquently demanded Helen's photograph of her, and got it from her the very next week, then it became my turn to say, *"There* now!" while Steve insisted that if he had only thought of doing such a thing himself, the situation had been different. And it was characteristic of our mutual relationship and of our attitude toward Helen that during the cotillion she was as much my partner as Steve's, and that my picture of her stood upon our common chest of drawers as a common shrine for adoration. Finally, by previous amicable agreement, we went to Helen both at once, and having seated ourselves on either side of her, flatly demanded that she decide between us. It is not likely that any word of hers could have altered our attitude toward her or toward each other. However Helen obviated even this slight possibility of discord by implying with charming candor and gratifying enthusiasm that not she nor any woman could ever make so difficult a choice. She hastened to add also that there was no one else within a hundred million miles of us. Somehow this satisfied us.

Reviewing the above paragraph in the light of a somewhat maturer experience, I am convinced that Helen, uncoached, could never have attained to such heights of wily impartiality. Her mother impressed me even at the time as an appallingly wise little lady. Her eyes, whenever they turned toward Steve and myself, giggled through her glasses at us and seemed to read the primer page of our psychology at a brief glance. But now, upon reflection, I am inclined to doubt, not the extent, but the profundity of her wisdom, which I think could not have been over-rich in understanding. There used always to be a very kindly mockery behind her glasses, a mockery that, as I now remember and interpret it, was compounded of affection and grown-up "amusement" which, analyzed, is plain contempt. And I would be willing to wager that to this day Helen's mother considers *Seventeen* or *Penrod* quite sound pediatry. . . . Could she have looked deeper into the hearts of those two small boys, I think she might have laughed as frequently, but with a more wistful and a less superior amusement. Her eyes behind her glasses might have twinkled every bit as bright, but not entirely with mirth.

But how look into those hearts now that they are changed beyond any recognition? In the loud confusion of the pulses which drum so tumultuously and so differently now, one can only remember a little and hope to keep a little of the truth. But I remember two very simple earnest spirits brimful of love, and of a love no less worthy and strong because there was in it none of that fierce hunger which breeds jealousy. Love without desire: Love without selfishness. And what greater love can any man have? . . . Still, to our elders it must have been laughable while it lasted, and it did not last so very long. All naïve earnestness is laughable to the grown sophisticates whom the years have taught to build up a wall of laughter and compromise against pain. And if that earnestness is driven by some generous power which shames the wise little subterfuges of maturity, the laughter rings all the louder for it. How short a time, too, the loves of childhood lasted. Yet was it the child's heart which was at fault, or nature who altered that heart with growth, and finally stole it and left a changeling in its place? Myself, I think that for a while those two small boys deserve to rank as lovers with Tristram and with Launcelot. And, for the worship she commanded of them, Helen was Helen indeed.

Well, now I must laugh a little too, considering how we must have appeared to the grown-ups around us. Either we were full of silly portentous earnestness, or else all giggles. To the British Latin-master who sometimes threw blackboard erasers at us, we represented merely exasperating vacuity. Our hair stood on end. Our clothes jutted away from our slim necks and everywhere else hung limp. Sometimes our ears were shadow-ringed. Our hands were grubby with chalk, pencil-lead, and other more miscellaneous grime. I remember how untidily Steve's nose used to run in cold weather. For myself I must have been an unbearable little prig with my look of conscious virtue and my small but constantly paraded store of erudition upon the subject of natural history. We were never beautiful. Sometimes positively hateful. Doubtless, we were always bothersome. And like all urchins we must always, by our very presence, have suggested vaguely the existence of natural processes only imperfectly controlled. . . . Still, though I despise Wordsworth, there was a glory in us.

I remember sitting drowsily in class of a spring afternoon. A slow sunny wind poured in at the windows, warm with sounds of an idle world. Presently my drowsiness entered deeper into me. It became spiritual. Then everything around me faded out of focus, and there remained only a background of sweet uncooling wind and bee-humming. I breathed slowly. I was aware of a pulse everywhere under my skin. I was thinking of Helen again; musing, praying, until I was abstracted almost out of consciousness; moving away onward, onward in a colored translucency, scarcely more sentient than the juices of spring moving through a sun-soaked leaf—until I was awakened rudely by the whack and puff of a hurled board-eraser or by the nausea of longing under my diaphragm. I glanced at Steve. Steve too! He rolled his eyes at me. We exchanged a weak smile. Ah, Helen!

We never brought much reality to our loving. Instead we ran to symbols. For instance there was Helen's cypher which we invented and cut into all available material such as hockey pucks, fence-rails, baseball bats, and our own fore-arms. This cypher, an N superimposed upon an E, contained all the letters of Helen's name and was meaningless to most people, so we delighted in using it. We employed other symbols also of speech and gesture and inscription, but I forget them now. . . . Outside of dancing school we saw Helen only by the merest chance, but even there we said little to her about our state of mind. I wonder what she could have thought of us, because we would rather have died than use the word "love" even in private. Actually we "did" nothing at all about the whole thing.

Of course Helen entered immediately and overwhelmingly into our treasured epic. But even here we were surprisingly ineffectual in our handling of the situation. With her coming the pagan spirit vapored out of our poem. Our voyages came to be like Sunday-school outings. One of us drove the plane while the other sat with Helen and rather embarrassedly pointed out the sights. Our lake held little magic now. The bears had hidden in the woods. The antelopes and dogs had all trooped away. Even the gorillas had migrated to haunt some paradise of richer enchantment. The Lady of the Lake and her nymphs, gone too. And on the whole that rather relieved us. So we simply rode around through the clear sunshine in our plane, wearing our Sunday clothes. . . . But we regretted nothing. We had discovered a greater magic. Our hearts were heavy as rain-drenched lilacs with love for her.

During the school term all our time was laid out for us so that there was no opportunity for Steve and me to seek Helen out. But my home was in the same town as hers, and one would naturally think I should have gone to see her during vacation time. Still I never did. I suppose, as I supposed then, that if I had expressed any desire to do so things would have "been made easy for me." Without a doubt there would have been amused telephone calls with Helen's mother. There might have ensued a party or some such horror from which I shrank. Or, if I had simply gone to her house, my return home would have been greeted with questions, and my anguished embarrassment would have been interpreted as guilt. An investigation of the mystery would have followed (I should have kept silence until the end) and at last relieved laughter for a crowd of grown-ups. So there was nothing for me to do even if I had really wanted to do anything, which I think I did not. I can remember seeing her only twice during vacations. Once in winter we encountered on the street car. We said "Hello." She was wearing a small fur hat which I think must have been mink. A dark tail hung down beside her cheek. I would have given my life then for the courage to join her. Instead, I left the trolley before I had intended to. Once in the summer I pedaled madly past her house on my bicycle. (An impressive sight, I thought, with my behind off the saddle, lurching as I pumped.) Helen was standing at her gate with a couple of other children, and she waved to me. I had hoped for this. I had intended stopping and speaking magnificently to her. But I pretended not to see, and dashed on. . . . And I loved her all day long, every day for three years.

I went to camp that summer, and while I was there my family moved away to a distant town. When I heard the news I thought regretfully of Helen, but the adventure of returning to a new home was a compensation. Helen and I began writing to each other occasionally after that, funny, banal little letters, signed "love." Her letters were a joy and a torment to me. I valued them too much to have the heart to destroy them, but when I was through reading them I was always faced with the problem of hiding them where no one would discover them and be moved to laughter. Having no more explicit privacy than most children, I was forced to the expedient of secreting them in the attic. Whenever any one went up to the attic after that I had miserably to go up too, and I would suffer horribly until whoever had been busy there came down again. Then I would rush to find a new cache for my little packet. I destroyed Helen's letters long ago in the ardor of a subsequent heart-spasm. But I have her picture still. I know exactly where it is, in what box in which trunk, but I am afraid to look at it any more. I should hate to find Helen plain or to catch myself snickering at her hair-ribbon.

That winter Helen wrote me asking me to be her partner at the dancing-school cotillion. The necessity of divulging this sacred and shameful news to grown people agonized me for days, and I think I should have let her letter go unanswered rather than face the ordeal but for the fear that her mother might communicate with my family and so discover my discourtesy. But when I had actually pricked myself to the point it was far pleasanter than I had dared to dream. No one even guffawed, and an older brother was even glad to bring me because he had friends to visit in the old town. I remember little about the cotillion, except that I had become noticeably taller than Helen and was very proud of the fact. Also, I was puzzled throughout the whole affair by an air of aloofness and mystery about her. It was as though some secret had been whispered in her ear since our last meeting, and for her the riddle of childhood had been solved. I felt myself left alone, wondering, wishful, and afraid.

The music, the sticky refreshments, the colored confetti, and lights of the children's party were over. We sat in the dark of a slowly rolling limousine which was first to take Helen to her house, and then deliver myself and my older brother back to New York. My brother sat in one corner, moody and abstracted. I suppose he had failed to catch the friends he had come to see, or else he was simply bored. Helen sat between us. None of us spoke. I peered at her. She seemed to be staring straight before her with her lips parted in a slight smile. I felt that she was expecting something of me, and I had a great longing to discover whatever thing it was that made her smile so in wise expectancy. I was puzzled and shaken. My mind groped for that magic gesture I must perform to cause the night to flower with flame and music. "I shall know then," I thought. "I shall know then what she knows." And I felt like crying. I thought, "I will kiss her cheek." But I had never dared. Besides my brother would see. Then the car stopped at her gate and we said good-by. She entered her house sedately, still smiling. . . . I never kissed her and I never saw her again. Still I wonder sometimes what magic must enter a man who has kissed his first love. Or is the greater magic never to have kissed her?

One further picture: It is autumn a year later. Now I too have learned that secret which in an instant illumines childhood and robs us of it forever. The earth is more terrible to me now, a thousand times more lovely. I have discovered the horror of reality and the drunken joy of true enchantment. I move alone through the world, sullen and shy with adolescence. Those in authority over me wonder whatever in the world has come over the boy. Nightmares, my good folk, nightmares and disastrous visions! Do not touch him now! He is a little mad and, therefore, holy.

A hot autumn night with rain on the garden leaves. I am alone in the house. My family is out somewhere for the evening. It is my study time. I find myself walking along the upper hallway past the stair-well. I have just lost my hold upon a vision. I am afraid to go up to my room on the third floor. I pause at the stair's foot and listen to the rain on the roof. Downstairs again. The house is silent. In the kitchen the clock beats. I can hear rain on the leaves in the garden. I go to my father's study and sit at his desk. I take a pencil and draw a foolish caricature. I toss it aside and try to draw the beautiful face of a girl, but the effort is grotesque, horrible. I cover it with a new sheet and begin to draw a monstrous obscenity. Before I am half finished I glance over my shoulder and quickly tear the three drawings into very small pieces, stirring them into the wastepaper basket. Then I am writing as I have never written: "Oh Helen, Helen! Help me! I love you. I know that secret now. Help me to bear it!" I cannot recall the letter that I wrote to her, but not those words surely. Yet my heart cried those words, and something of that cry must have sounded in the words I wrote. I ran out into the dark rain with my letter and posted it at the street corner before I should have time to be ashamed. . . . She answered me very promptly, a gentle affectionate letter. No, she had not forgotten me. She still thought of me very often.

But in five days I had traveled too far beyond my writing mood ever to recapture it. Before me lay the hollow land of adolescence where all things move and all things change. I never answered her kind letter.

All that is left now of my heart's green sickness is a photograph which I am afraid to look at any more, and a persistent magic which stirs me still at the name of Helen.

Frances Gray Patton

REMOLD IT NEARER

Mrs. Patton's story dramatizes an evening at home with the
Potter family—a family that might be your own, or your
professor's. Elinor's reaction to the sophisticated conversation
of her parents and their intellectual friends is calmly realistic
and characteristically teen-age, particularly so in response to
Professor Adams' comments on the atomic bomb and his
prophetic view of the fate of civilization.

To say that Elinor Potter was all duty and deference when her
mother told her, one raw, sleety Saturday night, that she'd best stay in
and coddle a cold would do less than justice to Elinor's alerted principles of self-determination and would strain the credulity of anyone who
had more than a passing acquaintance with the generality of fifteen-
year-old girls. Each Saturday at 8 P.M. (the afternoon having been
sacrificed, at the request of the local P.-T.A., to a program of animated
cartoons on the early-juvenile level), a new feature began a week's run
at the Criterion, the leading motion-picture theatre in the Potters'
home town. To Elinor and her cronies, the recurring occasion had a
significance beyond that of entertainment. For them, a fresh, charming
world full of coincidence, passionate contretemps, incorruptible coif-
fures, and other properties notably absent from public high schools and
private family bosoms was created every seven days. To miss the weekly
picture or to delay seeing it until, vulgarized by the gaze of hoi polloi,
it had lost its pristine quality was to break a link in the chain of existence.

Nor was the miracle confined to its own circle of time. As far into
the ensuing week as, say, Thursday, its trailing ribbons of light provided conversation in study halls and Donut Dinettes and—to the
despair of such subscribers to the telephone system as wished to consult
physicians or arrange bridge games—on the party lines; and even before the miracle occurred, its imminent presence, like the mysterious
palsy that affects a leafy tree in the moment before sunrise, trembled
in the air. Regularly on Saturday, as the hour for the movie approached,

Professor and Mrs. Potter watched a sort of spell descend upon their daughter.

After an early dinner, during which Elinor would withdraw into a trancelike state, she would retire to her boudoir. From that retreat she would presently emerge, varnished into something rich and strange, to await the arrival of the boy called Bucky, perhaps, or Choo-Choo, or Pat Junior, who was to be her squire for the evening. Perched on the edge of the old sofa in the living room and wrapped in a cloud of exotic scent that must soon, her troubled parents felt, assume her bodily into a higher sphere of experience, she would appear oddly dissociate from her surroundings—like Browning's famous bird that lit, in transit, upon a poor lowly spray. She wouldn't deign to speak except at intervals— her mother suspected that she was afraid of disarranging the painted outline of her lips—and then only to express fashionable dissatisfaction with her perfectly lovely yellow hair. ("It's falling," she would say—a complaint that had once wrung sympathetic alarm from her father, who was himself inclined to baldness, but that he'd long known referred merely to a certain relaxation of the ridges into which Elinor had pressed her locks.) Eventually, a motor horn would sound in the driveway. The elder Potters, having decreed that their daughter wasn't to be becked or called by any mechanical noise, would pretend to ignore the horn. They would pretend, as well, to ignore the gaze that Elinor trained upon them —a piteous gaze suggesting the glassy reproach in the eye of a shot dove—but they would speculate uneasily upon the mean position they would be left in if, as they'd been warned to expect, the honker of the unanswered summons should back away, discouraged, into the dark. Mercifully, however, the honker never did. In due course, a youth always condescended to present himself at the Potters' door, and under his protection Elinor would depart for the Criterion Theatre. There, one of a flock of similarly protected maidens, who looked and smelled uncannily like herself, she would again discover how marvellous life was meant to be.

Left behind, the Professor and his wife would open a few windows to let the fumes of My Sin or Tigress escape from the house, and as they shivered in the cleansing currents of air, they would exchange doleful comments upon the artificial excitement—the folly, they called it—that was in store for their child. But they never contemplated keeping her, by command or by strategy, from that excitement. The Potters, quiet as their tastes and habits were, were not unacquainted with folly. They had encountered it in the pages of history and poetry, in generations of college students, and among their most erudite friends. In a world bursting with sin and sorrow, they would, they felt, look rather priggish making a great fuss about Elinor's attachment to the cinema. Moreover, they weren't entirely at ease with Elinor. They loved her and were frequently refreshed by the artless comedy she introduced into their household, but the notion of spending several hours with her—a reluctant, injured, and possibly belligerent companion—scared them.

When, on the evening in question, Mrs. Potter decided that Elinor must not venture out, she was motivated solely by a regard for the girl's health.

"Do you mean you won't let me go to the show?" Elinor demanded in reply to her mother's tactfully worded suggestion that a heavy cold bore watching.

"I shouldn't like to put it that way," Mrs. Potter said. "Your own good sense will tell you . . ."

Elinor said that her mother's attitude was preposterous, that she had lounged around all day conserving her strength for the evening, that Bucky Weathers was celebrating the occasion of having secured his first driver's license by coming to fetch her in his father's personal car —an Oldsmobile eight with white sidewall tires that would do a hundred miles an hour—and that Tyrone Power was starring at the Criterion in a picture about guerrilla fighting that was highly educational, because the same sort of warfare would shortly obtain in every corner of the earth.

Mrs. Potter said that such a movie would be calculated to produce a rise in Elinor's temperature.

"Reality doesn't make me sick!" Elinor retorted.

"You're a remarkably tough-minded girl, then," Professor Potter said. "I congratulate you." He added consolingly that Mr. Power's vehicle would likely return to town and that Elinor could see it then.

"At a second-run house, I presume," Elinor said disdainfully, as if she'd been offered water from a public dipper.

"Daddy and I will stay here to keep you company," said Mrs. Potter.

Elinor was not impressed by the magnitude of her parents' sacrifice. "Where would you go if you didn't?" she inquired. "To a lecture, or over to the Adamses', just to talk?"

Mrs. Potter, who should have known better, felt called upon to defend the variety of their diversions. "Sometimes we go dancing," she said.

"Once a month, and this isn't the night," Elinor said. "And I don't believe you and Daddy enjoy dancing anyhow. You just do it because you think you ought to make a social effort."

"That's to our credit," her father said.

"Maybe," Elinor said, with a shrug. Her eyes glinted. Evidently she felt she could risk being impudent. "Know what Randy Adams calls that faculty cotillion group? The Charley Horse Club!"

"Young Adams is too clever by half," said the Professor. But he was obliged to smile when he thought of his colleague, Randy's father, as he appeared on the dance floor, pumping up and down and slinging plump matrons about with abandon, as if the object of his exercise were to generate a purifying sweat.

Unexpectedly, Elinor smiled, too—and very sweetly. She hadn't, her mother perceived, hoped to win more than a moral victory; she had wished simply to avoid setting a precedent for future submission, and with that prudent end accomplished she was ready to be affable.

"Bucky's mother probably won't let *him* out in this weather," she confessed. "He has a sore throat. I'll give him a ring, and then I'll catch up on my literature assignment."

Elinor completed her call with dispatch. In a few minutes, clad in flannel pajamas and a quilted dressing gown, she returned to the living room. She settled herself on the sofa with a novel by Jane Austen.

At ten o'clock, Mrs. Potter realized that she had seldom passed a pleasanter Saturday evening. She was sitting in a rocking chair with her shoes off when this happy thought occurred to her. She had her feet propped against the warm flank of Brandy, an ancient Irish setter, who lay catercorner to the hearth, dozing in the honorable repose one likes to associate with the fireside years of heroes; she was thumbing through an illustrated seed catalogue, letting her fancy run ahead of the season down the green lanes of spring. At a round, book-strewn table in the middle of the room, the Professor was writing letters to the two Potter boys, who were away at boarding school, and on the sofa, in the diffuse illumination of a floor lamp, Elinor lay under an afghan with her small brown-backed volume open in her hands. Her hair was brushed smoothly, without any attempt at effect, off her clear, untroubled brow; her face wore the look of calm absorption that had once—before Elinor had begun warily to disguise her native intelligence—been its prevailing expression; the sole fragrance emanating from her person was a faint odor of Vicks Vapo-Rub. It's a kind of pity that the child can't catch cold oftener, Mrs. Potter thought.

Beneath a composed exterior, Mrs. Potter had been low-spirited for some weeks. The financial inflation, an ever increasing threat to her small domestic economy; the animosities spreading like plague between nations; and each new morning's nagging reminder that her sons were one day closer to the age for military service weighed upon her mind, and although her anxiety was no worse than that of ten million other women, it was perhaps peculiarly hard for her to bear. She was so sanguine by nature that she hadn't acquired the usual cushions of callus against despair, nor did she possess the temperament, common in academic circles, that derives comfort from frilling a sorry prospect with words, elaborating its structure until it becomes too Gothic and fancy to appear more than the castle of an ogre in a fairy tale. In her simplicity, Mrs. Potter took the troubles of the world for what they were. Being a lady, with a lady's respect for tranquillity, she forbore to discuss these troubles (especially in the presence of children), as she would have forborne to recount the details of an unpleasant disease. But her silence was far from phlegmatic. At odd, solitary moments she was seized by an animal terror, an impulse, physical in intensity, toward panic flight.

But now, in this familiar room, with the fire burning, the curtains drawn, and all the creatures whose fortunes were hers within easy reach (for the Professor's epistolary activities seemed to bring the boys back into the fold), Mrs. Potter felt that life was snug and safe and scaled down to a manageable size that almost fitted in her hand. The banjo clock on the wall ticked complacently, as if it had Time trained to heel.

"This is a good book," Elinor said, "even if nothing happens in it that couldn't happen in ordinary life. People sit around in parlors, you know, and gossip, and go to walk. There's this girl named Emma, who's always messing in other people's romances, and her dumb friend, Harriet. And there's this man, Mr. Knightley, who sort of reminds me of Daddy."

Professor Potter looked up from his letter. "I'm charmed by the comparison," he said.

"It wouldn't make an A-grade movie, though," Elinor said ruefully. "Hollywood would ruin it. The trouble with the movies is—" She hesitated, like a medical man about to extract from a clutter of secondary symptoms the true diagnosis of his patient's malady.

Mrs. Potter and the Professor fixed their full attention upon their child. Never before had they heard her admit that anything at all ailed the film industry.

The doorbell rang.

Mrs. Potter put on her shoes. "Who on earth, at this hour?" she said.

Her husband laughed in the silent, affectionate way he reserved for the foibles of his friends. "The Adamses, probably," he said. "Under the circumstances, I've been half expecting them."

Mrs. Potter sighed. She knew that by "circumstances" her husband meant one of those spells of abstinence from the bottle with which the Adamses occasionally mortified their nerves. She was fond of her neighbors, but she thought them pompous about their habits. Neither of them drank enough to worry about (they were, in fact, among that elect of society in whom the moderate use of alcohol releases optimism and amiability), and yet from time to time they embraced austerity as desperate men fly to the arms of Bacchus. These "temperance toots," as Mrs. Potter termed them, never lasted long, but they were tiresome. They commenced with pious platitudes about plain living and high thinking and how alcohol numbed the cortex of the brain, progressed through a week or so of elevated and rather touchy temper, and ended in some friend's house, where the Adamses, after a broad hint and a feeble show of resistance, allowed, in Professor Adams' arch way of putting it, their arms to be twisted.

"I don't know what we can offer them," Mrs. Potter said. The Potters themselves had been enduring a dry season—not from choice but from the stodgy, middle-class ethics that had impelled them to pay a plumber's bill.

"I have my nest egg," her husband told her. "The pint I won from Adams on the election returns."

"We were saving that for an emergency," Mrs. Potter objected, "or until we had something to celebrate."

"Liquor in the bottle never solaced the soul," said the Professor. He went into the hall, toward the front door.

"I'd better scoot," Elinor said to her mother. "I look repulsive. No lipstick, and my hair's fallen."

"Please stay," Mrs. Potter said. "If you're here, they may leave early."

"Huh?" said Elinor.

"I mean they're afraid of germs," Mrs. Potter said. She added, not wishing to set Elinor an example of ungraciousness, "It's nice to have friends drop in, but, somehow, tonight . . ."

Elinor nodded. "It was so peaceful," she said.

There were voices in the hall—Professor Potter's hearty with welcome, and Professor Adams' saying that he'd breasted the storm to return a borrowed book and that on such a night Christians would have to give him shelter, even if he were their enemy's dog who had bitten them.

Elinor glanced significantly at her mother, allowing her eyes to droop in a recognizable, if somewhat ludicrous, imitation of Miss Bette Davis being cynical. "Randy says whenever Mr. Adams stops drinking, he gets on a talking jag," she said.

"That isn't very loyal of Randy," Mrs. Potter said. "I trust you wouldn't speak so of *your* father."

"Daddy doesn't talk phony," Elinor said.

From the hall, Mrs. Adams was heard explaining that she'd accompanied her husband out of a thirst for intellectual stimulation.

Elinor giggled. "Intellectual!" she muttered.

"Careful, now," said Mrs. Potter as her husband ushered the guests into the room.

The Adamses were a florid, fleshy couple who gave the impression, generally, of finding life juicy in the mouth. Professor Adams was a harmless exhibitionist—the kind of teacher who cultivates a mellow bonhomie with his students and poses before the camera with a pipe between his teeth and his hair mussy; his wife was a languid woman who still affected the vaguely Pre-Raphaelite style of dress that had symbolized sensibility in her youth. But this evening they both had a badgered look that might, to a stranger, have suggested the ravages of prolonged dissipation.

Mrs. Potter went forward to greet them. "Why, Madge! And George!" she exclaimed in accents of cordial surprise.

"*Carissima!*" said Mrs. Adams, making a noble try for airiness. "My, but you're cozy!"

"A quiet English evening at home, eh?" said Professor Adams. He kept his voice free of praise or blame, like a cagey theatregoer who hasn't read the reviews of a play he's been to and doesn't care to commit himself upon its merits until he has. He let his bright eyes rove the room. (He was hoping, Mrs. Potter guessed, to discover that the quiet evening was being enlivened by a festive glass.) "And behold proud Beauty on her sacred couch! Why aren't you with the other nymphs, Elinor, gathering rosebuds in the balcony of the Criterion?"

Elinor flushed. The girls who sat in the balcony were known as "cruds" to her set, and she thought, mistakenly, that Professor Adams was cognizant of that fact.

Adams interpreted Elinor's change of color as a bashful response to his gallantry. Bending forward from the waist and with the thumb and forefinger of his right hand describing a broken oval, like a crab's claw, he approached the sofa. He had reached an age that is marked in many men by a compulsive urge to pinch a blushing cheek.

Mrs. Potter recognized the tweaking reflex as an innocent manifestation of nature. She pitied George Adams much as she pitied his son, Randy, who suffered from adolescent acne, but she didn't expect like charity from her daughter. "Elinor has a respiratory infection," she said quickly.

Professor Adams stuck his hand in his pocket and backed away. "Can that be a *book* you are fondling?" he inquired, beaming at Elinor from a safe distance.

Elinor squirmed, as the young do when impaled upon the spit of an elder's approval. "It's a school parallel, sir," she said. (She had learned to say "sir" from her schoolboy brothers and, guessing that middle-aged men weren't flattered when a pretty girl used the stiff title of respect, she kept it for occasions upon which she wished to be offish and didn't dare be uncivil.) "Required outside reading. A dumb thing called 'Emma,' sir."

"But you were saying you liked 'Emma,' " her father said. "And you were about to tell us what was wrong with the movies."

"There's nothing wrong with the movies except that I'm not *at* them," Elinor said. She managed a perfunctory smile. "If you'll all excuse me, I'll just lie here and get on with this book. I'm supposed to report on it Monday."

"I bow to Jane," said Adams.

" '*Emma,*' sir," said Elinor.

Professor Adams moved toward the fire, near which the ladies were already seated. "Now, what, in this lurid twilight of the human experiment, can 'Emma' be said to parallel?" he asked rhetorically.

"What indeed!" murmured Mrs. Potter. She thought with envy of Miss Austen's power to hedge her fancy in bosky villages where placid pools of custom were scarcely rippled by the thought that a world might be ending just across the English Channel.

Professor Adams stooped to pat Brandy. The dog rose to his thin, rheumatic legs and stalked away; he sank down beside Elinor's sofa, muzzle on forepaws, eyes closed. Adams looked hurt. "Dogs and children seem not to like me," he said.

"Brandy's a very old party," Professor Potter apologized, drawing up a chair for his friend.

"So are we all," Adams said. He ran his fingers through his thick hair. He was, as he hoped to be reminded, a year the junior of Professor Potter.

Mrs. Potter was anxious to start the conversation on a rational plane. She retrieved the seed catalogue that she'd let slip to the floor and flicked it open to a colored photograph of an incredibly perfect spike of blossoms. "I've been planning my annual border," she said brightly. "Here's a new improved nicotiana called 'Starlight'—"

"What a joy you must find in gardening!" Mrs. Adams said. "To touch, at this time of confusion, the simple, elemental roots of things! How I wish I could do something with my hands!" Her tone implied that her mind, neither sleeping nor slumbering, was a hard mistress.

"You'll touch the elemental soon enough, my love, if the inflation continues, as it doubtless will," her husband said. He gave her a glittering look that was part malice and part gratitude for the opportunity to be unpleasant. "Those lily hands will be seamed with the grime of toil."

"Oh, George!" Mrs. Adams cried in real dismay. Her long, elegant hands were her great vanity. They lay on her lap, white against the dark velvet of her full skirt, looking more like possessions of sentimental value than useful members of her body.

"We have reached the peak of our standard of living," Professor Adams declared. "Now for the descent." He waved his arm in an inclusive gesture. "Consider the room in which we sit. Adequate. Decent. But no more than my own living room an apartment to boast of."

Inwardly, Mrs. Potter bridled. She thought her room far nicer than the Adamses', which was cluttered with cloisonné jars, Florentine boxes, and trailing sprays of jaundiced ivy.

"The day will dawn when we shall recall an hour in these modest surroundings as an hour in the lap of luxury," Adams continued.

"I'm comfortable now," his wife said politely.

He ignored her remark. "The Potters will still hug their hearth as they do tonight, but with a difference. Their furnace will have given up its ghost. Their roof will leak. A lone, naked bulb, giving a gibbous light, will dangle on a cord from the ceiling. The whole aspect of this room will be changed."

"I can feel it changing now," said Mrs. Potter.

Professor Adams gave her a sharp glance, as if to judge whether she was poking fun at him. He switched his attention to his host. "Those pants that clothe your nether limbs," he said, "—they aren't your best pants?"

Professor Potter looked down at his decent but baggy gray flannel slacks.

"No," he admitted. "Not quite."

"They will be," said Adams. "They'll be your only pants."

Professor Potter shifted in his chair.

"Are you afraid the seat of your trousers is already wearing through?" Mrs. Adams asked.

The ladies laughed. Brandy, stirred by some stray dream of love or prowess, growled in his sleep.

Professor Adams still smarted under the old dog's contempt. "Families won't keep pets then," he said. "Unless for food."

Elinor, who was constantly tormented by the knowledge that Brandy's days were numbered, reached out to scratch the setter between the eyes.

"When George is on the wagon, he thinks too much," said Mrs. Adams.

Professor Potter took his cue. "Let's have a drink to the status quo," he said. "We all need something to numb our cortexes."

"I don't know," Adams said. He grinned disarmingly. "Well—if you twist our arms!"

When four highballs had been mixed and served, there was an interlude of inconsequential chatter around the fire.

"Is your outlook brighter now?" Mrs. Adams asked her husband.

"My outlook has always been brighter than you seem to realize," he said. "My prophecy anent the decline was based upon the rosy and exceedingly flimsy assumption that any of us will be here to see it. The Russians will drop their first shower of bombs on the United States in 1952."

"Who slipped you the date?" Professor Potter asked.

"I thought it was common knowledge," Adams said. He took a swallow of whiskey-and-soda. "There's a plethora of conjecture about the bomb, much of it frivolous. I sometimes fancy that, of all my acquaintance, I alone take it seriously."

"*I* do," said Mrs. Potter. She couldn't, inoffensively, add that she took the possibility of total destruction far too seriously to want the idea of it bandied about in the presence of her daughter, who was vulnerable not only because of youth but because of a virus. Neither could she send Elinor off to bed. In this year of grace, parents didn't dismiss young girls from rooms in which the talk threatened to turn unsuitable for their ears. (And more's the pity that parents don't, thought Mrs. Potter.)

"Do you ever try to picture the effects of a bomb?" Professor Adams asked her. "A bomb of gigantic, moot proportions?"

"I try not to," Mrs. Porter said, truly enough.

"Exactly," said Professor Adams. "The illusion of immunity. The old, pathetic confidence in special providence and Maginot Lines. Tell me—if this city were struck, what would you do?"

"They say you should fall flat on your face," Mrs. Potter said.

"And when you got up—for you couldn't stay down forever—what would you do?"

"How should I know?" Mrs. Potter said with forced flippancy. "Stop asking the same question."

"You should ask it of yourself," Professor Adams said. "You should be prepared. Suppose you chanced to be on the periphery of the disaster. Suppose, as a limbering exercise for the imagination, that you were the only survivor for miles around."

Mrs. Potter's imagination required no limbering. Professor Adams had hit upon the hideous eventuality that haunted her dreams. "Me?" she said. "Why me?" She thought that in all fairness someone should volunteer to keep her company. But no one did. Her husband's face wore a mask of patience. Mrs. Adams seemed lost in contemplation of her hands. Elinor didn't raise her eyes from her book.

"Why not you?" said Professor Adams. "Are you so complacent that you believe it couldn't happen to you?"

"No," Mrs. Potter said.

"This house sits on a hill," Adams said. His voice became bland and deliberate. "From your garden, one can see, beyond trees and low rooftops, the so-called skyline of the city. That little cluster of tall buildings—the First National Bank, the Masonic Temple, the steeple of the Memorial Methodist Church. Ugly structures in themselves, but what enchantment distance lends them! They seem to have the poised serenity of clouds."

"I know," Mrs. Potter said dryly. She was quite familiar with the view from her own front yard.

"Let us set the day in June. Blue sky. Green leaves. A lustre of life on everything. You would be plucking a rose—one of those old-fashioned, bell-shaped roses that you brought me last year when I was laid up with kidney colic."

"Duchesse de Brabant," said Mrs. Potter.

"And as you raised the dainty blossom to your nose"—here Professor Adams raised his glass to his lips—"the explosion! The apocalyptic flash rending the curtain of Heaven but revealing, alas, no angels beyond it! The roar—for our world will end with a bang, not a whimper! You hurl yourself to the grass. Beneath you body you feel the earth tremble. You hear the bones of our planet grinding in their sockets."

This was stuff and nonsense, Mrs. Potter told herself. George Adams knew less than Elinor about atomic power. Why, he was downright vain of his scientific ignorance—flaunting it as evidence of aesthetic genius. But the palms of her hands were clammy.

"Then the ssstillness," Professor Adams said, lingering on his sibilants. "The vasty silence, as of death. Rising to your knees, to your feet, you would look upon a scene you had loved. Where our little city once stood you would see an enormous column of smoke and haze. A dense, vaporous tower composed of pulverized steel and stone and brick and the dreams of the Chamber of Commerce. Beautiful in its terrible way. Along the horizon, like sores on the lip of an open wound, sporadic fires would lick the sky. *What would you do?*"

"Search for my family, of course," Mrs. Potter said.

"We are assuming you know they are done for," Professor Adams reminded her gently, the way one might repeat a lesson to a backward child.

"Then I would—" Mrs. Potter began, and stopped. She had been about to say honestly that she would weep.

"You would run," Professor Adams said.

"Where?" Mrs. Potter asked him.

"West," he said. "Away from the center of destruction. Down through the woods behind your lot. The leaves would lie shrivelled at the feet of the trees—'bare ruin'd choirs, where late the sweet birds sang'—for vegetable matter is more pervious than our flesh to noxious air. You would stumble through briar and bog. Your breath would come in pants."

"Old pants, like mine," Professor Potter suggested, from the depths of his boredom.

Mrs. Potter thought her husband's hackneyed pun unworthy of his talents.

"The dust of the stricken city would pursue you like the ghost of an old sin," Professor Adams said. He paused long enough to down the remains of his drink.

Mrs. Potter glanced at Elinor. The girl appeared still to be reading; she had the aloof, chiselled look of a recumbent statue.

"Toward nightfall," Adams continued, dropping his voice to the pitch of quiet horror, "against a dwindling band of uncontaminated sunset, you would see a dark, moving figure. A human shape."

Elinor sat up against her sofa pillows. "Good God!" she said.

"Imagine your sensations," Professor Adams said to Mrs. Potter. "The spasm of hope—I am not alone, you would feel; here is my fellow, who will blow with me upon the ashes of poetry and faith!—and, on the heels of hope, the terror. The sense of strangeness vested in that unknown creature. And when you approached him—for your loneliness would oblige you to approach him—you would perceive the ineluctable truth that men are *not* brothers in misfortune. In his face, stripped of the veneer of civilization, you would see plainly those basic animal qualities that we smugly brand as criminal. Violence, lust, greed. There he would stand—a powerful brute with his great hands hanging down below his knees. And there you would stand, in a ruined world, with *him!*"

Professor Adams leaned back in his chair. His attitude, Mrs. Potter observed, was relaxed—as if the whiskey were at last taking hold and what Elinor might call "phony talk" had purged his mind of bile.

For an instant, Mrs. Potter hated him. She heard the clock ticking on the wall. It ticked faster, she imagined, than it had, like blood beating in the neck of a spent runner.

Mrs. Adams smiled archly at Professor Potter. "I was smart to get killed," she said.

"Let me sweeten the glasses all around," said Professor Potter.

Elinor arose from the sofa. She was a small-boned girl, and in her childish night clothes—the pink bathrobe zoned tightly at her waist, the polka-dot pajamas that were too short and revealed her skinny ankles, and the old beaded felt moccasins—she appeared fragile and wistful and even younger than she was. I should have sent her to the Criterion with my blessing, Mrs. Potter thought bitterly; guerrilla warfare is nothing compared to what she's hearing here at home. And suddenly the vision of Elinor and her ilk—poised and shining in all their absurd airs and graces—watching, from semi-darkness, while a dénouement as improbably satisfactory as a flower in a catalogue unfolded on a screen before them seemed the prettiest vision in the world.

"I guess I'll say good night," Elinor said.

"Did you finish 'Emma'?" Professor Adams inquired.

"No," she said, "but what I learned from you was more vital."

Professor Adams' fingers went into a pinching formation, but he stayed where he was. "Take me *cum grano salis,* Elinor," he said. "I'm no physicist." (He had the grace, Mrs. Potter noted, to look sheepish.)

"You were brilliant," Elinor said simply. "Mother, may Brandy sleep with me?"

"This once," said Mrs. Potter. Years before, when Brandy had left the foot of Elinor's bed to murder a guinea pig in the boys' room next door, and the night had been horrid with shrieks and laments and carnage, she had made a rule against pets in bedrooms. But she thought that now was a time to honor that rule in the breach. Elinor deserved what comfort she could command.

With the red dog in her wake, Elinor started across the room. She took delicate, hesitant steps on the patterned carpet, like a little bird picking its way among dead leaves. At the door, she turned. "Mr. Adams," she said, cocking her head to one side, "do you mind if I make a suggestion?"

"Of course not, honey," said Professor Adams.

"Well, in your final scene—the fade-out, you know—" Elinor said, "when Mother sees the dark human shape against the sunset?"

"Yes," he said.

"At first, she thinks of kneeling with him and blowing on the ashes of poetry and faith," Elinor went on in a husky voice. "That bit was sheer poetry itself!"

Professor Adams looked as uncomfortable as a man whose prenuptial letters to his wife are read aloud in public. "I don't believe I said they would *kneel,*" he objected. "But thank you."

Elinor gazed off into space. "I *see* them kneeling," she said. "But then you introduce a sour note. Mother goes up to him, and he turns out to be this repulsive beast, this degenerate, this—this underworld character." She paused. "Please, Mr. Adams, don't let him be like that!"

Elinor drew a deep, tremulous breath. She tilted her head back, so that her yellow hair foamed out like a nimbus around her face. She lifted her hands, palms cupped, as if to catch some precious substance that rained from Heaven.

"Oh!" she said. "Let's have him be Tyrone Power!"

THE GLASS WALL

Miss Lincoln's realistic portrayal of high-school life in a
medium-size and perhaps typical American city is effectively—
at times beautifully—presented. The story reveals a keen
insight into the thoughts and attitudes of two young people when
they begin to become aware of the glass wall of prejudice that
has somehow come into existence between them. Celia
Amberley is portrayed with rare understanding.

Dizzy Harris was the sports editor of the *New Rich,* the school
paper, and Joe Veneziano was the business manager. The board meetings always narrowed down, at their close, to Celia Amberley and
Louis Shapiro sitting together talking, the manuscripts between them
and forgotten. Celia, who was almost eighteen, sat at a desk; Louis
straddled the seat before it, facing her. He was a thin, awkward boy,
his neck too long and his Adam's apple prominent; and still, the immediate impression he made was one of remarkable good looks, because his thin-lipped face was sensitive and clear-cut, and his whole
person, the dark hair, the fine hands with their clean, square nails, the
excellent clothes, were kept with a meticulous cleanliness that gave him
a look, remarkable in New Richmond, of true, aristocratic elegance,
far removed from any foppery.

He was a boy of quick, mature mind, a mind with wit and taste.
Celia had always been a greedy reader, but he had read more than she,
more and better.

"I wish you could talk to Shapiro," she said to Stella. "He's really a
genius."

"Also," said Stella, "dippy, batty, and a nut."

It's no use, Celia thought. You couldn't make her see it.

There were still, in nineteen twenty-three, almost no wealthy Jews
in New Richmond. The Shapiros' big house on Elm Place was a curiosity, viewed by some with open resentment, by others with laughing
tolerance. Louis' father was referred to as "that Jew lawyer," and his
name produced frequent jokes about fire insurance and ambulance
chasing. His services were retained with laughing apology: "I need
someone plenty smart to keep an eye on you fellows." The fact that he
was a Harvard man, cultivated in manner and well read, was counted

simply as a further effrontery, an evidence of shameless pushing, like his good clothes, his expensive car, and the house on Elm Place.

Celia had met Louis' father. Once, when she was walking with her own father, the two men had spoken, stopping for a few words about a projected slum clearance in which both were actively interested. She had watched him closely, fascinated by his firm, pleasant voice, and his manner, which was so unlike Louis', so poised and decisive.

How could Louis bring home the Lubitsky kids? she thought now. Maybe he wanted to, maybe he tried, once. And his father would have looked at them the way Mother did that time I brought home little Monica Brien—as if she were nice, but not real. Only it would have been worse—his father isn't like Mother.

She gave it up. After all, it didn't matter what Stella thought; it wasn't as if Louis were part of their gang. And the year went on, and the meetings. "Celia, have you read—" "Louis, you must read—" "Did you ever use to think—" "Have you ever believed in—"

It was her mother, it was Anne, who first disturbed it.

"You're late home today, darling," Anne said.

"New Rich meeting."

"Did Joe Veneziano say anything funny?" Joe was famous for his bad puns.

"No. It was just Louis and me. Finishing up."

"All that time?"

"We get to talking."

"Oh." Anne hesitated, moistened her lips. "What do you talk about?"

"Oh, books. Religion. People. Stuff like that."

"Isn't there—well, a teacher around? Or someone?"

"Oh, Mother—millions of people all over the place, for goodness' sake."

"I only meant—well, I hate even to say it. I know it's unnecessary. After all, dear, I have the greatest confidence in your judgment and common sense; but you don't think that boy could ever get—well, you know, silly about you, do you, dear?"

Celia stared at her. "Mother, Louis Shapiro? You don't know what you're talking about."

The honest amazement, the unfeigned disgust in the wide blue eyes made Anne completely reassured and a little ashamed of herself. She was not at all annoyed when Celia stalked out of the room, slamming the door behind her.

But Celia did not look at Louis in quite the same way again. Something had been changed. She had always found his face handsome; but now when she looked at it, she felt a stirring. The eager, rich, exciting talk was unchanged, and her pleasure in it; but at the same time, she was conscious of his face, and of their hands lying on the manuscripts between them, close and not touching. And her mind, total in its acceptance of the small world that had made it, denied the stirring, the consciousness, drove it back. Proudly, by an extraordinary feat of will, she shut out of knowledge the stirring, the consciousness, and the guilt.

No one was allowed in the building after four.

"Meeting adjourned," he would say, looking at the clock, and hurry from the room, leaving her to gather up the papers, to put them away. When Celia left the school building, he was never in sight.

Elm Place was not far from Allen Road, where Celia lived. If he took the shortest way to his house, he would inevitably go the same way Celia took daily. A year before, she had often caught up with him and passed him; she would say, a little vacantly, "Hello, Louis," as she greeted all casual acquaintances. But a month or so after she joined the staff of the *New Rich,* she realized that she had not passed him in the street for some weeks.

She gave it little thought at the time, her feeling for him being then no more than friendly admiration, touched a little with her keen native curiosity, a curious admiration very like the curious pity that had led her into her painful blunder with Eadie Finch. But as the year went on, she did wonder. Four o'clock came quickly. There were tags of business left to be discussed and, more and more often, fragments of unfinished conversation: "Did you ever try any George Moore?" "What do you think a man should do if—" It would have been fun to discuss them on the way home. But he always tore off in such a hurry.

Celia left it at that. First casually, and later compulsively, she left it at that. It was not until a day quite late in the spring that her mind, one afternoon, tripped and betrayed itself.

He could have waited, she thought. We hadn't really settled it about the prize story. He could have walked with me.

The books she carried were heavy. She lowered her head, shifting their weight on her arm. And besides, her mind added, he has to turn off for Elm Place before he gets to my corner.

She stood quite still, hearing the words in her mind, feeling the belated realization with the abruptness of a physical blow. Why, of course, she thought. He goes home some other way. I must have known it all along, really. He's going some other way because he knows that if I lived in another house, if my house were the first one we passed, I wouldn't ask him in.

Her face turned white. "I knew it all along," she whispered. "I knew it all along."

And from that moment, she was unable to keep from herself, in the secrecy of wordlessness, all that she was coming to feel about Louis Shapiro.

Still, for a great deal of her time, she didn't think about him at all.

Life was departmentalized, and in every department it was absorbing and intense; the comprehensive examinations were coming closer; there were Ginger Club meetings; there were school dances. It had become a custom for ten or twelve of her friends to meet at Celia's house almost every Friday night.

"Shall I roll back the living-room rug for tonight?" Anne would ask. She was proud because Celia's house was the meeting place most frequently chosen.

"Three Fridays in a row," she said happily to Edwin, Celia's father. "It makes me feel as if I've learned something about being a good mother—their choosing this house, time after time."

"Well, they like you," said Edwin. "You treat them as if they were grown-up."

Celia, in the upstairs hall, heard them with a smile.

"It's wonderful at your house," Stella said that afternoon. "You have that upstairs sitting room. Everywhere else we have to have the mother and father flashing around all evening like I don't know what. Even a downstairs library doesn't help much."

And Celia replied, "I know. Isn't it funny? You know we don't do anything different. Even if they aren't there, if you were going to kiss somebody, you'd slip off to the butler's pantry or somewhere. Isn't it funny what a difference it makes the minute they go upstairs?"

"Yes, terribly. Especially, you know, under the circumstances."

"What circumstances?"

"You know—the way we never seem to get whopped up over any particular boy any more, the way we used to be about Palmer White and Gordon Lamb."

"Yes, I know. Stella—" very earnestly— "do you think we're getting hard? Just using boys, the way we do? Poor Nick Thomas—"

"Poor, heck. He got to be Class President, didn't he? What do you think they're *for,* Celia?"

"Stella, you're hard as nails."

And Stella, brushing back the deep black waves of her hair, now cut in the first bob the school had seen, laughed aloud. "You should talk!"

Yes, thought Celia gravely. She's right. It's true. There isn't a single boy in the school that I care anything about. And I let Graham Priestly kiss me after the last assembly, and I've let Nick Thomas kiss me at least once after every dance we've gone to. Yes, she's right. I am hard. As hard as nails.

Quite simply, quite without any suspicion of self-deceit, her mind excluded the thought of Louis Shapiro. Louis was not a part of the world that held the dances, the Friday nights. She knew him with another self.

It was quite otherwise that she excluded Jerry Manning. He was there, often, at the Friday nights. Though he was in the class behind them, he had come, in the last year, to be more and more included by their crowd. There was not often time, nowadays, for Celia's and Jerry's country walks; but on their rare occasions they were as good, as peaceful as ever. It was only that Celia's friendship with Jerry, so taken for granted, so curiously without flirtation or jealousy, had come to be accepted as a permanent condition in her life, as good and naturally accepted as the food she ate or the air she breathed. He was no longer just Jerry; but he was Jerry, and apart. He came to the parties, he passed for one of the crowd; but he belonged to the world of summer and the open fields, a world at once more innocent and more mature than any other Celia knew.

They went into the country together a fortnight before the end of the school year. They had been sitting in one of their accustomed silences, looking down the fields to the lighthouse and the bay, warmed with the late May sun, when Jerry spoke.

"How do you get on with Shapiro?" he said abruptly. "Last year you said he couldn't stand you."

Her heart jolted oddly. "Fine," she said. And then quickly, very quickly, "I like him. He's okay."

The warm, direct eyes rested seriously on her face. "Thought you would. I like him, always have, from that little Greek Club we're in. I always thought you were a lot alike, different ways."

Her small fingers worked in the grass. "Sometimes we get into arguments. Sometimes he's pretty insulting."

"Yep? I don't think he means it. Knowing him, and you—he doesn't mean it." The dark face lifted to the sky, changed. "Say, look up there!" He was smiling widely.

"What is it?"

"Marsh hawk. Watch him quarter that field."

"What's he doing?"

"Mousing."

"How does he coast like that? Watch his wings, so still. I wish I could do that."

"It would make talk."

They laughed. They got up. At the wall, they paused again.

"Say, Celia."

She looked up.

"About Louis," he said. "He's a nice kid. Well, look, what I'm trying to say is, it's awful easy to hurt his feelings."

"Do you think I don't know that?" she exclaimed. "Do you think I don't butter his darned feelings all the time?"

The kind, troubled face refused her anger. "That wasn't it," Jerry said slowly. "I meant—well, skip it. It's no good, fooling with other people's business."

"You know I wouldn't hurt anyone's feelings."

He looked down at the fair, angry face, the small hands working together. "Sure," he said, very gently. "I was dumb. I beg your pardon, Celia."

The spring sun was warm. A light air moved over the fields. The hawk balanced overhead.

I imagine things, Celia thought. He didn't mean anything, only what he said. I felt as if he meant something like what Mother meant that time I got home late. As if he thought that Louis—that I—that I might want to make him feel about me the way—the way Nicky—and then—

Jerry isn't like that; he couldn't think of things like that—not Jerry. Not Jerry.

Sharply, urgently, her mind made its denial. She turned her face to the moving air. She smiled. "He's still there, Jerry," she said. "The hawk."

Then it was Graduation Week. Celia and Stella had talked for a long time about their dresses. Marquisette? Georgette? Voile?

"I tell you what," Stella cried suddenly. "Let's have white dotted Swiss. Mother can make mine, and you get a dressmaker. And for Class Day, organdy, made just alike. I could have rose and soft pink, and you could have buttercup and pale, pale yellow, just like your hair. Oh, Celia, we'd be divine. So simple, and still, you know, striking and not like anyone else."

"Oh, Stel, you're wonderful!"

And the dresses, now hanging in their respective closets, were all that they had dreamed.

And the *Ode* was written, and printed. It was on the first page of the little white-and-gold Commencement Day booklets.

Mr. Ryder showed a copy of it to Celia. "Looks better in print, doesn't it, Miss Amberley? I hope you don't feel so downcast about it now."

And it did look better in print, though it was not what it should have been. It was not the four years of growing up and coming to the beginning of the great adventure, caught forever in a fire and a singing; it was not what she had wanted, sitting hour by hour in her room, with the poetry lump in her throat and her eyes strained on distances beyond distances. But it was not bad.

She read the last words. "It is the morning, and the door stands wide." With one fingertip she touched her printed name, *Celia Amberley*.

"Well," she said, "maybe it will pass in a crowd." And then, feeling that something more was expected of her, "Thank you for showing it to me, Mr. Ryder."

In the hall she met Louis Shapiro.

"I just saw that everlasting *Ode* in print," she said.

"What tune are they using?"

"Kreisler's *Old Refrain*."

"My Lord, why did they do a thing like that to you?"

"I chose it myself. I like it."

"You do?" He stared at her for a moment, his face incredulous. Then it softened to a look of extreme pleasure. "Well," he said gently, "you could have made a worse choice." He continued to look at her, the expression of his eyes wholly unfamiliar, direct and gentle, almost happy. "Be good," he said. "See you later." And he walked down the hall at his shambling gait.

Celia stood perfectly still. The hall was crowded with boys and girls passing from room to room, but she stood as if she were quite alone.

He meant, she thought, that I don't know any more about music than a cat, that I haven't any taste. But why did it make him happy, and kind to me? Why didn't he act like that time I said I liked Ernest Dowşon?

She did not see Stella until she felt her arm taken and heard the laughter in her ear.

"For Pete's sake, are you in a trance or something? You look like a mummy stood up on end."

She gave it up. "I was just thinking."

"Well, next time don't think so hard."

They walked down the corridor, arm in arm.

But that night, lying in bed, she understood. He thinks I know more about books than he does. He's crazy, but he thinks so. That's why it made him feel good, razzing me about Dowson, and quoting all those gummy lines, to make Joe and Diz laugh at me. There's so little he can be sure of, he can't bear to have anyone make it seem as if it were less.

And still he—he likes me, because I have yellow hair, and I'm not tall, and I don't let people kid him. Last week, that day it was so dark, and he turned the light on—

A feeble, insufficient gleam came from the high, dim light in the ceiling. Louis pointed upward. "Not light," he said, "but rather darkness visible."

Celia did not shout with laughter, as she did at Joe's bad puns or Dizzy's good-natured clowning. She drew a deep breath and exhaled it slowly. "Perfect," she said.

Dizzy looked puzzled. "What was that crack again?"

"Highbrow stuff," said Joe. "Out of our class, Diz."

Celia looked at Louis' face, then looked away. Once, long ago, in the schoolyard, she had heard the children talking about her. "She uses big words," they said. "She tries to be original. She's peculiar, I think." She had not forgotten. It was different now, but she had not forgotten: staring at the gravel path, pretending not to hear, her eyes held wide to prevent the awful betrayal of tears. She grinned at Joe. "Sure," she said. "You supply the looks, we supply the brains." Yes, that was it. It was all right. Two against two, not him alone. He was almost smiling. "Never mind, Joe," she said gaily. "You can't have everything."

She moved restlessly on her bed, her mind sharp and sorrowful with the new understanding. I was kind to him. I'm always kind to him. And he knows it, and he's grateful, and he hates me for it.

Only, about music it was different. It's a real thing to him, as real as poetry, and I showed him that I was stupid and ignorant. And all of a sudden, he could be kind to me. He could keep me from having my feelings hurt. He could be the one who is kind.

Tears began to flow from her eyes, wetting her loosened hair. She cried without knowing that she cried, soundlessly.

Then the words came, the words she had kept so long in the remotest fastness of her mind, unspoken. "I love him," she said aloud. "I love him. And I've never even touched his hands. I love him. And now we're going away, and it's all over."

She heard her voice, felt the chill of her tears, and turning on her face, she sobbed herself into quietness, her mouth buried in the pillow so that Anne should not hear her.

The next day, in the lunchroom, Stella set her tray on the table with an indignant thump. "That Shapiro!" she said. "This is the limit, Cee. This is sickening. Shapiro says he won't go to the banquet." She paused for effect.

"Well, go on," said Celia sharply. "Don't take all night."

"What's eating you, Cee? Listen, Nick asked him to be toastmaster, and Shapiro put on that look and said thank you for the honor, but he wouldn't go to any of the tiresome stuff if he could get out of it, and the so-called banquet was just one too much. Those were his exact words."

"But he has to go!"

"Well, naturally, if he wasn't such a pill, he'd feel obligated. Why, even if I was so sick I couldn't even raise my head, I'd feel it was my duty, as Class Historian. We have all these kids who look up to us and expect things of us. And after all, Cee, think, the Valedictorian, and playing the piano Class Day, and everything!"

"Yes."

"Well, aren't you going to say anything? Don't you think it's sickening?"

"Yes. Yes, he's got to go." Celia pushed the food about on her plate for a moment. Then she lifted her head. "I'll tell him he's got to go."

"He wouldn't listen. Everything Nicky said, he just sneered."

"I'll make him listen," said Celia. "I'll go out early and wait on the steps, so he can't get away ahead of me. I'll simply follow him and talk. I'll make him listen." She heard her voice, unfamiliar, light and high, tinged with hysterical laughter. What's got into me? she thought. What am I doing?

He had passed her as if she were not there, had gone down the full flight of steps before she stood up and called. "Louis!" Tension made her voice shrill. "Louis, wait for me!"

He turned and looked at her, his face startled, almost frightened, odd with bewilderment. "Celia, what's the matter?"

"Louis, listen. You've got to let me walk with you."

"I—I'm sorry. I was going downtown."

"All right. Then I'll go downtown."

"No, I've changed my mind. We may as well walk toward home." She hesitated for a moment. "Well, come on, then," she said.

She carried her books and her raincoat, but although his hands were empty, he did not offer to relieve her. He fell into his loose-hung, awkward pace beside her, his face still baffled.

"What's the trouble? What's up?"

"Louis, Stella says you aren't going to the banquet."

"That's right."

"But you have to go, Louis."

"Why do I have to go?"

"Why—why, because they expect it of you. It's an obligation."

"Then excuse me from obligations."

"But they look up to you."

"You know how much. So do I."

"But you're Valedictorian."

"As I understand it, the honor is automatic, going to the student with the best grades."

"But if you're the cleverest one in the class, how can you say they don't admire you, that they won't be hurt if you don't come and join in?"

His thin cheeks moved in and out. His color changed. "Yes," he said, "they admire me. Their fathers admire my father. They retain his services, don't they?"

And now it was out, the trouble, the unspoken thing between them. In their minds, at least, it had been put into words.

"A banquet," he said, "followed by a dance, is, unlike school exercises, a social function."

In the shock of hearing it spoken, the terrible thing, the focal point about which her mind had cast for so long its whole periphery of denial—oh, even last night, when it broke at last, so much had been left unworded, everything that mattered, really, everything— In the shock of desperation she was clumsier, more stupid than she would ever be again. "Is Miriam Lubinsky staying away?" she said. "Is David Garfinkle staying away?"

Mercifully, the anger that shot through his heart spared him the fullest measure of his suffering. The white face he turned on her blazed with intelligent scorn. "Is Elmer Hicks staying away?" he said quietly. "Is Eadie Finch? Do you know, and did the knowledge influence your decision?"

She stumbled at the curb, and he caught her arm.

"Look where you're going," he said. His voice was gentle. "Here," he said gently, "let me carry some of those things." He hung the raincoat over his arm; he took the heavy books, stacking them firmly in his arm. He stood before her for a moment, utterly gentled, utterly quieted, seeing the completeness of his triumph written on her blind, averted face. "Celia," he said.

The sight came back into her wide eyes; she turned them to him. "Yes?"

"I'm sorry. You didn't know what you were going to say."

They walked on in silence.

At the corner of Elm Place, Celia paused. "This is your corner," she said.

"I'll go a little farther. There's something I've been trying to say."

"What is it, Louis?"

He kept his face turned away from her, looking directly forward. "Remember this, Celia, if you ever remember me. I don't think it was your fault, any more than it was mine. It wasn't your fault, Celia. I never will think it was your fault."

She could not answer.

"And I'm glad it happened. Now we know everything, don't we?"

"Yes," she whispered. "Yes."

He turned his head and looked down at the trembling lips, at the fair face, so helpless in its open vulnerability, so moving in its soft-colored prettiness.

"And perhaps I was wrong about the banquet," he said. "I—I'll think it over."

Again she could not speak.

"Here's your house, Celia. Here, take your things." He thrust the coat, the books into her arms, turned, and was gone.

She glanced toward the windows of her house. She controlled the impulse to look back until she reached the door. He was at the corner walking with his head nearly erect and his hands hanging easily at his sides.

Celia went directly to her room, shut the door, and wept.

She wept again at night, but she woke with an unfamiliar feeling of inner quietness. There were presents at breakfast, graduation presents. Anne and Edwin sat facing her, their faces fond and eager, waiting. She opened the long envelope first. She looked uncomprehendingly at the printed paper.

"Mill stocks," said her father. "New Richmond preferred. It's as well for a woman your age to have something in her own name."

It meant little to her. Having no sense of insecurity, she had no interest in money that was not to be spent immediately in some complete extravagance, something beyond the new clothes, the theatre tickets, that were always hers for the asking. However, she found the gift adult and, as such, flattering. "Thank you, Papa." She picked up the other present, the narrow jeweler's box. "Oh, how lovely! How beautiful!" A watch, octagonal, green gold, deeply chased, in the height of the contemporary style. "Oh, Mother, it's even more beautiful than yours!"

Anne's eyes dropped affectionately to her own watch, of platinum, very large by the standards of this day. It had been Edwin's Christmas gift. Despite the recession, they had had a remarkably successful year. "I'm so glad you like it, darling."

The old silver Swiss watch in its leather case lay on the table; the new gold bracelet slipped over the narrow wrist.

"Is it too loose?" Anne asked.

"Oh, no, it's perfect! Oh, honestly, I could die of joy!"

But when she went to her room after breakfast, she was tense and restless, unwilling to be alone. She went to the telephone. "Stella, just wait till you see my watch. You'll honestly die."

"You wait till you see my ring. This heavenly white-gold basket setting. And the stone! Did you ever see a pink tourmaline?"

"No, I don't think so."

"Well, it is the most beautiful— Celia, listen, all this excitement, I forgot! How did you come out?"

"Come out?"

"Shapiro, idiot, Shapiro! I bet you never got up your nerve, after all."

She caught her breath. "Yes, I did."

"Tell me! What did he say?"

"He—he sort of got the point, I think. He—he said he'd see about it."

"Celia, you are simply marvelous. Good heavens, you are simply marvelous. Do you think he meant it?"

"I think so."

"Well, what are you so down in the mouth about?"

"I don't know," said Celia. She hesitated. "Nothing much," she said. "I was just sort of wishing that Jerry was going to graduate this year."

"Sure," said Stella. "Going with you so much, and all. He's got so he has more friends in our class than his own. Yes, I certainly see your point."

"I wish he was going to be at the banquet."

"Sure. Celia, are you terribly excited?"

"I feel funny. It's a funny feeling, having it all over."

"Yes, it is, isn't it? Celia, it's after ten. And I'm still in my kimono."

"Same here. Well, so long."

Anne came up the stairs. "Better start dressing, lamb."

"That's just what I said to Stella." She followed her mother into the bedroom.

Why did I think of Jerry like that? she wondered. It isn't as if I wouldn't see him all summer. I suddenly felt so. As if I'd give anything if he could be at the banquet, too. As if I were afraid to go if he wouldn't be there. It doesn't make any sense.

She stood in the middle of the room, staring before her. Jerry, she thought. And then sharply, overwhelmingly, Louis! Oh, Louis, Louis!

"Well, woolgatherer!" said Anne.

"I was thinking," said Celia. "I was just saying to Stella, it's such a funny feeling, having it all over. This morning. Mother, I'm graduating from high school."

"My darling," said Anne.

The school orchestra gave everything it had to the *Pilgrims' Chorus*. The boys entered from one door, the girls from another, two and two, Celia and Stella together, fresh and snowy and admired, as they had fully expected to be, in their identical fluttering of dotted Swiss. The *Ode* was sung, and everyone looked at Celia and smiled. The Congregational minister, Doctor Graham, made the address. The Valedictorian read his speech drawn from the class motto, "Always Faithful." She heard it quietly, feeling little. His face, his voice, reading, were unfamiliar, serious but quite composed, the face and the voice of a pleasant, adequate, undistinguished boy, reading a pleasant, adequate, undistinguished address to his graduating class in a public high school, as hundreds like him were doing on that same day all across the continent.

She heard him quietly; she joined with moderation in the friendly, moderate applause. For a first, brief moment, she clapped harder, as if she wanted, by her own effort, to swell the demonstration to ovation. Then her wrists slackened.

A graduation, she thought, is more like church. He knows it isn't like Class Day, where they cheer and whistle.

She walked across the platform and received in her hand the white roll with its ribbons of blue and buff. She returned to her place and heard the orchestra play *The March of the Priests* from *Aïda*. And then she was shaking hands with teachers, and kissing her parents, irrationally, as if she had returned from a long journey, or was setting out on one, and it was over. . . .

Anne had advised her against the pale-yellow organdy. "It's too much like your hair, darling," she had said. "Stella will look radiant, but you'll just fade right out."

But today she stood before her daughter, shaking her head with delight. "I must admit I was wrong," she said. "Just that tiny touch of rouge makes all the difference. You look like— Oh, Edwin, come and see her now!"

Celia stood before the long mirror. Yes, she thought, I look pretty. The prettiest I ever looked in my life. It doesn't show, the way I feel, so sick and shaky. Why didn't I feel like this yesterday? Nothing is different. Why did I feel so good and quiet all yesterday, and wake up this morning feeling as if I were going to die?

She touched the square neck of the dress, the billowing skirt, with light, cold fingertips. He'll remember me like this, she thought. I wish— I wish it weren't so pretty. And then, fiercely, No. I'm glad. Glad.

"Isn't it almost time?" she asked.

The auditorium was bright and hot with afternoon sun. The girls' faces were flushed. Mr. and Mrs. Wales, Mr. and Mrs. Amberley sat together. Happy, without jealousy, four faces lifted to the platform, seeing the adored only-daughter with her best friend. Everyone's whispering about them, their dresses, so pretty together—so dark, so fair. Celia—Stella—is a remarkably pretty child, said the faces, uplifted. Except for my Stella—my Celia—easily the prettiest child in the school.

Celia sat erect, her head lifted, her hands lying in her lap, one upon the other, palms up. Tim Kelly had almost finished reading the class poem.

"Miss Stella Wales, our Class Historian."

And Stella, standing at the very edge of the platform, directly before her, reading in her musical, stilted, reading-aloud voice, saying the words already familiar to Celia, but meaningless, unable to hold her attention. Stella was going to Ohio Wesleyan, where her mother had met her father. Out West, Celia thought vaguely. She's going out West. We're all going away.

The sad, pretty voice, the meaningless words fell into silence. Then the applause again, as it had been for Tim Kelly, loud, like waves of heat.

"The Class Prophet, Joseph Veneziano."

She leaned forward anxiously, hearing. She did not move her head; her eyes did not move toward the end of the line, where Louis Shapiro sat. She only waited, following every word, knowing he must say something about Louis. And he did; in a humorous scene, depicting Louis as a famous newspaper editor. There was no bite, no sting in his words. Then Joe's good-natured prediction went on to other classmates; Stella, Celia, Dizzy—

Celia sat back. I should have known, she thought gratefully. Joe's nice. He knows Louis. He wouldn't have said anything to make him feel unhappy and unwanted there, anything he would mind.

She heard no more until she felt her hands joining in the loud applause.

"And now Louis Shapiro will perform for us at the piano a rendition of Beethoven's *Sonata Pathétique*."

And Louis crossed the stage before her. His head was thrust forward, his face whiter than she had ever seen it before. He walked at a quick, shambling trot.

"The white rabbit," Stella whispered. "Oh, my ears and whiskers, how late it's getting."

Celia sat erect, so that Stella, beside her, could not see her face.

The six tragic chords, and six again, rising, filled the stage, the hall. And then six again, the same and changed, the last three repeated; and one, and one, rising in the great statement of human sorrow; and then the cascade of sound breaking, falling on her, falling.

She was ignorant of music, but not impervious to it. Perhaps, indeed it is likely, she would have been equally moved by any music sufficiently grandiose and passionate, a Lizst *Hungarian Rhapsody* or the Rachmaninoff *Prelude,* granted only that she was hearing it now, like this, for the first time.

To Anne, who was truly musical, the score unfolded itself, vitiated by familiarity, dulled by amateurish and uneven reading, and still remarkably moving. He really has excellent technique, she thought, for a boy taught as he must have been, and intense feeling. What a queer quality he gets into it, such unhappiness, and a total lack of serenity. But he's an interesting boy. He has a handsome face. I should think that Celia and Stella would have liked him better, Celia especially. She's been brought up with so much less prejudice than most of these poor little things.

Clear, free of guilt, her eyes moved from Louis' face to Celia's. She smiled. Bored to tears, she thought, poor little thing. Funny how she and Ed are both so dead to music; they love poetry,

For Celia, the pure moment of hearing was rapidly exhausted. It became false, self-conscious. For an instant she clutched at the dissolving ecstasy. And then, the music protracting itself beyond any possible term of her attention, she forgot even the pose, shifted uneasily in her chair, like Stella, like Joe Veneziano beside her.

Then her attention was caught again. Something had happened. He was playing differently; the sound was rapid and irritable. He was running off the final pages at unpleasant speed, accurately, with no false notes, but all in a single sustained voice of perfunctory irritability.

What's the matter? Celia thought. What hit him, what changed him, like that? As if—as if he suddenly said, Oh, what's the use! As if he were trying to say something—to himself—to me—yes, to me; and then he thought, Oh, what's the use.

And suddenly, from startled understanding, from pity, from love, she felt her heart go cold with anger.

I like the *Old Refrain,* she thought. I'm too dumb to bother with. No one in this room could possibly understand him. The great man alone in the throng. I hope they know he's insulting them, all of them. I hope they *know.*

But the school, as a body, was not at all interested in the music. "Classical," their minds had said at the first notes. They sat politely, unhearing. Still, they could see, the piece was hard. That was something, to know a hard piece as long as that by heart. And fast—why, near the end, his fingers just flew.

When he rose and stood before them, jerking his head in the stiff bow, unsmiling, the loud applause was augmented in part by the tension of their long, enforced quiet and boredom; but for the most part it sprang from an admiration that was wholly sincere.

Celia was more angry than ever. That makes it perfect for him, she thought, none of them knowing it was rotten. Standing there, taking all that kindness and despising them for it. He won't go to the banquet, not after this pretty little triumph. He wouldn't spoil it for himself. The perfect moment. And who cares? Who cares?

She stood with the others and lifted her light voice in the school song.

> *"Though other lands may claim us,*
> *Though we walk 'neath alien sky,*
> *We'll e'er be true to Buff and Blue,*
> *Dear old New Richmond High."*

Then everyone was clapping, standing up, moving from his seat. She turned quickly from side to side. "Stel, you were so wonderful. Joe, you were a sketch, you were simply swell!"

And quickly, quickly, before the line in which they stood could break, could close about her on the stage, become a crowd, before they could be about her, all of them within sight, within touch, she sprang down from the platform, first of them all, and was blessedly engulfed by the audience, thronging forward with its congratulations.

In her room, Celia pulled off the yellow dress and threw herself on the bed. "I'm so tired," she said. "When I think about that banquet, Mother, I have the cold shakes. Honestly, I'll die before it's over."

Anne went about the room quietly, closing the closet door, drawing the shades. "Of course," she soothed. "Of course. Why, your poor little hands are just like ice. Take a nice nap, darling pet. Don't be afraid to drop right off to sleep. I'll wake you in plenty of time. All this excitement! Of course you're worn out. Of course you are."

"I ache," said Celia.

And her mother's voice came back, light and cool, infinitely soothing. "Why, of course you do, dear. Let me get a cool cloth and sponge your face, and then you'll go right to sleep."

Her eyes closed, Celia lay on the bed, abandoning herself to her mother's ministrations. As, long ago, Anne had pushed back the day's failure and the night's fear, accepting, in her light voice, which was at once so blessedly sympathetic and matter-of-fact, the nightmare, the bout of feverish vomiting, exorcising the ghosts, dispelling the terror and the unwilling hate, speaking the magic formulas: "Dear, we must make it a rule that you don't eat any chocolate. . . . Dear, you mustn't read those dreadful, overstimulating stories at bedtime." So, now, she bent above the bed, sponging the flushed forehead, rubbing the cold hands, drawing up the light cover.

"All this excitement," she said again. "I should think you'd be dead. All of you." She patted the narrow fingers, touched the small wrist. "That is a pretty watch, dear, isn't it?" she said. "Well, now, go to sleep."

And Celia lay with closed eyes, quieted, and heard the closing of the door. She felt the aching slacken in her shoulders and the calves of her legs. She felt the choked, fluttering tension pass from her throat and breast.

It's nice, she thought, the tradition about the banquet. All the boys going stag, and no evening dresses. So many would stay away if a boy didn't ask them, if they had to get a new, long dress. Everyone going, everyone mixing together for the last time.

She stirred uneasily. What got into me this afternoon, taking it all to myself, his playing like that? As if it wasn't typical of the way he acts about everything, all the time. He'll come tonight. He'd have told us if he didn't mean to go. Just to get the good out of it, because he wouldn't be there to see us all hanging around, waiting for him. He'd have told us, just to have us all saying, Please.

He'll be there, to have us all say, Thank you, thank you for the great favor. Or he wouldn't have missed his chance, this afternoon, when he knows he may not see some of us again—hardly ever.

We're going to the country tomorrow.

And suddenly she sat up, looking around the room with eyes wide and startled. "Why," she said aloud, "except for Christmas and Easter vacations, I don't suppose I'll ever live in this house, live in New Richmond again!"

She lay back, covering her lips with her fingers.

"I never thought of that," she whispered. "It's more, it's much more, than just the end of school." She lay perfectly still, all the fluent color withdrawn from her face, staring at nothingness. "I never thought," she whispered again. "I never thought before."

And suddenly she threw herself over, hiding her face in the pillow. "Louis," she wept. "Louis, Louis, Louis. Oh, please come to the banquet. Please, please. Come tonight, Louis. Please."

A long, trembling sigh came from her lips; she moved her face to one side, and five minutes before Anne once more opened the door, she had fallen asleep.

The mezzanine of the hotel was a joyful madhouse. The tables, which would be pushed aside later for the dancing, now covered the ballroom floor. The upper lobby was crowded, incredibly noisy.

"Ouch," cried Stella. "My ears! Is this just the senior class? It sounds like the whole school."

"Some party!" shouted Dizzy Harris behind her. "Even before it begins, I'll say it's some party!"

"Celia, isn't it wonderful? Who got the idea of having all the boys wear a red carnation? When I saw them all with those blue jackets and ice-cream pants and those carnations, I thought I'd die. It's the cutest thing. Diz, who got it up?"

"You're talking to the great man himself."

"Diz, honestly? You know what I think? I bet they'll always do it after this. I bet you've started a school tradition!"

"Yep, the kid is clever. Say, someone pat my back for me. I ain't tall enough to reach it."

"Oh, Dizzy, you're a sketch!"

A small crowd had begun to surround him, pushing carelessly forward, catching Stella in the midst of it.

Celia, moving more slowly, found herself thrust back. She drew inconspicuously away. "He must be here," she told herself. "Off in a corner, probably. He must be here." But she could not find him.

At last, she stood at the head of the staircase that led down to the main lobby. "He is coming," she told herself. "Something happened, to make him late. When he comes, late like this, he will be glad because I am looking for him, waiting for him. If anyone notices me here, I'll say I left something down in the ladies' room. I'll go down and then come back."

Her fingers traced the ornate pattern of the carved balustrade. "He will come," she told herself again. "He will come. He'll be late, and afraid that they will say something. He'll think, 'I could back out, I could go home, even now.' He'll hear the noise. Then he'll look up the stairs and see me, waiting for him." *And if he doesn't come?* She closed her eyes for an instant. "He'll come," she told herself once more. "He simply must come."

She stood motionless except for the fingers of the hand that traced, over and over, the carved pattern on the balustrade. She felt a direction, a stir in the crowd behind her. They were moving toward the banqueting room.

"Celia?" She heard Stella's voice. "Where's Celia?"

And Fanny Allbright: "I think I saw her over on the other side, Stella. I think she's gone in."

"It's no use," she thought then. "It's no use. He's not coming. I'll have to give up. It's no use." She was turning away when she saw him. He was hurrying across the lobby. Once he stumbled a little in his haste. He started up the stairs without lifting his eyes, a poor figure of a boy, indeed, shy, ludicrously awkward, pitiable; but to Celia he was not pitiable. She saw his face, very white but composed, the eyes lowered but steady, the lips set, as if he were going to a grave ordeal. She felt a shock of joy in her arms, sharp as a shock of terror.

"Louis!" she cried. She did not think at all of being heard by the others, of controlling her voice, of being light or casual. He had come, he was there. "Oh, Louis!"

His startled face lifted. Halfway up the stairs he stopped still, seeing her, as she had wanted him to see her, in the yellow dress, waiting.

"I—I'm late," he said. "I'm sorry I'm late."

She saw him completely, then, as he moved closer. Oh, she thought, helplessly, oh, he—he even got a carnation, like the others. He even got a carnation. And suddenly her eyes filled with tears.

He drew even with her and put his hand on her arm, above the elbow. "Come on," he said. "Everyone's going in now, Celia. Come on."

They moved slowly forward, silent, perfectly still at heart, in the moment which was at once the declaration and the completion of their love.

Only the small fry, preempting places in their chosen groups, had begun to seat themselves. Around the head table they were milling and giggling. Hands snatched at place cards. "Where am *I*? Stella Wales, Joe Veneziano, Louis Shapiro—" "Say, did he ever come?"

And Diz was striking an attitude, singing, "We shall meet, but we shall miss him. There will be a va-cant chair."

Louis stood beside him. "That my seat, Harris?"

"Shapiro! Say, here's Shapiro! Say, where've you been?"

They were all good-natured, pleasant children. For a moment they stood silent, embarrassed because Diz had sung and they had laughed. Gee, what if he's sore, or thinks we don't want him?

But Louis stood at his place, smiling, his head erect, and his hands, as Celia had seen them only once before, hanging easily at his sides.

"We were lost in the shuffle," she said. And then, loudly, across the table, "Stella, where'd you get to? I couldn't find you out there." She took her marked place, by Nick. She smiled up, first at him, then to her left, at Joe Veneziano.

The babble rose again, the uncomfortable lull quickly passed.

It's all right, she thought. That fixed it. It's all right.

But the small deceit, the overswift protective gesture, had not been necessary. Across the table, Louis sat beside Stella. His head was bent toward her at an angle of courteous attention, his lips smiled; but his eyes were fixed quietly on another place, a timeless world where Celia Amberley stood at the top of a long flight of stairs, in her yellow dress, looking down, waiting.

If that had only been the end, if Celia had only been able to let it alone! But she could not let it alone.

After the speeches, after the dance with Nick, the dance with Diz (during which she exchanged speaking glances, over his shoulder, with the now faded Gordon Lamb), she looked about once more, as she had looked often since the music began, to see if Louis were still there. Several of the boys who did not dance, several of the shyest and least attractive girls had left already.

But he was standing by the wall, talking to Joe. His hands were by his side, and his face, directed toward her, was bright and quiet.

"Excuse me, Gordon," she said. "I've got to tell something to Joe." And she walked toward Louis.

He watched her come, as he had watched her dancing, with the same quiet face of bright composure. He looked at her as she had often seen Jerry Manning look at her, happily, fondly, desiring no more than what he already possessed. Although Louis did not realize it consciously, still, in the moment of looking up, of seeing her in the yellow dress, waiting, he had effected a renunciation. The mute declaration, the love given and returned, made itself felt in him as something all-sufficing, more than he had ever hoped for, all that he would ever again desire. It was the end; it was altogether likely that he would not see her again for more than a few casual instants. He had his possession.

She approached them. "Hi, Joe. Hi, Louis."

"Say, Celia, I've been getting after Louis to dance. Show himself a time and make a big night of it for once."

"You know I can't dance." His voice was easy, undisturbed.

"Aw, go on, Cee, drag him out and dance him around a couple of times. Change the whole course of his life. You're only young once, Shapiro."

"Drop it." But he spoke quietly, his voice tolerant and amused, the good-natured kidding at last incapable of hurting him.

"Don't be like that, Lou, old boy, old boy. Come on, Cee, swing him around."

And then she made her mistake; she committed, so far as our cruelties are ever unwitting, her unwitting cruelty. "Yes," she said, "Louis, come on. It's fun. Please dance with me."

"Celia, I can't dance."

"My goodness, neither can Jerry Manning, but he hasn't let it stop him yet. Just walk me backward."

The music had begun again.

"Grab him," said Joe, laughing. "Grab him, Cee, and swing him off his feet. What are you waiting for, a big, brawny woman like you?"

He seized Celia's slender waist and whirled her into position before Louis. He thrust Louis' arm around her and interlocked their hands, right and left.

"Now you got him, girl," he said. "Let's go."

She walked backward, drawing him after her, laughing. "Just once around," she said loudly, for everyone to hear, "just so that big ape will be satisfied, Louis."

He stumbled forward for a few steps.

"Why, you said you can't dance!" She lifted her face, her laughing, half-coy, dancer's face, to his, and her heart clogged and stood still.

He was looking down at her with utter contempt, contempt for her and for himself. She felt his open hand pressed against the softness of her side; she felt his fingers clutched on her own, working on them with fierce, involuntary concentration, as if it were necessary, immediately, urgently necessary, for him to determine through their smooth flesh the exact configuration of the bone beneath. She saw his face, a blind mask of contempt and despair, the despair of loss, of irrevocable loss.

She stumbled and stood still, feeling herself supported by the fierce, helpless pressure of his arm, his open hand hard against her side; feeling herself beaten down by the contempt, the awful contempt on his face.

Her own arm dropped from his shoulder. Her voice clogged in her throat. "Louis," she said. "I'm—I didn't think—"

He released her so abruptly that he appeared to thrust her away. "Louis, I meant—I didn't mean—"

She saw his lips work stiffly for an instant, as if he were finding his voice with difficulty; but when it came, it was perfectly normal, courteous, untouched by histrionics. "You see," he said. "I told you I can't dance. There's no use making an exhibition of ourselves just to please Joe. Will you excuse me, Celia?" Without waiting for an answer, he turned and left her.

She stood still, her face blank with shock.

In a moment Joe stood beside her. He scratched his black mop with unfeigned bewilderment. "Well, what's eating him now?"

She could hold herself in control, but she did not dare trust her voice. She shook her head.

"Well, feature that," said Joe. "Just left you standing. Well, can you tie that!" He scratched his head again. Then he shrugged, grinning his wide, good-natured grin. "Well, it takes all kinds to make a world. His loss, my gain. Come on, let's step and show them something."

He circled her unresisting waist, took her unresisting hand. Her feet, following his steps, moved with a life of their own. Swaying from side to side, moving like a girl hypnotized, Celia followed him. Over his shoulder she could see Louis leaving.

I could run after him, she thought desperately. I could catch up with him and tell him—tell him—

She remembered his face, at the bottom of the staircase, lifted to hers. She remembered the moment in which she had seen the carnation he wore, like all the others. She remembered his face, looking down at her, the look of rejection, the terrible mingling of tragic loss and contempt, brutal and murderous.

"Smooth," said Joe. "I'll tell the world we're smooth." He swung her in a circle. "The great night, hey?" he said. "The night we'll never forget."

But what had happened, really? What have I told you, in so many, many words, that you could not summarize in a casual three or four? There was a boy in her class—if things had been otherwise, if the mores of her city had been different, the tribal feelings of the in-group and the out-group a little less stringent, there might have been a story, something to tell, to remember.

But a potentiality is not a fact; nor can it be remembered like a fact. For a few days after she got to the country, she thought a great deal about Louis Shapiro, and wept a great deal, when she was alone; although in her parents' presence she managed to appear fairly cheerful and collected. For a few days longer, she was tired and restless, dreaming at night, confused dreams from which she woke sweating. She would lie, unable to remember what she had dreamed, able only to recall the strong effect of helpless guilt, of failure.

And then it was all over. She was her summer self, reading in the orchard, sunning on the float, walking in the countryside with Jerry; and when she thought of Louis at all, it was kindly, with objectivity. "He's such a nice kid," she said to Jerry. She picked a spray of clover and turned it slowly in her fingers as she talked; but her blue, unconcealing eyes were lifted honestly to his. "I—I hope he gets on all right. He sort of has a genius for making trouble for himself."

The dark, direct eyes looked back into hers. "I don't know," said Jerry quietly. "I thought he did all right, everything considered. In New York, at Columbia, it won't be the same." He stretched out on his back, looking away from her into the blue of the zenith, his wide dark eyes steady against the light. "It struck me that you had a lot in common," he went on slowly. "Not just the things you read. It used to hit me sometimes, when I was talking to him. Not so much that he was like you, maybe, as like the way you would have been if you hadn't always had the breaks. If New Richmond had been the same place for you that it was for him."

She looked at him sharply. It was surprising, unfamiliar, the slow voice, the troubled manner, the curious, personal probing, from Jerry, who was always so easy, so untroubled, so totally impersonal. "I didn't know you gave that kind of thought to people," she said.

"I don't, much." He rubbed his fingers over his broad forehead, in an unfamiliar, troubled gesture, as if some small, important fact had momentarily deserted him. "Only the last week of school there was something—something or other—that kept making me think—"

I could tell him, she thought suddenly. I could tell him. Only, there isn't anything to tell—not really. She leaned forward. "I liked him," she said. "As much as I ever got a chance to see of him. And then the last week of school—oh, I don't know, I just did everything all wrong, and made him feel awful."

"I'm sorry," he said. "Well, it was none of my business. Just knowing you, and him, and thinking things over, it hit me that it was a sort of shame, all that time, that you weren't better friends."

Her slender hands pressed together abruptly. "How could we? I only saw him in school."

He sat up, looking at her. He saw the direct, childish face, the fair, soft hair done in the recent modish fashion, now just passing. She was dressed more carefully than she had been a year ago. He looked at the pretty, womanly style of the blue voile dress, the white slippers with the baby-Louis heels, the silver locket on the long chain.

"What else could I have done?" she said sharply. "Had him to the house?"

He looked at her without censure or pity, his eyes perfectly kind, perfectly fond. But he could not find the heart to answer her.

The silence answered her.

She turned her head away. But when she spoke, at last, it was to forgive herself. "I don't belong in New Richmond, Jerry," she said. "I'm glad I'm getting out. I never belonged in New Richmond."

He nodded. He put out a hard brown hand and gave her arm a quick double pat. He smiled his broad, open smile. "Tide's coming in," he said. "Look out there, in the bay. All the boats are shifting."

Pamela Frankau

THE DUCHESS AND THE SMUGS

What are smugs? Penelope finds out. Penelope, a delightfully precocious child of fourteen, is as completely fascinating a young lady as the reader is ever likely to meet, in or out of the pages of literature. Her parents run an exclusive inn for tourists on the Riviera—exclusive, that is, after a fashion, for Penelope's father wishes to feel free to entertain only those who seem to him to be personally congenial. He has no use for people who are incapable of appreciating the haphazard, carefree atmosphere of his inn and the individualistic character of some of the guests. The Duchess is one of the more interesting guests who stay at the inn, and it is through Penelope's dramatic experience with her that the reader is enabled to share with Penelope a clearer view of the other characters in in the story, including "the smugs."

There had been two crises already that day before the cook's husband called to assassinate the cook. The stove caught fire in my presence; the postman had fallen off his bicycle at the gate and been bitten by Charlemagne, our sheep dog, whose policy it was to attack people only when they were down.

Whenever there were two crises my stepmother Jeanne said, *"Jamais deux sans trois."* This morning she and Francis (my father) had debated whether the two things happening to the postman could be counted as two separate crises and might therefore be said to have cleared matters up. I thought that they were wasting their time. In our household things went on and on and on happening. It was a hotel, which made the doom worse: it would have been remarkable to have two days without a crisis and even if we did, I doubted whether the rule would apply in reverse, so that we could augur a third. I was very fond of the word augur.

I was not very fond of the cook. But when I was sitting on the terrace in the shade working on my Anthology of Hates, and a man with a bristled chin told me in *patois* that he had come to kill her, I thought it just as well for her, though obviously disappointing for her husband, that she was off for the afternoon. He carried a knife that did not look particularly sharp; he smelt of licorice, which meant that he had been drinking Pernod. He stamped up and down, making speeches about his wife and Laurent the waiter, whom he called a *salaud* and many other words new to me and quite difficult to understand.

I said at last, "Look, you can't do it now, because she has gone over to St. Raphael in the bus. But if you wait I will fetch my father." I took the Anthology with me in case he started cutting it up.

I went down the red rock steps that sloped from the garden to the pool. The garden looked the way it always looked, almost as brightly colored as the post cards of it that you could buy at the desk. There was purple bougainvillaea splashing down the white walls of the hotel; there were hydrangeas of the exact shade of pink blotting paper; there were huge silver-gray cacti and green umbrella pines against a sky that was darker blue than the sky in England.

I could not love this garden. Always it seemed to me artificial, spiky with color, not quite true. My idea of a garden was a green lawn and a little apple orchard behind a gray stone house in the Cotswolds. I saw that garden only once a year, in September. I could conjure it by repeating inside my head—

> And autumn leaves of blood and gold
> That strew a Gloucester lane.

Then the homesickness for the place that was not my home would make a sharp pain under my ribs. I was ashamed to feel so; I could not talk about it; not even to Francis, with whom I could talk about most things.

I came to the top of the steps and saw them lying around the pool, Francis and Jeanne and the two novelists who had come from Antibes for lunch. They were all flat on the yellow mattresses, talking.

I said, "Excuse me for interrupting you, but the cook's husband has come to assassinate the cook."

Francis got up quickly. He looked like Mephistopheles. There were gray streaks in his black hair; all the lines of his face went upward and the pointed mustache followed the lines. His body was dark brown and hairy, except that the scars on his back and legs, where he was burned when the airplane was shot down, did not tan with the sun.

"It's a hot afternoon for an assassination," said the male novelist as they ran up the steps together.

"Perhaps," said Francis, "he can be persuaded to wait until the evening."

"He will have to," I said, "because the cook is in St. Raphael. I told him so."

"Penelope," said my stepmother, sitting up on the yellow mattress, "you had better stay with us."

"But I am working on my book."

"All right, *chérie;* work on it here."

The lady novelist, who had a sparkling, triangular face like a cat, said, "I wish you would read some of it to us. It will take our minds off the current bloodcurdling events."

I begged her to excuse me, adding that I did not anticipate any bloodcurdling events because of the battered look of the knife.

Jeanne said that the cook would have to go in any case, but that her love for Laurent was of a purely spiritual character.

I said, "Laurent is a smoothy, and I do not see how anybody could be in love with him."

"A certain smoothness is not out of place in a headwaiter," said the lady novelist.

I did not tell her my real reason for disliking Laurent; he made jokes. I hated jokes more than anything. They came first in the Anthology: they occupied whole pages: I had dozens and dozens: it was a loose-leaf book, so that new variations of hates already listed could be inserted at will.

Retiring from the conversation, I went to sit on the flat rock at the far end of the pool. Francis and the male novelist returned very soon. Francis came over to me. I shut the loose-leaf book.

"The cook's husband," he said, "has decided against it."

"I thought he would. I imagine that if you are really going to murder somebody you do not impart the intention to others."

"Don't you want to swim?" said Francis.

"No, thank you. I'm working."

"You couldn't be sociable for half an hour?"

"I would rather not."

"I'll write you down for RCI," he threatened.

RCI was Repulsive Children Incorporated, an imaginary foundation which Francis had invented a year before. It came about because a family consisting mainly of unusually spoiled children stayed at the hotel for two days, and were asked by Francis to leave on the third, although the rooms were booked for a month. According to Francis, RCI did a tremendous business and there were qualifying examinations wherein the children were tested for noise, bad manners, whining, and brutal conduct. I tried to pretend that I thought this funny.

"Will you please let me work for a quarter of an hour?" I asked him. "After all, I was disturbed by the assassin."

"All right. Fifteen minutes," he said. "After which you qualify."

In fact I was not telling him the truth. I had a rendezvous at this hour every day. At four o'clock precisely I was sure of seeing the people from the next villa. I had watched them for ten days and I knew how

Dante felt when he waited for Beatrice to pass him on the Ponte Vecchio. Could one, I asked myself, be in love with four people at once? The answer seemed to be Yes. These people had become a secret passion.

The villa was called La Lézardière; a large, stately pink shape with green shutters; there was a gravel terrace, planted with orange trees and descending in tiers, to a pool that did not sprawl in a circle of red rocks as ours did, but was of smooth gray concrete. At the tip of this pool there was a real diving board. A long gleaming speedboat lay at anchor in the deep water. The stage was set and I waited for the actors.

They had the quality of Vikings; the father and mother were tall, handsome, white-skinned, and fair-haired. The boy and girl followed the pattern. They looked as I should have preferred to look. (I was as dark as Francis, and, according to the never-ceasing stream of personal remarks that seemed to be my lot at this time, I was much too thin. And not pretty. If my eyes were not so large I knew that I should be quite ugly. In Francis' opinion, my face had character. "But this, as Miss Edith Cavell said of patriotism," I told him, "is not enough.")

Oh, to look like the Bradleys; to be the Bradleys, I thought, waiting for the Bradleys. They were fair, august, and enchanted; they wore the halo of being essentially English. They were Dad and Mum and Don and Eva. I spied on them like a huntress, strained my ears for their words, cherished their timetable. It was regular as the clock. They swam before breakfast and again at ten, staying beside the pool all the morning. At a quarter to one the bell would ring from the villa for their lunch. Oh, the beautiful punctuality of those meals! Sometimes we did not eat luncheon until three and although Jeanne told me to go and help myself from the kitchen, this was not the same thing at all.

In the afternoon the Bradleys rested on their terrace in the shade. At four they came back to the pool. They went fishing or waterskiing. They were always doing something. They would go for drives in a magnificent gray car with a white hood that folded back. Sometimes they played a catching game beside the pool; or they did exercises in a row, with the father leading them. They had cameras and butterfly nets and field-glasses. They never seemed to lie around and talk, the loathèd recreation in which I was expected to join.

I took Don and Eva to be twins; and perhaps a year younger than I. I was just fourteen. To be a twin would, I thought, be a most satisfying destiny. I would even have changed places with the youngest member of the Bradley family, a baby in a white perambulator with a white starched nurse in charge of it. If I could be the baby, I should at least be sure of growing up and becoming a Bradley, in a white shirt and gray shorts.

Their magic linked with the magic of my yearly fortnight in England, when, besides having the gray skies and the green garden, I had acquaintance with other English children not in the least like me: solid, pink-cheeked sorts with ponies, they came over to tea at my aunt's house and it was always more fun in anticipation than in fact, because I seemed to make them shy. And I could never tell them that I yearned for them.

So, in a way, I was content to watch the Bradleys at a distance. I felt that it was hopeless to want to be friends with them; to do the things that they did. I was not only different on the outside, but different on the inside, which was worse. On the front page of the Anthology I had written: "I was born to trouble as the sparks fly upward," one of the more consoling quotations because it made the matter seem inevitable.

Now it was four o'clock. My reverie of the golden Bradleys became the fact of the golden Bradleys, strolling down to the water. Dad and Don were carrying the water-skis. I should have only a brief sight of them before they took the speedboat out into the bay. They would skim and turn far off, tantalizing small shapes on the shiny silky sea. Up on the third tier of the terrace, between the orange trees, the neat white nurse was pushing the perambulator. But she was only faintly touched with the romance that haloed the others. I mourned.

Then a most fortunate thing happened. There was a drift of strong current around the rocks and as the speedboat moved out toward the bay, one of the water-skis slipped off astern, and was carried into the pool under the point where I sat. Don dived in after it; I ran down the slope of rock on their side, to shove it off from the edge of the pool.

"Thanks most awfully," he said. He held on to the fringed seaweed and hooked the water-ski under his free arm. Now that he was so close to me I could see that he had freckles; it was a friendly smile and he spoke in the chuffy, English boy's voice that I liked.

"It's rather fun, water-skiing."

"It looks fun. I have never done it."

"Would you like to come out with us?" he jerked his head towards the boat: "Dad's a frightfully good teacher."

I groaned within me, like the king in the Old Testament. Here were the gates of Paradise opening and I must let them shut again, or be written down for RCI.

"Painful as it is to refuse," I said, "my father has acquired visitors and I have sworn to be sociable. The penalty is ostracism." (Ostracism was another word that appealed to me.)

Don, swinging on the seaweed, gave a gurgle of laughter.

"What's funny?" I asked.

"I'm terribly sorry. Wasn't that meant to be funny?"

"Wasn't what meant to be funny?"

"The way you talked."

"No, it's just the way I talk," I said, drooping with sadness.

"I like it awfully," said Don. This was warming to my heart. By now the speedboat was alongside the rock point. I could see the Viking heads; the delectable faces in detail. Mr. Bradley called: "Coming aboard?"

"She can't," said Don. "Her father has visitors; she'll be ostracized." He was still giggling and his voice shook.

"Oh dear, that's too bad," said Mrs. Bradley. "Why don't you ask your father if you can come tomorrow?"

"I will, most certainly," I said, though I knew that I need never ask permission of Jeanne or Francis for anything that I wanted to do.

I felt as though I had been addressed by a goddess. Don gurgled again. He flashed through the water and they pulled him into the boat.

I had to wait for a few minutes alone, hugging my happiness, preparing a kind of vizor to pull down over it when I went back to the group on the yellow mattresses.

"Making friends with the Smugs?" Francis greeted me.

"What an enchanting name," said the lady novelist.

"It isn't their name; it's what they are," said Francis.

I heard my own voice asking thinly: "Why do you call them that?" He shocked me so much that my heart began to beat heavily and I shivered. I tried to conceal this by sitting crouched and hugging my knees. I saw him watching me.

"Well, aren't they?" he said gently. I had given myself away. He had guessed that they meant something to me.

"I don't know. I don't think so. I want to know why you think so."

"Partly from observation," said Francis. "Their gift for organized leisure; their continual instructions to their children; the expressions on their faces. And the one brief conversation that I've conducted with Bradley—he congratulated me on being able to engage in a commercial enterprise on French soil. According to Bradley, you can never trust the French." He imitated the chuffy English voice.

"Isn't 'commercial enterprise' rather an optimistic description of Chez François?" asked the lady novelist, and the male novelist laughed. Francis was still looking at me.

"Why do you like them, Penelope?"

I replied with chilled dignity: "I did not say that I liked them. They invited me to go water-skiing with them tomorrow."

Jeanne said quickly: "That will be fun. You know, Francis, you are becoming too intolerant of your own countrymen: it is enough in these days for you to meet an Englishman to make you dislike him." This was comforting; I could think this and feel better. Nothing, I thought, could make me feel worse than for Francis to attack the Bradleys. It was another proof that my loves, like my hates, must remain secret, and this was loneliness.

II

I awoke next morning full of a wild surmise. I went down early to the pool and watched Francis taking off for Marseilles in his small, ramshackle seaplane. He flew in a circle over the garden as he always did, and when the seaplane's long boots pointed for the west, I saw Don and Eva Bradley standing still on the gravel terrace to watch it. They were coming down to the pool alone. Offering myself to them, I went out to the flat rock. They waved and beckoned and shouted.

"Is that your father flying the seaplane?"

"Yes."

"Does he take you up in it?"

"Sometimes."

"Come and swim with us," Don called.

I ran down the rock slope on their side. I was shy now that we stood together. I saw that Eva was a little taller than Don; that she also was freckled; and that they had oiled their skins against sunburn as the grownups did. Don wore white trunks and Eva a white swimming suit. They laughed when I shook hands with them, and Don made me an elaborate bow after the handshake. Then they laughed again.

"Are you French or English?"

That saddened me. I said, "I am English, but I live here because my stepmother is a Frenchwoman and my father likes the Riviera."

"We know that," said Don quickly. "He was shot down and taken prisoner by the Germans and escaped and fought with the Resistance, didn't he?"

"Yes. That is how he met Jeanne."

"And he's Francis Wells, the poet?"

"Yes."

"And the hotel is quite mad, isn't it?"

"Indubitably," I said. It was another of my favorite words. Eva doubled up with laughter. "Oh, that's wonderful. I'm *always* going to say indubitably."

"Is it true," Don said, "that guests only get served if your father likes the look of them, and that he charges nothing sometimes, and that all the rooms stay empty for weeks if he wants them to?"

"It is true. It does not seem to me the most intelligent way of running an hotel, but that is none of my business."

"Is he very rich?" asked Eva.

Don said quickly: "Don't, Eva, that's not polite."

"He isn't rich or poor," I said. I could not explain our finances to the Bradleys any more than I could explain them to myself. Sometimes we had money. When we had not, we were never poor in the way that other people were poor. We were "broke" which, as far as I could see, meant being in debt but living as usual and talking about money.

"Do you go to school in England?"

"No," I said, handing over my chief shame. "I am a day boarder at a convent school near Grasse. It is called Notre Dame des Oliviers."

"Do you like it?"

"I find it unobjectionable," I said. It would have been disloyal to Francis and Jeanne to tell these how little I liked it.

"Do they teach the same things as English schools?"

"Roughly."

"I expect you're awfully clever," said Eva, "and top at everything."

How did she know that? Strenuously, I denied it. Heading the class in literature, composition, and English poetry was just one more way of calling attention to myself. It was part of the doom of being noticeable, of not being like Other People. At Les Oliviers, Other People were French girls, strictly brought up, formally religious, cut to a foreign pattern. I did not want to be they, as I wanted to be the Bradleys: I merely envied their uniformity.

God forbid that I should tell the Bradleys about winning a special prize for a sonnet; about being chosen to recite Racine to hordes of parents; about any of it. I defended myself by asking questions in my turn. Eva went to an English boarding school in Sussex; Don would go to his first term at public school this autumn. I had guessed their ages correctly. They were just thirteen. "Home" was Devonshire.

"I would greatly love to live in England," I said.

"I'd far rather live in an hotel on the French Riviera. Lucky Penelope."

"I am not lucky Penelope; I am subject to dooms."

"How heavenly. What sort of dooms?"

"For example, getting an electric shock in science class, and finding a whole nest of mice in my desk," I said. "And being the only person present when a lunatic arrived believing the school to be Paradise."

"Go on. Go on," they said. "It's wonderful. Those aren't dooms, they are adventures."

"Nothing that happens all the time is an adventure," I said. "The hotel is also doomed."

They turned their heads to look up at it; from here, through the pines and the cactus, we could see the red crinkled tiles of its roof, the bougainvillaea, the top of the painted blue sign that announced *"Chez François."*

"It can't be doomed," Don said. "Don't famous people come here?"

"Oh yes. But famous people are more subject to dooms than ordinary people."

"How?"

"In every way you can imagine. Important telegrams containing money do not arrive. Their wives leave them; they are recalled on matters of state."

"Does Winston Churchill come?"

"Yes."

"And Lord Beaverbrook and Elsa Maxwell and the Duke of Windsor and Somerset Maugham?"

"Yes. Frequently. All their signed photographs are kept in the bar. Would you care to see them?"

Here I encountered the first piece of Bradley dogma. Don and Eva, who were splashing water on each other's hair ("Dad is most particular about our not getting sunstroke"), looked doubtful.

"We *would* love to."

"I'm sure it's all right, Eva; because she lives there."

"I don't know. I think we ought to ask first. It is a bar, after all."

Ashamed, I hid from them the fact that I often served in the bar when Laurent was off duty.

"Oh, do let's chance it," said Don.

"I don't believe we ought to."

Mr. and Mrs. Bradley had gone over to Nice and would not return until the afternoon, so a deadlock threatened. The white starched nurse appeared at eleven o'clock with a Thermos-flask of cold milk and a plate of buns. I gave birth to a brilliant idea; I told her that my stepmother had invited Don and Eva to lunch with us.

It was a little difficult to convince them after the nurse had gone, that Jeanne would be pleased to have them to lunch without an invitation. When I led them up through our garden, they treated it as an adventure, like tiger shooting.

Jeanne welcomed them, as I had foretold, and the lunch was highly successful, although it contained several things, such as *moules,* which the Bradleys were not allowed to eat. We had the terrace to ourselves. Several cars drove up and their owners were told politely that lunch could not be served to them. This delighted Don and Eva. They were even more delighted when Jeanne told them of Francis' ambition, which was to have a notice: "Keep Out; This Means You," printed in seventeen languages. One mystery about the Bradleys was that they seemed to like jokes. They thought that I made jokes. When they laughed at my phrases they did not laugh as the grownups did, but in the manner of an appreciative audience receiving a comedian. Eva would hold her stomach and cry: "Oh *stop!* It hurts to giggle like this; it really hurts."

I took them on a tour of the hotel. The salon was furnished with some good Empire pieces. The bedrooms were not like hotel bedrooms, but more like rooms in clean French farmhouses, with pale walls and dark wood and chintz. All the rooms had balconies where the guests could eat their breakfast. There were no guests.

"And Dad says people *clamor* to stay here in the season," Don said, straddled in the last doorway.

"Yes, they do. Probably some will be allowed in at the end of the week," I explained, "but the Duchess is arriving from Venice at any moment and Francis always waits for her to choose which room she wants, before he lets any. She is changeable."

Eva said, "I can't get over your calling your father Francis. Who is the Duchess?"

"The Duchessa di Terracini. She is half Italian and half American."

"Is she very beautiful?"

"Very far from it. She is seventy and she looks like a figure out of a waxworks. She was celebrated for her lovers but now she only loves roulette." I did not wish to be uncharitable about the Duchess, whose visit was to be dreaded, and these were the nicest things that I could make myself say. The only thing in her favor was that she had been a friend of my mother, who was American and utterly beautiful and whom I did not remember.

"*Lovers?*" Eva said, looking half pleased and half horrified. Don flushed and looked at his feet. I had learned from talks at school that reactions to a mention of the facts of life could be like this. I knew also that Francis despised the expression, "the facts of life," because, he said, it sounded as though all the other things that happened in life were figments of the imagination.

"A great many people loved the Duchess desperately," I said. "She was engaged to an Austrian Emperor; he gave her emeralds, but somebody shot him."

"Oh well, then, she's practically history, isn't she?" Eva said, looking relieved.

III

I might have known that the end of the day would bring doom. It came hard upon the exquisite pleasure of my time in the speedboat with the Bradleys. This was even better than I had planned it in anticipation, a rare gift. I thought that the occasion must be under the patronage of a benign saint or what the Duchess would call a favorable aura; the only worry was Mrs. Bradley's worry about my having no dry clothes to put on after swimming; but with typical Bradley organization there were an extra white shirt and gray shorts in the boat. Dressed thus I felt like a third twin.

The sea changed color; the sea began to be white and the rocks a darker red.

"Would you like to come back and have supper with us, Penelope?"
I replied, "I can imagine nothing that I would like more."

"She *does* say wonderful things, doesn't she?" said Eva. I was drunk
by now on Bradley admiration and almost reconciled to personal remarks.

"Penelope speaks very nice English," said Mrs. Bradley.

"Will you ask your stepmother then?" she added as we tied up the
boat. I was about to say this was unnecessary when Don gave my ribs
a portentous nudge; he said quickly, "Eva and I will walk you up
there." It was obvious that the hotel exercised as much fascination for
them as they for me.

When the three of us set off across the rocks Mr. Bradley called,
"Seven o'clock sharp, now!" and Eva made a grimace. She said,
"Wouldn't it be nice not to have to be punctual for anything?"

"I never have to be," I said, "except at school, and I think that I
prefer it to having no timetable at all."

"Oh, my goodness! Why?"

"I like days to have a shape," I said.

"Can you just stay out to supper when you want to? Always? Without telling them?"

"Oh, yes."

"What would happen if you stayed away a whole night?"

I said that I had never tried. And now we went into the bar because
Don said that he wanted to see the photographs again. Laurent was
there; straw-colored and supercilious in his white coat. He began to
make his jokes: *"Mesdames, monsieur, bon soir.* What may I serve
you? A Pernod? A champagne cocktail?" He flashed along the shelves,
reading out the name of each drink, muttering under his breath, *"Mais
non; c'est terrible;* we have nothing that pleases our distinguished visitors." I saw that the Bradleys were enchanted with him.

We walked all round the gallery of photographs and were lingering
beside Winston Churchill when the worst thing happened. I heard it
coming. One could always hear the Duchess coming. She made peals of
laughter that sounded like opera; the words came fast and high between the peals.

And here she was, escorted by Francis. She cried, "Ah my love, my
love," and I was swept into a complicated, painful embrace, scratched
by her jewelry, crushed against her stays, and choked with her scent
before I got a chance to see her in perspective. When I did, I saw that
there were changes since last year and that these were for the worse.
Her hair, which had been dyed black, was now dyed bright red. Her
powder was whiter and thicker than ever; her eyelids were dark blue;
she had new false eyelashes of great length that made her look like a
Jersey cow.

She wore a dress of dark blue chiffon, sewn all over with sequin stars, and long red gloves with her rings on the outside; she tilted back on her heels, small and bony, gesticulating with the gloves. "Beautiful—beautiful—beautiful!" was one of her slogans. She said it now; she could not conceivably mean me; she just meant everything. The Bradleys had become awed and limp all over. When I introduced them they shook hands jerkily, snatching their hands away at once. Francis took from Laurent the bottle of champagne that had been on ice awaiting the Duchess; he carried it to her favorite table, the corner table beside the window. She placed upon the table a sequin bag of size, a long chiffon scarf, and a small jeweled box that held *bonbons au miel*, my least favorite sweets, reminding me of scented glue.

Francis uncorked the champagne.

"But glasses for all of us," the Duchess said. "A glass for each." The Bradleys said, "No thank you very much," so quickly that they made it sound like one syllable and I imitated them.

"But how good for you," cried the Duchess. "The vitalizing, the magnificent, the harmless grape. All children should take a little to combat the lassitude and depressions of growth. My mother used to give me a glass every morning after my fencing lesson. *Et toi*, Penelope? More than once last year you have taken your *petit verre* with me."

"Oh, didn't you know? Penelope is on the water wagon," said Francis, and the Duchess again laughed like opera. She cried, *"Santé, santé!"* raising her glass to each of us. Francis helped himself to a Pernod and perched on the bar, swinging his legs. The Bradleys and I stood in a straight, uncomfortable row.

"Of youth," said the Duchess, "I recall three things. The sensation of time seeming endless, as though one were swimming against a current; the insipid insincerity of one's teachers; and bad dreams, chiefly about giants."

Sometimes she expected an answer to statements of this character; at other times she went on talking: I had known her to continue without a break for fifteen minutes.

"I used to dream about giants," said Eva.

"How old are you, Miss?"

"Thirteen."

"At fifteen the dreams become passionate," said the Duchess, sounding lugubrious about it.

"What do you dream about now?" asked Don, who had not removed his eyes from her since she came.

"Packing; missing airplanes; losing my clothes," said the Duchess. "Worry—worry—worry; but one is never bored in a dream, which is more than can be said for real life. Give me your hand," she snapped at Eva. She pored over it a moment, and then said briskly, "You are going to marry very young and have three children; an honest life; always be careful in automobiles." Don's hand was already stretched out and waiting. She gave him two wives, a successful business career, and an accident "involving a horse between the ages of twenty and twenty-three."

"That is tolerably old for a horse," Francis interrupted.

"Sh-h," said the Duchess, "perhaps while steeplechasing; it is not serious." She blew me a little kiss: "Penelope I already know. She is as clear to me as a book written by an angel. Let me see if there is any change," she commanded, a medical note in her voice: "Beautiful—beautiful—beautiful! Genius and fame and passion are all here."

"Any dough?" asked Francis.

"I beg your pardon," said the Duchess, who knew perfectly well what dough meant, but who always refused to recognize American slang.

"I refer to cash," said Francis looking his most Mephistophelean: "My ambition for Penelope is that she acquire a rich husband, so that she may subsidize Papa in his tottering old age."

"Like so many creative artists, you have the soul of a fishmonger," said the Duchess. She was still holding my hand; she planted a champagne-wet kiss on the palm before she let it go. "I have ordered our dinner, Penelope. It is to be the *écrevisses au gratin* that you like, with small *goûters* of caviar to begin with and *fraises des bois* in kirsch afterward."

I had been anticipating this hurdle; she always insisted that I dine with her on her first evening, before she went to the Casino at nine o'clock.

"I am very sorry, Duchessa; you must excuse me. I am having supper with Don and Eva." I saw Francis raise one eyebrow at me. "I really didn't know you were coming tonight," I pleaded.

"No, that is true," said the Duchess, "but I am very disappointed. I have come to regard it as a regular tryst." She put her head on one side. "Why do you not all three stay and dine with me? We will make it a *partie carrée*. It could be managed, Francis? Beautiful—beautiful—beautiful! There. That is settled."

"I'm most awfully sorry; we'd love to," Eva said. "But we couldn't possibly. Supper's at seven and Mum's expecting us."

"Thank you very much, though," said Don, who was still staring at her. "Could we do it another time?"

"But of course! Tomorrow; what could be better? Except tonight," said the Duchess. "I was looking to Penelope to bring me good luck. Do you remember last year, how I took you to dine at the Carlton and won a fortune afterward?"

"And lost it on the following afternoon," said Francis. The Duchess said an incomprehensible Italian word that sounded like a snake hissing. She took a little ivory hand out of her bag and pointed it at him.

"I thought one never could win at roulette," said Don. "According to my father, the game is rigged in favor of the Casino."

"Ask your father why there are no taxes in Monaco," said the Duchess. "In a game of this mathematic there is no need for the Casino to cheat. The majority loses naturally, not artificially. And tell him further that all European Casinos are of the highest order of probity, with the possible exception of Estoril and Budapest. Do you know the game?"

When the Bradleys said that they did not, she took from her bag one of the cards that had upon it a replica of the wheel and the cloth. She embarked upon a roulette lesson. The Bradleys were fascinated and of course we were late for supper. Francis delayed me further, holding me back to speak to me on the terrace: "Do you have to have supper with the Smugs?"

"Please don't call them that. Yes, I do."

"It would be reasonable, I should think, to send a message saying that an old friend of the family had arrived unexpectedly."

Of course it would have been reasonable; Mrs. Bradley had expected me to ask permission. But nothing would have made me stay.

"I'm extremely sorry, Francis; I can't do it."

"You should know how much it means to her. She has ordered your favorite dinner. All right," he said, "I see that it is useless to appeal to your better nature. Tonight you qualify for RCI." He went back to the bar, calling, "The verdict can always be withdrawn if the candidate shows compensating behavior."

"Didn't you want to stay and dine with the Duchess?" asked Don, as we raced through the twilit garden.

"I did not. She embarrasses me greatly."

"I thought she was terrific. I do hope Mum and Dad will let us have dinner with her tomorrow."

"But *don't* say it's *écrevisses*, Don, whatever you do. There's always a row about shell fish," Eva reminded him.

"I wouldn't be such an ass," Don said. "And the only thing that would give it away would be if you were ill afterward."

"Why should it be me?"

"Because it usually is," said Don.

I awoke with a sense of doom. I lay under my mosquito curtain, playing the scenes of last evening through in my mind. A slight chill upon the Viking parents, due to our being late; smiles pressed down over crossness, because of the visitor. Don and Eva pouring forth a miscellany of information about the Duchess and the signed photographs; myself making mental notes, a devoted sociologist studying a favorite tribe: grace before supper; no garlic in anything; copies of *Punch* and the English newspapers; silver napkin rings; apple pie. The secret that I found in the Cotswold house was here, I told myself; the house in Devonshire took shape; on the walls there were photographs of it; a stream ran through the garden; they rode their ponies on Dartmoor; they had two wire-haired terriers called Snip and Snap. I collected more evidence of Bradley organization: an expedition tomorrow to the Saracen village near Brignoles; a Current-Affairs Quiz that was given to the family by their father once a month.

No, I said to myself, brooding under my mosquito net, nothing went wrong until after the apple pie. That was when Eva had said, "The Duchess told all our fortunes." The lines spoken were still in my head:

Don saying, "Penelope's was an absolute fizzer; the Duchess says she will have genius, fame, and passion." Mr. Bradley's Viking profile becoming stony; Mrs. Bradley's smooth white forehead puckering a little as she asked me gently, "Who is this wonderful lady?"

Myself replying, "The Duchessa de Terracini," and Mrs. Bradley remarking that this was a beautiful name. But Mr. Bradley's stony face growing stonier and his officer-to-men voice saying, "Have we all finished?"; then rising so that we rose too and pushed in our chairs and bowed our heads while he said grace.

After that there was a spirited game of Monopoly. "But the atmosphere," I said to myself, "went on being peculiar." I had waited for Don and Eva to comment on it when they walked me home, but they were in a rollicking mood and appeared to have noticed nothing.

"Indubitably there is a doom," I thought while I put on my swimming suit, "and since I shall not see them until this evening because of the Saracen village, I shall not know what it is."

As I crossed the terrace, the Duchess popped her head out of the corner window above me; she leaned like a little gargoyle above the bougainvillaea; she wore a lace veil fastened under her chin with a large diamond.

"Good morning, Duchessa. Did you win?"

"I lost consistently, and your friends cannot come to dine tonight, as you may know; so disappointing, though the note itself is courteous." She dropped it into my hands. It was written by Mrs. Bradley; fat, curly handwriting on paper headed

CROSSWAYS

CHAGFORD

DEVON

It thanked the Duchess and regretted that owing to the expedition, Don and Eva would not be able to accept her kind invitation to supper.

I knew that the Bradleys would be back by six.

IV

I spent most of the day alone working on the Anthology. I had found quite a new Hate, which was headed "Characters." People called the Duchess a character and this was said to others who came here. I made a brief description of each and included some of their sayings and habits.

There was the usual paragraph about the Duchess in the *Continental Daily Mail;* it referred to her gambling and her emeralds and her *joie-de-vivre. Joie-de-vivre* seemed to be a worthy subject for Hate and I entered it on a separate page, as a subsection of Jokes.

At half-past-four, to my surprise, I looked up from my rock writing desk and saw the Bradleys' car sweeping in from the road. Presently Eva came running down the tiers of terrace alone. When she saw me she waved, put her finger to her lips, and signaled to me to stay where I was. She came scrambling up.

"I'm so glad to see you. There's a row. I can't stay long. Don has been sent to bed."

"Oh, dear. I was conscious of an unfavorable aura," I said. "What happened?"

Eva looked miserable. "It isn't anything against you, of course. They like you terribly. Mum says you have beautiful manners. When Don and I said we wanted you to come and stop a few days with us at Crossways in September, it went down quite *well.* Would you like to?" she asked, gazing at me, "or would it be awfully boring?"

I was momentarily deflected from the doom and the row. "I cannot imagine anything that would give me greater pleasure," I said. She wriggled her eyebrows, as usual, at my phrases.

"That isn't just being polite?"

"I swear by yonder hornèd moon it isn't."

"But of course it may not happen now," she said in melancholy, "although it wasn't *your* fault. After all you didn't make us meet the Duchess on purpose."

"Was the row about the Duchess?"

"Mm—m."

"Because of her telling your fortunes and teaching you to play roulette? I did have my doubts, I admit."

"Apparently they were quite cross about that, but of course they couldn't say so in front of you. Daddy had *heard* of the Duchess, anyway. And they cracked down on the dinner party and sent a note. And Don kept on asking why until he made Daddy furious; and there seems to have been something in the *Continental Mail,* which we are not allowed to read."

"Here it is," I said helpfully. She glanced upward over her shoulder. I said, "Have no fear. We are invisible from the villa at this angle."

She raised her head from the paper and her eyes shone; she said, "Isn't it wonderful?" I had thought it a pedestrian little paragraph, but I hid my views.

"Mummy said that the Duchess wasn't at all the sort of person she liked us to mix with, and that no lady would sit in a bar drinking champagne when there were children present, and that we shouldn't have gone into the bar again anyway. And Don lost his temper and was quite rude. So that we came home early instead of having tea out; and Dad said that Don had spoiled the day and asked him to apologize. And Don said a word that we aren't allowed to use and now he's gone to bed. Which is awful for him because he's too big to be sent to bed. And I'll have to go back. I'm terribly sorry."

"So am I," I said. "Please tell your mother that I deplore the Duchess deeply, and that I always have."

As soon as I had spoken, I became leaden inside myself with remorse. It was true that I deplored the Duchess because she was possessive, overpowering, and embarrassing, but I did not disapprove of her in the way that the Bradleys did. I was making a desperate effort to salvage the thing that mattered most to me.

In other words, I was assuming a virtue though I had it not, and while Shakespeare seemed to approve of this practice, I was certain that it was wrong. (And I went on with it. I added that Francis would not have dreamed of bringing the Duchess into the bar if he had known that we were there. This was an outrageous lie. Francis would have brought the Duchess into the bar if the Archbishop of Canterbury were there—admittedly an unlikely contingency.)

When Eva said that this might improve matters and might also make it easier for Don to apologize, because he had stuck up for the Duchess, I felt lower than the worms.

Which is why I quarreled with Francis. And knew that was why. I had discovered that if one were feeling guilty one's instinct was to put the blame on somebody else as soon as possible.

Francis called to me from the bar door as I came up onto the terrace. I had been freed from RCI on the grounds of having replaced Laurent before lunch at short notice. He grinned at me. "Be an angel and take these cigarettes to Violetta's room, will you, please? I swear that woman smokes two at a time."

"I am sorry," I said. "I have no wish to run errands for the Duchess just now."

Francis, as usual, was reasonable. "How has she offended you?" he asked.

I told him about the Bradleys, about the possible invitation to Devonshire; I said that, thanks to the Duchess cutting such a pretty figure in the bar, not to mention the *Continental Mail,* my future was being seriously jeopardized. I saw Francis' eyebrows twitching.

He said, "Penelope, you are a thundering ass. These people are tedious *petits bourgeois,* and there is no reason to put on their act just because you happen to like their children. And I see no cause to protect anybody, whether aged seven or seventy, from the sight of Violetta drinking champagne."

"Mrs. Bradley said that no lady would behave in such a way."

"Tell Mrs. Bradley with my love and a kiss that if she were a tenth as much of a lady as Violetta she would have cause for pride. And I am not at all sure," he said, "that I like the idea of your staying with them in Devonshire."

This was, as the French said, the *comble.*

"Do you mean that you wouldn't let me go?" I asked, feeling as though I had been struck by lightning.

"I did not say that. I said I wasn't sure that I liked the idea."

"My God, why not?"

"Do not imagine when you say, 'My God,' " said Francis, "that you add strength to your protest. You merely add violence."

He could always make me feel a fool when he wanted to. And I could see that he was angry; less with me than with the Bradleys. He said, "I don't think much of the Smugs, darling, as you know. And I think less after this. Violetta is a very remarkable old girl, and if they knew what she went through in Rome when the Germans were there, some of that heroism might penetrate even their thick heads. Run along with those cigarettes now, will you please?"

I was trembling with rage; the worst kind of rage, hating me as well as everything else. I took the cigarettes with what I hoped was a dignified gesture, and went.

The Duchess was lying on the chaise longue under her window; she was swathed like a mummy in yards of cyclamen chiffon trimmed with marabou. She appeared to be reading three books at once: a novel by Ignazio Silone, Brewer's *Dictionary of Phrase and Fable,* and a *Handbook of Carpentry for Beginners.*

The room, the best of the rooms, having two balconies, had become unrecognizable. It worried me with its rampaging disorder. Three wardrobe trunks crowded it: many dresses, scarves, and pairs of small pointed shoes had escaped from the wardrobe trunks. The Duchess always brought with her large unexplained pieces of material; squares of velvet, crepe de chine, and damask, which she spread over the furniture. The writing table had been made to look like a table in a museum; she had put upon it a black crucifix and two iron candlesticks, a group of ivory figures, and a velvet book with metal clasps.

Despite the heat of the afternoon the windows were shut; the room smelled of smoke and scent.

"Beautiful—beautiful—beautiful!" said the Duchess, holding out her hands for the cigarettes. "There are the *bonbons au miel* on the bedside table. Help yourself liberally, and sit down and talk to me."

"No, thank you very much. If you will excuse me, Duchessa, I have to do some work now."

"I will not excuse you, darling. Sit down here. Do you know why I will not excuse you?"

I shook my head.

"Because I can see that you are unhappy, frustrated, and restless." She joined her fingertips and stared at me over the top of them. "Some of it I can guess," she said, "and some of it I should dearly like to know. Your mother would have known."

I was silent; she was hypnotic when she spoke of my mother, but I could not make myself ask her questions.

"Genius is not a comfortable possession. What do you want to do most in the world, Penelope?"

The truthful reply would have been, "To be like other people. To live in England; with an ordinary father and mother who do not keep a hotel. To stop having dooms; never to be told that I am a genius, and to have people of my own age to play with so that I need not spend my life listening to grownups."

I said, "I don't know."

The Duchess sighed and beat a tattoo with her little feet inside the marabou; they looked like clock-work feet.

"You are, beyond doubt, crying for the moon. Everybody at your age cries for the moon. But if you will not tell me which moon, I cannot be of assistance. What is the book that you are writing?"

"It is an Anthology of Hates," I said, and was much surprised that I had told her because I had not told anybody.

"Oho," said the Duchess. "Have you enough Hates to make an anthology?"

I nodded.

"Is freedom one of your hates?"

I frowned; I did not want to discuss the book with her at all and I could not understand her question. She was smiling in a maddening way that implied more knowledge of me than I myself had.

"Freedom is the most important thing that there is. You have more freedom than the average child knows. One day you will learn to value this and be grateful for it. I will tell you why." Her voice had taken on the singsong, lecturing note that preceded a fifteen-minute monologue. I stared at the figures on the writing table. She had let her cigarette lie burning in the ash tray, and a small spiral of smoke went up like incense before the crucifix; there was this, there was the hot scented room and the sound of her voice: "It is necessary to imprison children to a certain degree, for their discipline and their protection. In schools, they are largely hidden away from life, like bees in a hive. This means that they learn a measure of pleasant untruth; a scale of simple inadequate values that resemble the true values in life only as much as a plain colored poster of the Riviera resembles the actual coastline.

"When they emerge from the kindly-seeming prisons, they meet the world of true dimensions and true values. These are unexpectedly painful and irregular. Reality is always irregular and generally painful. To be unprepared for its shocks and to receive the shocks upon a foundation of innocence is the process of growing up. In your case, Penelope, you will be spared many of those pains. Not only do you have now a wealth of freedom which you cannot value because you have not experienced the opposite, but you are also endowing yourself with a future freedom; freedom from the fear and shock and shyness which make the transition from youth to maturity more uncomfortable than any other period of existence. Francis is bringing you up through the looking-glass, back-to-front. You are learning what the adult learns, and walking through these lessons toward the light-heartedness that is usually to be found in childhood but lost later. I wonder how long it will take you to find that out." She sat up on her elbows and stared at me again. "Do you know what I think will happen to your Anthology of Hates when you do find it out? You will read it through and find that these are not Hates any more."

By this last remark she had annoyed me profoundly, and now she clapped her hands and cried, "If young people were only allowed to gamble! It takes the mind off every anxiety. If I could take you to the Casino with me tonight, Penelope! Wouldn't that be splendid? Disguised as a young lady of fashion!" She sprang off the chaise longue, snatched the square of velvet from the bed and flung it over my shoulders. Its weight almost bore me to the ground; it was heavy as a tent and it smelled musty. "Look at yourself in the mirror!" cried the Duchess. "Beautiful—beautiful—beautiful! A Principessa!" She scuttled past me. "We will place this silver girdle here." She lashed it so tightly that it hurt my stomach; I was stifled; it felt like being dressed in a carpet. "Take this fan and these gloves." They were long white kid gloves, as hard as biscuits; she forced my fingers in and cajoled the gloves up my arms as far as the shoulders.

"The little amethyst circlet for your head."

She caught some single hairs as she adjusted it and put one finger in my eye. Sweat was trickling all over me.

"Now you have a very distinct resemblance to your mother," said the Duchess, standing before me and regarding me with her head on one side.

"This is the forecast of your womanhood. Will you please go downstairs at once and show yourself to Jeanne?"

I said that I would rather not. She was peevishly disappointed. I struggled out of the ridiculous costume; hot, dispirited, no fonder of myself than before, I got away.

V

My bedroom was on the ground floor, with a window that opened onto the far end of the terrace. It was late, but I was still awake and heard Francis and Jeanne talking outside. I did not mean to listen, but their voices were clear and when I heard the name "Bradley" I could not help listening.

"I agree with you," Jeanne said, "that it is all an outrageous fuss. But these Bradleys mean a great deal to Penelope."

"Wish I knew why," said Francis. "They represent the worst and dullest aspect of English 'county'; a breed that may soon become extinct and no loss, either."

"They are the kind of friends that she has never had; English children of her own age."

Their footsteps ceased directly outside my window. I heard Francis sigh. *"Ought* we to send her to school in England, do you think?"

"Perhaps next year."

"That will be too late, beloved."

I had heard him call Jeanne "beloved" before, but tonight the word touched my heart, perhaps because I was already unhappy; it made me want to cry. "She will be fifteen," Francis said. "First she'll kill herself trying to fit into the pattern and if she succeeds in the task, we shall never see her again. God knows what we'll get but it won't be Penelope."

"She will change in any case, whether she stays or goes, darling; they always do."

"Perhaps I've done a poor job with her from the beginning," Francis said: he spoke my mother's name. And then I was so sure I must listen no more, that I covered my ears with my hands. When I took them away Jeanne was saying, "You are always sad when your back is hurting you. Come to bed. Tomorrow I'll invite the Bradley children for lunch again; on Thursday when Violetta's in Monte Carlo."

"Why should we suck up to the Smugs?" Francis grumbled, and Jeanne replied, "Only because of Penelope, *tu le sais,*" and they walked away down the terrace.

I wept because they destroyed my defenses; my conscience still troubled me for the speeches of humbug that I had made to Eva, for quarreling with Francis, and for being uncivil to the Duchess. It was a weary load. If the Bradleys accepted the invitation to lunch, it would seem that God was not intending to punish me for it, but exactly the reverse, and that was a bewildering state of affairs.

By morning, however, God's plan became clear. Jeanne brought me my breakfast on the terrace. She sat with me while I ate it. I thought, as I had thought before, that she looked very young; more an elder sister than a stepmother, with her short, flying dark hair, the blue eyes in the brown face, the long slim brown legs. She smoked a *caporal* cigarette.

I could hardly wait for her to tell me whether she had healed the breach with the Bradleys. But I dared not ask. Their talk on the terrace had been too intimate for me to admit that I had heard it. She said, "Penelope, the situation with your friends at La Lézardière has become a little complex."

My heart beat downward heavily and I did not want to eat any more.

"I thought that it would give you pleasure if I asked them to lunch and would perhaps clear up any misunderstanding. But I have been talking to Mrs. Bradley and apparently she would prefer them not to visit the hotel."

I did not know whether I was blushing for the hotel, for my own disappointment, or for the Bradleys; I was only aware of the blush, flaming all over my skin, most uncomfortably.

"Mrs. Bradley was friendly and polite, you must not think otherwise. She wants you to swim with them as much as you like; she said that she hoped you would go out in the speedboat again. But her exact phrase was, 'We feel that the hotel surroundings are just a little too grown-up for Don and Eva.'"

I was silent.

"So, I thought that I would tell you. And ask you not to be unhappy about it. People are entitled to their views, you know, even when one does not oneself agree with them."

"Thank you, Jeanne: I am not at all unhappy," I said, wishing that my voice would not shake. "And if the Bradleys will not come to me, I am damned if I am going to them." And I rose from the table. She came after me, but when she saw that I was near to tears she gave me a pat on the back and left me alone.

This was the point at which I discovered that hate did not cast out love, but that it was, on the contrary, possible to hate and love at the same time. I could not turn off my infatuation for the Bradleys, much as I longed to do so. They were still the desirable Vikings. The stately pink villa above the orange trees, the gray rocks where the diving board jutted and the speedboat lay at anchor, remained the site of romance, the target of forlorn hopes. It hurt me to shake my head and retire from the flat rock when Don and Eva beckoned me. They seemed to understand quickly enough, more quickly than their parents did. Mr. Bradley still called, "Coming aboard?" and Mrs. Bradley waved to me elaborately on every possible occasion. The children turned their heads away. For two days I saw them all like figures set behind a glass screen; only the echo of their voices reached me; I gave up haunting the beach and worked in a corner of the garden; the regularity of their timetable made it easy to avoid the sight of them. I told myself that they were loathsome, that they were the Smugs, that Don and Eva were both candidates for RCI. I even considered including them in the Anthology of Hates, but I found it too difficult. Now they had indeed become the moon that the Duchess told me I cried for. I cherished dreams of saving Don's life or Eva's at great risk to myself, and being humbly thanked and praised by their parents. Then I hoped that they would all die in a fire, or better still that I would die and they would come to my funeral.

In these two days I found myself looking at my home differently; seeing it in Bradley perspective. I had been plagued by the crises and irregularities but never ashamed of them. Was I ashamed now? I could not be sure; the feeling was one of extra detachment and perception; I was more than ever aware of the garden's bright colors, of the garlic smells from the kitchen, of the dusky coolness in the bar; every time that I walked through the salon I looked at it with startled visitors' eyes; Bradleys' eyes:

"It's pretty, of course; it's like a little room in a museum, but it isn't the sort of place where one wants to *sit*." The terrace with the blue and white umbrellas above the tables, the stone jars on the balustrade, the lizards flickering along the wall, seemed as temporary as the deck of a ship on a short voyage. I felt as though I were staying here, not living here. And there was no consolation in my own room with my own books because here the saddest thoughts came and they seemed to hang in the room waiting for me, as palpable as the tented mosquito net above the bed.

I found that I was seeing Francis, Jeanne, and the Duchess through a grotesque lens; they were at once complete strangers and people whom I knew intimately. I could place them in a Bradley context, thinking, "That is Francis Wells, the poet, the poet who keeps the mad hotel. He always seems to wear the same red shirt. He looks like Mephistopheles when he laughs. And that is his wife, his *second* wife; younger than he is; very gay always, isn't she? What very *short* shorts. And there goes the Duchessa de Terracini, rather a terrible old lady who gambles at the Casino and drinks champagne; doesn't she look ridiculous in all that make-up and chiffon?" And then I would be talking to them in my own voice and with my own thoughts and feeling like a traitor.

I knew that they were sorry for me; that Francis above all approved my defiant refusal. I was aware of their hands held back from consoling gestures, to spare me too much overt sympathy. Even the Duchess did not speak to me of the Bradleys.

For once I welcomed the crises as diversion. And these two days naturally were not free from crisis; a British ambassador and his wife found themselves *en panne* at our gates. All the entrails of their car fell out upon the road and we were obliged to give them rooms for the night.

This would not of itself have been other than a mechanical crisis, because the ambassador and Francis were old friends. Unfortunately the ambassador and the press baron from Cap d'Ail, who was dining with the Duchess, were old enemies. So a fierce political fight was waged in the bar, with both elderly gentlemen calling each other poltroon, and they would have fought a duel had not the electric current failed and the hotel been plunged in darkness till morning. (My only grief was that Don and Eva had missed it. All roads led to the Bradleys.)

On the third morning, which was Thursday, doom accelerated. I woke to find Francis standing beside my bed.

"Sorry, darling; trouble," he said. "A telephone call just came through from Aix; Jeanne's mother is very ill and I'm going to drive her over there now. Can you take care of you for today?"

He never asked me such questions: this was like a secret signal saying, "I know you are miserable and I am sorry."

"But of course. Please don't worry."

"There are no guests, thank God. Violetta's going over to Monte Carlo; Laurent will be in charge tonight. You might see that he locks up, if I'm not back."

"I will do that."

"But don't let him lock Violetta out, for Heaven's sake."

"I will see that he does not. Can I help Jeanne or do anything for you?"

"No, my love. We are off now. I'll telephone you later." He ducked under the mosquito curtain to kiss me.

"You must pray rather than worry," the Duchess said to me, standing on the doorstep. For her expedition to Monte Carlo, she wore a coat and skirt of white shantung, a bottle-green frilly blouse, and the usual chiffon scarf. She was topped by a bottle-green tricorn hat with a green veil descending from it. "Death is a part of life," she added, pulling on her white gloves.

I could feel little emotion for my stepgrandmother who lived in seclusion near Aix-en-Provence, but I was sorry for Jeanne.

"The best thing that you could do, Penelope," said the Duchess, grasping her parasol like a spear, "would be to come over with me to

73

Monte Carlo. We will lunch delightfully on the balcony of the Hotel de Paris; then you shall eat ices while I am at the tables; then a little stroll and a little glass and we could dine on the port at Villefranche and drive home under the moon. The moon is at the full tonight and I look forward to it. *Viens, chérie, ça te changera les idées,"* she added, holding out her hand.

I thanked her very much and said that I would rather stay here.

When she was placed inside the high purple Isotta-Fraschini, I thought that she and her old hooky chauffeur looked like a Punch-and-Judy show. The car was box-shaped with a fringed canopy under the roof and they swayed as it moved off. I waved good-by.

The first part of the day seemed endless. I sat in the garden on a stone bench under the largest of the umbrella pines. That way I had my back to La Lézardière. I could hear their voices and that was all. When the bell rang for their lunch, I went down to the pool and swam. I swam for longer than usual; then I climbed to the flat rock and lay in the sun. I was almost asleep when I heard Eva's voice. "Penelope!"

She was halfway up the rock; she said, "Look; we are so miserable we've written you this note. I have to go back and rest now." She was like a vision out of the long past; the freckles, the sunburn, and the wet hair. I watched her scuttle down and she turned to wave to me from the lowest tier of the terrace. I gave her a half-wave and opened the note.

It said:

Dear Penelope,
Please don't be cross with us. Mum and Dad are going out to supper tonight. Don't you think that you could come? They have asked us to ask you.
Always your friends,
Don and Eva.

I wrote my reply at the *écritoire* in the salon. I wrote:

Much as I appreciate the invitation, I am unable to accept it. Owing to severe illness in the family my father and stepmother have left for Aix. I feel it necessary to stay here and keep an eye on things.
Penelope.

To run no risk of meeting them, I went into the bar and asked Laurent if he would be so kind as to leave this note at La Lézardière.

Laurent was in one of his moods; he replied sarcastically that it gave him great pleasure to run errands and do favors for young ladies who had not the energy to perform these for themselves. I echoed the former cook's husband, the assassin, and said, *"Salaud,"* but not until he was gone.

After I had answered the note, I alternated between wishing that I had accepted and wishing that I had given them more truthful reasons for my refusal.

Later, I sought comfort by writing to my aunt in England; I sat there conjuring the fortnight as it would be and putting in the letter long descriptions of the things that I wanted to see and do again. It helped. I had covered twelve pages when the telephone rang.

Francis' voice spoke over a bad line: "Hello, Child of Confusion. Everything all right?"

"Yes, indeed. Nothing is happening at all. What is the news?"

"Better," he said. "But Jeanne will have to stay. I may be very late getting back. See that Laurent gives you the cold lobster. Jeanne sends her love."

Nothing would have induced me to ask Laurent for my dinner, but I was perfectly capable of getting it myself and the reference to cold lobster had made me hungry. No reason why I should not eat my dinner at six o'clock. I was on my way to the kitchen by way of the terrace when I heard a voice calling me:

"Penelope!"

I turned, feeling that horrible all-over blush begin. Mrs. Bradley stood at the doorway from the salon onto the terrace. She looked golden and statuesque in a white dress with a scarlet belt. The sight of her was painful. It seemed as though I had forgotten how lovely she was.

"May I talk to you a moment, my dear?"

"Please do," I said, growing hotter and hotter.

"Shall we sit here?" She took a chair beneath one of the blue and white umbrellas. She motioned to me to take the other chair. I said, "Thank you, but I prefer to stand."

She smiled at me. I could feel in my heart the alarming collision of love and hate and now I could see her in two contexts; as a separate symbol, the enemy; as a beloved haunting of my own mind, the Mrs. Bradley of the first days, whom I had made my private possession. Her arms and hands were beautifully shaped, pale brown now against the white of her dress.

"Can't we be friends, Penelope? I think we can, you know, if we try. Don and Eva are so sad and it all seems such a pity."

I said, "But, Mrs. Bradley, you made it happen."

"No, dear. That is what I want to put right. When I talked to your stepmother, I made it quite clear that we all hoped to see much more of you."

"But," I said, "that Don and Eva couldn't come here. As though it were an awful place."

She put her hand on mine; she gave a soft low laugh. "Penelope, how foolish of you. Of course it isn't an awful place. You have just imagined our thinking that, you silly child."

"Did I imagine what you said about the Duchess?"

Still she smiled and kept her hand on mine. "I expect that what I said about the Duchess was quite a little exaggerated to you by Eva and Don. That was an uncomfortable day for all of us. We don't often quarrel in our family; I don't suppose that you do, either. Quarrels are upsetting to everybody and nobody likes them."

"Certainly," I said, "I don't like them."

"Let's try to end this one, Penelope."

Did she guess how badly I wanted to end it? I could not tell.

"Supposing," she said, "that you let me put my point of view to you, as one grown-up person to another. You are very grown-up for your age, you know."

"I do know, and I deplore it."

She gave another little low laugh. "Well, I shouldn't go on deploring it if I were you. Think what a dull world it would be if we were all made alike."

I winced inside at the cliché because Francis had taught me to wince at clichés. But I pretended that she had not said it. She went on: "Listen, dear. Just because you are so grown-up and this place is your home, you have a very different life from the life that Don and Eva have. I'm not saying that one sort of life is right and the other wrong. They just happen to be different. Now, my husband and I have to judge what is good for Don and Eva, don't we? You'll agree? Just as your father and stepmother have to judge what is good for you."

"Yes. I agree to that." It sounded reasonable; the persuasion of her manner was beginning to work.

"Well, we think that they aren't quite grown-up enough yet to understand and appreciate all the things that you understand and appreciate. That's all. It's as though you had a stronger digestion and could eat foods that might upset them. Do you see?"

When I was still silent, she added, "I think you should. Your stepmother saw perfectly."

"I suppose I see."

"Do try."

In fact I was trying hard; but the struggle was different from the struggle that she imagined. I felt as though I were being pulled over the line in a tug of war. Inside me there was a voice saying, "No, no. This is wrong. Nothing that she says can make it right. It is not a matter of seeing her point of view; you *can* see it; she has sold it to you. But you mustn't surrender." Oddly, the voice seemed to be the voice of the Duchess. I felt as though the Duchess were inside me, arguing.

I looked into the lovely, smiling face. "Do try," Mrs. Bradley repeated. "And do please come and have supper with the children tonight. Let's start all over again; shall we?"

When she held out both hands to me, she had won. I found myself in her arms and she was kissing my hair. I heard her say, "Poor little girl."

VI

Only the smallest shadow stayed in my heart and I forgot it for long minutes. We talked our heads off. It was like meeting them again after years. I found myself quoting in my head: "And among the grass shall find the golden dice wherewith we played of yore." They still loved me; they still laughed at everything I said. When I ended the description of the ambassador fighting the press baron and the failure of the electric lights, they were sobbing in separate corners of the sofa.

"Go on; go on. What did the Duchess do?"

"I think she enjoyed it mightily. She had an electric torch in her bag and she flashed it over them both like a searchlight."

"You do have the loveliest time," said Eva.

"Where is the Duchess tonight?" asked Don.

"In fact I think I heard her car come back about ten minutes ago." I began to describe the car and the chauffeur.

"*Older* than the Duchess? He can't be. I'd love to see them bouncing away under the fringe. Let's go out and look."

"Too late," I said. "At night he takes the car to the garage in Théoule."

"Hark, though," Don said. "There's a car now." He ran to the window; but I knew that it wasn't the Isotta-Fraschini. It was the putt-putt noise of Laurent's little Peugeot.

"How exactly like Laurent," I said. "As soon as the Duchess gets home, he goes out for the evening. And Francis has left him in charge."

It occurred to me now that I should go back. I reminded myself that Charlemagne was an effective watchdog. But I was not comfortable about it.

"D'you mean you ought to go and put the Duchess to bed? Undo her stays; help her off with her wig?"

"It isn't a wig; it's her own hair, and she requires no help. But I do think I should go back. The telephone may ring."

"Well then, the Duchess will answer it."

"She will not. She claims that she has never answered a telephone in her life. She regards them as an intrusion upon privacy."

"Isn't there anybody else in the hotel?"

"No."

"Oh you *can't* go yet," said Eva.

I sat on a little longer. Then I knew that it was no good. "I shall have remorse if I don't," I said, "and that is the worst thing."

"All right, then. We'll go with you."

"Oh, Don—" said Eva.

"Mum and Dad won't be back yet awhile," said Don, "and we'll only stay ten minutes."

"They'll be furious."

"We won't tell them."

Eva looked at me. I said, "I cannot decide for you. I only know I must go."

"Of course if you want to stay behind," Don said to Eva.

"Of course I don't. What shall we say to Nanny?"

"We can say we went down to the beach."

We crept out, silent in the spirit of adventure. The moon had risen, the full moon, promised by the Duchess, enormous and silver and sad; its light made a splendid path over the sea; the palms and the orange trees, the rock shapes on the water, were all sharp and black.

"Here we go on Tom Tiddler's ground," Eva sang. We took the short cut, scrambling through the oleander hedge instead of going round by the gate. I could hear Don panting with excitement beside me. Almost, their mood could persuade me that the hotel was an enchanted place. We came onto the terrace and darted into the empty bar; Laurent had turned off the lights; I turned them up for the Bradleys to look at the photographs.

"What'll we drink?" said Don facetiously, hopping onto a stool.

"Champagne," said Eva.

"If the Duchess was still awake, she'd give us some champagne."

"You wouldn't drink it," said Eva.

"I would."

"You wouldn't."

"I jolly well would."

"She's probably in the salon," I said. "She never goes to bed early."

I put out the lights again and led them to the salon by way of the terrace. The salon lights were lit. We looked through the windows.

"There she is," said Don. "She's lying on the sofa."

They bounded in ahead of me. I heard Don say, "Good evening, Duchessa," and Eva echoed it. There was no reply from the Duchess. With the Bradleys, I stood still staring at her. She was propped on the Empire sofa; her red head had fallen sideways on the stiff satin cushion. Her little pointed shoes and thin ankles stuck out from the hem of her shantung skirt and the skirt, which was of great width, drooped down over the edge of the sofa to the floor. On the table beside her she had placed the green tricorn hat, the green scarf, and her green velvet bag. A bottle of champagne stood in an ice pail; the glass had fallen to the floor; since one of her arms dangled limply, I thought that she must have dropped the glass as she went off to sleep.

"Please wake up, Duchessa; we want some champagne," said Don. He took a step forward and peered into her face, which was turned away from us.

"She looks sort of horrid," he said; "I think she's ill."

For no reason that I could understand I felt that it was impertinent of him to be leaning there so close to her. When he turned back to us, I saw that his face was pale; the freckles were standing out distinctly on the bridge of his nose.

"She is ill, I'm sure," he said. "She's unconscious." He looked at the bottle of champagne. "She must be—" He stopped. I saw that he thought that the Duchess was intoxicated and that he could not bring himself to say so.

"Let's go," Eva said in a thin scared voice. She grabbed Don's hand. "Come on, Penelope. Quick."

"But of course I'm not coming."

They halted. "You can't stay here," Don said. Eva was shivering. There was no sound nor movement from the figure on the sofa. I said, "Certainly I can stay here. What else can I do? If she is ill, I must look after her."

I saw them straining against their own panic. Suddenly they seemed like puppies, very young indeed.

"But *we* can't stay here," Eva said. "Oh, please, Penelope, come with us."

"No indeed. But you go," I said. "It's what you want to do isn't it?"

"It's what we ought to do," Eva stammered through chattering teeth. Don looked a little more doubtful. "Look here, Penelope, you needn't stay with her. When they—they get like that, they sleep it off."

Now I was angry with him. "Please go at once," I said. "This is my affair. And I know what you mean and it isn't true." I found that I had clapped my hands to shoo them off; they went; I heard the panic rush of their feet on the terrace. I was alone with the Duchess.

Now that they were gone, I had no hesitation in approaching her. I said softly, "Hello, Duchessa. It's only me," and I bent above her as Don had done. I saw what he had seen; the shrunken look of the white face with the false eyelashes. Indeed she looked shrunken all over, like a very old doll.

I lowered my head until my ear touched the green frilled chiffon at her breast. I listened for the beat of her heart. When I could not hear it, I lifted the little pointed hand and felt the wrist. There was no pulse here that I could find.

I despised myself because I began to shiver as Eva Bradley had shivered. My fingers would not stay still; it was difficult to unfasten the clasp of the green velvet bag. I thought that there would be a pocket mirror inside and that I must hold this to her lips. Searching for the mirror I found other treasures; the ivory hand that she had aimed at Francis, a cut-glass smelling-bottle, some colored plaques from the Casino, a chain holding a watch, and a cluster of seals.

The mirror, when I found it, was in a folding morocco case with visiting cards in the pocket on the other side. I said, "Excuse me, please, Duchessa," as I held it in front of her face. I held it there a long time; when I took it away the bright surface was unclouded. I knew that the Duchess was dead.

A profound curiosity took away my fear. I had never seen a person lying dead before. It was so strange to think of someone I knew well, as having stopped. But the more I stared at her, the less she looked as though she had stopped; rather, she had gone. This was not the Duchess lying here; it was a little old doll, a toy thing of which the Duchess had now no need. Where, I wondered, had she gone? What had happened to all the things that she remembered, the fencing lessons, and the child's dreams, and the Emperor? What happened, I wondered, to the memories that you carried around in your head? Did they go on with your soul or would a soul not want them? What did a soul want? Did the Duchess's soul like roulette? Theology had never been my strongest subject and I found myself baffled by the rush of abstract questions flowing through my mind.

Then I became aware of her in relation to me. It was impossible to believe that I would not talk to her again. I was suddenly deeply sorry that I had not dined with her on the first evening, that I had not gone down in the fancy-dress to show myself to Jeanne. She had asked me to do this; she had asked me to come to Monte Carlo with her. *"Viens, chérie, ça te changera les idées."* Always she had been kind. I had not. I had never been nice to her because she embarrassed me and now I should never have another chance to be nice to her.

Automatically I began to perform small meaningless services. I covered her face with the green scarf, drawing it round her head so that it made a dignified veil. I fetched a rug and laid it across her feet; I did not want to see the little shoes. I carried the untouched champagne back to the bar. I lifted her tricorn hat, her bag and gloves off the table; I took them up to her room. It was more difficult to be in her room, with the bed turned down and the night clothes laid there, than it was to be in the salon with her body. I put the hat, bag, and gloves down on the nearest chair and I was running out when I saw the crucifix on the table. I thought that she might be pleased to have this near her ("Although," I said to myself, "she isn't there any more, one still goes on behaving as if she is"), and I carried it down; I set it on the table beside her. There seemed to be too many lights here now. I turned off all but one lamp; this room became a suitable place for her to lie in state, the elegant little shell of a room with the Empire furnishings. I pulled a high-backed chair from the wall, set it at the foot of the sofa, and sat down to watch with her.

Outside the windows the moonlight lay in the garden. I heard her saying, "The moon is at the full tonight. I look forward to it." I heard her saying, "Naturally, you cry for the moon." I heard her saying, "Death is a part of life," as she pulled on her white gloves.

At intervals I was afraid again; the fear came and went like intermittent seasickness. I did not know what brought it. She was so small and still and gone that I could not fear her. But I felt as though I were waiting for a dreadful thing to walk upon the terrace, and the only poem that would stay in my head was one that had always frightened me a little, "The Lykewake Dirge":

>This ae nighte, this ae nighte,
>Everye nighte and alle,
>Fire and sleet and candlelyte,
>And Christe receive thy saule.

It made shivers down my back. I would have liked to fetch Charlemagne from his kennel, but I had heard that dogs howled in the presence of the dead and this I did not want.

Sitting there so stiffly I became terribly tired: "But it is a vigil," I said to myself, "and it is all that I can do for her." It was not much. It was no true atonement for having failed her in kindness; it could not remit my having betrayed her to the Bradleys. It seemed hours since I had thought of the Bradleys. Now I wondered whether the parents had returned, and with the question there came incredulity that Don and Eva should not have come back. They had simply run off and left me, because they were afraid. The memory of their scared faces made them small and silly in my mind. Beside it, I uncovered the memory of my talk with Mrs. Bradley: the talk that had left a shadow. I admitted the shadow now: it was the note of patronage at the end of all the spellbinding. She had called me "poor little girl."

"You never called me poor little girl," I said in my thoughts to the Duchess. She had called me fortunate and a genius. She had spoken to me of the world, of freedom and maturity. That was truly grown-up conversation. In comparison the echo of Mrs. Bradley saying, "As one grown-up person to another," sounded fraudulent. Some of the magic had left the Bradleys tonight.

I was so tired. I did not mean to sleep, because this was vigil. But I found my head falling forward and the moonlight kept vanishing and the Duchess' voice was quite loud in my ears. "Of death," she said, "I remember three things; being tired, being quiet, and being gone. That's how it is, Penelope." She seemed to think that I could not hear her. She went on calling, "Penelope! Penelope!"

I sat up with a start. Somebody was in fact calling "Penelope": a man's voice from the terrace. I climbed down stiffly from the chair. "Who's that?" I asked, my voice sounding cracked and dry. Mr. Bradley stood against the moonlight.

"Are you there, child? Yes, you are. Come along out of this at once." He looked large and golden and worried; he seized my hand; then he saw the Duchess on the sofa.

"Lord," he said. "She's still out, is she?" He started again. "Did you cover her up like that?"

"Yes. Please talk quietly," I said. "She is dead."

He dropped my hand, lifted the scarf a little way from her face, and put it back. I saw him looking at the crucifix.

"I put it there. I thought that she would like it. I am watching by her," I said.

He looked pale, ruffled, not the way, I thought, that grown-up people should look. "I'm terribly sorry," he said in a subdued voice. "Terribly sorry. Young Don came along to our room, said he couldn't sleep for knowing you were over here with her. Of course he didn't think—"

"I know what he thought, Mr. Bradley," I said coldly. "Don and Eva are only babies really. Thank you for coming, just the same."

He said, in his officer-to-men voice, "Out of here now. There's a good girl."

"I beg your pardon?"

"You're coming to our house. I'll telephone the doctor from there." He took my hand again; I pulled it free.

"I'll stay with her, please. You telephone the doctor."

He looked down at me, amazed, almost smiling. He dropped his voice again. "No, no, no, Penelope. You mustn't stay."

I said, "I must."

"No, you mustn't. You can't do her any good."

"It is a vigil."

"That's just morbid and foolish. You're coming over to our house now."

"I am not."

"Yes, you are," he said, and he picked me up in his arms. To struggle in the presence of the Duchess would have been unseemly. I remained tractable, staying in his arms until he had carried me onto the terrace. He began to put me down and at once I twisted free.

"I'm not coming with you. I'm staying with her. She is my friend and she is not your friend. You were rude about her, and stupid," I said to him.

He grabbed me again and I fought: he imprisoned me with my arms to my sides. For the moment he did not try to lift me. He simply held me there.

"Listen, Penelope, don't be hysterical. I'm doing what's best for you. That's all. You can't possibly sit up all night alone with the poor old lady; it's nearly one o'clock now."

"I shall stay with her till dawn; and she is not a poor old lady, just because she is dead. That is a ridiculous cliché."

I was aware of his face close to mine, the stony, regular features, the blue eyes and clipped mustache in the moonlight. The face seemed to struggle for speech. Then it said, "I don't want insolence any more than I want hysteria. You just pipe down and come along. This is no place for you."

"It is my home," I said.

He shook me gently. "Have some sense, will you? I wouldn't let my kids do what you're doing and I won't let you do it."

"Your children," I said, "wouldn't want to do it anyway; they are, in vulgar parlance, a couple of sissies."

At this he lifted me off my feet again and I struck at his face. I had the absurd idea that the Duchess had come to stand in the doorway and was cheering me on. And at this moment there came the miracle. The noise of the car sweeping in from the road was not the little noise of Laurent's car, but the roaring powerful engine that meant that Francis had come home.

The headlights swung yellow upon the moonlit garden. Still aloft in Mr. Bradley's clutch I said, "That is my father, who will be able to handle the situation with dignity."

He set me down as Francis braked the car and jumped out.

"That you, Bradley?" said Francis. "What, precisely, are you doing?"

Mr. Bradley said, "I am trying to make your daughter behave in a sensible manner. I'm very glad to see you."

Francis came up the steps onto the terrace. He sounded so weary that I knew his back hurt him: "Why should it be your concern to make my daughter behave in any manner whatsoever?"

"Really, Wells, you'll have to know the story. There's been a tragedy here tonight, I'm afraid. Just doing what I could to help."

"I will tell him," I said. I was grateful for Francis' arm holding me; my legs had begun to feel as though they were made of spaghetti.

"You let me do the talking, young woman," said Mr. Bradley.

"If you don't mind, I'd prefer to hear it from Penelope," said Francis.

I told him. I told him slowly, leaving out none of it; there seemed less and less breath in my lungs as I continued. "And Mr. Bradley called it morbid and foolish and removed me by force," I ended.

"Very silly of you, Bradley," said Francis.

"Damn it, look at the state she's in!"

"Part of which might be due to your methods of persuasion, don't you think? All right, Penelope, easy now." I could not stop shivering.

"Leaving her alone like that in a place like this. You ought to be ashamed of yourself," Mr. Bradley boomed.

"Quiet, please," said Francis in his most icy voice.

"Damned if I'll be quiet. It's a disgrace and I don't want any part of it."

"Nobody," I said, "asked you to take any part in it, Mr. Bradley."

"Hush," said Francis. "Mr. Bradley meant to be kind and you must be grateful."

"I am not in the least."

"Fine manners you teach her," said Mr. Bradley.

"Quiet, please," said Francis again. "Penelope has perfect manners, mitigated at the moment by perfect integrity and a certain amount of overstrain." Looking up at him, I could see the neat Mephistophelean profile, the delicate shape of his head. I loved him more than I had ever loved him. Mr. Bradley, large and blowing like a bull, was outside this picture, nothing to do with either of us.

Suddenly he looked as though he realized this. He said: "I don't want my wife or my kids mixed up in it either."

"Mixed up in what, precisely?" Francis asked.

I said, "It is possible that he is referring to the inquest. Or do you mean mixed up with me? Because if you do, no problem should arise. After tonight I have not the slightest wish to be mixed up with them or you."

It would have been more effective had I been able to stop shivering; I was also feeling rather sick, never a help when attempting to make dignified speeches.

Mr. Bradley faded away in the moonlight.

Francis said gently, "Did you mean it? It is easy to say those things in anger."

"I think I meant it. Was the vigil, in your opinion, the right thing to do?"

"It was. I am very pleased with you."

I said, "But I am not sure that I can continue with it for a moment. I feel funny."

Francis took me into the bar; he poured out a glass of brandy and a glass of water, making me drink them in alternate swallows.

"Of course," he said gloomily, "it may make you sick. In which event the last state will be worse than the first."

But it did not; it made me warm.

"They can't *help* being the Smugs, can they?" I said suddenly, and then for the first time I wanted to cry.

"They're all right," said Francis. "They are merely lacking in imagination."

I managed to say, "Sorry," and no more. I knew that he disliked me to cry. This time he said, watching me, "On some occasions it is better to weep."

I put my head down on the table and sobbed, "If only she could come back; I would be nice."

Francis said, "You gave her great pleasure always."

"Oh, not enough."

"Nobody can give anybody enough."

"Not ever?"

"No, not ever. But one must go on trying."

"And doesn't one ever value people until they are gone?"

"Rarely," said Francis.

I went on weeping; I saw how little I had valued him; how little I had valued anything that was mine. Presently he said, "Do you think that you can cry quite comfortably by yourself for a few minutes because I must telephone the doctor?"

Though I said, "Yes, indeed," I stopped crying immediately. As I sat waiting for him, I was saying good-by, to my first dead, to a love that was ended, and to my dream of being like other people.

The next day I tore the Anthology of Hates into pieces and cast the pieces into the sea. I did not read through the pages first, so certain was I that I had done with hating.

Aldous Huxley

YOUNG ARCHIMEDES

"Young Archimedes" is the youthful genius Guido, an attractive
little Italian boy who is gifted to an astonishing degree in both
music and mathematics. Guido's comprehension of symphonic
music and his unusual grasp of the principles of mathematics,
which would normally be far beyond the grasp of a boy twice his
age, are of compelling interest to Aldous Huxley, who is
well qualified not only to appreciate the extraordinary nature
of the boy's mental powers but also to see their interrelationship.
Against a background of desperate human conflict over the
exploitation of little Guido's musical abilities, the tragedy
develops. The course of true genius in this world is not
destined to run smooth.

Men cannot live at ease except where they have mastered
their surroundings and where their accumulated lives outnumber and
outweigh the vegetative lives about them. Stripped of its dark woods,
planted, terraced, and tilled almost to the mountains' tops, the Tuscan
landscape is humanised and safe. Sometimes upon those who live in the
midst of it there comes a longing for some place that is solitary, inhuman, lifeless, or peopled only with alien life. But the longing is soon
satisfied, and one is glad to return to the civilised and submissive scene.

I found that house on the hilltop the ideal dwelling-place. For there,
safe in the midst of a humanised landscape, one was yet alone; one could
be as solitary as one liked. Neighbours whom one never sees at close
quarters are the ideal and perfect neighbours.

Our nearest neighbours, in terms of physical proximity, lived very
near. We had two sets of them, as a matter of fact, almost in the same
house with us. One was the peasant family, who lived in a long, low
building, part dwelling-house, part stables, storerooms and cowsheds,
adjoining the villa. Our other neighbours—intermittent neighbours,
however, for they only ventured out of town every now and then, during the most flawless weather—were the owners of the villa, who had
reserved for themselves the smaller wing of the huge L-shaped house—
a mere dozen rooms or so—leaving the remaining eighteen or twenty
to us.

They were a curious couple, our proprietors. An old husband, grey, listless, tottering, seventy at least; and a signora of about forty, short, very plump, with tiny fat hands and feet and a pair of very large, very dark black eyes, which she used with all the skill of a born comedian. Her vitality, if you could have harnessed it and made it do some useful work, would have supplied a whole town with electric light. The physicists talk of deriving energy from the atom; they would be more profitably employed nearer home—in discovering some way of tapping those enormous stores of vital energy which accumulate in unemployed women of sanguine temperament and which, in the present imperfect state of social and scientific organisation, vent themselves in ways that are generally so deplorable: in interfering with other people's affairs, in working up emotional scenes, in thinking about love and making it, and in bothering men till they cannot get on with their work.

Signora Bondi got rid of her superfluous energy, among other ways, by "doing in" her tenants. The old gentleman, who was a retired merchant with a reputation for the most perfect rectitude, was allowed to have no dealings with us. When we came to see the house, it was the wife who showed us round. It was she who, with a lavish display of charm, with irresistible rollings of the eyes, expatiated on the merits of the place, sang the praises of the electric pump, glorified the bathroom (considering which, she insisted, the rent was remarkably moderate), and when we suggested calling in a surveyor to look over the house, earnestly begged us, as though our well-being were her only consideration, not to waste our money unnecessarily in doing anything so superfluous. "After all," she said, "we are honest people. I wouldn't dream of letting you the house except in perfect condition. Have confidence." And she looked at me with an appealing, pained expression in her magnificent eyes, as though begging me not to insult her by my coarse suspiciousness. And leaving us no time to pursue the subject of surveyors any further, she began assuring us that our little boy was the most beautiful angel she had ever seen. By the time our interview with Signora Bondi was at an end, we had definitely decided to take the house.

"Charming woman," I said, as we left the house. But I think that Elizabeth was not quite so certain of it as I.

Then the pump episode began.

On the evening of our arrival in the house we switched on the electricity. The pump made a very professional whirring noise; but no water came out of the taps in the bathroom. We looked at one another doubtfully.

"Charming woman?" Elizabeth raised her eyebrows.

We asked for interviews; but somehow the old gentleman could never see us, and the Signora was invariably out or indisposed. We left notes; they were never answered. In the end, we found that the only method of communicating with our landlords, who were living in the same house with us, was to go down into Florence and send a registered express letter to them. For this they had to sign two separate receipts and even, if we chose to pay forty centimes more, a third incriminating document, which was then returned to us. There could be no pretending, as there always was with ordinary letters or notes, that the communication had never been received. We began at last to get answers to our complaints. The Signora, who wrote all the letters, started by telling us that, naturally, the pump didn't work, as the cisterns were empty, owing to the long drought. I had to walk three miles to the post office in order to register my letter reminding her that there had been a violent thunderstorm only last Wednesday, and that the tanks were consequently more than half full. The answer came back: bath water had not been guaranteed in the contract; and if I wanted it, why hadn't I had the pump looked at before I took the house? Another walk into town to ask the Signora next door whether she remembered her adjurations to us to have confidence in her, and to imform her that the existence in a house of a bathroom was in itself an implicit guarantee of bath water. The reply to that was that the Signora couldn't continue to have communications with people who wrote so rudely to her. After that I put the matter into the hands of a lawyer. Two months later the pump was actually replaced. But we had to serve a writ on the lady before she gave in. And the costs were considerable.

One day, towards the end of the episode, I met the old gentleman in the road, taking his big maremman dog for a walk—or being taken, rather, for a walk by the dog. For where the dog pulled the old gentleman had perforce to follow. And when it stopped to smell, or scratch the ground, or leave against a gatepost its visiting-card or an offensive challenge, patiently, at his end of the leash, the old man had to wait. I passed him standing at the side of the road, a few hundred yards below our house. The dog was sniffing at the roots of one of the twin cypresses which grew one on either side of the entry to a farm; I heard the beast growling indignantly to itself, as though it scented an intolerable insult. Old Signor Bondi, leashed to his dog, was waiting. The knees inside the tubular grey trousers were slightly bent. Leaning on his cane, he stood gazing mournfully and vacantly at the view. The whites of his old eyes were discoloured, like ancient billiard balls. In the grey, deeply wrinkled face, his nose was dyspeptically red. His white moustache, ragged and yellowing at the fringes, drooped in a melancholy curve. In his black tie he wore a very large diamond; perhaps that was what Signora Bondi had found so attractive about him.

I took off my hat as I approached. The old man stared at me absently, and it was only when I was already almost past him that he recollected who I was.

"Wait," he called after me, "wait!" And he hastened down the road in pursuit. Taken utterly by surprise and at a disadvantage—for it was engaged in retorting to the affront imprinted on the cypress roots—the dog permitted itself to be jerked after him. Too much astonished to be anything but obedient, it followed its master. "Wait!"

I waited.

"My dear sir," said the old gentleman, catching me by the lapel of my coat and blowing most disagreeably in my face, "I want to apologise." He looked around him, as though afraid that even here he might be overheard. "I want to apologise," he went on, "about that wretched pump business. I assure you that, if it had been only my affair, I'd have put the thing right as soon as you asked. You were quite right: a bathroom is an implicit guarantee of bath water. I saw from the first that we should have no chance if it came to court. And besides, I think one ought to treat one's tenants as handsomely as one can afford to. But my wife"—he lowered his voice—"the fact is that she likes this sort of thing, even when she knows that she's in the wrong and must lose. And besides, she hoped, I dare say, that you'd get tired of asking and have the job done yourself. I told her from the first that we ought to give in; but she wouldn't listen. You see, she enjoys it. Still, now she sees that it must be done. In the course of the next two or three days you'll be having your bath water. But I thought I'd just like to tell you how . . ." But the Maremmano, which had recovered by this time from its surprise of a moment since, suddenly bounded, growling, up the road. The old gentleman tried to hold the beast, strained at the leash, tottered unsteadily, then gave way and allowed himself to be dragged off. ". . . how sorry I am," he went on, as he receded from me, "that this little misunderstanding . . ." But it was no use. "Goodbye." He smiled politely, made a little deprecating gesture, as though he had suddenly remembered a pressing engagement, and had no time to explain what it was. "Good-bye." He took off his hat and abandoned himself completely to the dog.

A week later the water really did begin to flow, and the day after our first bath Signora Bondi, dressed in dove-grey satin and wearing all her pearls, came to call.

"Is it peace now?" she asked, with a charming frankness, as she shook hands.

We assured her that, so far as we were concerned, it certainly was.

"But why *did* you write me such dreadfully rude letters?" she said, turning on me a reproachful glance that ought to have moved the most ruthless malefactor to contrition. "And then that writ. How *could* you? To a lady . . ."

I mumbled something about the pump and our wanting baths.

"But how could you expect me to listen to you while you were in that mood? Why didn't you set about it differently—politely, charmingly?" She smiled at me and dropped her fluttering eyelids.

I thought it best to change the conversation. It is disagreeable, when one is in the right, to be made to appear in the wrong.

A few weeks later we had a letter—duly registered and by express messenger—in which the Signora asked us whether we proposed to renew our lease (which was only for six months), and notifying us that, if we did, the rent would be raised 25 per cent, in consideration of the improvements which had been carried out. We thought ourselves lucky, at the end of much bargaining, to get the lease renewed for a whole year with an increase in the rent of only 15 per cent.

It was chiefly for the sake of the view that we put up with these intolerable extortions. But we had found other reasons, after a few days' residence, for liking the house. Of these, the most cogent was that, in the peasant's youngest child, we had discovered what seemed the perfect playfellow for our own small boy. Between little Guido—for that was his name—and the youngest of his brothers and sisters there was a gap of six or seven years. His two elder brothers worked with their father in the fields; since the time of the mother's death, two or three years before we knew them, the eldest sister had ruled the house, and the younger, who had just left school, helped her and in betweenwhiles kept an eye on Guido, who by this time, however, needed very little looking after; for he was between six and seven years old and as precocious, self-assured, and responsible as the children of the poor, left as they are to themselves almost from the time they can walk, generally are.

Though fully two and a half years older than little Robin—and at that age thirty months are crammed with half a life-time's experience —Guido took no undue advantage of his superior intelligence and strength. I have never seen a child more patient, tolerant, and untyrannical. He never laughed at Robin for his clumsy efforts to imitate his own prodigious feats; he did not tease or bully, but helped his small companion when he was in difficulties and explained when he could not understand. In return, Robin adored him, regarded him as the model and perfect Big Boy, and slavishly imitated him in every way he could.

These attempts of Robin's to imitate his companion were often exceedingly ludicrous. For by an obscure psychological law, words and actions in themselves quite serious become comic as soon as they are copied; and the more accurately, if the imitation is a deliberate parody, the funnier—for an overloaded imitation of someone we know does not make us laugh so much as one that is almost indistinguishably like the original. The bad imitation is only ludicrous when it is a piece of sincere and earnest flattery which does not quite come off. Robin's imitations were mostly of this kind. His heroic and unsuccessful attempts to perform the feats of strength and skill, which Guido could do with ease, were exquisitely comic. And his careful, longdrawn imitations of Guido's habits and mannerisms were no less amusing. Most ludicrous of all, because most earnestly undertaken and most incongruous in the imitator, were Robin's impersonations of Guido in the pensive mood. Guido was a thoughtful child, given to brooding and sudden abstractions. One would find him sitting in a corner by himself, chin in hand, elbow on knee, plunged, to all appearances, in the profoundest meditation. And sometimes, even in the midst of his play, he would suddenly break off, to stand, his hands behind his back, frowning and staring at the ground. When this happened Robin became overawed and a little disquieted. In a puzzled silence he looked at his companion. "Guido," he would say softly, "Guido." But Guido was generally too much preoccupied to answer; and Robin, not venturing to insist, would creep near him, and throwing himself as nearly as possible into Guido's attitude—standing Napoleonically, his hands clasped behind him, or sitting in the posture of Michelangelo's Lorenzo the Magnificent—would try to meditate too. Every few seconds he would turn his bright blue eyes towards the elder child to see whether he was doing it quite right. But at the end of a minute he began to grow impatient; meditation wasn't his strong point. "Guido," he called again and, louder, "Guido!" And he would take him by the hand and try to pull him away. Sometimes Guido roused himself from his reverie and went back to the interrupted game. Sometimes he paid no attention. Melancholy, perplexed, Robin had to take himself off to play by himself. And Guido would go on sitting or standing there, quite still; and his eyes, if one looked into them, were beautiful in their grave and pensive calm.

They were large eyes, set far apart and, what was strange in a dark-haired Italian child, of a luminous pale blue-grey colour. They were not always grave and calm, as in these pensive moments. When he was playing, when he talked or laughed, they lit up; and the surface of those clear, pale lakes of thought seemed, as it were, to be shaken into brilliant sun-flashing ripples. Above those eyes was a beautiful forehead, high and steep and domed in a curve that was like the subtle curve of a rose petal. The nose was straight, the chin small and rather pointed, the mouth drooped a little sadly at the corners.

I have a snapshot of the two children sitting together on the parapet of the terrace. Guido sits almost facing the camera, but looking a little to one side and downwards; his hands are crossed in his lap and his expression, his attitude are thoughtful, grave, and meditative. It is Guido in one of those moods of abstraction into which he would pass even at the height of laughter and play—quite suddenly and completely, as though he had all at once taken it into his head to go away and had left the silent and beautiful body behind, like an empty house, to wait for his return. And by his side sits little Robin, turning to look up at him, his face half averted from the camera, but the curve of his cheek showing that he is laughing; one little raised hand is caught at the top of a gesture, the other clutches at Guido's sleeve as though he were urging him to come away and play. And the legs dangling from the parapet have been seen by the blinking instrument in the midst of an impatient wriggle; he is on the point of slipping down and running off to play hide-and-seek in the garden. All the essential characteristics of both the children are in that little snapshot.

"If Robin were not Robin," Elizabeth used to say, "I could almost wish he were Guido."

And even at that time, when I took no particular interest in the child, I agreed with her. Guido seemed to me one of the most charming little boys I had ever seen.

We were not alone in admiring him. Signora Bondi when, in those cordial intervals between our quarrels, she came to call, was constantly speaking of him. "Such a beautiful, beautiful child!" she would exclaim with enthusiasm. "It's really a waste that he should belong to peasants who can't afford to dress him properly. If he were mine, I should put him into black velvet; or little white knickers and a white knitted silk jersey with a red line at the collar and cuffs! or perhaps a white sailor suit would be pretty. And in winter a little fur coat, with a squirrel skin cap, and possibly Russian boots . . ." Her imagination was running away with her. "And I'd let his hair grow, like a page's, and have it just curled up a little at the tips. And a straight fringe across his forehead. Everyone would turn round and stare after us if I took him out with me in Via Tornabuoni."

What you want, I should have liked to tell her, is not a child; it's a clock-work doll or a performing monkey. But I did not say so—partly because I could not think of the Italian for a clock-work doll and partly because I did not want to risk having the rent raised another 15 per cent.

"Ah, if only I had a little boy like that!" She sighed and modestly dropped her eyelids. "I adore children. I sometimes think of adopting one—that is, if my husband would allow it."

I thought of the poor old gentleman being dragged along at the heels of his big white dog and inwardly smiled.

"But I don't know if he would," the Signora was continuing, "I don't know if he would." She was silent for a moment, as though considering a new idea.

A few days later, when we were sitting in the garden after luncheon, drinking our coffee, Guido's father, instead of passing with a nod and the usual cheerful good-day, halted in front of us and began to talk. He was a fine handsome man, not very tall, but well-proportioned, quick and elastic in his movements, and full of life. He had a thin brown face, featured like a Roman's and lit by a pair of the most intelligent-looking grey eyes I ever saw. They exhibited almost too much intelligence when, as not infrequently happened, he was trying, with an assumption of perfect frankness and a childlike innocence, to take one in or get something out of one. Delighting in itself, the intelligence shone there mischievously. The face might be ingenuous, impassive, almost imbecile in its expression; but the eyes on these occasions gave him completely away. One knew, when they glittered like that, that one would have to be careful.

Today, however, there was no dangerous light in them. He wanted nothing out of us, nothing of any value—only advice, which is a commodity, he knew, that most people are only too happy to part with. But he wanted advice on what was, for us, rather a delicate subject: on Signora Bondi. Carlo had often complained to us about her. The old man is good, he told us, very good and kind indeed. Which meant, I dare say, among other things, that he could easily be swindled. But his wife . . . Well, the woman was a beast. And he would tell us stories of her insatiable rapacity: she was always claiming more than the half of the produce which, by the laws of the metayage [1] system, was the proprietor's due. He complained of her suspiciousness: she was forever accusing him of sharp practices, of downright stealing—him, he struck his breast, the soul of honesty. He complained of her short-sighted avarice: she wouldn't spend enough on manure, wouldn't buy him another cow, wouldn't have electric light installed in the stables. And we had sympathised, but cautiously, without expressing too strong an opinion on the subject. The Italians are wonderfully noncommittal in their speech; they will give nothing away to an interested person until they are quite certain that it is right and necessary and, above all, safe to do so. We had lived long enough among them to imitate their caution. What we said to Carlo would be sure, sooner or later, to get back to Signora Bondi. There was nothing to be gained by unnecessarily embittering our relations with the lady—only another 15 per cent, very likely, to be lost.

Today he wasn't so much complaining as feeling perplexed. The Signora had sent for him, it seemed, and asked him how he would like it if she were to make an offer—it was all very hypothetical in the cautious Italian style—to adopt little Guido. Carlo's first instinct had been to say that he wouldn't like it at all. But an answer like that would have been too coarsely committal. He had preferred to say that he would think about it. And now he was asking for our advice.

[1] share cropping

93

Do what you think best, was what in effect we replied. But we gave it distantly but distinctly to be understood that we didn't think that Signora Bondi would make a very good foster-mother for the child. And Carlo was inclined to agree. Besides, he was very fond of the boy.

"But the thing is," he concluded rather gloomily, "that if she has really set her heart on getting hold of the child, there's nothing she won't do to get him—nothing."

He too, I could see, would have liked the physicists to start on unemployed childless women of sanguine temperament before they tried to tackle the atom. Still, I reflected, as I watched him striding away along the terrace, singing powerfully from a brazen gullet as he went, there was force there, there was life enough in those elastic limbs, behind those bright grey eyes, to put up a good fight even against the accumulated vital energies of Signora Bondi.

It was a few days after this that my gramophone and two or three boxes of records arrived from England. They were a great comfort to us on the hilltop, providing as they did the only thing in which that spiritually fertile solitude—otherwise a perfect Swiss Family Robinson's island—was lacking: music. There is not much music to be heard nowadays in Florence. The times when Dr. Burney could tour through Italy, listening to an unending succession of new operas, symphonies, quartets, cantatas, are gone. Gone are the days when a learned musician, inferior only to the Reverend Father Martini of Bologna, could admire what the peasants sang and the strolling players thrummed and scraped on their instruments. I have travelled for weeks through the peninsula and hardly heard a note that was not "Salome" or the Fascists' song. Rich in nothing else that makes life agreeable or even supportable, the northern metropolises are rich in music. That is perhaps the only inducement that a reasonable man can find for living there. The other attractions—organised gaiety, people, miscellaneous conversation, the social pleasures—what are those, after all, but an expense of spirit that buys nothing in return? And then the cold, the darkness, the mouldering dirt, the damp and squalor. . . . No, where there is no necessity that retains, music can be the only inducement. And that, thanks to the ingenious Edison, can now be taken about in a box and unpacked in whatever solitude one chooses to visit. One can live at Benin, or Nuneaton, or Tozeur in the Sahara, and still hear Mozart quartets, and selections from the Well-Tempered Clavichord, and the Fifth Symphony, and the Brahms clarinet quintet, and motets by Palestrina.

Carlo, who had gone down to the station with his mule and cart to fetch the packing-case, was vastly interested in the machine.

"One will hear some music again," he said, as he watched me unpacking the gramophone and the disks. "It is difficult to do much one self."

Still, I reflected, he managed to do a good deal. On warm nights we used to hear him, where he sat at the door of his house, playing his guitar and softly singing; the eldest boy shrilled out the melody on the mandolin, and sometimes the whole family would join in, and the darkness would be filled with their passionate, throaty singing. Piedigrotta [2] songs they mostly sang; and the voices drooped slurringly from note to note, lazily climbed or jerked themselves with sudden sobbing emphases from one tone to another. At a distance and under the stars the effect was not unpleasing.

"Before the war," he went on, "in normal times" (and Carlo had a hope, even a belief, that the normal times were coming back and that life would soon be as cheap and easy as it had been in the days before the flood), "I used to go and listen to the operas at the Politeama. Ah, they were magnificent. But it costs five lire now to get in."

"Too much," I agreed.

"Have you got *Trovatore?*" he asked.

I shook my head.

"*Rigoletto?*"

"I'm afraid not."

"*Bohème? Fanciulla del West? Pagliacci?*"

I had to go on disappointing him.

"Not even *Norma?* Or the *Barbiere?*"

I put on Battistini in "La ci darem" out of *Don Giovanni*. He agreed that the singing was good; but I could see that he didn't much like the music. Why not? He found it difficult to explain.

"It's not like *Pagliacci,*" he said at last.

"Not palpitating?" I suggested, using a word with which I was sure he would be familiar; for it occurs in every Italian political speech and patriotic leading article.

"Not palpitating," he agreed.

And I reflected that it is precisely by the difference between *Pagliacci* and *Don Giovanni*, between the palpitating and the nonpalpitating, that modern musical taste is separated from the old. The corruption of the best, I thought, is the worst. Beethoven taught music to palpitate with his intellectual and spiritual passion. It has gone on palpitating ever since, but with the passion of inferior men. Indirectly, I thought, Beethoven is responsible for *Parsifal, Pagliacci,* and the *Poem of Fire;* still more indirectly for *Samson and Delilah* and "Ivy, cling to me." Mozart's melodies may be brilliant, memorable, infectious; but they don't palpitate, don't catch you between wind and water, don't send the listener off into erotic ecstasies.

Carlo and his elder children found my gramophone, I am afraid, rather a disappointment. They were too polite, however, to say so openly; they merely ceased, after the first day or two, to take any inter-

2 popular songs of Naples

est in the machine and the music it played. They preferred the guitar and their own singing.

Guido, on the other hand, was immensely interested. And he liked, not the cheerful dance tunes, to whose sharp rhythms our little Robin loved to go stamping round and round the room, pretending that he was a whole regiment of soldiers, but the genuine stuff. The first record he heard, I remember, was that of the slow movement of Bach's Concerto in D Minor for two violins. That was the disk I put on the turntable as soon as Carlo had left me. It seemed to me, so to speak, the most musical piece of music with which I could refresh my long-parched mind—the coolest and clearest of all draughts. The movement had just got under way and was beginning to unfold its pure and melancholy beauties in accordance with the laws of the most exacting intellectual logic, when the two children, Guido in front and little Robin breathlessly following, came clattering into the room from the loggia.

Guido came to a halt in front of the gramophone and stood there, motionless, listening. His pale blue-grey eyes opened themselves wide; making a little nervous gesture that I had often noticed in him before, he plucked at his lower lip with his thumb and forefinger. He must have taken a deep breath; for I noticed that, after listening for a few seconds, he sharply expired and drew in a fresh gulp of air. For an instant he looked at me—a questioning, astonished, rapturous look—gave a little laugh that ended in a kind of nervous shudder, and turned back towards the source of the incredible sounds. Slavishly imitating his elder comrade, Robin had also taken up his stand in front of the gramophone, and in exactly the same position, glancing at Guido from time to time to make sure that he was doing everything, down to plucking at his lip, in the correct way. But after a minute or so he became bored.

"Soldiers," he said, turning to me; "I want soldiers. Like in London." He remembered the rag-time and the jolly marches round and round the room.

I put my fingers to my lips. "Afterwards," I whispered.

Robin managed to remain silent and still for perhaps another twenty seconds. Then he seized Guido by the arm, shouting, "Vieni, Guido! Soldiers. Soldati. Vieni giuocare soldati."

It was then, for the first time, that I saw Guido impatient. "Vai!" he whispered angrily, slapped at Robin's clutching hand and pushed him roughly away. And he leaned a little closer to the instrument, as though to make up by yet intenser listening for what the interruption had caused him to miss.

Robin looked at him, astonished. Such a thing had never happened before. Then he burst out crying and came to me for consolation.

When the quarrel was made up—and Guido was sincerely repentant, was as nice as he knew how to be when the music had stopped and his mind was free to think of Robin once more—I asked him how he liked the music. He said he thought it was beautiful. But *bello* in Italian is too vague a word, too easily and frequently uttered, to mean very much.

"What did you like best?" I insisted. For he had seemed to enjoy it so much that I was curious to find out what had really impressed him.

He was silent for a moment, pensively frowning. "Well," he said at last, "I liked the bit that went like this." And he hummed a long phrase. "And then there's the other thing singing at the same time—but what are those things," he interrupted himself, "that sing like that?"

"They're called violins," I said.

"Violins." He nodded. "Well, the other violin goes like this." He hummed again. "Why can't one sing both at once? And what is in that box? What makes it make that noise?" The child poured out his questions.

I answered him as best I could, showing him the little spirals on the disk, the needle, the diaphragm. I told him to remember how the string of the guitar trembled when one plucked it; sound is a shaking in the air, I told him, and I tried to explain how those shakings get printed on the black disk. Guido listened to me very gravely, nodding from time to time. I had the impression that he understood perfectly well everything I was saying.

By this time, however, poor Robin was so dreadfully bored that in pity for him I had to send the two children out into the garden to play. Guido went obediently; but I could see that he would have preferred to stay indoors and listen to more music. A little while later, when I looked out, he was hiding in the dark recesses of the big bay tree, roaring like a lion, and Robin, laughing, but a little nervously, as though he were afraid that the horrible noise might possibly turn out, after all, to be the roaring of a real lion, was beating the bush with a stick, and shouting, "Come out, come out! I want to shoot you."

After lunch, when Robin had gone upstairs for his afternoon sleep, he reappeared. "May I listen to the music now?" he asked. And for an hour he sat there in front of the instrument, his head cocked slightly on one side, listening while I put on one disk after another.

Thenceforward he came every afternoon. Very soon he knew all my library of records, had his preferences and dislikes, and could ask for what he wanted by humming the principal theme.

"I don't like that one," he said of Strauss's *Till Eulenspiegel*. "It's like what we sing in our house. Not really like, you know. But somehow rather like, all the same. You understand?" He looked at us perplexedly and appealingly, as though begging us to understand what he meant and so save him from going on explaining. We nodded. Guido went on. "And then," he said, "the end doesn't seem to come properly out of the beginning. It's not like the one you played the first time." He hummed a bar or two from the slow movement of Bach's D Minor Concerto. "It isn't," I suggested, "like saying: All little boys like playing. Guido is a little boy. Therefore Guido likes playing."

He frowned. "Yes, perhaps that's it," he said at last. "The one you played first is more like that. But, you know," he added, with an excessive regard for truth, "I don't like playing as much as Robin does."

Wagner was among his dislikes; so was Debussy. When I played the record of one of Debussy's Arabesques, he said, "Why does he say the same thing over and over again? He ought to say something new, or go on, or make the thing grow. Can't he think of anything different?" But he was less censorious about the "Après-Midi d'un Faune." "The things have beautiful voices," he said.

Mozart overwhelmed him with delight. The duet from *Don Giovanni,* which his father had found insufficiently palpitating, enchanted Guido. But he preferred the quartets and the orchestral pieces.

"I like music," he said, "better than singing."

Most people, I reflected, like singing better than music; are more interested in the executant than in what he executes, and find the impersonal orchestra less moving than the soloist. The touch of the pianist is the human touch, and the soprano's high C is the personal note. It is for the sake of this touch, that note, that audiences fill the concert halls.

Guido, however, preferred music. True, he liked "La ci darem"; he liked "Deh vieni alla finestra"; he thought "Che soave zefiretto" so lovely that almost all our concerts had to begin with it. But he preferred the other things. The *Figaro* overture was one of his favourites. There is a passage not far from the beginning of the piece, where the first violins suddenly go rocketing up into the heights of loveliness; as the music approached that point, I used always to see a smile developing and gradually brightening on Guido's face, and when, punctually, the thing happened, he clapped his hands and laughed aloud with pleasure.

On the other side of the same disk, it happened, was recorded Beethoven's *Egmont* overture. He liked that almost better than *Figaro.*

"It has more voices," he explained. And I was delighted by the acuteness of the criticism; for it is precisely in the richness of its orchestration that *Egmont* goes beyond *Figaro.*

But what stirred him almost more than anything was the *Coriolan* overture. The third movement of the Fifth Symphony, the second movement of the Seventh, the slow movement of the Emperor Concerto—all these things ran it pretty close. But none excited him so much as *Coriolan.* One day he made me play it three or four times in succession; then he put it away.

"I don't think I want to hear that any more," he said.

"Why not?"

"It's too . . . too . . ." he hesitated, "too big," he said at last. "I don't really understand it. Play me the one that goes like this." He hummed the phrase from the D Minor Concerto.

"Do you like that one better?" I asked.

He shook his head. "No, it's not that exactly. But it's easier."

"Easier?" It seemed to me rather a queer word to apply to Bach.

"I understand it better."

One afternoon, while we were in the middle of our concert, Signora Bondi was ushered in. She began at once to be overwhelmingly affectionate towards the child; kissed him, patted his head, paid him the most outrageous compliments on his appearance. Guido edged away from her.

"And do you like music?" she asked.

The child nodded.

"I think he has a gift," I said. "At any rate, he has a wonderful ear and a power of listening and criticising such as I've never met with in a child of that age. We're thinking of hiring a piano for him to learn on."

A moment later I was cursing myself for my undue frankness in praising the boy. For Signora Bondi began immediately to protest that, if she could have the upbringing of the child, she would give him the best masters, bring out his talent, make an accomplished maestro of him—and, on the way, an infant prodigy. And at that moment, I am sure, she saw herself sitting maternally, in pearls and black satin, in the lee of the huge Steinway, while an angelic Guido, dressed like little Lord Fauntleroy, rattled out Liszt and Chopin, to the loud delight of a thronged auditorium. She saw the bouquets and all the elaborate floral tributes, heard the clapping and the few well-chosen words with which the veteran maestri, touched almost to tears, would hail the coming of the little genius. It became more than ever important for her to acquire the child.

"You've sent her away fairly ravening," said Elizabeth, when Signora Bondi had gone. "Better tell her next time that you made a mistake, and that the boy's got no musical talent whatever."

In due course, the piano arrived. After giving him the minimum of preliminary instruction, I let Guido loose on it. He began by picking out for himself the melodies he had heard, reconstructing the harmonies in which they were embedded. After a few lessons, he understood the rudiments of musical notation and could read a simple passage at sight, albeit very slowly. The whole process of reading was still strange to him; he had picked up his letters somehow, but nobody had yet taught him to read whole words and sentences.

I took occasion, next time I saw Signora Bondi, to assure her that

99

Guido had disappointed me. There was nothing in his musical talent, really. She professed to be very sorry to hear it; but I could see that she didn't for a moment believe me. Probably she thought that we were after the child too, and wanted to bag the infant prodigy for ourselves, before she could get in her claim, thus depriving her of what she regarded almost as her feudal right. For, after all, weren't they her peasants? If anyone was to profit by adopting the child it ought to be herself.

Tactfully, diplomatically, she renewed her negotiations with Carlo. The boy, she put it to him, had genius. It was the foreign gentleman who had told her so, and he was the sort of man, clearly, who knew about such things. If Carlo would let her adopt the child, she'd have him trained. He'd become a great maestro and get engagements in the Argentine and the United States, in Paris and London. He'd earn millions and millions. Think of Caruso, for example. Part of the millions, she explained, would of course come to Carlo. But before they began to roll in, those millions, the boy would have to be trained. But training was very expensive. In his own interest, as well as in that of his son, he ought to let her take charge of the child. Carlo said he would think it over, and again applied to us for advice. We suggested that it would be best in any case to wait a little and see what progress the boy made.

He made, in spite of my assertions to Signora Bondi, excellent progress. Every afternoon, while Robin was asleep, he came for his concert and his lesson. He was getting along famously with his reading; his small fingers were acquiring strength and agility. But what to me was more interesting was that he had begun to make up little pieces on his own account. A few of them I took down as he played them and I have them still. Most of them, strangely enough, as I thought then, are canons. He had a passion for canons. When I explained to him the principles of the form he was enchanted.

"It is beautiful," he said, with admiration. "Beautiful, beautiful. And so easy!"

Again the word surprised me. The canon is not, after all, so conspicuously simple. Thenceforward he spent most of his time at the piano in working out little canons for his own amusement. They were often remarkably ingenious. But in the invention of other kinds of music he did not show himself so fertile as I had hoped. He composed and harmonised one or two solemn little airs like hymn tunes, with a few sprightlier pieces in the spirit of the military march. They were extraordinary, of course, as being the inventions of a child. But a great many children can do extraordinary things; we are all geniuses up to the age of ten. But I had hoped that Guido was a child who was going to be a genius at forty; in which case what was extraordinary for an ordinary child was not extraordinary enough for him. "He's hardly a Mozart," we agreed, as we played his little pieces over. I felt, it must be confessed, almost aggrieved. Anything less than a Mozart, it seemed to me, was hardly worth thinking about.

*

He was not a Mozart. No. But he was somebody, as I was to find out, quite extraordinary. It was one morning in the early summer that I made the discovery. I was sitting in the warm shade of our westward-facing balcony, working. Guido and Robin were playing in the little enclosed garden below. Absorbed in my work, it was only, I suppose, after the silence had prolonged itself a considerable time that I became aware that the children were making remarkably little noise. There was no shouting, no running about; only a quiet talking. Knowing by experience that when children are quiet it generally means that they are absorbed in some delicious mischief, I got up from my chair and looked over the balustrade to see what they were doing. I expected to catch them dabbling in water, making a bonfire, covering themselves with tar. But what I actually saw was Guido, with a burnt stick in his hand, demonstrating on the smooth paving-stones of the path, that the square on the hypotenuse of a right-angled triangle is equal to the sum of the squares on the other two sides.

Kneeling on the floor, he was drawing with the point of his blackened stick on the flagstones. And Robin, kneeling imitatively beside him, was growing, I could see, rather impatient with this very slow game.

"Guido," he said. But Guido paid no attention. Pensively frowning, he went on with his diagram. "Guido!" The younger child bent down and then craned round his neck so as to look up into Guido's face. "Why don't you draw a train?"

"Afterwards," said Guido. "But I just want to show you this first. It's *so* beautiful," he added cajolingly.

"But I want a train," Robin persisted.

"In a moment. Do just wait a moment." The tone was almost imploring. Robin armed himself with renewed patience. A minute later Guido had finished both his diagrams.

"There!" he said triumphantly, and straightened himself up to look at them. "Now I'll explain."

And he proceeded to prove the theorem of Pythagoras—not in Euclid's way, but by the simpler and more satisfying method which was, in all probability, employed by Pythagoras himself. He had drawn a square and dissected it, by a pair of crossed perpendiculars, into two squares and two equal rectangles. The equal rectangles he divided up by their diagonals into four equal right-angled triangles. The two squares are then seen to be the squares on the two sides of any one of these triangles other than the hypotenuse. So much for the first diagram. In the next he took the four right-angled triangles into which the rectangles had been divided and rearranged them round the original square so that their right angles filled the corners of the square, the hypotenuses looked inwards and the greater and less sides of the triangles were in continuation along the sides of the square (which are each equal to the sum of these sides). In this way the original square is redissected into four right angled triangles and the square on the hypotenuse. The four triangles are equal to the two rectangles of the original dissection. Therefore the square on the hypotenuse is equal to the sum of the two squares—the squares on the other two sides—into which, with the rectangles, the original square was first dissected.

In very untechnical language, but clearly and with a relentless logic, Guido expounded his proof. Robin listened, with an expression on his bright, freckled face of perfect incomprehension.

"Treno," he repeated from time to time. "Treno. Make a train."

"In a moment," Guido implored. "Wait a moment. But do just look at this. *Do.*" He coaxed and cajoled. "It's so beautiful. It's so easy."

So easy. . . . The theorem of Pythagoras seemed to explain for me Guido's musical predilections. It was not an infant Mozart we had been cherishing; it was a little Archimedes with, like most of his kind, an incidental musical twist.

"Treno, treno!" shouted Robin, growing more and more restless as the exposition went on. And when Guido insisted on going on with his proof, he lost his temper. "Cattivo Guido," he shouted, and began to hit out at him with his fists.

"All right," said Guido resignedly. "I'll make a train." And with his stick of charcoal he began to scribble on the stones.

I looked on for a moment in silence. It was not a very good train. Guido might be able to invent for himself and prove the theorem of Pythagoras; but he was not much of a draughtsman.

"Guido!" I called. The two children turned and looked up. "Who taught you to draw those squares?" It was conceivable, of course, that somebody might have taught him.

"Nobody." He shook his head. Then, rather anxiously, as though he were afraid there might be something wrong about drawing squares, he went on to apologise and explain. "You see," he said, "it seemed to me so beautiful. Because those squares"—he pointed at the two small squares in the first figure—"are just as big as this one." And, indicating the square on the hypotenuse in the second diagram, he looked up at me with a deprecating smile.

I nodded. "Yes, it's very beautiful," I said—"it's very beautiful indeed."

An expression of delighted relief appeared on his face; he laughed with pleasure. "You see, it's like this," he went on, eager to initiate me into the glorious secret he had discovered. "You cut these two long squares"—he meant the rectangles—"into two slices. And then there are four slices, all just the same, because, because— oh, I ought to have said that before—because these long squares are the same, because those lines, you see . . ."

"But I want a train," protested Robin.

Leaning on the rail of the balcony, I watched the children below. I thought of the extraordinary thing I had just seen and of what it meant.

I thought of the vast differences between human beings. We classify men by the colour of their eyes and hair, the shape of their skulls. Would it not be more sensible to divide them up into intellectual species? There would be even wider gulfs between the extreme mental types than between a Bushman and a Scandinavian. This child, I thought, when he grows up, will be to me, intellectually, what a man is to a dog. And there are other men and women who are, perhaps, almost as dogs to me.

Perhaps the men of genius are the only true men. In all the history of the race there have been only a few thousand real men. And the rest of us—what are we? Teachable animals. Without the help of the real men, we should have found out almost nothing at all. Almost all the ideas with which we are familiar could never have occurred to minds like ours. Plant the seeds there and they will grow; but our minds could never spontaneously have generated them.

There have been whole nations of dogs, I thought; whole epochs in which no Man was born. From the dull Egyptians the Greeks took crude experience and rules of thumb and made sciences. More than a thousand years passed before Archimedes had a comparable successor. There has been only one Buddha, one Jesus, only one Bach that we know of, one Michelangelo.

Is it by a mere chance, I wondered, that a Man is born from time to time? What causes a whole constellation of them to come contemporaneously into being and from out of a single people? Taine thought that Leonardo, Michelangelo, and Raphael were born when they were because the time was ripe for great painters and the Italian scene congenial. In the mouth of a rationalising nineteenth-century Frenchman the doctrine is strangely mystical; it may be none the less true for that. But what of those born out of time? Blake, for example. What of those?

This child, I thought, has had the fortune to be born at a time when he will be able to make good use of his capacities. He will find the most elaborate analytical methods lying ready to his hand; he will have a prodigious experience behind him. Suppose him born while Stonehenge was building; he might have spent a lifetime discovering the rudiments, guessing darkly where now he might have had a chance of proving. Born at the time of the Norman Conquest, he would have had to wrestle with all the preliminary difficulties created by an inadequate symbolism; it would have taken him long years, for example, to learn the art of dividing MMMCCCCLXXXVIII by MCMXIX. In five years, nowadays, he will learn what it took generations of Men to discover.

And I thought of the fate of all the Men born so hopelessly out of time that they could achieve little or nothing of value. Beethoven born in Greece, I thought, would have had to be content to play thin melodies on the flute or lyre; in those intellectual surroundings it would hardly have been possible for him to imagine the nature of harmony.

From drawing trains, the children in the garden below had gone on to playing trains. They were trotting round and round; with blown round cheeks and pouting mouth, like the cherubic symbol of a wind, Robin puff-puffed, and Guido, holding the skirt of his smock, shuffled behind him, tooting. They ran forward, backed, stopped at imaginary stations, shunted, roared over bridges, crashed through tunnels, met with occasional collisions and derailments. The young Archimedes seemed to be just as happy as the little tow-headed barbarian. A few minutes ago he had been busy with the theorem of Pythagoras. Now, tooting indefatigably along imaginary rails, he was perfectly content to shuffle backwards and forwards among the flower-beds, between the pillars of the loggia, in and out of the dark tunnels of the laurel tree. The fact that one is going to be Archimedes does not prevent one from being an ordinary cheerful child meanwhile. I thought of this strange talent distinct and separate from the rest of the mind, independent, almost, of experience. The typical child-prodigies are musical and mathematical; the other talents ripen slowly under the influence of emotional experience and growth. Till he was thirty Balzac gave proof of nothing but ineptitude; but at four the young Mozart was already a musician, and some of Pascal's most brilliant work was done before he was out of his teens.

In the weeks that followed, I alternated the daily piano lessons with lessons in mathematics. Hints rather than lessons they were; for I only made suggestions, indicated methods, and left the child himself to work out the ideas in detail. Thus I introduced him to algebra by showing him another proof of the theorem of Pythagoras. In this proof one drops a perpendicular from the right angle on to the hypotenuse, and arguing from the fact that the two triangles thus created are similar to one another and to the original triangle, and that the proportions which their corresponding sides bear to one another are therefore equal, one can show in algebraical form that $c^2 + d^2$ (the squares on the other two sides) are equal to $a^2 + b^2$ (the squares on the two segments of the hypotenuse) $+ 2ab;$ which last, it is easy to show geometrically, is equal to $(a + b)^2$, or the square on the hypotenuse. Guido was as much enchanted by the rudiments of algebra as he would have been if I had given him an engine worked by steam, with a methylated spirit lamp to heat the boiler; more enchanted, perhaps—for the engine would have got broken, and remaining always itself, would in any case have lost its charm, while the rudiments of algebra continued to grow and blossom in his mind with an unfailing luxuriance. Every day he made the discovery of something which seemed to him exquisitely beautiful; the new toy was inexhaustible in its potentialities.

In the intervals of applying algebra to the second book of Euclid, we experimented with circles; we stuck bamboos into the parched earth, measured their shadows at different hours of the day, and drew exciting conclusions from our observations. Sometimes, for fun, we cut and folded sheets of paper so as to make cubes and pyramids. One afternoon Guido arrived carrying carefully between his small and rather grubby hands a flimsy dodecahedron.

"E tanto bello!" he said, as he showed us his paper crystal; and when I asked him how he managed to make it, he merely smiled and said it had been so easy. I looked at Elizabeth and laughed. But it would have been more symbolically to the point, I felt, if I had gone down on all fours, wagged the spiritual outgrowth of my *os coccyx,* and barked my astonished admiration.

It was an uncommonly hot summer. By the beginning of July our little Robin, unaccustomed to these high temperatures, began to look pale and tired; he was listless, had lost his appetite and energy. The doctor advised mountain air. We decided to spend the next ten or twelve weeks in Switzerland. My parting gift to Guido was the first six books of Euclid in Italian. He turned over the pages, looked ecstatically at the figures.

"If only I knew how to read properly," he said. "I'm so stupid. But now I shall really try to learn."

From our hotel near Grindelwald we sent the child, in Robin's name, various postcards of cows, Alp-horns, Swiss chalets, edelweiss, and the like. We received no answers to these cards; but then we did not expect answers. Guido could not write, and there was no reason why his father or his sisters should take the trouble to write for him. No news, we took it, was good news. And then one day, early in September, there arrived at the hotel a strange letter. The manager had it stuck up on the glass-fronted notice-board in the hall, so that all the guests might see it, and whoever conscientiously thought that it belonged to him might claim it. Passing the board on the way in to lunch, Elizabeth stopped to look at it.

"But it must be from Guido," she said.

I came and looked at the envelope over her shoulder. It was unstamped and black with postmarks. Traced out in pencil, the big uncertain capital letters sprawled across its face. In the first line was written: AL BABBO DI ROBIN, and there followed a travestied version of the name of the hotel and the place. Round the address bewildered postal officials had scrawled suggested emendations. The letter had wandered for a fortnight at least, back and forth across the face of Europe.

"Al Babbo di Robin. To Robin's father." I laughed. "Pretty smart of the postmen to have got it here at all." I went to the manager's office, set forth the justice of my claim to the letter and, having paid the fifty-centime surcharge for the missing stamp, had the case unlocked and the letter given me. We went in to lunch.

"The writing's magnificent," we agreed, laughing, as we examined the address at close quarters. "Thanks to Euclid," I added. "That's what comes of pandering to the ruling passion."

But when I opened the envelope and looked at its contents I no longer laughed. The letter was brief and almost telegraphical in style. "SONO DALLA PADRONA," it ran, "NON MI PIACE HA RUBATO IL MIO LIBRO NON VOGLIO SUONARE PIU VOGLIO TORNARE A CASA VENGA SUBITO GUIDO." [3]

"What is it?"

I handed Elizabeth the letter. "That blasted woman's got hold of him," I said.

*

Busts of men in Homburg hats, angels bathed in marble tears extinguishing torches, statues of little girls, cherubs, veiled figures, allegories and ruthless realisms—the strangest and most diverse idols beckoned and gesticulated as we passed. Printed indelibly on tin and embedded in the living rock, the brown photographs looked out, under glass, from the humbler crosses, headstones, and broken pillars. Dead ladies in the cubistic geometrical fashions of thirty years ago—two cones of black satin meeting point to point at the waist, and the arms: a sphere to the elbow, a polished cylinder below—smiled mournfully out of their marble frames; the smiling faces, the white hands, were the only recognisably human things that emerged from the solid geometry of their clothes. Men with black moustaches, men with white beards, young clean-shaven men stared or averted their gaze to show a Roman profile. Children in their stiff best opened wide their eyes, smiled hopefully in anticipation of the little bird that was to issue from the camera's muzzle, smiled sceptically in the knowledge that it wouldn't, smiled laboriously and obediently because they had been told to. In spiky Gothic cottages of marble the richer dead privately reposed; through grilled doors one caught a glimpse of pale Inconsolables weeping, of distraught Geniuses guarding the secret of the tomb. The less prosperous sections of the majority slept in communities, close-crowded but

[3] I am at the Padrona's—I don't like it—she has stolen my book—I don't want to play [the piano] any more—I want to return home—come quickly—Guido.

elegantly housed under smooth continuous marble floors, whose every flagstone was the mouth of a separate grave.

These continental cemeteries, I thought, as Carlo and I made our way among the dead, are more frightful than ours, because these people pay more attention to their dead than we do. That primordial cult of corpses, that tender solicitude for their material well-being, which led the ancients to house their dead in stone, while they themselves lived between wattles and under thatch, still lingers here; persists, I thought, more vigorously than with us. There are a hundred gesticulating statues here for every one in an English graveyard. There are more family vaults, more "luxuriously appointed" (as they say of liners and hotels) than one would find at home. And embedded in every tombstone there are photographs to remind the powdered bones within what form they will have to resume on the Day of Judgment; beside each are little hanging lamps to burn optimistically on All Souls' Day. To the Man who built the Pyramids they are nearer, I thought, than we.

"If I had known," Carlo kept repeating, "if only I had known." His voice came to me through my reflections as though from a distance. "At the time he didn't mind at all. How should I have known that he would take it so much to heart afterwards? And she deceived me, she lied to me."

I assured him yet once more that it wasn't his fault. Though, of course, it was, in part. It was mine too, in part; I ought to have thought of the possibility and somehow guarded against it. And he shouldn't have let the child go, even temporarily and on trial, even though the woman was bringing pressure to bear on him. And the pressure had been considerable. They had worked on the same holding for more than a hundred years, the men of Carlo's family; and now she had made the old man threaten to turn him out. It would be a dreadful thing to leave the place; and besides, another place wasn't so easy to find. It was made quite plain, however, that he could stay if he let her have the child. Only for a little to begin with; just to see how he got on. There would be no compulsion whatever on him to stay if he didn't like it. And it would be all to Guido's advantage; and to his father's, too, in the end. All that the Englishman had said about his not being such a good musician as he had thought at first was obviously untrue—mere jealousy and little-mindedness: the man wanted to take credit for Guido himself, that was all. And the boy, it was obvious, would learn nothing from him. What he needed was a real good professional master.

All the energy that, if the physicists had known their business, would have been driving dynamos, went into this campaign. It began the moment we were out of the house, intensively. She would have more chance of success, the Signora doubtless thought, if we weren't there. And besides, it was essential to take the opportunity when it offered itself and get hold of the child before we could make our bid—for it was obvious to her that we wanted Guido just as much as she did.

Day after day she renewed the assault. At the end of a week she sent her husband to complain about the state of the vines: they were in a shocking condition; he had decided, or very nearly decided, to give Carlo notice. Meekly, shamefacedly, in obedience to higher orders, the old gentleman uttered his threats. Next day Signora Bondi returned to the attack. The padrone, she declared, had been in a towering passion; but she'd do her best, her very best, to mollify him. And after a significant pause she went on to talk about Guido.

In the end Carlo gave in. The woman was too persistent and she held too many trump cards. The child could go and stay with her for a month or two on trial. After that, if he really expressed a desire to remain with her, she could formally adopt him.

At the idea of going for a holiday to the seaside—and it was to the seaside, Signora Bondi told him, that they were going—Guido was pleased and excited. He had heard a lot about the sea from Robin. "Tanta acqua!" It had sounded almost too good to be true. And now he was actually to go and see this marvel. It was very cheerfully that he parted from his family.

But after the holiday by the sea was over, and Signora Bondi had brought him back to her town house in Florence, he began to be homesick. The signora, it was true, treated him exceedingly kindly, bought him new clothes, took him out to tea in the Via Tornabuoni and filled him up with cakes, iced strawberryade, whipped cream, and chocolates. But she made him practise the piano more than he liked, and what was worse, she took away his Euclid, on the score that he wasted too much time with it. And when he said that he wanted to go home, she put him off with promises and excuses and downright lies. She told him that she couldn't take him at once, but that next week, if he were good and worked hard at his piano meanwhile, next week . . . And when the time came she told him that his father didn't want him back. And she redoubled her petting, gave him expensive presents, and stuffed him with yet unhealthier foods. To no purpose. Guido didn't like his new life, didn't want to practise scales, pined for his book, and longed to be back with his brothers and sisters. Signora Bondi, meanwhile, continued to hope that time and chocolates would eventually make the child hers; and to keep his family at a distance, she wrote to Carlo every few days letters which still purported to come from the seaside (she took the trouble to send them to a friend, who posted them back again to Florence), and in which she painted the most charming picture of Guido's happiness.

It was then that Guido wrote his letter to me. Abandoned, as he supposed, by his family—for that they shouldn't take the trouble to come to see him when they were so near was only to be explained on the hypothesis that they really had given him up—he must have looked to me as his last and only hope. And the letter, with its fantastic address, had been nearly a fortnight on its way. A fortnight—it must have seemed hundreds of years; and as the centuries succeeded one another, gradually, no doubt, the poor child became convinced that I too had abandoned him. There was no hope left.

"Here we are," said Carlo.

I looked up and found myself confronted by an enormous monument. In a kind of grotto hollowed in the flanks of a monolith of grey sandstone, Sacred Love, in bronze, was embracing a funerary urn. And in bronze letters riveted into the stone was a long legend to the effect that the inconsolable Ernesto Bondi had raised this monument to the memory of his beloved wife, Annunziata, as a token of his undying love for one whom, snatched from him by a premature death, he hoped very soon to join beneath this stone. The first Signora Bondi had died in 1912. I thought of the old man leashed to his white dog; he must always, I reflected, have been a most uxorious husband.

"They buried him here."

We stood there for a long time in silence. I felt the tears coming into my eyes as I thought of the poor child lying there underground. I thought of those luminous grave eyes, and the curve of that beautiful forehead, the droop of the melancholy mouth, of the expression of delight which illumined his face when he learned of some new idea that pleased him, when he heard a piece of music that he liked. And this beautiful small being was dead; and the spirit that inhabited this form, the amazing spirit, that too had been destroyed almost before it had begun to exist.

And the unhappiness that must have preceded the final act, the child's despair, the conviction of his utter abandonment—those were terrible to think of, terrible.

"I think we had better come away now," I said at last, and touched Carlo on the arm. He was standing there like a blind man, his eyes shut, his face slightly lifted towards the light; from between his closed eyelids the tears welled out, hung for a moment, and trickled down his cheeks. His lips trembled and I could see that he was making an effort to keep them still. "Come away," I repeated.

The face which had been still in its sorrow, was suddenly convulsed; he opened his eyes, and through the tears they were bright with a violent anger. "I shall kill her," he said, "I shall kill her. When I think of him throwing himself out, falling through the air . . ." With his two hands he made a violent gesture, bringing them down from over his head and arresting them with a sudden jerk when they were on a level with his breast. "And then crash." He shuddered. "She's as much responsible as though she had pushed him down herself. I shall kill her." He clenched his teeth.

To be angry is easier than to be sad, less painful. It is comforting to think of revenge. "Don't talk like that," I said. "It's no good. It's stupid. And what would be the point?" He had had those fits before, when grief became too painful and he had tried to escape from it. Anger had been the easiest way of escape. I had had, before this, to persuade him back into the harder path of grief. "It's stupid to talk like that," I repeated, and I led him away through the ghastly labyrinth of tombs, where death seemed more terrible even than it is.

By the time we had left the cemetery, and were walking down from San Miniato towards the Piazzale Michelangelo below, he had become calmer. His anger had subsided again into sorrow from which it had derived all its strength and its bitterness. In the Piazzale we halted for a moment to look down at the city in the valley below us. It was a day of floating clouds—great shapes, white, golden, and grey; and between them patches of a thin, transparent blue. Its lantern level, almost, with our eyes, the dome of the cathedral revealed itself in all its grandiose lightness, its vastness and aerial strength. On the innumerable brown and rosy roofs of the city the afternoon sunlight lay softly, sumptuously, and the towers were as though varnished and enamelled with an old gold. I thought of all the Men who had lived here and left the visible traces of their spirit and conceived extraordinary things, I thought of the dead child.

THE OTHER MARGARET

The people that Stephen Elwin meets and the things that
happen are all part of the experiences of a single day. The
author comments on the significance of Elwin's experiences and
reflects accordingly upon the uses of wisdom, for in each
instance Elwin himself realizes the need for a clearer
understanding of human behavior and of human relationships.
He is, in fact, constantly aware of the need for wisdom in his
effort to reconcile himself to the part he has played or must
play in the complex pattern of his life. The two bus conductors,
the boy who wants to ride on the bus, the maid with the
genteel malice, the young lieutenant in the art shop, and, yes,
Rouault's king in his frame—all play their part in the span of
this one day. It has been a day of varied and apparently
unrelated happenings and recollections, and the reader will
have a thoughtful time of it in sharing Elwin's reactions.

Mark Jennings stood the picture up on the wide counter and
he and Stephen Elwin stepped back and looked at it. It was one of
Rouault's kings. A person looking at it for the first time might find it re-
pellent, even brutal or cruel. It was full of rude blacks that might seem
barbarically untidy.

But the two men knew the picture well. They looked at it in silence.
The admiration they were sharing made a community between them
which at their age was rare, for they had both passed forty. Jennings
waited for Elwin to speak first—they were friends but Elwin was the
customer. Besides, the frame had been designed by Jennings and in
buying a reproduced picture the frame is of great importance, accounting for more than half the cost. Elwin had bought the picture some weeks
before but he was seeing it framed for the first time.

Elwin said, "The frame is very good, Mark. It's perfect." He was a
rather tall man with an attractive, competent face. He touched the frame
curiously with the tip of his forefinger.

Jennings replied in a judicious tone, as if it were not his own good taste but that of a very gifted apprentice of his. "*I* think so," he said. And he too touched the frame, but intimately, rubbing briskly up and down one moulding with an artisan's possessive thumb, putting an unneeded last touch. He explained what considerations of color and proportion made the frame right for the picture. He spoke as if these were simple rules anyone might find in a book.

The king, blackbearded and crowned, faced in profile to the left. He had a fierce quality that had modulated, but not softened, to authority. One could feel of him—it was the reason why Elwin had bought the picture—that he had passed beyond ordinary matters of personality and was worthy of the crown he was wearing. Yet he was human and tragic. He was not unlike the sculptured kings of Chartres. In his right hand he held a spray of flowers.

"Is he a favorite of yours?" Elwin said. He did not know whether he meant the king or the king's painter. Indeed, as he asked the question, it seemed to him that he had assumed that the painter was this archaic personage himself. He had never imagined the painter painting the canvas with a brush. It was the beginning of a new thought about the picture.

Jennings answered with a modified version of the Latin gesture of esteem, a single decisive shake of his lifted hand, thumb and forefinger touching in a circle.

Elwin acknowledged the answer with a nod but said nothing. He did not want Jennings' admiration, even though he had asked for it. Jennings would naturally give as much admiration to most of the fine pictures in fine reproduction with which his shop was filled. At that moment, Elwin was not interested in admiration or in art. But he liked what Jennings said next.

"It will give you a lot of satisfaction," Jennings said. It was exactly as if he had just sold Elwin a suit or a pair of shoes.

Elwin said, "Yes," a little hesitatingly, only politely agreeing, not committing himself in the matter of his money's worth until it should be proved.

From behind the partition that made Jennings' little office they had been hearing a man talking on the telephone. Now the conversation ended and a young soldier, a second lieutenant, came out into the shop. Jennings said to him, "Did the call get through?" and the young man said, "Oh yes, after some difficulty. It was eighty-five cents. Let me pay you for it." "Oh nonsense," said Jennings, and took him by the arm and quickly introduced him to Elwin as a cousin of his wife's. The young man offered Elwin the hand that had been reaching into his pocket and said, "I'm glad to meet you, sir."

He said it very nicely, with the niceness that new young officers are likely to have. Pleased with themselves, they are certain that every one will be nice to them. This young man's gold bar did a good deal for him, did perhaps more than rank ought to have to do for a man. He was not really much of a person. Yet Elwin, meeting him, felt the familiar emotion in which he could not distinguish guilt from envy. He knew it well, knew how to control it and it did not diminish, not much, the sense of holiday he was having. The holiday was made by his leaving his office a little early. He published scientific books in a small but successful way and the war had made a great pressure of work for him, but he had left his office early when Jennings phoned that the picture was back from the framer's.

The young lieutenant was looking at the picture. He so clearly did not like it that Jennings said quickly, "Mr. Elwin's just bought it."

The lieutenant regarded the picture thoughtfully. "Very nice," he said, with an enthusiastic and insincere shake of his head. He did not want to spoil things for Jennings by undermining the confidence of the customer. Elwin looked from the king to the lieutenant and back to the king. It was perfectly polite, only as if he had looked at the young man to hear his opinion more clearly and then had examined again the thing they were talking about.

But Jennings understood the movement of Elwin's glance, for when the lieutenant had shaken hands and left the shop, Jennings said stoutly, "He's a good kid."

"Yes he is," Elwin said serenely.

"It's funny seeing him an officer. He used to be against anything like that. But he was glad to go—he said he did not want to miss sharing the experience of his generation."

"A lot of them say that." Elwin had heard it often from the young men, the clever ones. Someone had started it and all the young men with the semi-political views said it. Their reasons for saying it were various. Elwin liked some of the reasons and disliked others, but whether he liked the reasons or not, he never heard the phrase without a twinge of envy. Now it comforted him to think that this man with the black beard and the flower had done his fighting without any remarks about experience and generations.

The idea of age and death did not present itself to Elwin in any horrifying way. It had first come to him in the form of a sentence from one of Hazlitt's essays. The sentence was, "No young man believes he shall ever die," and the words had come to him suddenly from the past, part of an elaborate recollection of a scene at high school. When he looked up the quotation, he found that he had remembered it with perfect accuracy, down to that very *shall* which struck his modern ear as odd and even ungrammatical. The memory had begun with the winter sunlight coming through the dirty windows of the classroom. Then there was the color, texture and smell of varnished wood. But these details were only pointing to the teacher himself and what he was saying. He was a Mr. Baxter, a heron-like man, esteemed as brilliant and eccentric, what some students called "a real person." Suddenly Mr. Baxter in a loud voice had uttered that sentence of Hazlitt's. He held the book in his hand but did not read from it. "No young man believes he shall ever die," he said, just as if he had thought of it himself.

It had been very startling to hear him say that, and this effect was of course just what the teacher wanted. It was the opening sentence of an essay called "On the Feeling of Immortality in Youth," and to Baxter it was important that the class should see what a bold and captivating way it was to begin an essay, how it was exactly as if someone had suddenly said the words, not written them after thought.

The chalky familiar classroom had been glorified by this moment of Mr. Baxter's. So many things had been said in the room, but here was one thing that had been said which was true. It was true in two ways. For Mr. Baxter it was true that no *young* man believes he shall ever die, but Mr. Baxter was not exactly a young man. For Stephen Elwin it was true that he would never die—he was scarcely even a young man yet, still only a boy. Between the student and the teacher the great difference was that the student would never die. Stephen Elwin had pitied Mr. Baxter and had been proud of himself. And mixed with the boy's feeling of immortality was a boy's pleasure at being involved with ideas which were not only solemn but complicated, for Mr. Baxter's mortality should have denied, but actually did not deny, the immortality that Stephen felt.

The Hazlitt sentence, once it had been remembered, had not left Elwin. Every now and then, sometimes just as he was falling asleep, sometimes just as he was waking up, sometimes right in the middle of anything at all, the sentence and the full awareness of what it meant would come to him. It felt like an internal explosion. It was not, however, an explosion of force but rather an explosion of light. It was not without pain but it was not wholly painful.

With the picture neatly wrapped in heavy brown paper, Elwin walked down Madison Avenue. It was still early. On a sudden impulse he walked west at 60th Street. Usually he came home by taxi, but this evening he thought of the Fifth Avenue bus, for some reason remembering that it was officially called a "coach" and that his father had spoken of it so, and had sometimes even referred to it as a "stage." The "coach" that he signaled was of the old kind, open wooden deck, platform at the rear, stairs connecting platform and deck with a big architectural curve. He saw it with surprise and affection. He had supposed that this model of bus had long been out of service and as he hailed it his mind sought for and found a word long unused. "DeDion," he said, pleased at having found it, "DeDion Bouton."

He pronounced it *Deedeeon,* the way he and his friends had said it in 1917 when they had discussed the fine and powerful motors from Europe that were then being used for the buses. Some of them had been Fiats, but the most powerful of all were said to be the DeDions from France. No one knew the authority for this superlative judgment, but boys finding a pleasure in firm opinions did not care. Elwin remembered the special note in his friends' voices as they spoke of the DeDions. They talked about the great Mediterranean motors with a respect that was not only technical but historical. There had never been more than a few of the DeDions in America. Even in 1917 they were no longer being imported and the boys thought of them as old and rare.

Elwin took his seat inside the bus, at the rear. As suddenly as the name DeDion, it came to him how the open deck had once been a deck indeed—how, as sometimes the only passenger braving the weather up there, he had been the captain of the adventure, facing into the cold wind, even into the snow or rain, stoic, assailed but unmoved by the elements, inhaling health, fortitude and growth, for he had a boy's certainty that the more he endured, the stronger he would become. And when he had learned to board the bus and alight from it while it was still moving—"board" and "alight" were words the company used in its notices—how far advanced in life he had felt. So many landmarks of Elwin's boyhood in the city had vanished but this shabby bus had endured since the days when it had taken him daily to school.

At 82nd Street the bus stopped for a red light. A boy stood at the curb near the iron stanchion that bore the bus-stop sign. He clutched something in his hand. It must have been a coin, for he said to the conductor, "Mister, how much does it cost to ride on this bus?"

Elwin could not be sure of the boy's age, but he was perhaps twelve, Elwin's own age when he had been touched by his friends' elegiac discussions of the DeDions. The boy was not alone, he had a friend with him, and to see this friend, clearly a follower, was to understand the quality of the chief. The subaltern was a boy like any other, but the face of his leader was alight with the power of mind and a great urgency. Perhaps he was only late and in a hurry, but in any case the urgency illuminated his remarkable face.

The conductor did not answer the question.

"Mister," the boy said again, "how much does it cost to ride on this bus?"

His friend stood by, sharing passively in the question but saying nothing. They did not dare "board" until they knew whether or not their resources were sufficient.

The boy was dressed sturdily enough, perhaps for a boy of his age he was even well dressed. But he had been on the town or in the park most of the afternoon, or perhaps he had been one of those boys who, half in awe, half in rowdy levity, troop incessantly through the Egyptian rooms of the Museum, repeatedly entering and emerging from and entering again the narrow slits of the grave vaults. His knickerbockers were sliding at the knees and his effort to control a drop at his nose further compromised but by no means destroyed his dignity. He had the clear cheeks and well-shaped head of a carefully reared child, but he seemed too far from home at this hour quite to be the child of very careful parents. There was an air about him which suggested that he had learned to expect at least a little resistance from the world and that he was ready to meet it.

The conductor did not reply to the second question. He had taken a large black wallet of imitation leather from some cranny of the rear platform and was making marks with a pencil on the cardboard trip-sheet it contained. He was an old man.

"Mister," said the boy again, and his voice, though tense, was reasonable. It was the very spirit of reasonableness. "Mister, how much does it cost to ride on this bus? A nickel or a dime?"

The conductor elaborately lifted his eyes from his record. He looked at the boy not hostilely nor yet quite facetiously, but with a certain quiet air of settled satisfaction. "What do you want to know for?" he said.

Elwin wanted to lower the window to tell the boy it was a dime. But he had waited too long. The conductor put his hand on the bell-button and gave the driver the signal. The light changed and the bus began to move.

"Mister!" the boy shouted. He may have been late to his supper but it was not this urgency that made his voice go up so loud and high. "For God's sake, mister!"

He of course did not bring in God by way of appeal. There was no longer any hope of his getting an answer. It was rather an expostulation with the unreasonable, the most passionate thing imaginable. Elwin looked back and saw the boy's hatred still following the conductor and, naturally, not only the conductor but the whole bus.

The conductor had now the modest look of a person who has just delivered a rebuke which was not only deserved but witty.

Well, Elwin thought, he is an old man and his pride is somewhere involved. Perhaps it was only that he could not at the moment bring himself to answer a question.

But he believed that in the past it could not have happened. When he was a boy the conductor might have said, "What do you want to know for?"—boys must always be teased a little by men. But the teasing would have stopped in time for him to board the bus. The bus was peculiarly safe. The people who rode in it and paid a dime after they had taken their seats were known to be nicer than the people who rode in the subway for a nickel which they paid before admission. It was the first public conveyance to which "nervous" parents entrusted their children —the conductors were known for their almost paternal kindness. For example, if you found on your trip to school that you had forgotten your money, the conductor would not fail to quiet the fear of authority that clutched your guilty heart. But this old man had outlived his fatherhood, which had once extended to all the bus-world of children. His own sons and daughters by now would have grown and gone and given him the usual causes for bitterness.

The old man's foolish triumph was something that must be understood. Elwin tried to know the weariness and sense of final loss that moved the old conductor to stand on that small dignity of his. He at once brought into consideration the conditions of life of the old man, especially the lack of all the advantages that he himself had had—the gentle rearing and the good education that made a man like Stephen Elwin answerable for all his actions. It had long been the habit of Elwin's mind to raise considerations of just this sort whenever he had reason to be annoyed with anyone who was not more powerful than himself.

But now, strangely, although the habit was in force, it did not check his anger. It was bewildering that he should feel anger at a poor ignorant man, a working man. It was the first time in his life that he had ever felt so. It shamed him. And he was the more bewildered and ashamed when he understood, as he did, that he was just as angry at the boy as at the old man. He was seeing the boy full grown and the self-pity and hatred taking root beside the urgency and power. The conductor and the boy were links in the great chain of the world's rage.

Clearly it was an unreasoning thing to feel. It was not what a wise man would feel. At this time in his life Stephen Elwin had the wish to be wise. He had never known a wise man. The very word sounded like something in a tale read to children. But the occasion for courage had passed. By courage Elwin meant something very simple, an unbending resistance of spirit under extreme physical difficulties. It was a boy's notion, but it had stayed with Elwin through most of his life, through his business and his pleasure, and nothing that he had ever done had given him the proof that he wanted. And now that the chance for that was gone—he was forty-one years old—it seemed to him that perhaps to be wise was almost as manly a thing as to be brave.

Two wars had passed Elwin by. For one he was too young, for the other too old, though by no means, of course, old. Had it not been for the war, and the consideration of age it so ruthlessly raised, the recollection of the sentence from Hazlitt would no doubt have been delayed by several years, and so too would the impulse to which it had given rise, the desire to have "wisdom." More and more in the last few months, Elwin had been able to experience the sensation of being wise, for it was indeed a sensation, a feeling of stamina, poise and illumination.

He was puzzled and unhappy as he "alighted" from the bus at 92nd Street. It seemed to him a great failure that his knowledge of death and his having reached the years of wisdom—they were the same thing —had not prevented him from feeling anger at an old man and a boy. It then occurred to him to think that perhaps he had felt his anger not in despite of wisdom but because of it. It was a disturbing, even a horrifying, fancy. Yet as he walked the two blocks to his home, he could not help recurring to it, with what was, as he had to see, a certain gratification.

In his pleasant living room, in his comfortable chair, Stephen Elwin watched his daughter as she mixed the drink he usually had before dinner. She was thirteen. About a month ago she had made this her job, almost her duty, and she performed it with an unspeakable seriousness. She measured out the whiskey and poured it into the tumbler. With the ice-tongs she reached the ice gently into the bottom of the glass so that there would not be the least splash of whiskey. She opened the bottle of soda. Holding up the glass for her father's inspection, she poured the soda slowly, ready to stop at her father's word. Elwin cried "Whoa!" and at the word he thought that his daughter had reached the stage of her growth where she did indeed look like a well-bred pony.

Now Margaret was searching for the stirring-spoon. But she had forgotten to put it on the tray with all the other paraphernalia and she gave a little cry of vexation and went to fetch it. Elwin did not tell her not to bother, that it did not matter if the drink was not stirred. He understood that this business had to proceed with a ceremonial completeness.

Margaret returned with the stirring-spoon. She stirred the highball and the soda foamed up. She waited until it subsided, meanwhile shaking the spoon dry over the glass with three precise little shakes. She handed her father the drink and put a coaster on the table by his chair. She watched while he took his first sip. He had taken the whole responsibility for the proportion of soda to whiskey. Still, she wanted to be told that she had made the drink just right. Elwin said, "Fine. Just right," and Margaret tried not to show the absurd pleasure she felt.

For this ritual of Margaret's there were, as Elwin guessed, several motives. The honor of her home required that her father not make his own highball in the pantry and bring it out to drink in his chair, not after she had begun to take notice that in the homes of some of her schoolmates, every evening and not only at dinner parties, a servant brought in, quite as a matter of course, a large tray of drinking equipment. But Margaret had other reasons than snobbishness—Elwin thought that she needed to establish a "custom," not only for now but for the future, against the time when she could say to her children, "And every night before dinner it was the *custom* in our family for me to make my father a drink." He supposed that this ritual of the drink was Margaret's first traffic with the future. It seemed to him that to know a thing like this about his daughter was one of the products of what could be called wisdom and he thought with irony but also with pleasure of his becoming a dim but necessary figure in Margaret's story of the past.

"I bought a picture today," Elwin said.

Margaret cocked an eye at him, as if to say, "Are you on the loose again?" She said, "What is it? Did you bring it home?"

"Oh, just a reproduction, a Rouault."

"Rouault?" she said. She shook her head decisively. "Don't know him." It quite settled Rouault for the moment.

"Don't know him?"

"Never heard of him."

"Well, take a look at it—it's over there."

She untied the string and took off the paper and sat there on the big hassock, her feet far out in front of her, holding the great king at arm's length. It was to Elwin strange and funny, this confrontation of the black, calm, tragic king and this blonde child in her sweater and skirt, in her moccasin shoes. She became abstracted and withdrawn in her scrutiny of the picture. Then Elwin, seeing the breadth and brightness of her brow, the steady intelligence of her gaze, understood that there was really no comic disproportion. What was funny was the equality. The young lieutenant had been quite neutralized by the picture. Even Mark Jennings had been a little diminished by it. But Margaret, with her grave, luminous brow, was able to meet it head on. And not in agreement either.

"You don't like it?" Elwin said.

She looked from the picture to him and said, "I don't think so."

She said it softly but it was pretty positive. She herself painted and she was in a very simple relation to pictures. She rose and placed the picture on the sofa as if to give it another chance in a different position and a better light. She stood at a distance and looked at it and Elwin stood behind her to get the same view of it that she had. He put his hand on her shoulder. After a moment she looked up at him and smiled. "I don't really *like* it," she said. The modulation of her voice was not apology, but simply a gesture of making room for another opinion. She did not think it was important whether she liked or disliked the picture. It said something to her that was not in her experience or that she did not want in her experience. Liking the picture would have given her pleasure. She got no pleasure from not liking it. It seemed to Elwin that in the little shake of her head, in her tone and smile, there was a quality, really monumental, by which he could explain his anger at the old conductor and the boy and forgive himself for having had it.

When Lucy Elwin came in, her face was flushed from the stove and she had a look of triumphant anticipation. She shamelessly communicated this to her family. "It's going to be ve-ry good," she said, not as if she were promising them a fine dinner, rather as if she were threatening them with a grim fate. She meant that her dinner was going to be so very good that if they did not extravagantly admire it, if they merely took it for granted, they would be made to feel sorry. "It will be ready in about ten minutes," she said. "Are you very hungry?"

"Just enough," Elwin said. "Are you tired?" For his wife had stretched out in the armchair and put back her head. She slouched with her long legs at full length, her skirt a little disordered, one ankle laid on the other. Her eyes being closed made her complicated face look simple and she seemed young and self-indulgent, like a girl who escapes from the embarrassment of herself into a broody trance. It was an attitude that had lately become frequent with Margaret.

Lucy Elwin said, "Yes, a little tired. But really, you know, I'd almost rather do the work myself than have that Margaret around."

She spoke with her eyes still closed, and so she did not see her daughter stiffen. But Elwin did. He knew that it was not because Margaret thought that her mother meant her but because of the feelings she had for the other Margaret, the maid. The other Margaret, as so often, had not come to work that day.

Margaret had mixed a drink for her mother and now she was standing beside Lucy's chair, waiting with exaggerated patience for Lucy to open her eyes. She said, "Here's your drink, mother!"

She said it as if she had waited quite long enough, using the lumpish, martyred, unsuccessful irony of thirteen, her eyebrows very weary, the expression of her mouth very dry. Lucy opened her eyes and sat 'up straight in her chair. She took the drink from Margaret and smiled. "Thank you, dear," she said. For the moment it was as if Margaret were the mother, full of rectitude and manners, and Lucy the careless daughter.

That Lucy was being careless even her husband felt. No one could say of their Negro maid, the other Margaret, that she was a pleasant person. Even Elwin would have to admit to a sense of strain in her presence. But surely Lucy took too passionate a notice of her. Elwin felt that this was not in keeping with his wife's nature. But no, that was really not so. It was often disquieting to Elwin, the willingness that Lucy had to get angry even with simple people when she thought they were not behaving well. And lately she had been full of stories about the nasty and insulted temper that was being shown by the people one daily dealt with. Only yesterday, for example, there had been her story of the soda-fountain man who made a point of mopping and puttering and changing the position of pieces of pie and only after he had shown his indifference and independence would take your order. Elwin had to balance against the notice his wife took of such things the deep, literal, almost childish way she spoke of them, the innocence of her passion. But this particular story of the soda-fountain clerk had really distressed him, actually embarrassing him for Lucy, and he had pointed out to her how frequent such stories had become. She had simply stared at him, the fact was so very clear. "Why, it's the war," she said. "People are just much meaner since the war." And when his rebuke had moved on to the matter of the maid Margaret, Lucy had said in the most matter-of-fact way, "Why, she just hates us." And she had shocked Elwin by giving, just like any middle-class housewife, a list of all the precious things Margaret had broken. "And observe," Lucy had said, "that never once has she broken anything cheap or ordinary, only the things I've pointed out to her that needed care."

Elwin had to admit that the list made a case. Still, even if the number of the green Wedgwood coffee cups had been much diminished, cups for which Elwin himself had a special fondness, and even if the Persian bowl had been dropped and the glass urn they had brought from Sweden had been cracked in the sink, they must surely not talk of such things. The very costliness of the objects which proved Margaret's animosity, the very affection which the Elwins felt for them, made the whole situation impossible to consider.

Lucy must indeed have been unaware of how deeply her husband resisted her carelessness in these matters and of what her daughter was now feeling. Otherwise she would not have begun her story, her eyes narrowing in anger at the recollection, "Oh, such a rotten thing happened on the way home on the bus."

It was Elwin who had had the thing happen on the bus, not quite "rotten" but sufficiently disturbing, and he was startled, as if his wife's consciousness had in some way become mixed up with his own in a clairvoyant experience. And this feeling was not diminished as Lucy told her story about a young woman who had asked the conductor a question. It was a simple, ordinary question, Lucy said, about what street one transferred at. The conductor at first had not answered, and then, when he came around again and the question was asked again, he had looked at the young woman—"looked her straight in the face," Lucy said—and had replied in a loud voice, "Vot deed you shay?"

"Mother!" cried Margaret. Her voice was all absolute childish horror.

Elwin at once saw what was happening, but Lucy, absorbed in what she had experienced, only said mildly, "What's the matter, dear?"

"Mother!" Margaret grieved, "you mustn't do that." Her face was quite aghast and she was standing stiff with actual fright.

"Why, do what, Margaret?" said Lucy. She was troubled for her daughter but entirely bewildered.

"Make fun of—fun of—" But Margaret could not say it.

"Of Jews?" said Elwin in a loud, firm, downright voice.

Margaret nodded miserably. Elwin said with enough sharpness, "Margaret, whatever makes you think that Lucy is making fun of Jews? She is simply repeating—"

"Oh," Margaret cried, her face a silly little moon of gratitude and relief. "Oh," she said happily, "what the woman said to the conductor!"

"No, Margaret. How absurd!" Lucy cried. *"Not* what the woman said to the conductor. What the conductor said to the woman."

Margaret just sat there glowering with silence and anger.

Elwin said to Margaret with a pedagogic clearness and patience, "The conductor was making fun of the woman for being Jewish."

"Not at all," Lucy said, beginning to be a little tried by so much misunderstanding. "Not at all, she wasn't Jewish at all. He was insulting her by pretending that she was Jewish."

Margaret had only one question to ask. "The *conductor?*" she cried with desperate emphasis.

And when Lucy said that it was indeed the conductor, Margaret said nothing, but shrugged her shoulders in an elaborate way and made with her hands a large grimace of despairing incomprehension. She was dismissing the grownups by this pantomime, appealing beyond all their sad nonsense to her own world of sure right reason. In that world one knew where one was, one knew that to say things about Jews was bad and that working men were good. And *therefore.*

Elwin, whose awareness was all aroused, wondered in tender amusement what his daughter would have felt if she had known that her gesture, which she had drawn from the large available stock of the folk-culture of children, had originally been a satiric mimicry of a puzzled shrugging Jew. The Margaret who stood there in sullenness was so very different from the Margaret who, only a few minutes before, had looked at the picture with him and had seemed, almost, to be teaching him something. Now he had to teach her. "That isn't a very pretty gesture," he said. "And what, please, is so difficult about Lucy's story? Don't you believe it?"

A mistake, as he saw at once. Margaret was standing there trapped— no, she did not believe it, but she did not dare say so. Elwin corrected himself and gave her her chance. "Do you think Lucy didn't hear right?"

Margaret nodded eagerly, humbly glad to take the way out that was being offered her.

"We studied the transit system," she said by way of explanation. "We made a study of it." She stopped. Elwin knew how her argument ran, but she herself was not entirely sure of it. She said tentatively, by way of a beginning, "They are underpaid."

Lucy was being really irresponsible, Elwin thought, for she said in an abstracted tone, as if she were musing on the early clues of an interesting scientific generalization, "They hate *women*—it's women they're always rude to. Never the men." Margaret's face flushed, and her eyes darkened at this new expression of her mother's moral obtuseness, and Elwin felt a quick impatience with his daughter's sensitivity—it seemed suddenly to have taken on a pedantic air. But he was annoyed with Lucy too, who ought surely be more aware of what her daughter was feeling. No doubt he was the more annoyed because his own incident of the bus was untold and would remain untold. But it was Lucy who saved the situation she had created. She suddenly remembered the kitchen. She hurried out, then came back, caught Margaret by the arm in a bustle of haste and said, "Come and hurl the salad." This was a famous new joke in the family. Elwin had made it, Margaret loved it. It had reference to a "tossed green salad" on a pretentious restaurant menu. Of the salad, when it was served to them in all its wiltedness, Elwin had said that apparently it needed to be more than tossed, it needed to be hurled.

And so all at once the family was restored, a family with a family joke. Margaret stood there grinning in the embarrassment of the voluptuous pleasure she felt at happiness returned. But she must have been very angry with her mother, for she came back and pulled Elwin's head down and whispered into his ear where he would be able to find and inspect the presents she had for Lucy's birthday next week.

He was to look for two things. In the top left-hand drawer of Margaret's desk he would find the "bought present" and on the shelf in the clothes closet he would find the "made present." The bought present was a wallet, a beautiful green wallet, so clearly expensive that Elwin understood why his daughter had had to tease him for money to supplement her savings, and so adult in its expensiveness that he had to understand how inexorably she was growing up.

The made present was also green, a green lamb, large enough to have to be held in two hands, with black feet and wide black eyes. The eyes stared out with a great charming question to the world, expressing the comic grace of the lamb's awkwardness. Elwin wondered if Margaret had been at all aware of how much the lamb was a self-portrait. When Elwin, some two years before, had listened to his daughter playing her first full piece on the recorder, he had thought that nothing could be more wonderful than the impervious gravity of her face as her eyes focussed on the bell of the instrument and on the music book while she blew her tune in a daze of concentration; yet only a few months later, when she had progressed so far as to be up to airs from Mozart, she had been able, in the very midst of a roulade, with her fingers moving fast, to glance up at him with a twinkling, sidelong look, her mouth puckering in a smile as she kept her lips pursed, amused by the music, amused by the frank excess of its ornamentation and by her own virtuosity. For Elwin the smile was the expression of gay and conscious life, of life innocently aware of itself and fond of itself, and, although there was something painful in having to make the admission, it was even more endearing than Margaret's earlier gravity. Life aware of itself seemed so much more life.

His daughter's room was full of life. His own old microscope stood on Margaret's desk and around it was a litter of slides and of the various objects from which she had been cutting sections, a prune and a dried apricot, a sliver of wood, a piece of cheese and what seemed to be a cockroach. There were tools for carving wood and for cutting linoleum blocks. The books were beginning to be too many for the small bookshelf, starting with *The Little Family* and going on to his own soiled copy of *The Light That Failed* that Margaret had unearthed. There was her easel and on one wall was a print of Picasso's trapeze people in flight, like fierce flames, and on another wall one of Benton's righteous stylizations, both at home, knowing nothing of their antagonism to each other. The dolls were no longer so much to the fore as they once were, but they were still about, and so was the elaborate doll's house which contained in precise miniature, accumulated over years, almost every object of daily living, tiny skillets, lamps, cups, kettles, packaged groceries. Surrounded by all that his daughter made and did and read, Elwin could not understand how she found the time. And then, on the thought of what time could be to a child, there came to him with more painful illumination than usual, the recurrent sentence. "No young man believes he shall ever die." And he stood contemplating the room with a kind of desolation of love for it.

Margaret burst in suddenly as if she were running away from something—as indeed she was, for her eyes blazed with the anger she was fleeing. She flung herself on the bed, ignoring her father's presence.

"Margaret, what's the matter?" Elwin said.

But she did not answer.

"Margaret!" There was the note of discipline in his voice. "Tell me what the matter is."

She was not crying, but her face, when she lifted it from the pillow, was red and swollen. "It's Mother," she said. "The way she talked to Margaret."

"To Margaret? Has Margaret come?"

"Yes, she came." The tone implied: through flood and fire. "And Mother—oh!" She broke off and shook her head in a rather histrionic expression of how impossible it was to tell what her mother had done.

"What did she say that was so terrible?"

"She said—she said, 'Look here—'" But Margaret could not go on.

Lucy strode into the room with quite as much impulse as Margaret had and with eyes blazing quite as fiercely as her daughter's. "Look here, Margaret," she said. "I've quite enough trouble with that Margaret without your nonsense. Nobody is being exploited in this house and nobody is being bullied and I'm not going to have you making situations about nothing. I'm sure your Miss Hoxie is very sweet and nice, but you seem to have got your ideas from her all mixed up. You weren't that way about Millie when she was with us. As a matter of fact," Lucy said with remorseless irony, "you were often not at all nice to her."

Margaret had not heard the end of Lucy's speech. At the mention of Miss Hoxie in the tone that Lucy had used—"your Miss Hoxie"—at the sacred name of her teacher blasphemously uttered, she looked at her mother with the horror of seeing her now in her true terrible colors. The last bond between them had snapped at this attack upon her heart's best loyalty.

But Lucy was taking no account of finer feelings. She closed the door and said firmly, "Now look here, the simple fact is that that Margaret is a thoroughly disagreeable person, a nasty, mean person."

"Oh, she is not," Margaret wailed. And then, despite all her passion, the simple fact broke in upon her irresistibly. Elwin's heart quite melted as he saw her confront the fact and struggle with it. For the fact was as Lucy had stated it, and he himself at that moment had to realize it. And it was wonderful to see that Margaret's mind, whatever the inclination of her will, was unable to resist a fact. But the mind that had momentarily deserted her will, came quickly again to its help. "She's not responsible," she said desperately. "It's not her fault. She couldn't help it. Society—" But at that big word she halted, unable to handle it. "We can't blame her," she said defiantly but a little lamely.

At that moment Lucy saw the green clay lamb that Elwin was still holding. She rushed to it and took it and cried, "Margaret, is this yours? I've never seen it, why didn't you show it to me?"

It was, of course, a decided point for Margaret that her birthday surprise was spoiled. She sat there looking dry and indifferent amid the ruins of family custom. Elwin said, "It's a birthday present for you, Lucy. You weren't supposed to see it," and their glances met briefly. He had been a little treacherous, for he could have managed to put the lamb out of sight, but some craftiness, not entirely conscious, had suggested its usefulness for peace.

"It's so *lovely*," Lucy said. "Is it really for me?"

Margaret had to acknowledge that it was, but with an elaborate ungraciousness from her bruised and empty heart. Her mother might have the gift, meaningless as it now was. But Lucy was in a flood of thanks and praise impossible to withstand—it was lovely, she said, to have a gift in advance of her birthday, it was something she had always wanted as a child and had never been able to induce her parents to allow, that she should have one, just one, of her presents before the others, and the lamb itself was simply beautiful, quite the nicest thing Margaret had ever made. "Oh, I love it," she said, stroking its face and then its rump. "Why darling!" she cried, "it looks exactly like you!" And Margaret had to submit to the child's pain at seeing the eminence of grief and grievance swept away. But at last, carried beyond the vacant moment when the forgiving and forgiven feeling had not yet come, she sat there in an embarrassed glow, beaming shyly as her mother kissed her and said quietly and finally, "Thank you."

When they were in the dining room, all three of them feeling chastened and purged, Lucy said, "I must have it here by my place." And she put the lamb by her at the table, touching its cheek affectionately.

The dinner that Lucy had cooked was served by the other Margaret. She was a tall, rather light colored girl, with a genteel manner and eyebrows that were now kept very high. As she presented the casserole to Lucy, she looked far off into a distance and stood a little too far away for convenience. Lucy sat there with the serving spoon and fork in her hand and then said, "Come a little closer, Margaret." Margaret Elwin sat rigid, watching. Margaret the maid edged a little closer and continued her gaze. She moved to serve Elwin but Lucy said, "It's Margaret you serve next." Her tone was a little dry. Margaret Elwin flushed and looked mortified. It had been a matter of some satisfaction that she was now of an age to be served at table just after her mother, but she hated to have a point made of it if Margaret objected, and Margaret did seem to object and would not accept the reassuring smile that was being offered her over the casserole.

In the interval between the serving of the casserole and the serving of the salad that had once that evening made the family peace, Margaret held her parents with a stern and desperate eye. But she was unable to suppress a glance her mother sent to her father, a glance that had in it a touch of mild triumph. And her father did not this time fortify himself against it. The odds were terribly against her and she looked from one to the other and said in an intense whisper, "It's not her fault. She's not responsible."

"Why not?" Elwin asked.

It was his voice that made the question baffling to Margaret. She did not answer, or try to. It was not merely that the question was, for the moment, beyond her powers. Nor was it that she was puzzled because her father had seemed to change sides. But she was touched by the sense, so little formulated, so fleeting as scarcely to establish itself in her memory, that something other than the question, or the problem itself, was involved here. She barely perceived, yet she did perceive, her mother's quick glance at her father under lowered lids. It was something more than a glance of surprise. Neither Margaret nor Lucy, of course, knew anything about the sentence from Hazlitt. But this was one of the moments when the sentence had occurred to Elwin and with it the explosion of light. And his wife and daughter had heard the event in his voice. For Elwin an illumination, but a dark illumination, was thrown around the matter that concerned them. It seemed to him—not suddenly, for it had been advancing in his mind for some hours now— that in the aspect of his knowledge of death, all men were equal in their responsibility. The two bus conductors, Lucy's and his own, the boy with his face contorted in rational rage against the injustice he suffered, Margaret the maid with her genteel malice—all of them, quite as much as he himself, bore their own blame. Exemption was not given by age or youth, or sex, or color, or condition of life. It was the sense of this that made his voice so strange at his own dinner table, as if it came not merely from another place but another time.

"Why not?" he said again. "Why not, Margaret?"

Margaret looked at her father's face and tried to answer. She seriously marshalled her thoughts and, as always, the sight of his daughter actually thinking touched Elwin profoundly. "It's because—because society didn't give her a chance," she said slowly. "She has a handicap. Because she's colored. She has to struggle so hard—against prejudice. It's so *hard* for her."

"It's true," Elwin said. "It's very hard for her. But it's hard for Millie too." Millie had been with the Elwins for nearly seven years. Some months ago she had left them to nurse a dying sister in the South.

Margaret of course knew what her father meant, that Millie, despite "society," was warm and good and capable. Her answer was quick, too quick. "Oh, Millie has a slave-psychology," she said loftily.

Really, Elwin thought, Miss Hoxie went too far. He felt a kind of disgust that a child should have been given such a phrase to use. It was a good school, he approved of its theory; but it must not give Margaret such things to say. He wondered if Margaret had submitted the question of Millie to Miss Hoxie. If she had, and if this was the answer she had been given, his daughter had been, yes, corrupted. He said, "You should not say such things about Millie. She is a good loyal person and you haven't any right to say she is not."

"Loyal!" said Margaret in triumph. "Loyal!"

"Why yes. To her sister in Alabama, Margaret, just as much as to us. Is it what you call slave-psychology to be loyal to your own sister?"

But Margaret was not to be put down. She kept in mind the main point, which was not Millie but the other Margaret.

"I notice," she said defiantly, "that when Millie sends you parts of the money you lent her, you take it all right."

Poor child, she had fumbled, and Elwin laid his hand on hers on the table. "But Margaret! Of course I do," he said. "If I didn't, wouldn't that be slave-psychology? Millie would feel very lowered if I didn't take it."

"But she can't afford it," Margaret insisted.

"No, she can't afford it."

"Well then!" and she confronted the oppressor in her father.

"But she can't afford not to. She needs it for her pride. She needs to think of herself as a person who pays her debts, as a responsible person."

"I wonder," Lucy said, "I wonder how Millie is. Poor thing!" She was not being irrelevant. She was successful in bringing her husband up short. Yes, all that his "wisdom" had done was to lead him to defeat his daughter in argument. And defeat made Margaret stupid and obstinate. She said, "Well, anyway, it's not Margaret's fault," and sat sulking.

Had he been truly the wise man he wanted to be, he would have been able to explain, to Margaret and himself, the nature of the double truth. As much as Margaret, he believed that "society is responsible." He believed the other truth too. He felt rather tired, as if the little debate with Margaret had been more momentous than he understood. Yet wisdom, a small measure of it, did seem to come. It came suddenly, as no doubt was the way of moments of wisdom, and he perceived what stupidly he had not understood earlier, that it was not the other Margaret but herself that his Margaret was grieving for, that in her foolish and passionate argument, with the foolish phases derived from the admired Miss Hoxie, she was defending herself from her own impending responsibility. Poor thing, she saw it moving toward her through the air at a great rate, and she did not want it. Naturally enough, she did not want it. And he, for what reason he did not know, was forcing it upon her.

He understood why Lucy, when they had risen from the table, made quiet haste to put her arm around Margaret's shoulders as they went into the living room.

They were sitting in the living room, a rather silent family for the moment, when the other Margaret stood in the doorway. "You may as well know," she said, "that I'm through here." And she added, "I've had enough."

There was a little cry, as of horror, from Margaret. She looked at her parents with a bitter and tragic triumph. Lucy said shortly, "Very well, Margaret. Just finish up and I'll pay you." The quick acceptance took the maid aback. Angrier than before, she turned abruptly back into the dining room.

For the third time that evening, Margaret Elwin sat in wretched isolation. Her father did not watch her, but he knew what she felt. She had been told *she* might go, never to return. She saw the great and frightening world before her. It was after all possible so to offend her parents that this expulsion would follow. Elwin rose to get a cigarette from the table near the sofa on which Margaret sat and he passed his hand over her bright hair. The picture of the king with the flower in his hand was in the other corner of the sofa.

It was as Elwin's hand was on his daughter's head that they heard the crash, and Elwin felt under his hand how Margaret's body experienced a kind of convulsion. He turned and saw Lucy already at the door of the dining room, while there on the floor, in many pieces, as if it had fallen with force, lay the smashed green lamb, more white clay showing than green glaze. Lucy stooped down to the fragments, examining them, delicately turning them over one by one, as if already estimating the possibility of mending.

The maid Margaret stood there, a napkin in her hand clutched to her breast. All the genteel contempt had left her face. She looked only frightened, as if something was now, at last, going to be done to her. For her, almost more than for his own Margaret, Elwin felt sad. He said, "It's all right, Margaret. Don't worry, it's all right." It was a foolish and weak thing to say. It was not all right, and Lucy was still crouching, heart-broken, over the pieces. But he had had to say it, weak and foolish as it was.

"Ah, darling, don't feel too bad," Lucy said to her daughter as she came back into the living room, tenderly holding the smashed thing in her hand.

But Margaret did not answer or even hear. She was staring into the dining room with wide, fixed eyes. "She meant to do it," she said. "She *meant* to do it."

"Oh, no," Lucy said in her most matter-of-fact voice. "Oh, no, dear. It was just an accident."

"She meant to do it, she meant to do it." And then Margaret said, "I *saw* her." She alone had been facing into the dining room and could have seen. "I saw her—with the napkin. She made a movement," and Margaret made a movement, "like this . . ."

Over her head her parents' eyes met. They knew that they could only offer the feeble lying of parents to a child. But they were determined to continue. "Oh, no," Elwin said, "it just happened." And he wondered if the king, within his line of vision as he stood there trying to comfort his daughter, would ever return to the old, fine, tragic power, for at the moment he seemed only quaint, extravagant and beside the point.

"She meant to. She didn't like me. She hated me," and the great sobs began to come. But Elwin knew that it was not because the other Margaret hated her that his Margaret wept, but because she had with her own eyes seen the actual possibility of what she herself might do, the insupportable fact of her own moral life. She was weeping bitterly now, her whole body shaking with the deepest of sobs, and she found refuge in a corner of the sofa, hiding her head from her parents. She had drawn up her knees, making herself as tight and inaccessible as she could, and Elwin, to comfort her, sat on what little space she allowed him on the sofa beside her, stroking her burrowing head and her heaving back, quite unable, whatever he might have hoped and wanted, to give her any better help than that.

THE JELLY-BEAN

This is a tale of luck and love and their effect upon one of the
more easygoing characters who live in a sleepy town in the
South and assuredly belong to the Jazz Age. There is a party
going on at the country club; the atmosphere is one in which
we can rightly expect the author to feel perfectly at home. Here
we meet Jim Powell, the hero of our story, and share his
reverie made sensuous at the moment by the night and "by the hot
smell of damp powder puffs, tucked in the fronts of low
dresses and distilling a thousand rich scents to float out through
the open door"—a door through which Nancy Lamar will walk
presently.

"Lucky in dice—unlucky in love!" The reader need not be
an accomplished crapshooter himself to follow the fortunes,
good and bad, attendant upon Nancy's—and Jim's—proficiency
in the art of the dice.

J im Powell was a Jelly-bean. Much as I desire to make him an
appealing character, I feel that it would be unscrupulous to deceive you
on that point. He was a bred-in-the-bone, dyed-in-the-wool, ninety-nine
three-quarters per cent Jelly-bean and he grew lazily all during Jelly-
bean season, which is every season, down in the land of the Jelly-beans
well below the Mason-Dixon line.

Now if you call a Memphis man a Jelly-bean he will quite possibly
pull a long sinewy rope from his pocket and hang you to a convenient
telegraph-pole. If you call a New Orleans man a Jelly-bean he will probably grin and ask you who is taking your girl to the Mardi Gras ball. The
particular Jelly-bean patch which produced the protagonist of this history lies somewhere between the two—a little city of forty thousand that
has dozed sleepily for forty thousand years in southern Georgia, occasionally stirring in its slumbers and muttering something about a war
that took place sometime, somewhere, and that everyone else has forgotten long ago.

Jim was a Jelly-bean. I write that again because it has such a pleasant sound—rather like the beginning of a fairy story—as if Jim were
nice. It somehow gives me a picture of him with a round, appetizing face

and all sorts of leaves and vegetables growing out of his cap. But Jim was long and thin and bent at the waist from stooping over pool tables, and he was what might have been known in the indiscriminating North as a corner loafer. "Jelly-bean" is the name throughout the undissolved Confederacy for one who spends his life conjugating the verb *to idle* in the first person singular—I am idling, I have idled, I will idle.

Jim was born in a white house on a green corner. It had four weather-beaten pillars in front and a great amount of lattice-work in the rear that made a cheerful criss-cross background for a flowery sun-drenched lawn. Originally the dwellers in the white house had owned the ground next door and next door to that and next door to that, but this had been so long ago that even Jim's father scarcely remembered it. He had, in fact, thought it a matter of so little moment that when he was dying from a pistol wound got in a brawl he neglected even to tell little Jim, who was five years old and miserably frightened. The white house became a boarding-house run by a tight-lipped lady from Macon, whom Jim called Aunt Mamie and detested with all his soul.

He became fifteen, went to high school, wore his hair in black snarls, and was afraid of girls. He hated his home where four women and one old man prolonged an interminable chatter from summer to summer about what lots the Powell place had originally included and what sort of flowers would be out next. Sometimes the parents of little girls in town, remembering Jim's mother and fancying a resemblance in the dark eyes and hair, invited him to parties, but parties made him shy and he much preferred sitting on a disconnected axle in Tilly's Garage, rolling the bones or exploring his mouth endlessly with a long straw. For pocket money, he picked up odd jobs, and it was due to this that he stopped going to parties. At his third party little Marjorie Haight had whispered indiscreetly and within hearing distance that he was a boy who brought the groceries sometimes. So instead of the two-step and polka, Jim had learned to throw any number he desired on the dice and had listened to spicy tales of all the shootings that had occurred in the surrounding country during the past fifty years.

He became eighteen. The war broke out and he enlisted as a gob and polished brass in the Charleston Navy-yard for a year. Then by way of variety, he went North and polished brass in the Brooklyn Navy-yard for a year.

When the war was over he came home. He was twenty-one, his trousers were too short and too tight. His buttoned shoes were long and narrow. His tie was an alarming conspiracy of purple and pink marvellously scrolled, and over it were two blue eyes faded like a piece of very good old cloth long exposed to the sun.

In the twilight of one April evening when a soft gray had drifted down along the cottonfields and over the sultry town, he was a vague figure leaning against a board fence, whistling and gazing at the moon's rim above the lights of Jackson Street. His mind was working persistently on a problem that had held his attention for an hour. The Jelly-bean had been invited to a party.

Back in the days when all the boys had detested all the girls, Clark Darrow and Jim had sat side by side in school. But, while Jim's social aspirations had died in the oily air of the garage, Clark had alternately fallen in and out of love, gone to college, taken to drink, given it up, and, in short, become one of the best beaux of the town. Nevertheless Clark and Jim had retained a friendship that, though casual, was perfectly definite. That afternoon Clark's ancient Ford had slowed up beside Jim, who was on the sidewalk, and, out of a clear sky, Clark had invited him to a party at the country club. The impulse that made him do this was no stranger than the impulse which made Jim accept. The latter was probably an unconscious ennui, a half-frightened sense of adventure. And now Jim was soberly thinking it over.

He began to sing, drumming his long foot idly on a stone block in the sidewalk till it wobbled up and down in time to the low throaty tune:

> *"One mile from Home in Jelly-bean town,*
> *Lives Jeanne, the Jelly-bean Queen.*
> *She loves her dice and treats 'em nice;*
> *No dice would treat her mean."*

He broke off and agitated the sidewalk to a bumpy gallop.

"Daggone!" he muttered, half aloud.

They would all be there—the old crowd, the crowd to which, by right of the white house, sold long since, and the portrait of the officer in gray over the mantel, Jim should have belonged. But that crowd had grown up together into a tight little set as gradually as the girls' dresses had lengthened inch by inch, as definitely as the boys' trousers had dropped suddenly to their ankles. And to that society of first names and dead puppy-loves Jim was an outsider—a running mate of poor whites. Most of the men knew him, condescendingly; he tipped his hat to three or four girls. That was all.

When the dusk had thickened into a blue setting for the moon, he walked through the hot, pleasantly pungent town to Jackson Street. The stores were closing and the last shoppers were drifting homeward, as if borne on the dreamy revolution of a slow merry-go-round. A street-fair farther down made a brilliant alley of vari-colored booths and contributed a blend of music to the night—an oriental dance on a calliope, a melancholy bugle in front of a freak show, a cheerful rendition of "Back Home in Tennessee" on a hand-organ.

The Jelly-bean stopped in a store and bought a collar. Then he sauntered along toward Soda Sam's, where he found the usual three or four cars of a summer evening parked in front and the little darkies running back and forth with sundaes and lemonades.

"Hello, Jim."

It was a voice at his elbow—Joe Ewing sitting in an automobile with Marylyn Wade. Nancy Lamar and a strange man were in the back seat.

The Jelly-bean tipped his hat quickly.

"Hi, Ben—" Then, after an almost imperceptible pause—"How y'all?"

Passing, he ambled on toward the garage where he had a room upstairs. His "How y'all?" had been said to Nancy Lamar, to whom he had not spoken in fifteen years.

Nancy had a mouth like a remembered kiss and shadowy eyes and blue-black hair inherited from her mother who had been born in Budapest. Jim passed her often in the street, walking small-boy fashion with her hands in her pockets, and he knew that with her inseparable Sally Carrol Hopper she had left a trail of broken hearts from Atlanta to New Orleans.

For a few fleeting moments Jim wished he could dance. Then he laughed and as he reached his door began to sing softly to himself:

> *Her Jelly Roll can twist your soul,*
> *Her eyes are big and brown,*
> *She's the Queen of the Queens of the Jelly-beans—*
> *My Jeanne of Jelly-bean town.*

I I

At nine-thirty Jim and Clark met in front of Soda Sam's and started for the Country Club in Clark's Ford.

"Jim," asked Clark casually, as they rattled through the jasmine-scented night, "how do you keep alive?"

The Jelly-bean paused, considered.

"Well," he said finally, "I got a room over Tilly's Garage. I help him some with the cars in the afternoon an' he gives it to me free. Sometimes I drive one of his taxis and pick up a little thataway. I get fed up doin' that regular though."

"That's all?"

"Well, when there's a lot of work I help him by the day—Saturdays usually—and then there's one main source of revenue I don't generally mention. Maybe you don't recollect I'm about the champion crap-shooter of this town. They make me shoot from a cup now because once I get the feel of a pair of dice they just roll for me."

Clark grinned appreciatively.

"I never could learn to set 'em so's they'd do what I wanted. Wish you'd shoot with Nancy Lamar some day and take all her money away from her. She *will* roll 'em with the boys and she loses more than her daddy can afford to give her. I happen to know she sold a good ring last month to pay a debt."

The Jelly-bean was noncommittal.

"The white house on Elm Street still belong to you?"

Jim shook his head.

"Sold. Got a pretty good price, seein' it wasn't in a good part of town no more. Lawyer told me to put it into Liberty bonds. But Aunt Mamie got so she didn't have no sense, so it takes all the interest to keep her up at Great Farms Sanitarium."

"H'm."

"I got an old uncle upstate an' I reckon I kin go up there if ever I get sure enough pore. Nice farm, but not enough niggers around to work it. He's asked me to come up and help him, but I don't guess I'd take much to it. Too doggone lonesome—" He broke off suddenly. "Clark, I want to tell you I'm much obliged to you for askin' me out, but I'd be a lot happier if you'd just stop the car right here an' let me walk back into town."

"Shucks!" Clark grunted. "Do you good to step out. You don't have to dance—just get out there on the floor and shake."

"Hold on," exclaimed Jim uneasily. "Don't you go leadin' me up to any girls and leavin' me there so I'll have to dance with 'em."

Clark laughed.

" 'Cause," continued Jim desperately, "without you swear you won't do that I'm agoin' to get out right here an' my good legs goin' carry me back to Jackson Street."

They agreed after some argument that Jim, unmolested by females, was to view the spectacle from a secluded settee in the corner where Clark would join him whenever he wasn't dancing.

So ten o'clock found the Jelly-bean with his legs crossed and his arms conservatively folded, trying to look casually at home and politely uninterested in the dancers. At heart he was torn between overwhelming self-consciousness and an intense curiosity as to all that went on around him. He saw the girls emerge one by one from the dressing room, stretching and pluming themselves like bright birds, smiling over their powdered shoulders at the chaperones, casting a quick glance around to take in the room and, simultaneously, the room's reaction to their entrance—and then, again like birds, alighting and nestling in the sober arms of their waiting escorts. Sally Carrol Hopper, blonde and lazy-eyed, appeared clad in her favorite pink and blinking like an awakened rose. Marjorie Haight, Marylyn Wade, Harriet Cary, all the girls he had seen loitering down Jackson Street by noon, now, curled and brilliantined and delicately tinted for the overhead lights, were miraculously strange Dresden figures of pink and blue and red and gold, fresh from the shop and not yet fully dried.

He had been there half an hour, totally uncheered by Clark's jovial visits which were each one accompanied by a "Hello, old boy, how you making out?" and a slap at his knee. A dozen males had spoken to him or stopped for a moment beside him, but he knew that they were each one surprised at finding him there and fancied that one or two were even slightly resentful. But at half past ten his embarrassment suddenly left him and a pull of breathless interest took him completely out of himself—Nancy Lamar had come out of the dressing room.

She was dressed in yellow organdie, a costume of a hundred cool corners, with three tiers of ruffles and a big bow in back until she shed black and yellow around her in a sort of phosphorescent lustre. The Jelly-bean's eyes opened wide and a lump arose in his throat. For a minute she stood beside the door until her partner hurried up. Jim recognized him as the stranger who had been with her in Joe Ewing's car that afternoon. He saw her set her arms akimbo and say something in a low voice, and laugh. The man laughed too and Jim experienced the quick pang of a weird new kind of pain. Some ray had passed between the pair, a shaft of beauty from that sun that had warmed him a moment since. The Jelly-bean felt suddenly like a weed in a shadow.

A minute later Clark approached him, bright-eyed and glowing.

"Hi, old man," he cried with some lack of originality. "How you making out?"

Jim replied that he was making out as well as could be expected.

"You come along with me," commanded Clark. "I've got something that'll put an edge on the evening."

Jim followed him awkwardly across the floor and up the stairs to the locker room where Clark produced a flask of nameless yellow liquid.

"Good old corn."

Ginger ale arrived on a tray. Such potent nectar as "good old corn" needed some disguise beyond seltzer.

"Say, boy," exclaimed Clark breathlessly, "doesn't Nancy Lamar look beautiful?"

Jim nodded.

"Mighty beautiful," he agreed.

"She's all dolled up to a fare-you-well tonight," continued Clark. "Notice that fellow she's with?"

"Big fella? White pants?"

"Yeah. Well, that's Ogden Merritt from Savannah. Old man Merritt makes the Merritt safety razors. This fella's crazy about her. Been chasing after her all year.

"She's a wild baby," continued Clark, "but I like her. So does everybody. But she sure does do crazy stunts. She usually gets out alive, but she's got scars all over her reputation from one thing or another she's done."

"That so?" Jim passed over his glass. "That's good corn."

"Not so bad. Oh, she's a wild one. Shoots craps, say, boy! And she do like her highball. Promised I'd give her one later on."

"She in love with this—Merritt?"

"Damned if I know. Seems like all the best girls around here marry fellas and go off somewhere."

He poured himself one more drink and carefully corked the bottle.

"Listen, Jim, I got to go dance and I'd be much obliged if you just stick this corn right on your hip as long as you're not dancing. If a man notices I've had a drink he'll come up and ask me and before I know it it's all gone and somebody else is having my good time."

So Nancy Lamar was going to marry. This toast of a town was to become the private property of an individual in white trousers—and all because white trousers' father had made a better razor than his neighbor. As they descended the stairs Jim found the idea inexplicably depressing. For the first time in his life he felt a vague and romantic yearning. A picture of her began to form in his imagination—Nancy walking boylike and debonnaire along the street, taking an orange as tithe from a worshipful fruit dealer, charging a dope on a mythical account at Soda Sam's, assembling a convoy of beaux and then driving off in triumphal state for an afternoon of splashing and singing.

The Jelly-bean walked out on the porch to a deserted corner, dark between the moon on the lawn and the single lighted door of the ballroom. There he found a chair and, lighting a cigarette, drifted into the thoughtless reverie that was his usual mood. Yet now it was a reverie made sensuous by the night and by the hot smell of damp powder puffs, tucked in the fronts of low dresses and distilling a thousand rich scents to float out through the open door. The music itself, blurred by a loud trombone, became hot and shadowy, a languorous overtone to the scraping of many shoes and slippers.

Suddenly the square of yellow light that fell through the door was obscured by a dark figure. A girl had come out of the dressing room and was standing on the porch not more than ten feet away. Jim heard a low-breathed "doggone" and then she turned and saw him. It was Nancy Lamar.

Jim rose to his feet.

"Howdy?"

"Hello—" She paused, hesitated, and then approached. "Oh, it's— Jim Powell."

He bowed slightly, tried to think of a casual remark.

"Do you suppose," she began quickly, "I mean—do you know anything about gum?"

"What?"

"I've got gum on my shoe. Some utter ass left his or her gum on the floor and of course I stepped in it."

Jim blushed, inappropriately.

"Do you know how to get it off?" she demanded petulantly. "I've tried every damn thing in the dressing room. I've tried soap and water —and even perfume and I've ruined my powder puff trying to make it stick to that."

Jim considered the question in some agitation.

"Why—I think maybe gasoline—"

The words had scarcely left his lips when she grasped his hand and pulled him at a run off the low veranda, over a flower bed and at a gallop toward a group of cars parked in the moonlight by the first hole of the golf course.

"Turn on the gasoline," she commanded breathlessly.

"What?"

"For the gum, of course. I've got to get it off. I can't dance with gum on."

Obediently Jim turned to the cars and began inspecting them with a view to obtaining the desired solvent. Had she demanded a cylinder he would have done his best to wrench one out.

"Here," he said after a moment's search. "Here's one that's easy. Got a handkerchief?"

"It's upstairs wet. I used it for the soap and water."

Jim laboriously explored his pockets.

"Don't believe I got one either."

"Doggone it! Well, we can turn it on and let it run on the ground."

He turned it on fuller. The dripping became a flow and formed an oily pool that glistened brightly, reflecting a dozen tremulous moons on its quivering bosom.

"Ah," she sighed contentedly, "let it all out. The only thing to do is to wade in it."

In desperation he turned on the tap full and the pool suddenly widened, sending tiny rivers and trickles in all directions.

"That's fine. That's something like."

Raising her skirts she stepped gracefully in.

"I know this'll take it off," she murmured.

Jim smiled.

"There's lots more cars."

She stepped daintily out of the gasoline and began scraping her slippers, side and bottom, on the running-board of the automobile. The Jelly-bean contained himself no longer. He bent double with explosive laughter and after a second she joined in.

"You're here with Clark Darrow, aren't you?" she asked as they walked back toward the veranda.

"Yes."

"You know where he is now?"

"Out dancin', I reckin."

"The deuce. He promised me a highball."

"Well," said Jim, "I guess that'll be all right. I got his bottle right here in my pocket."

She smiled at him radiantly.

"I guess maybe you'll need ginger ale though," he added.

"Not me. Just the bottle."

"Sure enough?"

She laughed scornfully.

"Try me. I can drink anything any man can. Let's sit down."

She perched herself on the side of a table and he dropped into one of the wicker chairs beside her. Taking out the cork, she held the flask to her lips and took a long drink. He watched her, fascinated.

"Like it?"

She shook her head breathlessly.

"No, but I like the way it makes me feel. I think most people are that way."

Jim agreed.

"My daddy liked it too well. It got him."

"American men," said Nancy gravely, "don't know how to drink."

"What?" Jim was startled.

"In fact," she went on carelessly, "they don't know how to do anything very well. The one thing I regret in my life is that I wasn't born in England."

"In England?"

"Yes. It's the one regret of my life that I wasn't."

"Do you like it over there?"

"Yes. Immensely. I've never been there in person, but I've met a lot of Englishmen who were over here in the army, Oxford and Cambridge men—you know, that's like Sewanee and University of Georgia are here —and of course I've read a lot of English novels."

Jim was interested, amazed.

"D'you ever hear of Lady Diana Manners?" she asked earnestly.

No, Jim had not.

"Well, she's what I'd like to be. Dark, you know, like me, and wild as sin. She's the girl who rode her horse up the steps of some cathedral or church or something and all the novelists made their heroines do it afterwards."

Jim nodded politely. He was out of his depths.

"Pass the bottle," suggested Nancy. "I'm going to take another little one. A little drink wouldn't hurt a baby."

"You see," she continued, again breathless after a draught. "People over there have style. Nobody has style here. I mean the boys here aren't really worth dressing up for or doing sensational things for. Don't you know?"

"I suppose so—I mean I suppose not," murmured Jim.

"And I'd like to do 'em an' all. I'm really the only girl in town that has style."

She stretched out her arms and yawned pleasantly.

"Pretty evening."

"Sure is," agreed Jim.

"Like to have boat," she suggested dreamily. "Like to sail out on a silver lake, say the Thames, for instance. Have champagne and caviar sandwiches along. Have about eight people. And one of the men would jump overboard to amuse the party and get drowned like a man did with Lady Diana Manners once."

"Did he do it to please her?"

"Didn't mean to drown himself to please her. He just meant to jump overboard and make everybody laugh."

"I reckin they just died laughin' when he drowned."

"Oh, I suppose they laughed a little," she admitted. "I imagine she did, anyway. She's pretty hard, I guess—like I am."

"You hard?"

"Like nails." She yawned again and added, "Give me a little more from that bottle."

Jim hesitated but she held out her hand defiantly.

"Don't treat me like a girl," she warned him. "I'm not like any girl *you* ever saw." She considered. "Still, perhaps you're right. You got— you got old head on young shoulders."

She jumped to her feet and moved toward the door. The Jelly-bean rose also.

"Good-bye," she said politely, "good-bye. Thanks, Jelly-bean."

Then she stepped inside and left him wide-eyed upon the porch.

III

At twelve o'clock a procession of cloaks issued single file from the women's dressing room and, each one pairing with a coated beau like dancers meeting in a cotillion figure, drifted through the door with sleepy happy laughter—through the door into the dark where autos backed and snorted and parties called to one another and gathered around the water-cooler.

Jim, sitting in his corner, rose to look for Clark. They had met at eleven; then Clark had gone in to dance. So, seeking him, Jim wandered into the soft-drink stand that had once been a bar. The room was deserted except for a sleepy Negro dozing behind the counter and two boys lazily fingering a pair of dice at one of the tables. Jim was about to leave them when he saw Clark coming in. At the same moment Clark looked up.

"Hi, Jim!" he commanded. "C'mon over and help us with this bottle. I guess there's not much left, but there's one all around."

Nancy, the man from Savannah, Marylyn Wade, and Joe Ewing were lolling and laughing in the doorway. Nancy caught Jim's eye and winked at him humorously.

They drifted over to a table and arranging themselves around it waited for the waiter to bring ginger ale. Jim, faintly ill at ease, turned his eyes on Nancy, who had drifted into a nickel crap game with the two boys at the next table.

"Bring them over here," suggested Clark.

Joe looked around.

"We don't want to draw a crowd. It's against club rules."

"Nobody's around," insisted Clark, "except Mr. Taylor. He's walking up and down like a wild man trying to find out who let all the gasoline out of his car."

There was a general laugh.

"I bet a million Nancy got something on her shoe again. You can't park when she's around."

"O Nancy, Mr. Taylor's looking for you!"

Nancy's cheeks were glowing with excitement over the game. "I haven't seen his silly little flivver in two weeks."

Jim felt a sudden silence. He turned and saw an individual of uncertain age standing in the doorway.

Clark's voice punctuated the embarrassment.

"Won't you join us, Mr. Taylor?"

"Thanks."

Mr. Taylor spread his unwelcome presence over a chair. "Have to, I'm waiting till they dig me up some gasoline. Somebody got funny with my car."

His eyes narrowed and he looked quickly from one to the other. Jim wondered what he had heard from the doorway—tried to remember what had been said.

"I'm right tonight," Nancy sang out, "and my four bits is in the ring."

"Faded!" snapped Taylor suddenly.

"Why, Mr. Taylor, I didn't know you shot craps!" Nancy was overjoyed to find that he had seated himself and instantly covered her bet. They had openly disliked each other since the night she had definitely discouraged a series of rather pointed advances.

"All right, babies, do it for your mama. Just one little seven." Nancy was *cooing* to the dice. She rattled them with a brave underhand flourish, and rolled them out on the table.

"Ah-h! I suspected it. And now again with the dollar up."

Five passes to her credit found Taylor a bad loser. She was making it personal, and after each success Jim watched triumph flutter across her face. She was doubling with each throw—such luck could scarcely last.

"Better go easy," he cautioned her timidly.

"Ah, but watch this one," she whispered. It was eight on the dice and she called her number.

"Little Ada, this time we're going South."

Ada from Decatur rolled over the table. Nancy was flushed and half-hysterical, but her luck was holding. She drove the pot up and up, refusing to drag. Taylor was drumming with his fingers on the table, but he was in to stay.

Then Nancy tried for a ten and lost the dice. Taylor seized them avidly. He shot in silence, and in the hush of excitement the clatter of one pass after another on the table was the only sound.

Now Nancy had the dice again, but her luck had broken. An hour passed. Back and forth it went. Taylor had been at it again—and again and again. They were even at last—Nancy lost her ultimate five dollars.

"Will you take my check," she said quickly, "for fifty, and we'll shoot it all?" Her voice was a little unsteady and her hand shook as she reached to the money.

Clark exchanged an uncertain but alarmed glance with Joe Ewing. Taylor shot again. He had Nancy's check.

"How 'bout another?" she said wildly. "Jes' any bank'll do—money everywhere as a matter of fact."

Jim understood—the "good old corn" he had given her—the "good old corn" she had taken since. He wished he dared interfere—a girl of that age and position would hardly have two bank accounts. When the clock struck two he contained himself no longer.

"May I—can't you let me roll 'em for you?" he suggested, his low, lazy voice a little strained.

Suddenly sleepy and listless, Nancy flung the dice down before him.

"All right—old boy! As Lady Diana Manners says, 'Shoot 'em, Jelly-bean'— My luck's gone."

"Mr. Taylor," said Jim, carelessly, "we'll shoot for one of those there checks against the cash."

Half an hour later Nancy swayed forward and clapped him on the back.

"Stole my luck, you did." She was nodding her head sagely.

Jim swept up the last check and putting it with the others tore them into confetti and scattered them on the floor. Someone started singing, and Nancy, kicking her chair backward, rose to her feet.

"Ladies and gentlemen," she announced. "Ladies—that's you, Marylyn. I want to tell the world that Mr. Jim Powell, who is a well-known Jelly-bean of this city, is an exception to a great rule—'lucky in dice—unlucky in love.' He's lucky in dice, and as matter of fact I—I *love* him. Ladies and gentlemen, Nancy Lamar, famous dark-haired beauty often featured in the *Herald* as one th' most popular members of younger set as other girls are often featured in this particular case. Wish to announce—wish to announce, anyway, gentlemen—" She tipped suddenly. Clark caught her and restored her balance.

"My error," she laughed, "she stoops to—stoops to—anyways— We'll drink to Jelly-bean . . . Mr. Jim Powell, King of the Jelly-beans."

And a few minutes later as Jim waited hat in hand for Clark in the darkness of that same corner of the porch where she had come searching for gasoline, she appeared suddenly beside him.

"Jelly-bean," she said, "are you here, Jelly-bean? I think—" and her slight unsteadiness seemed part of an enchanted dream—"I think you deserve one of my sweetest kisses for that, Jelly-bean."

For an instant her arms were around his neck—her lips were pressed to his.

"I'm a wild part of the world, Jelly-bean, but you did me a good turn."

Then she was gone, down the porch, over the cricket-loud lawn. Jim saw Merritt come out the front door and say something to her angrily —saw her laugh and, turning away, walk with averted eyes to his car. Marylyn and Joe followed, singing a drowsy song about a Jazz baby.

Clark came out and joined Jim on the steps. "All pretty lit, I guess," he yawned. "Merritt's in a mean mood. He's certainly off Nancy."

Over east along the golf course a faint rug of gray spread itself across the feet of the night. The party in the car began to chant a chorus as the engine warmed up.

"Good night, everybody," called Clark.

"Good night, Clark."

"Good night."

There was a pause, and then a soft, happy voice added, "Good night, Jelly-bean."

The car drove off to a burst of singing. A rooster on a farm across the way took up a solitary mournful crow, and behind them a last Negro waiter turned out the porch light. Jim and Clark strolled over toward the Ford, their shoes crunching raucously on the gravel drive.

"O boy!" sighed Clark softly, "how you can set those dice!"

It was still too dark for him to see the flush on Jim's thin cheeks— or to know that it was a flush of unfamiliar shame.

IV

Over Tilly's Garage a bleak room echoed all day to the rumble and snorting downstairs and the singing of the Negro washers as they turned the hose on the cars outside. It was a cheerless square of a room punctuated with a bed and a battered table on which lay half a dozen books —Joe Miller's *Slow Train through Arkansas; Lucile,* in an old edition very much annotated in an old-fashioned hand; *The Eyes of the World,* by Harold Bell Wright, and an ancient prayerbook of the Church of England with the name Alice Powell and the date 1831 written on the fly-leaf.

The East, gray when the Jelly-bean entered the garage, became a rich and vivid blue as he turned on his solitary electric light. He snapped it out again, and going to the window rested his elbows on the sill and stared into the deepening morning. With the awakening of his emotions, his first perception was a sense of futility, a dull ache at the utter grayness of his life. A wall had sprung up suddenly around him, hedging him in, a wall as definite and tangible as the white wall of his bare room. And with his perception of this wall all that had been the romance of his existence, the casualness, the light-hearted improvidence, the miraculous open-handedness of life faded out. The Jelly-bean strolling up Jackson Street humming a lazy song, known at every shop and street stand, cropfull of easy greeting and local wit, sad sometimes for only the sake of sadness and the flight of time—that Jelly-bean was suddenly vanished. The very name was a reproach, a triviality. With a flood of insight he knew that Merritt must despise him, that even Nancy's kiss in the dawn would have awakened not jealousy but only a contempt for Nancy so lowering herself. And on his part the Jelly-bean had used for her a dingy subterfuge learned from the garage. He had been her moral laundry; the stains were his.

As the gray became blue, brightened and filled the room, he crossed to his bed and threw himself down on it, gripping the edges fiercely.

"I love her," he cried aloud. "God!"

As he said this something gave way within him like a lump melting in his throat. The air cleared and became radiant with dawn, and turning over on his face he began to sob dully into the pillow.

In the sunshine of three o'clock Clark Darrow chugging painfully along Jackson Street was hailed by the Jelly-bean, who stood on the curb with his fingers in his vest pockets.

"Hi!" called Clark, bringing his Ford to an astonishing stop alongside. "Just get up?"

The Jelly-bean shook his head.

"Never did go to bed. Felt sorta restless, so I took a long walk this morning out in the country. Just got into town this minute."

"Should think you *would* feel restless. I been feeling thataway all day—"

"I'm thinkin' of leavin' town," continued the Jelly-bean, absorbed by his own thoughts. "Been thinkin' of goin' up on the farm, and takin' a little that work off Uncle Dun. Reckin I been bummin' too long."

Clark was silent and the Jelly-bean continued:

"I reckin maybe after Aunt Mamie dies I could sink that money of mine in the farm and make somethin' out of it. All my people originally came from that part up there. Had a big place."

Clark looked at him curiously.

"That's funny," he said. "This—this sort of affected me the same way."

The Jelly-bean hesitated.

"I don't know," he began slowly, "somethin' about—about that girl last night talkin' about a lady named Diana Manners—an English lady, sorta got me thinkin'!" He drew himself up and looked oddly at Clark. "I had a family once," he said defiantly.

Clark nodded.

"I know."

"And I'm the last of 'em," continued the Jelly-bean, his voice rising slightly, "and I ain't worth shucks. Name they call me by means jell-weak and wobbly like. People who weren't nothin' when my folks was a lot turn up their noses when they pass me on the street."

Again Clark was silent.

"So I'm through. I'm goin' today. And when I come back to this town it's going to be like a gentleman."

Clark took out his handkerchief and wiped his damp brow.

"Reckon you're not the only one it shook up," he admitted gloomily. "All this thing of girls going round like they do is going to stop right quick. Too bad, too, but everybody'll have to see it thataway."

"Do you mean," demanded Jim in surprise, "that all that's leaked out?"

"Leaked out? How on earth could they keep it secret? It'll be announced in the papers tonight. Doctor Lamar's got to save his name somehow."

Jim put his hands on the sides of the car and tightened his long fingers on the metal.

"Do you mean Taylor investigated those checks?"

It was Clark's turn to be surprised.

"Haven't you heard what happened?"

Jim's startled eyes were answer enough.

"Why," announced Clark dramatically, "those four got another bottle of corn, got tight and decided to shock the town—so Nancy and that fella Merritt were married in Rockville at seven o'clock this morning."

A tiny indentation appeared in the metal under the Jelly-bean's fingers.

"Married?"

"Sure enough. Nancy sobered up and rushed back into town, crying and frightened to death—claimed it'd all been a mistake. First, Doctor

Lamar went wild and was going to kill Merritt, but finally they got it patched up some way, and Nancy and Merritt went to Savannah on the two-thirty train."

Jim closed his eyes and with an effort overcame a sudden sickness.

"It's too bad," said Clark philosophically. "I don't mean the wedding —reckon that's all right, though I don't guess Nancy cared a darn about him. But it's a crime for a nice girl like that to hurt her family that way."

The Jelly-bean let go the car and turned away. Again something was going on inside him, some inexplicable but almost chemical change.

"Where you going?" asked Clark.

The Jelly-bean turned and looked dully back over his shoulder.

"Got to go," he muttered. "Been up too long; feelin' right sick."

"Oh."

The street was hot at three and hotter still at four, the April dust seeming to enmesh the sun and give it forth again as a world-old joke forever played on an eternity of afternoons. But at half past four a first layer of quiet fell and the shades lengthened under the awnings and heavy foliaged trees. In this heat nothing mattered. All life was weather, a waiting through the hot where events had no significance for the cool that was soft and caressing like a woman's hand on a tired forehead. Down in Georgia there is a feeling—perhaps inarticulate—that this is the greatest wisdom of the South—so after a while the Jelly-bean turned into a pool-hall on Jackson Street where he was sure to find a congenial crowd who would make all the old jokes—the ones he knew.

DENRY AT THE DANCE

This story will stir the imagination of more than one reader
with a secret desire to occupy the center of the stage for once,
to rise like Denry "from nonentity into renown." Denry here
proves himself to be audacious indeed, realizing—for he picks
things up easily—that more than a five-pound note is at
stake. He displays wisdom that is not often attained in the
years of one's youth and knowledge "more precious than a
knowledge of geography."

He had never been to a dance. He had no dress-suit, and no
notion of dancing.

He was a strange inconsequent mixture of courage and timidity. You
and I are consistent in character; we are either one thing or the other;
but Denry Machin had no consistency.

For three days he hesitated, and then, secretly trembling, he slipped
into Sillitoe's, the young tailor who had recently set up and who was
gathering together the *jeunesse dorée* of the town.

"I want a dress-suit," he said.

Sillitoe, who knew that Denry earned only eighteen shilling a week,
replied with only superficial politeness that a dress-suit was out of the
question; he had already taken more orders than he could execute without killing himself. The whole town had uprisen as one man and demanded a dress-suit.

"So you're going to the ball, are you?" said Sillitoe, trying to conde-
scend, but in fact slightly impressed.

"Yes," said Denry, "are you?"

Sillitoe started and then shook his head. "No time for balls," said he.

"I can get you an invitation, if you like," said Denry, glancing at the
door precisely as he had glanced at the door before adding 2 to 7.

"Oh!" Sillitoe cocked his ears. He was not a native of the town, and
had no alderman to protect his legitimate interests.

To cut a shameful story short, in a week Denry was being tried on.
Sillitoe allowed him two years' credit.

The prospect of the ball gave an immense impetus to the study of the
art of dancing in Bursley, and so put quite a nice sum of money into

the pocket of Miss Earp, a young mistress in that art. She was the daughter of a furniture dealer with a passion for the bankruptcy court. Miss Earp's evening classes were attended by Denry, but none of his money went into her pocket. She was compensated by an expression of the Countess's desire for the pleasure of her company at the ball.

The Countess had aroused Denry's interest in women as a sex. Ruth Earp quickened the interest. She was plain, but she was only twenty-four, and very graceful on her feet. Denry had one or two strictly private lessons from her in reversing. She said to him one evening, when he was practising reversing and they were entwined in the attitude prescribed by the latest fashion: "Never mind me! Think about yourself. It's the same in dancing as it is in life—the woman's duty is to adapt herself to the man." He did think about himself. He was thinking about himself in the middle of the night, and about her too. There had been something in her tone . . . her eye . . . ! At the final lesson he enquired if she would give him the first waltz at the ball. She paused, then said yes.

On the evening of the ball, Denry spent at least two hours in the operation which was necessary before he could give the Countess the pleasure of his company. This operation took place in his minute bedroom at the back of the cottage in Brougham Street, and it was of a complex nature. Three weeks ago he had innocently thought that you had only to order a dress-suit and there you were! He now knew that a dress-suit is merely the beginning of anxiety. Shirt! Collar! Tie! Studs! Cuff-links! Gloves! Handkerchief! (He was very glad to learn authoritatively from Sillitoe that handkerchiefs were no longer worn in the waistcoat opening, and that men who so wore them were barbarians and the truth was not in them. Thus, an everyday handkerchief would do.) Boots! . . . Boots were the rock on which he had struck. Sillitoe, in addition to being a tailor, was a hosier, but by some flaw in the scheme of the universe hosiers do not sell boots. Except boots Denry could get all he needed on credit; boots he could not get on credit, and he could not pay cash for them. Eventually he decided that his church boots must be dazzled up to the level of this great secular occasion. The pity was that he forgot—not that he was of a forgetful disposition in great matters; he was simply over-excited—he forgot to dazzle them up until after he had fairly put his collar on and his necktie in a bow. It is imprudent to touch blacking in a dress-shirt. So Denry had to undo the past and begin again. This hurried him. He was not afraid of being late for the first waltz with Miss Ruth Earp, but he was afraid of not being out of the house before his mother returned. Mrs. Machin had been making up a lady's own materials all day, naturally—the day being what it was! If she had had twelve hands instead of two, she might have made up the own materials of half a dozen ladies instead of one, and earned twenty-four shillings instead of four. Denry did not want his mother to see him ere he departed. He had lavished an enormous amount of brains and energy to the end of displaying himself in this refined and novel attire to the gaze of two hundred persons, and yet his secret wish was to deprive his mother of the beautiful spectacle!

However, she slipped in, with her bag and her seamy fingers and her rather sardonic expression, at the very moment when Denry was putting on his overcoat in the kitchen (there being insufficient room in the passage). He did what he could to hide his shirt-front (though she knew all about it) and failed.

"Bless us!" she exclaimed briefly, going to the fire to warm her hands.

A harmless remark. But her tone seemed to strip bare the vanity of human greatness.

"I'm in a hurry," said Denry importantly, as if he was going forth to sign a treaty involving the welfare of nations.

"Well," said she, "happen ye are, Denry. But the kitchen table's no place for boot-brushes."

He had one piece of luck. It froze. Therefore, no anxiety about the condition of boots!

The Countess was late; some trouble with a horse. Happily the Earl had been in Bursley all day and had dressed at the Conservative Club; and his lordship had ordered that the programme of dances should be begun. Denry learned this as soon as he emerged, effulgent, from the gentlemen's cloak-room into the broad red-carpeted corridor which runs from end to end of the ground-floor of the Town Hall. Many important townspeople were chatting in the corridor—the innumerable Sweetnam family, the Stanways, the great Etches, the Fearnses, Mrs. Clayton Vernon, the Suttons, including Beatrice Sutton. Of course everybody knew him for Duncalf's shorthand clerk and the son of the incomparable flannel-washer; but universal white kid gloves constitute a democracy, and Sillitoe could put more style into a suit than any other tailor in the Five Towns.

"How do?" the eldest of the Sweetnam boys nodded carelessly.

"How do, Sweetnam?" said Denry with equal carelessness.

The thing was accomplished! That greeting was like a masonic initiation, and henceforward he was the peer of no matter whom. At first he had thought that four hundred eyes would be fastened on him, their glance saying: "This youth is wearing a dress-suit for the first time, and it is not paid for, either!" But it was not so. And the reason was that the entire population of the Town Hall was heartily engaged in pretending that never in its life had it been seen after seven o'clock of a night apart from a dress-suit. Denry observed with joy that, while numerous middle-aged and awkward men wore red or white silk handkerchiefs in their waistcoats, such people as Charles Fearns, the Sweetnams, and Harold

Etches did not. He was, then, in the shyness of his handkerchief, on the side of the angels.

He passed up the double staircase (decorated with white or pale frocks of unparalleled richness) and so into the grand hall. A scarlet orchestra was on the platform, and many people strolled about the floor in attitudes of expectation. The walls were festooned with flowers. The thrill of being magnificent seized him, and he was drenched in a vast desire to be truly magnificent himself. He dreamt of magnificence; bootbrushes kept sticking out of this dream like black mud out of snow. In his reverie he looked about for Ruth Earp, but she was invisible. Then he went down-stairs again, idly; gorgeously feigning that he spent six evenings a week in ascending and descending monumental staircases, appropriately clad. He was determined to be as sublime as any one.

There was a stir in the corridor, and the sublimest consented to be excited.

The Countess was announced to be imminent. Everybody was grouped round the main portal, careless of temperatures. Six times was the Countess announced to be imminent before she actually appeared, expanding from the narrow gloom of her black carriage like a magic vision. Aldermen received her, and they did not do it with any excess of gracefulness. They seemed afraid of her, as though she was recovering from influenza and they feared to catch it. She had precisely the same high voice, and precisely the same efficient smile as she had employed to Denry, and these instruments worked marvels on Aldermen; they were as melting as salt on snow. The Countess disappeared up-stairs in a cloud of shrill apologies and trailing Aldermen. She seemed to have greeted everybody except Denry. Somehow he was relieved that she had not drawn attention to him. He lingered, hesitating, and then he saw a being in a long yellow overcoat, with a bit of peacock's feather at the summit of a shiny high hat. This being held a lady's fur mantle. Their eyes met. Denry had to decide instantly. He decided.

"Hello, Jock!" he said.

"Hello, Denry!" said the other, pleased.

"What's been happening?" Denry enquired, friendly.

Then Jock told him about the antics of one of the Countess's horses.

He went up-stairs again, and met Ruth Earp coming down. She was glorious in white. Except that nothing glittered in her hair, she looked the very equal of the Countess, at a little distance, plain though her features were.

"What about that waltz?" Denry began, informally.

"That waltz is nearly over," said Ruth Earp, with chilliness. "I suppose you've been staring at her ladyship with all the other men."

"I'm awfully sorry," he said. "I didn't know the waltz was—"

"Well, why didn't you look at your programme?"

"Haven't got one," he said naïvely.

He had omitted to take a programme. Ninny! Barbarian!

"Better get one," she said, cuttingly, somewhat in her rôle of dancing mistress.

"Can't we finish the waltz?" he suggested, crestfallen.

"No!" she said, and continued her solitary way downwards.

She was hurt. He tried to think of something to say that was equal to the situation, and equal to the style of his suit. But he could not. In a moment he heard her, below him, greeting some male acquaintance in the most effusive way. . . .

He got a programme, and with terror gripping his heart he asked sundry young and middle-aged women whom he knew by sight and by name for a dance. (Ruth had taught him how to ask.) Not one of them had a dance left. Several looked at him as much as to say: "You must be a goose to suppose that my programme is not filled up in the twinkling of my eye!"

Then he joined a group of despisers of dancing near the main door. Harold Etches was there, the wealthiest manufacturer of his years (barely twenty-four) in the Five Towns. Also Sillitoe, cause of another of Denry's wicked crimes. The group was taciturn, critical, and very doggish.

The group observed that the Countess was not dancing. The Earl was dancing (need it be said with Mrs. Jos. Curtenly, second wife of the Deputy Mayor?), but the Countess stood resolutely smiling, surrounded by Aldermen. Possibly she was getting her breath; possibly nobody had had the pluck to ask her. Anyhow she seemed to be stranded there, on a bench of Aldermen. Very wisely she had brought with her no members of a house-party from Sneyd Hall. Members of a house-party, at a municipal ball, invariably operate as a bar between greatness and democracy; and the Countess desired to participate in the life of the people.

"Why don't some of those johnnies ask her?" Denry burst out. He had hitherto said nothing in the group, and he felt that he must be a man with the rest of them.

"Well, *you* go and do it. It's a free country," said Sillitoe.

"So I would, for two pins!" said Denry.

Harold Etches glanced at him, apparently resentful of his presence there. Harold Etches was determined to put the extinguisher on *him*.

"I'll bet you a fiver you don't," said Etches, scornfully.

"I'll take you," said Denry very quickly, and very quickly walked off.

"She can't eat me. She can't eat me!"

This was what he said to himself as he crossed the floor. People seemed to make a lane for him, divining his incredible intention. If he had not started at once, if his legs had not started of themselves, he would never have started; and, not being in command of a fiver, he would afterwards have cut a preposterous figure in the group. But started he was, like a piece of clockwork that could not be stopped! In the grand crisis of his life something not himself, something more powerful than himself, jumped up in him and forced him to do things. Now for the first time he seemed to understand what had occurred within him in previous crises.

In a second—so it appeared—he had reached the Countess. Just behind her was his employer, Mr. Duncalf, whom Denry had not previously noticed there. Denry regretted this, for he had never mentioned to Mr. Duncalf that he was coming to the ball, and he feared Mr. Duncalf.

"Could I have this dance with you?" he demanded bluntly, but smiling and showing his teeth.

No ceremonial title! No mention of "pleasure" or "honour." Not a trace of the formula in which Ruth Earp had instructed him! He forgot all such trivialities.

("I've won that fiver, Mr. Harold Etches," he said to himself.)

The mouths of Aldermen inadvertently opened. Mr. Duncalf blenched.

"It's nearly over, isn't it?" said the Countess, still efficiently smiling. She did not recognise Denry. In that suit he might have been a Foreign Office attaché.

"Oh! that doesn't matter, I'm sure!" said Denry.

She yielded, and he took the paradisiacal creature in his arms. It was her business that evening to be universally and inclusively polite. She could not have begun with a refusal. A refusal might have dried up all other invitations whatsoever. Besides, she saw that the Aldermen wanted a lead. Besides, she was young, though a Countess, and adored dancing.

Thus they waltzed together, while the flower of Bursley's chivalry gazed in enchantment. The Countess's fan, depending from her arm, dangled against Denry's suit in a rather confusing fashion which withdrew his attention from his feet. He laid hold of it gingerly between two unemployed fingers. After that he managed fairly well. Once they came perilously near the Earl and his partner; nothing else. And then the dance ended, exactly when Denry had begun to savour the astounding spectacle of himself enclasping the Countess.

The Countess had soon perceived that he was the merest boy.

"You waltz quite nicely!" she said, like an aunt, but with more than an aunt's smile.

"Do I?" he beamed. Then something compelled him to say: "Do you know, it's the first time I've ever waltzed in my life, except in a lesson, you know?"

"Really!" she murmured. "You pick things up easily, I suppose?"

"Yes," he said. "Do you?"

Either the question or the tone sent the Countess off into carillons of amusement. Everybody could see that Denry had made the Countess laugh tremendously. It was on this note that the waltz finished. She was still laughing when he bowed to her (as taught by Ruth Earp). He could not comprehend why she had so laughed, save on the supposition that he was more humorous than he had suspected. Anyhow he laughed too, and they parted laughing. He remembered that he had made a marked effect (though not one of laughter) on the tailor by quickly returning the question, "Are you?" And his unpremeditated stroke with the Countess was similar. When he had got ten yards on his way towards Harold Etches and a fiver he felt something in his hand. The Countess's fan was sticking between his fingers. It had unhooked itself from her chain. He furtively pocketed it.

"Just the same as dancing with any other woman!"—he told this untruth in reply to a question from Sillitoe. It was the least he could do. And any other young man in his place would have said as much or as little.

"What was she laughing at?" somebody else asked.

"Ah!" said Denry judiciously, "wouldn't you like to know?"

"Here you are!" said Etches, with an inattentive, plutocratic gesture handing over a five-pound note. He was one of those men who never venture out of sight of a bank without a banknote in their pockets—"because you never know what may turn up."

Denry accepted the note with a silent nod. In some directions he was gifted with astounding insight. And he could read in the faces of the haughty males surrounding him that in the space of a few minutes he had risen from nonentity into renown. He had become a great man. He did not at once realise how great, how renowned. But he saw enough in those eyes to cause his heart to glow, and to rouse in his brain those ambitious dreams which stirred him upon occasion. He left the group; he had need of motion, and also of that mental privacy which one may enjoy while strolling about on a crowded floor, in the midst of a considerable noise. He noticed that the Countess was now dancing with an Alderman, and that the Alderman, by an oversight inexcusable in an Alderman, was not wearing gloves. It was he, Denry, who had broken the ice so that the Aldermen might plunge into the water! He first had danced with the Countess, and had rendered her up to the Alderman with delicious gaiety upon her countenance. By instinct he knew Bursley, and he knew that he would be talked of. He knew that, for a time at any rate, he would displace even Jos. Curtenly, that almost professional "card" and amuser of burgesses, in the popular imagination. It would not be: "Have ye heard Jos.'s latest?" It would be: "Have ye heard about young Machin, Duncalf's clerk?"

Then he met Ruth Earp, strolling in the opposite direction with a young girl, one of her pupils, of whom all he knew was that her name was Nellie, and that this was her first ball: a childish little thing with a wistful face. He could not decide whether to look at Ruth or to avoid her glance. She settled the point by smiling at him in a manner that could not be ignored.

"Are you going to make it up to me for that waltz you missed?" said Ruth Earp. She pretended to be vexed and stern, but he knew that she was not. "Or is your programme full?" she added.

"I should like to," he said simply.

"But perhaps you don't care to dance with us poor ordinary people, now you've danced with the *Countess!*" she said, with a certain lofty and bitter pride.

He perceived that his tone had lacked eagerness.

"Don't talk like that," he said, as if hurt.

"Well," she said, "you can have the supper dance."

He took her programme to write on it.

"Why!" he said, "there's a name down here for the supper dance. 'Herbert' it looks like."

"Oh!" she replied carelessly, "that's nothing. Cross it out."

So he crossed Herbert out.

"Why don't you ask Nellie here for a dance," said Ruth Earp.

And Nellie blushed. He gathered that the possible honour of dancing with the supremely great man had surpassed Nellie's modest expectations.

"Can I have the next one?" he said.

"Oh, yes!" Nellie timidly whispered.

"It's a polka, and you aren't very good at polking, you know," Ruth warned him. "Still, Nellie will pull you through."

Nellie laughed, in silver. The naïve child thought that Ruth was trying to joke at Denry's expense. Her very manifest joy and pride in being seen with the unique Mr. Machin, in being the next after the Countess to dance with him, made another mirror in which Denry could discern the reflection of his vast importance.

At the supper, which was worthy of the hospitable traditions of the Chell family (though served standing-up in the police-court), he learnt all the gossip of the dance from Ruth Earp; amongst other things that more than one young man had asked the Countess for a dance, and had been refused, though Ruth Earp for her part declined to believe that Aldermen and Councillors had utterly absorbed the Countess's programme. Ruth hinted that the Countess was keeping a second dance open for him, Denry. When she asked him squarely if he meant to request another from the Countess, he said, No, positively. He knew when to let well alone, a knowledge which is more precious than a knowledge of geography. The supper was the summit of Denry's triumph. The best people spoke to him without being introduced. And lovely creatures mysteriously and intoxicatingly discovered that programmes which had been crammed two hours before were not after all quite, quite full.

"Do tell us what the Countess was laughing at?" This question was shot at him at least thirty times. He always said he would not tell. And one girl who had danced with Mr. Stanway, who had danced with the Countess, said that Mr. Stanway had said that the Countess would not tell, either. Proof, here, that he was being extensively talked about!

Toward the end of the festivity the rumour floated abroad that the Countess had lost her fan. The rumour reached Denry, who maintained a culpable silence. But when all was over, and the Countess was departing, he rushed down after her, and in a dramatic fashion which demonstrated his genius for the effective, he caught her exactly as she was getting into her carriage.

"I've just picked it up," he said, pushing through the crowd of worshippers.

"Oh! thank you so much!" she said. And the Earl also thanked Denry. And then the Countess, leaning from the carriage, said with archness in her efficient smile: "You do pick things up easily, don't you?"

And both Denry and the Countess laughed without restraint, and the pillars of Bursley society were mystified.

Denry winked at Jock as the horses pawed away. And Jock winked back.

The envied of all, Denry walked home, thinking violently. At a stroke he had become possessed of more than he could earn from Duncalf in a month. The faces of the Countess, of Ruth Earp, and of the timid Nellie mingled in exquisite hallucinations before his tired eyes. He was inexpressibly happy.

A STUDENT IN ECONOMICS

This story has become a classic case history; it might have
been taken from the files of a dean's office in a large state
university. Life is real and life is earnest on any campus for
the unsung majority who must work for a living as well as
study. (Script-writers for Hollywood and television, if they
haven't heard, would do well to note this!) When the dean says
to Charlie, "Always keep in mind that the University is a social
as well as an educational institution, Wingate," the words
have a hollow sound.

All of the boys on the third floor of Mrs. Gooch's approved
rooms for men had been posted to get Charlie Wingate up that afternoon. He had to go to see the Dean. Two or three of them forgot about
it and two or three of them had other things to do, but Eddie Barbour
liked waking people up. Eddie stuck his weasel face in at Charlie's door
just as the alarm clock was giving one last feeble tap. The clock stood
on the bottom of a tin washpan that was set upside-down on a wooden
chair beside the bed. The alarm had made a terrific din. Eddie had heard
it far down the hall. The hands showed two o'clock. Pale needles from
a December sun were piercing the limp green window shade in a hundred places.

Eddie Barbour yelled, "Aw right, Charlie! Snap out of it!" He came
into the chilly room and stood for a moment staring vaguely at the ridge
of quilts on the sagged iron bed. The only sound was the long, regular
sough of Charlie Wingate's breathing. He hadn't heard a thing. Eddie
made a sudden grab for the top of the covers, stripped them back and
began jouncing the sleeper by the shoulders. Charlie grunted every time
the bed springs creaked, but he nuzzled his pillow and went on sleeping.
Eddie went over to the study table where a large, white-enameled water
pitcher stood and he came back to the bed with the water, breathing
giggles. He tipped the water pitcher a little and a few drops fell on the
back of Charlie's neck without waking him. Eddie sloshed the icy water

up over the pitcher's mouth. A whole cupful splashed on Charlie's head. Charlie sat up quickly, batting his arms about, and Eddie Barbour whinnied with laughter.

"Arise, my lord, for the day is here," he said, going across and ceremoniously raising the crooked window shade. Charlie sat straight up among the rumpled quilts with his head cocked on one side, staring dully. He had slept with his clothes on. He sat up in bed all dressed, in a soldier's brown uniform, all but his shoes and roll puttees.

"You got army today?" Eddie asked, putting the pitcher down. Charlie looked at him for a moment and blinked. Then he said in a voice stuffy with sleep, "Naw. I had army yesterday. I got army make-up today." He worked his mouth, making clopping noises.

"What time you got army make-up, Charlie? When you come in from class you said get you up because you had to go see the Dean at two-thirty."

"Yeah, I do have to go see the Dean at two-thirty. But I got army make-up too. I got to make up drill cuts from three till six." All at once he flopped back down on the bed, sound asleep again.

"Hey!" Eddie cried, jumping forward. "Come out of that! Wake up there, Charlie! You can't sleep no more if you got to see the Dean at two-thirty. You just about got time to make it." He jerked him back up in bed.

"Damn the Dean," Charlie said; "two hours' sleep ain't enough."

"Is two hours all the sleep you got last night?"

"Where you get the 'last night'? I worked all night last night. I had classes till noon. Two hours' sleep was all I got today. And darn little more yesterday or the day before. When is Sunday? Sunday's the first day I'm due to get any real sleep. Two hours' sleep is not enough sleep for a man to get."

He plumped his stockinged feet onto the cold floor and got up stiffly. He went over to the washstand, where he picked up his tooth brush and tooth paste and a bar of soap and slowly took his face towel down from beside the warped looking-glass. He came back to where his shoes lay and stood looking at the toilet articles in his hands as if he had forgotten what he meant to do with them. He dumped them on the bed, took the pan with the alarm clock on it and set it on the floor. Then he sat down on the chair and picked up one of the heavy army shoes, held it and felt it and studied it carefully before he put it on. He put on the other shoe with equal deliberation and stood up without lacing either of them. He took his things up from the bed and started off for the bathroom, his loose shoes clogging. Eddie Barbour followed him down the drafty hall.

The creosote disinfectant that Mrs. Gooch used in her bathrooms gave off a strong odor. "Dag gum bathroom smells just like a hen coop," Charlie said thickly as he stood in front of the white-specked mirror twisting his face. He wouldn't need a shave for another day. He had a fairly good-looking face, tan and thin, with ringlets of black hair tumbling down over his forehead. His large ears stuck straight out. He looked at his image with dark eyes made narrow by two purplish puffs under them, and he yawned widely.

Eddie Barbour stood leaning against the jamb of the bathroom door. He said, "You ought to try and get more sleep, Charlie."

"Are you telling *me?*" Charlie said, running water in the face bowl. Eddie Barbour was a freshman too.

II

Charlie Wingate came walking along University Boulevard toward the campus, hunched up in his army overcoat. The raw December wind whipped his face and made him feel wide awake. He passed a bunch of fraternity men pitching horseshoes in the drive beside the K.A. house. Two or three, sprucely dressed, gave him impersonal glances as he passed. They did not speak, and he walked past self-consciously, seeing them without looking toward them.

When he reached the business section opposite the campus he turned in at the white-tiled front of The Wigwam. The noon rush was over and Nick was not at the cash register. A few noon "dates" were still sitting in the booths along the wall. Charlie walked straight back along the white-tile counter and sat down on the end stool. Red Hibbert was standing by the coffee urns reading the sports section. When Charlie sat down Red folded his newspaper slowly and came over to wait on him. Charlie sat with his cheeks resting on the heels of his hands.

"How's it, Chollie, old boy, old boy?" Red Hibbert said.

"Not bad. Give me a cup of javy without and a couple of them Grandma's oatmeal cookies over there, Red. Where's Nick?"

Red scooted the plate with the cookies on it down the glassy white counter top and came along with the cup of black coffee. "This is Nick's day for Kiwanis," he said. "It looks to me like you'd stay home and get some sleep once in a while. You're dyin' on your feet."

"I am going to get some sleep Sunday, don't you never worry. I have to go see the Dean this afternoon. And I got make-up drill at three o'clock. I've got to make up some drill cuts."

"What you got to go see the Dean about?"

"I don't know what about; here's all it said." Charlie reached in his overcoat pocket and pulled out a jagged window envelope and a mimeographed postal card. He pushed the envelope across the counter along with the postal card. "I got that other in the morning mail too."

Red took the printed form from the Dean of Men's office out of the envelope and glanced at it. Then he picked up the postal card. It was headed

FOURTH AND FINAL NOTICE

You are hereby summoned to appear before the chairman of the Student Senate Committee on Freshman Activities, Rm 204 Student Union Bldg., not later than 4 P.M., Friday afternoon. It will be to your advantage not to ignore this summons as you have three previous ones. This is positively the last opportunity you will be given to rectify your delinquency. Should you fail to appear this time, steps will be taken to bring you.

(Signed) Aubrey H. Carson, Chrmn.
Com. on Frshmn
Actvts.

Red waggled the postal card. "What you going to do about this?"

"Tear it up like I did the others, I guess. I know what they want. They want to try and make me buy one of them damn' freshman caps."

"Take a tip from me, Charlie: I'd go see them. It won't hurt nothing, and it might be a lot easier on you in the long run."

"Hell, what can they do?"

"Plenty. They could sick the Black Hoods onto you."

"Ah! The Black Hoods, that bunch of amateur ku kluckers!"

"Call 'em amateurs if you want to, Charlie, but it wasn't only but last Friday night they took that little Jew-boy, Sol Lewis, out of the rooming house where I stay. It looked to me like they did a pretty professional job on him. They used the buckle-end of a belt on him. They claim he was a stool pigeon for the University."

"Stool pigeon! Ah, you know that guy wasn't a stool pigeon, Red."

"We-ell, I'm not saying one way or the other. Anyhow, that's what you're up against when you take to fooling with that Student Committee on Freshman Activities, Charlie."

"Prexy claimed in his opening address at the first of school that he had put a stop to these masked frats and all this hazing."

"Yeah, he said he had; but how's he going to put a stop to the Black Hoods? He can't kick out all the biggest shots in the University, can he? All the big shots on the campus are Black Hoods. Football stars and fellas like that. You won't see the President kicking guys like that out of the University."

"Maybe not, but—why, hell, that freshman cap business is nothing but a racket. That's all it is. Damn' if I let 'em scare me into paying a dollar for a little sleazy green cloth cap!"

"O.K., Charlie; I guess you know what you want to do."

"Anyway, how could I get around to see that committee before four o'clock this afternoon, and see the Dean at two-thirty, and go to make-up drill from three till six? I'll be late to drill and get bawled out by the captain again. The captain's already about to flunk me for cuts. That's what's getting me down—Military. It's this Military that's getting me down."

159

"Jees, I don't know, Charlie; seems like I get a bigger kick out of army than I do any other course I got. They sure learn you more in army than they do in anything else *in* this University."

"Yeow, you learn plenty in army, all right. But what I don't like is the compulsory part. I don't think they ought to be allowed to make it compulsory for freshmen and sophomores. That's just like they had it over in Germany before they got rid of the Kaiser."

The red-haired boy gave him a startled look. He frowned heavily. "Charlie," he exclaimed, "where are you getting all these radical ideas you been spouting around here lately?" Charlie peered at him. Red's face was set in earnestness.

"Why, that's not a radical idea," Charlie said, pushing back his empty coffee cup. "That's just a plain historical fact, that's all that is. I don't see where they got any right to make Military Training compulsory. This is supposed to be a *free* country. That compulsory stuff is what Mussle-leany and birds like that pull."

"But, Charlie, it's all for your own benefit. The University is just looking out after your own interests."

"How do you figure they're looking out for *my* interests?"

"Well, for one thing, when the next war comes we'll all be officers, us fellas that got this training in college. We'll go right into the regular army as officers. There's where we'll have the edge on guys that never did take advantage of a college education. Person'ly, when the next war comes along, I'm not hankerin' after any front-line trenches. And you know darn' well they're not going to stick their college-trained officers into front-line trenches to get shot. So there's where I figure us guys in R.O.T.C. will have a big advantage."

"Yeah, you might be right, at that, Red. But I'm not kicking about R.O.T.C. It's just the compulsory part I'm kicking against."

Red perked his head and scowled impatiently. "Charlie, they *got* to make it compulsory. If it wasn't compulsory, how many of the fellas would enroll in it? They have to make Military compulsory in order to give the fullest benefits. What good could they do if only a few of the fellas was taking it?"

"Anyway, I know some it's not compulsory for," Charlie said stubbornly. "Last night there was a Phi Gam pledge in here bragging about how he got out of Military. He told them at the first of school he didn't want to take Military. They told him he *had* to take it—required of all able-bodied freshmen. Couldn't get his degree without it. So he had to go buy his army shoes. Well, he got the shoe store to send the bill to his old man. His old man is one of these they call 'em pacifists. When his old man gets the bill for his kid's army shoes, maybe you think he don't get the President of this University on long distance and tell him where to head in at. And this kid didn't have to take Military, neither. His old man's a big shot lawyer in the City."

"Yeah, but you got to have pull to get away with that, Charlie."

"That's what I mean, Red. You can get away with plenty in this University if you got the pull."

III

Charlie Wingate loped up the steps of the Administration Building, hurried through the revolving doors, and walked past hissing steam radiators down the long hall to the Dean of Men's office. He was ten minutes late. Before he opened the frosted-glass door he took out a pair of amber-colored spectacles and put them on. Then he went in and handed his summons to the secretary.

"The Dean will see you in a moment," she said. "Please take a chair."

Charlie sat down and gave an amber-hued glance about the outer office. Three dejected freshmen, holding their green caps, were waiting with him. He recognized none of them, so he picked up a week-old copy of the *Christian Science Monitor* and started to read it. But the room was warm and he immediately went to sleep. He had his head propped back against the wall. The newspaper slipped down into his lap. His amber-colored glasses hid his eyes and no one could see that they were closed. He was awakened by the secretary shaking him. She was smiling and the freshmen were all snickering.

"Wake up and pay for your bed, fella!" one of the freshmen called, and everyone laughed heartily.

"I sort of drowsed off. It's so nice and warm in here," Charlie said, apologizing to the pretty secretary.

The Dean of Men got up as he entered and, with his eyes on the slip bearing Charlie's name, said, "Ah, this is Charles Wingate, isn't it?" He grasped Charlie's hand as if it were an honor and pressed a button under the edge of his desk with his other hand. The secretary appeared at the door. "Miss Dunn, will you bring in Wingate's folder—Charles W-i-n-g-a-t-e. How do you like college by now, Wingate? Eyes troubling you?"

"Pretty well, sir. Yes, sir, a little. I wear these glasses."

The secretary came back with the folder and the Dean looked through it briefly. "Well, Wingate, I suppose you're anxious to know why I sent for you. The unpleasant truth is, Wingate, you don't seem to be doing so well in your college work. Your freshman adviser conferred with you twice about this, and this week he turned your case over to me. My purpose, of course, is to help you. Now, to be quite frank, Wingate, you're on the verge of flunking out. Less than a third of the semester remains, and you have a failing grade in English 101, conditional grades in Psychology 51 and Military Training; three hours of F and four hours of D, almost half your total number of hours. On the other hand, you have an A average in Spanish I and a B in Economics 150. Wingate, how do you account for your failing English when you are an A student in Spanish?"

"To tell you the truth, sir, I got behind on my written work in English, and I've never been able to catch up. And I don't really have to study Spanish. My father is a railway section foreman in my home town, and he's always had a gang of Mexicans working for him. I've been speaking Mexican ever since I was a kid. It's not the pure, what they call Castilian, Spanish, but I probably know almost as much Spanish as my professor."

"How about this B in Economics? That's a fairly high grade."

"Yes, sir. Doctor Kenshaw—he's my Ec professor—doesn't give exams. Instead he gives everyone a B until he calls for our term papers. We don't recite in his class. We just listen to him lecture. And the grade you get on your term paper is your semester grade."

"Ah! What you students term a pipe course, eh, Wingate?"

"Not exactly, sir. We have to do a lot of outside reading for the term paper. But I'm counting on keeping that B in Ec."

"That's fine, Wingate. But it appears to me that it's high time you were getting busy on some of these other grades, too. Why can't you dig in and pull these D's up to B's, and this F up to at least a C? You've got it in you. You made an unusually high grade on your entrance exams, your record shows. Graduated from high school with honors. What's the trouble, Wingate? Tell me!"

"I don't know, sir, except I work at night and—"

"Oh, I see it here on your enrollment card now. Where do you work?"

"I work nights for Nick Pappas, down at The Wigwam."

"How many hours a night do you work?"

"Ten hours, sir. From nine till seven. The Wigwam stays open all night. I eat and go to eight o'clock class when I get off."

"Very interesting, Wingate. But don't you suppose that it would be advisable to cut down a bit on this outside work and attend a little more closely to your college work? After all, that's what you're here for, primarily—to go to college, not work in a café."

"I couldn't work fewer hours and stay in school, sir. I just barely get by as it is. I get my board at The Wigwam, and I pay my room rent, and I've been paying out on a suit of clothes. That leaves only about a dollar a week for all the other things I have to have."

"Wingate, shouldn't you earn more than that, working ten hours?"

"I get the regular, first-year-man rate, sir. Twenty cents an hour. It's set by the University. Nick takes out a dollar a day for board. Pays me five dollars a week in cash."

"Can't you arrange for a little financial support from home?"

"No, sir, I'm afraid I couldn't. I have two brothers and two sisters at home younger than I am. It wouldn't be right for me to ask my father to send money out of what he makes."

"But surely you could get out and land something a little more lucrative than this all-night restaurant job, Wingate."

"No, sir. Twenty cents an hour is standard rate for working students, and I haven't found anything better. Nick says he has at least thirty men on the waiting list for this job I have."

"Well, there's this about it, Wingate. The University is here, supported by the taxpayers of this State, for the purpose of giving the young men and women of this State educational opportunities. The University is not here for the purpose of training young men to be waiters in all-night restaurants. And, so far as I can see, that's about all you are deriving from your University career. So it occurs to me that you should make a choice: either find some way to devote more attention to your college work or drop out of school altogether. We are very loath to encourage students who are *entirely* self-supporting. And yet, I will admit that I know any number of first rate students who are entirely self-supporting. There's Aubrey Carson, for example. Quarterback on the football team, delegate to the Olympics, president of the Student Senate, and he's a straight A student. Aubrey Carson was telling me only last week that he hasn't had any financial assistance from home since he enrolled as a freshman. Aubrey is a fine example of the working student."

"Yes, sir; but look at the job Carson has. He works for a big tobacco company, and all he has to do is hand out Treasure Trove cigarettes to other students. The tobacco company pays him a good salary for passing out samples of their cigarettes."

"Why, Wingate, you surely must be mistaken about that. I don't believe Aubrey Carson smokes. In fact, I know he doesn't smoke. He's one of the finest all-'round athletes in this country."

"No, sir; I don't say he smokes either. But that's the straight stuff about his job with the cigarette company. They figure it's a good advertisement to have a popular guy like Aubrey Carson passing out Treasure Troves. Sort of an endorsement."

"All the same, Wingate, it doesn't reflect a very good attitude on your part, criticizing the way one of your fellow students earns his college expenses."

"Oh, I didn't mean to criticize him, sir. I was only saying—"

"Yes, yes, I know; but all this is beside the point. We're here to discuss the state of your grades, Wingate. The fact is, you are on probation right now. As you must know, any student who is passing in less than half his work is automatically suspended from the University and must return to his home. Now one F more and out you'll go, Wingate. That's just being frank with you."

"I'd hate to have to go back home like that, sir."

"Well, you'd have to. If you flunk out, the University authorities are obliged to see that you return to your home immediately."

"I'd hate that, sir. I'd hate to go back home and have to live off my family, and that's probably what I'd have to do. I had a letter from mother yesterday, and she says that nearly all the boys who graduated from high school with me are still there, loafing on the streets and living off their old folks. I don't like that idea. Mother's proud of me because I'm working my way through college. You know there are not many jobs to be had nowadays, sir, and I'd hate to have to go back home and loaf."

"It *is* a problem, I'll confess, Wingate. But what's the point in your coming to the University and working all night in a café and then flunking your class work? Moreover, your freshman adviser reports that you make a practice of sleeping in class. Is that true?"

"Well, yes, sir. I suppose I do drop off sometimes."

"Pretty impossible situation, isn't it, Wingate? Well, I've given you the best advice I can. Unless you can alter your circumstances I suggest that you withdraw from the University at once. We have six thousand other students here who need our attention, and the University has to be impartial and impersonal in dealing with these problems. Unless you can find some means to avoid flunking out I suggest withdrawing beforehand."

"Withdrawal would be a disgrace to me, sir. If I withdrew and went back home now, everyone at home would say that I had been expelled. You know how small towns are."

"Ah, now, Wingate, when you begin dealing with small-town gossip, I fear you're really getting outside my province. But I should think you'd prefer honorable withdrawal to flunking out."

"I believe I'll try to stick it through, sir. I'll try to remove the conditional grades, and maybe I can luck through on my finals."

"I hope you can, Wingate. As long as you feel that way about it, good luck to you." The Dean of Men stood up. Charlie stood up too. The Dean put out his hand and showed his teeth in a jovial smile and bore down hard on Charlie's knuckles. "I'm counting on you strong, old man," he said, encircling Charlie's shoulders with his left arm. "I know you have the stuff and that you'll come through with flying colors one of these days."

"Thank you, sir," Charlie said, grinning tearfully while the Dean gave his shoulder little pats. He edged toward the door as soon as the Dean released him, but when he reached it he hesitated and pulled the postal card out of his pocket. "Oh, pardon me, sir, but there's something I forgot to ask you. I got this in the mail today. I've been a little bothered about what to do about it."

The Dean of Men took the mimeographed card and read it quickly. "Why, I should say that you ought to go see what they want, Wingate. You shouldn't ignore things of this sort, you know. It's all a part of the normal activities of college life. No reason for antagonizing your fellow-students by ignoring a request of this kind."

"All right, sir; I'll go see them."

"Why, to be sure, go see them! Always keep in mind that the University is a social as well as an educational institution, Wingate."

I V

Room 204, Student Union Building, was a newly finished, rather barren office that smelled dankly of lime in the fresh plaster. It was fitted with a metal desk painted to imitate painted walnut, a large brass spittoon, a square metal waste-paper basket, a green metal filing cabinet, a large bank calendar, a huge pasteboard shipping case, and Aubrey H. Carson, who had the freshman cap concession.

Charlie Wingate hesitantly opened the door and saw Aubrey H. Carson tilted back in a chair, his feet on the metal walnut desk, reading a copy of *Ballyhoo*.

"Co-ome in! Co-ome in!" Aubrey Carson called loudly without putting down his magazine. "All right, old timer. What's on your mind?"

Charlie held out the mimeographed card. Carson held his magazine a moment longer before accepting the card. He shoved his hat down over one eye, turning the card, looking first at the back, then at the name on the front. "Um-m-m," he grunted. He reached over to a drawer in the filing cabinet without taking his feet down and flipped through the cards. He looked at the name on the postal card again, pulled a card out of the file, and drew his thick lips up into a rosette. He looked at the file card in silence.

"Wingate," he said at last in a severe tone, "you have been dilatory. Indeed, Wingate, I might even go so far as to say you have been remiss. At the beginning of this semester you applied for and received a refund on your student ticket fee. That signifies that you have not attended a single football game this season, and that you have no intention of honoring any of the University's athletic spectacles with your presence this season. Also, the record discloses that you did not register at the Y.M.C.A. freshman mixer. Neither did you respond to polite solicitation for a trifling monetary pledge to the Memorial Stadium Fund. And, most heinous offense of all, Wingate, we find that you have yet to pay in one dollar for your freshman cap, prescribed by your seniors and purveyed to you on a non-profit basis by the Student Committee on Freshman Activities. And yet, Wingate, I find you duly enrolled and attending classes in this here now University. Wingate, what possible excuse do you have for such gross neglect of University tradition? Speak up!"

Charlie said meekly, "Well, I work nights and it's hard for me to get here in the daytime, and I can't afford to buy a cap."

"What's this!" Carson exclaimed, jerking his legs down from the desk top and banging the desk with two flat hands. "Why, boy, this is treason! You mean you can't afford *not* to buy a freshman cap."

"No, I just came to tell you that a dollar has to go a long way with me and that I need every cent I earn to stay in school. So I wish you'd please excuse me from buying a freshman cap."

Carson's lean, florid face suddenly became rigid and he stuck his jaw out with his lower teeth showing and, in spite of his marcelled taffy pompadour and his creased tailored suit, he again looked very much as he did in all the sporting section photographs. "See here, Wingate," he said, hard-lipped, "you're still a freshman at this University. You'll have to wait another year before you can start saying what you will do and won't do, see? Now we've been patient with you. You've been in school here three months without putting on a freshman cap. Do you realize that over eighty-five per cent of the freshman class came in here and bought their caps before the first week of school ended? Now who do you think *you* are, Wingate—Mr. God? You're going to get you a cap, and you're going to wear it. See? No ifs, ands, or buts about it. And if you don't leave this office with a green cap on your head then I don't mind telling you that we've got ways of getting one on you before another day passes."

"Well, if I buy one it's going to put me in a bad hole. All the money I've got is what I saved out to pay my room rent this week."

"Listen, fella, if we let horsefeathers like that go here, half the freshman class wouldn't be wearing freshman caps right now. Now I've said all I'm going to to you. Do you want your green cap now or will you wait till later? That's all I want to know. I don't aim to give you any high-pressure sales talk on something that's already been decided for you. Take it or leave it."

Carson reached over into the large pasteboard box, groped far down in it, and brought forth a small green monkey cap. He tossed it on the desk. Charlie Wingate stuck his forefinger in his watch pocket and pulled out a small pad of three carefully folded dollar bills. He unfolded them and laid one on the desk and picked up the cap. Carson put the dollar in his pocket and stood up.

Charlie stood holding his cap. He scuffed the cement floor with his shoe toe and began doggedly, "The only thing is—"

"Aw, that's O.K., Wingate, old man," Carson said suavely. "No hard feelings whatsoever." He held out a freshly opened pack of cigarettes. "Here, have a Treasure Trove on me before you go."

V

That night all the stools along the counter at The Wigwam were filled when Charlie Wingate came in, still dusty from the drill field. He got himself a set-up back of the counter and went into the kitchen. He moved about the steam-table, dishing up his dinner. He dragged a stool over to a zinc-covered kitchen table and sat down to eat. The kitchen was warm and steamy and the air was thick with the odors of sour chili grease and yellow soap melting in hot dishwater. Charlie's fork slipped through his fingers, and he began nodding over his plate.

Fat Kruger, the night dishwasher and short-order cook, yelled, "Hey, there, wake up and pay for your bed!" Charlie jerked his head up and looked at the ponderous, good-humored cook with half-lidded eyes. "Why'n't you try sleeping in bed once in a w'ile, Charlie?" Fat said in a friendly tone. "You're going to kill yourself if you don't watch out, trying to go without sleep."

"Don't worry, Fat. I can take it," Charlie said.

Almost two hours had to pass before it would be the hour for him to come on, but not time enough for him to walk back to his room and catch a nap, so he took the book on which he had to make an outside reading report in Economics 150 and went up to the last booth to study until nine o'clock. He fell asleep and he did not wake up until Red Hibbert, going off, shook him and told him that it was almost time for him to come on. He closed his book and went back to the washroom. The acrid stench of the mothballs that Nick used to deodorize the latrine cleared his head. He took down his apron and tied it on over his army breeches. Then he slipped into a white coat.

The usual black-coffee addicts came dribbling in. When the telephone rang, Charlie answered it, jotting down short orders to go. The delivery boy came in and went out and banged off on his motorcycle with paper bags full of "red hots" and nickel hamburgers and coffee in paper cylinders. The Wigwam's white tile shone under the inverted alabaster urns. There was a pale pink reflection in the plate-glass window as the Neon sign outside spelled and respelled "Wigwam Eats. Open All Night." A party of drunken Betas came in at ten-thirty and seated themselves noisily in the last booth. They tossed Charlie's economics book out into the aisle with a whoop, and he came and picked it up and took their orders in silence while they kidded him about his flap ears and the grease on his white coat. At eleven o'clock the last whistle at the University power house blew for the closing hour, and a couple of lingering "dates" scurried out. Finally, the drunks left, after one had been sick in a corner of the booth. The delivery boy came coasting up at midnight and checked in and roared away again on his motorcycle. The long small hours began inching past.

At one o'clock Charlie finished cleaning up the drunk's mess and he had cleared off the last of the tables. The Wigwam was empty, so he opened the book he must read for Ec 150. He had read a few lines when a bunch of girls from the Theta house down the street came charging in, giggling and talking in gasps and screams, their fur coats clutched over their sleeping pajamas. It was long after the closing hour, and they told Charlie to keep an eye out for the University night watchman. They took up the two back booths and they consulted The Wigwam's printed menu card without failing to read aloud the lines "Nick (Pericles) Pappas," "We Employ Student Help Exclusively" and "Please Do Not Tip. A Smile Is Our Reward" with the customary shrieks. Nearly all ordered filet mignon and French fries, which were not on the menu, but two or three ordered pecan waffles and coffee, which were. When he had served their orders Charlie went back to his book again, but the low buzz of their talk and their sudden spurts of laughter disturbed him and he could not read. At a quarter of two they began peering round corners of their booths. They asked Charlie in stage-whispers if the coast were clear.

Charlie went to the door and looked out on the street and beckoned widely with his arms. They trooped out with their fur coats pulled tight, their fur-trimmed silken mules slapping their bare heels. Charlie went on back to clear away their dishes. They had left about thirty cents as a tip, all in cents and nickels. The coins were carefully imbedded in the cold steak grease and gluey syrup and putty-colored cigarette leavings on their plates. Charlie began stacking the plates without touching the money. He carried the dirty dishes back and set them through the opening in the kitchen wall. Fat Kruger came to the opening and Charlie went back to his book.

Fat called, "Hey, Charlie, you leavin' this tip again?"

"You're damn' right, I'm leaving it!" Charlie said. "I can get along without their tips. They leave it that way every time. I guess they think I'll grabble on their filthy plates to get a lousy thirty cents. It takes a woman to think up something like that."

"Charlie, you're too proud. I don't see where you can afford to be so proud. The way I figure it, thirty cents is thirty cents."

"Hell, I'm not proud, Fat. I just try to keep my self-respect. When those sorority sows come in and plant their tips in the dirt and grease of their plates, damn' if I'll lower myself to grub it out."

He sat down on a counter stool with the economics book before him, trying to fix his mind on it. He read a page. The print became thin blurred parallels of black on the page. His eyelids kept drooping shut and he propped the muscles with his palms at his temples, trying to keep his eyes open. His head jerked forward and he caught it and began reading again. Soon his face lowered slowly through his hands and came to rest on the open book.

Fat Kruger came through the kitchen swinging door and tiptoed up front. Fat stood grinning, watching Charlie sleep. Cramped over with his head on the counter, Charlie snored softly. Fat gave his head a gentle shove, and Charlie started up to catch his balance.

"For God sakes, guy, you're *dead!*" Fat howled. "Don't you never get no sleep except like that?"

"What time is it?" Charlie said, yawning and arching his back.

"Half-past two."

"Jees, is that all?"

"Charlie, go back there and lay down on the kitchen table. I'll watch the front for you. Nobody'll be coming in for a while."

As he was talking old Uncle Jim Hudson ambled in, a bundle of sweaters, overcoats, and grizzled dewlaps, his black timeclock slung over one shoulder by a leather lanyard. Uncle Jim laid his long, nickeled flashlight carefully on the counter and eased himself onto a stool. He ordered a cup of black coffee and in a lecherous wheeze began telling dirty stories selected from his twenty years' experience as a campus night watchman. Fat Kruger nickered loudly after each telling, and Charlie jerked his eyes open and smiled sleepily. It was three-thirty when Uncle Jim left. Charlie opened his book again.

"Charlie, I wouldn't put my eyes out over that damn' book if I was you, when you're dyin' for sleep," Fat said.

"I've got to get it read, Fat. It's my outside reading in Economics and the whole semester grade depends on it. It's the hardest book to keep your mind on you ever saw. I've been reading on it for over a month and I'm only half through, and he's going to call for these reports any day now. If I flunk Ec I flunk out of school."

"Why mess with reading it? I know a guy over at the Masonic Dorm who'll read it and write your report for two bucks. He writes all my English themes for me, and I'm making a straight A in English. He only charges fifty cents for short themes and two bucks for term papers. You ought to try him."

"Hell, Fat, you get five dollars a week from home. Where am I going to get two dollars for hiring a guy to read this book?"

"Charlie, I just can't figure you out. You never do get any real sleep. You sure must want a college education bad. It don't look to me like you would figure it's worth it."

"Oh, it's worth it! It's a big satisfaction to my folks to have me in college. And where can a man without a college degree get nowadays? But I'll tell you the truth, I didn't know it was going to be like this when I came down here last Fall. I used to read *College Humor* in high school, and when fellows came home from University for the holidays, all dressed up in snappy clothes, talking about dates and football and dances, and using college slang—well, I had a notion I'd be like that when I got down here. The University publicity department sent me a little booklet showing how it was easy to work your way through college. So here I am. I haven't had a date or been to a dance or seen a football game since I enrolled. And there are plenty of others just like me. I guess I'm getting a college education, all right—but the only collegiate thing I've been able to do is go to sleep in class."

"How you get by with sleeping in class, Charlie?"

"I wear those colored spectacles and prop myself, and the profs can't see I've got my eyes closed."

Fat waggled his heavy face mournfully. "Boy, it sure is tough when a man don't get his sleep."

"Yeah, it is," Charlie said, looking down at his book again. "I'll get a break pretty soon, though. I'd rather chop off a hand than to flunk out of University before I'd even finished one semester."

VI

The tardiest of the hundred students enrolled in Dr. Sylvester C. O. Kenshaw's Economics 150 straggled into the lecture room and made their ways to alphabetically-assigned chairs with much scuffling and trampling of toes and mumbled apologies. Ec 150, renowned as a pipe course, was always crowded. Doctor Kenshaw was the celebrated author of seven textbooks on economics, five of which his students were required to buy each semester. Doctor Kenshaw's national reputation as an economist permitted him to be erratic about meeting his classes, but fame had never dimmed his fondness for student flattery. The only students who ever flunked Ec 150 were those who gave affront to Doctor Kenshaw by neglecting to buy his textbooks or by not laughing at his wit or by being outrageously inattentive to his lectures.

Doctor Kenshaw was late that morning. Charlie Wingate sat in his chair on the back row in an agony of waiting. He had on his amber glasses and he could fall asleep as soon as Doctor Kenshaw opened his lecture. But he had to stay awake until then. There was a slow ache in the small of his back. The rest of his body was numb. He had not taken off his army shoes for twenty hours, and his feet were moist and swollen. Every time he shifted position his arms and legs were bathed in prickling fire. He kept his eyes open behind the amber lenses, watching the clock. Small noises of the classroom came to him as a low, far-off humming.

When the clock on the front wall showed nine after eleven the seated class began stirring as if it were mounted on some eccentric amusement-park device. Excited whispers eddied out on the warm air of the steam-heated lecture room. "He's giving us another cut!" "He's not meeting this class today!" "He's got one more minute to make it!" "Naw; six more! You have to wait fifteen minutes on department heads."

There was a seething argument on this point, but when the clock showed fourteen minutes after eleven a bold leader sprang up and said, "Come on, everybody!" All but five or six especially conscientious students rose and milled after him toward the door. Charlie Wingate followed, thoroughly awakened by the chance of getting to bed so soon. The leader yanked the door open and Doctor Kenshaw stumbled in, all out of breath, his eyeglasses steamed, his pointed gray beard quivering, a vain little man in a greenish-black overcoat.

"Go back to your seats!" Doctor Kenshaw commanded sternly as soon as he could get his breath. He marched over to his lecture table and planked down his leather brief case. He took off his overcoat and began wiping the steam from his eyeglasses while the students hurried back to their chairs. "It does seem to me," he said, his voice quavering with anger, "that it would be no more than courteous for this class to await my arrival on those rare occasions when I am delayed. Day after day you come lagging into my classes, and I have always been extremely lenient in giving credit for attendance, no matter how tardy your arrival. Certainly it is no more than my privilege to ask that you wait for me occasionally."

A few students exchanged meaning glances. They meant, "Now we're in for it. The old boy has on one of his famous mads."

"Today, I believe I shall forego delivering my prepared lecture," Doctor Kenshaw went on in a more even voice, but with elaborate sarcasm, "and let *you* do the talking. Perhaps it would be meet to hear a few outside reading reports this morning. All of you doubtless are aware that these reports were due last week, although I had not expected to call for them at once. I trust that I have impressed you sufficiently with the importance of these reports. They represent to me the final result of your semester's work in this course. The grades you receive on these reports will be your grades for the semester. Let us begin forthwith. When your name is called, you will rise and read your report to the class." He opened his roll book.

"Mr. Abbott!" he called. Mr. Abbott stammered an excuse. Doctor Kenshaw passed coldly on to Miss Adams, making no comment. All through the A's it was the same. But with the B's an ashen, spectacled Miss Ballentyne stood up and began reading in a droning voice her report on *The Economic Consequences of the Peace*. Obviously Doctor Kenshaw was not listening to her. His hard little eyes under craggy brows were moving up one row and down the other, eager for a victim. On the back row, Charlie Wingate's propped legs had given way and he had slipped far down into his seat, fast asleep. When Doctor Kenshaw's preying eyes reached Charlie they stopped moving. Someone tittered nervously and then was silent as Doctor Kenshaw jerked his head round in the direction of the noise. Miss Ballentyne droned on.

When she had finished, Doctor Kenshaw said dryly, "Very good, Miss Ballentyne, very good, indeed. Er—ah—would someone be kind enough to arouse the recumbent young gentleman in the last row?"

There was a murmur of laughter while everyone turned to look at Milton Weismann nudging Charlie Wingate. Doctor Kenshaw was running down the list of names in his small record book. Milton Weismann gave Charlie another stiff poke in the ribs, and Charlie sprang up quickly. Everyone laughed loudly at that.

"Mr.—ah—*Wingate,* isn't it? Mr. Wingate, your report."

"Pardon me, sir?"

"Mr. Wingate, what was the title of the book assigned to you for report in this class?"

"Theory of the Leisure Class by Veblen, sir."

"Ah, then, that's the explanation. So you were assiduously engaged in evolving your own theory of the leisure class. Is that right, Mr. Wingate? You have evidently concluded that Economics 150 is the leisure class."

The class rocked with laughter. Doctor Kenshaw, pleased with his pun and flattered by the response to it, found it hard to keep his face straight. Suddenly he was back in good humor. "Mr. Wingate's theory is quite apparently one to which the majority of this class subscribes. Now I try to be lenient with students in this class. Surely no one could describe me as a hard task-master. But I resent your implication that I have been too easy-going. Now these reading reports were assigned to you last September, and you have had ample time to prepare them. I'll not call for any more of them today, but at the next session of this class I expect every one of these papers in. As for you, Mr. Wingate, if you'll see me directly after class, I'll be glad to hear any explanation or apology that you may wish to make. I want most of all to be fair. I have always given every student the benefit of the doubt until a student deliberately flouts me with his indifference. But I am capable of being quite ruthless, I assure you."

"Thank you, sir," Charlie mumbled. He suffered a slow torture, trying to keep awake until the class bell rang. He rolled his hot, red-veined eyes up with drunken precision to see the clock. Fifteen minutes had to pass before the bell would ring.

When the bell rang the class arose quickly and began clumping out. Several co-eds and men, politickers and apple-polishers wangling for A's, crowded about the lecture table. Doctor Kenshaw always remained behind after each class to accept their homage. But today he looked up over the heads of the eager group. He silenced their inane questions and flagrant compliments by placing his right forefinger against his thin, unsmiling lips. "Sh-h-h!" he said. The apple-polishers turned their heads in the direction of his gaze and then, giggling softly, tiptoed away. When the last had gone out, Doctor Kenshaw unscrewed his fountain pen and opened his roll book. He ran his finger down the list until he came to "Wingate, C." and in the space opposite under "Smstr Grd" he marked a precise little F.

A whiffling snore escaped Charlie Wingate in the back of the room. Doctor Kenshaw looked back across the varnished chair rows with a frown of annoyance. He took his overcoat from its hanger, slipped into it, and strapped up his brief case. He jammed on his hat and strode out of the lecture room, slamming the door. The noise made a hollow echo in the empty room, but it did not disturb Charlie Wingate. He slept on behind his amber glasses.

THE PROFESSOR OF DREAMS

In this poetic story from the author's *Notes for a New
Mythology,* we are carried away from the economics student's
all-night restaurant and from the office of a very prosaic dean
to a classroom like none, sad to say, that we have ever sat in.
But a professor can dream, as Greenlaw does when he appears
in this story—a fugitive, no doubt, from the living mythology
of the present, of which he is a glorious part—and at times a
professor can realize a dream by setting his students on the quest
for literature, "the world of the passionate mind." Who is this
ambiguous Greenlaw, this poet, this professor? More than
one student, untouched by the dream, is sure to ask.

President Burbage was inclined to be discouraged. Was college
education a success or a failure? If a success, how came it that among
his students was never a poet, a dreamer? History had indicated a certain usefulness for such persons; colleges, thought President Burbage,
should produce them now and then, if only out of reverence. But how?
As he thought of such matters, his heart grew heavy.

One day he was aware of a stranger. Where he was at the time or
what doing he could never afterward remember; somehow his path had
crossed another's, and his suddenly hesitant eyes had beheld a young
man with indelineable features.

The stranger introduced himself as Greenlaw by name, a writer, a
traveler, a teacher of the art of dreams. Burbage was pleased with the
young man, and they conversed, though whether for minutes or hours
the president was later unable to calculate. The upshot was that Burbage tendered Greenlaw the professorship of dreams, and that Greenlaw accepted.

Dr. Greenlaw had escaped the hand of time, as one would put it; one
felt that he was not so young as he appeared to be. Indeed, he appeared
regrettably young. But to grow accustomed to his youth was not to grow
accustomed to him. He was apart from his youth, was more than youth.
And how, unless he had somehow duped time?

His was the lurking smile of centuries, which waited and waited. It
was a smile hard to abandon; a smile which, when one saw it no more,

left the world celibate and poor. His eyes, even more, made one suspect Greenlaw of years fraudulently obtained: they were not contemporary. The Woolworth tower crumbled before their gaze, in them the jungle grew upon the streets of Nineveh, and the ancient sea beat on its ruined shores.

The young man could hardly be mistaken for a commercial traveler selling electric flat-irons. The streets of our age were not at home with him. His speech was that of nations and of ages. His clothes—but no one ever looked. Horses and dogs liked him. He had ways of enticing.

President Burbage had said to the young man:

"Observation, imagination—these, above all, I want my students to see, to feel. Go at the matter as you desire, but produce the results."

"You are a man after my own heart," returned Dr. Greenlaw, with his slow smile.

The teacher kept his students from slumber. Sometimes he entered the classroom through the window with an agility that made him admired. Sometimes, wishing to stretch his legs, he would say, "Let us walk out to the wood and talk."

Dr. Greenlaw opened pages of the heritage of literature which had never been opened in a classroom. Where he obtained the old volumes, the time-stained manuscripts, no one knew. Before his students he unrolled the fabulous, the beautiful, the tragic. He kindled the imagination. Leaning upon the broad desk, his face toward his class, he would read a ballad with commentary that made the students vibrate to dialogue dead three hundred years. He would rehabilitate a demigod, a god, as old as history. To his classes, Prometheus, with the vultures at his breast, became a fierce symbol.

One day the doctor appeared with a strange lady in a leafy hat, who had come, he said, from the ends of the earth. The visitor smiled oddly. Then she spoke to them as follows:

"Lads and maidens, it does not matter that the university is built on the profits of iron bath-tubs, that the town is the junction of railroads, that it has such and such a number of hotels, garages, and warehouses. It matters not at all that you sleep in beds, eat at tables, that your teachers make you study, that your friends and parents give you advice. What does matter is that you live in the light of the sun and its companion stars, and shrink not from the moon of dreams, or from shaggy music in the woods at daybreak.

"Youths and maidens, nothing can harm you so long as you are will-o'-the-wisps, animated alibis, averted faces, dwellers in your own wildernesses, saviors of yourselves and others."

She smiled oddly again, and the class, which had hardly caught the import of her words, smiled oddly back. A dark-haired boy in the back row looked at her and quivered.

Greenlaw's students began to write, and they were not frugal with their fire. The teacher read aloud to them with spirit the best of what they wrote, pointing out how the description of a certain ghost could be made more disturbing; how the head-lights of a doomed motor-car could be brought more uncannily to bear on the lurking terror of a midnight road; by what verbal insinuations the mood of the woods in autumn could be thrust into the mind of the reader.

The students withdrew more and more from the everyday world; the neighboring streams, the little hills, the elm-trees along the highways, the moon, began to have for them an agitating import. One boy wrote home of a conversation he had held with the night, and was withdrawn by his father, a manufacturer of dentifrice, who put the boy under the care of a physician. A girl sent her landlady into hysterics by narrating to her truthfully what she had heard voices say under her eaves at daybreak.

Boys went about with "Doctor Faustus" in their pockets. Girls recited to one another Shakspere and the dirges of Li Po. The booksellers were pestered by orders for rare and unheard-of volumes, while the "best-sellers" of the day, conveniently at hand, lay unsold.

Other teachers began to complain. One touch of imagination made the whole university tremble. Late hours made it impossible for Dr. Greenlaw's students to be prompt at early classes; in afternoon classes they were apt to sleep. Surreptitiously reading "Hydriotaphia," "The Marriage of Heaven and Hell," or "The City of the Sun," they survived lectures on the history of American business and the psychology of salesmanship. For Dr. Greenlaw's class that uncertain teacher became the college, and the world from which he had abducted them was superseded by literature, the world of the passionate mind.

But when Dr. Greenlaw was alone? Walking restlessly before his fire on cold November and December evenings or stamping his heels before a book-case, with a hovering hand unable to choose where any choice would exclude so much, he would say:

"It seems to be getting rather long. Is the seed being sowed?" he would ask himself. When he had glanced through the latest sheaf of papers, he would run his hands through the locks that vined above his forehead and murmur:

"Not yet. But excessive stimulation in an American college cannot differ from excessive stimulation in the groves of Thebes or the gardens of Bagdad."

Before the evening passed, he habitually wandered into the night along the bank of a river, where there were great trees. Late pedestrians might have seen his ambiguous form there, and heard him whisper in a voice like wind-swept trees:

"What is your substance, whereof are you made, that millions of strange shadows on you tend?"

He came back sometimes as late as daybreak. His landlady said he slept amazingly little, occasionally not for three or four nights running. It was beyond her how a body could get along so. Yet Greenlaw was always alert, as resurgent as the dawn.

Before school he would select books from his shelves, and perhaps a picture or two from an overflowing store. As he did, he would say with that most perplexing smile:

"Mixed drafts of stronger potency, 'wine that never grew in the belly of the grape.' By Zeus! I shall make these youths stagger, whether I persuade them to my ends or not."

The doctor little guessed to what extent the liquors he distilled had affected his students in their other studies. He hardly knew by sight his confrères of the faculty, but it had pleased him had he known how Rogers, sent to the board in calculus, stood like an idiot, his tongue forming the words of *Rosalind,* "I could shake them off my coat: these burs are in my heart." Or how behind the dark brows of young Burbage, the president's son, *Sancho Panza* jostled *Falstaff,* and *Desdemona* wept upon the bosom of *Scheherazade.*

Of these things he knew nothing. Nor did he meet young Burbage prowling about among the trees at night. He never heard of the landlady who had hysterics or of the slender lad who conversed with the night, and was therefore under the doctor's eye.

Otherwise it is doubtful whether he would have said absently to his class one morning late in March:

"At dawn there were cloven prints in the soft garden ground beneath my window. Yet I have found no cloven imprint on all you have written since last September." Young Burbage changed his attitude, and searched his teacher's face with a sidelong eye.

The days grew longer, and the first flowers bloomed in the wood. Breezes soft with moisture and the smell of springing vegetation stole through the open windows of bedrooms at morning and evening.

Dr. Greenlaw sat beneath his oak-tree late one afternoon in a somewhat melancholy mood.

"The year will soon be over," he said to himself. "Strange that I am unable to spread the magic carpet; that I send no spy across the walls of the magic city."

He glanced through the papers he held on his knee. He opened one that bore no name. He leaped to his feet with a suppressed sound. Within was the black imprint of a hoof, a goat's hoof, neat, small, and cloven. He brought the paper close, his fingers trembling.

"Is it a jest," he asked himself, "or is it the word of the wood?"

Now he noticed a few lines of verse faintly inscribed at the bottom of the page. He read them:

> I sat me down to write for you,
>   And write for you I did;
> And now, across the close-knit page,
>   My written words are hid
> Beneath an unexpected hoof
>   That stamped itself unbid.

"Burbage, beyond a doubt," said Greenlaw; "but Burbage writing verse, and trampled by the cloven hoofs of spring?"

At the conclusion of the next class Greenlaw asked Burbage to wait. Burbage lingered warily.

"My dear boy," said the teacher, curving about a chair, "what is the meaning of this?"

Young Burbage, with an eye remoter than Arabia, answered:

"If they dance below your window, sir, why cannot they dance across my page?"

There was a pause, a long pause, rich in mysterious things.

"I am not doubting you, foolish boy," said Dr. Greenlaw at last; "I merely ask how it happened."

"I fell asleep, I dare say; when I awoke, the mark was there."

Dr. Greenlaw was on his feet, walking up and down the classroom with his hands up, as though holding something to his lips. The boy sent a piercing look after him. There ensued another remarkable pause.

The teacher became quiet, and pursued his eager inquiry:

"Have you had other intimations of them?"

"Not before you came,"—the youth gave a long sigh,—"but this spring five or six times."

"What other marks have they left?" The teacher put an impetuous hand on Burbage.

The boy considered the question, perplexed. He could not answer it directly, but he pulled a note-book out of his pocket, and handed it to Dr. Greenlaw.

The doctor seized it and read:

> The goat that rubbed my knees last night
>   And left his ancient smell
> Maddened my heart that I was what
>   A hornèd goat could tell.
>
> For if his favor singled me
>   Out of the passing crowd,
> I know I'm not too well disguised
>   Nor yet too worldly proud.

Most difficult it is to-day
      Beneath a coat and vest;
I feared my old identity
      Might fade with all the rest.

But I'll go back to hill and sky,
      And hold a colloquy;
I need those ancient presences
      Whose tumult still is me.

Dr. Greenlaw smiled in a way one hardly dared to look at. It had the brightness of the sun.

"I'm glad you caught the real language of the goat," he said. "The goat, like the lizard and the lion, speaks in the tongue of dreams."

Burbage walked over to the open window and sniffed the breeze.

"Speak," said Dr. Greenlaw, dropping into his chair.

The boy went on, with no change of posture:

      "When spring came on,
      Why did the satyrs dance, and who were they?
      Last night I thought a satyr danced in me:
      The curtains of a hundred centuries
      Were drawn away; and as he stood revealed,
      I started, for the satyr's limbs were mine!"

Dr. Greenlaw smiled again.

"The satyr, too, has been misunderstood," he said. "One strain more, brother, and I shall be satisfied."

"I'll tell you of an adventure." And the boy began:

      "Oh, the night was mist enfolded,
      And my body wasn't molded
      To resist it.
      So it twisted,
      So it tiptoed down the stairs,
      And on the porch I found it, unawares."

"Absolutely true," interrupted Greenlaw, imperiously. "Go on!"

      "The mist was dense and blinded me,
      The mist was silk and winded me;
      Oh, it was everywhere upon me,
      Folding me and holding me.
      So I laughed and I danced and I wept and I sung;
      And I kissed the leaves where syringas hung."

Dr. Greenlaw rose, and took the boy in his arms.

"Another star has risen," he said. "You are mad, charmingly, evasively mad. I have sown it, the ancient seed. Nothing now can do you hurt. Now you will grow; you will throw this head back and sing like a myriad birds; you will bellow like— But enough." A shade of sadness went across his face. "I must go."

The boy searched his teacher's ancient eyes, chilled by the words.

"Go away?"

"Yes; for nothing now remains to do," he replied.

The boy stood silent.

"Where will you go?"

"Up and down the earth," answered Greenlaw.

"Shall I go with you?"

"No, lad."

The boy's eyes filled with tears.

"I shall come back," said Greenlaw, softly.

With a tremendous cry of liberation, and before Burbage knew what he was about, Dr. Greenlaw had leaped through the open window and was gone. Burbage stood riveted to the floor. A moment later he rushed to the window, but his strange teacher had disappeared. The boy searched the ground to see where he had alighted; and when he found the marks, he remained a long time, staring.

Nancy G. Chaikin

BACHELOR OF ARTS

The emotions of Anne Lupoff must be experienced in some measure to be fully appreciated. She has walked out of her dormitory and across the campus for the last time. College is all over, and she feels the misery of being "wedged between two clashing worlds." As the author says, she is "caught in the only half-understood moment of having just received a diploma, a degree, the sad consummation of sixteen years." Commencement is literally the beginning of something, and the reader is given an admirable opportunity to live through this chapter in Anne Lupoff's life, to share Anne's mood of "strange incomprehensible fears and longings." It is a mood so well sustained throughout as to give to the entire story an effective unity of impression.

From the window of her dormitory room, Anne Lupoff could see across to the windows of the faculty offices in Mackey Hall, those little cubicles of light and dark that even in the nighttime smelled comfortably of tobacco and old books. She had got into the habit of looking across every night, as she sat at her desk, to see whether Russell Slater was working late; and now, on the night before graduation, she noted, with a sudden electric shock at her stomach, that the light was on in his office. She had promised herself that she would not go through the foolishness of trying to see him that night, that her eagerness was all out of proportion to what she had a right to expect from him—that there was, in fact, nothing to expect. But as surely as she had resolved and known, even while she was doing it, that she was deceiving herself, she felt now the old, strong impulse driving over her; it was the last night, the very last night. Slowly she turned from the window and took the pins out of her hair, walking toward the dresser where she had left her comb. It had been a simple, if fond, professor-student relationship—absolutely nothing more. But now the comb was racing through her hair, and her heart was beating audibly, and she was thinking, "What if he leaves before I get there, what if he leaves, what if he leaves?"

The final, irrevocable, beautiful, warm spring night on this campus. The air flowed softly around her head as she left the dormitory, and there was the slightest sound of it in the trees; and over in the bell tower, a darkening shaft against the late spring sky, the carillonist was playing "Gaudeamus Igitur." She looked up again at the office window—she knew so well which one, counting from left to right until she hit number four—the light was still there, all alone, surrounded on either side by long dark rectangles, the windows of deserted rooms. The others had all gone home—indeed, there was no reason for anyone to be there now; the grades were in, most of the students had left. Why should Russell be working at night in his office? Perhaps he knew, perhaps he had known all along that she would have to come; perhaps that was why he had said nothing, not a word, up to now.

The elevator was closed down for the night and she walked the two flights of stairs slowly, hearing the echo of her footsteps carrying hollowly into the halls, thinking that maybe he could hear them too, there in his office—would know that it was she, and smile to himself, that strange reluctant half smile that did not quite close his small dark eyes. But when she reached his office there was no sign that he had expected her. His head was bent over some papers—familiar, ugly, balding head that inclined itself to one side when he lectured—and his chair creaked back and forth, back and forth as he read. She knew that she could have stood there for some time while he read, could even have turned and left and he would not have noticed. But, having done the foolish, childish, inevitable thing, she wanted it now to be inescapable. So she stood there only for several seconds before she made the final, efficient, deliberate sounds which would give her away. It was silly—as silly as a grammar school adolescent waiting around the corner for her crush—but she was too close to the end of it to care how it looked, what he would think or had been thinking. She wanted only to know whether he welcomed it, whether there was anything there at all.

At last he looked up, and smiled the smile she had imagined, predicted, craved. At last the head came up from the papers, the eyes half closed, and the large dry lips said quietly, "Please come in."

"I can't imagine why you're working tonight," she said, annoyed with herself because, as usual, the words came out flippant, intrusive—not gentle, and softly sympathetic, as she had wanted them to sound. "Everyone else has gone home."

"Everyone else has less to do," he said, offering her a cigarette across the desk, then leaning back and waiting for her to speak.

She shifted uncomfortably in the chair she had taken automatically, and wondered what on earth, what in the name of heaven she could possibly say now that would make sense. In a panic of foolishness, she realized that there wasn't anything at all.

"Out late tonight, aren't you?" he said.

"It doesn't matter the night before graduation—no hours at the dorm.

I could stay out and sleep anywhere tonight." My God, of all the things to say! But he spared her any signs of misapprehension.

"Of course," he said quietly. "The night before graduation. At last. Have you stopped mourning?"

She was determined to disregard his amusement. "I'll never stop mourning," she said quickly. "I want to stay here, dammit all. I don't want to graduate."

"So you've said. But, as I've told you, there's nothing to stop you from coming back eventually. They might even give you a teaching fellowship."

"Eventually," she said with disgust. "By the end of the summer I'll have gone crazy."

He laughed out loud, holding his cigarette up in the air in front of him, leaning way back in his swivel chair.

"This is most unwholesome of you, my dear. You're supposed to *want* to graduate. But that's nothing," still laughing, with his ridiculously short legs coming up in front of him, "you'll find out what you want—one of these days."

She grew hot and red under his "my dear," his paternal amusement, his fifteen years of seniority, and hated herself for even hoping that he might have known how important he was to the whole thing.

"I don't know," was all she could say. "I just don't know." And, after a long silence in which he simply pulled on his cigarette and she thought of all the crazy stories in which she might have thrown herself upon his gentle, true, unrevealed love for her—"My parents will be here in the morning. They'd like to meet you. Will you have lunch with us after the exercises?"

"Of course I will, Anne. And thank you."

She got up and went to the door. "Good night then," she said, turning for just a minute on the threshold. "Good night, Professor Slater."

He blew her a kiss with his small hand, and she ran down the hall like a little child, her head pounding, not wanting to give him a chance to spoil that tiny, harmless gesture.

Back at the dormitory she stopped for a moment before going in. The air was cooler now, and the carillon had stopped playing. But she imagined that she could still hear the strong prophetic chords of its clear, sad music—"Gaudeamus igitur, juvenes dum summus . . ." She rubbed the remembered echo of it like salt into her consciousness and wished that she could cry loudly, uncontrollably, as she had cried in her bed when she was a little girl. But nothing would come, except the realization that this, at last, was it—that tomorrow she would have to leave, with her regret sifting inside of her like grey ashes—a strange combination of incomprehensible fears and longings. She did not even know what she wanted from Russell; surely there was nothing she could rightfully expect. She did not know where along the way he had come to represent some sort of solution—a last desperate straw at which she might clutch. But that was what had happened, and now, looking back over it, she saw that it was an empty, innocent way—a filmy world of literature and abstraction—and that there was nothing she could hope for from it to sustain her. The world, the real world, loomed like an ugly unpassable giant and now, after all the years of loving school, her only refuge from it, she was being cast forth against it—out of this balmy, un-real, spring-washed campus, into its evil, waiting arms. Russell had re-fused to be the slayer—had he offered, she realized now, she did not know what she would have done. And she did not know now, what she would do, how she could bear it. Perhaps that was the way people died, too, crying to life "Keep me, keep me," but finding no refuge anywhere. Suddenly she felt cold and tired, so she opened the door to the dormitory and went in.

Inside the halls were strangely quiet and empty, with the voices of the few graduates who were in their rooms scarcely able to break the unac-customed silence. She knew that they were playing bridge down the hall on her floor, and one of the girls had a turkey which she had been invited to help eat. But she did not go down the hall at all. Instead, she lay awake for a long time, hearing their voices.

"I pass." The slap of the cards on the floor of somebody's room.

"Oh no you don't! That's my trick!"

"My God, fellers, think of getting out of here at last!"

"Tomorrow, no less, my fine feathered graduate!" And all the others laughed loudly, genuinely, feverish in the excitement of having finished the four years.

You see, she thought to herself, I'm unnatural. I'm probably the only one in the whole place who doesn't want to graduate. They don't even care, they don't even care. They'd think I was crazy. I can't even explain it to myself—how could I explain it to them?

She fell asleep long after the bridge game had broken up, after the turkey had been noisily eaten. When one of the girls came down the hall yelling, "Lupoff, hey Anne—your turkey!" she closed her eyes and breathed deeply and loudly, until the girl went away. Finally it was all over, the doors closed on the other rooms, and there was only the heavy silence in which she fell asleep at last.

In the morning, with the sun slanting hotly across the floor of her room, she put on her cap and gown and stood before the mirror looking at herself, pleased with how right they looked on her—how sensible and bright and wise they made her seem. She could never remember which way the tassel went, but she'd see when she got down to the procession. Now she would only have to come back to this room to collect her bags— they were all packed—and they stood alone in the middle of the floor of the half empty room, with its stripped bed and cleared, glass top dresser, and dust-covered study lamp. She looked across to Mackey Hall, but the window glared in reflected sunlight and hurt her eyes— then, down to the street, where the black-robed figures were already hurrying to have breakfast before the procession formed.

She thought of calling the Union, where her parents had presumably spent the night after arriving very late, but decided, instead, to go directly over there and meet them for breakfast. They had said that they would be sitting in the lobby that morning, before the exercises, but she was afraid they would get mixed up and go to the wrong place.

She knew they would expect her to be excited and pleased and loving, that they would not understand. She prayed for patience with them, but knew, even before she went to meet them, that she would not have it. To them, her degree was their stamp of having succeeded in the demanding, difficult New World to which they had come together thirty years ago. She was their only child—the next best thing to a son; if she could not be a professional (my son, the doctor . . .) she could at least be a Bachelor of Arts. In their letters to her—long, affectionate, awkward letters which begged her silently to fulfill their hopes and prayers—they had betrayed their longing for a tall capable son who would do them honor in a profession. And she, with the academic honors which came to her as a by-product of her furious love for the place and the life, had given them the next best thing. They were unbearably proud of her, and she was embarrassed by their open, unashamed European pride, their overstated affection, their naïve conviction that in giving her a college education they had attained the peak of parental obligation. Instead, she thought sadly, they had driven her further and further from them—with their strange emotional way of life, their pathetic ignorance of everything she had come to love. She was not ashamed of them—she had never attempted to cover up for their uncertain, fumbling ways—but they had widened the gap immeasurably, and she was ashamed, not of them, but of herself, for having betrayed them by growing so unattainable, by spending these years in slipping further and further out of their reach. And now, the cruelest blow surely, that she could not honestly say she was glad to be going home with them, could not even try to fool them by celebrating, savoring, loving the meaning of this day.

She walked slowly over to the Union Building, feeling the unfamiliar folds of the black robe about her legs, the pressure of the four-cornered hat upon her brow. And they were there in the lobby of the tall white building, huddled close to one another on a leather sofa, watching anxiously for her through the crowds of noisy alumni and polished, expectant-looking fathers and mothers, and eager black-gowned graduates. Her mother looked beautiful—that dark Balkan beauty seeming out of place amidst the athletic trophies and plaidy, collegiate trimmings which characterized the big room; the dark blue eyes looking very deep and sorrowful under the pale brim of her hat, the black hair curling softly all around her face, the white of her blouse pointing up the incredible, natural foreign coloring. Her father, small and very white-haired, turning his summer hat around and around in his fingers, looked only worried and afraid, as he always looked in a crowd. But when they saw her, when they saw her, they clasped their hands simultaneously in front of them, like one person, and smiled broadly, looking slowly down her, from the stiff top of her cap with its ridiculous displaced tassel, to her shoes, just showing from beneath the gown—their glance sweeping with love and wonder over her face, her body, her hands, tentatively outstretched to them. Then they were kissing her and saying the things she had known they would say.

"My Anna—" they would never call her Anne—"our own girl—to think this day would come, that we are here, so far away, to see you with your college graduation."

"Hello Momma—Pa. Did you have a good trip?"

"Such a long trip. You never told us how long—and we sat up all night." Her mother shook her head slowly.

"Well my gosh, you should have taken a Pullman. I *told* you to take a Pullman, Poppa."

"I didn't know. The man said the chairs were comfortable. It wasn't so bad, Momma, was it?"

"I don't know, I don't know. I only know we're here—and soon our girl will graduate." It was all that mattered. She looked eagerly around the crowding room. "You want breakfast first, yes Anna?"

"Yes, Momma, first we have breakfast and then I'll tell you where to go for your seats and where to meet me afterwards."

They had their breakfast in the big oak-paneled dining room of the Union, but no one was very hungry. Her parents simply kept shaking their heads and looking curiously, proudly, about the big room. And for Anne, it was an intolerable imposition of one of her worlds upon the other—they simply did not go together; they had nothing to do with one another. She did not even know what there was for her to say to her parents—but they did a good deal of the talking themselves. She had almost forgotten how odd their conversation could sound.

"You know, Anna, what a great day this is for us—our own daughter graduating. We want you to know how proud it is for us." Her father laid his cool, old hand over her perspiring one, then passed it swiftly, lightly over her cheek.

"Yes, Pa, I know, *I* know." She was stifling with their pride, their misplaced joy.

"And we want, your momma and I, you should come home now and rest and read and do whatever you want till the fall. All summer you shouldn't work. You should just stay home with us and be—" he laughed loudly—"a loafer!"

It was an attempt, a pitiful attempt. And an image of the long, unfilled, intolerable summer days consumed her, filled her eyes with tears. Her mother saw them and turned to the little man, with bewilderment in her own eyes.

"Leave her, Joe," she said, "plenty of time for talk later."

Later, later, later—the shocking, desolating recognition of how much time there would be, how much of later, sent her sobbing out of the dining room. After several seconds of hesitation, the other two people followed her, and they all walked together in silence to the point at which the academic procession was to start. She left them there, indicating the building to which they were to go and arranging to meet them again at the Union for lunch. She hoped they remembered that Russell would be with her—they had told her to invite him, as many as she wanted, they had said—but she did not want to bring it up now. So she stood in line with the others, under the blazing sun, her head throbbing beneath the cap—and watched their figures disappear toward the doorway of Blane Auditorium, their legs very short, moving quickly, firmly, their hands clasped together between them. Then the procession started and she felt nothing except the burning of the sun through her gown, the hot pavement through the soles of her thin summer shoes.

She was grateful that, in the huge auditorium, with the visitors all sitting behind the graduates, she could not see the faces of her parents or hear their murmured wonder and pride when the honors were announced. But on the platform she could make out Russell's face, saw the familiar, noncommittal half smile when her name was announced for the work she had done under his tutelage. At least she had done him proud —at least that; it meant a lot to a man appointed as a Special Studies Tutor to have his student come out on top. Even now some silly, overeager, bright young sophomore was plotting to take her place. And maybe he was thinking that there would be others who would do just as well as she had—someone else he could treat to lunch and Aristotle. She brightened a little—he *had* treated her to lunch, hadn't he—often. And today, today at least was hers. She would make the most of it.

Then, at last, they were singing the Alma Mater—and she sobbed as if she were a slobbering old alumnus at a reunion dinner who had too much to drink.

When the ceremonies were over, she stood outside in the milling mixed throng of graduates and parents, all of them kissing, calling, perspiring—caught in the only half-understood moment of having just received a diploma, a degree, the sad consummation of sixteen years. The high noon sun was incredibly strong, a summer sun now, sudden, uncompromising, with no hint of the balminess and promise of spring in a college town. She stood there for some time, waiting for the faculty to file out, hoping to catch Russell before he started for the Union. Then she spotted him, talking over in a corner to Bill Daimler, a young teaching fellow who was always following him around. Wondering whether he had forgotten, she hurried over to them.

"Behold," shouted Bill, when he saw her coming, "the sweet girl graduate."

"Who mourneth as she comes," said Russell, holding out his hand in a congratulatory gesture.

She shook his hand, and Bill's. "My parents are going to go on ahead and meet us at the Union," she said. "I hope you'll have lunch with us too, Bill. They'd be happy to meet you."

"I'll come gladly—if nobody minds—provided you promise to smile all the way there." Bill looked at Russell sternly. "One thing you haven't taught your prize student, Professor Slater, is how to accept the facts of graduation."

Russ rolled his tongue over into one cheek and looked at her carefully. "She doesn't want to learn," he said at last.

Anne felt terribly foolish again now, and turned her head away quickly. But Bill grabbed her shoulder and was steering her out of the crowd. "Enough of such trifling conversation," he said cheerfully, "on to the Union and the parents of the sweet girl graduate."

She looked around to be sure that her parents were not waiting in front of the auditorium, but she did not see them anywhere. So they walked together, the three of them, down the suddenly busy, crowded, excited streets of the town to the Union Building. Now everything was beginning to lose its meaning, and the only thing, in all this strange turmoil, that seemed to have any real relation to her was the sight of her parents, small and anxious, standing together near the front entrance of the Union lobby, looking once again for their daughter. She felt a renewed sweep of pleasure in her mother's beauty, as she introduced them to her, and in the way her father, suddenly secure in the pride of his daughter's success, shook their hands quietly and firmly, looked brightly into their faces.

"We have heard so much about you—all of you professors," her mother said.

"The faculty, no less," her father said laughing, his too even false teeth showing in the pink face. "If you love her like she loves you. . . ."

"Poppa! Oh Poppa!" She made a gesture of impatience, and the rest of them laughed with the old man.

Then they climbed the marble stairs to the busy dining room and took seats together at a table near one of the big windows. The dining room was almost filled already, and it was some time before their orders were taken. Waiting there at the table, only half-hearing her parents' questions and the answers, some flippant, some serious and respectful, which came from Russell and Bill, she began to feel again the misery of being wedged between two clashing worlds. They were all strangers now, and there was nothing she could say to any of them that would bring them together, or her closer to them. Slowly she allowed herself to be wrapped again in self-pity, wanting to cry out to them that one of them—one of the two worlds, lives, homes—should claim her, keep her, hold her safe against the other. But there was no sign that anyone knew what she was thinking, could have understood what she meant; and the meal was a miserable, confused ceremony of farewell.

"When does your train leave, Mrs. Lupoff?"

"Soon, I think. What time, Joe?"

"This afternoon, three o'clock. Maybe you and Anna should go ahead back for her bags, Momma, there's not much time."

Anne looked at her watch. It was true, there wasn't much time.

"No, no. We'll all go," her mother said.

But Bill had to leave before dessert had been served. To her great relief, Anne noted that Russell was making no move to leave with him. She wanted him with her until the last possible minute. And, thank goodness, he knew it.

"If nobody minds," he said, "I'll string along until train time. Can't see my best pupil leaving without a proper sendoff."

Both parents laughed with pleasure.

"Mind?" her mother said, inclining her head slightly toward him. "Why I think we love having you. Isn't it, Poppa?"

"Delighted," said her father, with a funny little bow from the shoulders.

Her mother and father waited in the parlor of the dormitory, while she and Russell went up to get her bags. He had never seen her room before—but now there was nothing of her left in it—not the cute little cartoons she had tacked up on a bulletin board near the door, or the snapshots stuck under the glass dresser top, or the sonnet from Keats, framed delicately on the wall. Only her bags—sitting miserably, coldly in the middle of the floor—and a coat for traveling flung across the stripped bed.

Russell looked around the room carefully, as if he could see it all, all that had been there—then walked slowly over to her desk—empty, dusty, untelling—near the window.

"And this," he said, running a finger over the surface, "is where you sat, turning out those themes of yours." She nodded. "And there—" he looked out the open window and pointed across the street—"is where I sat and read them." He turned and faced her again.

"So you knew that I could see your window from here."

"You forget that as a member of the faculty, I know everything."

He smiled at her—but softly, gently, touching her chin lightly with his finger. "Someday you'll know everything too. And you'll see what a little goose you're being and how important it is for you to leave now and give yourself a summer to think things through." He did not say what things —only "things . . . ."

Then, unexpectedly, he drew out of his pocket a small volume—a thin edition of Shakespeare's sonnets, bound in rich red supple leather.

"From me to you," he said, handing it to her.

She opened to the flyleaf. "For Anne, my favorite," he had written, "to remind her gently of her salad days." Then, after watching her as she read the inscription, he walked out of the room. Slowly, closing the book without a word, she followed him down the stairs to where her parents waited.

In the taxi, on the way to the station, she watched her town rush by, wondering how she could be expected to throw it over, demolish it, forget it, after four years of living only from semester to semester, return to return. As the familiar streets and structures stretched out behind them, she found herself coping unsuccessfully with that incomprehensible prospect—that she would not ever see them again and that they, in turn, would go on about their business of standing, being, aging, as if she had never been there at all. She remembered how ugly they had all seemed at first—the streets busier than she had thought college-town streets should be, and the buildings, old and baroque, spread out all over them. And now, how beautiful, with their smell of pipes, their old halls and rooms, their windows and mottoes and walls.

She turned to Russell, who sat beside her holding her small traveling case.

"You're used to graduations by now, aren't you?" He was something like the buildings—a permanent, steady figure, unmoved and unmoving against the incoming and outflowing tide of students.

"I'm used to them. But some I regret more than others."

"Oh—you'll have another Honors student. Next year it will be someone else to do you proud. You're used to that too, aren't you?"

"Perhaps," he said. "But by next year that won't matter to you."

She wanted to say, "Will it matter to you?" But she only sat there silently, until the cab pulled up in front of the station house, at the foot of a long sweeping hill. From the bottom, you could see only the bell tower and the wonderful blue sky behind it. She had had her last glimpse of the buildings now, and of the town.

While her father paid the driver, her mother waiting beside him, she and Russell went into the station house with her bags. He set them down near the door to the tracks and pulled her over into a corner, near a candy machine.

"Never mind, Anne honey," he said. He put a nickel into the machine and pulled the plunger under a chocolate bar. "Sweets to the sweet," he said, handing it to her.

"Hardly worthy of you, that old cliché," she said. She could feel the tears starting to roll softly down her cheeks.

He swept his fingers lightly over them—first one side, then the other. "Or of you," he said.

They shook hands slowly, and she felt that his hand, like hers, was warm and sweating.

Her parents joined them, then, looking embarrassed and outcast, and there was the sound of the train, eastbound, rushing in upon the track. They all walked silently out of the station house and, as she mounted the steep little flight of steps to the coach, she could hear him saying good-bye to her parents. They were telling him over and over how much he had done for her, how he must visit them if he ever came east, how much, how very much, they knew she would miss him. He thanked them and helped them on to the train.

As the train quickly gathered its speed, she could see him standing on the platform—still waving—his small form becoming smaller and smaller—his hand at last going down to his side.

She pressed her head hard against the window then, sobbing softly, letting the wetness and the smooth pane of glass cool her flushed face. In the seat in front of her, her parents sat wordlessly together, looking at each other and at her. Finally, when the sobbing had stopped, her mother turned around tentatively, apologetically.

"Such a nice man," she said. "So brilliant. How lucky for you to have him."

And her father turned around too. "You are spoiled by such smart men," he said. "You only shouldn't look for too much now in the ones at home."

"Oh Poppa, Poppa." It was too much.

"Never mind, never mind." Her mother slapped her father impatiently on the shoulder. "Poppa will see now if we can get berths for the night. Go, Joe. When we get home we talk—when we get home."

Anne turned her head again toward the window, renewing the effort to escape the bewilderment in their eyes. Now she resented having to cope with it, with any of it, and she tried hard to push herself once again back into the world in which she had so recently succeeded. Silently she reviewed the last few days and hours, flushing again under the triumph of her oral examination, feeling again the weight of her thick, careful thesis manuscript as she handed it to the head of the department, accepting again, from a high, crowded platform, the academic honors which had come to her. She thought of everything Russell had said, everything he might have meant to say; and she stood with him again in her empty, bereft room, taking from his hands the smooth, leather-covered volume with his farewell on the flyleaf. But something had changed, thinned, lost its earlier impact; and against the even mechanical counterpoint of the noisy eastbound train, the meaning seemed to slip away from her. She was again strongly conscious of her mother's eyes upon her.

The older woman turned further around in her seat. "Anna," she said quietly, "Anna." She waited for her daughter to look at her. "We think now we should fix up the house for you—the way you want it. Then maybe you can entertain all your friends."

Anne smiled briefly at her. It was natural, after all, that even as she had been looking backward, in a last desperate effort to hold on, her parents, with the same measure of desperation, were looking ahead to home, the only place they understood, the only place in which she was —or seemed to be—wholly theirs.

Now she thought of her home, substantial, middle class brick house that stood solidly on the corner of a city street, having nothing to do with classes or Honors or midnight discussions of philosophy—but only with the strong rich smells of foreign cooking, the sounds of steady, quiet domesticity, the small passing exultations of family life. It was, after all, the only place to which she had always been able to return. Now, sud-denly, she felt curiously relieved by its simplicity, its lack of complication, its demonstrative, basic, unashamed warmth. For the first time in her life she was not embarrassed by it.

She wished that there was something she could say to her parents to make up for the last few hours. But she knew that they did not expect any such compensation from her—and that their surprise and delight at getting it would be more than she could bear, would only push her back again into her shell of remorse and longing for something else.

So she sat there alone, saying nothing, struggling with the changing tides of her emotions, pressing hard against the images which had so easily brought tears. At last, after a long time, with the flat landscape darkening against the sky of summer evening, she was able to picture, clearly and with a sudden sharp knowledge of how it felt to be there, her own room at home—with its windows wide and flung open over a long, green lawn, its bed, large and soft, that had stood there, in that corner of that room, as long as she could possibly remember.

Mark Schorer

BOY IN THE SUMMER SUN

Many a young man must learn, often under conditions far less favorable than those portrayed here, what this young man learns in the pleasant heat of the summer sun. Somewhat painfully he awakens to the state of mind often experienced by the college graduate when he leaves the campus and says good-bye to what used to be called the sheltered years. He finds that his world can never be the same again; he learns to his sorrow that all things, including women, change.

Unalloyed, summer had lingered miraculously into late September without a suggestion that autumn was at hand. Leaves and grass were green still, smoke had not yet come into the air, and the lake was calm, almost sapphire blue. Mid-mornings were hot, like mornings in July. So they walked where the woods were thickest, where the air was always slightly damp and the cool of night never quite gone. They did not speak much but went silently along the path, almost shoulder to shoulder, their hands touching, or their arms, as they moved. Now and then the girl spoke, quietly, briefly pointed out a bird, a flower, once a green snake gliding through the grass, and the boy answered with a nod or a monosyllable, his face touched with abstraction and a slight worry. After they came to a place in the wood where they stretched out now with their arms about each other lightly as if the place and this gesture were habitual, they did not speak at all until at last the girl, Rachel, asked suddenly, "Why are you so quiet? Is it Max? Are you angry because he's coming, Will?"

The boy started and looked into her face. "Angry? No, I'm not angry . . . I was just thinking about that lousy job. When I'm out here it's hard to believe that a job like that can be waiting for me when I get back."

The girl looked away into the depth of the wood. "Is it, Will?" she asked. "Or is it just that in college we never learn that for most people life finally comes down to work?"

"Maybe that's it."

"Or is it foul, Will? Is it worse then most jobs in the city, in summer?"

"Maybe not. But it's still foul."

They were quiet again, and it seemed a long time later, to him, when Rachel said, "Anyway, I'm glad it isn't Max."

His arms tightened around her shoulders. Then he sat up, his eyes narrowed in the shade, and he asked, "Why should it be?"

She said, "It shouldn't."

He lay down beside her again. He stared up into the lace-work of green leaves arched above them, and at the rare patches of blue sky that the leaves did not cover. Why should it be Max? Or why should she think it might be?

He had been awakened that morning by the ringing telephone, and lay sleepily in bed listening to Rachel's voice talking to someone in a way that did disturb him vaguely then, although now it seemed only mildly irritating that this week-end should be intruded upon. "But darling!" her voice had cried over the telephone. "What are you doing here? Come over at once! Mind? Of course not! We'll love it! In two hours? Good!"

When he came to breakfast, she smiled brightly and cried,

"Guess who's coming, Will! Max Garey! He got bored and started out early this morning, and just now called from the village. Isn't it grand? Mother's so fond of him—she'll take care of him."

"Does your mother know him? I didn't know she did."

"Oh, yes! I must have told you."

"No, you didn't," he said. And now he wondered why she had not told him.

Then Mrs. Harley came out on the porch. "Good morning, Will," she said brightly as she patted her white hair. "Isn't it *nice* that Mr. Garey can come! I'm so fond of Mr. Garey!"

"Yes, isn't it?" Will said into his coffee, and looked across the table into Rachel's eyes, which, shining with pleasure, were heedless of the question in his.

"Did you have any work with Mr. Garey, Will? Rachel thought him such a splendid teacher."

"No, I didn't," Will said. "His classes were always filled with girls."

Rachel looked at him quickly. "Now you're being unfair, Will. Everybody thinks he's a good teacher."

"I'm sorry," he said, and felt suddenly lonely in the bright morning with Rachel only across the table from him.

He was feeling that loneliness again now. "Maybe it's more than the job," he said. "Everything's different since June. I don't know why."

"What do you mean, Will?"

"Just a feeling that everything's breaking up."

They were quiet then until Rachel said, "I know. I'm different, too. Something's changed in me. There's something sad, some ache . . ."

Will knew that something had changed in her. She was older than she had been in June. There was something about her now that bewildered him, the feeling that she had lived without him, an aloofness and self-sufficiency which was new. She was like a woman, sometimes, putting up with a boy. He had felt it almost every week-end, and this and the more general sadness of the summer had darkened otherwise bright hours. Yet her kisses, her sweet arms around him, her yielding body, all denied his feeling. With him, there still came from her throat a little moan of pain and passion which he knew no one else had ever heard. And yet, now in the deep cool wood as she lay in his arms, he felt that she had forgotten him beside her.

She spoke at last as with an effort, as if recalling herself from a dream. "You know, Will, after you left college, in that week I stayed on, I saw Max rather often. Then mother met him. She invited him to come up. He was here earlier in the summer. Didn't I tell you?"

"No," he said, his throat contracting. "You must have forgotten."

His sadness knotted in his throat intensely, and he remembered then very clearly, almost as if she were saying it again now, something she had said before he left her in June. "Sometimes I wonder if this can last. We know each other as I think people almost never do. Now it begins to seem a little unreal, perhaps because it's been too lovely, part of this unreal life we're leaving. I wonder if that sometimes happens, Will."

Then he had laughed; but now, as he remembered, his arms tightened around her suddenly, as if from fright, and he leaned down and kissed her. Her lips were quiet, without response. He saw that her eyes were fixed on some remote object in the arch of trees or beyond, some dream, something far from him. He stood up and moved away. "Let's go back," he said, and without waiting for her started quickly up the path, toward the house.

All the afternoon they lay on the raft, Rachel between them. Max talked, his voice reflective and lazy, mixing with the sun of that afternoon and the endless laziness in the sounds that insects made in the woods and in the long grass along the shore, his voice spinning itself out, pausing now and then to listen to itself, and going on again, with Rachel lying quiet between them, her eyes closed and the oil gleaming on her brown skin. Will's head was turned toward her, his eyes wandering back and forth from her parted lips and her gleaming lashes to the swell of her breasts under her white swimming suit, to her long browned legs and her crossed feet at the end of the raft.

All the time Max's voice went on, the lazy, professor's voice. Will could tell as he heard it that it was a voice that always talked and that always had listeners, and yet, now, it did not irritate him. He was almost content to lie in the sun with the sensation of burning on his skin, the soft warm glow of skin absorbing bright sun enough in the afternoon to allay for the moment the morning's inarticulate fears, even though it was Max who was lying stretched out beyond Rachel, who was talking, pausing, talking, sometimes falling silent and no word coming from Rachel or himself, and then starting up again, the voice spinning itself out softly in the afternoon sun, with all the laziness of the afternoon in his slow words.

". . . and so in Donne the central factor is death . . . death, of course . . . he, more than any of the poets, built what he wrote upon what may be called a metaphysic of death . . . death as the great leveler on the one hand, the great destroyer of everything, beauty, love . . . and death as the figure at the gate of Heaven . . . these two, this one . . . the central factor, always present . . ."

His voice was slow, modulated, a little affected, quite soft, and in it, Will knew as he looked at Rachel's face, there was some magic of wisdom and experience that enthralled her.

Rachel's voice began, slow and soft as if infected by Max's voice, as warm as the sun, and speaking lines that Max first spoke to her, perhaps—only perhaps—in the classroom:

"When I died last, and, Dear, I die
    As often as from thee I go,
    Though it be but an hour ago,
And Lovers hours be full eternity,
    I can remember yet, that I
    Something did say, and something did bestow. . . ."

Max laughed. "But darling," he said, "that's still another kind of death, not so serious."

Rachel said nothing. And the sun wove around them its bright and golden web, and the whole world then as they lay there had slipped away and left the three of them stranded together in an unreality of sunlight on burning skin and closed eyelids, and nothing more. And Will, too, felt out of the world of fact, was empty of feeling, as if pure sensation had replaced it. And only slowly did a faint jangling come into his mind, the jangle of Max's word *darling,* like something shaken in a metal box, some harsh sound, or a feeling perhaps, shaking him abruptly from the web. He stirred. He turned. And in turning the web was broken, and he was free of it again, his hand plunged in the cold blue water of the lake and left to dangle there, his eyes turned from Rachel and Max for the moment but seeing nothing in the indeterminable depths of the blue water that gently lapped his hand.

"Not nearly so serious," Max said. "Only a metaphor, a way of speaking . . ."

Will turned toward them again and he saw in Rachel's face how serious it was, for she looked suddenly ill for all the glow of her skin, her face turned away from him and her lips fallen apart, and every line in her face and body taut suddenly, yearning, aching suddenly with sharp longing, sharp pain, she quite sick for love. Will's hands closed at his sides and opened again, turned empty to the sun.

"Poetry is full of such conventions, formalized short cuts to express familiar sentiments," Max was saying. "In Donne, of course, there's enough fire, usually, to vitalize them, but in others . . . mere metaphors . . ."

Something in Will's mind snapped, then seemed to shout, *Who cares? For God's sake, who cares?* He was enraged beyond endurance by the man's pompous classroom manner, his easy presence, his way of excluding Will, as if he were alone with Rachel and no one else existed. He hated him, and the very presence of Rachel there made his throat ache with something like the pressure of tears coming. The sun had lost its spell. The buzz of insects on the shore seemed for a moment unbearably loud, and the sun no longer warm, but hot, searing, parching his throat and mouth, blinding him. For now he hated Max, and he knew as he remembered Rachel's voice speaking those lines, that she was lost to him, that he had nothing more for her, that Max had all. And there Max lay, as if he belonged there, had every right to be there, talking and priding himself in his talk, delighting to hear his own words, lecturing as though he were in the classroom and Rachel in the front row looking up at him with wide eyes, lecturing as though Rachel and he were alone in the room and Will did not exist.

Will's eyes clouded in anger as he stared down into the water disturbed by his hand. He tried not to hear what their low voices said, and only when they were silent did he turn again suddenly on the raft to see how their bodies had moved together, so that their legs touched, and Max's hand lay quite near Rachel's hair. He stood abruptly, stirring the raft in the water, and then dived deep, swam quickly out and away from them, his arms beating the water in his anger, in a frantic effort to forget the hurt which came from Rachel's willing reception of the man's intolerable arrogance.

He struck out into the lake. The water was cold on his skin, and as he swam his anger cooled. But when his anger was gone, he felt sad and futile again, swam more slowly, felt helpless and wounded, felt almost weak in the water, so that he grew angry with himself instead and wished that he could hold that other anger. When he turned back and swam slowly toward the shore, only the hurt remained, and he did not go to the raft. There Max's words would still be spinning themselves out in the sunlight, catching Rachel's mind in their spell, catching her heart firmly and her whole mind and life, and holding them there, as if the words were really magic.

He walked up the beach and stretched out on the sand. He lay on his back and looked up into the blue sky, and as he lay there he felt suddenly that this was the last time in his life that he would be doing quite this. All summer he had been coming from the sweltering, grimy city, and in seeing Rachel in the country, in living in her mother's friendly house, in swimming and dancing and drinking and finding cool spots in the woods where the moss was thick and only the trees and birds made sound—in all of this it had seemed that nothing had changed or was ending. And this in spite of the fact that when they parted in June, when they walked for the last time along familiar walks between familiar buildings, they had vaguely felt that an end had come to a period, that a new life was waiting for both of them, and that (Rachel felt) somehow they were therefore ending for one another. But then Max was nothing to him, only a professor whom she liked; so for him nothing really ended.

Now the golden day was unbearable. He turned over on his stomach and put his face in his arms. Almost at once he could feel the sun burning his neck, his back. But it alleviated nothing. There was the dull ache in his chest and throat, the constant feeling that at any moment he would cry out like a child in sobs. It was a pressure in his body that he could not put into thoughts, only the feeling that something was ending, inevitably ending. He thought of his past and it was all gold, all brightness and gold, all magic landscape, all an idyl, all a bright day, and all ending.

He thought he must cry. All his youth was gathered into a knot of pain that choked him, that, dull and heavy, pressed against his heart. He thought of going back to the city, to the hot office, to stupid work sweating over accounts, of the years he had ahead of him in which to slave there. And he knew as he lay in the sand, really *knew* for the first time, that all of that was no mere interlude.

He felt a touch on his shoulder, turned, and looked up. It was Rachel, brown in the sun, saying, "Darling, don't be rude."

He sat up. "Am I being rude?"

"Does he bore you?"

"Yes. I don't like him much."

"Well, I'm sorry he came, Will, but I couldn't help it. Come back and try to bear him. He's not bad, you know."

"No?" Will asked as he got up.

She looked at him swiftly, then smiled. "Don't be silly, darling."

"No, *darling.*"

"Good."

Then they went up the shore, back to the raft where Max still lay in the lessening glare of the sun.

Then finally he could put up with him no longer. The whole thing, suddenly, was impossible, too much for him. He sat at the table for a minute more and fought against the impulse to leave. But Mrs. Harley, cooing in a voice that almost made him ill ("But how *interesting*, Mr. Garey. *Do* go on! Do you *really* believe that?") and Max, toying with his fork and smiling with what Will supposed was great "charm" before continuing his monologue, decided him. He looked quickly at Rachel. She sat at the end of the table, opposite her mother. She looked very cool in a white dress, brown throat and arms cool and lovely, her lips slightly parted, her eyes fixed—lost to him.

Then he rose quickly to his feet. "Excuse me, please," he said, and went to the porch, and then outside, down the steps, stumbled down toward the shore under the pines. He sat down in the grass. His fingers fumbled for a cigarette and a match in his pocket. Then he stared out at the water and the new moon hanging close over the opposite shore. In the reeds the frogs sang. From above came the ring of silver on china. He bit hard into his lower lip when he knew suddenly that the salt he tasted was of tears.

Then everything broke, collapsed in him like a sail when the wind dies. He wept as he had not wept since he was a small boy; and there, for a time in the night, he felt that he was a small boy still, alone in the dark and empty night. He lay on the grass and sobbed, and there was a violence in his weeping as of a body tortured. He smothered the sound in the grass.

But he could not smother the pain in his chest. It was like a live thing in his heart, heavy and pressing, torturing, not relieved by sobs. It came over him in waves of torment, and now it was no longer anything of the mind, but of the body alone, a physical pressure, wracking and violent, eruptive and convulsive, as if his very life, well-loved, were ending in the torment.

He did not feel Rachel's hand on his shoulder. It was her voice that recalled him: "Will—darling—please!"

Even then he could not prevent his sobs from coming. It was as if they were something separate from him, separate from his will, as if they had their own life, must come to their own slow end. He felt no shame before her, had no feelings at all, no thoughts, was given over entirely to what seemed wholly a physical act. Then slowly, at last, his shoulders grew quieter. Slowly his breathing quieted. Slowly his eyes dried. And it was over at last. He felt empty, weak, desolate as he turned slowly over on his back to look at her.

The moon was almost in the water. He could see it, touching the opposite shore. The sky was dark, sprinkled with cold stars. These too he saw, blurred and faint, unsteady in the darkness. Beside him knelt Rachel, her white dress a vague lightness, her face above him a blur. She spoke again: "Darling, what is it, what's *wrong?*"

He swallowed hard but could not speak. He lay on his back and looked at the blur of her face. His hand reached out and seized hers, held it tightly. Then she lay down beside him suddenly, put her arms around him, and her cheek to his mouth. He smelled the familiar perfume of her hair and moved away from her a little. Now he could see the stars more clearly; their light was brighter, harder, they were steadier in the sky, fixed and remote. Then, although Rachel's arms were around him and her face so close that he could feel her warm breath sweet on his face, he was alone, desolate, empty, alone on the shore under the stars. He did not say this then, nor did he even quite feel it, but he knew it, his body, empty and quiet, knew it—the cold loneliness of the stars even on a summer night. He lay still and looked up. Something momentous had happened.

"I felt sick," he said at last, though Rachel had not spoken again.

She said nothing for a while, then whispered, "I'm sorry."

"It's all right now."

As if startled by the deadly quiet of his voice, she sat up and looked closely into his face. "*Are* you all right now, Will?"

"Yes, it's all right now." He said it clearly.

"What was it, though?" she asked.

"You know."

"No."

"Yes, you do."

"Not *Max,* Will?"

"What else?"

"Oh, but *darling—*"

"It doesn't matter, Rachel."

"What do you mean—doesn't matter? Do you think—"

"I know, Rachel. I knew it this morning. But only tonight, suddenly, at the table, when I saw your face while he was talking—it took that long until I really could believe it. But it doesn't matter now."

"You think I love him?"

"You do love him."

Then she did not answer.

"Yesterday I wouldn't have believed that things like this happen. For over a year . . ." He paused. Then, "Nothing will ever be the same again—love, or anything."

"Please, Will. Nothing's happened."

"Everything's happened. Now it's over."

She looked at him closely. Then she said, "I've never heard you talk like that. You're different. Your voice—it's . . ."

"What?"

"You're different. Your voice frightens me. It's so quiet and cold and far away, so different—" She spoke jerkily. "So dead!"

He sat up, leaned back on his elbows. The moon was gone, sunk under the water. The sky was darker, and the stars seemed brighter still, separate, and farther away. Then he lay down again and she beside him. They were both very quiet. Finally she said, "Do you hate me?"

He turned to her. "No," he answered. He watched her face. He saw her eyes sparkling with tears. He said, "What are you crying for?"

"I can't tell you why, I can't say, I don't know. I'm afraid. I do love you, Will. Only now I'm afraid, because I do love someone else—more. I don't want to. But I do. It frightens me!"

Now she was no longer older than he. She was a girl again, her woman's poise, given her briefly by this new love, taken from her again by that same love because, in the face of it, she was afraid. She was afraid of its swiftness, of what it might hold, of her own heart, turning. Now he felt older than she, felt that he could tell her something. He said, "I know what it is. It isn't just that we've been in love. We've had such a fine time. I don't know if I can say this, but it's something like this anyway—you weren't just yourself for me, and I wasn't just myself for you. We were both in love with much more than each other. You were all of that life for me, and maybe I was that for you, too. We were that whole life for each other, and we didn't want to lose it, but we couldn't help ourselves, we couldn't keep it any longer."

She was crying. She put her face on his shoulder and he felt her tears on his neck. Then he put his arms around her and held her close. But he felt no less alone. And he thought then that this aloneness would never entirely leave him again, but that when he got back to the city next day, after he had been there a while, working in the office, after a week or two or perhaps a whole year, finally anyway, it would have left him somewhat less empty, less deadly calm. Then this day and this summer and all the golden days would have become the dream; and the other life would be real.

"How did your poem go, Rachel? 'When I last died, and, dear, I die whenever you go from me . . .' ?"

"Please—don't," she said.

He began to stroke her hair. She was quiet now, no longer crying, held close in his arms. He said, "Maybe it's always like this. Maybe the end of every love is a kind of little death, when you have to put behind more than just the love itself, but all the life, too, in which the love was wrapped. Maybe living is really a lot of little dyings."

For a moment more they sat together and then she said, "We must go back. They'll wonder . . ."

"All right," he said.

Then, clinging together like children still under the stars, helping each other up the slope, they went back to the house, where the lights were and the sounds of voices.

Love is so many things . . .

Clifford R. Bragdon

LOVE'S SO MANY THINGS

In the stories of Part II the common denominator is love.
Only an editor, or a professor, would use such a prosaic
term to describe the line of narrative interest which runs
through each of these selections. Love manifests itself in many
ways, as we shall see. In fact only a few of the stories
brought together here—like Katherine Mansfield's "Mr. and
Mrs. Dove"—may be conventionally classified as love stories in
the popular sense. For these there is at least one tried and
true approach. "Woman," said Saint Chrysostom, "is a
desirable calamity." Stories may often be classified according to
the attitude of their authors toward this profound observation.
Which of the two final words of the quotation, for instance,
does an author consider the more important? Here there
is ground for speculation, as the reader will discover in seeking
the answer in, say, Joseph Conrad's "The Lagoon" and then in
D. H. Lawrence's "Tickets, Please." In Katherine Mansfield's
amusing little purview (or is it a preview?) of marriage, the
reader can divine clearly enough what the venerable Saint
Chrysostom probably had in mind.

"Love's so many things"—as Clifford Bragdon found out on a
Greyhound bus between Youngstown, Ohio, and Harrisburg,
Pennsylvania. His story catches the tragic irony in what is,
superficially, just the usual coarse comedy of an all-night bus
ride. He tells about the man sitting next to him, "the man
with the wife," Mary, who, except for her coughing, is
silent all through the singing and the wisecracking. This man
is as crude as anybody on the bus, and talks as tough; he is
pretty offensive—except where she is concerned. This
is not a laugh–clown–laugh situation, though, for Pagliacci
must play a somewhat self-conscious role. The clown on the bus,
unaware of his role, calls for truer tears.

The first four hours out of Cleveland were not bad. The bus
was hot as the devil, but almost empty, and I had the whole back
seat alone where I could make myself comfortable stretched out. But
when we hit Youngstown, it was all over. Everybody in eastern Ohio

got on there—fat women with bundles, slick boys with panama hats and several suitcases, girls in couples, and a sailor. I had to sit up to make room for a fellow and his wife.

The man looked as if he thought he were pretty hard—tight blue suit and long hair plastered back and parted in the middle—like a million others; all they seem to care about is how smooth their hair is. When he smoked, he pulled his lips tight and made the smoke spurt out of the corner of his mouth, first up and then down. They all do that, millions of them. They want you to think they are pretty hard. This one's eyes were little and grey. His wife was pretty, poor kid, though sort of pale and thin, it seemed to me.

Anyway, every chair was taken, and the heat was terrific. I began to wonder whether it was worth the twelve or fifteen I would save on it. If it had not been for the sailor and a couple of girls, I don't know how we could have stood it. As it was, everyone was glad to have them along. They sang songs and giggled and carried on almost all night. Sitting right in back of them, I got the benefit of the really good part, the hot give and take, so to speak. For instance, the sailor asked the thinnest one where they were going, and she said, "No place, friend. We're just travelling for our health." Then the other one began singing,

"I wonder how the old folks are to-night.
Do they miss the little girl who ran away?"

It was like that almost till morning. Sometimes one would sing, sometimes both—harmony—and it really wasn't bad, except once in a while. Then the sailor would groan, and they would laugh it off and get talking.

The fellow next to me—the fellow with the wife—was all ears. Every time one of them would make a wisecrack, he would haw-haw and stamp his feet. His wife would look up at him now and then and smile as if she thought it was pretty good too, and blink her eyes. But as a matter of fact, I don't think she was even listening, because the minute she got on the bus she just curled up in a corner—coughed a few times—she had a pretty bad cough—and closed her eyes. Her husband didn't seem to mind, though. He ate three or four plums and took in the entertainment. He was sitting so that his wife could rest her head on his lap and he had to lean over on me to hear everything the sailor and the girls said.

As soon as he finished the plums, he got friendly. First he winked at me after he had nearly fallen over from laughing once, and then he leaned even closer than he was already, nudging me.

"They're rich, ain't they?" he whispered. His voice didn't sound at all the way he looked.

"Yeah," I said. "Your wife mind if I smoke?"

"No. Where you from?" he said. "Youngstown?"

I told him, no, I was from Cleveland, and he mentioned how bad the Indians were doing. Just then his wife sat up and coughed. She asked him for a cigarette, but he shook his head. Then he kissed her.

When she was curled up again, he turned to me. "It must be swell being a sailor," he said. "Lots of fun, them fellows."

"Yeah," I said, "but they don't get on land only once in so often."

"That's right," he answered, nudging me again, "but when they do, oh, boy—uh?"

I moved over a little. "It's pretty good, I guess."

"You bet," he said. "You know I used to be pretty quick on the pickup myself. I used to have a pretty good line—and they fell for it, too, if I do say it."

Neither of us spoke for a while then. We were scrouging around trying to get a little less cramped and hot than we were, or else listening to the clowns in front of us. Everybody else was doing the same thing or just sitting still with their heads back and their mouths open—especially the fat women. All the women on this bus were fat—except the little girl on the back seat—and they appeared not to mind the heat as much as the thin men. They sat as if they had been dumped down and a few yards of crumpled stuff thrown around them.

My new friend seemed to be turning something over in his mind, and so I had a chance to take a peek at his wife. I couldn't see her very well unless we were passing under a light. It gave a funny effect then, as if she were alive for a second and then dead, about to wake up and then just dropped asleep again. I was getting so I could hardly keep my eyes off her.

When we were pulling out of Pittsburgh where someone got off, leaving us three the back seat to ourselves, he started in again. "Where you bound for, Bud?" he asked me.

I told him New York and asked him where he was going.

"Harrisburg. I got an aunt," he said. "Well, we're getting off the bus at Harrisburg, that is, but we're going up to the Pocono Mountains. We been over two thousand miles on the roads in the last five days. We been out to Denver."

"Is that so?" I said. "Nice out there, they tell me."

He laughed a little. "Well," he said, "yeah, it's a nice enough place, but no work."

I asked him what he'd been doing out there then, thinking he might be one of these auto-hoboes. Neither he nor his wife looked like money at all—even cheap money. He didn't answer my question, so I said, "What did you do, drive out and then take the busses back?"

"No," he answered, "we took the busses both ways. Was you ever in Harrisburg?"

"No," I said.

It was getting late, and the entertainment was off for a while because one of the girls, the less fat one, had paired off with the sailor. The other pretended she didn't care and sang by herself for a minute but not for long. She tried to get hold of a red-headed fellow across the aisle, but there was nothing doing, so she flopped around and pretended to go to sleep. I was ready for sleep myself, but didn't like to sleep sitting up, and besides, I kept glancing over at the girl curled up in the corner. I lit another cigarette and asked the girl's husband what he was going to do in Pocono.

"I don't know," he said.

"A little vacation, maybe?"

"No, I'll get work up there if I can," he said. "One reason for going up there is maybe my uncle can get me some work. I got a trade—glass worker, but I don't care much what I do." He settled himself a little. "It don't make any difference," he went on. "There are some good farms up there—Dutch. Maybe I'd make a good farmer. Yeah, a swell farmer—not. But it's O.K. with me." He stepped carefully on the cigarette I had just tossed on the floor, and smiled.

"Well, but what's the idea going up into the hills though?" I asked him. It was about two in the morning. The time and the heat both must have made me feebleminded. Anyway he didn't answer my question, because his wife woke up just then and sat up and put her fingers through his hair as if she liked the stuff. She was just a kid. He must have been about thirty-one or -two; hard to tell exactly. But she didn't look more than twenty at the most.

Well, for a while then he didn't even know I was alive. A big change came over him. He took out his handkerchief and fanned her like they do a fighter. It seemed funny to see this tiny little kid sitting in a corner of the back seat on a bus, all slumped down like a fighter just saved by the bell, and being fanned like one, too. It made me feel sore at something because I wanted to do something for her. Of course there wasn't anything I could do—I just felt like it ought to have been somebody else fanning her and kissing her. Not that there was anything wrong with this fellow exactly; she ought to have been married to somebody else, that's all. The poor kid must have been boiling hot—though it had cooled off a little by this time—because there were little beads of sweat all over her forehead, and she coughed so much I finally had the sense to quit smoking.

Her husband fanned her like that until she smiled at him and closed her eyes. Then she curled up again, and her husband made her as comfortable as he could. At about the same time the sailor and the girl split up. The girl came back and sat with her friend. At first the fat one pretended she was still asleep, but she soon got over that, and the two of them started in singing again. It was late, and some man up front didn't like it.

"Aw, pipe down, lady," he hollered, "and go to sleep."

The girls came right back at him. "If you don't like it, why don't you get out?" one of them said.

This got a good laugh; we were in the mountains without a house in sight. Just the same the girls quit singing.

"If he was back here, I'd slap his mouth," the fat one said.

The sailor turned around. "Well," he said, "your friend here bit mine."

"Oh, hush up, you big liar," answered the girl he had been sitting with. Then they all three laughed and started another conversation.

The fellow sitting with me laughed so hard at what the sailor said, I thought he would roll off onto the floor.

"That was a fast one," he said, rubbing his nose. "Like I said to a girl friend once." He reached in his pocket as if he wanted a cigarette, but changed his mind. He slid down in his seat so that he was talking up sideways at my chin. "This girl was in swimming, see?" he went on, grinning all over, "so I come up behind her under water and pinched her on the—well, you get me, haw, haw, haw—just kidding, see, but she made out she didn't notice it, and she says to her friend who was standing there with her, she says, 'Oh, wasn't that a big wave, Betty— or Beth, or whatever her name was.' I heard her and came right back, 'Yeah, that was swell,' I says. Swell, see, me pinching her," and he laughed hard and nudged me for the hundredth time. He was looking the way people usually do when they tell a joke—like a kid watching someone else eating a piece of candy. I thought it was a pretty bum joke, but we got talking along those lines for a while. He told a few pretty fair ones about his adventures—just the usual stuff, and then I asked him again how he happened to be going up to the mountains with the hill-billies. I preferred hearing about that though I guess it was really his wife I was interested in.

Every now and then I would look over at her, but she made me feel so foolish, I kept trying to listen to her dumb husband instead. She made me feel like I wanted to hold her like a little kid and give her a drink of water—in little sips. She would sip, I thought, and then look up and catch her breath and smile with her eyes. It made me feel foolish, thinking like that.

Well, her husband said something after a minute, answering me, I guess, but I missed it. Then I heard him say,

"I said she's pretty, ain't she?"

Of course I felt like even a bigger yap then than before; he couldn't have helped noticing me staring at her, not even him. But he didn't seem sore. I said, "Yes, but she don't look very well."

"No," he said, "she's got a cold."

He turned so that he could look at her, and patted her arm. "She's only twenty-two," he went on. "We been married five years, would you believe it? She was seventeen then."

"Is that a fact?" I answered, not knowing what else to say.

"Yeah. She's Irish. Look at that nose and you can tell she's a little mick all right. She's only been in this country five and a half years. She come over six months before I married her."

He just seemed to be talking for talking's sake. I guess he didn't want to fall asleep, either. But I wanted him to keep on about her, so I said, "What's her name? Colleen?"

"No," he said, "Mary. She's not really Irish I guess though. She says she's Manx from the Isle of Man. Sounds like a cat, don't it? There's a cat name Manx, ain't there? Anyway I tell her she ain't got it right. She's a minx, not a Manx, I tell her."

He stopped suddenly and looked at me as if he was afraid I might think he was a sap, and yet as if he wanted me to laugh at the same time. One dirty, stubby hand was still on her arm, stroking it. It was dark, and he didn't know I could see that. But I could. Her arm was so white. It was impossible now to keep from looking at her; I was beginning to think she was the prettiest girl I had ever seen.

Pretty soon her husband started talking again. "She was working at my aunt's house when I was there for a while. They lived in Brooklyn then. That's how I come to meet her. Ever been in Brooklyn?"

"Love at first sight, uh?" I said.

He chuckled. "Hell, no," he said. "She wouldn't have a thing to do with me at first. I was carrying on around there with some other girls at the time. But, you know, I cut all that out. It's funny, ain't it, how you'll do that."

All I wanted to do was to keep on asking him questions. "How did you finally bring her around then?" I asked him.

"Oh, she come around all right in the end," he whispered, winking at me. "You can't keep the girls away from a good-looking fellow, uh?" His little grey eyes opened wide, and he nudged me. "Ain't that right?" he added, laughing when I looked at him. "Of course I was just kidding, Bud," he said. "I guess I ain't no John Barrymore, all right."

He sounded so serious I had to laugh. "Sure, I knew that," I said.

I didn't mean it the way it sounded, but I was just as glad to let it go. I was so sick of his nudging me I could have hit him anyway. Besides, as I said, looking at his wife made me sore at things in general, and I guess I was taking it out on him. He wasn't really such a bad guy.

But he got over it all right, and pretty soon he laughed. "We was married in Brooklyn. She's a Catholic," he said.

"But how did it all happen?" I broke in on him, wanting to hear all I could. It seemed as if I had to.

"Well, I'll tell you how it was, Bud," he answered, sitting up again and crossing his legs, but keeping one hand on his wife's arm, "we got to keep awake, huh? But there ain't much to tell. There wasn't anything romantic about it or anything. I'd just been kidding around with her for a while—you know how it is—taking her to a show now and then without meaning much. She never let on one way or the other till the very end—but—but she said then she'd been crazy about me. Anyway I didn't hardly believe it myself for a long while. She was just a kid, see?"

"Oh, yeah, I see," I said.

He went right on. "She would be around the house cooking and dusting and so on and I'd just sneak up behind her and kiss her on the neck —that's about all. She was too tired for much gallavanting around most of the time usually."

I didn't like him telling me all this, and yet I kept egging him on. "Didn't she mind you kissing her like that?" I asked.

"Oh, no," he answered. "She wouldn't stand for a lot of fooling, but I wasn't never rough with her. I—I—she seemed to take it all right. Anyway we didn't court long. In fact it was just a month before I popped the question, like they say. It come on me like a bolt of lightning, but Mary said afterward the only thing that surprised her was— and worried her too, she said—was why I didn't get on to myself earlier."

"Yeah, go on," I said.

"Well, one night she was out in the kitchen and I was sort of helping around when my aunt come in. 'Mary,' she says, 'Mrs. Link's out here with her baby. Come on out and take care of him while me and her go to the show, will you?' she says.

"So Mary and I went out and played with this kid for about half an hour. It was a cute kid—falling around. And then all of a sudden I felt something sort of come over me. It was the funniest feeling I ever had— like—like I wanted to pick her up and . . . Oh, well, anyway I stood up, see?—we were sitting on the floor—and Mary looked up at me as if she was surprised—the little bum. She wasn't no more surprised— but believe me I was. I was so surprised I was afraid if I opened my mouth I'd holler and act crazy. But then the first thing I knew I heard myself talking—like I was way away.

" 'Well, Kid,' I says, 'I guess you better set the date.' Right like that. 'Make it whenever you like,' I says, 'but the sooner the better.' That was all there was to it. I didn't mean to say it that way, believe me, but that's the way it was. Funny, how things happen so different from what you'd have said they would when you were thinking about it, ain't it? That was May, and we was married the following September. Mary carried roses."

I didn't say anything. I just took a quick look at his wife. Apparently the poor kid was sound asleep.

We were coming into a small town at the moment and stopped to gas up. Everybody that was awake piled out for a cup of coffee. I drank two. I was trying to think straight, but I guess I was too sleepy. The fellow and his wife both stayed in the bus.

When it came time to climb in again, I noticed it had gotten quite chilly while we were talking, so when I'd picked my way back to my seat, I told the fellow I was going to try to get a little sleep on the floor and his wife could stretch out and make herself comfortable. She was sitting up then and heard me. Neither one of them said anything, but the girl did stretch out, and he sat crunched up in one corner. I was hoping the girl would smile or something, but she didn't.

Pretty soon everybody else piled in and we started out again. The sailor and the two girls were just as full of pep as ever and began kidding around out loud. One of them said something funny, and my talkative friend let out another one of his horse laughs. I was feeling foolish still, so I took off my coat and put it over the girl's feet; she was coughing a little. Her husband already had his over her shoulders. He had the window open and I was glad it was warm on the floor. I asked him why he didn't put the window down, but he pointed to his wife, and shook his head. He was laughing so hard at the wisecrack from the scat in front he couldn't speak, but when he got through, he leaned over—I was stretched out on the floor in front of him then.

"Say, Bud, listen," he whispered, "did you ever hear the one about the Irishman and the girl in Hoboken?"

Well, I couldn't see him, but I knew just what he looked like. Something jumped up inside me, and I said, "No, damn it, and I don't want to, either."

He didn't say anything, but I could hear him sit back and move around trying to get comfortable. I was feeling so bad I could have killed him. Pretty soon I heard a kiss and some whispering, but from where I was, I couldn't tell whether it was in front or in back of me. That was all I knew for about three hours.

It was light when I woke up. I sat up on the floor and looked around. The girl was lying stretched out, fast asleep with her head in her husband's lap. When he saw me sit up, he winked at me, and grinned. I almost felt sorry for him—he looked so cold. I said, "How is she?"

He looked down at her and put his hand on her forehead. "Her cold's pretty bad," he whispered.

They got out at Harrisburg.

A SICK CALL

Here the author poses a deep, unanswerable question. Philosophers and churchmen have found it so through the ages. Upon completing the story—and it has a familiar, domestic setting—the reader will ponder Father Macdowell's thoughts regarding sacred and profane love. The old priest feels "inexpressibly sad." Why?

Sometimes Father Macdowell mumbled out loud and took a deep wheezy breath as he walked up and down the room and read his office. He was a huge old priest, white-headed except for a shiny baby-pink bald spot on the top of his head, and he was a bit deaf in one ear. His florid face had many fine red interlacing vein lines. For hours he had been hearing confessions and he was tired, for he always had to hear more confessions than any other priest at the cathedral: young girls who were in trouble, and wild but at times repentant young men, always wanted to tell their confessions to Father Macdowell, because nothing seemed to shock or excite him, or make him really angry, and he was even tender with those who thought they were most guilty.

While he was mumbling and reading and trying to keep his glasses on his nose, the house girl knocked on the door and said, "There's a young lady here to see you, Father. I think it's about a sick call."

"Did she ask for me especially?" he said in a deep but slightly cracked voice.

"Indeed she did, Father. She wanted Father Macdowell and nobody else."

So he went out to the waiting room, where a girl about thirty years of age, with fine brown eyes, fine cheek bones, and rather square shoulders, was sitting daubing her eyes with a handkerchief. She was wearing a dark coat with a gray wolf collar. "Good evening, Father," she said. "My sister is sick. I wanted you to come and see her. We think she's dying."

"Be easy, child; what's the matter with her? Speak louder. I can hardly hear you."

"My sister's had pneumonia. The doctor's coming back to see her in an hour. I wanted you to anoint her, Father."

"I see, I see. But she's not lost yet. I'll not give her extreme unction now. That may not be necessary. I'll go with you and hear her confession."

"Father, I ought to let you know, maybe. Her husband won't want to let you see her. He's not a Catholic, and my sister hasn't been to church in a long time."

"Oh, don't mind that. He'll let me see her," Father Macdowell said, and he left the room to put on his hat and coat.

II

When he returned, the girl explained that her name was Jane Stanhope, and her sister lived only a few blocks away. "We'll walk and you tell me about your sister," he said. He put his black hat square on the top of his head, and pieces of white hair stuck out awkwardly at the sides. They went to the avenue together.

The night was mild and clear. Miss Stanhope began to walk slowly, because Father Macdowell's rolling gait didn't get him along the street very quickly. He walked as if his feet hurt him, though he wore a pair of large, soft, specially constructed shapeless shoes. "Now, my child, you go ahead and tell me about your sister," he said, breathing with difficulty, yet giving the impression that nothing could have happened to the sister which would make him feel indignant.

There wasn't much to say, Miss Stanhope replied. Her sister had married John Williams two years ago, and he was a good, hard-working fellow, only he was very bigoted and hated all church people. "My family wouldn't have anything to do with Elsa after she married him, though I kept going to see her," she said. She was talking in a loud voice to Father Macdowell so he could hear her.

"Is she happy with her husband?"

"She's been very happy, Father. I must say that."

"Where is he now?"

"He was sitting beside her bed. I ran out because I thought he was going to cry. He said if I brought a priest near the place he'd break the priest's head."

"My goodness. Never mind, though. Does your sister want to see me?"

"She asked me to go and get a priest, but she doesn't want John to know she did it."

III

Turning into a side street, they stopped at the first apartment house, and the old priest followed Miss Stanhope up the stairs. His breath came with great difficulty. "Oh dear, I'm not getting any younger, not one day younger. It's a caution how a man's legs go back on him," he said. As Miss Stanhope rapped on the door, she looked pleadingly at the old priest, trying to ask him not to be offended at anything that might happen, but he was smiling and looking huge in the narrow hallway. He wiped his head with his handkerchief.

The door was opened by a young man in a white shirt with no collar, with a head of thick black wavy hair. At first he looked dazed, then his eyes got bright with excitement when he saw the priest, as though he were glad to see someone he could destroy with pent-up energy. "What do you mean, Jane?" he said. "I told you not to bring a priest around here. My wife doesn't want to see a priest."

"What's that you're saying, young man?"

"No one wants you here."

"Speak up. Don't be afraid. I'm a bit hard of hearing." Father Macdowell smiled rosily. John Williams was confused by the unexpected deafness in the priest, but he stood there, blocking the door with sullen resolution as if waiting for the priest to try to launch a curse at him.

"Speak to him, Father," Miss Stanhope said, but the priest didn't seem to hear her; he was still smiling as he pushed past the young man, saying, "I'll go in and sit down, if you don't mind, son. I'm here on God's errand, but I don't mind saying I'm all out of breath from climbing those stairs."

John was dreadfully uneasy to see he had been brushed aside, and he followed the priest into the apartment and said loudly, "I don't want you here."

Father Macdowell said, "Eh, eh?" Then he smiled sadly. "Don't be angry with me, son," he said. "I'm too old to try and be fierce and threatening." Looking around, he said, "Where's your wife?" and he started to walk along the hall, looking for the bedroom.

John followed him and took hold of his arm. "There's no sense in your wasting your time talking to my wife, do you hear?" he said angrily.

Miss Stanhope called out suddenly, "Don't be rude, John."

"It's he that's being rude. You mind your business," John said.

"For the love of God let me sit down a moment with her, anyway. I'm tired," the priest said.

"What do you want to say to her? Say it to me, why don't you?"

IV

Then they both heard someone moan softly in the adjoining room, as if the sick woman had heard them. Father Macdowell, forgetting that the young man had hold of his arm, said, "I'll go in and see her for a moment, if you don't mind," and he began to open the door.

"You're not going to be alone with her, that's all," John said, following him into the bedroom.

Lying on the bed was a white-faced, fair girl, whose skin was so delicate that her cheek bones stood out sharply. She was feverish, but her eyes rolled toward the door, and she watched them coming in. Father Macdowell took off his coat, and as he mumbled to himself he looked around the room at the mauve-silk bed light and the light wallpaper with the tiny birds in flight. It looked like a little girl's room. "Good evening, Father," Mrs. Williams whispered. She looked scared. She didn't glance at her husband. The notion of dying had made her afraid. She loved her husband and wanted to die loving him, but she was afraid, and she looked up at the priest.

"You're going to get well, child," Father Macdowell said, smiling and patting her hand gently.

John, who was standing stiffly by the door, suddenly moved around the big priest, and he bent down over the bed and took his wife's hand and began to caress her forehead.

"Now if you don't mind, my son, I'll hear your wife's confession," the priest said.

"No, you won't," John said abruptly. "Her people didn't want her, and they left us together, and they're not going to separate us now. She's satisfied with me." He kept looking down at her face as if he could not bear to turn away.

Father Macdowell nodded his head up and down and sighed. "Poor boy," he said. "God bless you." Then he looked at Mrs. Williams, who had closed her eyes, and he saw a faint tear on her cheek. "Be sensible, my boy," he said. "You'll have to let me hear your wife's confession. Leave us alone awhile."

"I'm going to stay right here," John said, and he sat down on the end of the bed. He was working himself up and staring savagely at the priest. All of a sudden he noticed the tears on his wife's cheeks, and he muttered as though bewildered, "What's the matter, Elsa? What's the matter, darling? Are we bothering you? Just open your eyes and we'll go out of the room and leave you alone till the doctor comes." Then he turned and said to the priest, "I'm not going to leave you here with her, can't you see that? Why don't you go?"

"I could revile you, my son. I could threaten you; but I ask you, for the peace of your wife's soul, leave us alone." Father Macdowell spoke with patient tenderness. He looked very big and solid and immovable as he stood by the bed. "I liked your face as soon as I saw you," he said to John. "You're a good fellow."

John still held his wife's wrist, but he rubbed one hand through his thick hair and said angrily, "You don't get the point, sir. My wife and I were always left alone, and we merely want to be left alone now. Nothing is going to separate us. She's been content with me. I'm sorry, sir; you'll have to speak to her with me here, or you'll have to go."

"No, you'll have to go for awhile," the priest said patiently.

V

Then Mrs. Williams moved her head on the pillow and said jerkily, "Pray for me, Father."

So the old priest knelt down by the bed, and with a sweet unruffled expression on his florid face he began to pray. At times his breath came with a whistling noise as though a rumbling were inside him, and at other times he sighed and was full of sorrow. He was praying that young Mrs. Williams might get better, and while he prayed he knew that her husband was more afraid of losing her to the Church than losing her to death.

All the time Father Macdowell was on his knees, with his heavy prayer book in his two hands, John kept staring at him. John couldn't understand the old priest's patience and tolerance. He wanted to quarrel with him, but he kept on watching the light from overhead shining on the one baby-pink bald spot on the smooth white head, and at last he burst out, "You don't understand, sir! We've been very happy together. Neither you nor her people came near her when she was in good health, so why should you bother her now? I don't want anything to separate us now; neither does she. She came with me. You see you'd be separating us, don't you?" He was trying to talk like a reasonable man who had no prejudices.

Father Macdowell got up clumsily. His knees hurt him, for the floor was hard. He said to Mrs. Williams in quite a loud voice, "Did you really intend to give up everything for this young fellow?" and he bent down close to her so he could hear.

"Yes, Father," she whispered.

"In Heaven's name, child, you couldn't have known what you were doing."

"We loved each other, Father. We've been very happy."

"All right. Supposing you were. What now? What about all eternity, child?"

"Oh, Father, I'm very sick and I'm afraid." She looked up to try to show him how scared she was, and how much she wanted him to give her peace.

He sighed and seemed distressed, and at last he said to John, "Were you married in the church?"

"No, we weren't. Look here, we're talking pretty loud and it upsets her."

"Ah, it's a crime that I'm hard of hearing, I know. Never mind, I'll go." Picking up his coat, he put it over his arm; then he sighed as if he were very tired, and he said, "I wonder if you'd just fetch me a glass of water. I'd thank you for it."

John hesitated, glancing at the tired old priest, who looked so pink and white and almost cherubic in his utter lack of guile.

"What's the matter?" Father Macdowell said.

John was ashamed of himself for appearing so sullen, so he said hastily, "Nothing's the matter. Just a moment. I won't be a moment." He hurried out of the room.

VI

The old priest looked down at the floor and shook his head; and then, sighing and feeling uneasy, he bent over Mrs. Williams, with his good ear down to her, and he said, "I'll just ask you a few questions in a hurry, my child. You answer them quickly and I'll give you absolution." He made the sign of the cross over her and asked if she repented for having strayed from the Church, and if she had often been angry, and whether she had always been faithful, and if she had ever lied or stolen —all so casually and quickly as if it hadn't occurred to him that such a young woman could have serious sins. In the same breath he muttered, "Say a good act of contrition to yourself and that will be all, my dear." He had hardly taken a minute.

When John returned to the room with the glass of water in his hand, he saw the old priest making the sign of the cross. Father Macdowell went on praying without even looking up at John. When he had finished, he turned and said, "Oh, there you are. Thanks for the water. I needed it. Well, my boy, I'm sorry if I worried you."

John hardly said anything. He looked at his wife, who had closed her eyes, and he sat down on the end of the bed. He was too disappointed to speak.

Father Macdowell, who was expecting trouble, said, "Don't be harsh, lad."

"I'm not harsh," he said mildly, looking up at the priest. "But you weren't quite fair. And it's as though she turned away from me at the last moment. I didn't think she needed you."

"God bless you, bless the both of you. She'll get better," Father Macdowell said. But he felt ill at ease as he put on his coat, and he couldn't look directly at John.

VII

Going along the hall, he spoke to Miss Stanhope, who wanted to apologize for her brother-in-law's attitude. "I'm sorry if it was unpleasant for you, Father," she said.

"It wasn't unpleasant," he said. "I was glad to meet John. He's a fine fellow. It's a great pity he isn't a Catholic. I don't know as I played fair with him."

As he went down the stairs, puffing and sighing, he pondered the question of whether he had played fair with the young man. But by the time he reached the street he was rejoicing amiably to think he had so successfully ministered to one who had strayed from the faith and had called out to him at the last moment. Walking along with the rolling motion as if his feet hurt him, he muttered, "Of course they were happy as they were . . . in a worldly way. I wonder if I did come between them?"

He shuffled along, feeling very tired, but he couldn't help thinking, "What beauty there was to his staunch love for her!" Then he added quickly, "But it was just a pagan beauty, of course."

As he began to wonder about the nature of this beauty, for some reason he felt inexpressibly sad.

James Joyce

EVELINE

Eveline's stream of consciousness develops a good deal of genuine feeling on the part of the reader, who shares her vivid recollections of the difficult life she has led. Now that she is about to leave home, however, she does not find that her life there has been wholly undesirable. There are always emotional reservations; one never does anything, knowingly, without such reservations. (The ultimate release from earth to heaven, one suspects, must be accompanied by ambivalent reflections.) Eveline knows well enough that her time is running out, that she may "never see again those familiar objects from which she had never dreamed of being divided." But, no matter how we react to this conflict of love and honor, we surely bless the sailor chap.

She sat at the window watching the evening invade the avenue. Her head was leaned against the window curtains and in her nostrils was the odor of dusty cretonne. She was tired.

Few people passed. The man out of the last house passed on his way home; she heard his footsteps clacking along the concrete pavement and afterwards crunching on the cinder path before the new red houses. One time there used to be a field there in which they used to play every evening with other people's children. Then a man from Belfast bought the field and built houses in it—not like their little brown houses but bright brick houses with shining roofs. The children of the avenue used to play together in that field—the Devines, the Waters, the Dunns, little Keogh the cripple, she and her brothers and sisters. Ernest, however, never played: he was too grown up. Her father used often to hunt them in out of the field with his blackthorn stick; but usually little Keogh used to keep *nix* and call out when he saw her father coming. Still they seemed to have been rather happy then. Her father was not so bad then; and besides, her mother was alive. That was a long time ago; she and her brothers and sisters were all grown up; her mother was dead. Tizzie Dunn was dead, too, and the Waters had gone back to England. Everything changes. Now she was going to go away like the others, to leave her home.

Home! She looked round the room, reviewing all its familiar objects which she had dusted once a week for so many years, wondering where on earth all the dust came from. Perhaps she would never see again those familiar objects from which she had never dreamed of being divided. And yet during all those years she had never found out the name of the priest whose yellowing photograph hung on the wall above the broken harmonium beside the colored print of the promises made to Blessed Margaret Mary Alacoque. He had been a school friend of her father. Whenever he showed the photograph to a visitor her father used to pass it with a casual word:

"He is in Melbourne now."

She had consented to go away, to leave her home. Was that wise? She tried to weigh each side of the question. In her home anyway she had shelter and food; she had those whom she had known all her life about her. Of course she had to work hard, both in the house and at business. What would they say of her in the Stores when they found out that she had run away with a fellow? Say she was a fool, perhaps; and her place would be filled up by advertisement. Miss Gavan would be glad. She had always had an edge on her, especially whenever there were people listening.

"Miss Hill, don't you see these ladies are waiting?"

"Look lively, Miss Hill, please."

She would not cry many tears at leaving the Stores.

But in her new home, in a distant unknown country, it would not be like that. Then she would be married—she, Eveline. People would treat her with respect then. She would not be treated as her mother had been. Even now, though she was over nineteen, she sometimes felt herself in danger of her father's violence. She knew it was that that had given her the palpitations. When they were growing up he had never gone for her, like he used to go for Harry and Ernest, because she was a girl; but latterly he had begun to threaten her and say what he would do to her only for her dead mother's sake. And now she had nobody to protect her. Ernest was dead and Harry, who was in the church decorating business, was nearly always down somewhere in the country. Besides, the invariable squabble for money on Saturday nights had begun to weary her unspeakably. She always gave her entire wages—seven shillings—and Harry always sent up what he could but the trouble was to get any money from her father. He said she used to squander the money, that she had no head, that he wasn't going to give her his hard-earned money to throw about the streets, and much more, for he was usually fairly bad on Saturday night. In the end he would give her the money and ask her had she any intention of buying Sunday's dinner. Then she had to rush out as quickly as she could and do her marketing, holding her black leather purse tightly in her hand as she elbowed her way through the crowds and returning home late under her load of provisions. She had hard work to keep the house together and to see that the two young children who had been left to her charge went to school regularly and got their meals regularly. It was hard work—a hard life—but now that she was about to leave it she did not find it a wholly undesirable life.

She was about to explore another life with Frank. Frank was very kind, manly, open-hearted. She was to go away with him by the night-boat to be his wife and to live with him in Buenos Ayres where he had a home waiting for her. How well she remembered the first time she had seen him; he was lodging in a house on the main road where she used to visit. It seemed a few weeks ago. He was standing at the gate, his peaked cap pushed back on his head and his hair tumbled forward over a face of bronze. Then they had come to know each other. He used to meet her outside the Stores every evening and see her home. He took her to see *The Bohemian Girl* and she felt elated as she sat in an unaccustomed part of the theater with him. He was awfully fond of music and sang a little. People knew that they were courting and, when he sang about the lass that loves a sailor, she always felt pleasantly confused. He used to call her Poppens out of fun. First of all it had been an excitement for her to have a fellow and then she had begun to like him. He had tales of distant countries. He had started as a deck boy at a pound a month on a ship of the Allan Line going out to Canada. He told her the names of the ships he had been on and the names of the different services. He had sailed through the Straits of Magellan and he told her stories of the terrible Patagonians. He had fallen on his feet in Buenos Ayres, he said, and had come over to the old country just for a holiday. Of course, her father had found out the affair and had forbidden her to have anything to say to him.

"I know these sailor chaps," he said.

One day he had quarreled with Frank and after that she had to meet her lover secretly.

The evening deepened in the avenue. The white of two letters in her lap grew indistinct. One was to Harry; the other was to her father. Ernest had been her favorite but she liked Harry too. Her father was becoming old lately, she noticed; he would miss her. Sometimes he could be very nice. Not long before, when she had been laid up for a day, he had read her out a ghost story and made toast for her at the fire. Another day, when their mother was alive, they had all gone for a picnic to the Hill of Howth. She remembered her father putting on her mother's bonnet to make the children laugh.

Her time was running out but she continued to sit by the window, leaning her head against the window curtain, inhaling the odor of dusty cretonne. Down far in the avenue she could hear a street organ playing. She knew the air. Strange that it should come that very night to remind her of the promise to her mother, her promise to keep the home together as long as she could. She remembered the last night of her mother's illness; she was again in the close dark room at the other side of the hall and outside she heard a melancholy air of Italy. The organ-player had been ordered to go away and given sixpence. She remembered her father strutting back into the sickroom saying:

"Damned Italians! coming over here!"

As she mused the pitiful vision of her mother's life laid its spell on the very quick of her being—that life of commonplace sacrifices closing in final craziness. She trembled as she heard again her mother's voice saying constantly with foolish insistence:

"Derevaun Seraun! Derevaun Seraun!"

She stood up in a sudden impulse of terror. Escape! She must escape! Frank would save her. He would give her life, perhaps love, too. But she wanted to live. Why should she be unhappy? She had a right to happiness. Frank would take her in his arms, fold her in his arms. He would save her.

She stood among the swaying crowd in the station at the North Wall. He held her hand and she knew that he was speaking to her, saying something about the passage over and over again. The station was full of soldiers with brown baggage. Through the wide doors of the sheds she caught a glimpse of the black mass of the boat, lying in beside the quay wall, with illumined portholes. She answered nothing. She felt her cheek pale and cold and, out of a maze of distress, she prayed to God to direct her, to show her what was her duty. The boat blew a long mournful whistle into the mist. If she went, tomorrow she would be on the sea with Frank, steaming towards Buenos Ayres. Their passage had been booked. Could she still draw back after all he had done for her? Her distress awoke a nausea in her body and she kept moving her lips in silent fervent prayer.

A bell clanged upon her heart. She felt him seize her hand:

"Come!"

All the seas of the world tumbled about her heart. He was drawing her into them: he would drown her. She gripped with both hands at the iron railing.

"Come!"

No! No! No! It was impossible. Her hands clutched the iron in frenzy. Amid the seas she sent a cry of anguish!

"Eveline! Evvy!"

He rushed beyond the barrier and called to her to follow. He was shouted at to go on but he still called to her. She set her white face to him, passive, like a helpless animal. Her eyes gave him no sign of love or farewell or recognition.

Frank O'Connor

THE MAD LOMASNEYS

We are tempted to drop the *s* from the title of this story, so
completely does Rita Lomasney capture and retain our
interest, occupying the center of the stage from beginning to end.
There are, of course, many other sharply-drawn characters
—including thin and spectacled Ned of the precise and tranquil
manner, "the best man in Cork, the best in Ireland"—
who share the stage with her. It is a story which can be likened
to a drama, in six acts; it is at once a realistic portrayal of Irish
characters and a love story dramatically presented, or rather
two or three love stories blended into one. Foreseeable as
we may believe the denouement to be when we come to the
end of the third act, the drama at that point is far from over.
Suspense of various sorts is beautifully sustained.
   "Love—the only sort of thing that you can call love—is
something that comes with experience," one character, who
doesn't know what he is talking about, says to another.
And there is considerable irony in the remark, as the final scene
clearly shows.

Ned Lowry and Rita Lomasney had, one might say, been
lovers from childhood. The first time they had met was when he was
fourteen and she a year or two younger. It was on the North Mall on a
Saturday afternoon, and she was sitting on a bench under the trees; a
tall, bony string of a girl with a long, obstinate jaw. Ned was a studious
young fellow in a blue and white college cap, thin, pale, and spectacled.
As he passed he looked at her owlishly and she gave him back an
impudent stare. This upset him—he had no experience of girls—so he
blushed and raised his cap. At that she seemed to relent.
   "Hullo," she said experimentally.
   "Good afternoon," he replied with a pale smile.
   "Where are you off to?" she asked.
   "Oh, just up the Dyke for a walk."
   "Sit down," she said in a sharp voice, laying her hand on the bench
beside her, and he did as he was told. It was a lovely summer evening,

and the white quay walls and tall, crazy, claret-coloured tenements under a blue and white sky were reflected in the lazy water, which wrinkled only at the edges and seemed like a painted carpet.

"It's very pleasant here," he said complacently.

"Is it?" she asked with a truculence that startled him. "I don't see anything very pleasant about it."

"Oh, it's very nice and quiet," he said in mild surprise as he raised his fair eyebrows and looked up and down the Mall at the old Georgian houses and the nursemaids sitting under the trees. "My name is Lowry," he added politely.

"Oh, are ye the ones that have the jeweller's shop on the Parade?" she asked.

"That's right," replied Ned with modest pride.

"We have a clock we got from ye," she said. " 'Tisn't much good of an old clock either," she added with quiet malice.

"You should bring it back to the shop," he said in considerable concern. "It probably needs overhauling."

"I'm going down the river in a boat with a couple of chaps," she said, going off at a tangent. "Will you come?"

"Couldn't," he said with a smile.

"Why not?"

"I'm only left go up the Dyke for a walk," he said complacently. "On Saturdays I go to Confession at St. Peter and Paul's, then I go up the Dyke and back the Western Road. Sometimes you see very good cricket matches. Do you like cricket?"

"A lot of old sissies pucking a ball!" she said shortly. "I do not."

"I like it," he said firmly. "I go up there every Saturday. Of course, I'm not supposed to talk to anyone," he added with mild amusement at his own audacity.

"Why not?"

"My mother doesn't want me to."

"Why doesn't she?"

"She comes of an awfully good family," he answered mildly, and but for his gentle smile she might have thought he was deliberately insulting her. "You see," he went on gravely in his thin, pleasant voice, ticking things off on his fingers and then glancing at each finger individually as he ticked it off—a tidy sort of boy—"there are three main branches of the Hourigan family: the Neddy Neds, the Neddy Jerrys, and the Neddy Thomases. The Neddy Neds are the Hayfield Hourigans. They are the oldest branch. My mother is a Hayfield Hourigan, and she'd have been a rich woman only for her father backing a bill for a Neddy Jerry. He defaulted and ran away to Australia," he concluded with a contemptuous sniff.

"Cripes!" said the girl. "And had she to pay?"

"She had. But, of course," he went on with as close as he ever seemed likely to get to a burst of real enthusiasm, "my grandfather was a very well-behaved man. When he was eating his dinner the boys from the National School in Bantry used to be brought up to watch him, he had such beautiful table manners. Once he caught my uncle eating cabbage with a knife and he struck him with a poker. They had to put four stitches in him after," he added with a joyous chuckle.

"Cripes!" the girl said again. "What did he do that for?"

"To teach him manners," Ned said earnestly.

"He must have been dotty."

"Oh, I wouldn't say so," Ned exclaimed in mild surprise. Everything this girl said came as a shock to him. "But that's why my mother won't let us mix with other children. On the other hand, we read a good deal. Are you fond of reading, Miss—I didn't catch the name."

"You weren't told it," she said, showing her claws. "But if you want to know, it's Rita Lomasney."

"Do you read much, Miss Lomasney?"

"I couldn't be bothered."

"I read all sorts of books," he said enthusiastically. "And as well as that, I'm learning the violin from Miss Maude on the Parade. Of course, it's very difficult, because it's all classical music."

"What's classical music?" she asked with sudden interest.

"*Maritana* is classical music," he replied eagerly. He was a bit of a puzzle to Rita. She had never before met anyone with such a passion for handing out instruction. "Were you at *Maritana* in the opera house, Miss Lomasney?"

"I was never there at all," she said curtly.

"And *Alice Where Art Thou* is classical music," he added. "It's harder than plain music. You see," he went on, composing signs in the air, "it has signs on it like this, and when you see the signs, you know it's after turning into a different tune, though it has the same name. Irish music is all the same tune and that's why my mother won't let us learn it."

"Were you ever at the opera in Paris?" she asked suddenly.

"No," said Ned. "I was never in Paris. Why?"

"That's where you should go," she said with airy enthusiasm. "You couldn't hear any operas here. The staircase alone is bigger than the whole opera house here."

It seemed as if they were in for a really informative conversation when two fellows came down Wyse's Hill. Rita got up to meet them. Lowry looked up at them and then rose too, lifting his cap politely.

"Well, good afternoon," he said cheerfully. "I enjoyed the talk. I hope we meet again."

"Some other Saturday," said Rita.

"Oh, good evening, old man," one of the two fellows said in an affected drawl, pretending to raise a top hat. "Do come and see us soon again."

"Shut up, Foster!" Rita said sharply. "I'll give you a puck in the gob."

"Oh, by the way," Ned said, coming back to hand her a number of the *Gem* which he took from his coat pocket, "you might like to look at this. It's not bad."

"Thanks, I'd love to," she said insincerely, and he smiled and touched his cap again. Then with a polite and almost deferential air he went up to Foster. "Did you say something?" he asked.

Foster looked as astonished as if a kitten had suddenly got on its hind legs and challenged him to fight.

"I did not," he said, and backed away.

"I'm glad," Ned said, almost purring. "I was afraid you might be looking for trouble."

It came as a surprise to Rita as well. Whatever opinion she might have formed of Ned Lowry, fighting was about the last thing she would have associated him with.

I I

The Lomasneys lived in a house on Sunday's Well, a small house with a long, sloping garden and a fine view of the river and city. Harry Lomasney, the builder, was a small man who wore grey tweed suits and soft collars several sizes too big for him. He had a ravaged brick-red face with keen blue eyes, and a sandy, straggling moustache with one side going up and the other down, and his workmen said you could tell his humour by the side he pulled. He was nicknamed "Hasty Harry." "Great God!" he fumed when his wife was having her first baby. "Nine months over a little job like that! I'd do it in three weeks if I could only get started." His wife was tall and matronly and very pious, but her piety never got much in her way. A woman who had survived Hasty would have survived anything. Their eldest daughter, Kitty, was loud-voiced and gay and had been expelled from school for writing indecent letters to a boy. She had copied the letters out of a French novel but she failed to tell the nuns that. Nellie was placider and took more after her mother; besides, she didn't read French novels.

Rita was the exception among the girls. There seemed to be no soft-ness in her. She never had a favourite saint or a favourite nun; she said it was soppy. For the same reason she never had flirtations. Her friend-ship with Ned Lowry was the closest she ever got to that, and though Ned came regularly to the house, and the pair of them went to the pictures together, her sisters would have found it hard to say whether she cared any more for him than she did for any of her girl ac-quaintances. There was something in her they didn't understand, something tongue-tied, twisted, and unhappy. She had a curious raw, almost timid smile as though she felt people desired no better sport than hurting her. At home she was reserved, watchful, almost mocking. She could listen for hours to her mother and sisters without once opening her mouth, and then suddenly mystify them by dropping a well-aimed jaw-breaker—about classical music, for instance—before relapsing into a sulky silence; as though she had merely drawn back the veil for a moment on depths in herself which she would not permit them to explore.

After taking her degree, she got a job in a convent school in a provincial town in the west of Ireland. She and Ned corresponded and he even went to see her there. He reported at home that she seemed quite happy.

But this didn't last. A few months later the Lomasney family were at supper one evening when they heard a car stop, the gate squeaked, and steps came up the long path to the front door. Then came the sound of a bell and a cheerful voice from the hall.

"Hullo, Paschal, I suppose ye weren't expecting me?"

" 'Tis never Rita!" said her mother, meaning that it was but that it shouldn't be.

"As true as God, that one is after getting into trouble," Kitty said prophetically.

The door opened and Rita slouched in, a long, stringy girl with a dark, glowing face. She kissed her father and mother lightly.

"Hullo," she said. "How's tricks?"

"What happened you?" her mother asked, rising.

"Nothing," replied Rita, an octave up the scale. "I just got the sack."

"The sack?" said her father, beginning to pull the wrong side of his moustache. "What did you get the sack for?"

"Give us a chance to get something to eat first, can't you?" Rita said laughingly. She took off her hat and smiled at herself in the mirror over the mantelpiece. It was a curious smile as though she were amused by the spectacle of what she saw. Then she smoothed back her thick black hair. "I told Paschal to bring in whatever was going. I'm on the train since ten. The heating was off as usual. I'm frizzled."

"A wonder you wouldn't send us a wire," said Mrs. Lomasney as Rita sat down and grabbed some bread and butter.

"Hadn't the tin," replied Rita.

"Can't you tell us what happened?" Kitty asked brightly.

"I told you. You'll hear more in due course. Reverend Mother is bound to write and tell ye how I lost my character."

"But what did you do, child?" her mother asked placidly. Her mother had been through all this before, with Hasty and Kitty, and she knew God was very good and nothing much ever happened.

"Fellow that wanted to marry me," said Rita. "He was in his last year at college, and his mother didn't like me, so she got Reverend Mother to give me the push."

"And what has it to do with Reverend Mother?" Nellie asked indignantly. "What business is it of hers?"

"That's what I say," said Rita.

But Kitty looked suspiciously at her. Rita wasn't natural; there was something wild about her, and this was her first real love affair. Kitty just couldn't believe that Rita had gone about it the same as anyone else.

"Still, I must say you worked pretty fast," she said.

"You'd have to in that place," said Rita. "There was only one possible man in the whole village and he was the bank clerk. We called him 'The One.' I wasn't there a week when the nuns ticked me off for riding on the pillion of his motor-bike."

"And did you?" asked Kitty.

"I never got the chance, girl. They did it to every teacher on principle to give her the idea that she was well watched. I only met Tony Donoghue a fortnight ago—home after a breakdown."

"Well, well, well!" her mother exclaimed without rancour. "No wonder his poor mother was upset. A boy that's not left college yet! Couldn't ye wait till he was qualified anyway?"

"Not very well," said Rita. "He's going to be a priest."

Kitty sat back with a superior grin. Of course, Rita could do nothing like anyone else. If it wasn't a priest it would have been a Negro, and Rita would have made theatre of it in precisely the same deliberate way.

"A what?" asked her father, springing to his feet.

"All right, don't blame me!" Rita said hastily. "It wasn't my fault. He told me he didn't want to be a priest. It was his mother was driving him into it. That's why he had the breakdown."

"Let me out of this," said her father, "before I—"

"Go on!" Rita said with tender mockery (she was very fond of her father). "Before you what?"

"Before I wish I was a priest myself," he snarled. "I wouldn't be saddled with a family like I am."

He stumped out of the room, and the girls laughed. The idea of their father as a priest appealed to them almost as much as the idea of him as a mother. Hasty had a knack of stating his grievances in such a way that they inevitably produced laughter. But Mrs. Lomasney did not laugh.

"Reverend Mother was perfectly right," she said severely. "As if it wasn't hard enough on the poor boys without girls like you throwing temptation in their way. I think you behaved very badly, Rita."

"All right, if you say so," Rita said shortly with a boyish shrug of her shoulders, and refused to answer any more questions.

After her supper she went to bed, and her mother and sisters sat on in the front room discussing the scandal. Someone rang and Nellie opened the door.

"Hullo, Ned," she said. "I suppose you came up to congratulate us on the good news?"

"Hullo," Ned said, smiling with his mouth primly shut. With a sort of automatic movement he took off his coat and hat and hung them on the rack. Then he emptied the pockets with the same thoroughness. He hadn't changed much. He was thin and pale, spectacled and clever, with the same precise and tranquil manner, "like an old Persian cat," as Nellie said. He read too many books. In the last year or two something seemed to have happened him. He didn't go to Mass any longer. Not going to Mass struck all the Lomasneys as too damn clever. "What good news?" he added, having avoided any unnecessary precipitation.

"You didn't know who was here?"

"No," he replied, raising his brows mildly.

"Rita!"

"Oh!" The same tone. It was part of his cleverness not to be surprised at anything.

"She's after getting the sack for trying to run off with a priest," said Nellie.

If Nellie thought that would shake him she was mistaken. He merely tossed his head with a silent chuckle and went in, adjusting his pince-nez. For a fellow who was supposed to be in love with her since they were kids, he behaved in a very peculiar manner. He put his hands in his trousers pockets and stood on the hearth with his legs well apart.

"Isn't it awful, Ned?" Mrs. Lomasney asked in her deep voice.

"Is it?" Ned purred, smiling.

"With a priest?" cried Nellie.

"Now, he wasn't a priest, Nellie," said Mrs. Lomasney reprovingly. " 'Tis bad enough as it is without making it any worse."

"Suppose you tell me what happened," suggested Ned.

"But we don't know, Ned," cried Mrs. Lomasney. "You know what that one is like in one of her sulky fits. Maybe she'll tell you. She's up in bed."

"I'll try," said Ned.

Still with his hands in his pockets, he rolled after Mrs. Lomasney up the thickly carpeted stairs to Rita's little bedroom on top of the house. She left him on the landing and he paused for a moment to look out over the river and the lighted city behind it. Rita, wearing a pink dressing-jacket, was lying with one arm under her head. By the bed was a table with a packet of cigarettes she had been using as an ashtray. He smiled and shook his head reprovingly at her.

"Hullo, Ned," she cried, reaching him a bare arm. "Give us a kiss. I'm quite kissable now."

He didn't need to be told that. He was astonished at the change in her. Her whole bony, boyish face seemed to have gone mawkish and soft and to be lit up from inside. He sat on an armchair by the bed, carefully pulling up the bottoms of his trousers, then put his hands in his trousers pockets again and sat back with crossed legs and shoulders slightly hunched.

"I suppose they're all in a floosther downstairs?" Rita asked with amusement.

"They seem a little excited," said Ned with bowed head cocked a little sideways, looking like a wise old bird.

"Wait till they hear the details and they'll have something to be excited about," said Rita grimly.

"Why?" he asked mildly. "Are there details?"

"Masses of them," said Rita. "Honest to God, Ned, I used to laugh at the glamour girls in the convent. I never knew you could get like that about a fellow. It's like something busting inside you. Cripes, I'm as soppy as a kid!"

"And what's the fellow like?" Ned asked curiously.

"Tony Donoghue? His mother had a shop in the Main Street. He's decent enough, I suppose. I don't know. He kissed me one night coming home. I was furious. I cut the blooming socks off him. Next evening he came round to apologize. I never got up or asked him to sit down or anything. I suppose I was still mad with him. He said he never slept a wink. 'Didn't you?' said I. 'It didn't trouble me much.' Bloody lies, of course. 'I did it because I was fond of you,' says he. 'Is that what you told the last one too?' said I. Then he got into a wax too. Said I was calling him a liar. 'And aren't you?' said I. Then I waited for him to hit me, but, begor, he didn't, and I ended up sitting on his knee. Talk about the Babes in the Wood! First time he ever had a girl on his knee, he said, and you know how much of it I did."

They heard a step on the stairs and Mrs. Lomasney smiled benevolently at them both round the door.

"I suppose 'tis tea Ned is having?" she asked in her deep voice.

"No, I'm having the tea," said Rita. "Ned says he'd sooner a drop of the hard tack."

"Oh, isn't that a great change, Ned?" cried Mrs. Lomasney.

" 'Tis the shock," Rita explained lightly, throwing him a cigarette. "He didn't think I was that sort of girl."

"He mustn't know much about girls," said Mrs. Lomasney.

"He's learning now," said Rita.

When Paschal brought up the tray, Rita poured out tea for Ned and whisky for herself. He made no comment. Things like that were a commonplace in the Lomasney household.

"Anyway," she went on, "he told his old one he wanted to chuck the

Church and marry me. There was ructions, of course. The people in the shop at the other side of the street had a son a priest. She wanted to be as good as them. So away with her up to Reverend Mother, and Reverend Mother sends for me. Did I want to destroy the young man's life and he on the threshold of a great calling? I told her 'twas they wanted to destroy him. I asked her what sort of priest Tony would make. Oh, 'twas a marvellous sacrifice, and after it he'd be twice the man. Honest to God, Ned, the way that woman went on, you'd think she was talking about doctoring an old tomcat. I told her that was all she knew about Tony, and she said they knew him since he was an altar boy in the convent. 'Did he ever tell you how he used to slough the convent orchard and sell the apples in town?' says I. So then she dropped the Holy Willie stuff and told me his ma was after getting into debt to put him in for the priesthood, and if he chucked it, he'd never be able to get a job at home to pay it back. Three hundred quid! Wouldn't they kill you with style?"

"And what did you do then?" asked Ned with amusement.

"I went to see his mother."

"You didn't!"

"I did. I thought I might work it with the personal touch."

"You don't seem to have been very successful."

"I'd as soon try the personal touch on a traction engine, Ned. That woman was too tough for me altogether. I told her I wanted to marry Tony. 'I'm sorry,' she said; 'you can't.' 'What's to stop me?' said I. 'He's gone too far,' says she. 'If he was gone farther it wouldn't worry me,' says I. I told her then what Reverend Mother said about her being three hundred pounds in debt and offered to pay it back to her if she let him marry me."

"And had you the three hundred?" Ned asked in surprise.

"Ah, where would I get three hundred?" she replied ruefully. "And she knew it too, the old jade! She didn't believe a word I said. After that I saw Tony. He was crying; said he didn't want to break his mother's heart. As true as God, Ned, that woman had as much heart as a traction engine."

"Well, you seem to have done it in style," Ned said approvingly as he put away his teacup.

"That wasn't the half of it. When I heard the difficulties his mother was making, I offered to live with him instead."

"Live with him?" asked Ned. Even he was startled.

"Well, go away on holidays with him. Lots of girls do it. I know they do. And, God Almighty, isn't it only natural?"

"And what did he say to that?" asked Ned curiously.

"He was scared stiff."

"He would be," said Ned, wrinkling up his nose and giving his superior little sniff as he took out a packet of cigarettes.

"Oh, it's all very well for you," Rita cried, bridling up. "You may think you're a great fellow, all because you read Tolstoy and don't go to Mass, but you'd be just as scared if a girl offered to go to bed with you."

"Try me," Ned said sedately as he lit her cigarette for her, but somehow the notion of suggesting such a thing to Ned only made her laugh.

He stayed till quite late, and when he went downstairs the girls and Mrs. Lomasney fell on him and dragged him into the sitting-room.

"Well, doctor," said Mrs. Lomasney, "how's the patient?"

"Oh, I think the patient is coming round nicely," said Ned.

"But would you ever believe it, Ned?" she cried. "A girl that wouldn't look at the side of the road a fellow was at, unless 'twas to go robbing orchards with him. You'll have another drop of whisky?"

"I won't."

"And is that all you're going to tell us?" asked Mrs. Lomasney.

"Oh, you'll hear it all from herself."

"We won't."

"I dare say not," he said with a hearty chuckle, and went for his coat.

"Wisha, Ned," said Mrs. Lomasney, "what'll your mother say when she hears it?"

"'All *quite* mad,'" said Ned, sticking his nose in the air and giving an exaggerated version of what Mrs. Lomasney called "his Hayfield sniff."

"The dear knows, I think she's right," she said with resignation, helping him with his coat. "I hope your mother doesn't notice the smell of whisky from your breath," she added dryly, just to show him that she couldn't be taken in, and then stood at the door, looking up and down, as she waited for him to wave from the gate.

"Ah," she sighed as she closed the door behind her, "with the help of God it might be all for the best."

"If you think he's going to marry her, I can tell you now he's not," said Kitty. "I'd like to see myself trying it on Bill O'Donnell. He'd have my sacred life. That fellow only enjoys it."

"Ah, God is good," her mother said cheerfully, kicking a mat into place. "Some men might like that."

I I I

Inside a week Kitty and Nellie were sick to death of the sight of Rita round the house. She was bad enough at the best of times, but now she just brooded and mooned and snapped the head off you. In the afternoons she strolled down the Dyke and into Ned's little shop, where she sat on the counter, swinging her legs and smoking, while Ned leaned against the side of the window, tinkering at the insides of a watch with some delicate instrument. Nothing seemed to rattle him. When he had finished work, he changed his coat and they went out to tea. He sat at the back of the teashop in a corner, pulled up the legs of his trousers, and took out a packet of cigarettes and a box of matches, which he placed on the table before him with a look that almost commanded them to stay there and not get lost. His face was pale and clear and bright, like an evening sky when the last light has drained from it.

"Anything wrong?" he asked one evening when she was moodier than usual.

"Just fed up," she said, thrusting out her jaw.

"What is it?" he asked gently. "Still fretting?"

"Ah, no. I can get over that. It's Kitty and Nellie. They're bitches, Ned; proper bitches. And all because I don't wear my heart on my sleeve. If one of them got a knock from a fellow she'd take two aspirins and go to bed with the other one. They'd have a lovely talk—can't you imagine? 'And was it then he said he loved you?' I can't do that sort of stuff. And it's all because they're not sincere, Ned. They couldn't be sincere."

"Remember, they have a long start on you," Ned said smiling.

"Is that it?" she asked without interest. "They think I'm batty. Do you?"

"I've no doubt that Mrs. Donoghue, if that's her name, thought something of the sort," replied Ned with a tight-lipped smile.

"And wasn't she right?" asked Rita with sudden candour. "Suppose she'd agreed to take the three hundred quid, wouldn't I be in a nice pickle? I wake in a sweat whenever I think of it. I'm just a blooming chancer, Ned. Where would I get three hundred quid?"

"Oh, I dare say someone would have lent it to you," he said with a shrug.

"They would like fun. Would you?"

"Probably," he said gravely after a moment's thought.

"Are you serious?" she whispered earnestly.

"Quite."

"Cripes," she gasped, "you must be very fond of me."

"It looks like it," said Ned, and this time he laughed with real heartiness, a boy's laugh of sheer delight at the mystification he was causing her. It was characteristic of Rita that she should count their friendship of years as nothing, but his offer of three hundred pounds in cash as significant.

"Would you marry me?" she asked frowningly. "I'm not proposing to you, only asking," she added hastily.

"Certainly," he said, spreading out his hand. "Whenever you like."

"Honest to God?"

"Cut my throat."

"And why didn't you ask me before I went down to that kip? I'd have married you then like a shot. Was it the way you weren't keen on me then?"

"No," he replied matter-of-factly, drawing himself together like an old clock preparing to strike. "I think I've been keen on you as long as I know you."

"It's easily seen you're a Neddy Ned," she said with amusement. "I go after mine with a scalping knife."

"I stalk mine," said Ned.

"Cripes, Ned," she said with real regret, "I wish you'd told me sooner. I couldn't marry you now."

"No?"

"No. It wouldn't be fair to you."

"Isn't that my look-out?"

"It's my look-out now." She glanced round the restaurant to make sure no one was listening and then went on in a dry voice, leaning one elbow on the table. "I suppose you'll think this is all cod, but it's not. Honest to God, I think you're the finest bloody man I ever met—even though you do think you're an atheist or something," she added maliciously with a characteristic Lomasney flourish in the cause of Faith and Fatherland. "There's no one in the world I have more respect for. I think I'd nearly cut my throat if I did something you really disapproved of—I don't mean telling lies or going on a skite," she added hastily, to prevent misunderstandings. "They're only gas. Something that really shocked you is what I mean. I think if I was tempted to do anything like that I'd ask myself: 'What would that fellow Lowry think of me now?' "

"Well," Ned said in an extraordinarily quiet voice, squelching the butt of his cigarette on his plate, "that sounds to me like a very good beginning."

"It is not, Ned," she said sadly, shaking her head. "That's why I say it's my look-out. You couldn't understand it unless it happened to yourself; unless you fell in love with a girl the way I fell in love with Tony. Tony is a scut, and a cowardly scut, but I was cracked about him. If he came in here now and said: 'Come on, girl, we're going to Killarney for the week-end,' I'd go out and buy a nightdress and toothbrush and be off with him. And I wouldn't give a damn what you or anybody thought. I might chuck myself in the lake afterwards, but I'd go. Christ, Ned," she exclaimed, flushing and looking as though she might burst into tears, "he couldn't come into a room but I went all mushy inside. That's what the real thing is like."

"Well," Ned said sedately, apparently not in the least put out—in fact, looking rather pleased with himself, Rita thought—"I'm in no hurry. In case you get tired of scalping them, the offer will still be open."

"Thanks, Ned," she said absent-mindedly, as though she weren't listening.

While he paid the bill, she stood in the porch, doing her face in the big mirror that flanked it, and paying no attention to the crowds, coming homeward through streets where the shop windows were already lit. As he emerged from the shop she turned on him suddenly.

"About that matter, Ned," she said, "will you ask me again, or do I have to ask you?"

Ned just refrained from laughing outright. "As you like," he replied with quiet amusement. "Suppose I repeat the proposal every six months."

"That would be the hell of a long time to wait if I changed my mind," she said with a thoughtful scowl. "All right," she said, taking his arm. "I know you well enough to ask you. If you don't want me by that time, you can always say so. I won't mind."

I V

Ned's proposal came as a considerable comfort to Rita. It bolstered up her self-esteem, which was always in danger of collapse. She might be ugly and uneducated and a bit of a chancer, but the best man in Cork—the best in Ireland, she sometimes thought—wanted to marry her, even after she had been let down by another man. That was a queer one for her enemies! So while her sisters made fun of her, Rita considered the situation, waiting for the best possible moment to let them know she had been proposed to and could marry before either of them if it suited her. Since her childhood Rita had never given anything away without extracting the last ounce of theatrical effect from it. She would tell her sisters, but not before she could make them sick with the news.

That was a pity, for it left Rita unaware that Ned, whom she respected, was far from being the only one who liked her. For instance, there was Justin Sullivan, the lawyer, who had once been by way of being engaged to Nellie. He hadn't become engaged to her, because she was as slippery as an eel, and her fancy finally lit on a solicitor called Fahy whom Justin despised with his whole heart and soul as a light-headed, butterfly sort of man. But Justin continued to visit the house as a friend of the girls. There happened to be no other house that suited him half as well, and besides he knew that sooner or later Nellie would make a mess of her life with Fahy, and his services would be required.

Justin, in other words, was a sticker. He was a good deal older than Rita, a tall, burly man with a broad face, a brow that was rising from baldness as well as brains, and a slow, watchful, ironic air. Like many lawyers, he tended to conduct conversation as though the person he was speaking to were a hostile witness who had either to be coaxed into an admission of perjury or bullied into one of mental deficiency. When Justin began, Fahy simply clutched his head and retired to sit on the stairs. "Can't anyone shut that fellow up?" he would moan with a martyred air. Nobody could. The girls shot their little darts at him, but he only brushed them aside. Ned Lowry was the only one who could even stand up to him, and when the pair of them argued about religion, the room became a desert. Justin, of course, was a pillar of orthodoxy. "Imagine for a moment," he would declaim in a throaty rounded voice that turned easily to pomposity, "that I am Pope." "Easiest thing in the world, Justin," Kitty assured him. He drank whisky like water, and the more he drank, the more massive and logical and orthodoxly Catholic he became.

At the same time, under his truculent air he was exceedingly gentle, patient, and understanding, and disliked the ragging of Rita by her sisters.

"Tell me, Nellie," he asked one night in his lazy, amiable way, "do you talk like that to Rita because you like it, or because you think it's good for her?"

"How soft you have it!" Nellie cried. "We have to live with her. You haven't."

"That may be my misfortune, Nellie," said Justin with a broad smile.

"Is that a proposal, Justin?" asked Kitty shrewdly.

"Scarcely, Kitty," said Justin. "You're not what I might call a good jury."

"Better be careful or you'll have her dropping in on your mother, Justin," Kitty said maliciously.

"Thanks, Kitty," Rita said with a flash of cold fury.

"I hope my mother would have sufficient sense to realize it was an honour, Kitty," Justin said severely.

When he rose to go, Rita accompanied him to the hall.

"Thanks for the moral support, Justin," she said in a low voice, and then threw her overcoat over her shoulders to go as far as the gate with him. When he opened the door they both stood and gazed about them. It was a moonlit night; the garden, patterned in black and silver, sloped to the quiet roadway, where the gas lamps burned with a dim green light, and in the farther walls gateways shaded by black trees led to flights of steps or to steep-sloping avenues which led to moonlit houses on the river's edge.

"God, isn't it lovely?" Rita said in a hushed voice.

"Oh, by the way, Rita," he said, slipping his arm through hers, "that was a proposal."

"Janey Mack, they're falling," she said, giving his arm a squeeze. "What are falling?"

"Proposals."

"Why? Had you others?"

"I had one anyway."

"And did you accept it?"

"No," Rita said doubtfully. "Not quite. At least, I don't think I did."

"You might consider this one," Justin said with unusual humility. "You know, of course, that I was very fond of Nellie. At one time I was very fond of her indeed. You don't mind that, I hope. It's all over and done with now, and there are no regrets on either side."

"No, Justin, of course I don't mind. If I felt like marrying you I wouldn't give it a second thought. But I was very much in love with Tony too, and that's not all over and done with yet."

"I know that, Rita," he said gently. "I know exactly what you feel. We've all been through it." If he had left it at that everything might have been all right, but Justin was a lawyer, which meant that he liked to keep things absolutely shipshape. "But that won't last forever. In a month or two you'll be over it, and then you'll wonder what you saw in that fellow."

"I don't think so, Justin," she said with a crooked little smile, not altogether displeased to be able to enlighten him on the utter hopelessness of her position. "I think it will take a great deal longer than that."

"Well, say six months, even," Justin went on, prepared to yield a point to the defence. "All I ask is that in one month or six, whenever you've got over your regrets for this—this amiable young man" (momentarily his voice took on its familiar ironic ring), "you'll give me a thought. I'm old enough not to make any more mistakes. I know I'm fond of you, and I feel pretty sure I could make a success of my end of it."

"What you really mean," said Rita, keeping her temper with the greatest difficulty, "is that I wasn't in love with Tony at all. Isn't that it?"

"Not quite," Justin said judiciously. Even if he'd had a serenade as well as the moonlight and the girl, it couldn't have kept him from correcting what he considered to be a false deduction. "I've no doubt you were very much attracted by this—this clerical Adonis; this Mr. Whatever-his-name-is, or that at any rate you thought you were, which in practice comes to the same thing, but I also know that that sort of thing, though it's painful enough while it lasts, doesn't last very long."

"You mean yours didn't, Justin," Rita said tartly.

"I mean mine or anybody else's," Justin said pompously. "Because love—the only sort of thing you can really call love—is something that comes with experience. You're probably too young yet to know what the real thing is."

As Rita had only recently told Ned that he didn't yet know what the real thing was, she found this rather hard to stomach.

"How old would you say you'd have to be?" she asked viciously. "Thirty-five?"

"You'll know soon enough—when it hits you," said Justin.

"Honest to God, Justin," she said, withdrawing her arm and looking at him with suppressed fury, "I think you're the thickest man I ever met."

"Good night, my dear," said Justin with perfect good humour, and he raised his cap and took the few steps to the gate at a run.

Rita stood gazing after him with folded arms. At the age of eighteen to be told that there is anything you don't know about love is like a knife in your heart.

V

Kitty and Nellie grew so tired of her moodiness that they persuaded her mother that the best way of distracting her mind was to find her another job. A new environment was also supposed to be good for her complaint, so Mrs. Lomasney wrote to her sister who was a nun in England, and the sister found her work in a convent there. Rita let on to pay no attention, though she let Ned see something of her resentment.

"But why England?" he asked wonderingly.

"Why not?" replied Rita challengingly.

"Wouldn't any place nearer do you?"

"I suppose I wouldn't be far enough away from them."

"But why not make up your own mind?"

"I'll probably do that too," she said with a short laugh. "I'd like to see what's in theirs first though."

On Friday she was to leave for England, and on Wednesday the girls gave a farewell party. This, too, Rita affected to take no great interest in. Wednesday was the half-holiday, and it rained steadily all day. The girls' friends all turned up. Most were men: Bill O'Donnell of the bank, who was engaged to Kitty; Fahy, the solicitor, who was Justin's successful rival for Nellie; Justin himself, who simply could not be kept out of the house by anything short of an injunction, Ned Lowry, and a few others. Hasty soon retired with his wife to the dining-room to read the evening paper. He said all his daughters' young men looked exactly alike and he never knew which of them he was talking to.

Bill O'Donnell was acting as barman. He was a big man, bigger even than Justin, with a battered boxer's face and a Negro smile, which seemed to well up from depths of good humour with life rather than from any immediate contact with others. He carried on loud conversations with everyone he poured out drink for, and his voice overrode every intervening tête-à-tête, and challenged even the piano, on which Nellie was vamping music-hall songs.

"Who's this one for, Rita?" he asked. "A bottle of Bass for Paddy. Ah, the stout man! Remember the New Year's Day in Bandon, Paddy? Remember how you had to carry me up to the bank in evening dress and jack me up between the two wings of the desk? Kitty, did I ever tell you about that night in Bandon?"

"Once a week for the past five years, Bill," said Kitty philosophically.

"Nellie," said Rita, "I think it's time for Bill to sing his song. 'Let Me like a Soldier Fall,' Bill!"

"My one little song!" Bill said with a roar of laughter. "My one and only song, but I sing it grand. Don't I, Nellie? Don't I sing it fine?"

"Fine!" agreed Nellie, looking up at his big, beaming moonface shining at her over the piano. "As the man said to my mother, 'Finest bloody soprano I ever heard.' "

"He did not, Nellie," Bill said sadly. "You're making that up. . . . Silence, please!" he shouted joyously, clapping his hands. "Ladies and gentlemen, I must apologize. I ought to sing something like Tosti's 'Good-bye,' but the fact is, ladies and gentlemen, that I don't know Tosti's 'Good-bye.' "

"Recite it, Bill," said Justin amiably.

"I don't know the words of it either, Justin," said Bill. "In fact, I'm not sure if there's any such song, but if there is, I ought to sing it."

"Why, Bill?" Rita asked innocently. She was wearing a long black dress that threw up the unusual brightness of her dark, bony face. She looked happier than she had looked for months. All the evening it was as though she were laughing to herself.

"Because 'twould be only right, Rita," said Bill with great melancholy, putting his arm about her and drawing her closer to him. "You know I'm very fond of you, don't you, Rita?"

"And I'm mad about you, Bill," said Rita candidly.

"I know that, Rita," he said mournfully, pulling at his collar as though to give himself air. "I only wish you weren't going, Rita. This place isn't the same without you. Kitty won't mind my saying that," he added with a nervous glance at Kitty, who was flirting with Justin on the sofa.

"Are you going to sing your blooming old song or not?" Nellie asked impatiently, running her fingers over the keys.

"I'm going to sing now in one minute, Nellie," Bill said ecstatically, stroking Rita fondly under the chin. "I only want Rita to know the way we'll miss her."

"Damn it, Bill," Rita said, snuggling up to him with her dark head on his chest, "if you go on like that I won't go at all. Tell me, would you really prefer me not to go?"

"I would prefer you not to go, Rita," he replied, stroking her cheeks and eyes. "You're too good for the fellows over there."

"Oh, go on doing that," she said hastily, as he dropped his hand. "It's gorgeous, and you're making Kitty mad jealous."

"Kitty isn't jealous," Bill said fondly. "Kitty is a lovely girl and you're a lovely girl. I hate to see you go, Rita."

"That settles it, Bill," she said, pulling herself free of him with a determined air. "I simply couldn't cause you all that suffering. As you put it that way, I won't go."

"Won't you, just?" said Kitty with a grin.

"Now, don't worry your head about it any more, Bill," said Rita briskly. "It's all off."

Justin, who had been quietly consuming large whiskies, looked round lazily.

"Perhaps I ought to have mentioned," he boomed, "that the young lady has just done me the honour of proposing to me and I've accepted her."

Ned Lowry, who had been enjoying the scene between Bill and Rita, looked at him for a moment in surprise.

"Bravo! Bravo!" cried Bill, clapping his hands with childish delight. "A marriage has been arranged and all the rest of it—what? I must give you a kiss, Rita. Justin, you don't mind if I give Rita a kiss?"

"Not at all, not at all," replied Justin with a lordly wave of his hand. "Anything that's mine is yours, old man."

"You're not serious, Justin, are you?" Kitty asked incredulously.

"Oh, I'm serious all right," said Justin. "I'm not quite certain whether your sister is. Are you, Rita?"

"What?" Rita asked as though she hadn't heard.

"Serious," repeated Justin.

"Why?" asked Rita. "Trying to give me the push already?"

"We're much obliged for the information," Nellie said ironically as she rose from the piano. "Now, maybe you'd oblige us further and tell us does Father know."

"Hardly," said Rita coolly. "It was only settled this evening."

"Well, maybe 'twill do with some more settling by the time Father is done with you," Nellie said furiously. "The impudence of you! How dare you! Go in at once and tell him."

"Keep your hair on, girl," Rita advised with cool malice and then went jauntily out of the room. Kitty and Nellie began to squabble viciously with Justin. They were convinced that the whole scene had been arranged by Rita to make them look ridiculous, and in this they weren't very far out. Justin sat back and began to enjoy the sport. Then Ned Lowry struck a match and lit another cigarette, and something about the slow, careful way in which he did it drew everyone's attention. Just because he was not the sort to make a fuss, people realized from his strained look that his mind was very far away. The squabble stopped as quickly as it had begun and a feeling of awkwardness ensued. Ned was too old a friend of the family for the girls not to feel that way about him.

Rita returned, laughing.

"Well?" asked Nellie.

"Consent refused," growled Rita, bowing her head and pulling the wrong side of an imaginary moustache.

"What did I say?" exclaimed Nellie, but without rancour.

"You don't think it makes any difference?" Rita asked dryly.

"I wouldn't be too sure of that," said Nellie. "What else did he say?"

"Oh, he hadn't a notion who I was talking about," Rita said lightly. " 'Justin who?' " she mimicked. " 'How the hell do you think I can remember all the young scuts ye bring to the house?' "

"Was he mad?" asked Kitty with amusement.

"Hopping."

"He didn't call us scuts?" asked Bill in a wounded tone.

"Oh, begor, that was the very word he used, Bill," said Rita.

"Did you tell him he was very fond of me the day I gave him the tip for Golden Boy at the Park Races?" asked Justin.

"I did," said Rita. "I said you were the stout block of a fellow with the brown hair that he said had the fine intelligence, and he said he never gave a damn about intelligence. He wanted me to marry the thin fellow with the specs. 'Only bloody gentleman that comes to the house.' "

"Is it Ned?" cried Nellie.

"Who else?" said Rita. "I asked him why he didn't tell me that before and he nearly ate the head off me. 'Jesus Christ, girl, don't I feed ye and clothe ye? Isn't that enough without having to coort for ye as well? Next thing, ye'll be asking me to have a few babies for ye.' Anyway, Ned," she added with a crooked, almost malicious smile, "you can always say you were Pa's favourite."

Once more the attention was directed to Ned. He put his cigarette down with care and sprang up with a broad smile, holding out his hand.

"I wish you all the luck in the world, Justin," he said.

"I know that well, Ned," boomed Justin, catching Ned's hand in his own two. "And I'd feel the same if it was you."

"And you too, Miss Lomasney," Ned said gaily.

"Thanks, Mr. Lowry," she replied with the same crooked smile.

VI

Justin and Rita got married, and Ned, like all the Hayfield Hourigans, behaved in a decorous and sensible manner. He didn't take to drink or break the crockery or do any of the things people are expected to do under the circumstances. He gave them a very expensive clock as a wedding present, went once or twice to visit them, permitted Justin to try and convert him, and took Rita to the pictures when Justin was away from home. At the same time he began to walk out with an assistant in Halpin's; a gentle, humorous girl with a great mass of jet-black hair, a snub nose, and a long, pointed melancholy face. You saw them everywhere together.

He also went regularly to Sunday's Well to see the old couple and Nellie, who wasn't yet married. One evening when he called, Mr. and Mrs. Lomasney were at the chapel, but Rita was there, Justin being again away. It was months since she and Ned had met; she was having a baby and very near her time, and it made her self-conscious and rude. She said it made her feel like a yacht that had been turned into a cargo boat. Three or four times she said things to Ned which would have maddened anyone else, but he took them in his usual way, without resentment.

"And how's little Miss Bitch?" she asked insolently.

"Little Miss who?" he asked mildly.

"Miss—how the hell can I remember the names of all your dolls? The Spanish-looking one who sells the knickers at Halpin's."

"Oh, she's very well, thanks," Ned said primly.

"What you might call a prudent marriage," Rita went on, all on edge.

"How's that, Rita?"

"You'll have the ring and the trousseau at cost price."

"How interested you are in her!" Nellie said suspiciously.

"I don't give a damn about her," Rita said with a shrug. "Would Señorita What's-her-name ever let you stand godfather to my footballer, Ned?"

"Why not?" Ned asked mildly. "I'd be delighted, of course."

"You have the devil's own neck to ask him after the way you treated him," said Nellie. Nellie was interested; she knew Rita and knew that she was in one of her emotional states, and was determined on finding out what it meant. Ordinarily Rita, who also knew her sister, would have delighted in thwarting her, but now it was as though she wanted an audience.

"How did I treat him?" she asked with amusement.

"Codding him along like that for years, and then marrying a man that was twice your age."

"Well, how did he expect me to know?"

Ned rose and took out a packet of cigarettes. Like Nellie he knew that Rita had deliberately staged the scene and was on the point of telling him something. She was leaning very far back in her chair and laughed up at him while she took a cigarette and waited for him to light it.

"Come on, Rita," he said encouragingly. "As you've said so much you might as well tell us the rest."

"What else is there to tell?"

"What you had against me."

"Who said I had anything against you? Didn't I distinctly tell you when you asked me to marry you that I didn't love you? Maybe you thought I didn't mean it."

He paused for a moment and then raised his brows.

"I did," he said quietly.

She laughed.

"The conceit of that fellow!" she said to Nellie, and then with a change of tone: "I had nothing against you, Ned. This was the one I had the needle in. Herself and Kitty were forcing me into it."

"Well, the impudence of you!" cried Nellie.

"Isn't it true for me?" Rita said sharply. "Weren't you both trying to get me out of the house?"

"We weren't," Nellie replied hotly, "and anyway that has nothing to do with it. It was no reason why you couldn't have married Ned if you wanted to."

"I didn't want to. I didn't want to marry anyone."

"And what changed your mind?"

"Nothing changed my mind. I didn't care about anyone, only Tony, but I didn't want to go to that damn place, and I had no alternative. I had to marry one of you, so I made up my mind that I'd marry the first of you that called."

"You must have been mad," Nellie said indignantly.

"I felt it. I sat at the window the whole afternoon, looking at the rain. Remember that day, Ned?"

He nodded.

"The rain had a lot to do with it. I think I half hoped you'd come first. Justin came instead—an old aunt of his was sick and he came for supper. I saw him at the gate and he waved to me with his old brolly. I ran downstairs to open the door for him. 'Justin,' I said, grabbing him by the coat, 'if you still want to marry me, I'm ready.' He gave me a dirty look—you know Justin! 'Young woman,' he said, 'there's a time and place for everything.' And away with him up to the lavatory. Talk about romantic engagements! Damn the old kiss did I get off him, even!"

"I declare to God!" said Nellie in stupefaction.

"I know," Rita cried, laughing again over her own irresponsibility. "Cripes, when I knew what I was after doing I nearly dropped dead."

"Oh, so you came to your senses?" Nellie asked ironically.

"What do you think? That's the trouble with Justin; he's always right. That fellow knew I wouldn't be married a week before I didn't give a snap of my fingers for Tony. And me thinking my life was over and that it was either that or the river! God, the idiots we make of ourselves over men!"

"And I suppose 'twas then you found out you'd married the wrong man?" Nellie asked.

"Who said I married the wrong man?" Rita asked hotly.

"I thought that was what you were telling us," Nellie said innocently.

"You get things all wrong, Nellie," Rita replied shortly. "You jump to conclusions too much. If I did marry the wrong man I wouldn't be likely to tell you—or Ned Lowry either."

She looked mockingly at Ned, but her look belied her. It was plain enough now why she wanted Nellie as an audience. It kept her from admitting more than she had to admit, from saying things which, once said, might make her own life impossible. Ned rose and flicked his cigarette ash into the fire. Then he stood with his back to it, his hands behind his back, his feet spread out on the hearth.

"You mean if I'd come earlier you'd have married me?" he asked quietly.

"If you'd come earlier, I'd probably be asking Justin to stand godfather to your brat," said Rita. "And how do you know but Justin would be walking out the señorita, Ned?"

"Then maybe you wouldn't be quite so interested whether he was or not," said Nellie, but she didn't say it maliciously. It was now only too plain what Rita meant, and Nellie was sorry for her.

Ned turned and lashed his cigarette savagely into the fire. Rita looked up at him mockingly.

"Go on!" she taunted him. "Say it, blast you!"

"I couldn't," he said bitterly.

A month later he married the señorita.

D. H. Lawrence

TICKETS, PLEASE

The reader will recognize in the subtle antagonism that
exists between Annie Stone and John Thomas one manifestation
of the age-old war between the sexes that is never lost,
never won. This time it is a war within a war, for after all
aren't the girls here fighting their country's war—
World War I—on the home front, by replacing the men
conductors on this "most dangerous tram-service in England"?
These girls are "fearless young hussies" in all truth, as the
outcome of the story shows them to be: "they fear nobody—
and everybody fears them." And all the normal emotions
are intensified aboard the careening little world of the tram
car as it plunges ahead through the stormy night, up hill and
down, over bridges and across long stretches of the countryside
of the Midlands.

Aboard the trams there is "wild romance," between the girls
and their good-looking inspector. And it is with this romance
that the story deals. Blame the lawlessness of wartime for what
happens; better still, attach the blame where it belongs, if
you can, and seek within the inner recesses of the female
heart for the motivation of the terrifying final scene.

There is in the Midlands a single-line tramway system which
boldly leaves the country town and plunges off into the black, industrial
countryside, up hill and down dale, through the long, ugly villages of
workmen's houses, over canals and railways, past churches perched
high and nobly over the smoke and shadows, through stark, grimy, cold
little market-places, tilting away in a rush past cinemas and shops down
to the hollow where the collieries are, then up again, past a little rural
church, under the ash trees, on in a rush to the terminus, the last little
ugly place of industry, the cold little town that shivers on the edge of
the wild, gloomy country beyond. There the green and creamy coloured
tram-car seems to pause and purr with curious satisfaction. But in a
few minutes—the clock on the turret of the Coöperative Wholesale Society's Shops gives the time—away it starts once more on the adventure.
Again there are the reckless swoops down hill, bouncing the loops:
again the chilly wait in the hill-top market-place: again the breathless

slithering round the precipitous drop under the church: again the patient halts at the loops, waiting for the outcoming car: so on and on, for two long hours, till at last the city looms beyond the fat gas-works, the narrow factories draw near, we are in the sordid streets of the great town, once more we sidle to a standstill at our terminus, abashed by the great crimson and cream-coloured city cars, but still perky, jaunty, somewhat daredevil, green as a jaunty sprig of parsley out of a black colliery garden.

To ride on these cars is always an adventure. Since we are in wartime, the drivers are men unfit for active service: cripples and hunchbacks. So they have the spirit of the devil in them. The ride becomes a steeple-chase. Hurray! we have leapt in a clear jump over the canal bridges—now for the four-lane corner. With a shriek and a trail of sparks we are clear again. To be sure, a tram often leaps the rails—but what matter! It sits in a ditch till other trams come to haul it out. It is quite common for a car, packed with one solid mass of living people, to come to a dead halt in the midst of unbroken blackness, the heart of nowhere on a dark night, and for the driver and the girl conductor to call, "All get off—car's on fire!" Instead, however, of rushing out in a panic, the passengers stolidly reply: "Get on—get on! We're not coming out. We're stopping where we are. Push on, George." So till flames actually appear.

The reason for this reluctance to dismount is that the nights are howlingly cold, black, and windswept, and a car is a haven of refuge. From village to village the miners travel, for a change of cinema, of girl, of pub. The trams are desperately packed. Who is going to risk himself in the black gulf outside, to wait perhaps an hour for another tram, then to see the forlorn notice "Depot Only," because there is something wrong! or to greet a unit of three bright cars all so tight with people that they sail past with a howl of derision. Trams that pass in the night.

This, the most dangerous tram-service in England, as the authorities themselves declare, with pride, is entirely conducted by girls, and driven by rash young men, a little crippled, or by delicate young men, who creep forward in terror. The girls are fearless young hussies. In their ugly blue uniform, skirts up to their knees, shapeless old peaked caps on their heads, they have all the *sang-froid* of an old non-commissioned officer. With a tram packed with howling colliers, roaring hymns downstairs and a sort of antiphony of obscenities upstairs, the lasses are perfectly at their ease. They pounce on the youths who try to evade their ticket-machine. They push off the men at the end of their distance. They are not going to be done in the eye—not they. They fear nobody—and everybody fears them.

"Hello, Annie!"

"Hello, Ted!"

"Oh, mind my corn, Miss Stone. It's my belief you've got a heart of stone, for you've trod on it again."

"You should keep it in your pocket," replies Miss Stone, and she goes sturdily upstairs in her high boots.

"Tickets, please."

She is peremptory, suspicious, and ready to hit first. She can hold her own against ten thousand. The step of that tram-car is her Thermopylæ.

Therefore, there is a certain wild romance aboard these cars—and in the sturdy bosom of Annie herself. The time for soft romance is in the morning, between ten o'clock and one, when things are rather slack: that is, except market-day and Saturday. Thus Annie has time to look about her. Then she often hops off her car and into a shop where she has spied something, while the driver chats in the main road. There is very good feeling between the girls and the drivers. Are they not companions in peril, shipments aboard this careering vessel of a tram-car, forever rocking on the waves of a stormy land?

Then, also, during the easy hours, the inspectors are most in evidence. For some reason, everybody employed in this tram-service is young: there are no grey heads. It would not do. Therefore the inspectors are of the right age, and one, the chief, is also good-looking. See him stand on a wet, gloomy morning, in his long oil-skin, his peaked cap well down over his eyes, waiting to board a car. His face is ruddy, his small brown moustache is weathered, he has a faint impudent smile. Fairly tall and agile, even in his waterproof, he springs aboard a car and greets Annie.

"Hello, Annie! Keeping the wet out?"

"Trying to."

There are only two people in the car. Inspecting is soon over. Then for a long and impudent chat on the footboard, a good, easy, twelve-mile chat.

The inspector's name is John Thomas Raynor—always called John Thomas, except sometimes, in malice, Coddy. His face sets in fury when he is addressed, from a distance, with this abbreviation. There is considerable scandal about John Thomas in half a dozen villages. He flirts with the girl conductors in the morning, and walks out with them in the dark night, when they leave their tram-car at the depôt. Of course, the girls quit the service frequently. Then he flirts and walks out with the newcomer: always providing she is sufficiently attractive, and that she will consent to walk. It is remarkable, however, that most of the girls are quite comely, they are all young, and this roving life aboard the car gives them a sailor's dash and recklessness. What matter how they behave when the ship is in port? To-morrow they will be aboard again.

Annie, however, was something of a Tartar, and her sharp tongue had kept John Thomas at arm's length for many months. Perhaps, therefore, she liked him all the more: for he always came up smiling, with impudence. She watched him vanquish one girl, then another. She could tell by the movement of his mouth and eyes, when he flirted with her in the morning, that he had been walking out with this lass, or the other, the night before. A fine cock-of-the-walk he was. She could sum him up pretty well.

In this subtle antagonism they knew each other like old friends, they were as shrewd with one another almost as man and wife. But Annie had always kept him sufficiently at arm's length. Besides, she had a boy of her own.

The Statutes fair, however, came in November, at Bestwood. It happened that Annie had the Monday night off. It was a drizzling ugly night, yet she dressed herself up and went to the fair ground. She was alone, but she expected soon to find a pal of some sort.

The roundabouts were veering round and grinding out their music, the side shows were making as much commotion as possible. In the cocoanut shies there were no cocoanuts, but artificial war-time substitutes, which the lads declared were fastened into the irons. There was a sad decline in brilliance and luxury. None the less, the ground was muddy as ever, there was the same crush, the press of faces lighted up by the flares and the electric lights, the same smell of naphtha and a few fried potatoes, and of electricity.

Who should be the first to greet Miss Annie, on the show ground, but John Thomas. He had a black overcoat buttoned up to his chin, and a tweed cap pulled down over his brows, his face between was ruddy and smiling and handy as ever. She knew so well the way his mouth moved.

She was very glad to have a "boy." To be at the Statutes without a fellow was no fun. Instantly, like the gallant he was, he took her on the Dragons, grim-toothed, round-about switchbacks. It was not nearly so exciting as the tram-car, actually. But, then, to be seated in a shaking green dragon, uplifted above the sea of bubble faces, careering in a rickety fashion in the lower heavens, whilst John Thomas leaned over her, his cigarette in his mouth, was after all the right style. She was a plump, quick, alive little creature. So she was quite excited and happy.

John Thomas made her stay on for the next round. And therefore she could hardly for shame repulse him when he put his arm round her and drew her a little nearer to him, in a very warm and cuddly manner. Besides, he was fairly discreet, he kept his movement as hidden as possible. She looked down, and saw that his red, clean hand was out of sight of the crowd. And they knew each other so well. So they warmed up to the fair.

After the Dragons they went on the horses. John Thomas paid each time, so she could but be complaisant. He, of course, sat astride on the outer horse—named "Black Bess"—and she sat sideways, towards him, on the inner horse—named "Wildfire." But of course John Thomas was not going to sit discreetly on "Black Bess," holding the brass bar. Round they spun and heaved, in the light. And round he swung on his wooden steed, flinging one leg across her mount, and perilously tipping up and down, across the space, half lying back, laughing at her. He was perfectly happy; she was afraid her hat was on one side, but she was excited.

He threw quoits on a table, and won for her two large, pale-blue hat-pins. And then, hearing the noise of the cinemas, announcing another performance, they climbed the boards and went in.

Of course, during these performances pitch darkness falls from time to time, when the machine goes wrong. Then there is a wild whooping, and a loud smacking of simulated kisses. In these moments John Thomas drew Annie towards him. After all, he had a wonderfully warm, cosy way of holding a girl with his arm, he seemed to make such a nice fit. And after all, it was pleasant to be so held: so very comforting and cosy and nice. He leaned over her and she felt his breath on her hair; she knew he wanted to kiss her on the lips. And after all, he was so warm and she fitted in to him so softly. After all, she wanted him to touch her lips.

But the light sprang up; she also started electrically, and put her hat straight. He left his arm lying nonchalantly behind her. Well, it was fun, it was exciting to be at the Statutes with John Thomas.

When the cinema was over they went for a walk across the dark, damp fields. He had all the arts of love-making. He was especially good at holding a girl, when he sat with her on a stile in the black, drizzling darkness. He seemed to be holding her in space, against his own warmth and gratification. And his kisses were soft and slow and searching.

So Annie walked out with John Thomas, though she kept her own boy dangling in the distance. Some of the tram-girls chose to be huffy. But there, you must take things as you find them, in this life.

There was no mistake about it, Annie liked John Thomas a good deal. She felt so rich and warm in herself whenever he was near. And John Thomas really liked Annie, more than usual. The soft, melting way in which she could flow into a fellow, as if she melted into his very bones, was something rare and good. He fully appreciated this.

But with a developing acquaintance there began a developing intimacy. Annie wanted to consider him a person, a man; she wanted to take an intelligent interest in him, and to have an intelligent response. She did not want a mere nocturnal presence, which was what he was so far. And she prided herself that he could not leave her.

Here she made a mistake. John Thomas intended to remain a nocturnal presence; he had no idea of becoming an all-round individual to her. When she started to take an intelligent interest in him and his life and his character, he sheered off. He hated intelligent interest. And he knew that the only way to stop it was to avoid it. The possessive female was aroused in Annie. So he left her.

It is no use saying she was not surprised. She was at first startled, thrown out of her count. For she had been so *very* sure of holding him. For a while she was staggered, and everything became uncertain to her. Then she wept with fury, indignation, desolation, and misery. Then she had a spasm of despair. And then, when he came, still impudently, on to her car, still familiar, but letting her see by the movement of his head that he had gone away to somebody else for the time being, and was enjoying pastures new, then she determined to have her own back.

She had a very shrewd idea what girls John Thomas had taken out. She went to Nora Purdy. Nora was a tall, rather pale, but well-built girl, with beautiful yellow hair. She was rather secretive.

"Hey!" said Annie, accosting her; then softly, "Who's John Thomas on with now?"

"I don't know," said Nora.

"Why tha does," said Annie, ironically lapsing into dialect. "Tha knows as well as I do."

"Well, I do, then," said Nora. "It isn't me, so don't bother."

"It's Cissy Meakin, isn't it?"

"It is, for all I know."

"Hasn't he got a face on him!" said Annie. "I don't half like his cheek. I could knock him off the footboard when he comes round at me."

"He'll get dropped-on one of these days," said Nora.

"Ay, he will when somebody makes up their mind to drop it on him. I should like to see him taken down a peg or two, shouldn't you?"

"I shouldn't mind," said Nora.

"You've got quite as much cause to as I have," said Annie. "But we'll drop on him one of these days, my girl. What? Don't you want to?"

"I don't mind," said Nora.

But as a matter of fact, Nora was much more vindictive than Annie.

One by one Annie went the round of the old flames. It so happened that Cissy Meakin left the tramway service in quite a short time. Her mother made her leave. Then John Thomas was on the *qui-vive*. He cast his eyes over his old flock. And his eyes lighted on Annie. He thought she would be safe now. Besides, he liked her.

She arranged to walk home with him on Sunday night. It so happened that her car would be in the depôt at half-past nine: the last car would come in at 10:15. So John Thomas was to wait for her there.

At the depôt the girls had a little waiting-room of their own. It was quite rough, but cosy, with a fire and an oven and a mirror, and table and wooden chairs. The half dozen girls who knew John Thomas only too well had arranged to take service this Sunday afternoon. So, as the cars began to come in, early, the girls dropped into the waiting-room. And instead of hurrying off home, they sat around the fire and had a cup of tea. Outside was the darkness and lawlessness of wartime.

John Thomas came on the car after Annie, at about a quarter to ten. He poked his head easily into the girls' waiting-room.

"Prayer-meeting?" he asked.

"Ay," said Laura Sharp. "Ladies only."

"That's me!" said John Thomas. It was one of his favourite exclamations.

"Shut the door, boy," said Muriel Baggaley.

"On which side of me?" said John Thomas.

"Which tha likes," said Polly Birkin.

He had come in and closed the door behind him. The girls moved in their circle, to make a place for him near the fire. He took off his great-coat and pushed back his hat.

"Who handles the teapot?" he said.

Nora Purdy silently poured him out a cup of tea.

"Want a bit o' my bread and drippin'?" said Muriel Baggaley to him.

"Ay, give us a bit."

And he began to eat his piece of bread.

"There's no place like home, girls," he said.

They all looked at him as he uttered this piece of impudence. He seemed to be sunning himself in the presence of so many damsels.

"Especially if you're not afraid to go home in the dark," said Laura Sharp.

"Me! By myself I am."

They sat still till they heard the last tram come in. In a few minutes Emma Houselay entered.

"Come on, my old duck!" cried Polly Birkin.

"It *is* perishing," said Emma, holding her fingers to the fire.

"But—I'm afraid to, go home in, the dark," sang Laura Sharp, the tune having got into her mind.

"Who're you going with to-night, John Thomas?" asked Muriel Baggaley, coolly.

"To-night?" said John Thomas. "Oh, I'm going home by myself to-night—all on my lonely-O."

"That's me!" said Nora Purdy, using his own ejaculation.

The girls laughed shrilly.

"Me as well, Nora," said John Thomas.

"Don't know what you mean," said Laura.

"Yes, I'm toddling," said he, rising and reaching for his overcoat.

"Nay," said Polly. "We're all here waiting for you."

"We've got to be up in good time in the morning," he said, in the benevolent official manner.

They all laughed.

"Nay," said Muriel. "Don't leave us all lonely, John Thomas. Take one!"

"I'll take the lot, if you like," he responded, gallantly.

"That you won't, either," said Muriel. "Two's company; seven's too much of a good thing."

"Nay—take one," said Laura. "Fair and square, all above board, and say which."

"Ay," cried Annie, speaking for the first time. "Pick, John Thomas; let's hear thee."

"Nay," he said. "I'm going home quiet to-night. Feeling good, for once."

"Whereabouts?" said Annie. "Take a good un, then. But tha's got to take one of us!"

"Nay, how can I take one," he said, laughing uneasily. "I don't want to make enemies."

"You'd only make *one,*" said Annie.

"The chosen *one,*" added Laura.

"Oh, my! Who said girls!" exclaimed John Thomas, again turning, as if to escape. "Well—good-night."

"Nay, you've got to make your pick," said Muriel. "Turn your face to the wall, and say which one touches you. Go on—we shall only just touch your back—one of us. Go on—turn your face to the wall, and don't look, and say which one touches you."

He was uneasy, mistrusting them. Yet he had not the courage to break away. They pushed him to a wall and stood him there with his face to it. Behind his back they all grimaced, tittering. He looked so comical. He looked around uneasily.

"Go on!" he cried.

"You're looking—you're looking!" they shouted.

He turned his head away. And suddenly, with a movement like a swift cat, Annie went forward and fetched him a box on the side of the head that sent his cap flying, and himself staggering. He started round.

But at Annie's signal they all flew at him, slapping him, pinching him, pulling his hair, though more in fun than in spite or anger. He, however, saw red. His blue eyes flamed with strange fear as well as fury, and he butted through the girls to the door. It was locked. He wrenched at it. Roused, alert, the girls stood round and looked at him. He faced them, at bay. At that moment they were rather horrifying to him, as they stood in their short uniforms. He was distinctly afraid.

"Come on, John Thomas! Come on! Choose!" said Annie.

"What are you after? Open the door," he said.

"We sha'n't—not till you've chosen!" said Muriel.

"Chosen what?" he said.

"Chosen the one you're going to marry," she replied.

He hesitated a moment.

"Open the blasted door," he said, "and get back to your senses." He spoke with official authority.

"You've got to choose!" cried the girls.

"Come on!" cried Annie, looking him in the eye. "Come on! Come on!"

He went forward, rather vaguely. She had taken off her belt, and swinging it, she fetched him a sharp blow over the head with the buckle end. He sprang and seized her. But immediately the other girls rushed upon him, pulling and tearing and beating him. Their blood was now thoroughly up. He was their sport now. They were going to have their own back, out of him. Strange, wild creatures, they hung on him and rushed at him to bear him down. His tunic was torn right up the back, Nora had hold at the back of his collar, and was actually strangling him. Luckily the button burst. He struggled in a wild frenzy of fury and terror, almost mad terror. His tunic was simply torn off his back, his shirt-sleeves were torn away, his arms were naked. The girls rushed at him, clenched their hands on him and pulled at him: or they rushed at him and pushed him, butted him with all their might: or they struck him wild blows. He ducked and cringed and struck sideways. They became more intense.

At last he was down. They rushed on him, kneeling on him. He had neither breath nor strength to move. His face was bleeding with a long scratch, his brow was bruised.

Annie knelt on him, the other girls knelt and hung on to him. Their faces were flushed, their hair wild, their eyes were all glittering strangely. He lay at last quite still, with face averted, as an animal lies when it is defeated and at the mercy of the captor. Sometimes his eye glanced back at the wild faces of the girls. His breast rose heavily, his wrists were torn.

"Now, then, my fellow!" gasped Annie at length. "Now then—now—"

At the sound of her terrifying, cold triumph, he suddenly started to struggle as an animal might, but the girls threw themselves upon him with unnatural strength and power, forcing him down.

"Yes—now, then!" gasped Annie at length.

And there was a dead silence, in which the thud of heart-beating was to be heard. It was a suspense of pure silence in every soul.

"Now you know where you are," said Annie.

The sight of his white, bare arm maddened the girls. He lay in a kind of trance of fear and antagonism. They felt themselves filled with super-natural strength.

Suddenly Polly started to laugh—to giggle wildly—helplessly—and Emma and Muriel joined in. But Annie and Nora and Laura remained the same, tense, watchful, with gleaming eyes. He winced away from these eyes.

"Yes," said Annie, in a curious low tone, secret and deadly. "Yes! You've got it now! You know what you've done, don't you? You know what you've done."

He made no sound nor sign, but lay with bright, averted eyes, and averted, bleeding face.

"You ought to be *killed,* that's what you ought," said Annie, tensely. "You ought to be *killed.*" And there was a terrifying lust in her voice.

Polly was ceasing to laugh, and giving long-drawn Oh-h-hs and sighs as she came to herself.

"He's got to choose," she said vaguely.

"Oh, yes, he has," said Laura, with vindictive decision.

"Do you hear—do you hear?" said Annie. And with a sharp move-ment, that made him wince, she turned his face to her.

"Do you hear?" she repeated, shaking him.

But he was quite dumb. She fetched him a sharp slap on the face. He started, and his eyes widened. Then his face darkened with de-fiance, after all.

"Do you hear?" she repeated.

He only looked at her with hostile eyes.

"Speak!" she said, putting her face devilishly near his.

"What?" he said, almost overcome.

"You've got to *choose!*" she cried, as if it were some terrible menace, and as if it hurt her that she could not exact more.

"What?" he said, in fear.

"Choose your girl, Coddy. You've got to choose her now. And you'll get your neck broken if you play any more of your tricks, my boy. You're settled now."

There was a pause. Again he averted his face. He was cunning in his overthrow. He did not give in to them really—no, not if they tore him to bits.

"All right, then," he said, "I choose Annie." His voice was strange and full of malice. Annie let go of him as if he had been a hot coal.

"He's chosen Annie!" said the girls in chorus.

"Me!" cried Annie. She was still kneeling, but away from him. He was still lying prostrate, with averted face. The girls grouped uneasily around.

"Me!" repeated Annie, with a terrible bitter accent.

Then she got up, drawing away from him with strange disgust and bitterness.

"I wouldn't touch him," she said.

But her face quivered with a kind of agony, she seemed as if she would fall. The other girls turned aside. He remained lying on the floor, with his torn clothes and bleeding, averted face.

"Oh, if he's chosen—" said Polly.

"I don't want him—he can choose again," said Annie, with the same rather bitter hopelessness.

"Get up," said Polly, lifting his shoulder. "Get up."

He rose slowly, a strange, ragged, dazed creature. The girls eyed him from a distance, curiously, furtively, dangerously.

"Who wants him?" cried Laura, roughly.

"Nobody," they answered, with contempt. Yet each one of them waited for him to look at her, hoped he would look at her. All except Annie, and something was broken in her.

He, however, kept his face closed and averted from them all. There was a silence of the end. He picked up the torn pieces of his tunic, without knowing what to do with them. The girls stood about uneasily, flushed, panting, tidying their hair and their dress unconsciously, and watching him. He looked at none of them. He espied his cap in a corner, and went and picked it up. He put it on his head, and one of the girls burst into a shrill, hysteric laugh at the sight he presented. He, however, took no heed, but went straight to where his overcoat hung on a peg. The girls moved away from contact with him as if he had been an electric wire. He put on his coat and buttoned it down. Then he rolled his tunic-rags into a bundle, and stood before the locked door, dumbly.

"Open the door, somebody," said Laura.

"Annie's got the key," said one.

Annie silently offered the key to the girls. Nora unlocked the door.

"Tit for tat, old man," she said. "Show yourself a man, and don't bear a grudge."

But without a word or sign he had opened the door and gone, his face closed, his head dropped.

"That'll learn him," said Laura.

"Coddy!" said Nora.

"Shut up, for God's sake!" cried Annie fiercely, as if in torture.

"Well, I'm ready to go, Polly. Look sharp!" said Muriel.

The girls were anxious to be off. They were tidying themselves hurriedly, with mute, stupefied faces.

Katherine Mansfield

MR. AND MRS. DOVE

Katherine Mansfield succeeds in getting a good deal of
incidental exposition and characterization into this delicately
shaded little story of Reggie's courtship. With her usual
artistry she tells of Reggie's farewell visit to "dear little Anne"
and of the circumstances of his leave-taking. The reader
will live through Reggie's emotional turmoil on this quiet
afternoon—disturbed on occasion only by the gentle cooing of
the doves—and will understand Reggie's feelings about his
mother and even his reaction to what Anne says about
Mr. and Mrs. Dove.

Of course he knew—no man better—that he hadn't a ghost
of a chance, he hadn't an earthly. The very idea of such a thing was
preposterous. So preposterous that he'd perfectly understand it if her
father—well, whatever her father chose to do he'd perfectly understand. In fact, nothing short of desperation, nothing short of the fact
that this was positively his last day in England for God knows how
long, would have screwed him up to it. And even now . . . He chose
a tie out of the chest of drawers, a blue and cream check tie, and sat
on the side of his bed. Supposing she replied, "What impertinence!"
would he be surprised? Not in the least, he decided, turning up his soft
collar and turning it down over the tie. He expected her to say something like that. He didn't see, if he looked at the affair dead soberly,
what else she could say.

Here he was! And nervously he tied a bow in front of the mirror,
jammed his hair down with both hands, pulled out the flaps of his
jacket pockets. Making between £500 and £600 a year on a fruit farm
in—of all places—Rhodesia. No capital. Not a penny coming to him.
No chance of his income increasing for at least four years. As for looks
and all that sort of thing, he was completely out of the running. He
couldn't even boast of top-hole health, for the East Africa business had
knocked him out so thoroughly that he'd had to take six months' leave.

He was still fearfully pale—worse even than usual this afternoon, he thought, bending forward and peering into the mirror. Good heavens! What had happened? His hair looked almost bright green. Dash it all, he hadn't green hair at all events. That was a bit too steep. And then the green light trembled in the glass; it was the shadow from the tree outside. Reggie turned away, took out his cigarette case, but remembering how the mater hated him to smoke in his bedroom, put it back again and drifted over to the chest of drawers. No, he was dashed if he could think of one blessed thing in his favour, while she . . . Ah! . . . He stopped dead, folded his arms, and leaned hard against the chest of drawers.

And in spite of her position, her father's wealth, the fact that she was an only child and far and away the most popular girl in the neighbourhood; in spite of her beauty and her cleverness—cleverness!—it was a great deal more than that, there was really nothing she couldn't do; he fully believed, had it been necessary, she would have been a genius at anything—in spite of the fact that her parents adored her, and she them, and they'd as soon let her go all that way as . . . In spite of every single thing you could think of, so terrific was his love that he couldn't help hoping. Well, was it hope? Or was this queer, timid longing to have the chance of looking after her, of making it his job to see that she had everything she wanted, and that nothing came near her that wasn't perfect—just love? How he loved her! He squeezed hard against the chest of drawers and murmured to it, "I love her, I love her!" And just for the moment he was with her on the way to Umtali. It was night. She sat in a corner asleep. Her soft chin was tucked into her soft collar, her gold-brown lashes lay on her cheeks. He doted on her delicate little nose, her perfect lips, her ear like a baby's, and the gold-brown curl that half covered it. They were passing through the jungle. It was warm and dark and far away. Then she woke up and said, "Have I been asleep?" and he answered, "Yes. Are you all right? Here, let me—" And he leaned forward to . . . He bent over her. This was such bliss that he could dream no further. But it gave him the courage to bound downstairs, to snatch his straw hat from the hall, and to say as he closed the front door, "Well, I can only try my luck, that's all."

But his luck gave him a nasty jar, to say the least, almost immediately. Promenading up and down the garden path with Chinny and Biddy, the ancient Pekes, was the mater. Of course Reginald was fond of the mater and all that. She—she meant well, she had no end of grit, and so on. But there was no denying it, she was rather a grim parent. And there had been moments, many of them, in Reggie's life, before Uncle Alick died and left him the fruit farm, when he was convinced that to be a widow's only son was about the worst punishment a chap could have. And what made it rougher than ever was that she was positively all that he had. She wasn't only a combined parent, as it were, but she had quarrelled with all her own and the governor's relations before Reggie had won his first trouser pockets. So that whenever Reggie was homesick out there, sitting on his dark veranda by starlight, while the gramophone cried, "Dear, what is Life but Love?" his only vision was of the mater, tall and stout, rustling down the garden path, with Chinny and Biddy at her heels. . . .

The mater, with her scissors outspread to snap the head of a dead something or other, stopped at the sight of Reggie.

"You are not going out, Reginald?" she asked, seeing that he was.

"I'll be back for tea, mater," said Reggie weakly, plunging his hands into his jacket pockets.

Snip. Off came a head. Reggie almost jumped.

"I should have thought you could have spared your mother your last afternoon," said she.

Silence. The Pekes stared. They understood every word of the mater's. Biddy lay down with her tongue poked out; she was so fat and glossy she looked like a lump of half-melted toffee. But Chinny's porcelain eyes gloomed at Reginald, and he sniffed faintly, as though the whole world were one unpleasant smell. Snip, went the scissors again. Poor little beggars; they were getting it!

"And where are you going, if your mother may ask?" asked the mater.

It was over at last, but Reggie did not slow down until he was out of sight of the house and half-way to Colonel Proctor's. Then only he noticed what a top-hole afternoon it was. It had been raining all the morning, late summer rain, warm, heavy, quick, and now the sky was clear, except for a long tail of little clouds, like ducklings, sailing over the forest. There was just enough wind to shake the last drops off the trees; one warm star splashed on his hand. Ping!—another drummed on his hat. The empty road gleamed, the hedges smelled of briar, and how big and bright the hollyhocks glowed in the cottage gardens. And here was Colonel Proctor's—here it was already. His hand was on the gate, his elbow jogged the syringa bushes, and petals and pollen scattered over his coat sleeve. But wait a bit. This was too quick altogether. He'd meant to think the whole thing out again. Here, steady. But he was walking up the path, with the huge rose bushes on either side. It can't be done like this. But his hand had grasped the bell, given it a pull, and started it pealing wildly, as if he'd come to say the house was on fire. The housemaid must have been in the hall, too, for the front door flashed open, and Reggie was shut in the empty drawing-room before that confounded bell had stopped ringing. Strangely enough, when it did, the big room, shadowy, with some one's parasol lying on top of the grand piano, bucked him up—or rather, excited him. It was so quiet, and yet in one moment the door would open, and his fate be decided. The feeling was not unlike that of being at the dentist's; he was almost reckless. But at the same time, to his immense surprise, Reggie heard himself saying, "Lord, Thou knowest, Thou hast not done *much* for me. . . ." That pulled him up; that made him realize again how dead serious it was. Too late. The door handle turned. Anne came in, crossed the shadowy space between them, gave him her hand, and said, in her small, soft voice, "I'm so sorry, father is out. And mother is having a day in town, hat-hunting. There's only me to entertain you, Reggie."

Reggie gasped, pressed his own hat to his jacket buttons, and stammered out, "As a matter of fact, I've only come . . . to say good-bye."

"Oh!" cried Anne softly—she stepped back from him and her grey eyes danced—"what a *very* short visit!"

Then, watching him, her chin tilted, she laughed outright, a long, soft peal, and walked away from him over to the piano, and leaned against it, playing with the tassel of the parasol.

"I'm so sorry," she said, "to be laughing like this. I don't know why I do. It's just a bad ha-habit." And suddenly she stamped her grey shoe, and took a pocket-handkerchief out of her white woolly jacket. "I really must conquer it, it's too absurd," said she.

"Good heavens, Anne," cried Reggie, "I love to hear you laughing! I can't imagine anything more—"

But the truth was, and they both knew it, she wasn't always laughing; it wasn't really a habit. Only ever since the day they'd met, ever since that very first moment, for some strange reason that Reggie wished to God he understood, Anne had laughed at him. Why? It didn't matter where they were or what they were talking about. They might begin by being as serious as possible, dead serious—at any rate, as far as he was concerned—but then suddenly, in the middle of a sentence, Anne would glance at him, and a little quick quiver passed over her face. Her lips parted, her eyes danced, and she began laughing.

Another queer thing about it was, Reggie had an idea she didn't herself know why she laughed. He had seen her turn away, frown, suck in her cheeks, press her hands together. But it was no use. The long, soft peal sounded, even while she cried, "I don't know why I'm laughing." It was a mystery. . . .

Now she tucked the handkerchief away.

"Do sit down," said she. "And smoke, won't you? There are cigarettes in that little box beside you. I'll have one too." He lighted a match for her, and as she bent forward he saw the tiny flame glow in the pearl ring she wore. "It is to-morrow that you're going, isn't it?" said Anne.

"Yes, to-morrow as ever was," said Reggie, and he blew a little fan of smoke. Why on earth was he so nervous? Nervous wasn't the word for it.

"It's—it's frightfully hard to believe," he added.

"Yes—isn't it?" said Anne softly, and she leaned forward and rolled the point of her cigarette round the green ash-tray. How beautiful she looked like that!—simply beautiful—and she was so small in that immense chair. Reginald's heart swelled with tenderness, but it was her voice, her soft voice, that made him tremble. "I feel you've been here for years," she said.

Reginald took a deep breath of his cigarette. "It's ghastly, this idea of going back," he said.

"Coo-roo-coo-coo-coo," sounded from the quiet.

"But you're fond of being out there, aren't you?" said Anne. She hooked her finger through her pearl necklace. "Father was saying only the other night how lucky he thought you were to have a life of your own." And she looked up at him. Reginald's smile was rather wan. "I don't feel fearfully lucky," he said lightly.

"Roo-coo-coo-coo," came again. And Anne murmured, "You mean it's lonely."

"Oh, it isn't the loneliness I care about," said Reginald, and he stumped his cigarette savagely on the green ash-tray. "I could stand any amount of it, used to like it even. It's the idea of—" Suddenly, to his horror, he felt himself blushing.

"Roo-coo-coo-coo! Roo-coo-coo-coo!"

Anne jumped up. "Come and say good-bye to my doves," she said. "They've been moved to the side veranda. You do like doves, don't you, Reggie?"

"Awfully," said Reggie, so fervently that as he opened the French window for her and stood to one side, Anne ran forward and laughed at the doves instead.

To and fro, to and fro over the fine red sand on the floor of the dove house, walked the two doves. One was always in front of the other. One ran forward, uttering a little cry, and the other followed, solemnly bowing and bowing. "You see," explained Anne, "the one in front, she's Mrs. Dove. She looks at Mr. Dove and gives that little laugh and runs forward, and he follows her, bowing and bowing. And that makes her laugh again. Away she runs, and after her," cried Anne, and she sat back on her heels, "comes poor Mr. Dove, bowing and bowing . . . and that's their whole life. They never do anything else, you know." She got up and took some yellow grains out of a bag on the roof of the dove house. "When you think of them, out in Rhodesia, Reggie, you can be sure that is what they will be doing. . . ."

Reggie gave no sign of having seen the doves or of having heard a word. For the moment he was conscious only of the immense effort it took to tear his secret out of himself and offer it to Anne. "Anne, do you think you could ever care for me?" It was done. It was over. And in the little pause that followed Reginald saw the garden open to the light, the blue quivering sky, the flutter of leaves on the veranda poles, and Anne turning over the grains of maize on her palm with one finger. Then slowly she shut her hand, and the new world faded as she murmured slowly, "No, never in that way." But he had scarcely time to feel anything before she walked quickly away, and he followed her down the steps, along the garden path, under the pink rose arches, across the lawn. There, with the gay herbaceous border behind her, Anne faced Reginald. "It isn't that I'm not awfully fond of you," she said. "I am. But"—her eyes widened—"not in the way"—a quiver passed over her face—"one ought to be fond of—" Her lips parted, and she couldn't stop herself. She began laughing. "There, you see, you see," she cried, "it's your check t-tie. Even at this moment, when one would think one really would be solemn, your tie reminds me fearfully of the bow-tie that cats wear in pictures! Oh, please forgive me for being so horrid, please!"

Reggie caught hold of her little warm hand. "There's no question of forgiving you," he said quickly. "How could there be? And I do believe I know why I make you laugh. It's because you're so far above me in every way that I am somehow ridiculous. I see that, Anne. But if I were to—"

"No, no." Anne squeezed his hand hard. "It's not that. That's all wrong. I'm not far above you at all. You're much better than I am. You're marvellously unselfish and . . . and kind and simple. I'm none of those things. You don't know me. I'm the most awful character," said Anne. "Please don't interrupt. And besides, that's not the point. The point is"—she shook her head—"I couldn't possibly marry a man I laughed at. Surely you see that. The man I marry—" breathed Anne softly. She broke off. She drew her hand away, and looking at Reggie she smiled strangely, dreamily. "The man I marry—"

And it seemed to Reggie that a tall, handsome, brilliant stranger stepped in front of him and took his place—the kind of man that Anne and he had seen often at the theatre, walking on to the stage from nowhere, without a word catching the heroine in his arms, and after one long, tremendous look, carrying her off to anywhere . . .

Reggie bowed to his vision. "Yes, I see," he said huskily.

"Do you?" said Anne. "Oh, I do hope you do. Because I feel so horrid about it. It's so hard to explain. You know I've never—" She stopped. Reggie looked at her. She was smiling. "Isn't it funny?" she said. "I can say anything to you. I always have been able to from the very beginning."

He tried to smile, to say "I'm glad." She went on. "I've never known any one I like as much as I like you. I've never felt so happy with any one. But I'm sure it's not what people and what books mean when they talk about love. Do you understand? Oh, if you only knew how horrid I feel. But we'd be like . . . like Mr. and Mrs. Dove."

That did it. That seemed to Reginald final, and so terribly true that he could hardly bear it. "Don't drive it home," he said, and he turned away from Anne and looked across the lawn. There was the gardener's cottage, with the dark ilex-tree beside it. A wet, blue thumb of transparent smoke hung above the chimney. It didn't look real. How his throat ached! Could he speak? He had a shot. "I must be getting along home," he croaked, and he began walking across the lawn. But Anne ran after him. "No, don't. You can't go yet," she said imploringly. "You can't possibly go away feeling like that." And she stared up at him frowning, biting her lip.

"Oh, that's all right," said Reggie, giving himself a shake. "I'll . . . I'll—" And he waved his hand as much to say "get over it."

"But this is awful," said Anne. She clasped her hands and stood in front of him. "Surely you do see how fatal it would be for us to marry, don't you?"

"Oh, quite, quite," said Reggie, looking at her with haggard eyes.

"How wrong, how wicked, feeling as I do. I mean, it's all very well for Mr. and Mrs. Dove. But imagine that in real life—imagine it!"

"Oh, absolutely," said Reggie, and he started to walk on. But again Anne stopped him. She tugged at his sleeve, and to his astonishment, this time, instead of laughing, she looked like a little girl who was going to cry.

"Then why, if you understand, are you so un-unhappy?" she wailed. "Why do you mind so fearfully? Why do you look so aw-awful?"

Reggie gulped, and again he waved something away. "I can't help it," he said, "I've had a blow. If I cut off now, I'll be able to—"

"How can you talk of cutting off now?" said Anne scornfully. She stamped her foot at Reggie; she was crimson. "How can you be so cruel? I can't let you go until I know for certain that you are just as happy as you were before you asked me to marry you. Surely you must see that, it's so simple."

But it did not seem at all simple to Reginald. It seemed impossibly difficult.

"Even if I can't marry you, how can I know that you're all that way away, with only that awful mother to write to, and that you're miserable, and that it's all my fault?"

"It's not your fault. Don't think that. It's just fate." Reggie took her hand off his sleeve and kissed it. "Don't pity me, dear little Anne," he said gently. And this time he nearly ran, under the pink arches, along the garden path.

"Roo-coo-coo-coo! Roo-coo-coo-coo!" sounded from the veranda. "Reggie, Reggie," from the garden.

He stopped, he turned. But when she saw his timid, puzzled look, she gave a little laugh.

"Come back, Mr. Dove," said Anne. And Reginald came slowly across the lawn.

Elizabeth Hardwick

THE GOLDEN STALLION

This quietly subtle story tells of the singular relationship
between Martha Fiske and Tony Jones—a baffling relationship
that was to result in a most unusual love affair. Martha Fiske
herself is baffled at first by the "obliqueness" of Tony Jones's
talk and by the "indefinable singularity" of his appeal. It is
on the occasion of their first meeting—at the time when
Tony accepts Martha's suggestion of the golden stallion as
a good enough symbol for the town—that he says, "There
are certain hidden qualities that give a place its meaning.
Just like a person." He does not realize the applicability
of this remark to himself.

The development of a close relationship between this
oddly matched pair has its origin in the most unpromising
beginnings. Martha knew by instinct, the author tells us, that
"theirs was one of those haphazard meetings that must
mean something to both, either for evil or for good."
And her instinct is true. Certainly the story's suspense is due to a
continuing uncertainty in the reader's mind, right up to the
final sentence, as to which of these alternatives is to be their
destiny. In the "warm golden rectangle of security" which
is Martha's living room, an unspoken tragedy is foreshadowed,
but it is not revealed until the whole story has been told.

Martha Fiske met the young soldier at a party. There were
several other soldiers present, but he was the only one she noticed. He
was about six feet tall and had the gracefully heavy body of an athlete.
His face was large and handsome with prominent, well-shaped features,
but his mouth and eyes were curiously small. Perhaps it was the remarkable alertness of those small eyes that made him look like a
wicked little urchin. A narrow, white scar was just barely visible on his
cheek. At first she couldn't identify the special quality that drew her to
him. And then he smiled and she knew. His smile was tender and childlike and made him appear momentarily helpless. This smile—it was
hardly more than a downward twisting of his mouth—had the effect
of an apology, as if he meant to say that though he might be good looking and confident there was an inviolable delicacy in him. The young

soldier quickly became the center of attention. Perhaps this was natural since he was sitting in the middle of the room, but she didn't think it such an accident as that. To her he assumed authority because he was a specimen of manhood far removed from the husbands who were telling stories heard many times before and exhibiting the limitations of their interests. He was also unlike his fellow soldiers. They were rawboned, commonplace boys who seemed extremely uncomfortable and kept saying, "Thank you, Ma'm," at every turn. The handsome soldier ingeniously disowned any possible connection with the other boys and never acknowledged, by a reference to the army, their common identity. In thus cutting himself off from his comrades, he also repudiated the generosity of the hospitable civilians. He seemed to accept his presence at the party as a natural tribute to his personality, rather than his soldier status.

She watched him all through the evening and noted that he did not get drunk and that his moods alternated between boredom of a tolerant, not unpleasant, sort and amusement which was, she felt, a bit patronizing. He said nothing about himself, at least not where he was from, what he had been or hoped to be. It is true he was asked, but he simply did not bother to answer. And yet, for all his lack of interest, she noticed he became distressed when the conversation lagged and it was always he who started it again. At such times he would look down at his glass, cough, as if to get attention, and then say, "Are the autumns in Kentucky always cool?" She observed he was not the least interested in the question. He looked away, in the manner of a faithful servant who had performed an expected duty and could now retire, when the men started to give comparative figures on cold and hot spells and to mention frozen pipes or prolonged summer droughts. He would then be silent and withdrawn until the next break in the conversation provided the opportunity to pay someone a casual compliment. The compliments, also, were presented as an obligation to some mysterious source.

Only once did Martha Fiske speak directly to the soldier, because she was both shy and aloof and did not talk much except with those seated next to her. When she was with more than one person she hardly spoke above a whisper and, though she was exceedingly civil and much given to sympathetic inquiries about the health and happiness of her friends, she knew her conversation lacked animation because of her reticence about her own affairs. From the first, the soldier's talent for asking the question most likely to appeal to the listeners had interested her. She put it down as an instinctive affability not unlike her own automatic courtesy. The soldier abruptly left his chair and went to the window. He stood there for some time in silence, as if he were absorbed in the view. Immediately she saw the paradox of his body that was similar to the strength and weakness of his face. Though he was strong, his movements were slow and deliberate. It was not that he appeared physically weak, but that he seemed to be burdened with an inner fatigue that was at once elegant and rather absurd. The guests were visibly startled when he suddenly said, "I've been lots of places and a new town is like a new person to me. There are certain hidden qualities that give a place its meaning. Just like a person." He paused and everyone stared at him. What other young man would have the daring to speak as he did? He spoke as an actor, more or less formally, without joking, mumbling or qualifying. "There is always some symbol, if you have the sort of mind that likes those things. I mean something that will recall the town. Even *here* there must be a distinctive thing." He hadn't a definite accent, but one would have guessed from the general nature of his behavior that he came from a large city. It occurred to Martha Fiske—she felt herself a bit more understanding of odd young men than the others—that he might be thoroughly artificial. She didn't object. On the contrary, it gave his personality a gloss she admired.

The men seemed particularly embarrassed by his question and for a moment no one attempted an answer. Then she, from the comparative isolation of the corner in which she was sitting, said, "There is a golden stallion weather vane on top of the courthouse."

The soldier stretched and yawned before he actually turned to look at her. "I beg your pardon?" he said, though she felt certain he had understood her. He moved away from the window and again took the chair in the middle of the room. Martha Fiske knew he was looking at her and she allowed herself the briefest glance at his face. At first she saw only that stubbornly maintained composure which distinguished him, but, as she continued to stare at him, she noticed that his lips trembled slightly.

"A golden stallion," he said, after forcing her to repeat. And then he laughed and turned his head around the room so that he brought everyone into his amusement. "Perhaps that's it." His laughter was nothing more than a few staccato grunts and there was not a trace of mirth in it. Again she looked up at him in her guarded way. Their eyes met and an odd feeling came over her. She believed he had tried to give her some personal attention he had denied the others.

He seemed distracted and annoyed when someone said, "Martha knows everything of that sort. She knows all about antiques and the names of historical places. If it's a symbol you want, she can give it to you."

"I wasn't thinking of historical symbols," he replied, "but something a bit less traditional. However, the golden stallion will do very well." He put his hand over his eyes and sighed very deeply. He was taller and stronger than anyone else in the room, and yet when he sighed there was a general flash of self-conscious laughter meant to reprimand him for the pose he had assumed. He made no response to the laughter and it vanished.

She found, later, that she was not clear about the rest of the evening. The conversation with the soldier had changed her from an observer to a participant in the party and this, because of her spontaneous interest in him, put her under a strain. The only thing she was certain of was that something had been established on this night. His head inclined in her direction when he spoke and when he was silent his eyes were fastened upon her face. In her usual way, she left just as the evening reached its peak. Though there was no particular reason for her departure, she, too, had her eccentricities and being the first to leave a party was a convention of her behavior. She was aware there was something planned in the act beyond the mere fatigue of social life. It was, she supposed, one of the tiny, harmless ways in which she sought to distinguish herself and had, no doubt, been inherited from her father who had said that in order not to be a mediocrity one had either to arrive places late or to leave them early. Also she had developed a certain technique for getting away with the least confusion. She merely slipped behind the circle of chairs, disappeared into the bedroom and then, almost on tiptoe and with her head down, came back to wave a vague and apologetic good night to her friends. Her way was so shy that people instinctively let her get away without the usual chatter. She was at the door before the hostess had time to reach her. To her surprise the soldier was standing beside her in the half-darkness of the hall.

"Good-night," she said.

She watched him for a moment. He was standing very close to her. And there it was—that way he had of pleading with her without saying a word. Already she was thinking of their exceedingly good possibilities for friendship. He continued to look at her and she felt obliged to give him some evidence of her feeling. She said, "I live very close to the college where you are stationed. Right across the street, in fact."

"I know," he said, quite softly. "I know."

His hand had fallen on her sleeve and she, from timidity, drew away. Still he said nothing, though there was the suggestion of impatience in his silence. "Will you come over sometime? Will you?" she said.

He smiled and nodded.

She started down the steps and was almost to the street when she heard him, as if he were laughing, call to her, "What is your name?"

"Martha Fiske," she answered.

"Mrs.?" he asked.

She stopped and turned around. However, there was no need for her to answer, because the door of the house had closed and she could no longer see the soldier.

Martha Fiske did not sleep well that night. She was disturbed by her thoughts of the soldier. It was not that she feared she had been too eager in her invitation. (She had long ago realized that a quiet, timid life gave one all sorts of privileges.) It did not matter that she might have been overheard and, since she was a married woman living alone, reproved for entertaining male visitors. Actually she was blessed with an extraordinary independence. She had always lived in her own way and the fact that this way was undramatic was merely the accident of her nature. Had she had emotions of another sort, those, too, would have been expressed without fear. In thinking of the soldier she concluded that she liked him because he was similar to the other young men who had come, too late, into her life and who were the only people she had ever truly cared for. Indeed he was not, as the others had been, somewhat girlish, but he shared with them an indefinable singularity. She was almost thirty—it occurred to her the soldier might be older than she, but for some perverse reason she liked to think him younger—and had not discovered until a few years ago that there were men with whom she could have both security and excitement. Her youth had been as normal as possible for a shy, almost taciturn girl. Her mother had once told her she was not hearty enough for most men's taste and she readily admitted her difficulty in overcoming that period of semiformality that precluded even the most superficial intimacy. Yet, she had had many friends and there had always been men who were, in an unspecified way, her suitors. As a rule these men were themselves fainthearted and unequal to the rigors of romance, but they seemed to find her a pleasant and acceptable companion. And, as she had expected, she had married one of the men for whom she felt neither friendship nor love, but only a high degree of tolerance. She had married a doctor, Robert Fiske, because he had asked her to do so. They had lived together one month before he was called away to the army. He had been gone more than a year now.

The mainstay of her existence was her flair for decorations and her limited knowledge of period architecture, furniture and the like. Though this was largely a hobby, she sometimes accepted money for the selection of frames and drapes or the evaluation of an old piece of furniture some circumspect buyer had discovered on the back porch of a Negro shack. Her interest deepened and she had decided, several years before, to take classes in art appreciation at the College. For the most part this was an unhappy decision. Her life became miserable the moment she stepped into the classroom. She hadn't the slightest notion what was going on, couldn't understand a thing the teacher said or spell more than one out of a dozen names under discussion. She knew hardly a fact about art history except that certain buildings in the town were part of something called the Greek Revival and that Henry Clay's garden had been laid out by L'Enfant. Her pretensions were slight, but this daily reminder of her ignorance threatened to destroy the little confidence she had and so, after a few months, she discontinued the classes and fell back upon her familiarity with corner cupboards, antique glassware, and portraits by the Kentuckian, Jouett. However, her excursion into study bore some fruit in that she made a number of new friends. She was a strikingly handsome woman, tall, with long, almost black, hair which she wore in a severe and rather out-of-date fashion. Her clothes were ordered from New York and were too odd to please the bachelor doctors, lawyers, and tobacco buyers with whom she associated, but they found immediate approval among several of the young male students. Perhaps her face was something like a monkey's, as one of the boys had said, but at the same time there was real distinction in her fine eyebrows and prominent cheek bones. She learned from these young men that she had *style* and, though she maintained her extensive reserve, her heart was deeply touched by their enthusiasm and friendship. It was not long before the young men started to come to her house and even her mother, with whom she had lived until the latter's death, found them interesting and lively. For two or three years Martha Fiske had experienced a sweetness of male companionship that was the most satisfactory thing in her life. The house was frequently noisy with the sound of records by Beatrice Lillie and Marlene Dietrich and obscurely bawdy songs by night club performers whose names she could not remember. She heard of great stage performances, of public characters who drank or took dope and had fabulous love affairs with other public characters. The boys knew an astonishing number of details about the lives of famous people. She heard a lot about Dorothy Parker, though she could not, to her great distress, remember any of the anecdotes. She was happy to experience the lives of the famous, but that alone would not have given her satisfaction. She liked best to hear the intimate difficulties of her new friends and to brood over their accounts of family dissension. She learned their secret spirit, hurt pride and petulant iconoclasm. Never had she come so close to another person and never had she been so serenely impersonal. Her life was enriched, also, by the boys' ambitions to take singing, dancing or acting lessons and, in those days, her acquaintanceship seemed to be a catalogue of great people to come. But one by one the boys had disappeared, usually with one of her checks in his pocket, either to New York or to the army. She was driven back to her old life and to the friends who seemed now unusually lethargic. Again she felt odd and timid and said yes when Robert Fiske asked her to marry him. Often she thought she would have consented to the proposal of any respectable man, because she believed women should marry and also because she felt her chances for making other friends like the young boys were over.

When her husband went away, she didn't miss him much. Their one month together had been uncomfortable, because he was more or less inhibited by her silence which he took as evidence of an artistic temperament. She was aware her manner made her husband less communicative than he might otherwise have been, but she didn't know how to bring him into her life. Sometimes she dreamed she would get to know him as intimately as she had known the young boys. She hoped he might tell her his fears, angers and ambitions, his memories of childhood. When a certain amount of time had passed without his indicating a need to unburden himself, she decided he was happy and had nothing to say. This conclusion made her, on the contrary, very melancholy because it deprived her of the opportunity to exercise her talent for sympathy. Writing letters to her husband had been, from the first, an almost intolerable burden. She never knew if she had put in enough *dears* or if her desire for his return seemed sincere. When she had, as all decorum demanded, to write "I love you" her fingers began to quiver. The months passed and she found it impossible to think of him as anything except a man who was away and to whom she had to write.

On the morning after the party she felt unusually alert and happy. Though she almost always slept well, she superstitiously considered the restless night a good omen. She sat at her window and watched the soldiers drilling on the grounds across from her house. The rows of brown uniforms had never before seemed particularly romantic; but, today, with the bright sun covering the field and the flags flying on the building, she found herself thinking of the old-fashioned comic operetta encampments and the rough gaiety of movies about the Foreign Legion. (There was no rôle in these ready-made day dreams she could play, for there was nothing of the ragamuffin, gypsy coquette in her. In all her dreams she remained the same: a dignified, Southern woman who was the sympathetic observer of life's exciting frivolities.) She did not think very much about the soldier, except to regret not having set a definite date for their meeting. However, her way was naturally slow and untroubled and she could let things happen as they would. As usual she went out in the afternoon to attend to shopping and business. When she returned there was a note in her mail box saying the soldier would visit her at eight in the evening. It was signed with the initials, T. J., and she realized she had forgot his name. For some minutes she studied his handwriting. The script was exceedingly large and irregular, like that of a child.

The soldier didn't arrive at eight. The night outside was clear and cool. She was pleased the wind had risen, because it gave her an excuse to make a fire in the grate and that was the domestic duty she most loved. She waited for him, but without impatience. Her mind was beautifully empty and tranquil when she was alone. She gave herself so completely to her solitary dreaming that she was startled when the bell finally rang. It was well past nine o'clock. She did not hurry to answer; instead she stopped and observed, as if the first time, the rather commonplace austerity of her living room. Though she was not often critical of herself or of others, she did in brief moments of tension, such as the arrival of the soldier, experience the wildest and most agonizing sense of personal inferiority. Tonight this fleeting sensation of inadequacy gave her a capricious desire to destroy all the things she had so painstakingly collected. Suddenly she was skeptical of the value of her tables, frames and bird prints. They became the undeniable emblems of her provincialism. The aspect of the soldier she remembered most vividly was his way of making things *small*. Now that she was to see him she felt herself diminished. The town in which she lived shrank and all her possibilities were worthless.

When she opened the door, her first impression was that the man standing before her was a stranger. Of course, she knew the next moment it was the young soldier, but she was unprepared for the change in him. What could it be? A kind of general shabbiness, she decided. When he saw her look at him his expression changed and he managed to recover some of his former self-possession.

"Am I late?" he said, hesitantly.

"Yes, you are," she answered. She pointed to the living room and he walked past her.

She did not immediately ask him to sit down and he, in some confusion, said, "I'm sorry. I didn't realize it was so late." He shrugged his shoulders in a vague gesture of repentance. She was rather annoyed that he should think her angry about the time, because she wasn't at all responsive to the conventions of social behavior. Her curtness came out of her surprise that the soldier had so many personalities. He had only to change his posture to be another human being. One moment he was impressive and the next he was guarded, feeble, second rate. He seemed a little less in every way than she had thought him. The fine color of the personality she had seen the night before had faded. What she saw meant to her that he was, after all, *nobody*, really nothing exceptional. She was glad and it gave her the courage to be open with him. Very quickly she organized her new impressions of his appearance. His hair grew low on his forehead; his face, at times extremely handsome, could also be merely ordinary. At the door he had reminded her of nothing so much as an appealing little beggar who, with cap in hand and eyes downcast, made the most of the pathos and contempt he aroused.

"I have no memory for names," she said, ignoring his apology. "Perhaps I didn't hear yours clearly last night."

"My name is Tony," he said. "Tony Jones. It suits me, doesn't it?"

"I don't know," she said seriously. When he said nothing, she asked him to sit down.

There was, certainly, an initial measure of awkwardness in their meeting. She, however, saw it as only a surface coolness and was surprised that she felt little real discomfort with Tony Jones. Perhaps they could not talk freely, and yet their very lack of crisp, nervous brightness seemed to her a miracle. They had the melancholy ease of friends. The soldier took off his coat and lighted a cigarette. She watched, without any embarrassment at all, this real entrance into her life which was symbolized by his coat on her sofa and the leisurely way he was settling himself for the evening. A wave of excitement came over her when she realized how deeply the image of the soldier had impressed her. It did not matter that the image was as yet blurred. What she had responded to was the man himself, that part of his nature which was naked and unalterable and which she felt mysteriously destined to discover. She knew by instinct theirs was one of those haphazard meetings that must mean something to both, either for evil or for good. The mere fact that she had been very deeply touched by him, without even being sure she liked him, was enough to draw them into some common history, however short.

When they were comfortably seated before the fire, Tony Jones, with the polite incaution that had stamped all their brief conversations, said, "I like you. I suppose you noticed it."

"If you do, I'm glad you told me," she said. No matter what he said, his eyes were always cold. They seemed to belong to another face.

"We don't need to begin in the usual way, then," he went on. "I don't see any reason why we shouldn't accept each other from the start." When she did not comment he added, "As friends only. You needn't fear anything else."

The neatness of his speech oppressed her slightly. The flat clarity of his conversation succeeded only in making his character, that which she was extremely anxious to comprehend, more and more obscure. She remembered now something told her at the party: the soldier had been *nowhere,* in the military sense. He was a recent recruit and had, therefore, probably suffered none of the currently possible disasters.

"Do you mind the army very much?" she asked. He lifted his shoulders to indicate it meant nothing one way or another. She had not supposed it would. His absorptions, whatever they were, went far back into his life and could not be displaced by public history. This she also accepted with relief, because she was unskilled in the specific anxieties that war might produce in intricate personalities; and, further, it was additional proof that he was nothing beyond himself, nothing he hadn't always been.

He looked carefully around the room and she thought his eyes stayed for an unnecessarily long time upon a collection of old fans visible through the glass doors of her cupboard. At last he said, "Well, your house is very nice. If it is necessary to be away from really exciting places, then certainly it isn't too much to ask for a little comfort and ease."

She didn't know whether or not he meant to compliment her house and, thereby, to show a similarity of taste. Since she had decided he was only a compelling nonentity, it didn't matter much that he seemed to turn her more important preoccupations into casual whimsicalities.

"What exciting places are you missing?" she asked. She took a cigarette from the box on the table and he came to her with a light. His savage little eyes met hers over the flame.

"Lots of places," he said. He was smiling brightly and turning his head to show the good line of his profile. "I was silly at the party, wasn't I?" he asked, looking at her attentively. "I often put on acts. It doesn't do to let everyone get close to you. With people I like, I'm different." The soldier had very short teeth that were somehow too square and regular. He smoked one cigarette after another and there was always a cloud of smoke around him. For the first time he noticed the portrait of Martha Fiske on the side wall. It had been done when she was in her teens by an itinerant painter who had flourished sketches of the Morgan and Vanderbilt families before the eyes of every prospective customer in the county and had, thereby, got many commissions. The portrait was elegantly sober. The planes in her face had been rejected for a perfectly smooth, oval-shaped countenance and an exquisitely proportioned gloominess of expression that had delighted her mother. Martha Fiske recalled the painter's stories of the great banquets his wealthy patrons had given in appreciation of his work. He was a liar, she thought now. Something in Tony Jones's manner, his way of appraising, made her skeptical. When the soldier had finished with the picture, he went to the desk and took down a volume which her father, at some expense, had had printed. It was titled, *Stories of Our Family*. He flipped through the pages and stopped over photographs of Martha Fiske in the arms of a Negro nurse, her parents in their wedding clothes, and a reproduction of a French menu around which an anecdote, very dear to her father, was told.

He put the book away and sat down again. "What do you think of me?" she asked.

"Nobody is as typical as you would seem to be," he said. He was looking at her now with the same unabashed calculation in which he had examined her belongings. When she put her hand, self-consciously, on her forehead, he said, "What are you afraid of? Don't hide."

"I'm not hiding," she said.

273

She saw now his cautious, despairing smile. "You want to suffer, don't you?" he said, almost tenderly. He didn't wait for her reply. "Well, you can't because that's my rôle."

"Why should you suffer?" she said. Actually she had not been prepared for the obliqueness of his conversation. The young boys to whom she had become attached had been far simpler than this and she had understood them on their own terms.

"I just do," he said. His voice rose in dramatic enthusiasm and she listened to him, not as if he were telling the truth, but as if he were repeating speeches he had learned for particular occasions. "There are so many things. Things you don't know about me now and won't know later. You may think I'm well-adjusted and all that, but I'm not. God, if you could only imagine what life is for some people. You think you worry and suffer and conceal, don't you?" He had moved closer to her and she wanted to draw away until she noticed he was totally preoccupied with the contemplation of his marvelously diversified self. "You don't wake up not wanting to live, do you?" he insisted.

"No, I suppose I don't," she said.

He nodded impatiently. "You will never know, I hope, what it is to feel that your whole life has been a mistake that can never be rectified. Have you had such an experience?"

She was, for all practical purposes, incapable of thought about general attitudes. If he had spoken to her of a particular, even a dreadful, event, she might have been able to make it a part of herself and to give him her peculiarly somber compassion; but here in this room which was, to her, a warm, golden rectangle of security she found it impossible to think of his diffuse sorrows. Instead she was listening to the familiar sounds of her life: the crackling of the coals as they broke apart and the fearful screams of a cat who had roamed into her yard.

"You didn't answer me," Tony Jones said. "You aren't always uneasy like I am, are you?"

"I can't say. I'm not sure I know what you mean," she said at last. She had not been looking at him and when she did turn his way she was puzzled to see how calm he was, how boyishly relaxed by his own thoughts.

"What mistakes have you made?" she said. He smiled in an impudent way she didn't like. "Tell me," she said, rather imperiously.

He looked down at the carpet and, with those unmotivated variations in mood she had noticed before, seemed to withdraw from her. "Not so fast, Mrs. Fiske. Not so fast," he said.

"I'm sorry," she said.

"Sorry?" The word seemed to please him, for he brushed his hand lightly over hers.

They fell into a lengthy silence which pleased her by providing the opportunity for further impressions of him. His hands, she saw, were short and tough and his fingers had the efficient strength of a workman's. And yet these same fingers could tremble furiously in evidence that his physical strength was often assaulted and nullified by his delicate nervous system. Though he made no effort to talk, she believed silence tormented him. He could be as motionless as an icon and yet betray a need that the world around him be active. After a time he took a sheaf of papers out of his pocket. There were letters, cards, snapshots, an address book and the usual loose scraps of paper. He turned each item over slowly, at times scowling and again smiling in what seemed to be the memory of the contents. Here, evidently, were the numerous odds and ends of his private life. Here were the remnants of the wandering he had done and the places to which he might return. He stacked the papers neatly and put them back in his pocket. "Have you a telephone, Mrs. Fiske?" he asked.

"My name is Martha," she said, not looking at him.

"Have you a telephone?" he repeated. She pointed to the hall and he got up without a word of explanation. His voice was loud enough when he requested the number, but during his conversation nothing was audible to her except his occasional effort to laugh. She did not wish to overhear him; in a fact, a kind of numbness had come over her. She went to the bedroom to get the fringed, pink shawl she sometimes wore in the house and when she returned he was waiting for her.

"You are very nice," he said brightly. "If only all of us had the sense to confine ourselves to nice people. And you are very good looking, even if you don't show yourself off enough. You must consider yourself a beautiful, desirable woman. It will make you more confident." He threw himself into this speech with the zeal of a hopeful salesman.

Who are you and how and where were you given form? she longed to ask. She was fiercely eager to invade the grave in which he had willfully buried himself and to disinter what she believed was a pathetically anguished heart. She wondered why she felt obliged to check herself. Why? Because she believed he would lie to her if she asked him for the kind of information she cherished. Instead she was cold to him and said reproachfully, "Do you consider yourself a handsome man?"

"I guess so," he answered quickly. "But to make you feel better I'll admit I'm not always certain." There was a mirror over the mantel and he, as if to annoy her, got up to look at his reflection. When he turned around again, he gave her his short-lipped, abbreviated smile and said, "What do you think I'll look like when I'm older? I often worry about it. Thank God, my hair is thick!"

To her surprise, she saw that he was not altogether jesting. He waited for her response. "You will always be handsome," she said. She did not care that he was, apparently, vain, mendacious and counterfeit. These matters were outside her interest; she sought something in him not above the traits he had revealed, but below them. She sought the open wound which gave off the poisons.

Again he drew the packet of letters and papers out of his pocket. Perhaps he was not interested in them, she thought, and only wished to make himself seem important. "Do you write so much?" she said, hesitantly.

"God no! I never write. People write to me. Lots of people."

"Does that make you proud?" she asked. A trace of anger had defiled her usually indifferent manner.

"Not at all," he said, dryly. "It's just a fact. People like me and I can't believe that's wrong. You are probably afraid people won't love you, but I happen to be afraid they will care too much. I have a fear of being loved, yet I can't disregard affection. Whenever I have it I hold on to it, because I'm not sure it will come again."

"I thought you didn't want it," she said.

"I want it in general. It's only in particular instances that it begins to suffocate me."

She took in his words one by one, as if there were no connection between them. Her mind was powerfully obstinate and she could sit there with an orderly and discreet smile on her lips even though she could not assimilate these fragments of his soul. As she listened to him, she thought that if he had any judgment at all it was only an animal shrewdness acquired for protection. She knew herself to be uninformed and at times she was aware of the large amount of indolence that constituted the very core of her nature; but she was without fear and, therefore, was quick to recognize it in others.

Tony Jones was now speaking very softly. By an act of will he seemed to be able to throw himself into a gentle hypnosis and to linger there in a submissive dream. "Do you know what I want more than anything in the world?" he said. "I want to love someone. That's all I ask . . . to fall in love."

"To fall in love? That shouldn't be difficult." She spoke in an unemphatic whisper for she, too, had fallen under a spell, the wonderful hallucination their meeting had been from the first moment.

Her answer seemed to distract him. "Perhaps it is easy for you, but that lack is the greatest terror of my life. It won't happen to me. Can't happen, ever." His voice broke at the end of the sentence. And then he did a very strange thing. His eyes filled with tears and he began quite suddenly to sob. She had never before heard a cry like it. It was a dry, fretful whimper such as a child might make in a disturbed sleep.

"Tony . . ." she said helplessly. She could not bring herself to touch him. She could only repeat his name over and over, "Tony Jones. . . . Tony Jones. . . ." He buried his face in his hands and, after a moment, the sobs disappeared. He did not look at her and remained so still she could hardly hear his breathing.

"What do you want to tell me?" she asked, unable to bear the terrible quiet that followed his crying. During their silences he seemed to be alone in the world; he was that orphan she had adopted the first time she saw him smile.

Finally he said, "Would you believe I cry often? It may not seem like me, but I've always done it. Naturally, I would never reveal this to anyone except you."

She thought of the warm purity of his dark skin and the strong line of his jaw. She kept looking at him and he seemed to find solace in her presence, because he began to talk about himself. In a way that was at once halting and eager, he told her that he was the son of a Detroit factory worker, a tired, simple-minded man. His life had been lived in the shadow of The Company for which his father, brothers, aunts, uncles and neighbors worked. He spoke cautiously of his mother and said that she had given herself to God with the same ferocity in which the others offered themselves up to the factory. Her days and nights were a furious tirade against dancing, picture shows and card playing. She was delicate, thin and angry from too much feeling, and he remembered best her light brown hair that fell to her waist—she didn't believe in cutting it—and the pale softness of her skin. When asked he admitted that he never wrote to her, even though he always wanted to do so. It seemed that his real break with his home dated from his meeting with a red-haired German jeweler who had extensive connections in a more cultivated and fastidious society. He hated this man passionately and could not think of him without anger. Tony Jones left home to live in Chicago, New York and St. Louis where, as he said vaguely, he had friends.

Where were those parents? Martha Fiske wondered. In some little, grey box of a house upon which the sun shone all day long without relief? And where was the red-haired man with the rings and silver bracelets, the man who stood behind the glass counters and brushed the dust from the velvet mats? She, by comparison with Tony Jones, had experienced nothing. Her greatest awareness—it had persisted until her middle twenties—had been of her parents rather than herself. She had been only the daughter of a man and woman whose character freed her from the obligation to develop personality. If she told anecdotes about her youth, they concerned something her parents did or said, or their parents before them. Tony Jones's childhood seemed utterly incomprehensible to her.

At last he had consumed the random crumbs of his life. (That was the way it worked for him. He gave out nothing; instead he let her watch him devour himself.) He said, sheepishly, "You like furniture, don't you? Everyone should have interests and that is your choice."

"Yes, I suppose it is," she said. If she had dared she would have told him that she had no real interests and that this fact gave their association its grave urgency. She was, and believed him to be, a person with a few needs and many habits, but without that which could be called a mind.

When the time came for him to leave they were both rather stiff. He put on his coat and she followed him to the door. Somewhat sadly they looked at each other. His weary movements, the slight way his shoulders dropped, gave his appearance an old-fashioned solemnity. How strange and dark his face is, she thought—dark like her own hair and brows. We might have come from any country, she said to herself. The little scar on his cheek seemed to twitch as a patch of light from the living room fell on his face.

He grasped her hand tightly before he left. The moon was still high and she watched him make his slow way across the street. She stood at the door until she began to shiver from the cold and until Tony Jones had disappeared into the black fields that surrounded his quarters.

During the weeks that followed, the routine of Martha Fiske's life was somewhat altered. The days had become tiresomely long and she found it difficult to occupy herself with household duties. Her yard was covered with fallen leaves and she made no move to sweep them away or to hire someone to do it for her. In some ways her house was brighter than ever and she was more and more conscious of her appearance. (Her clothes had now become rather bizarre. She ordered several lemon yellow dresses and wore them with long strands of jet beads draped around her neck and jeweled combs in her hair. She had red, Japanese style shoes, studded with shining yellow and green nails.) She was negligent, however, of that which presupposed a settled life and about which she had to make plans. She did only those things necessary for the pleasure and comfort of a particular day. With the soldier she drifted along in a remarkably uneventful fashion that was much to her liking. Their conversation was repetitious; their meetings lacked atmosphere and drama. He asked nothing of her and did not even try to discover the old and hidden motives of her behavior. She mentioned, on an occasion, one of the young boys and he became so scornful she could not continue. "Oh, God," he said. "You don't need to tell me anything more. They turn up everywhere . . . always the same." She and the soldier were locked in the present, because they shared no past and mentioned no future. Yet, sometimes when she was alone in the house, she knew that something was happening. It was neither an event nor a feeling, but a kind of corrosion they both had to undergo. Slowly and painlessly, they were wearing down into slightly different shapes.

Not long after her meeting with Tony Jones she gave the first of a long series of parties. The guests were usually bold young people she didn't like at all. The girls had halos of crimped, blonde hair and their faces were covered with a heavy powder mask that made them look like mummies. They laughed all the time, but not as she had thought young people laughed. Instead every sound they made carried the habitual innuendo of a burlesque barker. The boys were sometimes soldiers and most often bleached-skin young men who worked all day and drank all night. She sat there among them and was always rather conscious of her brilliant dresses, her smooth dark hair and the angularity of her face. Being absolutely lifeless when confronted with this violently meaningless activity, she began to think of herself as not a person at all, but the stationary object on a stage set, the powerful, inanimate image around which all action revolved.

The more informal of these parties grew out of the soldier's insatiable lust for company. For a stranger, he knew a surprising number of people and he no sooner came into her house than he began to telephone everyone in his address book. Though he considered these acquaintances unusually dull, he evidently felt no need to explain or to justify his desire for their company. After a time even these numerous, if haphazard, gatherings failed to satisfy him and he could find excitement only in more ambitious parties to which he would invite a different sort of person, this time trim salesgirls and stenographers, young men who sold insurance policies or worked in banks, and again a few soldiers from the barracks. He seemed to have met some of his friends in bars and they had, in turn, introduced him to others. At the parties he was very restless and kept stirring the fire and lighting cigarettes for everyone, but he did not talk unless he had to in order to keep the conversation going. She began to suspect he deliberately censored himself out of some notion that the less he said the more impression he made. In this he was not altogether mistaken, because his detachment did perplex his friends and his gentleness could be rather frightening. She came to understand the parties and to see that he was frantically trying to reproduce the apartment life of unattached, young city people. She even knew now the sudden pallors and tremblings that attacked him came out of his recurrent fears that he wasn't living at all.

The moments that followed the departure of the guests made the evenings worth the trouble. Then Martha Fiske had the most of Tony Jones. He faced each day as a crisis and at the end, having come through, he always experienced a relaxation that softened and warmed him. He became talkative and was even gay in his condemnation of those who had just left. These ordinary people became either pathetic or strikingly comical by his precise, talented mimicry. He sighed and yawned and talked, as she went about emptying the ashtrays and gathering up the glasses. When she was alone with him she felt as if she were thrown back into a remembered childhood existence of great purity. Her adult life, up until their meeting, seemed merely a kind of loitering in a half-human state.

He said to her one evening, "You see how meaningless life is? I told you I only wanted someone I could love, but where is that to be found?" In the end he always came face to face with his private gloom: the inability to love.

"Maybe you are too hard on people," she said.

"I'm not hard on them," he said. "I'm more interested than you are and that makes me critical."

She was standing by the window, absent-mindedly fingering the folds in the curtains. "I'm not interested in people, but I'm interested in you," she said. "You might as well tell me everything. I don't even know how you've lived."

"Money?" he said. She hadn't meant that exactly, but she nodded. "You won't hate me if I tell you? Well, suppose you do. I can't be anything except myself." He took a deep breath. "I don't need to worry about money. I think I've said before that people like me. It's true and it pays."

"What sort of people?"

"Oh, women . . . and men. Don't give me any lectures, please. I've been nice to them. I'm never cruel or selfish. If I had money I'd give it to anyone, but I don't have it. Everyone prefers the giving."

She smiled at him and he, foolishly, took it as a reproach. (When would he learn that she pitied him as she would a mutilated animal and therefore did not scold, but nursed and indulged?) "Why are you smiling?" he demanded.

"It means nothing," she said. He came to her and put his hand on her shoulder, again demanding. "I meant nothing," she repeated.

How could she mean anything when she was thinking at this moment of the powerful contentment they shared? Didn't he sometimes take a nap while she sat beside him and gazed sweetly at his relaxed, dreaming face and his fine dark hair? No doubt there were a thousand places in which he might be tense with the clash of personalities; here they knew the beauty of an undemanding affection.

"Why do you like me? Why do you come to see me?" she asked.

He laughed, possibly to indicate to her that his answer would not be serious. "It's always my policy to tell the truth. Or maybe I should say to tell the truth when I can get by with it. I see you because you are near my quarters and I like company. Of course, if I weren't fond of you, you wouldn't be a good companion. You have helped me."

"Have I?"

"Yes, you have. And I have helped you by knowing what you want out of life."

"What do I want?" she said.

"You want to look after me, or someone like me. I need looking after." There was nothing in his voice. It was flat and dead.

"Are you weak?" she asked.

"Oh, very," he said.

She thought, later, a great deal about their conversation and though she remembered the words she hadn't any definite frame to fit them into. The weeks went by and she was more or less happy. Sometimes his visits were separated by several days. Once he was gone for an entire week end and he later told her he had been in Cincinnati. He gave her a detailed account of a house party and spoke quite contemptuously of the people at whose house it had been given. Something in his manner, a nervousness and loss of confidence, made her think the week end hadn't gone particularly well. This grieved her deeply and it may have been from that moment she started to love him fiercely. She tried to imagine people for whom Tony Jones would be an ordinary man, one to be treated without special favor, and she ended by despising those who could thus reduce him. Once she had admitted her love, a mysterious and lawless power burst forth in her. It was stronger than his humiliations and moods, stronger than his indifference. It came up on her so quickly and with such force it almost wiped him out of her thoughts, since it was her love, and not Tony Jones himself, that startled and invigorated her.

He was deeply absorbed in the details of his personality and these were gradually revealed to her. Oddly enough, he believed himself to be in poor health. He spoke of diseases, approaching blindness and the like. She took these revelations lightly, partly out of her knowledge of his temptation to exaggerate and partly from her belief she could work miracles if any of these dread expectations came true. At times he seemed to her ridiculous and worthless, but she was patient because she had always accepted him as a sort of underworld hero. Nothing he could do touched her feelings. Had she not known these evils from the first? She waited one evening for him to come, waited until midnight and he had not appeared. When the clock struck twelve, she started to put out the lights, but was actually powerless to do so. During the past months she had, like the soldier, developed that tenacious self-assurance of a desperado. If she left her light on, he could not pass her house without stopping. This was an act of extortion, done for itself alone, and without regard for the value of seeing him.

It was almost dawn when she heard a rap on her door. He looked stern and unpleasant as he entered the house and it was not until he had removed his coat that she noticed he was bleeding. The blood was thick on his chin and a few dark drops stained his collar.

"What is it?" she said. He evidently had forgot the wound, because his face was deeply set in that strangely peasant-like haughtiness that always astonished her with its fierceness.

"I shouldn't have come here, but I saw the light," he said severely. "You are a fool. It's very late." His inflamed eyes were almost hidden in the dark cave of his eyelids. "Why are you up at this hour?"

"You let me know you, wanted me to know you," she said softly. He seemed confused when she smiled at him. His anger did not alarm her. Here he was, that choleric, tyrannical waif who might at this moment have broken out of an institution and come to her for refuge. They were indeed conspirators. "You let me know you," she repeated.

"My God! My God!" he said impatiently. Again she saw the little clump of blood on his chin. "What happened?" she said.

He brushed his hand over the wound. "Just a fight. It's nothing."

She led him to the chair and got a pan of water and a towel from the kitchen. "I have to touch your face," she said. "It will be the first time."

"You needn't do it, you know. I don't ask you to." She trembled a bit as she approached him, because his body seemed as rigid as if he were in a cataleptic state. He did not move at all when she unbuttoned his collar.

Very gently she worked the towel over his face and neck. His skin was still cold from the wind. "Don't you want to tell me what happened?" she said.

"I was downtown," he said. "I got into a fight with two men."

"They hurt you," she said, her voice almost vanishing over these terrible words. "They hurt you."

"Yes, they did." He opened his eyes widely now and stared at her curiously. She tried to imagine where this had taken place, the beginning and end of it. Nothing came to her except a vision of Tony Jones wandering in and out of dark streets. She could not conceive of this secretive, forbidding figure in conflict with the ordinary hoodlums of the town.

"I'm sorry," she said.

"Don't be sorry," he said quickly. "I wanted them to." He continued to stare at her until she wondered what outrages of feeling he was attempting to hide. Her fingers touched his forehead and brushed against his hair.

"Wanted them to hurt you?" she asked.

"Yes."

"Why?" She drew away from him. His face was now clean and she saw that there was only a slight scratch on his chin.

"I like it," he said. His voice seemed hollow and tired now and she too felt suddenly weary. She heard an old truck rattling up the street. It was now passing her dreary, cold house and she had a longing to see the face of the driver, to see how some other human being might look in this hour or so before daylight.

"I will take care of you," she said at last. She said it simply, as she might have said that she would take the ashes out of the grate in the morning or pick up the magazine that had fallen to the floor.

"You will have lots of wounds to nurse if you take care of me," he said insistently.

At this moment he looked rather lonely and she too felt cut off from all familiarities. He was old and wise in ways unknown to her. "Will there be more?" she asked.

"There will be when I feel like it." His head was thrown back against the chair and her limp arm touched his shoulder. "You might even make a few wounds of your own if you love me. Do you think you could love me that much?"

"I might do anything almost, if I could learn what you mean." She pulled his head down on her chest. Her hands were long and rather bony. She had always thought them ugly, but now as they smoothed his hair they seemed to have a peculiar beauty all their own. "If I knew . . ." she repeated. Though her voice was soft and calm, she was overpowered by a kind of inner frenzy. She could not even make the effort to understand what he had told her because of the wild beating of her heart. "My love! My love!" she said over and over to herself.

The time came for the departure of the soldiers. It was rumored that the entire camp was to be disbanded. Martha Fiske accepted the fact, though she did not connect it with Tony Jones. It was not easy to imagine him subject to orders not of his own making. She gave little thought to his leaving, largely because her mind was occupied with other matters. Her mother's death, seven months ago, began to worry her. Whenever she remembered the old lady she fell into a torpor that often lasted for hours. At times she thought of her father and then, again, of her husband. She had written her husband that she didn't love him and he had not answered. In this instance she felt neither pity nor anxiety. He was fit for something better than the life they had had together and she believed he would easily discover a new one. More than anything else she brooded over her own hardness. In the strictest terms, she had done nothing that couldn't have been known by all; yet she fretted, not because of guilt but because she was no longer innocent. Considering her hardness, or rather the inflexibility of her will, she often pitied Tony Jones. Her determination operated only with regard to the soldier and she was able to see it for what it was: a perilous heresy that must be accepted without reservation if she were ever to have peace again. In other respects, she was still timid and indefinite, still a soft-spoken, prudent woman. She often wondered how she had managed to out-balance him and she found no explanation except in her love.

Finally the night of their last meeting arrived. Even this event did not fully enter her consciousness. She approached it as if it were an obligatory ritual which had for her no personal content. Tony Jones came to her house in the evening. The night was dark and cold and for some hours there had been intermittent rainstorms. "We have always met at night," she said to him.

"Have we?" His hands were busy folding and unfolding his cap. She saw that he was not going to take off his coat, that he had come only to say goodbye and to leave her forever. "Well, it's been nice," he said uneasily. "It hasn't been quite like anything else." He turned to look at her living room. As he did so, he tried rather unsuccessfully to smile. "Well . . ." he said again. Beads of perspiration stood out on his lip and his voice was unsteady.

She had left the front door open and was watching the night outside. "We have never been in the sun together," she said. It had been a long time since she had actually had conversations with him; instead her whole mind was absorbed in her own delirious monologue.

Her coat was hanging in the hall and she put it on. "At least we shall have been in the rain together," she said.

He stepped back from her. "It's cold and damp. I hate this weather," he said without a pretense of good humor.

She smiled at him as she tied a scarf over her hair. "Where will you be sent from here?" she asked. Together they went through the door and out into the rain. The sky was low and dark and the streets were slippery. She put her arm through his. His damp coat brushed against her cheek as they walked.

"It's better that you don't know where I'm going," he said. "I think this sort of thing demands that I disappear. I always used to do that as a civilian and I can, in a sense, do it again."

"Disappear? Why should you want to do such a thing?" She tried to see his face, but it was almost hidden by his coat collar. Is it possible, she asked herself, that he doesn't know what has taken place between us? Does he think he can leave the town as he came into it?

"I hate the rain," he repeated desperately. "I must go back. We're leaving early in the morning." He was begging now. She had grown accustomed to his sorry, trapped little whine, to his bent head and angry breathing. But even when he was most childish there was a cunning energy in him. At times she thought his real strength lay in his hesitations, his anxiety and lack of will. They protected him.

"Where are you being sent?" she repeated. She felt him slow his pace to prepare an answer. (He could hardly take a breath now that she didn't anticipate.)

"Pray for me," he said with exaggerated lightness. "I could use a little of your courage. I'm not young enough to get by so easily now." He looked at her and his eyes widened with astonishment. She knew he was frightened by her calm, persistent questioning, her tearless face, and he seemed at that moment to realize that this was not the end, but the beginning with her.

She had no interest at all in his ridiculous verbal games. What little there was to be said must come out now. "You didn't answer my question," she said impatiently.

He began then to abuse her and to try, as his last means of escape, to hurt her. "So there's a golden stallion weather vane on the courthouse," he said crossly. "Yes, I think that suits you."

"What do you mean?" she said.

"There will be another . . . There are lots of golden stallions."

"I don't think so," she said.

They walked on past the houses until she turned into the park that surrounded the public library. The caretaker's cottage was almost hidden by the darkness, but she could hear the rain beating on the roof and pouring out of the gutters. They stepped now on soggy ground and made their way through the trees that led up to the library. One tiny corridor light glowed in the square stone building. When they came to the porch she said, "It will be dry here." They climbed the steps to the shelter and stood there for a long time looking at the circular darkness of the park out of which a few scanty tree branches pointed up to the sky. He was behind her, breathing heavily, waiting . . .

"Tell me where you are going!" she said in a sudden fury. Her voice was sharp and clear.

"You are married. Remember that," he said. He was wearing his soldier's cap, that article of clothing he most despised because it seemed to reduce him to the common herd. The cap had slipped down to his eyebrows.

"I'm not. You know I'm not. The marriage never touched me." She spoke with a flat finality that sent him into a violent, but hopeless, anger.

"It's these damned small towns," he groaned. Before her view his face seemed to vanish. In the dim light he had no features at all— only those vigilant, untamed little eyes. "They aren't good for me, these places! People are too serious. You don't know when to stop."

"Perhaps that's it," she said calmly. The town clock struck eleven. She counted the strokes wearily, for she had suddenly lost her energy. The quiet that followed the striking of the hour depressed her. Here there was nothing of his past or of hers. They might have been two tramps wrestling with some ugly destiny on the steps of a public building. She had heard of the vagrants who prowled about the park. There were none here now. Only she and Tony Jones were out in the night.

"Tony . . . I have money," she said softly, offering it to him openly as compensation for his losses. For a long time she had known that he, in asking her to understand him, had suffered a kind of accident that had left him powerless. "I have more than people realize. Wherever you go there will be a nice place for you and when the war is over we can live as you like. Any city will do for me." She put her body in front of him and forced him to look at her. He bit his lip deeply and with a clenched fist brushed the rain from his face. For a moment she had thought he might strike her.

"I don't care," he said. His voice was so low and broken it was almost a growl. "Damn you and this place! Damn you!"

He drew back from her and started for the steps. Suddenly he was running away, through the park, back to his barracks. She watched him from the porch. At the edge of the park he passed through the street light, into the darkness and then back to the light, like a rabbit startled by an automobile. He stopped now, his back toward her. The rain was pelting down on him. She hardly breathed as she waited for him to move again. It seemed hours before he turned around and looked in the direction of the shelter. He will wait, she thought. He is mine. She walked forward to meet him in the darkness.

MAIDEN IN A TOWER

What is it like for Kimball Harris to return to the scene, the
identical setting, of one long-remembered chapter of his
youth? A quarter of a century has gone by since then. When
Kim Harris returns to Salt Lake City and the street of
tall stone and brick houses with high porches and lawns, he
remembers that one of those houses, the one that Holly
once lived in, had a three-story stone tower. His
memories are focused on Holly, the maiden within that
tower. She was the center of a crew of friends and acquaintances
and hangers-on whom only the haphazard and often
irresponsible generation of the twenties, his own generation,
could have assembled in one place.

Kim Harris was trapped now in this old tower—trapped by
the past; it "held him like pain," having overtaken him most
poignantly in the room that had once been Holly's. The
past had come to life in what was quite literally a house of the
dead, for nostalgia is no respecter of person or place
or circumstance.

Τhe highway entering Salt Lake City from the west curves
around the southern end of Great Salt Lake past Black Rock and its
ratty beaches, swings north away from the spouting smoke of the smelter
towns, veers toward the onion-shaped domes of the Saltair Pavilion,
and straightens out eastward again on the speedway. Ahead, across the
white flats, the city and its mountains are a mirage, or a mural: metro-
politan towers, then houses and trees and channeled streets, and then
the mountain wall.

Driving into that, Kimball Harris began to feel like the newsreel
diver whom the reversed projector sucks feet first out of his splash. Perhaps fatigue from the hard day and a half across the desert explained
both the miragelike look of the city and his own sense that he was being
run backward toward the beginning of the reel. But the feeling grew as
he bored townward along the straight road, the same road out which, as
a high-school boy, he had driven much too fast in a stripped-down Ford
bug with screaming companions in the rumble seat. They must have

driven back, too, but he remembered only the going out. To see the city head-on, like this, was strange to him.

Middle-aged, rather tired, but alert with the odd notion that he was returning both through distance and through time, he passed the airport and the fair grounds and slowed for the first streets of the city.

Twenty-five years had made little difference. The city had spread some, and he was surprised, after the desert, by the green luxuriance of the trees, but the streets were still a half mile wide, and water still ran in the gutters. It was a really good town, clean, with a freshness about it that revived him. Circling the Brigham Young monument, he nodded gravely to the figure with the outstretched hand, and like a native returning he went through the light and turned around the button in the middle of the block and came back to park before the Utah Hotel, careful to park well out from the curb so as not to block the flowing gutter. They gave you a ticket for that. It tickled him that he had remembered.

The doorman collared his bag, a bellhop climbed in to take the car around to the garage. Still running pleasantly backward into the reel, he went into the unchanged lobby and registered, and was carried up the unchanged elevators to the kind of room he remembered, such a room as they used to take when they held fraternity parties in the hotel, back in Prohibition times. During those years he had been on a diet for ulcers, and couldn't drink, but he had retired religiously with the boys, gargled raw Green River redeye, and spit it out again in the washbowl, only for the pleasure of lawbreaking and of carrying a distinguished breath back to the ballroom and the girls.

He shook his head, touched for a moment with his giddy and forgotten youth.

Later, fresh from the shower, with a towel around him, he picked up the telephone book, so dinky and provincial-seeming after the ponderous San Francisco directory that he caught himself feeling protective about it. But when he found the Merrill Funeral Parlors in the yellow pages he sat thinking, struck by the address. 363 East South Temple. On the Avenues side, just below Fourth East. He tried to visualize that once familiar street but it was all gone except for a general picture of tall stone and brick houses with high porches and lawns overtaken by plantain weeds. One, the one Holly had lived in, had a three-story stone tower.

That tower! With all the Jazz Age Bohemians crawling in and out. Havelock Ellis, Freud, Mencken, *The Memoirs of Fanny Hill, Love's Coming of Age, The Well of Loneliness,* Harry Kemp, Frank Harris. My Lord.

He was flooded with delighted recollection, they were all before him: reed-necked aesthetes, provincial cognoscenti, sad sexy yokels, lovers burning with a hard gemlike flame, a homosexual or two trying to look blasted and corroded by inward sin. Painters of bile-green landscapes, cubist photographers, poets and iconoclasts, scorners of the bourgeoisie, makers of cherished prose, dream-tellers, correspondence school psychoanalysts, they had swarmed through Holly's apartment and eddied around her queenly shape with noises like breaking china. He remembered her in her gold gown, a Proserpine or a Circe. For an instant she was slim and tall in his mind and he saw her laughing in the midst of the excitement she created, and how her hair was smooth black and her eyes very dark blue and how she wore massive gold hoops in her ears.

He wrote the number down and tucked it in the pocket of the suit laid out on the bed. But when he had dressed and gone down and was walking up South Temple past Beehive House, Lion House, Eagle Gate, the old and new apartment buildings, he began to look at numbers with a feeling that approached suspense, and he searched not so much for the Merrill Funeral Parlors as for the house with the round stone tower. Finally he saw it, lifting across the roof of a mansion gone to seed, and in another thirty paces he could see the sign and the new brass numbers on the riser of the top porch step. It was the very house.

Quickly he looked around for landmarks to restore and brace his memory. Some of the old maples and hickories he remembered along the sidewalk were gone, the terrace rolled down with an unfamiliar smooth nap of grass. The porch no longer carried its sagging swing, and porch and steps had been renewed and painted. The door was as he remembered it, with lozenges of colored glass above it, and the door knob's massive handful was an almost startling familiarity. But inside all was changed. Partitions had been gutted out. The stairs now mounted, or levitated, a spiral of white spokes and mahogany rails. from an expanse of plum-colored carpet. Instead of the cupping old parquetry his feet found softness, hushedness. The smells were of paint and flowers.

He was eying the stairs when a young man came out of an office on the left and bent his head a little leftward and said softly and pleasantly, "Yes, sir. Can I help?"

Harris brought himself dryly back to what he had driven eight hundred miles to do. He said, "I'm Kimball Harris. My aunt, Mrs. George Webb, died day before yesterday at the Julia Hicks Home. They telephoned me she would be here."

"We've been expecting you," the young man said, and put out his hand. "My name is McBride." A brief handshake, a moment when the young man regarded Harris with his head tilted. "Did you fly in?" he asked.

"Drove."

"All the way from San Francisco?"

"I slept a few hours in Elko."

"It wasn't so bad, then."

"Oh, no," Harris said. "Not bad at all."

In his mind was a faint amusement: this young man might have been left over from one of Holly's parties. He looked better equipped to write fragile verses than deal with corpses.

"She's in the parlor just back here," McBride said. "Would you like to see her? She looks very nice."

That would be young McBride's function, of course. He would be the one who made them look nice. "Maybe later," Harris said. "I expect there are some details we ought to settle."

"Of course," McBride said. "If you'll just step in here. We can look at caskets after a minute. You have a family cemetery plot, I believe? It will only take a minute for this. The details you can leave to us." He held the door wide, standing gracefully and deferentially back, and ushered Harris through.

A very few minutes seemed to settle the details. They rose, facing each other across the desk coolly glimmering in muted afternoon light. "Now would you like to see her?" McBride said.

Why, he takes pride, Harris thought. He probably stands back estimating his effects like a window dresser. Mister McBride, the Mortuary Max Factor. "All right," he said, "though it's not as if I had any tears to shed. I haven't seen her for twenty-five years, and she's been senile for ten."

McBride guided him around the unfamiliar stairs to where the plum carpet flowed smoothly into what had evidently once been a dining room. "She does look nice," he said. "Very sweet and peaceful."

Which is more than she did alive, Harris thought, and went forward to the table with the basket of chrysanthemums at its foot. To remind himself that this was his mother's sister, his last near relative, made him feel nothing. Not even a deliberate attempt to squeeze sentimental recollections out of the past and remember suppers at Aunt Margaret's, Christmas visits at Aunt Margaret's, times when Aunt Margaret had unexpectedly given him a quarter, made the wax figure any dearer or realer. His indifference was so marked that he separated it and noticed it, wondering with a tinge of shame if he was callous. He supposed that if he had been attached to the dead woman he might think her peaceful, touching, even terrible. All he could think as he looked at her was that she looked well-embalmed—but then she had probably been close to mummified before she died.

Old Aunt Margaret, never very lovable, never dear to him in his childhood, and in his maturity only a duty and an expense, thrust her sharp nose, sharp cheekbones, withered lips, up through the rouge and lipstick and was, if she was not a total stranger, only old Aunt Margaret mercifully dead at eighty-three. Harris did not even feel the conventional disgust with young McBride, who tampered with the dead. Considering what he had had to work with, McBride had done reasonably well.

Back in the hall again, he stood looking up the spiral stairs, apparently as unsupported as the Beanstalk, and remembered a time when Holly and three roommates—which three didn't matter, they changed so fast—came down the old shabby steps arguing about the proportions of the perfect female figure, and he met them on the second landing and like a chorus line they raised their skirts and thrust out their right legs before him, clamoring to know which was the most shapely. An undergraduate Paris and four demanding goddesses. He had picked Holly: why would he not?

McBride was in the office doorway. "We've just redone the whole place," he said. "It was the home of a Park City silver king originally, but it was all run down." ·

Harris was still looking up the stairs. McBride's words were no more important than the decorative changes, but upstairs there was something that *was* important, that pulled at him like an upward draft.

"I used to know this house twenty-five years ago," he said. "Some people I knew had an apartment on the third floor."

"Really? The front one or the back?"

"Front. The one with the round tower window."

"Oh yes," said McBride. "We haven't done much to that yet—just painted it."

"I wonder," Harris said, and made a little shrugging deprecatory motion and felt irritably ashamed, like a middle-aged man recalling last night's revels and his own unseemly capers and his pawing of the host's wife. It was fatuous to want to go up there, yet he did.

"Go on up if you want," McBride said. "The only thing, there's a woman laid out there."

"Well, then . . ."

"That wouldn't matter, if you don't mind. She's . . . presentable."

For a moment Harris hung on the word, and on the thought that McBride's professional vanity was one of the odder kinds, and on a little fit of irritability that a corpse should intrude upon a sentimental but perfectly legitimate impulse. Then he put his hand on the mahogany rail. "Maybe I will."

The second-floor hall, at whose doors he had knocked or entered, was as much changed as the ground floor, but up the second flight of stairs he mounted into a growing familiarity. And he climbed against the pressure of a crowd of ghosts. The carpet ended at the stairhead; he put his feet down softly and held back his breath with the wild notion that he heard voices from the door of Holly's old apartment. Up these stairs, a hundred, two hundred, three hundred times, through how long? a year? two years? he had come with books or bottles or manuscripts in his hands and (it seemed to him now) an incomparable capacity for enthusiasm in his heart. From the high burlap-hung windows of the apartment inside they had let their liquid ridicule fall on the streets of the bourgeois city. He half expected, as he moved into the doorway, to see their faces look up inquiringly from chair and couch and floor.

But in the room there was only the dead woman, and she was not looking at him.

She lay on a wheeled table, with beside her one stiff chair and a taboret bearing a bowl of flowers, all of it composed as if for a macabre still life. Looking toward the windows across the woman's body he saw how the gray light of the afternoon blurred in her carefully-waved hair.

For a minute or two, perhaps, he stood in the doorway, stopped partly by the body, and partly by the feeling of an obscure threat: he must summon and gather and recreate his recollections of this room; he was walking in a strange neighborhood and needed his own gang around him.

In Holly's time the tower bay had held an old upright piano, its backside exposed to the room like the hanging seat of a child's sleepers. Afternoons, evenings, Sunday and holiday mornings, there had been loud four-hand renderings of "Twelfth Street Rag," "St. Louis Blues," "Mood Indigo." On at least one Christmas morning they had even sung carols around it, syncopating them wickedly. That was the morning when he brought Holly the facsimile copy of *The Marriage of Heaven and Hell*—a mutinous book full of mottoes for their personalities and their times.

But what he remembered now, hanging in the doorway, was how in some lull in the bedlam that always went on there they had found themselves smiling foolishly at each other by the piano and she had put up her hands to his face and kissed him sweet and soft, a kiss like a happy child's. He realized now that he had recalled that kiss before, waking or sleeping, and that the memory of it had acquired a kind of caption, a fragment of the world's wisdom contributed to his adolescent store by a returned Mormon missionary: *"Das ewig Weibliche fuehrt uns hinan,"* that remembered moment said.

How they had flocked and gathered there, debated, kissed, lied, shocked and astonished and delighted each other, there in the tower with Holly at their center, there by the vanished piano: poets and athletes, Renaissance heroes, fearless Stoics and impassioned Epicureans and abandoned Hedonists, girls with the bloom on their loveliness, goddesses with Perfect Proportions, artists and iconoclasts, as delighted with their own wickedness as if it had meant something.

He felt the stairs in his legs, the years in his mind, as he went in softly past the woman who lay so quietly on her back, and when he had passed her he turned and searched her face, almost as if he might surprise in it some expression meaningful to this wry and confusing return.

She was a plain woman, perhaps fifty. McBride had not yet made her look nice with rouge and lipstick. She lay in a simple black dress, but she had a Navajo squash-blossom necklace around her throat. It struck him as a remarkable piece of realism—perhaps something she had especially liked and had stubbornly worn even past the age when costume jewelry became her. It gave her a touching, naïvely rakish air.

Yet she shed a chill around her, and her silence spread to fill the room. Hardly a sound came through the stone walls. In the old days there had always been the piano banging, the phonograph going, two or six or sixteen voices making cosmic conversation. And he never remembered daylight in the apartment. Holly had affected a romantic gloom; the windows were always shrouded by the artistically-frayed burlap, and the light was from lamps, most of them low on the floor and some of them at least with red globes in them. And always the smell of sandalwood.

Like a Chinese whorehouse. He shook his head, pitying and entranced, and sat down on the window seat overlooking the reach of South Temple. Directly across was a Five Minute Car Wash with a big apron of concrete and a spick dazzle of white paint and red tiles. In the times he remembered, that lot had held a Peewee Golf Course where men in shirt sleeves, women in summer dresses, young couples loud with laughter, putted little white balls along precise green alleys and across precise circles of green artificial grass and over gentle and predictable bridges and causeways into numbered holes.

"Look at them," Holly said to him once as they sat in the tower looking down at the after-dinner golfers moving under the bright floodlights. *"Toujours gai,* my God. Some day I'm going to build a miniature golf course with fairways six inches wide and rough all over the place. I'll fill the water holes with full-sized crocodiles and sow the sandtraps with sidewinders. How would it be to hide a black widow spider in every hole so that holing out and picking up your ball would earn you some excitement? What if you sawed the supports of all the little bridges nearly in two?"

Live it dangerously. It was strange to recall how essential that had seemed. Go boom, take chances. He touched the casement windows, thinking that this was the pose, sitting right here and looking out, that Holly had assumed when Tom Stead painted her in her gold velvet gown.

Probably that portrait wasn't anything special. It couldn't have been. The chances were that Tom Stead was painting signs somewhere now, if he hadn't drunk himself to death. But then, in this room, in the presence of its subject whose life overflowed upon them all, that slim golden shape with the velvet highlights was Lilith, Helen, Guenevere, *das ewig Weibliche*. And it was hardly a day before other girls, less fortunately endowed or graced, had begun dropping comments on how *warm* that Stead-Holly romance was getting, and hinting that there was hidden away somewhere a companion portrait—a nude.

Well, well, what a bunch of Bohemian puritans. Harris did not believe in any nude, or in its importance if there had been one, though at the time it had bothered him, and he had been malely offended, surprised that she would *lower* herself, you know?

Now, sitting bemused in the window, he reflected that what had truly shone out of that golden portrait, as out of Holly herself, was not so much glamour as innocence. Under the sheath she was positively virginal; if you cracked the enamel of her sophistication you found a delighted little girl playing Life.

Again he remembered the soft, childlike kiss by the piano on a Christmas morning, and he stood up so sharply that he startled himself with the sight of the dead woman. It *was* innocence. She could put away the predatory paws of college boys, twist laughing from the casual kiss, pass among the hot young Freudians as untouched as a nun, shed like water the propositions that were thrown at her seven to the week. There she sat in her gold gown by her window opening on the foam: a maiden in a tower.

He crossed the room and tried the bedroom door, wanting to look in on her intimately. In this room, now completely bare, aseptically painted, he had sat dozens of times when she was ill or when on Sunday mornings she made it a charming point of her sophistication to entertain in bed. While she lay propped with pillows he had read to her, talked to her, kissed her, had his hands fended away. The empty room was still charged with the vividness with which she invested everything. There was one night very late, two or three o'clock, when he had sat on one side of the bed and a mournful and lovesick jazz trumpeter had sat on the other, neither willing to leave the other alone there, and all that night he had read aloud into the smell of sandalwood the life story of a mad woman from Butte, Montana. *I, Mary MacLean,* that one was called.

What an occasion she made of it, laid up by flu, hemmed in by rival young men, covered to the chin in an absurd, high-necked, old-fashioned nightgown, taking aspirin with sips of ginger beer, laughing at them alternately or together with that face as vivid on the pillow as a flower laid against the linen. It was innocence. In that crackpot Bohemian pre-crash wonderful time, it was innocence.

How he and the trumpeter broke the deadlock, what had ever happened to the Tom Stead flurry, what had happened to any of Holly's string of admirers—all gone. She sent them away, or they quarreled at her over their bruised egos, or they grew huffy at finding her always in a crowd. Plenty of self-appointed humming-bird catchers, but no captures.

And yet, maybe . . .

Summer and winter, day and night, were telescoped in his memory. How old would he have been? Twenty? Twenty-one? It must have been near the end of Holly's reign in this apartment, before everything went sour and the delayed wave of the crash reached them and he left school to go to work and Holly herself went away. There was neither beginning nor end nor definite location in time to what he most vividly remembered. What they were doing, whether there had been a party there or whether they had been out on a date, whether she had roommates then or was living alone, none of that came back. But they were alone in a way they had seldom been.

They must have been talking, something must have led up to it, for there she was with the clarity of something floodlighted in his mind, Holly pressing against him and crying with her face against his chest, clinging and crying and saying—he heard only the refrain, not the garble against his chest—"Kim, Kim, get me out of here! I want to get out of this. This is all no good, I've got to, Kim, please!"

Both the tears and the way she clung excited him. But the game had been played so long by other rules that he went on in the old way, laughing, burlesquing gestures of consolation, patting the crow-wing hair, saying. "There there, little girl." Inanities, idiocies. . . . She wore an evening dress cut very low in the back, and he played his fingers up and down her spine. He slid his hand against her skin, slid it further, expecting the competent twist and shrug and fending and the laugh that would mean the emotional fit was over. But his hand went on around, clear around, and with a shock like an internal explosion he found it cupping the frantic softness of her breast.

Even remembering, all his sensations were shocking to him. He remembered how smoothly the curve of her side swelled upward, how astonishingly *consecutive* her body seemed. Also, also, and almost with revulsion, how rigid and demanding the nipple of her breast. Innocence —he had never touched a girl there, never imagined, or rather had imagined wrong. Stupefied by the sudden admission to her flesh, made uneasy by the way she crowded and clung, he stood wrapping her awkwardly, and kissed her and tasted her tears, and thought with alarm and conviction of Tom Stead and the rumored nude, and was anguished with eagerness to escape.

He could remember not a scrap, not a detail, of how he got away.

She offered herself passionately in his memory, and that was all. The Peewee Golfer putting his little white ball up the little green alley of his youth came suddenly upon the sidewinder in the sandtrap, the crocodile in the artificial lake.

Harris closed the door on the ridiculous and humiliating memory. It had begun to occur to him that he had been an extraordinary young man, and very little of what had been extraordinary about himself pleased him. Innocence? Well, maybe, though there were more contemptuous names for it. He had been a fraud, a gargler of whiskey he would obediently not drink. A great yapper with the crowd, but when the cat stopped running, what a frantic sliding to a stop, what digging not to catch what he was after.

Weakly he tried to prop up the slack thing he had been. He told himself that it was a pose with all of them, the life that revolved around Holly was an absurd and perhaps touching and certainly unimportant part of growing up. Or was it? What might he be at this moment, would he have more or less to regret, if he had taken Holly at her passionate word, married her, lived it, as she was determined to live it in her innocence, dangerously?

The last time he saw Holly she was boarding a train for Seattle, on her way to Shanghai and a job they all publicly envied but would probably not have risked taking themselves. Her life, whatever happened to her, would not have been dull. And yet it might have been more thoroughly wasted than at that moment he thought his own had been.

He had played it the other way, not so much from choice as from yielding to pressures, and he had done the best he could with it. How would he look to Holly now, at this very minute? How had he looked then?

Like a bubble of gas from something submerged and decaying in deep water there rose to the surface of his mind one of Blake's proverbs of Hell that they had admired together that long-gone Christmas morning. It burst, and it said, "Prudence is a rich ugly old maid courted by Incapacity."

It shamed him to remember, though he half repudiated it. From the life of prudence he had got a wife he loved and respected, children he adored, a job he could do with interest and almost with content. He regretted none of them. But he stood here remembering that moment when Holly stopped playing make-believe, and it seemed to him that his failure to take her when she offered herself was one of the saddest failures of his life. The fact that he might make all the same crucial choices the same way if he had them to make again helped not at all; it did him no good to remind himself that no one could turn in any direction without turning his back on something. The past had trapped him, and it held him like pain.

Angrily he looked at his watch. Past five. Starting for the door, he passed the dead woman's table and saw her calm pale face, the skin delicately wrinkled like the skin of a winter-kept apple, but soft-looking, as if it would be not unpleasant to touch. What was her name, what had she died of, what had she looked like when she wore expressions? Who mourned her, who had loved her, what things in her life did they regret or had she regretted? Would they think it disagreeable that a total stranger had been alone with her here staring into her dead face? And in that face what was it that the caution of death enclosed and hid?

The barbaric silver necklace seemed somehow to define her. What it said of frivolity, girlishness, love or ornament and of gaiety and of life, made him like her; the way it lay on the sober black crepe breast preached the saddest lesson he had ever derived.

He thought of how she had been transported and tampered with by McBride, and how further touches of disguise would complete her transfiguration from something real and terrible and lost to something serene, removed, bearable. Alone with her here, before the arrival of the others, before she went forth to be forgotten, he could feel a strange, real anguish for this woman he had never known, and a strange gratitude that he had been permitted to see her.

Gratitude, or something near it. And yet as he started for the door he threw a sick, apologetic glance around the room as quiet and empty as a chapel, and at the woman who lay so quietly at its center. He meant to tiptoe out, but he heard, almost with panic, the four quick raps his heels made on the bare floor before they found the consoling softness of the stairs.

THE LAGOON

"The Lagoon" is one of Conrad's best-known stories. Running through this tale, with its moments of breathless excitement, stolen love, death, and retribution, is a theme as old as the recorded spiritual trials of man. Letting Arsat tell his own story, Conrad translates it into language which preserves the native's passionate intensity as well as the poetic rhythms of his speech.

"Therefore I shall speak to you of love. Speak in the night. Speak before night and love are gone—and the eye of day looks upon my sorrow and my shame; upon my blackened face; upon my burnt-up heart." Thus Arsat, the Malayan, begins his tale, for—as he says to Tuan, the white man— a man must speak of war and love. And he must speak, too, of brotherly love, for it is this strong attachment which compels him in the end to act in accordance with his own code of honor.

T he white man, leaning with both arms over the roof of the little house in the stern of the boat, said to the steersman—

"We will pass the night in Arsat's clearing. It is late."

The Malay only grunted, and went on looking fixedly at the river. The white man rested his chin on his crossed arms and gazed at the wake of the boat. At the end of the straight avenue of forests cut by the intense glitter of the river, the sun appeared unclouded and dazzling, poised low over the water that shone smoothly like a band of metal. The forests, somber and dull, stood motionless and silent on each side of the broad stream. At the foot of big, towering trees, trunkless nipa palms rose from the mud of the bank, in bunches of leaves enormous and heavy, that hung unstirring over the brown swirl of eddies. In the stillness of the air every tree, every leaf, every bough, every tendril of creeper and every petal of minute blossoms seemed to have been bewitched into an immobility perfect and final. Nothing moved on the river but the eight paddles that rose flashing regularly, dipped together with a single splash; while the steersman swept right and left with a periodic and sudden flourish of his blade describing a glinting semicircle above his head. The churned-up water frothed alongside with a confused murmur. And the white man's canoe, advancing upstream in the short-lived disturbance of its own making, seemed to enter the portals of a land from which the very memory of motion had forever departed.

The white man, turning his back upon the setting sun, looked along the empty and broad expanse of the sea-reach. For the last three miles of its course the wandering, hesitating river, as if enticed irresistibly by the freedom of an open horizon, flows straight into the sea, flows straight to the east—to the east that harbors both light and darkness. Astern of the boat the repeated call of some bird, a cry discordant and feeble, skipped along over the smooth water and lost itself, before it could reach the other shore, in the breathless silence of the world.

The steersman dug his paddle into the stream, and held hard with stiffened arms, his body thrown forward. The water gurgled aloud; and suddenly the long straight reach seemed to pivot on its center, the forests swung in a semicircle, and the slanting beams of sunset touched the broadside of the canoe with a fiery glow, throwing the slender and distorted shadows of its crew upon the streaked glitter of the river. The white man turned to look ahead. The course of the boat had been altered at right-angles to the stream, and the carved dragon-head of its prow was pointing now at a gap in the fringing bushes of the bank. It glided through, brushing the overhanging twigs, and disappeared from the river like some slim and amphibious creature leaving the water for its lair in the forests.

The narrow creek was like a ditch: tortuous, fabulously deep; filled with gloom under the thin strip of pure and shining blue of the heaven. Immense trees soared up, invisible behind the festooned draperies of creepers. Here and there, near the glistening blackness of the water, a twisted root of some tall tree showed amongst the tracery of small ferns, black and dull, writhing and motionless, like an arrested snake. The short words of the paddlers reverberated loudly between the thick and somber walls of vegetation. Darkness oozed out from between the trees, through the tangled maze of the creepers, from behind the great fantastic and unstirring leaves; the darkness, mysterious and invincible; the darkness scented and poisonous of impenetrable forests.

The men poled in the shoaling water. The creek broadened, opening out into a wide sweep of a stagnant lagoon. The forests receded from the marshy bank, leaving a level strip of bright green, reedy grass to frame the reflected blueness of the sky. A fleecy pink cloud drifted high above, trailing the delicate coloring of its image under the floating leaves and the silvery blossoms of the lotus. A little house, perched on high piles, appeared black in the distance. Near it, two tall nibong palms, that seemed to have come out of the forests in the background, leaned slightly over the ragged roof, with a suggestion of sad tenderness and care in the droop of their leafy and soaring heads.

The steersman, pointing with his paddle, said, "Arsat is there. I see his canoe fast between the piles."

The polers ran along the sides of the boat glancing over their shoulders at the end of the day's journey. They would have preferred to spend the night somewhere else than on this lagoon of weird aspect and ghostly reputation. Moreover, they disliked Arsat, first as a stranger, and also because he who repairs a ruined house, and dwells in it, proclaims that he is not afraid to live amongst the spirits that haunt the places abandoned by mankind. Such a man can disturb the course of fate by glances or words; while his familiar ghosts are not easy to propitiate by casual wayfarers upon whom they long to wreak the malice of their human master. White men care not for such things, being unbelievers and in league with the Father of Evil, who leads them unharmed through the invisible dangers of this world. To the warnings of the righteous they oppose an offensive pretense of disbelief. What is there to be done?

So they thought, throwing their weight on the end of their long poles. The big canoe glided on swiftly, noiselessly, and smoothly, towards Arsat's clearing, till, in a great rattling of poles thrown down, and the loud murmurs of "Allah be praised!" it came with a gentle knock against the crooked piles below the house.

The boatmen with uplifted faces shouted discordantly, "Arsat! O Arsat!" Nobody came. The white man began to climb the rude ladder giving access to the bamboo platform before the house. The juragan of the boat said sulkily, "We will cook in the sampan, and sleep on the water."

"Pass my blankets and the basket," said the white man, curtly.

He knelt on the edge of the platform to receive the bundle. Then the boat shoved off, and the white man, standing up, confronted Arsat, who had come out through the low door of his hut. He was a man young, powerful, with broad chest and muscular arms. He had nothing on but his sarong. His head was bare. His big, soft eyes stared eagerly at the white man, but his voice and demeanor were composed as he asked, without any words of greeting—

"Have you medicine, Tuan?"

"No," said the visitor in a startled tone. "No. Why? Is there sickness in the house?"

"Enter and see," replied Arsat, in the same calm manner, and turning short round, passed again through the small doorway. The white man, dropping his bundles, followed.

In the dim light of the dwelling he made out on a couch of bamboos a woman stretched on her back under a broad sheet of red cotton cloth.

She lay still, as if dead; but her big eyes, wide open, glittered in the gloom, staring upwards at the slender rafters, motionless and unseeing. She was in a high fever, and evidently unconscious. Her cheeks were sunk slightly, her lips were partly open, and on the young face there was the ominous and fixed expression—the absorbed, contemplating expression of the unconscious who are going to die. The two men stood looking down at her in silence.

"Has she been long ill?" asked the traveler.

"I have not slept for five nights," answered the Malay, in a deliberate tone. "At first she heard voices calling her from the water and struggled against me who held her. But since the sun of today rose she hears nothing—she hears not me. She sees nothing. She sees not me—me!"

He remained silent for a minute, then asked softly—

"Tuan, will she die?"

"I fear so," said the white man, sorrowfully. He had known Arsat years ago, in a far country in times of trouble and danger, when no friendship is to be despised. And since his Malay friend had come unexpectedly to dwell in the hut on the lagoon with a strange woman, he had slept many times there, in his journeys up and down the river. He liked the man who knew how to keep faith in council and how to fight without fear by the side of his white friend. He liked him—not so much perhaps as a man likes his favorite dog—but still he liked him well enough to help and ask no questions, to think sometimes vaguely and hazily in the midst of his own pursuits, about the lonely man and the long-haired woman with audacious face and triumphant eyes, who lived together hidden by the forests—alone and feared.

The white man came out of the hut in time to see the enormous conflagration of sunset put out by the swift and stealthy shadows that, rising like a black and impalpable vapor above the tree-tops, spread over the heaven, extinguishing the crimson glow of floating clouds and the red brilliance of departing daylight. In a few moments all the stars came out above the intense blackness of the earth and the great lagoon gleaming suddenly with reflected lights resembled an oval patch of night sky flung down into the hopeless and abysmal night of the wilderness. The white man had some supper out of the basket, then collecting a few sticks that lay about the platform, made up a small fire, not for warmth, but for the sake of the smoke, which would keep off the mosquitoes. He wrapped himself in the blankets and sat with his back against the reed wall of the house, smoking thoughtfully.

Arsat came through the doorway with noiseless steps and squatted down by the fire. The white man moved his outstretched legs a little.

"She breathes," said Arsat in a low voice, anticipating the expected question.. "She breathes and burns as if with a great fire. She speaks not; she hears not—and burns!"

He paused for a moment, then asked in a quiet, incurious tone—
"Tuan . . . will she die?"

The white man moved his shoulders uneasily and muttered in a hesitating manner—

"If such is her fate."

"No, Tuan," said Arsat, calmly. "If such is my fate. I hear, I see, I wait. I remember . . . Tuan, do you remember the old days? Do you remember my brother?"

"Yes," said the white man. The Malay rose suddenly and went in. The other, sitting still outside, could hear the voice in the hut. Arsat said: "Hear me! Speak!" His words were succeeded by a complete silence. "O Diamelen!" he cried, suddenly. After that cry there was a deep sigh. Arsat came out and sank down again in his old place.

They sat in silence before the fire. There was no sound within the house, there was no sound near them; but far away on the lagoon they could hear the voices of the boatmen ringing fitful and distinct on the calm water. The fire in the bows of the sampan shone faintly in the distance with a hazy red glow. Then it died out. The voices ceased. The land and the water slept invisible, unstirring and mute. It was as though there had been nothing left in the world but the glitter of stars streaming, ceaseless and vain, through the black stillness of the night.

The white man gazed straight before him into the darkness with wide-open eyes. The fear and fascination, the inspiration and the wonder of death—of death near, unavoidable, and unseen, soothed the unrest of his race and stirred the most indistinct, the most intimate of his thoughts. The ever-ready suspicion of evil, the gnawing suspicion that lurks in our hearts, flowed out into the stillness round him—into the stillness profound and dumb, and made it appear untrustworthy and infamous, like the placid and impenetrable mask of an unjustifiable violence. In that fleeting and powerful disturbance of his being the earth enfolded in the starlight peace became a shadowy country of inhuman strife, a battle-field of phantoms terrible and charming, august or ignoble, struggling ardently for the possession of our helpless hearts. An unquiet and mysterious country of inextinguishable desires and fears.

A plaintive murmur rose in the night; a murmur saddening and startling, as if the great solitudes of surrounding woods had tried to whisper into his ear the wisdom of their immense and lofty indifference. Sounds hesitating and vague floated in the air round him, shaped themselves slowly into words; and at last flowed on gently in a murmuring stream of soft and monotonous sentences. He stirred like a man waking up and changed his position slightly. Arsat, motionless and shadowy, sitting with bowed head under the stars, was speaking in a low and dreamy tone—

". . . for where can we lay down the heaviness of our trouble but in a friend's heart? A man must speak of war and of love. You, Tuan, know what war is, and you have seen me in time of danger seek death as other men seek life! A writing may be lost; a lie may be written; but what the eye has seen is truth and remains in the mind!"

"I remember," said the white man, quietly. Arsat went on with mournful composure—

"Therefore I shall speak to you of love. Speak in the night. Speak before both night and love are gone—and the eye of day looks upon my sorrow and my shame; upon my blackened face; upon my burnt-up heart."

A sigh, short and faint, marked an almost imperceptible pause, and then his words flowed on, without a stir, without a gesture.

"After the time of trouble and war was over and you went away from my country in the pursuit of your desires, which we, men of the islands, cannot understand, I and my brother became again, as we had been before, the sword-bearers of the Ruler. You know we were men of family, belonging to a ruling race, and more fit than any to carry on our right shoulder the emblem of power. And in the time of prosperity Si Dendring showed us favor, as we, in time of sorrow, had showed to him the faithfulness of our courage. It was a time of peace. A time of deer-hunts and cock-fights; of idle talks and foolish squabbles between men whose bellies are full and weapons are rusty. But the sower watched the young rice-shoots grow up without fear, and the traders came and went, departed lean and returned fat into the river of peace. They brought news, too. Brought lies and truth mixed together, so that no man knew when to rejoice and when to be sorry. We heard from them about you also. They had seen you here and had seen you there. And I was glad to hear, for I remembered the stirring times, and I always remembered you, Tuan, till the time came when my eyes could see nothing in the past, because they had looked upon the one who is dying there—in the house."

He stopped to exclaim in an intense whisper, "O Mara bahia! O Calamity!" then went on speaking a little louder:

"There's no worse enemy and no better friend than a brother, Tuan, for one brother knows another, and in perfect knowledge is strength for good or evil. I loved my brother. I went to him and told him that I could see nothing but one face, hear nothing but one voice. He told me: 'Open your heart so that she can see what is in it—and wait. Patience is wisdom. Inchi Midah may die or our Ruler may throw off his fear of a woman!' . . . I waited! . . . You remember the lady with the veiled face, Tuan, and the fear of our Ruler before her cunning and temper. And if she wanted her servant, what could I do? But I fed the hunger of my heart on short glances and stealthy words. I loitered on the path to the bath-houses in the daytime, and when the sun had fallen behind the forest I crept along the jasmine hedges of the women's courtyard. Unseeing, we spoke to one another through the scent of flowers, through the veil of leaves, through the blades of long grass that stood still before our lips; so great was our prudence, so faint was the murmur of our great longing. The time passed swiftly . . . and there were whispers amongst women—and our enemies watched—my brother was gloomy, and I began to think of killing and of a fierce death. . . . We are of a people who take what they want—like you whites. There is a time when a man should forget loyalty and respect. Might and authority are given to rulers, but to all men is given love and strength and courage. My brother said, 'You shall take her from their midst. We are two who are like one.' And I answered, 'Let it be soon, for I find no warmth in sunlight that does not shine upon her.' Our time came when the Ruler and all the great people went to the mouth of the river to fish by torch-light. There were hundreds of boats, and on the white sand, between the water and the forests, dwellings of leaves were built for the households of the Rajahs. The smoke of cooking-fires was like a blue mist of the evening, and many voices rang in it joyfully. While they were making the boats ready to beat up the fish, my brother came to me and said, 'Tonight!' I looked to my weapons, and when the time came our canoe took its place in the circle of boats carrying the torches. The lights blazed on the water, but behind the boats there was darkness. When the shouting began and the excitement made them like mad we dropped out. The water swallowed our fire, and we floated back to the shore that was dark with only here and there the glimmer of embers. We could hear the talk of slave-girls amongst the sheds. Then we found a place deserted and silent. We waited there. She came. She came running along the shore, rapid and leaving no trace, like a leaf driven by the wind into the sea. My brother said gloomily, 'Go and take her; carry her into our boat.' I lifted her in my arms. She panted. Her heart was beating against my breast. I said, 'I take you from those people. You came to the cry of my heart, but my arms take you into my boat against the will of the great!' 'It is right,' said my brother. 'We are men who take what we want and can hold it against many. We should have taken her in daylight.' I said, 'Let us be off'; for since she was in my boat I began to think of our Ruler's many men. 'Yes. Let us be off,' said my brother. 'We are cast out and this boat is our country now—and the sea is our refuge.' He lingered with his foot on the shore, and I entreated him to hasten, for I remembered the strokes of her heart against my breast and thought that two men cannot withstand a hundred. We left, paddling downstream close to the bank; and as we passed by the creek where they were fishing, the great shouting had ceased, but the murmur of voices was loud like the humming of insects flying at noonday. The boats floated, clustered together, in the red light of torches, under a black roof of smoke; and men talked of their sport. Men that boasted, and praised, and jeered—men that would have been our friends in the morning, but on that night were already our enemies. We paddled swiftly past. We had no more friends in the country of our birth. She sat in the middle of the canoe with covered face; silent as she is now; unseeing as she is now—and I had no regret at what I was leaving because I could hear her breathing close to me—as I can hear her now."

He paused, listened with his ear turned to the doorway, then shook his head and went on:

"My brother wanted to shout the cry of challenge—one cry only—to let the people know we were freeborn robbers who trusted our arms and the great sea. And again I begged him in the name of our love to be silent. Could I not hear her breathing close to me? I knew the pursuit would come quick enough. My brother loved me. He dipped his paddle without a splash. He only said, 'There is a half a man in you now—the other half is in that woman. I can wait. When you are a whole man again, you will come back with me here to shout defiance. We are sons of the same mother.' I made no answer. All my strength and all my spirit were in my hands that held the paddle—for I longed to be with her in a safe place beyond the reach of men's anger and of women's spite. My love was so great, that I thought it could guide me to a country where death was unknown, if I could only escape from Inchi Midah's fury and from our Ruler's sword. We paddled with haste, breathing through our teeth. The blades bit deep into the smooth water. We passed out of the river; we flew in clear channels amongst the shallows. We skirted the black coast; we skirted the sand beaches where the sea speaks in whispers to the land; and the gleam of white sand flashed back past our boat, so swiftly she ran upon the water. We spoke not. Only once I said, 'Sleep, Diamelen, for soon you may want all your strength.' I heard the sweetness of her voice, but I never turned my head. The sun rose and still we went on. Water fell from my face like rain from a cloud. We flew in the light and heat. I never looked back, but I knew that my brother's eyes, behind me, were looking steadily ahead, for the boat went as straight as a bushman's dart, when it leaves the end of the sumpitan. There was no better paddler, no better steersman than my brother. Many times, together, we had won races in that canoe. But we never had put out our strength as we did then—then, when for the last time we paddled together! There was no braver or stronger man in our country than my brother. I could not spare the strength to turn my head and look at him, but every moment I heard the hiss of his breath getting louder behind me. Still he did not speak. The sun was high. The heat clung to my back like a flame of fire. My ribs were ready to burst, but I could no longer get enough air into my chest.

And then I felt I must cry out with my last breath, 'Let us rest!' . . .
'Good!' he answered; and his voice was firm. He was strong. He was
brave. He knew not fear and no fatigue . . . My brother!"

A murmur powerful and gentle, a murmur vast and faint; the murmur of trembling leaves, of stirring boughs, ran through the tangled
depths of the forests, ran over the starry smoothness of the lagoon, and
the water between the piles lapped the slimy timber once with a sudden
splash. A breath of warm air touched the two men's faces and passed on
with a mournful sound—a breath loud and short like an uneasy sigh of
the dreaming earth.

Arsat went on in an even, low voice.

"We ran our canoe on the white beach of a little bay close to a long
tongue of land that seemed to bar our road; a long wooded cape going
far into the sea. My brother knew that place. Beyond the cape a river
has its entrance, and through the jungle of that land there is a narrow
path. We made a fire and cooked rice. Then we lay down to sleep on the
soft sand in the shade of our canoe, while she watched. No sooner had I
closed my eyes than I heard her cry of alarm. We leaped up. The sun
was halfway down the sky already, and coming in sight in the opening
of the bay we saw a prau manned by many paddlers. We knew it at
once; it was one of our Rajah's praus. They were watching the shore,
and saw us. They beat the gong, and turned the head of the prau into
the bay. I felt my heart become weak within my breast. Diamelen sat
on the sand and covered her face. There was no escape by sea. My
brother laughed. He had the gun you had given him, Tuan, before you
went away, but there was only a handful of powder. He spoke to me
quickly: 'Run with her along the path. I shall keep them back, for they
have no firearms, and landing in the face of a man with a gun is certain
death for some. Run with her. On the other side of that wood there is
a fisherman's house—and a canoe. When I have fired all the shots I will
follow. I am a great runner, and before they can come up we shall be
gone. I will hold out as long as I can, for she is but a woman—that can
neither run nor fight, but she has your heart in her weak hands.' He
dropped behind the canoe. The prau was coming. She and I ran, and as
we rushed along the path I heard shots. My brother fired—once—twice
—and the booming of the gong ceased. There was silence behind us.
That neck of land is narrow. Before I heard my brother fire the third
shot I saw the shelving shore, and I saw the water again; the mouth of a
broad river. We crossed a grassy glade. We ran down to the water. I
saw a low hut above the black mud, and a small canoe hauled up. I
heard another shot behind me. I thought, 'That is his last charge.' We
rushed down to the canoe; a man came running from the hut, but I
leaped on him, and we rolled together in the mud. Then I got up, and
he lay still at my feet. I don't know whether I had killed him or not. I

and Diamelen pushed the canoe afloat. I heard yells behind me, and I saw my brother run across the glade. Many men were bounding after him. I took her in my arms and threw her into the boat, then leaped in myself. When I looked back I saw that my brother had fallen. He fell and was up again, but the men were closing round him. He shouted, 'I am coming!' The men were close to him. I looked. Many men. Then I looked at her. Tuan, I pushed the canoe! I pushed it into deep water. She was kneeling forward looking at me, and I said, 'Take your paddle,' while I struck the water with mine. Tuan, I heard him cry. I heard him cry my name twice; and I heard voices shouting, 'Kill! Strike!' I never turned back. I heard him calling my name again with a great shriek, as when life is going out together with the voice—and I never turned my head. My own name! . . . My brother! Three times he called—but I was not afraid of life. Was she not there in that canoe? And could I not with her find a country where death is forgotten—where death is unknown!"

The white man sat up. Arsat rose and stood, an indistinct and silent figure above the dying embers of the fire. Over the lagoon a mist drifting and low had crept, erasing slowly the glittering images of the stars. And now a great expanse of white vapor covered the land: it flowed cold and gray in the darkness, eddied in noiseless whirls round the tree-trunks and about the platform of the house, which seemed to float upon a restless and impalpable illusion of a sea. Only far away the tops of the trees stood outlined on the twinkle of heaven, like a somber and forbidding shore—a coast deceptive, pitiless and black.

Arsat's voice vibrated loudly in the profound peace.

"I had her there! I had her! To get her I would have faced all mankind. But I had her—and—"

His words went out ringing into the empty distances. He paused, and seemed to listen to them dying away very far—beyond help and beyond recall. Then he said quietly—

"Tuan, I loved my brother."

A breath of wind made him shiver. High above his head, high above the silent sea of mist the drooping leaves of the palms rattled together with a mournful and expiring sound. The white man stretched his legs. His chin rested on his chest, and he murmured sadly without lifting his head—

"We all love our brothers."

Arsat burst out with an intense whispering violence—

"What did I care who died? I wanted peace in my own heart."

He seemed to hear a stir in the house—listened—then stepped in noiselessly. The white man stood up. A breeze was coming in fitful puffs. The stars shone paler as if they had retreated into the frozen depths of immense space. After a chill gust of wind there were a few seconds of perfect calm and absolute silence. Then from behind the black and wavy line of the forests a column of golden light shot up into the heavens and spread over the semicircle of the eastern horizon. The sun had risen. The mist lifted, broke into drifting patches, vanished into thin flying wreaths; and the unveiled lagoon lay, polished and black, in the heavy shadows at the foot of the wall of trees. A white eagle rose over it with a slanting and ponderous flight, reached the clear sunshine and appeared dazzlingly brilliant for a moment, then soaring higher, became a dark and motionless speck before it vanished into the blue as if it had left the earth forever. The white man, standing gazing upwards before the doorway, heard in the hut a confused and broken murmur of distracted words ending with a loud groan. Suddenly Arsat stumbled out with outstretched hands, shivered, and stood still for some time with fixed eyes. Then he said—

"She burns no more."

Before his face the sun showed its edge above the tree-tops rising steadily. The breeze freshened; a great brilliance burst upon the lagoon, sparkled on the rippling water. The forests came out of the clear shadows of the morning, became distinct, as if they had rushed nearer—to stop short in a great stir of leaves, of nodding boughs, of swaying branches. In the merciless sunshine the whisper of unconscious life grew louder, speaking in an incomprehensible voice round the dumb darkness of that human sorrow. Arsat's eyes wandered slowly, then stared at the rising sun.

"I can see nothing," he said half aloud to himself.

"There is nothing," said the white man, moving to the edge of the platform and waving his hand to his boat. A shout came faintly over the lagoon and the sampan began to glide towards the abode of the friend of ghosts.

"If you want to come with me, I will wait all the morning," said the white man, looking away upon the water.

"No, Tuan," said Arsat, softly. "I shall not eat or sleep in this house, but I must first see my road. Now I can see nothing—see nothing! There is no light and no peace in the world; but there is death—death for many. We are sons of the same mother—and I left him in the midst of enemies; but I am going back now."

He drew a long breath and went on in a dreamy tone:

"In a little while I shall see clear enough to strike—to strike. But she has died, and . . . now . . . darkness."

He flung his arms wide open, let them fall along his body, then stood still with unmoved face and stony eyes, staring at the sun. The white man got down into his canoe. The polers ran smartly along the sides of the boat, looking over their shoulders at the beginning of a weary journey. High in the stern, his head muffled up in white rags, the juragan sat moody, letting his paddle trail in the water. The white man, leaning with both arms over the grass roof of the little cabin, looked back at the shining ripple of the boat's wake. Before the sampan passed out of the lagoon into the creek he lifted his eyes. Arsat had not moved. He stood lonely in the searching sunshine; and he looked beyond the great light of a cloudless day into the darkness of a world of illusions.

America is so many things . . .

A MAN FROM FORT NECESSITY

America has meant many things to so many well-known American writers—as the titles and names in Part III suggest —that it would be hard to decide on the best order of presentation of these stories, or at least where to begin, were it not for "A Man from Fort Necessity." This story should come first. It is history, and the year is not long after 1776.

Here Benét, speaking in the person of Aeneas Todkill, a veteran of the French and Indian war, recreates the character of a great Revolutionary War hero in the early days of his untried leadership. The character reminds us of the words of one of the keenest of American biographers, Gamaliel Bradford, who made this observation regarding the native tendency of Americans to allow "a silly legendary atmosphere" to envelop their national heroes: If a hero "is really great, nothing will make him more so than to prove that he was really human." The hero of Todkill's story is really human—and so is Todkill.

You can say that he wants to make himself a king or a dictator, if you like—every man to his own brand of politics. But you'll have to say it outside; not in my house. He's a man that likes his own way; yes, I'll grant you that. I don't give a shinplaster for a man that don't, myself; other people may be otherwise minded. But as for that New York newsletter and what it says about him, you can put that right back in your pocket while you're drinking my liquor. I can't refuse travelers refreshment for man or beast, because that's the law, and a reasonable one. But you come in here with your new buckskin pantaloons and the rest of it, talking as if you owned the state of Virginia. Well, my name's Aeneas Todkill and I've heard that kind of talk before.

I suppose you never heard of the little affair we had here before you ever had breeches on. They called it "the Seven Years' War" in the benighted monarchies of Europe, and I've heard it called "the French and Indian" by the sort of folks who write your newsletter. But here on the frontier we just knew it was blood and fire and fighting. We just knew that.

'Taint settled yet, and it won't be till we clear them out along the rivers and push to the west. But it's different, yes. You don't appreciate that difference—not if you're from tidewater. You think this is the backwoods, and maybe it is. But I've ridden forty miles with a light rein, whistling, where I wouldn't have dared to ride, or walk either, when I was your age. Not that I didn't do it, but I did it because I didn't dare to, if you can understand that. A young man's that way. You try clearing your ground and raising your cabin, and looking back over your shoulder, day and night. Because, if you're off in the forest after a deer, you never know what you'll come back to. It may be your wife, washing out her skirt, and everything peaceful; and it may be a heap of cinders and the bloody-headed dead. I tell you, they were pushing us in those days—Frenchies and Indians both. Folks forget about days like that, once they're past, just the way you forget about a bullet, once the wound's skinned over. But it aches you sometimes in cold wind. That's why I spoke as I did.

Well, if you're bound for Kentucky, that's a horse of another color. You'll find what you're looking for there—they say it's a fine country— but maybe you'll find something else too. That's why I'm talking to you. I was twenty, myself, in those days, but I was used to the woods. And the French were stirring up the Indians and going where they'd no right. So, when Governor Dinwiddie called for troops and money—a queer old codger he was, with his laced hat and his silk stockings, but an honest man for all that—I joined up in the Virginia regiment. At least they called it that. For uniforms, we had the shirts on our backs, and for rations we had what we could forage. But most of us were backwoodsmen and used to that way of living. It wasn't Dinwiddie's fault we weren't better provided; he had to squeeze the money out of the Assembly, and you know what Assemblies are.

A lifetime ago it was, but you don't forget youth. No, nor bad rations neither—especially when you don't even get 'em. But we could have stood that well enough, if they hadn't put that youngster in to command us. I'd meant to go with Fry—Colonel Josh Fry—and I know I kicked like a steer when I found I was in this other fellow's detachment. It's queer, but I can see that long-legged youngster just as plain as I'm seeing you today. A tall, stiff-necked, rawboned young'un of twenty-one or so —excuse me!—with gray-blue eyes and a big nose he hadn't grown up to yet, dressed up in a militia uniform and ordering folks around that knew a lot more than he did. We didn't take to it very well, we backwoodsmen. No, not at first. He wanted to teach us discipline, for one thing, and we figured it was shooting, not discipline, that was going to lick the Frenchies. We might have stood that kind of thing from Colonel Josh Fry, but then Josh was an Englishman. This man wasn't. He was a Virginian, all right, but one of the gentry, with a family that had land claims on the Ohio to boot. We didn't like the sound of him or the smell of him. We didn't, for a fact.

I remember turning to Joe Lightbucket—Joe and I were raised in the same neck of the woods—and saying "Joe, what's your idea of this elegant campstool colonel they've settled down on us?"

"Got a temper," said Joe. "See it in the white of his eye. Same with men as horses."

He was always a sparing man with words, was Joe Lightbucket.

"Temper?" I said. "I know he's got a temper. Told me my shirttail was out. Who gives a damn about a shirttail in the backwoods? We can't all have cambric shirts and a servant to wash 'em, the way he was back home."

Joe chewed for a while. "Hot-headed feller," he said. "Or looks hot-headed. Good man in a fight, I reckon—got big hands. Knows the woods, some. But thinks he knows more than he does know. Well, we'll see."

"See?" I said. "Well, if they think that any fox-hunting, gentryfied colonial jackanapes is good enough to command—"

"Colonial?" said Joe, and chuckled. "And who do you think you are? King George?"

Well, that shut me up, as he meant it to, but it didn't shut up my feelings. And yet, all the same, as the expedition went on, I couldn't help feeling sorry for the boy.

He was pleased and excited and worried, all at once; the way anybody is bound to be with his first sizable command. He had a good hold over himself, but you could see it just the same. He'd go along, with his big nose in front of him, and he'd give us orders without a crack in his big voice, but, nevertheless and notwithstanding, you could see that half of him was itching to win a big, celebrated victory and the other half wondering desperately if he'd forgotten to do things he ought to have done. But he didn't forget very much. And work! He worked like a beaver. He might be commanding officer, but he didn't take it easy for that. There was something in him you couldn't get very close to; and yet, as we went along, I began to take quite a fancy to him. He came from the gentry—the kind that like cards and wine and dancing, and think they're the top of the earth. And yet, he was out here with all of us backwoodsmen, and not doing so badly, either. I thought it was ambition, then.

First thing gave me some hope about him was, he seemed to have an eye for ground. He noticed it, if you know what I mean. Not like one of your British regulars that goes crashing through the woods like a lost bull calf and about as noisy. He walked light and he knew where he was and he noticed things—and you have to do that on the frontier, if you want to keep your hair. So that seemed, to me, a good sign. But then something happened that floored me. We'd been going through some right pretty country, for a wonder—I remember that, for most of that march was plain hell. And we'd shaken down into shape and the sun was shining and, in spite of young sobersides and his dignified notions, we were most of us feeling pretty good. I know I was, for a fact. Well, we'd halted for a spell—give him his due, he didn't wear men out without reason—and I happened to stroll up to him, feeling pretty spunky. "Well, colonel," I said, "nice weather for the time of year."

He stiffened up into his collar the way he always did when you talked to him without all the proper salutes and fumadiddles. But he was getting used to us by now and he tried to take it in good part.

"Yes, Private Todkill," he said. "We'd call it good growing weather, on the Rappahannock." And he gave a queer little sigh.

"Noticed you looking over the lay of the land, colonel," I said, in a free way. Oh yes, I'd have known better afterward, but in those days it took more than general orders to make a freeborn Virginian touch his hat to a colonel. "Wondered if there was anything around that struck your eye in particular." I just wanted to be friendly, you know.

"Why, yes, Private Todkill," he said, in his gentleman's voice. "If we wrest this region—and it is rightfully ours—from our gallant adversaries, the French, such country as this will be a great source of increase for our Virginians. It is noble ground."

"Yes, sir," I said, though I couldn't make out what in the world he was talking about.

"Yes," he said, "once the land is cleared, I can see it will be most fertile." He shaded his eyes with his hand and looked down the little valley. "Now," he said, "for a field such as that one, I wonder whether it would be of greater advantage to plant it to oats or rye."

"Oats or rye?" I said, with my mouth open.

"Oats or rye," he said, perfectly serious—I could see he'd forgotten I was there. "There are two opinions, I grant you. But I think I should plump for the oats. At least the first year."

Well, that was enough for me. And I made myself scarce and hunted up Joe Lightbucket.

"Joe," I said, "do you know what sort of hay-headed imbecile we've got in command of this expedition?"

"I've heard you talk," said Joe, "but I notice he's always had scouts out and we ain't been ambushed yet. That's something."

"Ambushed?" I said. "If we ain't, it's just God's providence! He ain't even a military man, Joe. He's a farmer—and a gentleman farmer to boot. All he thinks of, when he looks at the country, is whether to plant it to oats or rye!"

"H'm," said Joe. "Well, that's looking pretty far ahead. I wouldn't think a man could do that."

315

"A man with any sense to him couldn't," I said. "And yet—hell, he looks like a fighter! But oats and rye! Why couldn't they send us a man?"

Well, the story got around and, after that, some of us used to call him Oats-and-Rye behind his back. Particularly when he'd go along so serious, with his big nose in front of him. I don't think he ever knew about it, though. I hope he didn't.

That was just before we got to the Great Meadows. We'd heard, by then, that the French were out from Fort Duquesne, and we were a little nervous. I wondered how Oats-and-Rye would take the news, but he didn't seem to scare. Fact was, when we did get to the Great Meadows, he looked it all over and said it was "a charming field for an encounter." Yes, that's what he wrote home. Ain't it beautiful? I wondered if he'd think it was so charming when the French started shooting real lead bullets out of the bushes. But I didn't know him yet.

I guess a man never quite forgets his first fight. That sobersided, big-nosed gentleman farmer of ours took forty of us all night through the rain—and it was raining pitchforks and grindstones, and you couldn't see your hand in front of your face—picked up his friendly Indians at the Half King's camp and hit the French the next morning before they had any idea we were that close. And all the time he was just as serious as a boy playing wooden soldiers. But it worked.

I remember the look of that rocky gully where we found them, and a big, dark Frenchy with his hair all tousled, shouting "Ozarm! Ozarm!"—which is French for "Hell's breakfast! They've got us!"—and how queer it was, having white men trying to kill you that you'd never even seen before. And then it was over, and as quick as that, and our Indians were taking scalps. It's their religion and we didn't feel called upon to hinder. But we'd killed ten Frenchies, including the commander—fellow called Jumonville—and captured twenty-two. Which wasn't bad for a farmer. Afterward, the Frenchies tried to make out that it wasn't fair fighting—but the losing side generally does. They claimed this Jumonville was on a mission and ought to have been treated respectful. Well, all I can say is, they acted like a war party the minute they saw us. And if we did wrong, we got paid for it later, as you'll see.

Now, if Oats-and-Rye had been just a little older—but he wasn't. We knew he was all right in a fight, by then. But fighting isn't all there is to a war. And after he'd won his first victory he didn't seem to know quite what to do with it, which is often the case. I don't think he'd have stuck at Great Meadows, twenty years later. The Frenchies were bound to come out in force, once they'd heard about friend Jumonville. But our big-nosed youngster played it according to his own best notions. And if it turned out unlucky, that wasn't all his fault. He asked for reinforcements and he got them. They weren't any good when they came, but he couldn't have told about that.

We got on as far as Gist's place, and then we couldn't hold it and had to fall back on Great Meadows again. And when we got back there we were clean frazzled out. The wilderness didn't care what happened to us or who won the fight, and it seemed as if whatever we did was the wrong thing to do. And yet we'd started out well and struck the first blow—that was the worst of it. But now it was just as if we were fighting shadows, and you could see, by the way the men walked, how they felt. You could see the confidence sweat out of them, day by day. It weighed upon Oats-and-Rye, as it would be bound to. It's a time like that takes the pith out of boy or man. Or else it does another thing. He called the place Fort Necessity in the end—he was right in calling it that.

I don't say he didn't make mistakes—he made plenty of them. I've been wet and hungry and miserable in my life, but I've never been wetter or hungrier or miserabler than inside that damned earthwork we'd scrabbled up, with the rain sloshing down and turning the world to mud, and the French marksmen picking us off from the woods till we couldn't even work the swivel guns. All the same, when they came, five hundred of them, we fought them ten hours in the rain. Then, that evening, they offered us terms, and there was just the one thing to do.

Oh, yes, they let us march out with the honors of war and the guns. But we'd surrendered, and we knew it. It was fifty-two miles back to Will's Creek, and we carried our sick and wounded on our backs. And that was the fourth of July.

I carried Joe Lightbucket till he died, though he was a hefty man, and, when he thought he was going, I put him down by the roadside and sat beside him. There wasn't anything else a man could do for him, and I didn't know what day it was. I didn't, for a fact. I knew Joe Lightbucket and me had been neighbors, but that seemed a long time ago. All I could think about now was that it kept raining on his face, and I wished I could stop that. I knew I'd seen our big-nosed youngster going by, once or twice, squelching along in the wet with an old skin cap on his head, and he looked as tired and hungry and wretched as the rest of us. I felt sorry for him, but I felt a kind of resentment too. He'd failed and he'd had to surrender, and nobody likes that. But he'd go back to his big easy farm, with servants to wait on him and powder his hair, and ride to hounds and tell the girls about his adventures. But beating the Frenchies was life and death to us backwoodsmen. And yet they'd licked us in spite of it, and killed my friend, Joe Lightbucket. Or at least that's the way I thought of it. I was pretty tired myself.

Then somebody was shaking me by the shoulder, and I looked up through the rain, and it was the big-nosed youngster.

"Wake up, man, wake up!" he said. "You'll die if you lie there in the rain."

"Joe Lightbucket's here, and he's dead," I said. That was all I thought of to say and I didn't thank him for rousing me. He looked at me sort of hopeless, and I saw how gray his face was, in spite of his youth. His big hands closed and unclosed—I can see the strong fingers opening and shutting.

"We can't take the dead," he said. "They've scalped two of our wounded already. But I'll give them no more. These men were put in my charge by the colony of Virginia. I had thought to do well with them once. By the Lord God Almighty, man, get up!"

I got up then because I had to, and Joe Lightbucket was dead and didn't mind. I wanted to say "Oats-and-Rye" at the big-nosed young-ster, but my mouth wouldn't find the words. He might get back to his farm and his servants and the rest of it, but that didn't seem to matter any more, in the rain. He'd got us licked, but he hadn't pretended any different. Well, I reckoned I could stand a thing as well as he could, al-though I wasn't gentry. I was sorry to leave Joe Lightbucket, but we had to do that. And we were a sorry lot when we got to Will's Creek. But we'd started a seven years' war and things besides a war, though none of us knew it then.

Oh, I know that was twenty years before—don't I know it, young man! But there's a man and a time. And sometimes they come together, like two streams from different hills. You don't know they're going to meet, when you stand by the sources, but meet they do. And as they get nearer each other, the look of the land starts changing. I know us back-woodsmen never thought so much of the British after Braddock got thrashed next year. They went fighting in the woods as if they were on parade—and very pretty they looked—but they got shot down the same way.

I wasn't there—I'd married—but my big-nosed youngster was, and that surprised me. You'd have thought he'd have had enough of it—espe-cially when you could see he was unlucky and always getting licked. I didn't bear him a grudge, but how was it his affair? We kept more to ourselves in those days—the tidewater men thought we were pretty tough customers. And I might like a Pennsylvanian, but I didn't feel he was any particular countryman of mine. I don't wonder the British thought we couldn't make a revolution. All I wonder is how we did.

Why did I join up, when it came? Well, it's hard for me to say. It wasn't because of the young imps who got themselves drunk on bad rum and called themselves Sons of Liberty—I was a grown man, then, with sons. I reckon, as much as anything else, it was feeling I had to pay somebody back for killing Joe Lightbucket—and as long as the French weren't handy, the British would have to do. Funny how a thing like that will stick in your mind. And when I did, it was just about what I'd expected. We got licked and retreated and the rest of it, and Congress muddled around and the Pennsylvania men despised the Connecticut ters and us Virginians despised them both. Yes, a tag-rag army, with a lot of our own folks against us, set to fight the trained troops of one of the greatest powers on earth. All the same, I'd drawn my line, and I meant to toe it. But once the first whooping's over, it takes more than handsome speeches to make a revolution.

That's another thing I won't forget—I don't reckon any of us will. I won't forget that winter valley and the hills that ringed us round. I've felt cold, before and since, but not like that cold. And, God, how the wet wood smoked and spit when you did get to make a fire. Army? We weren't an army that we could see—not then. We were just a lot of hungry perishers caught in a trap of winter, and half the time wondering why we were there. I know sometimes I'd wake up in the freezing morning and think: *Is this me? Aeneas Todkill? It can't be. Why, I've got a hundred acres on Split Run and a wife I'm considerable fond of, not to speak of the children—and what in the name of glory am I doing here in Pennsylvania with my left ear froze? If it's independence I want, I had plenty of that before, and as for a United States, that's a big word, but does it mean anything?*

Then, of course, there'd be orders to give and the wood to get and some dumb fool to keep from deserting because he was homesick, and by the time it was night, you were too bone-tired to think of anything at all. Which was just as well, because all the time the British were in Philadelphia, taking it easy, with the taverns open and the Tories giving balls for them. Till, now and then, you'd wonder if the Tories mightn't be right. That's the thing that takes the heart out of you.

I was feeling pretty sick that evening—not sick in the body, but sick in the mind. We'd had a fight with some Maryland men over a rabbit— nothing that sane and sensible men would fight about, but men on the edge of dying ain't sane or sensible. It was going to make bad blood. My best sergeant and my best corporal were both of them down with dysentery, and the sergeant had the pinched face you don't like to see. And then, after all, and just as we were cooking the rabbit, that fool, Willy Grimes, had tilted a pail of snow water on the fire. I wanted to get away from the lot of 'em. If I didn't, I was likely to start cursing my own men. So I left George Baker to clean up the mess and went off to the edge of the woods. The sun was setting, early and red, and the light looked like blood on the snow. And I thought that was right and it was our blood and we'd spilt it and got no good of it.

For who had we got to lead us and train us and make us win—twenty years from Fort Necessity and the first time I'd gone to war? A parcel of windbags in Congress and a Prussian drill sergeant, a Virginia gentleman farmer and a nice little red-haired French boy that smiled like a girl. That was all we had to put against the great and the strong. Why, half our own gentry were against us, in places like New York and Philadelphia! And there was worse than that. For the British, at least, knew they were British, and proud of it. But how were you going to make one thing or one nation out of folks as different as folks from Massachusetts and Virginia and York State when, even the way we were, we'd quarrel over a rabbit? How was it ever going to be done?

I was thinking like this and looking down at the valley—at the makeshift huts and the mean little smokes from the fires, and the hard snow. There were four men bringing a log of wood along—two men ought to have been able to carry it. But they moved slow—you could see their knees wobble as they walked. One fellow had his feet wrapped in rags and another's pants were splitting. It was comic, in a way—they'd have laughed at it in Philadelphia. But it wasn't comic to me.

I didn't hear him come along—it was getting dark and he always walked light for a big man. He usually had the Frenchman with him, or the New Yorker, or some of his staff, but this time he was all by himself. I saw the big nose the minute I turned around, and the eyes that could burn a hole in you when they felt like it. Things had happened to him since he was a big-boned youngster—and they were in his face. I suppose they'll make statues of him, but he wasn't marble—I heard him curse Lee at Monmouth, and he did it high and fancy. I saluted and said, "Captain Todkill, general." I'd learned that much in twenty years.

"Observing our dispositions, Captain Todkill?" he said in his stiffnecked way. "I'm glad to find you so alert."

"No, general," I said. "To tell you the truth, the dispositions weren't in my mind. I just thought I'd get out of the clutter for a minute, and think about something else; for sometimes a man gets sick of the whole blamed business."

I looked at him for a minute and wondered if I dared. I didn't feel as if I cared any more, and yet, somehow, I had to know.

"They tell me this used to be pretty good farming country before we got here, general," I said. "Well, now, that bottom field—I was just wondering if, when the folks come back, they'd plant it to oats or rye."

He swept his eye down the valley. But if he remembered anything, he didn't let on.

"An interesting question, Captain Todkill," he said. "There is a new vetch that is very well spoken of. My overseer is trying it at Mount Vernon, but I yet have had no definite news as to the success or failure of the experiment." And he sighed for a moment, as if that was the biggest thing in the world to him. Most likely it was, when he thought of it—he'd always been a farmer.

But I'd been looking at him and then looking down the valley. And there was the line of an earthwork and a trench behind it—and suddenly it all seemed to come together. You know how a sound or a smell or a sight will take you back twenty years. Like the blow of a hammer it was, and just as sudden. I must have been tuckered, all right. For just for a second, I wasn't there any more; I was sitting beside Joe Lightbucket and the rain was falling on my face.

"It's Fort Necessity!" I said, in a queer, loud voice, and a black, drowning wave came over me. For this was the second time.

He looked at me very steady. They say you can tell by the lines in a man's forehead what he's been through. But I say you can tell by his eyes.

"No, Captain Todkill," he said, and his voice was as stiff as ever, but there was a ring to it, and his big hands shut and opened as I'd seen them do once before. "This is not Fort Necessity. It is a bigger field than ever man plowed before. But we shall yet make a nation."

It was dark now in the valley, and the poor little lights were beginning. He looked at them once more.

"I fear we must go back, captain," he said. "I have guests for supper. Colonel Hamilton has promised the Marquis a bowl of cornmeal mush, and the Marquis seems all agog for the experience."

"Well, we've got a rab—we've got mush ourselves," I said. "It's a damned tiresome sort of food when you get it so constant, but as long as it sticks to you, I reckon we can't complain."

"I am much of the same opinion, captain," he said. "It is damned tiresome. But it does—er—stick to you."

Then he went his way and I went mine, and that was all there was to it. Yes, I reckon that was all. But I'd seen what I wanted to see, when he talked about Fort Necessity. I knew what I wanted to know. I'd been thinking back, but he'd been thinking ahead—same as he did at first, only then I didn't know it. You can't beat a man who's been to Fort Necessity and learned from it—you can't beat that man at all. We didn't know we were getting to be an army, much less a nation, and it kind of surprised us. But I guess he'd had some thoughts on the subject.

Oh, yes, I went through to the surrender—saw the redcoats come out of Yorktown, with the drums beating and the field music playing The World Turned Upside Down. And that was quite a sight, but not to compare. We didn't make the country then. We made it that freezing winter, in spite of Philadelphia and Billy Howe and the Tories. And that's what I say—if you're talking kings and dictators, you're talking bellywash. They'd have cheered to have a man like that come over to their side, but he and Tom Jefferson wouldn't. And yet, all he had to do was sit back and take it easy. At the worst, he could have sneaked off to Nova Scotia or England, the way a lot of gentry did. But he threw it all in on our side—the plain folks' side—and he stuck by it, too, the stiff-necked, big-nosed old man. Let him ride in a coach and four if he likes —coaches and fours won't change him. He's going to have manners till he dies, and every now and then he's bound to lose his temper. But that doesn't make any difference. He ain't going to be George the First or George the Emperor. He's going to stay George Washington and look after his oats and rye. No, we ain't seen the full crop yet. But we're going to remember who planted it. You remember that, in Kentucky, when you come to break your own ground.

THE DORYMEN

This thrilling story, portraying as it does the great seafaring
tradition of New England, deserves a pre-eminent place among
the Americana here. The author, a native of Massachusetts
who spent much of his boyhood near the fishing port of
Gloucester, writes about the men who give their days and
nights, and their lives, to the sea. "The Dorymen," if it
were filmed for the movies—it would require a wide screen—
would make an impressive documentary of the Yankee sailing
ships that once carried the fishermen and their dories to the
Sable Island Banks. The first settlers, as the author observes,
followed the cod fishery. They were fishermen; that was
their trade—the most ancient in our history. From long before
the time of Queen Elizabeth, Englishmen had come to fish
off the Newfoundland Banks. And when the early English
settlers sailed westward to America, they came to the
Massachusetts shore for the same reason.

Here is retold in vivid detail the story of two days on
the open seas off the Sable Island Banks.

Riding a poorly-broken wild horse of the Sable Island herds, I
passed one September morning along the eastern beaches of that rift
of dunes, the "graveyard of the Atlantic"—so called because of the
sprawled hulls and tipping spars of wrecks new and old: iron freighters,
square-rigged vessels, and schooners of the Grand Banks. A north-
easterly gale had blown itself out after three days of unbroken mauling
by combers that, more than once, had breached clear across the island.

A flood tide now heaved between the ruins of the lost vessels. Ancient
spars had fallen in the night past. Other masts had risen into the morning
sun, for the peculiar action of the gales plows the bars and shoals
asunder; and the ruins of vessels, lost a century before, may then emerge.
A British-built Greek freighter, wallowing in a sea grave she had come
far to find, had been beaten so far over that the green tide, roaring into

her shattered hatchways, came gushing out in streams blackened by the coal dust of her bunkers.

Half a mile ahead of me, two seamen of the Canadian coast guard rode at a trot, their heads constantly turning to the left and right. Now and then, one reined up to bend over a swath of seaweed or a spar rolled up by the surf. They were seeking drowned men, or men still living that may have come ashore from one of the vessels whose signals of distress had been read from the lighthouses, the West Bar Light and the East Bar Light.

It is a standing order in that efficient establishment that the beaches must be constantly patrolled during gales and after them. Since it was a task too severe for men on foot, the coast guard had long since captured the wild horses, had broken them to the saddle and to the great wagon that hauled the lifesaving gear up and down the dune tracks. It is well known that those horses, malformed now by poor forage and inbreeding, are the descendants of Arabian herds put on that island in Columbian times by Portuguese adventurers. Those men intended to kill and eat the horses if stores ran short on that uncharted coast or if a gale swept their vessels onto the frightful lee shore.

Bursting holds, and rusted anchor chains clanging on twisted deck plates, and the screech of timbers parting: all these, added to the din of the swirling tide and the incessant clamor of terns, overhead, kept the beaches in an uproar. Bitter cold and keen against my face, the spray struck so hard that I turned the horse into a shelter between two dunes. One of them had been split by the gale. This furious alteration had uncovered a boat; that is, its bow and its port gunwale lay bare to the sun. It stirred me to see the familiar bottle green still vivid under the gunwale. The dory had been well preserved by the avalanche of sand that had overwhelmed it on a long-gone day or night when a gale had harried the Banks and the Gloucester schooners hove to.

I rode slowly around the boat, holding my horse down with difficulty, because this relic made him uneasy, although such things were well known to him. In the end, I dismounted and let him stand at ease some distance away.

I knew this dory. By its blunt prow and stern, high sides, its strong, good wood and traditional color, I made it out to be a dory of the old Yankee fleet. I knelt at the bow and struck away a crust of sand and seaweed clumped there by the pressure of the dune. There I read her vessel's name: *Adventurer* of Gloucester. I took up the blade of an oar, sea-bitten, and drew it across the drifted sand within her. The toe of an upturned boot appeared. I shoveled a bit more, and thus uncovered the other boot. The wrinkled cowhide had turned to a coppery hue. It seemed improper to dig farther, to find out whether a man really lay there. With my hands, I threw the sand back over the boots. And I asked myself: "Is his dorymate there, too? Stretched on bottom boards, where they fought it out together against the gale and cold and thirst? And lost the fight?"

If it was true that the dorymates lay in their dory tomb, who had they been and what their trade? And how did they come to lie there in the ancient graveyard of their kind?

They had been dorymen of a Gloucester schooner, perhaps the first to bear that memorable name. I myself had sailed in a topsail schooner of the same name; in fact, she was working on Sable Island Bank that very season, one of the last of our schooners to fish under sail only. The two dorymen had been driven ashore long before our time. There is no record of their loss. Indeed, if the vessel herself was killed in that gale, there would be only this record: Schooner *Adventurer*, lost with all hands, on Sable Island Bank, September, 18—. Something like that; and, nearby, a note about the memorial service, the funeral masses for the unfound dead.

They were fishermen; that was their trade. It is the most ancient in our history, because the first settlers followed the cod fishery, lived by it, and, in fact, came to the Massachusetts shore because they knew they could kill cod. And how did they acquire that knowledge? This way: long before the time of Queen Elizabeth and her Walter Raleigh, the Englishman of the West Country ports—Bristol among them—had fished the Grand Bank of Newfoundland. They built curing establishments and cooking rooms on that shore. Before them, the Bretons had killed cod there, using the islands of Saint Pierre and Miquelon for their bases. Because the cod were fat and abundant, because they were less oily than the European fish, they could be well cured. Cod thus became a prized food among the Portuguese, whose historians assert, with good reason, that the ships of Portugal fished there long before Columbus was born.

The settlers on the New England shores followed that trade. Their descendants pushed it vigorously to new banks and to the old ones. They were the first men to pitch their energy and thought into the improvement of gear. They replaced the hand lines with the trawls: long lines from which shorter lines, bearing baited hooks, were sent down to the bottom to reach the cod and haddock. While other nations patiently jigged for cod off Newfoundland, the Yankees added more and more hooks until, at last, the schooners were setting trawls a mile long, a hook every six feet, a rich harvest for every haul.

Century by century, those fishermen created the dory. By changes big and infinitely small, they altered the design until, in the end, they had created the perfect craft for their trade. Its high sides withstood the assaults of waves; its flat bottom let the dory fall off before such combers;

its sideboards, strengthened cunningly in the boatyards of home, made it so sturdy that it could stand almost any weather if the right kind of men were in it.

They created the fishery and the gear, and they made history. They fed the slaves of the Spanish New World and fed the towns of the Atlantic coast. Under sail and at the oars, they fought the wars. It was the Yankee dorymen who carried Washington's army away from the Long Island disaster and set it on the desperate road to Yorktown. When, in our day, the U-boats surfaced on the banks to shell the schooners, the shells that split their conning towers were fired by dorymen.

Backed by a craftsmanship richer than all the trades of the sea, the two dorymen of the Sable Island grave had, on that fatal day, started the last rounds of a task that can be accurately reconstructed because it never changed.

Here it is:

The *Adventurer,* clearing out of Gloucester under a whole mainsail and topsails, too, had driven across to Nova Scotia, her rail under, her dories upside down in two nests on either side the foremast. In the shelter of the nests, and elsewhere, the dorymen set to their first work: sharpening hooks in hook sets, fastening them to the main trawl by short lines called gangins (variously spelled), and mending the trawl tubs, actually canvas baskets into which the readied trawls were coiled.

Those men, in storm hats and oil clothing, were of all the Atlantic peoples: Nova Scotians, Newfoundlanders, Irishmen of Gloucester and Boston, Italians, and, as always, the skilled Portuguese. The skipper came from the ranks. A good man in a dory, he had become competent in directing them, in hard sailing home to the lively Wednesday markets, and in selling his fare of fish. By the old fifty-fifty lay, half the gross profit went to the captain and crew, the balance to the owners.

The dorymen paid for all the food and, to a degree, for lost gear. The skipper purchased the stores and took a commission, which is why he bought the best, and established the high character of the table set in the schooners. The men ate three big meals a day: prime beef, spring lamb, bread out of the Shipmate stove, vegetables and choice fruits, pies and cakes. In the shack locker were always the cheese, crackers, and cookies for those coming off night watches. On the stove there were tea kettles always brewing. The dorymen never ate fish.

"Sit ye down, chum," was the traditional greeting to greenhorns. "Eat, and give the vessel a good name."

Eastward the *Adventurer* swept into the rose-colored evening of Nova Scotia, and by the time the lighthouses began to flash she steered up the Roseway River, dropping sail after sail, and made fast to the herring wharf of Shelburne. There, in the morning, the herring men brought aboard a few samples from their icehouse; and the skipper, a mnnuur at buying bait, ran his thumbnail down a herring belly to test its firmness, snuffed it to mark its freshness. He bought. The baskets went swinging over the rail, and down the herring flowed onto the ice of pens below decks, soon to be filled with cod.

On the first tide that serves, away she flies. Now the skipper's other skills come into play. Ancient charts are studied: "Western Bank— 69,000 mixed fish, June 7, 1892; Banquereau—90,000 cod, Sept. 4, 1911," and so forth until, at last, the dorymen hear the word:

"On fish! He says we're on fish!"

"He" is the skipper again, straddled near the helm, watching the sails come off the schooner until she glides under headsails only. How does he know there are cod below in tens of thousands? The sea isn't full of fish—not by a long shot. They must have their forage. It isn't everywhere. His charts have guided him so far. His memory helps. Now he must learn one more fact: the character of the sea bottom right below her keel. He has seen on his charts the symbols "VFGS." He calls for the deep-sea lead, armed with tallow or butter. When it is hauled and handed to him, he rolls the caught particles between thumb and forefinger. Should his trained fingers fail to assure him, he tastes the butter and his tongue gives him the news. It repeats: "On fish!" It is, indeed, the very fine gray sand signified in the chart letters.

"Bait up! Bait up!" he says, "Bait up!"

The herring, chopped by the dorymen into chunks of a certain size, are set on the hooks, and the hooks are again coiled into the baskets.

"Number one dory!"

This is the dory of Sable Island.

Her two men are not specifically named in the records. It may be well to let them bear, for a short time, the names of men well remembered on the Grand Banks for their courage and devotion: Dick Murphy, Colin Bell. They are men in their forties: great shoulders rounded by life at the oars, dark eyes sobered by a labor that was not much more than enslavement. Dick is an inch taller than Colin; otherwise, they are alike in their oil clothing, storm hats, cowhide boots, well oiled by the oil of cod livers.

They swing out the top dory of the starboard nest. Into it they place oars and blackball buoys—small kegs with black flags marked "No. 1." Dick climbs into the dory. Colin passes up the tubs of baited trawls, the willow wand for heaving the trawl, the water bottle, the food tin. These, most likely, contain a little water, a few pilot biscuits. They are stowed in the sideboards.

"Dory away!"

The men on deck lower the dory. The skipper points to the southeast, the direction of the set. The vessel glides on, dropping dories as she goes.

Colin sits at the oars and pulls easily away. In the stern, Dick heaves over the first buoy and its anchor; and then, in a smooth, strong action, lifts the top coil with the wand and flips it over. Thus the bait sinks to the very fine gray sand, twenty fathoms down.

Continually they raise their heads to measure the wind, try the wintry air for snow smell, the sky for its changes. This is late in the season. If winter comes to pay a visit, there'll be no notice before a howling arrival.

The vessel is out of sight. They are alone, these two, in a lonely wilderness, heaving black to the rim of the world. They have only each other. It is enough. They are dorymates and have been so a score of seasons. Each depends thoroughly on the other. There's no need of talk or shouts or warnings. They think as one alert, crafty man, immensely strong, fighters against the Atlantic now holding them in a cold, steel-blue embrace.

The last hook goes gleaming down. The second buoy goes over. Its anchor slants bubbling away.

"Stay here?"

"Aye, chum!"

They thus agree to lay on the ends; which is to say, they will tie up to the buoy and wait for the *Adventurer* to come around and blow the fishing signal—two hours hence. It is too cold to row back to her. They might sail the dory. They choose to lie down out of the wind, gossip a bit about home, and then, perhaps, "take a kink"—a nap on the bottom boards while the cod swallow hooks far below.

"Hoo-oo! Hoo-oo!" Silence; and then again: "Hoo-oo! Hoo-oo!"

Back at the starting place, the skipper cranks the horn. The cod have had time for breakfast. They have found it a little on the steely side. But they've had it. The fishing signal bowls across the sea, and in each of the ten dories the dorymates rise to their toil.

Colin takes his place in the bow, hauls the blackball and anchor, passes them to Dick, and then lays the trawl line on a small iron wheel in a frame, set on the gunwale forward. This is the gurdy. Turning as he hauls, it lightens his labor.

He strains to it. The first hooks come up empty; then he yields to the heavy tug of fish. Up comes the first cod, a fat twenty-pounder, a "steaker." Harvest is under way. He slats the fish off by a deft whirl backward. The cod falls into the middle place. Colin coils the empty hooks into an empty basket.

Hour after hour, the task goes on. The dory fills slowly. Salt and freezing wind bite at the dorymates. In silence, they rise and bend, haul and coil; and change places, rise and bend, until the last hook is coiled, the dory loaded.

The wind being fair for the dory, they hoist the blue sail—blue, black, or whatever—and steer for the schooner. Sail after sail rises beyond; other dories answer to the great oars and the short, deep stroke. No. 1 comes alongside first. The cook hands down the pitchforks. In the last action of the fishing itself, Dick and Colin pitch the cod over the rail and into the deck pens. Up their dory goes, its plug pulled to let brine and cod-blood drain.

On deck, the toil hits a harder pace. One as gutter, the other as ripper, Dick and Colin take their places at the troughs. Colin rips down with the knife, Dick seizes the cod and tears out the gut, and the refuse flows into the sea for the waiting gulls. The dressed cod fly backward into a tub, where water runs. An "idler"—first man handy—stirs the fish in a circular, cleansing motion and sends them below to the pens of cracked ice, where other men pack the cod between layers of ice.

It is barely noon, yet the two dorymates have done a terrible day's work already. They now turn and haul up other dories, gut and split other loads, and—

"Dinner! Dinner! First table!"

They eat slowly, thoroughly, steak after steak, cleaning the deep plate with bread, eating it, swallowing mugs of tea, and thus stoke the inner fires that must burn hot far into the night. Another set is made. Night falls over the returning dories. Oil torches blaze along the decks. Knives click and slice until the cod are down below. The night watch is set: two hours. Dick and Colin stand it, ceaselessly watching, listening. They call the relief, tumble into their forecastle bunks, and tumble out at daybreak for another eighteen-hour day, give or take an hour.

What do they get for it? Two dollars? Three? At times, four or five. They cannot know. Forces working thousands of miles away—West Indies, California, Alaska, Boston—determine what the dealers will bid at Gloucester or at Boston. Four cents a pound? Five? As much as eight? Perhaps. They cannot know until it's done and the vessel sold "right through." They can take it. They can't leave it. They are masters of a high skill. They have no other. They must fish or go hungry, houseless. There are no longshore jobs for them while fish can be killed. The Yankee packers see to that.

Day breaks, and with it comes the familiar cry: "Number one! Dory away!"

Again the heaving, again the hauling until late in the afternoon. Once more, Dick and Colin stretch out on the bottom boards, bodies strained now to the utmost. This is the last set. By midnight, if all goes well, the *Adventurer* will be under a whole mainsail again or, most likely, on a hard, dead beat to windward, until the lights of home greet them kindly.

Vapor curls from their snoring mouths. Frost creeps along their oil-skins. It is uneasy sleep. A flurry of snow floats over them. The water blackens and a roller passes under the dory, knocks at it. These changes pass without notice.

"Hoo-oo-oo!"

They rise and haul until the dory fills. The sun slants down, far snow squalls glittering on the long rays; then, right out of the sun, a hailstorm blows, rattles, stops. These two have no barometer, only the barometer of skilled hearts. Deep in twisting cod, they labor until a word or two must be passed.

"I don't like this."

That's all.

"No, Dick. We'd best look sharp."

Far to the north, too far to be heard in the rising racket, the *Adventurer* sounds the gale warning. Sharp and close calls of her horn blare out: "Hoot! Hoot! Hoot!" Which is to say: "Cut gear! Stand by! I am coming. Gale! Gale!"

Darting unseen in the snowy dusk, the schooner takes in the first dory, No. 10, and No. 9 and No. 8; and, fearful of the rising gale, she sails faster and begins taking them "on the fly," a dangerous, heartbreaking job.

No. 1 must be the last, having been the first. Stolidly, Dick and Colin peer into the darkness, waiting for the torches to gleam, the horn to sound. The gale does not wait. Rising in true September fashion, the Atlantic suddenly hurls wave after wave against the dory. A blinding drive of snow beats between the dory and the schooner's position. She drives past unseen. Half a mile onward, the skipper begins the traditional circle of search, closing in, point by point, to the place where the dory must be.

It is not there. Dick, at the approving nod, cuts the buoy and anchor, lets them go. They wait, listening, staring. A sea strikes against the high side and rams the dory into a whirling motion, a hurtling drive down into a trough.

Without a word, without a murmur, the dorymen open the battle. Over goes the other buoy and anchor, then the trawl baskets, and, one by one, two by two, the hard-won cod. They clear for action. They do not know what that action must be. All they know is that they must have room at the oars, room to bail. A sea leaps over the gunwale, half fills the boat. Dick bails. Colin sits to the oars to keep her head into it. He gives to the gale the only answer he can give: the short, deep stroke.

The dory joins the battle like a living thing. All she needs is men— and she has the best of them on her thwart, on the bottom boards bailing.

An hour passes in the first desperate effort to stay there, to keep the place known to the *Adventurer*. Too far in the black sky hammers on their heads, their arms, their stretching, straining hands. They know that soon the skipper must ask himself: "Can I keep her under sail in this blow? How long before I must heave her to and save what men I've got?"

In the end, Colin gives the verdict.

"Chum, we're in for it."

"Aye, Colin! Where to, would you say?"

Dick is bent over the pocket compass, striving to read it in the gloom. Colin answers: "Sable Island?"

"We can try, chum. Due west. I'll spell you when you say so." He bails.

How far before the lights of Sable Island will flash their candle power across that sea? Neither Dick nor Colin can tell exactly. They are in for it. That is all.

Hail falls again, succeeding the snow. The hail turns to rain. It freezes on them and at their feet. The oars strike and rise. The bailer matches the action. They gain a few lengths, fall back. The gale keeps hauling until it stands in the northeast for good. The tide swings and helps the dory a little. At midnight, Dick goes to the oars. Colin takes up the bailer. Yet he is so far gone that he must lie down awhile. A boarding sea brings him up again at once.

"Think we're doing anything, Dick?"

"Aye."

By midnight, they know they're on the way. The flood tide, rolling toward the island, holds them high at times, drops them down into ever-deepening troughs. Now the stroke of the oars droops to a lower stroke. The wind is piping up in real earnest; the gale is following after the dory, hammering at it, and the rollers are higher, higher. Hunger and thirst begin to weaken hearts used to great supplies of rich food. The sips of water, bits of cracker, carefully taken, serve them poorly.

The day breaks. Colin rises, clinging to the gunwale, and looks around the compass, hoping that even now, even so late, the wily skipper may have figured out their course and be after them. He sees nothing, nothing but the whirling spray of the empty sea. He falls to bailing.

Long since, the keen knife of the wind has cut through their oil clothing and into the layers of wool beneath. They have no heat within to keep the blizzard out of their hearts.

"I'll spell you now, chum." Dick totters from the thwart, nearly losing the oars. Colin falls upon them and begins to row. The tide turns against them, snatches at the blades. The sky, not much lighter even so far into the morning, is a mass of heaving gray-black clouds, another image of the sea.

"You got any idea now, Dick?" Colin leans far down to shout his question, because his dorymate has not stirred at all.

"By nightfall we should make out the light. East Bar."

331

Slewing snow and freezing spray before it, the night falls on them; and the gale, blowing harder now that the sun is out of the way, hammers the dory down into the deepening troughs, hammers her harder when the failing oars drive her to the crests. The ice begins to make. It forms on the bottom boards, thickens there. White, frosty bands glitter on the sideboards. Frost hangs from the brims of storm hats.

Dick clears the dory of water again and goes to the oars to relieve his dorymate. Once free of the whitening thwart, Colin falls dumbly and sprawls. Those first strokes of the oars, which must be hard and strong to straighten the boat out, take a toll of Dick's waning strength. He rows now with his eyes shut, his mouth gasping out the story of his emptying heart.

Unstirring and slowly whitening along his twisted back and shoulders, Colin lies unseen by his dorymate. In the next two hours, the strokes grow feebler, the dory wavers and at times falls swirling down from the crest of a battering sea. It is midnight again before, faint and far, very far, to the eastward, a light shoots out a yellow flash, drowned by the sea before it reaches them. Dick has long since given up the life-long habit of glancing over his shoulder at every fifth stroke. He cannot see, can only try for one more stroke of the oars.

A crosswise sea, bolting in against the wind, snatches at the oar in his right hand and bears it down and away. He is so far gone, in the delirium of frost and weariness, that he fails to change his stroke. His frozen right hand still seems to hold the oar. At last, when wind and tide and gale combine to upend the dory, whirl it higher and faster, he topples and falls by his dorymate's side.

Increasing to full force, the gale sweeps over the island, drowning the wrecks, the shores, the dunes, and screening the two lights. And it draws along with it, sea after following sea, a dory made of crystal, a bright thing lightly whirling, all afire with ice and frost. In the shoaler water, among the bars, the gale breaks even higher, making such billows that the crystal dory is picked up and hurled upon the beach. There the breakers push it to the high-water mark, then beyond it, until it swirls into the hollow between the two dunes. Before daybreak, the shifting sands cover it. The earth receives it, hides it from the guardsmen on their horses.

So their story ends. So their names—whatever they may be—are added to the centuries' toll of dorymen, a toll that, in some opinions, is ten thousand.

These were the dorymen. Those were the days of their lives and deaths. Days that are gone forever—and a good thing, too. In all that enormous coast line, from Gloucester to Fortune Bay, there is not now a vessel fishing under sail. There is not one dory carried out of the ports, except for a few used in an obscure halibut fishery out of Nova Scotian ports.

The dragger has displaced the trawl. Cod are now taken in vast nets, handled by powerful winches, set on great, steel plates. The fishermen of Gloucester still toil hard. Their job is not one that ever causes envy. The best that can be said of it is this: they need never leave the deck.

William Faulkner

SKIRMISH AT SARTORIS

The "skirmish" shows as dramatically as the rebel yell, the note
on which this revealing episode concludes, that the spirit of
men like the Colonel was not to be defeated on the home
front, no matter what might have happened on the field of
battle. The issue of the ballot box was the proposed election
of Benbow to the office of Marshal of Jefferson, for it
symbolized an unforgivable affront to Southern pride as
well as the end of whatever toleration there might have been
otherwise for Yankees. But the story of what happened at
Sartoris is also the story of Drusilla, Colonel Sartoris, and
Aunt Louisa, whose ideals of Southern womanhood were
not to be defeated either.

When I think of that day, of Father's old troop on their horses
drawn up facing the house, and Father and Drusilla standing on the
ground with that Carpet Bagger voting box in front of them, and opposite them the ladies on the porch and the two sets of them, the men
and the ladies, facing one another like they were both waiting for the
sound to charge, I think I know the reason. I think it was because
Father's troop (like all the other Southern soldiers too), even though
they had surrendered and said that they were whipped, were still soldiers. Maybe from the old habit of doing everything as one man; maybe
when you have lived for four years in a world ordered completely by
men's doings, even when it is danger and fighting, you don't want to
quit that world: maybe the danger and the fighting are the reasons, because men have been pacifists for every reason under the sun except to
avoid danger and fighting. And so now Father's troop and all the other
men in Jefferson, and Aunt Louisa and Mrs. Habersham and all the
ladies in Jefferson were actually enemies for the reason that the men
had given in and admitted that they belonged to the United States but
the ladies had never surrendered.

I remember the night we got the letter and found out at last where
Drusilla was. It was just before Christmas in 1864, after the Yankees
had burned Jefferson and gone away, and we didn't even know for
sure if the war was still going on or not. All we knew was that for three

years the country had been full of Yankees, and then all of a sudden they were gone and there were no men there at all any more. We hadn't even heard from Father since July, from Carolina, so that now we lived in a world of burned towns and houses and ruined plantations and fields inhabited only by women. Ringo and I were fifteen; we felt almost exactly like we had to eat and sleep and change our clothes in a hotel built only for ladies and children.

The envelope was worn and dirty and it had been opened once and then glued back, but Ringo and I could still make out *Hawkhurst, Gihon County, Alabama,* on it even though we didn't recognize Aunt Louisa's hand at first. It was addressed to Granny, and that showed how long ago it had been written because Aunt Louisa didn't even know that Granny was dead now. It was six pages cut with scissors from wallpaper and written on both sides with pokeberry juice, and I thought about the time two years ago when Granny and Ringo and I went to Hawkhurst on the way to catch the Yankee army that stole our silver and we found how the Yankees had come and burned Hawkhurst too after Uncle Dennison and Gavin Breckbridge were killed at Shiloh, and Aunt Louisa and Drusilla and Denny were living in a Negro cabin just like we did at Sartoris in Mississippi. And Drusilla had cut her hair off short like mine almost and she wore a shirt and jeans pants just like Ringo and me and her hands were rough from working too, and Aunt Louisa began to cry and tell us how Drusilla had cut her hair and put on man's clothes the day the news came that Gavin Breckbridge was dead too. But Drusilla didn't cry; it was just that night we were there; the Negroes were still passing in the road all night long, and she waked me and we went down to the road and listened to them passing in the darkness, singing, trying to catch the Yankee army and get free. Then they were gone and Drusilla told me to go on back to bed and I asked her if she wasn't going to bed too and she said she didn't sleep any more, that she had to stay up and keep a dog quiet; it wasn't a bad dog only she just had to get up now and then and show it the stick and then it would be quiet, and I said, "What dog? I haven't seen any dog." And then she turned and put her hand on my shoulder (I was already taller than she was) and said:

"Listen. When you see Cousin Johnny again, ask him to let me ride in his troop with him. Tell him I can ride and maybe I can learn to shoot and that I won't be afraid. Will you tell him?" But I didn't tell Father. Maybe I forgot it. Then the Yankees went away, and Father and his troop went away too. Then, six months later, we had a letter from him about how they were fighting in Carolina, and a month after that we had one from Aunt Louisa that Drusilla was gone too, a short letter on the wallpaper that you could see where Aunt Louisa had cried in the pokeberry juice about how she did not know where Drusilla was but that she had expected the worst ever since Drusilla had deliberately tried to unsex herself by refusing to feel any natural grief at the death not only of her affianced husband but of her own father and that she took it for granted that Drusilla was with us and though she did not expect Drusilla to take any steps herself to relieve a mother's anxiety, she hoped that Granny would. But we didn't know where Drusilla was either. She had just vanished. It was like the Yankees in just passing through the South had not only taken along with them all living men blue and gray and white and black, but even one young girl who had happened to try to look and act like a man after her sweetheart was killed.

So then the next letter came. Only Granny wasn't there to read it, and so for a while Ringo and I couldn't make out what Aunt Louisa was trying to tell us. This one was on the same wallpaper too, six pages this time, only Aunt Louisa hadn't cried in the pokeberry juice this time: Ringo said because she must have been writing too fast:

DEAR SISTER:

I think this will be news to you as it was to me though I both hope and pray it will not be the heart-rending shock to you it was to me as naturally it cannot since you are only an aunt while I am the mother. But it is not myself I am thinking of since I am a woman, a mother, a Southern woman, and it has been our lot during the last four years to learn to bear anything. But when I think of my husband who laid down his life to protect a heritage of courageous men and spotless women looking down from heaven upon a daughter who had deliberately cast away that for which he died, and when I think of my half-orphan son who will one day ask of me why his martyred father's sacrifice was not enough to preserve his sister's good name. . . .

That's how it sounded. Ringo was holding a pineknot for me to read by, but after a while he had to light another pineknot and all the far we had got was how when Gavin Breckbridge was killed at Shiloh before he and Drusilla had had time to marry, there had been reserved for Drusilla the highest destiny of a Southern woman—to be the bride-widow of a lost cause—and how Drusilla had not only thrown that away, she had not only become a lost woman and a shame to her father's memory but she was now living in a word that Aunt Louisa would not even repeat but that Granny knew what it was, though at least thank God that Father and Drusilla were not actually any blood kin, it being Father's wife who was Drusilla's cousin by blood and not Father himself. So then Ringo lit the other pineknot and then we put the sheets of wallpaper down on the floor and then we found out what it was: how Drusilla had been gone for six months and no word from her except she was alive, and then one night she walked into the cabin where Aunt Louisa and Denny were (and now it had a line drawn under it, like this:) in the garments not alone of a man but of a common private soldier and told them how she had been a member of Father's troop for six months, bivouacking at night surrounded by sleeping men and not even bothering to put up the tent for her and Father except when the weather was bad, and how Drusilla not only showed neither shame nor remorse but actually pretended she did not even know what Aunt Louisa was talking about; how then Aunt Louisa told her that she and Father must marry at once, Drusilla said, "Can't you understand that I am tired of burying husbands in this war? That I am riding in Cousin John's troops not to find a man but to hurt Yankees?" and how Aunt Louisa said:

"At least don't call him *Cousin* John where strangers can hear you."

The third letter did not come to us at all. It came to Mrs. Compson. Drusilla and Father were home then. It was in the spring and the war was over now, and we were busy getting the cypress and oak out of the bottom to build the house and Drusilla working with Joby and Ringo and Father and me like another man, with her hair shorter than it had been at Hawkhurst and her face sunburned from riding in the weather and her body thin from living like soldiers lived. After Granny died Ringo and Louvinia and I all slept in the cabin, but after Father came Ringo and Louvinia moved back to the other cabin with Joby and now Father and I slept on Ringo's and my pallet and Drusilla slept in the bed behind the quilt curtain where Granny used to sleep. And so one night I remembered Aunt Louisa's letter and I showed it to Drusilla and Father, and Father found out that Drusilla had not written to tell Aunt Louisa where she was and Father said she must, and so one day Mrs. Compson came out with the third letter. Drusilla and Ringo and Louvinia too were down in the bottom at the sawmill and I saw that one too, on the wallpaper with the pokeberry juice and the juice not cried on this time either, and this the first time Mrs. Compson had come out since Granny died and not even getting out of her surrey but sitting there holding to her parasol with one hand and her shawl with the other and looking around like when Drusilla would come out of the house or from around the corner it would not be just a thin sunburned girl in a man's shirt and pants but maybe something like a tame panther or bear. This one sounded just like the others: about how Aunt Louisa was addressing a stranger to herself but not a stranger to Granny and that there were times when the good name of one family was the good name of all and that she naturally did not expect Mrs. Compson to move out and live with Father and Drusilla because even that would be too late now to preserve the appearance of that which had never existed anyway. But that Mrs. Compson was a woman too, Aunt Louisa believed, a Southern woman too, and had suffered too, Aunt Louisa didn't doubt, only she did hope and pray that Mrs. Compson had been spared the sight of her own daughter if Mrs. Compson had one flouting and outraging all

337

Southern principles of purity and womanhood that our husbands had died for, though Aunt Louisa hoped again that Mrs. Compson's husband (Mrs. Compson was older than Granny and the only husband she had ever had had been locked up for crazy a long time ago because in the slack part of the afternoons he would gather up eight or ten little niggers from the quarters and line them up across the creek from him with sweet potatoes on their heads and he would shoot the potatoes off with a rifle; he would tell them he might miss a potato but he wasn't going to miss a nigger, and so they would stand mighty still) had not made one of the number. So I couldn't make any sense out of that one too and I still didn't know what Aunt Louisa was talking about and I didn't believe that Mrs. Compson knew either.

Because it was not her: it was Mrs. Habersham, that never had been out here before and that Granny never had been to see that I knew of. Because Mrs. Compson didn't stay, she didn't even get out of the surrey, sitting there kind of drawn up under the shawl and looking at me and then at the cabin like she didn't know just what might come out of it or out from behind it. Then she begun to tap the nigger driver on his head with the parasol and they went away, the two old horses going pretty fast back down the drive and back down the road to town. And the next afternoon when I came out of the bottom to go to the spring with the water bucket there were five surreys and buggies in front of the cabin and inside the cabin there were fourteen of them that had come the four miles out from Jefferson, in the Sunday clothes that the Yankees and the war had left them, that had husbands dead in the war or alive back in Jefferson helping Father with what he was doing, because they were strange times then. Only like I said, maybe times are never strange to woman: that it is just one continuous monotonous thing full of the repeated follies of their menfolks. Mrs. Compson was sitting in Granny's chair, still holding the parasol and drawn up under her shawl and looking like she had finally seen whatever it was she had expected to see, and it had been the panther. It was Mrs. Habersham who was holding back the quilt for the others to go in and look at the bed where Drusilla slept and then showing them the pallet where Father and I slept. Then she saw me and said, "And who is this?"

"That's Bayard," Mrs. Compson said.

"You poor child," Mrs. Habersham said. So I didn't stop. But I couldn't help but hear them. It sounded like a ladies' club meeting with Mrs. Habersham running it, because every now and then Mrs. Habersham would forget to whisper: "—Mother should come, be sent for at once. But lacking her presence . . . we, the ladies of the community, mothers ourselves . . . child probably taken advantage of by gallant romantic . . . before realizing the price she must—" and Mrs. Compson said, "Hush! Hush!" and then somebody else said, "Do you really suppose—" and then Mrs. Habersham forgot to whisper good: "What else? What other reason can you name why she should choose to conceal herself down there in the woods all day long, lifting heavy weights like logs and—"

Then I went away. I filled the bucket at the spring and went back to the log-yard where Drusilla and Ringo and Joby were feeding the bandsaw and the blindfolded mule going round and round in the sawdust. And then Joby kind of made a sound and we all stopped and looked and there was Mrs. Habersham, with three of the others kind of peeping out from behind her with their eyes round and bright, looking at Drusilla standing there in the sawdust and shavings, in her dirty sweated overalls and shirt and brogans, with her face sweat-streaked with sawdust and her short hair yellow with it. "I am Martha Habersham," Mrs. Habersham said. "I am a neighbor and I hope to be a friend." And then she said, "You poor child."

We just looked at her; when Drusilla finally spoke, she sounded like Ringo and I would when Father would say something to us in Latin for a joke. "Ma'am?" Drusilla said. Because I was just fifteen; I still didn't know what it was all about; I just stood there and listened without even thinking much, like when they had been talking in the cabin. "My condition?" Drusilla said. "My—"

"Yes," Mrs. Habersham said. "No mother, no woman to . . . forced to these straits—" kind of waving her hand at the mules that hadn't stopped and at Joby and Ringo goggling at her and the three others still peeping around her at Drusilla. "—to offer you not only our help, but our sympathy."

"My condition," Drusilla said. "My con . . . Help and sym—" Then she began to say, "Oh. Oh. Oh," standing there, and then she was running. She began to run like a deer, that starts to run and then decides where it wants to go; she turned right in the air and came toward me, running light over the logs and planks, with her mouth open, saying "John, John" not loud; for a minute it was like she thought I was Father until she waked up and found I was not; she stopped without even ceasing to run, like a bird stops in the air, motionless yet still furious with movement. "Is that what you think too?" she said. Then she was gone. Every now and then I could see her footprints, spaced and fast, just inside the woods, but when I came out of the bottom, I couldn't see her. But the surreys and buggies were still in front of the cabin and I could see Mrs. Compson and the other ladies on the porch, looking out across the pasture toward the bottom, so I did not go there. But before I came to the other cabin, where Louvinia and Joby and Ringo lived, I saw Louvinia come up the hill from the spring, carrying her cedar water bucket and singing. Then she went into the cabin and the singing stopped short off and so I knew where Drusilla was. But I didn't hide. I went to the window and looked in and saw Drusilla just turning from where she had been leaning her head in her arms on the mantel when Louvinia came in with the water bucket and a gum twig in her mouth and Father's old hat on top of her headrag. Drusilla was crying. "That's what it is, then," she said. "Coming down there to the mill and telling me that in my condition—sympathy and help— Strangers; I never saw any of them before and I don't care a damn what they— But you and Bayard. Is that what you believe? that John and I—that we—" Then Louvinia moved. Her hand came out quicker than Drusilla could jerk back and lay flat on the belly of Drusilla's overalls, then Louvinia was holding Drusilla in her arms like she used to hold me and Drusilla was crying hard. "That John and I—that we— And Gavin dead at Shiloh and John's home burned and his plantation ruined, that he and I— We went to the war to hurt Yankees, not hunting women!"

"I knows you ain't," Louvinia said. "Hush now. Hush."

And that's about all. It didn't take them long. I don't know whether Mrs. Habersham made Mrs. Compson send for Aunt Louisa or whether Aunt Louisa just gave them a deadline and then came herself. Because we were busy, Drusilla and Joby and Ringo and me at the mill, and Father in town; we wouldn't see him from the time he would ride away in the morning until when he would get back, sometimes late, at night. Because they were strange times then. For four years we had lived for just one thing, even the women and children who could not fight: to get Yankee troops out of the country; we thought that when that happened, it would be all over. And now that had happened, and then before the summer began I heard Father say to Drusilla, "We were promised Federal troops; Lincoln himself promised to send us troops. Then things will be all right." That, from a man who had commanded a regiment for four years with the avowed purpose of driving Federal troops from the country. Now it was as though we had not surrendered at all, we had joined forces with the men who had been our enemies against a new foe whose aim we could not always fathom but whose means we could always dread. So he was busy in town all day long. They were building Jefferson back, the courthouse and the stores, but it was more than that which Father and the other men were doing; it was something which he would not let Drusilla or me or Ringo go into town to see. Then one day Ringo slipped off and went to town and came back and he looked at me with his eyes rolling a little.

"Do you know what I ain't?" he said.

"What?" I said.

"I ain't a nigger any more. I done been abolished." Then I asked him what he was, if he wasn't a nigger any more and he showed me what he had in his hand. It was a new scrip dollar; it was drawn on the United States Resident Treasurer, Yoknapatwpha County, Mississippi, and signed "Cassius Q. Benbow, Acting Marshal" in a neat clerk's hand, with a big sprawling X under it.

"Cassius Q. Benbow?" I said.

"Co-rect," Ringo said. "Uncle Cash that druv the Benbow carriage twell he run off with the Yankees two years ago. He back now and he gonter be elected Marshal of Jefferson. That's what Marse John and the other white folks is so busy about."

"A nigger?" I said. "A nigger?"

"No," Ringo said. "They ain't no more niggers, in Jefferson nor nowhere else." Then he told me about the two Burdens from Missouri, with a patent from Washington to organize the niggers into Republicans, and how Father and the other men were trying to prevent it. "Naw, suh," he said. "This war ain't over. Hit just started good. Used to be when you seed a Yankee you knowed him because he never had nothing but a gun or a mule halter or a handful of hen feathers. Now you don't even know him and stid of the gun he got a clutch of this stuff in one hand and a clutch of nigger voting tickets in the yuther." So we were busy; we just saw Father at night and sometimes then Ringo and I and even Drusilla would take one look at him and we wouldn't ask him any questions. So it didn't take them long, because Drusilla was already beaten; she was just marking time without knowing it from that afternoon when the fourteen ladies got into the surreys and buggies and went back to town until one afternoon about two months later when we heard Denny hollering even before the wagon came in the gates, and Aunt Louisa sitting on one of the trunks (that's what beat Drusilla: the trunks. They had her dresses in them that she hadn't worn in three years, and Ringo and I never had seen her in a dress until Aunt Louisa came) in mourning even to the crepe bow on her umbrella handle, that hadn't worn mourning when we were at Hawkhurst two years ago though Uncle Dennison was just as dead then as he was now. She came to the cabin and got out of the wagon, already crying and talking just like the letters sounded, like even when you listened to her you had to skip around fast to make any sense:

"I have come to appeal to them once more with a mother's tears though I don't think it will do any good though I had prayed until the very last that this boy's innocence might be spared and preserved but what must be must be and at least we can all three bear our burden together"; sitting in Granny's chair in the middle of the room, without even laying down the umbrella or taking her bonnet off, looking at the pallet where Father and I slept and then at the quilt nailed to the rafter to make a room for Drusilla, dabbing at her mouth with a handkerchief that made the whole cabin smell like dead roses. And then Drusilla came in from the mill, in the muddy brogans and the sweaty shirt and overalls and her hair sunburned and full of sawdust, and Aunt Louisa looked at her once and begun to cry again, saying, "Lost, lost. Thank God in His mercy that Dennison Hawk was taken before he lived to see what I see."

She was already beaten. Aunt Louisa made her put on a dress that night; we watched her run out of the cabin in it and run down the hill toward the spring while we were waiting for Father. And he came and walked into the cabin where Aunt Louisa was still sitting in Granny's chair with the handkerchief before her mouth. "This is a pleasant surprise, Miss Louisa," Father said.

"It is not pleasant to me, Colonel Sartoris," Aunt Louisa said. "And after a year, I suppose I cannot call it surprise. But it is still a shock." So Father came out too and we went down to the spring and found Drusilla hiding behind the big beech, crouched down like she was trying to hide the skirt from Father even while he raised her up. "What's a dress?" he said. "It don't matter. Come. Get up, soldier."

But she was beaten, like as soon as she let them put the dress on her she was whipped; like in the dress she could neither fight back nor run away. And so she didn't come down to the log-yard any more, and now that Father and I slept in the cabin with Joby and Ringo, I didn't even see Drusilla except at mealtime. And we were busy getting the timber out, and now everybody was talking about the election and how Father had told the two Burdens before all the men in town that the election would never be held with Cash Benbow or any other nigger in it and how the Burdens had dared him to stop it. And besides, the other cabin would be full of Jefferson ladies all day; you would have thought that Drusilla was Mrs. Habersham's daughter and not Aunt Louisa's. They would begin to arrive right after breakfast and stay all day, so that at supper Aunt Louisa would sit in her black mourning except for the bonnet and umbrella, with a wad of some kind of black knitting she carried around with her and that never got finished and the folded handkerchief handy in her belt (only she ate fine; she ate more than Father even because the election was just a week off and I reckon he was thinking about the Burdens) and refusing to speak to anybody except Denny; and Drusilla trying to eat, with her face strained and thin and her eyes like somebody's that had been whipped a long time now and is going just on nerve.

Then Drusilla broke; they beat her. Because she was strong; she wasn't much older than I was, but she had let Aunt Louisa and Mrs. Habersham choose the game and she had beat them both until that night when Aunt Louisa went behind her back and chose a game she couldn't beat. I was coming up to supper; I heard them inside the cabin before I could stop: "Can't you believe me?" Drusilla said. "Can't you understand that in the troop I was just another man and not much of one at that, and since we came home here I am just another mouth for John to feed, just a cousin of John's wife and not much older than his own son?"

And I could almost see Aunt Louisa sitting there with that knitting that never progressed:

"You wish to tell me that you, a young woman, associated with him, a still young man, day and night for a year, running about the country with no guard nor check of any sort upon— Do you take me for a complete fool?" So that night Aunt Louisa beat her; we had just sat down to supper when Aunt Louisa looked at me like she had been waiting for the noise of the bench to stop: "Bayard, I do not ask your forgiveness for this because it is your burden too; you are an innocent victim as well as Dennison and I—" Then she looked at Father, thrust back in Granny's chair (the only chair we had) in her black dress, the black wad of knitting beside her plate. "Colonel Sartoris," she said, "I am a woman; I must request what the husband whom I have lost and the man son which I have not would demand, perhaps at the point of a pistol.—Will you marry my daughter?"

I got out. I moved fast; I heard the light sharp sound when Drusilla's head went down between her flungout arms on the table, and the sound the bench made when Father got up too; I passed him standing beside Drusilla with his hand on her head. "They have beat you, Drusilla," he said.

I I

Mrs. Habersham got there before we had finished breakfast the next morning. I don't know how Aunt Louisa got word in to her so quick. But there she was, and she and Aunt Louisa set the wedding for the day after tomorrow. I don't reckon they even knew that that was the day Father had told the Burdens Cash Benbow would never be elected marshal in Jefferson. I don't reckon they paid any more attention to it than if all· the men had decided that day after tomorrow all the clocks in Jefferson were to be set back or up an hour. Maybe they didn't even know there was to be an election, that all the men in the county would be riding toward Jefferson tomorrow with pistols in their pockets, and that the Burdens already had their nigger voters camped in a cotton gin on the edge of town under guard. I don't reckon they even cared. Because like Father said, women cannot believe that anything can be right or wrong or even be very important that can be decided by a lot of little scraps of scribbled paper dropped into a box.

It was to be a big wedding; all Jefferson was to be invited and Mrs. Habersham planning to bring the three bottles of Madeira she had been saving for five years now when Aunt Louisa began to cry again. But they caught on quick now; now all of them were patting Aunt Louisa's hands and giving her vinegar to smell and Mrs. Habersham saying, "Of course. You poor thing. A public wedding now, after a year, would be a public notice of the . . ." So they decided it would be a reception, because

Mrs. Habersham said how a reception could be held for a bridal couple at any time, even ten years later. So Drusilla was to ride into town, meet Father and be married as quick and quiet as possible, with just me and one other for witnesses to make it legal; none of the ladies themselves would even be present. Then they would come back home and we would have the reception.

So they began to arrive early the next morning, with baskets of food and tablecloths and silver like for a church supper. Mrs. Habersham brought a veil and a wreath and they all helped Drusilla to dress, only Aunt Louisa made Drusilla put on Father's big riding cloak over the veil and wreath too, and Ringo brought the horses up, all curried and brushed, and I helped Drusilla on with Aunt Louisa and the others all watching from the porch. But I didn't know that Ringo was missing when we started, not even when I heard Aunt Louisa hollering for Denny while we rode down the drive. It was Louvinia that told about it, about how after we left the ladies set and decorated the table and spread the wedding breakfast and how they were all watching the gate and Aunt Louisa still hollering for Denny now and then when they saw Ringo and Denny come up the drive riding double on one of the mules at a gallop, with Denny's eyes round as doorknobs and already hollering, "They kilt um! They kilt um!"

"Who?" Aunt Louisa hollered. "Where have you been?"

"To town!" Denny hollered. "Them two Burdens! They kilt um!"

"Who killed them?" Aunt Louisa hollered.

"Drusilla and Cousin John!" Denny hollered. Then Louvinia said how Aunt Louisa hollered sure enough.

"Do you mean to tell me that Drusilla and that man are not married yet?"

Because we didn't have time. Maybe Drusilla and Father would have, but when we came into the square we saw the crowd of niggers kind of huddled beyond the hotel door with six or eight strange white men herding them, and then all of a sudden I saw the Jefferson men, the men that I knew, that Father knew, running across the square toward the hotel with each one holding his hip pocket like a man runs with a pistol in his pocket. And then I saw the men who were Father's troop lined up before the hotel door, blocking it off. And then I was sliding off my horse too and watching Drusilla struggling with George Wyatt. But he didn't have hold of her, he just had hold of the cloak, and then she was through the line of them and running toward the hotel with her wreath on one side of her head and the veil streaming behind. But George held me. He threw the cloak down and held me. "Let go," I said. "Father."

"Steady, now," George said, holding me. "John's just gone in to vote."

"But there are two of them!" I said. "Let me go!"

"John's got two shots in the derringer," George said. "Steady, now."
But they held me. And then we heard the three shots and we all
turned and looked at the door. I don't know how long it was. "The last
two was that derringer," George said. I don't know how long it was. The
old nigger that was Mrs. Holston's porter, that was too old even to be
free, stuck his head out once and said "Gret Gawd" and ducked back.
Then Drusilla came out, carrying the ballot box, the wreath on one side
of her head and the veil twisted about her arm, and then Father came
out behind her, brushing his new beaver hat on his sleeve. And then it
was loud; I could hear them when they drew in their breath like when
the Yankees used to hear it begin:

"Yaaaaa—" But Father raised his hand and they stopped. Then you
couldn't hear anything.

"We heard a pistol too," George said. "Did they touch you?"

"No," Father said. "I let them fire first. You all heard. You boys can
swear to my derringer."

"Yes," George said. "We all heard." Now Father looked at all of
them, at all the faces in sight, slow.

"Does any man here want a word with me about this?" he said. But
you could not hear anything, not even moving. The herd of niggers stood
like they had when I first saw them, with the Northern white men herding them together. Father put his hat on and took the ballot box from
Drusilla and helped her back onto her horse and handed the ballot box
up to her. Then he looked around again, at all of them. "This election
will be held out at my home," he said. "I hereby appoint Drusilla Hawk
voting commissioner until the votes are cast and counted. Does any man
here object?" But he stopped them again with his hand before it had
begun good. "Not now, boys," he said. He turned to Drusilla. "Go home.
I will go to the sheriff, and then I will follow you."

"Like hell you will," George Wyatt said. "Some of the boys will ride
out with Drusilla. The rest of us will come with you."

But Father would not let them. "Don't you see we are working for
peace through law and order?" he said. "I will make bond and then
follow you. You do as I say." So we went on; we turned in the gates with
Drusilla in front, the ballot box on her pommel—us and Father's men
and about a hundred more, and rode on up to the cabin where the buggies and surreys were standing, and Drusilla passed the ballot box to
me and got down and took the box again and was walking toward the
cabin when she stopped dead still. I reckon she and I both remembered
at the same time and I reckon that even the others, the men, knew all of
a sudden that something was wrong. Because like Father said, I reckon
women don't ever surrender: not only victory, but not even defeat. Because that's how we were stopped when Aunt Louisa and the other
ladies came out on the porch, and then Father shoved past me and

jumped down beside Drusilla. But Aunt Louisa never even looked at him.

"So you are not married," she said.

"I forgot," Drusilla said.

"You forgot? You *forgot?*"

"I . . ." Drusilla said. "We . . ."

Now Aunt Louisa looked at us; she looked along the line of us sitting there in our saddles; she looked at me too just like she did at the others, like she had never seen me before. "And who are these, pray? Your wedding train of forgetters? Your groomsmen of murder and robbery?"

"They came to vote," Drusilla said.

"To vote," Aunt Louisa said. "Ah. To vote. Since you have forced your mother and brother to live under a roof of license and adultery you think you can also force them to live in a polling booth refuge from violence and bloodshed, do you? Bring me that box." But Drusilla didn't move, standing there in her torn dress and the ruined veil and the twisted wreath hanging from her hair by a few pins. Aunt Louisa came down the steps; we didn't know what she was going to do: we just sat there and watched her snatch the polling box from Drusilla and fling it across the yard. "Come into the house," she said.

"No," Drusilla said.

"Come into the house. I will send for a minister myself."

"No," Drusilla said. "This is an election. Don't you understand? I am voting commissioner."

"So you refuse?"

"I have to. I must." She sounded like a little girl that has been caught playing in the mud. "John said that I—"

Then Aunt Louisa began to cry. She stood there in the black dress, without the knitting and for the first time that I ever saw it, without even the handkerchief, crying, until Mrs. Habersham came and led her back into the house. Then they voted. That didn't take long either. They set the box on the sawchunk where Louvinia washed, and Ringo got the pokeberry juice and an old piece of window shade, and they cut it into ballots. "Let all who want the Honorable Cassius Q. Benbow to be Marshal of Jefferson write Yes on his ballot; opposed, No," Father said.

"And I'll do the writing and save some more time," George Wyatt said. So he made a pack of the ballots and wrote them against his saddle and fast as he would write them the men would take them and drop them into the box and Drusilla would call their names out. We could hear Aunt Louisa still crying inside the cabin and we could see the other ladies watching us through the window. It didn't take long. "You needn't bother to count them," George said. "They all voted No."

And that's all. They rode back to town then, carrying the box, with

Father and Drusilla in the torn wedding dress and the crooked wreath and veil standing beside the sawchunk, watching them. Only this time even Father could not have stopped them. It came back high and thin and ragged and fierce, like when the Yankees used to hear it out of the smoke and the galloping:

"Yaaaaay, Drusilla!" they hollered. "Yaaaaaay, John Sartoris! Yaaaa-aaay!"

SHOWER OF GOLD

The charm of the story of Snowdie MacLain—and what a
story it is, once it has been pieced together!—comes from Mrs.
Rainey's manner of telling it, as well as from the almost
legendary atmosphere surrounding King MacLain, who is,
in a sense, its hero. The narrative comes to the reader
through several persons, and the result is a masterpiece of
indirection—completely unverifiable but somehow believable.
We hear from Mrs. Rainey what Old Plez has told Mrs. Stark.
Old Plez was *there* on Hallowe'en, and he saw what
happened . . . It takes our storyteller some time to put the
whole thing together; but the reader, diverted if not immediately
enlightened by Mrs. Rainey's digressions and asides, will
stay with her to the end, and then, having come to appreciate its
many subtleties, will want to read the story again for
greater understanding of what it was all about.

That was Miss Snowdie MacLain.

She comes after her butter, won't let me run over with it from just
across the road. Her husband walked out of the house one day and left
his hat on the banks of the Big Black River.—That could have started
something, too.

We might have had a little run on doing that in Morgana, if it had
been so willed. What King did, the copy-cats always might do. Well,
King MacLain left a new straw hat on the banks of the Big Black and
there are people that consider he headed West.

Snowdie grieved for him, but the decent way you'd grieve for the
dead, more like, and nobody wanted to think, around her, that he
treated her that way. But how long can you humor the humored? Well,
always. But I could almost bring myself to talk about it—to a passer-by,
that will never see her again, or me either. Sure I can churn and talk.
My name's Mrs. Rainey.

You seen she wasn't ugly—and the little blinky lines to her eyelids
comes from trying to see. She's an albino but nobody would ever try to
call her ugly around here—with that tender, tender skin like a baby.

Some said King figured out that if the babies started coming, he had a chance for a nestful of little albinos, and that swayed him. No, I don't say it. I say he was just willful. *He* wouldn't think ahead.

Willful and outrageous, to some several. Well: he married Snowdie. Lots of worse men wouldn't have: no better sense. Them Hudsons had more than MacLains, but none of 'em had enough to count or worry over. Not by then. Hudson money built that house, and built it for *Snowdie* . . . they prayed over that. But take King: marrying must have been some of his showing off—like man never married at all till *he* flung in, then had to show the others how he could go right on acting. And like, "Look, everybody, this is what I think of Morgana and Mac-Lain Courthouse and all the way between"—further, for all I know— "marrying a girl with pink eyes." "I swan!" we all say. Just like he wants us to, scoundrel. And Snowdie as sweet and gentle as you find them. Of course gentle people aren't the ones you lead best, he had that to find out, so know-all. No, sir, she'll beat him yet, balking. In the meantime children of his growing up in the County Orphan's, so say several, and children known and unknown, scattered-like. When he does come, he's just as nice as he can be to Snowdie. Just as courteous. Was from the start.

Haven't you noticed it prevail, in the world in general? Beware of a man with manners. He never raised his voice to her, but then one day he walked out of the house. Oh, I don't mean once!

He went away for a good spell before he come back that time. She had a little story about him needing the waters. Next time it was more than a year, it was two—oh, it was three. I had two children myself, enduring his being gone, and one to die. Yes, and that time he sent her word ahead: "Meet me in the woods." No, he more invited her than told her to come—"Suppose you meet me in the woods." And it was night time he supposed to her. And Snowdie met him without asking "What for?" which I would want to know of Fate Rainey. After all, they were married—they had a right to sit inside and talk in the light and comfort, or lie down easy on a good goosefeather bed, either. I would even consider he might not be there when I came. Well, if Snowdie went without a question, then I can tell it without a question as long as I love Snowdie. Her version is that in the woods they met and both decided on what would be best.

Best for him, of course. We could see the writing on the wall.

"The woods" was Morgan's Woods. We would any of us know the place he meant, without trying—I could have streaked like an arrow to the very oak tree, one there to itself and all spready: a real shady place by *day,* is all I know. Can't you just see King MacLain leaning his length against that tree by the light of the moon as you come walking through Morgan's Woods and you hadn't seen him in three years? "Suppose you meet me in the woods." My foot. Oh, I don't know how poor Snowdie stood it, crossing the distance.

Then, twins.

That was where I come in, I could help when things got to there. I took her a little churning of butter with her milk and we took up. I hadn't been married long myself, and Mr. Rainey's health was already a little delicate so he'd thought best to quit heavy work. We was both hard workers fairly early.

I always thought twins might be nice. And might have been for them, by just the sound of it. The MacLains first come to Morgana bride and groom from MacLain and went into that new house. He was educated off, to practice law—well needed here. Snowdie was Miss Lollie Hudson's daughter, well known. Her father was Mr. Eugene Hudson, a storekeeper down at Crossroads past the Courthouse, but he was a lovely man. Snowdie was their only daughter, and they give her a nice education. And I guess people more or less expected her to teach school: not marry. She couldn't see all that well, was the only thing in the way, but Mr. Comus Stark here and the supervisors overlooked that, knowing the family and Snowdie's real good way with Sunday School children. Then before the school year even got a good start, she got took up by King MacLain all of a sudden. I think it was when jack-o'-lanterns was pasted on her window I used to see his buggy roll up right to the schoolhouse steps and wait on her. He courted her in Morgana and MacLain too, both ends, didn't skip a day.

It was no different—no quicker and no slower—than the like happens every whipstitch, so I don't need to tell you they got married in the MacLain Presbyterian Church before you could shake a stick at it, no matter how surprised people were going to be. And once they dressed Snowdie all in white, you know she was whiter than your dreams.

So—he'd been educated in the law and he traveled for somebody, that was the first thing he did—I'll tell you in a minute what he sold, and she stayed home and cooked and kept house. I forget if she had a Negro, she didn't know how to tell one what to do if she had. And she put her eyes straight out, almost, going to work and making curtains for every room and all like that. So busy. At first it didn't look like they would have any children.

So it went the way I told you, slipped into it real easy, people took it for granted mighty early—him leaving and him being welcomed home, him leaving and him sending word, "Meet me in the woods," and him gone again, at last leaving the hat. I told my husband I was going to quit keeping count of King's comings and goings, and it wasn't long after that he did leave the hat. I don't know yet whether he meant it kind or cruel. Kind, I incline to believe. Or maybe she was winning. Why do I try to figure? Maybe because Fate Rainey ain't got a surprise in him, and proud of it. So Fate said, "Well now, let's have the women to settle down and pay attention to homefolks a while." That was all he could say about it.

So, you wouldn't have had to wait long. Here come Snowdie across the road to bring the news. I seen her coming across my pasture in a different walk, it was the way somebody comes down an aisle. Her sunbonnet ribbons was jumping around her: springtime. Did you notice her little dainty waist she has still? I declare it's a mystery to think about her having the strength once. Look at me.

I was in the barn milking, and she come and took a stand there at the head of the little Jersey, Lady May. She had a quiet, picked-out way to tell news. She said, "I'm going to have a baby too, Miss Katie. Congratulate me."

Me and Lady May both had to just stop and look at her. She looked like more than only the news had come over her. It was like a shower of something had struck her, like she'd been caught out in something bright. It was more than the day. There with her eyes all crinkled up with always fighting the light, yet she was looking out bold as a lion that day under her brim, and gazing into my bucket and into my stall like a visiting somebody. Poor Snowdie. I remember it was Easter time and how the pasture was all spotty there behind her little blue skirt, in sweet clover. He sold tea and spices, that's what it was.

It was sure enough nine months to the day the twins come after he went sallying out through those woods and fields and laid his hat down on the bank of the river with "King MacLain" on it.

I wish I'd seen him! I don't guess I'd have stopped him. I can't tell you why, but I wish I'd seen him! But nobody did.

For Snowdie's sake—here they come bringing the hat, and a hullaballoo raised—they drug the Big Black for nine miles down, or was it only eight, and sent word to Bovina and on, clear to Vicksburg, to watch out for anything to wash up or to catch in the trees in the river. Sure, there never was anything—just the hat. They found everybody else that ever honestly drowned along the Big Black in this neighborhood. Mr. Sissum at the store, he drowned later on and they found him. I think with the hat he ought to have laid his watch down, if he wanted to give it a better look.

Snowdie kept just as bright and brave, she didn't seem to give in. She must have had her thoughts and they must have been one of two things. One that he was dead—then why did her face have the glow? It had a glow—and the other that he left her and meant it. And like people said, if she smiled *then,* she was clear out of reach. I didn't know if I liked the glow. Why didn't she rage and storm a little—to me, anyway, just Mrs. Rainey? The Hudsons all hold themselves in. But it didn't seem to me, running in and out the way I was, that Snowdie had ever got a real good look at life, maybe. Maybe from the beginning. Maybe she just doesn't know the *extent*. Not the kind of look I got, and away back when I was twelve year old or so. Like something was put to my eye.

She just went on keeping house, and getting fairly big with what I told you already was twins, and she seemed to settle into her content. Like a little white kitty in a basket, making you wonder if she just mightn't put up her paw and scratch, if anything was, after all, to come near. At her house it was like Sunday even in the mornings, every day, in that cleaned-up way. She was taking a joy in her fresh untracked rooms and that dark, quiet, real quiet hall that runs through her house. And I love Snowdie. I love her.

Except none of us felt very *close* to her all the while. I'll tell you what it was, what made her different. It was the not waiting any more, except where the babies waited, and that's not but one story. We were mad at her and protecting her all at once, when we couldn't be close to her.

And she come out in her pretty clean shirt waists to water the ferns, and she had remarkable flowers—she had her mother's way with flowers, of course. And give just as many away, except it wasn't like I or you give. She was by her own self. Oh, her mother was dead by then, and Mr. Hudson fourteen miles down the road away, crippled up, running his store in a cane chair. We was every bit she had. Everybody tried to stay with her as much as they could spare, not let a day go by without one of us to run in and speak to her and say a word about an ordinary thing. Miss Lizzie Stark let her be in charge of raising money for the poor country people at Christmas that year, and like that. Of course we made all her little things for her, stitches like that was way beyond her. It was a good thing she got such a big stack.

The twins come the first day of January. Miss Lizzie Stark—she hates all men, and is real important: across yonder's her chimney—made Mr. Comus Stark, her husband, hitch up and drive to Vicksburg to bring back a Vicksburg doctor in her own buggy the night before, instead of using Dr. Loomis here, and stuck him in a cold room to sleep at her house; she said trust any doctor's buggy to break down on those bridges. Mrs. Stark stayed right by Snowdie, and of course several, and I, stayed too, but Mrs. Stark was not budging and took charge when pains commenced. Snowdie had the two little boys and neither one albino. They were both King all over again, if you want to know it. Mrs. Stark had so hoped for a girl, or two *girls*. Snowdie clapped the names on them of Lucius Randall and Eugene Hudson, after her own father and her mother's father.

It was the only sign she ever give Morgana that maybe she didn't think the name King MacLain had stayed beautiful. But not much of a sign; some women don't name after their husbands, until they get down to nothing else left. I don't think with Snowdie even *two* other names meant she had changed yet, not towards King, that scoundrel.

Time goes like a dream no matter how hard you run, and all the time we heard things from out in the world that we listened to but that still didn't mean we believed them. You know the kind of things. Somebody's cousin saw King MacLain. Mr. Comus Stark, the one the cotton and timber belongs to, he goes a little, and he claimed three or four times he saw his back, and once saw him getting a haircut in Texas. Those things you will hear forever when people go off, to keep up a few shots in the woods. They might mean something—might not.

Till the most outrageous was the time my husband went up to Jackson. He saw a man that was the spit-image of King in the parade, my husband told me in his good time, the inauguration of Governor Vardaman. He was right up with the big ones and astride a fine animal. Several from here went but as Mrs. Spights said, why wouldn't they be looking at the Governor? Or the New Capitol? But King MacLain could steal anyone's glory, so he thought.

When I asked the way he looked, I couldn't get a thing out of my husband, except he lifted his feet across the kitchen floor like a horse and man in one, and I went after him with my broom. I knew, though. If it was King, he looked like, "Hasn't everybody been wondering, though, been out of their minds to know, where I've been keeping myself!" I told my husband it reasoned to me like it was up to Governor Vardaman to get hold of King and bring something out of him, but my husband said why pick on one man, and besides a parade was going on and what all. Men! I said if I'd been Governor Vardaman and spied King MacLain from Morgana marching in my parade as big as I was and no call for it, I'd have had the whole thing brought to a halt and called him to accounts. "Well, what good would it have done you?" my husband said. "A plenty," I said. I was excited at the time it happened. "That was just as good a spot as any to show him forth, right in front of the New Capitol in Jackson with the band going, and just as good a man to do it."

Well, sure, men like that need to be shown up before the world, I guess—not that any of us would be surprised. "Did you go and find him after the Governor got inaugurated to suit you then?" I asked my husband. But he said no, and reminded me. He went for me a new bucket; and brought me the wrong size. Just like the ones at Holifield's. But he said he saw King or his twin. What twin!

Well, through the years, we'd hear of him here or there—maybe two places at once. New Orleans and Mobile. That's people's careless way of using their eyes.

I believe he's been to California. Don't ask me why. But I picture him there. I see King in the West, out where it's gold and all that. Everybody to their own visioning.

II

Well, what happened turned out to happen on Hallowe'en. Only last week—and seems already like something that couldn't happen at all. My baby girl, Virgie, swallowed a button that same day—later on —and that *happened,* it seems like still, but not this. And not a word's been spoke out loud, for Snowdie's sake, so I trust the rest of the world will be as careful.

You can talk about a baby swallowing a button off a shirt and having to be up-ended and her behind pounded, and it sounds reasonable if you can just see the baby—there she runs—but get to talking about something that's only a kind of *near* thing—and hold your horses.

Well, Hallowe'en, about three o'clock, I was over at Snowdie's helping her cut out patterns—she's kept on sewing for those boys. Me, I have a little girl to sew for—she was right there, asleep on the bed in the next room—and it hurts my conscience being that lucky over Snowdie too. And the twins wouldn't play out in the yard that day but had hold of the scraps and the scissors and the paper of pins and all, and there underfoot they were dressing up and playing ghosts and boogers. Uppermost in their little minds was Hallowe'en.

They had on their masks, of course, tied on over their Buster Brown bobs and pressing a rim around the back. I was used to how they looked by then—but I don't like masks. They both come from Spights' store and cost a nickel. One was the Chinese kind, all yellow and mean with slant eyes and a dreadful thin mustache of black horsy hair. The other one was a lady, with an almost scary-sweet smile on her lips. I never did take to that smile, with all day for it. Eugene Hudson wanted to be the Chinaman and so Lucius Randall had to be the lady.

So they were making tails and do-lollies and all kinds of foolishness, and sticking them on to their little middles and behinds, snatching every scrap from the shirts and flannels me and Snowdie was cutting out on the dining room table. Sometimes we could grab a little boy and baste something up on him whether or no, but we didn't really pay them much mind, we was talking about the prices of things for winter, and the funeral of an old maid.

So we never heard the step creak or the porch give, at all. That was a blessing. And if it wasn't for something that come from outside us all to tell about it, I wouldn't have the faith I have that it come about.

But happening along our road—like he does every day—was a real trustworthy nigger. He's one of Mrs. Stark's mother's niggers, Old Plez Morgan everybody calls him. Lives down beyond me. The real old kind, that knows everybody since time was. He knows more folks than

I do, who they are, and all the *fine* people. If you wanted anybody in Morgana that wouldn't be likely to make a mistake in who a person is, you would ask for Old Plez.

So he was making his way down the road, by stages. He still has to do a few people's yards won't let him go, like Mrs. Stark, because he don't pull up things. He's no telling how old and starts early and takes his time coming home in the evening—always stopping to speak to people to ask after their health and tell them good evening all the way. Only that day, he said he didn't see a soul *else*—besides you'll hear who in a minute—on the way, not on porches or in the yards. I can't tell you why, unless it was those little gusts of north wind that had started blowing. Nobody likes that.

But yonder ahead of him was walking a man. Plez said it was a white man's walk and a walk he knew—but it struck him it was from away in another year, another time. It wasn't just the walk of anybody supposed to be going along the road to MacLain right at that *time*—and yet it was too—and if it was, he still couldn't think what business that somebody would be up to. That was the careful way Plez was putting it to his mind.

If you saw Plez, you'd know it was him. He had some roses stuck in his hat that day, I saw him right after it happened. Some of Miss Lizzie's fall roses, big as a man's fist and red as blood—they were nodding side-to-side out of the band of his old black hat, and some other little scraps out of the garden laid around the brim, throwed away by Mrs. Stark; he'd been cleaning out her beds that day, it was fixing to rain.

He said later he wasn't in any great hurry, or he would have maybe caught up and passed the man. Up yonder ahead he went, going the same way Plez was going, and not much more interested in a race. And a real familiar stranger.

So Plez says presently the familiar stranger paused. It was in front of the MacLains'—and sunk his weight on one leg and just stood there, posey as statues, hand on his hip. Ha! Old Plez says, according, he just leaned himself against the Presbyterian Church gate and waited a while.

Next thing, the stranger—oh, it was King! By then Plez was calling him Mr. King to himself—went up through the yard and then didn't go right in like anybody else. First he looked around. He took in the yard and summerhouse and skimmed from cedar to cedar along the edge of where he lived, and under the fig tree at the back and under the wash (if he'd counted it!) and come close to the front again, sniffy like, and Plez said though he couldn't swear to seeing from the Presbyterian Church exactly what Mr. King was doing, he knows as good as seeing it that he looked through the blinds. He would have looked in the dining room—have mercy. We shut the West out of Snowdie's eyes of course.

At last he come full front again, around the flowers under the front bedroom. Then he settled himself nice and started up the front steps.

The middle step sings when it's stepped on, but we didn't hear it. Plez said, well, he had on fine tennis shoes. So he got across the front porch and what do you think he's fixing to do but knock on that door? Why wasn't he satisfied with outdoors?

On his own front door. He makes a little shadow knock, like trying to see how it would look, and then puts his present behind his coat. Of course he had something there in a box for her. You know he constitutionally brought home the kind of presents that break your heart. He stands there with one leg out pretty, to surprise them. And I bet a nice smile on his face. Oh, don't ask me to go on!

Suppose Snowdie'd took a notion to glance down the hall—the dining room's at the end of it, and the folding-doors pushed back—and seen him, all "Come-kiss-me" like that. I don't know if she could have seen that good—but I could. I was a fool and didn't look.

It was the twins seen him. Through those little bitty mask holes, those eagle eyes! There ain't going to be no stopping those twins. And he didn't get to knock on the door, but he had his hand raised the second time and his knuckles sticking up, and out come the children on him, hollering "Boo!" and waving their arms up and down the way it would scare you to death, or it ought to, if you wasn't ready for them.

We heard them charge out, but we thought it was just a nigger that was going by for them to scare, if we thought anything.

Plez says—allowing for all human mistakes—he seen on one side of King come rolling out Lucius Randall all dressed up, and on the other side, Eugene Hudson all dressed up. Could I have forgotten to speak of their being on skates? Oh, that was all afternoon. They're real good skaters, the little fellows, not to have a sidewalk. They sailed out the door and circled around their father, flying their arms and making their fingers go scarey, and those little Buster Brown bobs going in a circle.

Lucius Randall, Plez said, had on something pink, and he did, the basted flannelette teddy-bears we had tried on on top of his clothes and he got away. And said Eugene was a Chinaman, and that was what he was. It would be hard to tell which would come at you the more outrageous of the two, but to me it would be Lucius Randall with the girl's face and the big cotton gloves falling off his fingers, and oh! he had on *my hat*. This one I milk in.

And they made a tremendous uproar with their skates, Plez said, and that was no mistake, because I remember what a hard time Snowdie and me had hearing what each other had to say all afternoon.

Plez said King stood it a minute—he got to turning around too. They were skating around him and saying in high birdie voices, "How do you do, Mister Booger?" You know if children *can* be monkeys, they're going to be them. (Without the masks, though, those two children would have been more polite about it—there's enough Hudson in them.) Skating around and around their papa, and just as ignorant! Poor little fellows. After all, they'd had nobody to scare all day for Hallowe'en, except one or two niggers that went by, and the Y. & M.V. train whistling through at two-fifteen, they scared that.

But monkeys—! Skating around their papa. Plez said if those children had been black, he wouldn't hesitate to say they would remind a soul of little nigger cannibals in the jungle. When they got their papa in their ring-around-a-rosy and he couldn't get out, Plez said it was enough to make an onlooker a little uneasy, and he called once or twice on the Lord. And after they went around high, they crouched down and went around low, about his knees.

The minute come, when King just couldn't get out quick enough. Only he had a hard time, and took him more than one try. He gathered himself together and King is a man of six foot height and weighs like a horse, but he was confused, I take it. But he got aloose and up and out like the Devil was after him—or in him—finally. Right up over the bannister and the ferns, and down the yard and over the ditch and gone. He plowed into the rough toward the Big Black, and the willows waved behind him, and where he run then, Plez don't know and I don't and don't nobody.

Plez said King passed right by him, that time, but didn't seem to know him, and the opportunity had gone by then to speak. And where he run then, nobody knows.

He should have wrote another note, instead of coming.

Well then, the children, I reckon, just held openmouth behind him, and then something got to mounting up after it was all over, and scared them. They come back in the dining room. There were innocent ladies visiting with each other. The little boys had to scowl and frown and drag their skates over the carpet and follow us around the table where we was cutting out Eugene Hudson's underbody, and pull on our skirts till we saw.

"Well, speak," said their mother, and they told her a booger had come up on the front porch and when they went out to see him he said, "I'm going. You stay," so they chased him down the steps and run him off. "But he looked back like this!" Lucius Randall said, lifting off his mask and showing us on his little naked face with the round blue eyes. And Eugene Hudson said the booger took a handful of pecans before he got through the gate.

And Snowdie dropped her scissors on the mahogany, and her hand just stayed in the air as still, and she looked at me, a look a minute long. And first she caught her apron to her and then started shedding it in the hall while she run to the door—so as not to be caught in it, I suppose, if anybody was still there. She run and the little glass prisms shook in the parlor—I don't remember another time, from *her*. She didn't stop at the door but run on through it and out on the porch, and she looked both ways and was running down the steps. And she run out in the yard and stood there holding to the tree, looking towards the country, but I could tell by the way her head held there wasn't nobody.

When I got to the steps—I didn't like to follow right away—there was nobody at all but Old Plez, who was coming by raising his hat.

"Plez, did you see a gentleman come up on my porch just now?" I heard Snowdie call, and there was Plez, just ambling by with his hat raised, like he was just that minute passing, like we thought. And Plez, of course, he said, "No'm, Mistis, I don't recollect one soul pass me, whole way from town."

The little fellows held on to me, I could feel them tugging. And my little girl slept through it all, inside, and then woke up to swallow that button.

Outdoors the leaves was rustling, different from when I'd went in. It was coming on a rain. The day had a two-way look, like a day will at change of the year—clouds dark and the gold air still in the road, and the trees lighter than the sky was. And the oak leaves scuttling and scattering, blowing against Old Plez and brushing on him, the old man.

"You're real positive, I guess, Plez?" asks Snowdie, and he answers comforting-like to her, *"You* wasn't looking for nobody to come today, was you?"

It was later on that Mrs. Stark got hold of Plez and got the truth out of him, and I heard it after a while, through her church. But of course he wasn't going to let Miss Snowdie MacLain get hurt now, after we'd all watched her so long. So he fabricated.

After he'd gone by, Snowdie just stood there in the cool without a coat, with her face turned towards the country and her fingers pulling at little threads on her skirt and turning them loose in the wind, making little kind deeds of it, till I went and got her. She didn't cry.

"Course, could have been a ghost," Plez told Mrs. Stark, "but a ghost—I believe—if he had come to see the lady of the house, would have waited to have word with her."

And he said he had nary doubt in his mind, that it was Mr. King MacLain, starting home once more and thinking better of it. Miss Lizzie said to the church ladies, "I, for one, trust the Negro. I trust him the way you trust me, Old Plez's mind had remained clear as a bell. I trust his story implicitly," she says, "because that's just what *I know* King MacLain'd do—run." And that's one time I feel in agreement about something with Miss Lizzie Stark, though she don't know about it, I guess.

358 *Welty*

And I live and hope *he* hit a stone and fell down running, before he got far off from here, and took the skin off his handsome nose, the devil.

And so that's why Snowdie comes to get her butter now, and won't let me bring it to her any longer. I think she kind of holds it against me, because I was there that day when he come; and she don't like my baby any more.

And you know, Fate says maybe King did know it was Hallowe'en. Do you think he'd go that far for a prank? And his own come back to him? Fate's usually more down to earth than that.

With men like King, your thoughts are bottomless. He was going like the wind, Plez swore to Miss Lizzie Stark; though he couldn't swear to the direction—so he changed and said.

But I bet my little Jersey calf King tarried long enough to get him a child somewhere.

What makes me say a thing like that? I wouldn't say it to my husband, you mind you forget it.

Peter Taylor

VENUS, CUPID, FOLLY AND TIME

This story, which concerns the time that Ned and Emily
Meriwether and Tom Bascomb attended the famous Dorsets'
children's party, calls for a closer reading than might seem
necessary at the outset. It is a leisurely story, told with careful
attention to detail, for Mr. Taylor cares about his characters and
lavishes much personal attention upon them. (One has a
feeling that such well-drawn characters must have had an
actual existence in the author's experience.) And the author
cares about Mero, the city, too. Paul Engle (the editor of the
O. Henry Prize Awards stories for 1959) observes in
introducing the story that the author's "particular triumph is the
story of people in a place, a social as well as geographical
place." Toward the end, Ned's wife asks the author to tell
her about Mero and to tell her about the Dorsets. Then
the reader learns about the history of Mero, "one of the first
English-speaking settlements west of the Alleghenies," and
about the lineage of the Dorsets—and particularly about the last
two members of the Dorset line, Miss Louisa and Mr.
Alfred. It was as descendants of Mero's first family that they
held a divine right to play the role of social arbiters among
the younger generations as they grew up and came of age. This
final part of the story, then, establishes its claim to being
rightfully placed among the Americana here. For, viewed in a
certain light, the story of Mero—of the Dorsets and of
their relationship to other families in the city—is an aspect of the
social history of our pioneer civilization.

The story's human interest lies primarily in the relationship
that develops between Emily and Ned Meriwether. This
relationship, in a way, gives point to the whole story, and it
provides the occasion for the author's talk with Ned's wife in the
closing scene. The reader will no doubt want to review the
whole story in the light of it.

Their house alone would not have made you think there was
anything so awfully wrong with Mr. Dorset or his old maid sister. But
certain things about the way both of them dressed had, for a long time,
annoyed and disturbed everyone. We used to see them together at the

grocery store, for instance, or even in one of the big department stores downtown, wearing their bedroom slippers. Looking more closely we would sometimes see the cuff of a pyjama top or the hem of a hitched up nightgown showing from underneath their ordinary daytime clothes. Such slovenliness in one's neighbors is so unpleasant that even husbands and wives in West Vesey Place, which was the street where the Dorsets lived, had got so they didn't like to joke about it with each other. Were the Dorsets, poor old things, losing their minds? If so, what was to be done about it? Some neighbors got so they would not even admit to themselves what they saw. And a child coming home with an ugly report on the Dorsets was apt to be told that it was time he learned to curb his imagination.

Mr. Dorset wore tweed caps and sleeveless sweaters. Usually he had his sweater stuffed down inside his trousers with his shirt tails. To the women and young girls in West Vesey Place this was extremely distasteful. It made them feel as though Mr. Dorset had just come from the bathroom and had got his sweater inside his trousers by mistake. There was, in fact, nothing about Mr. Dorset that was not offensive to the women. Even the old touring car he drove was regarded by most of them as a disgrace to the neighborhood. Parked out in front of his house, as it usually was, it seemed a worse violation of West Vesey's zoning than the house itself. And worst of all was seeing Mr. Dorset wash the car.

Mr. Dorset washed his own car! He washed it not back in the alley or in his driveway but out there in the street of West Vesey Place. This would usually be on the day of one of the parties which he and his sister liked to give for young people or on a day when they were going to make deliveries of the paper flowers or the home grown figs which they sold to their friends. Mr. Dorset would appear in the street carrying two buckets of warm water and wearing a pair of skin-tight coveralls. The skin-tight coveralls, of khaki material but faded almost to flesh color, were still more offensive to the women and young girls than his way of wearing his sweaters. With sponges and chamois cloths and a large scrub brush (for use on the canvas top) the old fellow would fall to and scrub away, gently at first on the canvas top and more vigorously as he progressed to the hood and body, just as though the car were something alive. Neighbor children felt that he went after the headlights exactly as if he were scrubbing the poor car's ears. There was an element of brutality in the way he did it and yet an element of tenderness too. An old lady visiting in the neighborhood once said that it was like the cleansing of a sacrificial animal. I suppose it was some such feeling as this that made all women want to turn away their eyes whenever the spectacle of Mr. Dorset washing his car presented itself.

As for Mr. Dorset's sister, her behavior was in its way just as offensive as his. To the men and boys in the neighborhood it was she who seemed quite beyond the pale. She would come out on her front terrace at midday clad in a faded flannel bathrobe and with her dyed black hair all undone and hanging down her back like the hair of an Indian squaw. To us whose wives and mothers did not even come downstairs in their negligees, this was very unsettling. It was hard to excuse it even on the grounds that the Dorsets were too old and lonely and hard-pressed to care about appearances any more.

Moreover, there was a boy who had gone to Miss Dorset's house one morning in the early fall to collect for his paper route and saw this very Miss Louisa Dorset pushing a carpet sweeper about one of the downstairs rooms without a stitch of clothes on. He saw her through one of the little lancet windows that opened on the front loggia of the house, and he watched her for quite a long while. She was cleaning the house in preparation for a party they were giving for young people that night, and the boy said that when she finally got hot and tired she dropped down in an easy chair and crossed her spindly, blue veined, old legs and sat there completely naked, with her legs crossed and shaking one scrawny little foot, just as unconcerned as if she didn't care that somebody was likely to walk in on her at any moment. After a little bit the boy saw her get up again and go and lean across a table to arrange some paper flowers in a vase. Fortunately he was a nice boy, though he lived only on the edge of the West Vesey Place neighborhood, and he went away without ringing the doorbell or collecting for his paper that week. But he could not resist telling his friends about what he had seen. He said it was a sight he would never forget! And she an old lady more than sixty years old who, had she not been so foolish and self-willed, might have had a house full of servants to push the carpet sweeper for her!

This foolish pair of old people had given up almost everything in life for each other's sake. And it was not at all necessary. When they were young they could have come into a decent inheritance, or now that they were old they might have been provided for by a host of rich relatives. It was only a matter of their being a little tolerant—or even civil —toward their kinspeople. But this was something that old Mr. Dorset and his sister could never consent to do. Almost all their lives they had spoken of their father's kin as "Mama's in-laws" and of their mother's kin as "Papa's in-laws." Their family name was Dorset, not on one side but on both sides. Their parents had been distant cousins. As a matter of fact, the Dorset family in the city of Mero had once been so large and was so long established there that it would have been hard to estimate how distant the kinship might be. But still it was something that the old couple never liked to have mentioned. Most of their mother's kin had, by the time I am speaking of, moved off to California, and most of their father's people lived somewhere up east. But Miss Dorset and her old bachelor brother found any contact, correspondence, even an exchange of Christmas cards with these in-laws intolerable. It was a case, so they said, of the in-laws respecting the value of the dollar above all else, whereas they, Miss Louisa and Mr. Alfred Dorset, placed importance on other things.

They lived in a dilapidated and curiously mutilated house on a street which, except for their own house, was the most splendid street in the entire city. Their house was one that you or I would have been ashamed to live in—even in the lean years of the early thirties. In order to reduce taxes the Dorsets had had the third story of the house torn away, leaving an ugly, flat-topped effect without any trim or ornamentation. Also they had had the south wing pulled down and had sealed the scars not with matching brick but with a speckled stucco that looked raw and naked. All this the old couple did in violation of the strict zoning laws of West Vesey Place, and for doing so they would most certainly have been prosecuted except that they were the Dorsets and except that this was during the depression when zoning laws weren't easy to enforce in a city like Mero.

To the young people whom she and her brother entertained at their house once each year Miss Louisa Dorset liked to say: "We have given up everything for each other. Our only income is from our paper flowers and our figs." The old lady, though without showing any great skill or talent for it, made paper flowers. During the winter months her brother took her in that fifteen-year-old touring car of theirs, with its steering wheel on the wrong side and with isinglass side-curtains that were never taken down, to deliver these flowers to her customers. The flowers looked more like sprays of tinted potato-chips than like any real flowers. Nobody could possibly have wanted to buy them except that she charged next to nothing for them and except that to people with children it seemed important to be on the Dorsets' list of worthwhile people. Nobody could really have wanted Mr. Dorset's figs either. He cultivated a dozen little bushes along the back wall of their house, covering them in the wintertime with some odd looking boxes which he had had constructed for the purpose. The bushes were very productive, but the figs they produced were dried up little things without much taste. During the summer months he and his sister went about in their car, with the side-curtains still up, delivering the figs to the same customers who bought the paper flowers. The money they made could hardly have paid for the gas it took to run the car. It was a great waste and it was very foolish of them.

And yet, despite everything, this foolish pair of old people, this same Miss Louisa and Mr. Alfred Dorset, had become social arbiters of a kind in our city. They had attained this position entirely through their fondness for giving an annual dancing party for young people. To *young* people—to *very* young people—the Dorsets' hearts went out. I don't mean to suggest that their hearts went out to orphans or to the children of the poor, for they were not foolish in that way. The guests at their little dancing parties were the thirteen and fourteen year-olds from families like the one they had long ago set themselves against, young people from the very houses to which, in season, they delivered their figs and their paper flowers. And when the night of one of their parties came round, it was in fact the custom for Mr. Alfred to go in the same old car and fetch all the invited guests to his house. His sister might explain to reluctant parents that this saved the children the embarrassment of being taken to their first dance by mommy and daddy. But the parents knew well enough that for twenty years the Dorsets had permitted no adult person, besides themselves, to put foot inside their house.

At those little dancing parties which the Dorsets gave, peculiar things went on—unsettling things to the boys and girls who had been fetched round in the old car. Sensible parents wished to keep their children away. Yet what could they do? For a Mero girl to have to explain, a few years later, why she never went to a party at the Dorsets' was like having to explain why she had never been a debutante. For a boy it was like having to explain why he had not gone up East to school or even why his father hadn't belonged to the Mero Racquet Club. If when you were thirteen or fourteen you got invited to the Dorsets' house, you went; it was the way of letting people know from the outset who you were. In a busy, modern city like Mero you cannot afford to let people forget who you are—not for a moment, not at any age. Even the Dorsets knew that.

Many a little girl, after one of those evenings at the Dorsets', was heard to cry out in her sleep. When waked, or half waked, her only explanation might be: "It was just the fragrance from the paper flowers." Or: "I dreamed I could really smell the paper flowers." Many a boy was observed by his parents to seem "different" afterward. He became "secretive." The parents of the generation that had to attend those parties never pretended to understand what went on at the Dorsets' house. And even to those of us who were in that unlucky generation it seemed we were half a lifetime learning what really took place during our one evening under the Dorsets' roof. Before our turn to go ever came round we had for years been hearing about what it was like from older boys and girls. Afterward, we continued to hear about it from those who followed us. And, looking back on it, nothing about the one evening when you were actually there ever seemed quite so real as the glimpses and snatches which you got from those people before and after you—the second-hand impressions of the Dorsets' behavior, of things they said, of looks that passed between them.

Since Miss Dorset kept no servants she always opened her own door. I suspect that for the guests at her parties the sight of her opening her door, in her astonishing attire, came as the most violent shock of the whole evening. On these occasions she and her brother got themselves up as we had never seen them before and never would again. The old lady invariably wore a modish white evening gown, a garment perfectly fitted to her spare and scrawny figure and cut in such high fashion that it must necessarily have been new that year. And never to be worn but that one night! Her hair, long and thick and newly dyed for the occasion, would be swept upward and forward in a billowy mass which was topped by a corsage of yellow and coral paper flowers. Her cheeks and lips would be darkly rouged. On her long bony arms and her bare shoulders she would have applied some kind of sun-tan powder. Whatever else you had been led to expect of the evening, no one had warned you sufficiently about the radical change to be noted in her appearance—or in that of her brother, either. By the end of the party Miss Louisa might look as dowdy as ever, and Mr. Alfred a little worse than usual. But at the outset, when the party was assembling in their drawing room, even Mr. Alfred appeared resplendent in a nattily tailored tuxedo, with exactly the shirt, the collar, and the tie which fashion prescribed that year. His grey hair was nicely trimmed, his puffy old face freshly shaven. He was powdered with the same dark powder that his sister used. One felt even that his cheeks had been lightly touched with rouge.

A strange perfume pervaded the atmosphere of the house. The moment you set foot inside, this awful fragrance engulfed you. It was like a mixture of spicy incense and sweet attar of roses. And always, too, there was the profusion of paper flowers. The flowers were everywhere —on every cabinet and console, every inlaid table and carved chest, on every high, marble mantel piece, on the book shelves. In the entrance hall special tiers must have been set up to hold the flowers, because they were there in overpowering masses. They were in such abundance that it seemed hardly possible that Miss Dorset could have made them all. She must have spent weeks and weeks preparing them, even months, perhaps even the whole year between parties. When she went about delivering them to her customers, in the months following, they were apt to be somewhat faded and dusty; but on the night of the party the colors of the flowers seemed even more impressive and more unlikely than their number. They were fuchsia, they were chartreuse, they were coral, aquamarine, brown, they were even black.

Everywhere in the Dorsets' house too were certain curious illuminations and lighting effects. The source of the light was usually hidden and its purpose was never obvious at once. The lighting was a subtler element than either the perfume or the paper flowers, and ultimately it was more disconcerting. A shaft of lavender light would catch a young visitor's eye and lead it, seemingly without purpose, in among the flowers. Then just beyond the point where the strength of the light would begin to diminish, the eye would discover something. In a small aperture in the mass of flowers, or sometimes in a larger grotto-like opening, there would be a piece of sculpture—in the hall a plaster replica of Rodin's *The Kiss,* in the library an antique plaque of Leda and the Swan. Or just above the flowers would be hung a picture, usually a black and white print but sometimes a reproduction in color. On the landing of the stairway leading down to the basement ballroom was the only picture that one was likely to learn the title of at the time. It was a tiny color print of Bronzino's *Venus, Cupid, Folly and Time*. This picture was not even framed. It was simply tacked on the wall, and it had obviously been torn—rather carelessly, perhaps hurriedly—from a book or magazine. The title and the name of the painter were printed in the white margin underneath.

About these works of art most of us had been warned by older boys and girls; and we stood in painful dread of that moment when Miss Dorset or her brother might catch us staring at any one of their pictures or sculptures. We had been warned, time and again, that during the course of the evening moments would come when she or he would reach out and touch the other's elbow and indicate, with a nod or just the trace of a smile, some guest whose glance had strayed among the flowers.

To some extent the dread which all of us felt of that evening at the Dorsets' cast a shadow over the whole of our childhood. Yet for nearly twenty years the Dorsets continued to give their annual party. And even the most sensible of parents were not willing to keep their children away.

But a thing happened finally which could almost have been predicted. Young people, even in West Vesey Place, will not submit forever to the prudent counsel of their parents. Or some of them won't. There was a boy named Ned Meriwether and his sister Emily Meriwether, who lived with their parents in West Vesey Place just one block away from the Dorsets' house. In November Ned and Emily were invited to the Dorsets' party, and because they dreaded it they decided to play a trick on everyone concerned—even on themselves, as it turned out. . . . They got up a plan for smuggling an uninvited guest into the Dorsets' party.

The parents of this Emily and Ned sensed that their children were concealing something from them and suspected that the two were up to mischief of some kind. But they managed to deceive themselves with the thought that it was only natural for young people—"mere children"

—to be nervous about going to the Dorsets' house. And so instead of questioning them during the last hour before they left for the party, these sensible parents tried to do everything in their power to calm their two children. The boy and the girl, seeing that this was the case, took advantage of it.

"You must not go down to the front door with us when we leave," the daughter insisted to her mother. And she persuaded both Mr. and Mrs. Meriwether that after she and her brother were dressed for the party they should all wait together in the upstairs sitting room until Mr. Dorset came to fetch the two young people in his car.

When, at eight o'clock, the lights of the automobile appeared in the street below, the brother and sister were still upstairs—watching from the bay window of the family sitting room. They kissed Mother and Daddy goodbye and then they flew down the stairs and across the wide, carpeted entrance hall to a certain dark recess where a boy named Tom Bascomb was hidden. This boy was the uninvited guest whom Ned and Emily were going to smuggle into the party. They had left the front door unlatched for Tom, and from the upstairs window just a few minutes ago they had watched him come across their front lawn. Now in the little recess of the hall there was a quick exchange of overcoats and hats between Ned Meriwether and Tom Bascomb; for it was a feature of the plan that Tom should attend the party as Ned and that Ned should go as the uninvited guest.

In the darkness of the recess Ned fidgeted and dropped Tom Bascomb's coat on the floor. But the boy, Tom Bascomb, did not fidget. He stepped out into the light of the hall and began methodically getting into the overcoat which he would wear tonight. He was not a boy who lived in the West Vesey Place neighborhood (he was in fact the very boy who had once watched Miss Dorset cleaning house without any clothes on), and he did not share Emily's and Ned's nervous excitement about the evening. The sound of Mr. Dorset's footsteps outside did not disturb him. When both Ned and Emily stood frozen by that sound, he continued buttoning the unfamiliar coat and even amused himself by stretching forth one arm to observe how high the sleeve came on his wrist.

The doorbell rang, and from his dark corner Ned Meriwether whispered to his sister and to Tom: "Don't worry. I'll be at the Dorsets' in plenty of time."

Tom Bascomb only shrugged his shoulders at this reassurance. Presently when he looked at Emily's flushed face and saw her batting her eyes like a nervous monkey, a crooked smile played upon his lips. Then, at a sign from Emily, Tom followed her to the entrance door and permitted her to introduce him to old Mr. Dorset as her brother.

From the window of the upstairs sitting room the Meriwether parents watched Mr. Dorset and this boy and this girl walking across the lawn toward Mr. Dorset's peculiar looking car. A light shone bravely and protectively from above the entrance of the house, and in its rays the parents were able to detect the strange angle at which Brother was carrying his head tonight and how his new fedora already seemed too small for him. They even noticed that he seemed a bit taller tonight.

"I hope it's all right," said the mother.

"What do you mean 'all right'?" the father asked petulantly.

"I mean—," the mother began, and then she hesitated. She did not want to mention that the boy out there did not look like their own Ned. It would have seemed to give away her feelings too much. "I mean that I wonder if I should have put Sister in that long dress at this age and let her wear my cape. I'm afraid the cape is really inappropriate. She's still young for that sort of thing."

"Oh," said the father, "I thought you meant something else."

"Whatever else did you think I meant, Edwin?" the mother said, suddenly breathless.

"I thought you meant the business we've discussed before," he said, although this was of course not what he had thought she meant. He had thought she meant that the boy out there did not look like their Ned. To him it had seemed even that the boy's step was different from Ned's. "The Dorsets' parties," he said, "are not very nice affairs to be sending your children off to, Muriel. That's all I thought you meant."

"But we *can't* keep them away," the mother said defensively.

"Oh, it's just that they are growing up faster than we realize," said the father, glancing at his wife out of the corner of his eye.

By this time Mr. Dorset's car had pulled out of sight, and from downstairs Muriel Meriwether thought she heard another door closing. "What was that?" she said, putting one hand on her husband's.

"Don't be so jumpy," her husband said irritably, snatching away his hand. "It's the servants closing up in the kitchen."

Both of them knew that the servants had closed up in the kitchen long before this. Both of them had heard quite distinctly the sound of the side door closing as Ned went out. But they went on talking and deceiving themselves in this fashion during most of that evening.

Even before she opened the door to Mr. Dorset, little Emily Meriwether had known that there would be no difficulty about passing Tom Bascomb off as her brother. In the first place, she knew that without his spectacles Mr. Dorset could hardly see his hand before his face and knew that due to some silly pride he had he never put on his spectacles except when he was behind the wheel of his automobile. This much was common knowledge. In the second place, Emily knew from experience that neither he nor his sister ever made any real pretense of knowing one child in their general acquaintance from another. And so, standing in the doorway and speaking almost in a whisper, Emily had merely to introduce first herself and then her pretended brother to Mr. Dorset. After that the three of them walked in silence from her father's house to the waiting car.

Emily was wearing her mother's second best evening wrap, a white lapin cape which, on Emily, swept the ground. As she walked between the boy and the man, the touch of the cape's soft silk lining on her bare arms and on her shoulders spoke to her silently of a strange girl she had seen in her looking glass upstairs tonight. And with her every step toward the car the skirt of her long taffeta gown whispered her own name to her: *Emily . . . Emily.* She heard it distinctly, and yet the name sounded unfamiliar. Once during this unreal walk from house to car she glanced at the mysterious boy, Tom Bascomb, longing to ask him—if only with her eyes—for some reassurance that she was really she. But Tom Bascomb was absorbed in his own irrelevant observations. With his head tilted back he was gazing upward at the nondescript winter sky where, among drifting clouds, a few pale stars were shedding their dull light alike on West Vesey Place and on the rest of the world. Emily drew her wrap tightly about her, and when presently Mr. Dorset held open the door to the back seat of his car she shut her eyes and plunged into the pitch-blackness of the car's interior.

Tom Bascomb was a year older than Ned Meriwether and he was nearly two years older than Emily. He had been Ned's friend first. He and Ned had played baseball together on Saturdays before Emily ever set eyes on him. Yet according to Tom Bascomb himself, with whom several of us older boys talked just a few weeks after the night he went to the Dorsets, Emily always insisted that it was she who had known him first. On what she based this false claim Tom could not say. And on the two or three other occasions when we got Tom to talk about that night, he kept saying that he didn't understand what it was that had made Emily and Ned quarrel over which of them knew him first and knew him better.

We could have told him what it was, I think. But we didn't. It would have been too hard to say to him that at one time or another all of us in West Vesey had had our Tom Bascombs. Tom lived with his parents in an apartment house on a wide thoroughfare known as Division Boulevard, and his only real connection with West Vesey Place was that that street was included in his paper route. During the early morning hours he rode his bicycle along West Vesey and along other quiet streets like it, carefully aiming a neatly rolled paper at the dark loggia, at the colonnaded porch, or at the ornamented doorway of each of the palazzos and chateaux and manor houses that glowered at him in the dawn. He was well thought of as a paper boy. If by mistake one of his papers went astray and lit on an upstairs balcony or on the roof of a porch, Tom would always take more careful aim and throw another. Even if the paper only went into the shrubbery, Tom got off his bicycle and fished it out. He wasn't the kind of boy to whom it would have occurred that the old fogies and the rich kids in West Vesey could very well get out and scramble for their own papers.

Actually a party at the Dorsets' house was more a grand tour of the house than a real party. There was a half hour spent over very light refreshments (fruit Jell-o, English tea biscuits, lime punch). There was another half hour ostensibly given to general dancing in the basement ballroom (to the accompaniment of victrola music). But mainly there was the tour. As the party passed through the house, stopping sometimes to sit down in the principal rooms, the host and hostess provided entertainment in the form of an almost continuous dialogue between themselves. This dialogue was famous and was full of interest, being all about how much the Dorsets had given up for each other's sake and about how much higher the tone of Mero society used to be than it was nowadays. They would invariably speak of their parents, who had died within a year of each other when Miss Louisa and Mr. Alfred were still in their teens; they even spoke of their wicked in-laws. When their parents died, the wicked in-laws had first tried to make them sell the house, then had tried to separate them and send them away to boarding schools, and had ended by trying to marry them off to "just anyone." Their two grandfathers had still been alive in those days and each had had a hand in the machinations, after the failure of which each grandfather had disinherited them. Mr. Alfred and Miss Louisa spoke also of how, a few years later, a procession of "young nobodies" had come of their own accord trying to steal the two of them away from each other. Both he and she would scowl at the very recollection of those "just anybodies" and those "nobodies," those "would-be suitors" who always turned out to be misguided fortune-hunters and had to be driven away.

The Dorsets' dialogue usually began in the living room the moment Mr. Dorset returned with his last collection of guests. (He sometimes had to make five or six trips in the car.) There, as in other rooms afterward, they were likely to begin with a reference to the room itself or perhaps to some piece of furniture in the room. For instance, the extraordinary length of the drawing room—or reception room, as the Dorsets called it—would lead them to speak of an even longer room which they had had torn away from the house. "It grieved us, we wept," Miss Dorset would say, "to have Mama's French drawing room torn away from us."

"But we tore it away from ourselves," her brother would add, "as we tore away our in-laws—because we could not afford them." Both of them spoke in a fine declamatory style, but they frequently interrupted themselves with a sad little laugh which expressed something quite different from what they were saying and which seemed to serve them as an aside not meant for our ears.

"That was one of our greatest sacrifices," Miss Dorset would say, referring still to her mother's French drawing room.

And her brother would say: "But we knew the day had passed in Mero for entertainments worthy of that room."

"It was the room which Mama and Papa loved best, but we gave it up because we knew, from our upbringing, which things to give up."

From this they might go on to anecdotes about their childhood. Sometimes their parents had left them for months or even a whole year at a time with only the housekeeper or with trusted servants to see after them. "You could trust servants then," they explained. And: "In those days parents could do that sort of thing, because in those days there was a responsible body of people within which your young people could always find proper companionship."

In the library, to which the party always moved from the drawing room, Mr. Dorset was fond of exhibiting snapshots of the house taken before the south wing was pulled down. As the pictures were passed around, the dialogue continued. It was often there that they told the story of how the in-laws had tried to force them to sell the house. "For the sake of economy!" Mr. Dorset would exclaim, adding an ironic, "Ha ha!"

His sister would repeat the exclamation, "For the sake of economy!" and also the ironic "Ha ha!"

"As though money—" he would begin.

"As though money ever took the place," his sister would come in, "of living with your own kind."

"Or of being well born," said Mr. Dorset.

After the billiard room, where everyone who wanted it was permitted one turn with the only cue that there seemed to be in the house, and after the dining room, where it was promised refreshments would be served later, the guests would be taken down to the ballroom— purportedly for dancing. Instead of everyone's being urged to dance, however, once they were assembled in the ballroom, Miss Dorset would announce that she and her brother understood the timidity which young people felt about dancing and that all that she and he intended to do was to set the party a good example. . . . It was only Miss Louisa and Mr. Alfred who danced. For perhaps thirty minutes, in a room without light excepting that from a few weak bulbs concealed among the flowers, the old couple danced; and they danced with such grace and there was such perfect harmony in all their movements that the guests stood about in stunned silence, as if hypnotized. The Dorsets waltzed,

they two-stepped, they even fox-trotted, stopping only long enough between dances for Mr. Dorset, amid general applause, to change the
victrola record.

But it was when their dance was ended that all the effects of the
Dorsets' careful grooming that night would have vanished. And, alas,
they made no effort to restore themselves. During the remainder of the
evening Mr. Dorset went about with his bow tie hanging limply on his
damp shirtfront, a gold collar button shining above it. A strand of
grey hair, which normally covered his bald spot on top, now would have
fallen on the wrong side of his part and hung like fringe about his ear.
On his face and neck the thick layer of powder was streaked with perspiration. Miss Dorset was usually in an even more dishevelled state,
depending somewhat upon the fashion of her dress that year. But always
her powder was streaked, her lipstick entirely gone, her hair falling
down on all sides, and her corsage dangling somewhere about the nape
of her neck. In this condition they led the party upstairs again, not
stopping until they had reached the second floor of the house.

On the second floor we—the guests—were shown the rooms which
the Dorsets' parents had once occupied (the Dorsets' own rooms were
never shown). We saw, in glass museum cases along the hallway, the
dresses and suits and hats and even the shoes which Miss Louisa and
Mr. Alfred had worn to parties when they were very young. And now
the dialogue, which had been left off while the Dorsets danced, was
resumed. "Ah, the happy time," one of them would say, "was when we
were *your* age!" And then, exhorting us to be happy and gay while we
were still safe in the bosom of our own kind and before the world came
crowding in on us with its ugly demands, the Dorsets would recall the
happiness they had known when they were very young. This was their
pièce de résistance. With many a wink and blush and giggle and shake
of the forefinger—and of course standing before the whole party—they
each would remind the other of his or her naughty behavior in some
old-fashioned parlor game or of certain silly little flirtations which they
had long ago caught each other in.

They were on their way downstairs again now, and by the time they
had finished with this favorite subject they would be downstairs.
They would be in the dark, flower bedecked downstairs hall and just
before entering the dining room for the promised refreshments: the
fruit Jell-o, the English tea biscuits, the lime punch.

And now for a moment Mr. Dorset bars the way to the dining room
and prevents his sister from opening the closed door. "Now, my good
friends," he says, "let us eat, drink and be merry!"

"For the night is yet young," says his sister.

"Tonight you must be gay and carefree," Mr. Dorset enjoins.

"Because in this house we are all friends," Miss Dorset says. "We are all young, we all love one another."

"And love can make us all young forever," her brother says. "Remember!"

"Remember this evening always, sweet young people!" "Remember!"

"Remember what our life is like here!"

And now Miss Dorset, with one hand on the knob of the great door which she is about to throw open, leans a little toward the guests and whispers hoarsely: "This is what it is like to be young forever!"

Ned Meriwether was waiting behind a big japonica shrub near the sidewalk when, about twenty minutes after he had last seen Emily, the queer old touring car drew up in front of the Dorsets' house. During the interval, the car had gone from the Meriwether house to gather a number of other guests, and so it was not only Emily and Tom who alighted on the sidewalk before the Dorsets' house. The group was just large enough to make it easy for Ned to slip out from his dark hiding place and join them without being noticed by Mr. Dorset. And now the group was escorted rather unceremoniously up to the door of the house, and Mr. Dorset departed to fetch more guests.

They were received at the door by Miss Dorset. Her eyesight was no doubt better than her brother's, but still there was really no danger of her detecting an uninvited guest. Those of us who had gone to that house in the years just before Ned and Emily came along, could remember that during a whole evening, when their house was full of young people, the Dorsets made no introductions and made no effort to distinguish which of their guests was which. They did not even make a count of heads. Perhaps they did vaguely recognize some of the faces, because sometimes when they had come delivering figs or paper flowers to a house they had of necessity encountered a young child there, and always they smiled sweetly at it, asked its age, and calculated on their old fingers how many years must pass before the child would be eligible for an invitation. Yet at those moments something in the way they had held up their fingers and in the way they had gazed *at* the little face instead of into it had revealed their lack of interest in the individual child. And later when the child was finally old enough to receive their invitation he found it was still no different with the Dorsets. Even in their own house it was evidently to the young people as a group that the Dorsets' hearts went out; while they had the boys and girls under their roof they herded them about like so many little thoroughbred calves. Even when Miss Dorset opened the front door she did so exactly as though she were opening a gate. She pulled it open very slowly, standing half behind it to keep out of harm's way. And the children, all huddled together, surged in.

How meticulously this Ned and Emily Meriwether must have laid their plans for that evening! And the whole business might have come out all right if only they could have foreseen the effect which one part of their plan—rather a last minute embellishment of it—would produce upon Ned himself. Barely ten minutes after they entered the house Ned was watching Tom as he took his seat on the piano bench beside Emily. Ned probably watched Tom closely, because certainly he knew what the next move was going to be. The moment Miss Louisa Dorset's back was turned Tom Bascomb slipped his arm gently about Emily's little waist and commenced kissing her all over her pretty face. It was almost as if he were kissing away tears.

This spectacle on the piano bench, and others like it which followed, had been an inspiration of the last day or so before the party. Or so Ned and Emily maintained afterward when defending themselves to their parents. But no matter when it was conceived, a part of their plan it was, and Ned must have believed himself fully prepared for it. Probably he expected to join in the round of giggling which it produced from the other guests. But now that the time had come—it is easy to imagine— the boy Ned Meriwether found himself not quite able to join in the fun. He watched with the others, but he was not quite infected by their laughter. He stood a little apart, and possibly he was hoping that Emily and Tom would not notice his failure to appreciate the success of their comedy. He was no doubt baffled by his own feelings, by the failure of his own enthusiasm, and by a growing desire to withdraw himself from the plot and from the party itself.

It is easy to imagine Ned's uneasiness and confusion that night. And I believe the account which I have given of Emily's impressions and her delicate little sensations while on the way to the party has the ring of truth about it, though actually the account was supplied by girls who knew her only slightly, who were not at the party, who could not possibly have seen her afterward. It may, after all, represent only what other girls imagined she would have felt. As for the account of how Mr. and Mrs. Meriwether spent the evening, it is their very own. And they did not hesitate to give it to anyone who would listen.

It was a long time, though, before many of us had a clear picture of the main events of the evening. We heard very soon that the parties for young people were to be no more, that there had been a wild scramble and chase through the Dorsets' house, and that it had ended by the Dorsets locking some boy—whether Ned or Tom was not easy to determine at first—in a queer sort of bathroom in which the plumbing had been disconnected, and even the fixtures removed, I believe. (Later I learned that there was nothing literally sinister about the bathroom, it self. By having the pipes disconnected to this, and perhaps other bath-rooms, the Dorsets had obtained further reductions in their taxes.) But a clear picture of the whole evening wasn't to be had—not without considerable searching. For one thing, the Meriwether parents im-mediately, within a week after the party, packed their son and daughter off to boarding schools. Accounts from the other children were con-tradictory and vague—perversely so, it seemed. Parents reported to each other that the little girls had nightmares which were worse even than those which their older sisters had had. And the boys were se-cretive and elusive, even with us older boys when we questioned them about what had gone on.

One sketchy account of events leading up to the chase, however, did go the rounds almost at once. Ned must have written it back to some older boy in a letter, because it contained information which no one but Ned could have had. The account went like this: When Mr. Dorset returned from his last round-up of guests, he came hurrying into the drawing room where the others were waiting and said in a voice trem-bling with excitement: "Now, let us all be seated, my young friends, and let us warm ourselves with some good talk."

At that moment everyone who was not already seated made a dash for a place on one of the divans or love seats or even in one of the broad window seats. (There were no individual chairs in the room.) Everyone made a dash, that is, except Ned. Ned did not move. He remained standing beside a little table rubbing his fingers over its polished surface. And from this moment he was clearly an object of suspicion in the eyes of his host and hostess. Soon the party moved from the drawing room to the library, but in whatever room they stopped Ned managed to isolate himself from the rest. He would sit or stand looking down at his hands until once again an explosion of giggles filled the room. Then he would look up just in time to see Tom Bascomb's cheek against Emily's or his arm about her waist.

For nearly two hours Ned didn't speak a word to anyone. He en-dured the Dorsets' dialogue, the paper flowers, the perfumed air, the works of art. Whenever a burst of giggling forced him to raise his eyes he would look up at Tom and Emily and then turn his eyes away. Before looking down at his hands again he would let his eyes travel slowly about the room until they came to rest on the figures of the two Dorsets. That, it seems, was how he happened to discover that the Dorsets un-derstood, or thought they understood, what the giggles meant. In the great mirror mounted over the library mantel he saw them exchanging half suppressed smiles. Their smiles lasted precisely as long as the giggling continued, and then, in the mirror, Ned saw their faces change and grow solemn when their eyes—their identical, tiny, dull, amber colored eyes—focussed upon himself.

From the library the party continued on the regular tour of the house. At last when they had been to the ballroom and watched the Dorsets dance, had been upstairs to gaze upon the faded party clothes in the museum cases, they descended into the downstairs hall and were just before being turned into the dining room. The guests had already heard the Dorsets teasing each other about the silly little flirtations and about their naughtiness in parlor games when they were young and had listened to their exhortations to be gay and happy and carefree. Then just when Miss Dorset leaned toward them and whispered, "This is what it is like to be young forever," there rose a chorus of laughter, breathless and shrill, yet loud and intensely penetrating.

Ned Meriwether, standing on the bottom step of the stairway, lifted his eyes and looked over the heads of the party to see Tom and Emily half hidden in a bower of paper flowers and caught directly in a ray of mauve light. The two had squeezed themselves into a little niche there and stood squarely in front of the Rodin statuary. Tom had one arm placed about Emily's shoulders and he was kissing her lightly first on the lobe of one ear and then on the tip of her nose. Emily stood as rigid and pale as the plaster sculpture behind her and with just the faintest smile on her lips. Ned looked at the two of them and then turned his glance at once on the Dorsets.

He found Miss Louisa and Mr. Alfred gazing quite openly at Tom and Emily and frankly grinning at the spectacle. It was more than Ned could endure. "Don't you *know?*" he fairly wailed, as if in great physical pain. "Can't you *tell?* Can't you see who they *are?* They're *brother* and *sister!*"

From the other guests came one concerted gasp. And then an instant later, mistaking Ned's outcry to be something he had planned all along and probably intended—as they imagined—for the very cream of the jest, the whole company burst once again into laughter—not a chorus of laughter this time but a volley of loud guffaws from the boys, and from the girls a cacophony of separately articulated shrieks and trills.

None of the guests present that night could—or would—give a satisfactory account of what happened next. Everyone insisted that he had not even looked at the Dorsets, that he, or she, didn't know how Miss Louisa and Mr. Alfred reacted at first. Yet this was precisely what those of us who had gone there in the past *had* to know. And when finally we did manage to get an account of it, we knew that it was a very truthful and accurate one. Because we got it, of course, from Tom Bascomb.

Since Ned's outburst came after the dancing exhibition, the Dorsets were in their most dishevelled state. Miss Louisa's hair was fallen half over her face, and that long, limp strand of Mr. Alfred's was dangling about his left ear. Like that, they stood at the doorway to the dining room grinning at Tom Bascomb's antics. And when Tom Bascomb, hearing Ned's wail, whirled about, the grins were still on the Dorsets' faces even though the guffaws and the shrieks of laughter were now silenced. Tom said that for several moments they continued to wear their grins like masks and that you couldn't really tell how they were taking it all until presently Miss Louisa's face, still wearing the grin, began turning all the queer colors of her paper flowers. Then the grin vanished from her lips and her mouth fell open and every bit of color went out of her face. She took a step backward and leaned against the doorjamb with her mouth still open and her eyes closed. If she hadn't been on her feet, Tom said he would have thought she was dead. Her brother didn't look at her, but his own grin had vanished just as hers did, and his face, all drawn and wrinkled, momentarily turned a dull copperish green.

Presently, though, he too went white, not white in faintness but in anger. His little brown eyes now shone like rosin. And he took several steps toward Ned Meriwether. "What we know is that you are not one of us," he croaked. "We have perceived that from the beginning! We don't know how you got here or who you are. But the important question is, What are you doing here among these nice children?"

The question seemed to restore life to Miss Louisa. Her amber eyes popped wide open. She stepped away from the door and began pinning up her hair which had fallen down on her shoulders, and at the same time addressing the guests who were huddled together in the center of the hall. "Who is he, children? He is an intruder, that we know. If you know who he is, you must tell us."

"Who *am* I? Why, I am Tom Bascomb!" shouted Ned, still from the bottom step of the stairway. "I am Tom Bascomb, your paper boy!"

Then he turned and fled up the stairs toward the second floor. In a moment Mr. Dorset was after him.

To the real Tom Bascomb it had seemed that Ned honestly believed what he had been saying; and his own first impulse was to shout a denial. But being a levelheaded boy and seeing how bad things were, Tom went instead to Miss Dorset and whispered to her that Tom Bascomb was a pretty tough guy and that she had better let *him* call the police for her. She told him where the telephone was in the side hall, and he started away.

But Miss Dorset changed her mind. She ran after Tom telling him not to call. Some of the guests mistook this for the beginning of another chase. Before the old lady could overtake Tom, however, Ned himself had appeared in the doorway toward which she and Tom were moving. He had come down the back stairway and he was calling out to Emily, "We're going *home,* Sis!"

A cheer went up from the whole party. Maybe it was this that caused Ned to lose his head, or maybe it was simply the sight of Miss Dorset rushing at him that did it. At any rate, the next moment he was running up the front stairs again, this time with Miss Dorset in pursuit.

When Tom returned from the telephone, all was quiet in the hall. The guests—everybody except Emily—had moved to the foot of the stairs and they were looking up and listening. From upstairs Tom could hear Ned saying, "All right. All right. All right." The old couple had cornered him.

Emily was still standing in the little niche among the flowers. And it is the image of Emily Meriwether standing among the paper flowers that tantalizes me whenever I think or hear someone speak of that evening. That, more than anything else, can make me wish that I had been there. I shall never cease to wonder what kind of thoughts were in her head to make her seem so oblivious to all that was going on while she stood there, and, for that matter, what had been in her mind all evening while she endured Tom Bascomb's caresses. When, in years since, I have had reason to wonder what some girl or woman is thinking —some Emily grown older—my mind nearly always returns to the image of that girl among the paper flowers. Tom said that when he returned from the telephone she looked very solemn and pale still but that her mind didn't seem to be on any of the present excitement. Immediately he went to her and said, "Your dad is on his way over, Emily." For it was the Meriwether parents he had telephoned, of course, and not the police.

It seemed to Tom that so far as he was concerned the party was now over. There was nothing more he could do. Mr. Dorset was upstairs guarding the door to the strange little room in which Ned was locked up. Miss Dorset was serving lime punch to the other guests in the dining room, all the while listening with one ear for the arrival of the police whom Tom pretended he had called. When the doorbell finally rang and Miss Dorset hurried to answer it, Tom slipped quietly out through the pantry and through the kitchen and left the house by the back door as the Meriwether parents entered by the front.

There was no difficulty in getting Edwin and Muriel Meriwether, the children's parents, to talk about what happened after they arrived that night. Both of them were sensible and clearheaded people, and they were not so conservative as some of our other neighbors in West Vesey. Being fond of gossip of any kind and fond of reasonably funny stories on themselves, they told how their children had deceived them earlier in the evening and how they had deceived themselves later. They tended to blame themselves more than the children for what had happened. They tried to protect the children from any harm or embarrassment that might result from it by sending them off to boarding school. In their talk they never referred directly to Tom's reprehensible conduct or to the possible motives that the children might have had for getting up their plan. They tried to spare their children and they tried to spare Tom, but fortunately it didn't occur to them to try to spare the poor old Dorsets.

When Miss Louisa opened the door, Mr. Meriwether said, "I'm Edwin Meriwether, Miss Dorset. I've come for my son, Ned."

"And for your daughter Emily, I hope," his wife whispered to him.

"And for my daughter Emily."

Before Miss Dorset could answer him Edwin Meriwether spied Mr. Dorset descending the stairs. With his wife, Muriel, sticking close to his side Edwin now strode over to the foot of the stairs. "Mr. Dorset," he began, "my son Ned—"

From behind them, Edwin and Muriel now heard Miss Dorset saying, "All the invited guests are gathered in the dining room." From where they were standing the two parents could see into the dining room. Suddenly they turned and hurried in there. Mr. Dorset and his sister of course followed them.

Muriel Meriwether went directly to Emily, who was standing in a group of girls. "Emily, where is your brother?"

Emily said nothing, but one of the boys answered: "I think they've got him locked up upstairs somewhere."

"Oh, no!" said Miss Louisa, a hairpin in her mouth—for she was still rather absent-mindedly working at her hair. "It is an intruder that my brother has upstairs."

Mr. Dorset began speaking in a confidential tone to Edwin. "My dear neighbor," he said, "our paper boy saw fit to intrude himself upon our company tonight. But we recognized him as an outsider from the start."

Muriel Meriwether asked: "Where *is* the paper boy? Where is the paper boy, Emily?"

Again one of the boys volunteered: "He went out through the back door, Mrs. Meriwether."

The eyes of Mr. Alfred and Miss Louisa searched the room for Tom. Finally their eyes met and they smiled coyly. "*All* the children are being mischievous tonight," said Miss Louisa, and it was quite as though she had said, "all *we* children." Then, still smiling, she said, "Your tie has come undone, Brother. Mr. and Mrs. Meriwether will hardly know what to think."

Mr. Alfred fumbled for a moment with his tie but soon gave it up. Now with a bashful glance at the Meriwether parents, and giving a nod in the direction of the children, he actually said, "I'm afraid we've all decided to play a trick on Mr. and Mrs. Meriwether."

Miss Louisa said to Emily: "We've hidden our brother somewhere, haven't we?"

Emily's mother said firmly: "Emily, tell me where Ned is."

"He's upstairs, Mother," said Emily in a whisper.

Emily's father said: "I wish you to take me to the boy upstairs, Mr. Dorset."

The coy, bashful expressions vanished from the two Dorsets' faces. Their eyes were little dark pools of incredulity, growing narrower by the second. And both of them were now trying to put their hair in order. "Why, *we* know nice children when we see them," Miss Louisa said peevishly. There was a pleading quality in her voice, too. "We knew from the beginning that that boy upstairs didn't belong amongst us," she said. "Dear neighbors, it isn't just the money, you know." All at once she sounded like a little girl about to burst into tears.

"It isn't just the money?" Edwin Meriwether repeated.

"Miss Dorset," said Muriel with new gentleness in her tone, as though she had just sensed that she was talking to a little girl, "there has been some kind of mistake—a misunderstanding."

Mr. Alfred Dorset said: "Oh, we wouldn't make a mistake of that kind! People *are* different. It isn't something you can put your finger on, but it isn't the money."

"I don't know what you're talking about," Edwin said, exasperated. "But I'm going upstairs and find that boy." He left the room with Mr. Dorset following him with quick little steps—steps like those of a small boy trying to keep up with a man.

Miss Louisa now sat down in one of the high-backed dining chairs which were lined up along the oak wainscot. She was trembling, and Muriel came and stood beside her. Neither of them spoke, and in almost no time Edwin Meriwether came downstairs again with Ned. Miss Louisa looked at Ned, and tears came into her eyes. "Where is my brother?" she asked accusingly, as though she thought possibly Ned and his father had locked Mr. Dorset in the bathroom.

"I believe he has retired," said Edwin. "He left us and disappeared into one of the rooms upstairs."

"Then I must go up to him," said Miss Louisa. For a moment she seemed unable to rise. At last she pushed herself up from the chair and walked from the room with the slow, steady gait of a somnambulist. Muriel Meriwether followed her into the hall and as she watched the old woman ascending the steps, leaning heavily on the rail, her impulse was to go and offer to assist her. But something made her turn back into the dining room. Perhaps she imagined that her daughter, Emily, might need her now.

The Dorsets did not reappear that night. After Miss Louisa went upstairs, Muriel promptly got on the telephone and called the parents of some of the other boys and girls. Within a quarter of an hour a dozen parents had arrived. It was the first time in many years that any adult had set foot inside the Dorset house. It was the first time that any parent had ever inhaled the perfumed air or seen the masses of paper flowers and the illuminations and the statuary. In the guise of holding consultations over whether or not they should put out the lights and lock up the house the parents lingered much longer than was necessary before taking the young people home. Some of them even tasted the lime punch. But in the presence of their children they made no comment on what had happened and gave no indication of what their own impressions were—not even their impressions of the punch. At last it was decided that two of the men should see to putting out the lights everywhere on the first floor and down in the ballroom. They were a long time in finding the switches for the indirect lighting. In most cases they simply resorted to unscrewing the bulbs. Meanwhile the children went to the large cloak closet behind the stairway and got their wraps. When Ned and Emily Meriwether rejoined their parents at the front door to leave the house, Ned was wearing his own overcoat and held his own fedora in his hand.

Miss Louisa and Mr. Alfred Dorset lived on for nearly ten years after that night, but they gave up selling their figs and paper flowers and of course they never entertained young people again. I often wonder if growing up in Mero can ever have seemed quite the same since. Some of the terror must have gone out of it. Half the dread of coming of age must have vanished with the dread of the Dorsets' parties.

After that night, their old car would sometimes be observed creeping about town, but it was never parked in front of their house any more. It stood usually at the side entrance where the Dorsets could climb in and out of it without being seen. They began keeping a servant too—mainly to run their errands for them, I imagine. Sometimes it would be a man, sometimes a woman, never the same one for more than a few months at a time. Both of the Dorsets died during the Second World War while many of us who had gone to their parties were away from Mero. But the story went round—and I am inclined to believe it—that after they were dead and the house was sold, Tom Bascomb's coat and hat were found still hanging in the cloak closet behind the stairs.

Tom himself was a pilot in the War and was a considerable hero. He was such a success and made such a name for himself that he never came back to Mero to live. He found bigger opportunities elsewhere I suppose, and I don't suppose he ever felt the ties to Mero that people with Ned's kind of upbringing do. Ned was in the War too, of course. He was in the navy and after the War he did return to Mero to live, though actually it was not until then that he had spent much time here since his parents bundled him off to boarding school. Emily came home and made her debut just two or three years before the War, but she was already engaged to some boy in the East; she never comes back any more except to bring her children to see their grandparents for a few days during Christmas or at Easter.

I understand that Emily and Ned are pretty indifferent to each other's existence nowadays. I have been told this by Ned Meriwether's own wife. Ned's wife maintains that the night Ned and Emily went to the Dorsets' party marked the beginning of this indifference, that it marked the end of their childhood intimacy and the beginning of a shyness, a reserve, even an animosity between them that was destined to be a sorrow forever to the two sensible parents who had sat in the upstairs sitting room that night waiting until the telephone call came from Tom Bascomb.

Ned's wife is a girl he met while he was in the navy. She was a Wave, and her background isn't the same as his. Apparently she isn't too happy with life in what she refers to as "Mero proper." She and Ned have recently moved out into a suburban development, which she doesn't like either and which she refers to as "greater Mero." She asked me at a party one night how Mero ever got its absurd name, and when I told her that it was named for the last Spanish governor of Louisiana she burst out laughing. I don't know why exactly. But what interests me most about her is that after a few drinks she likes to talk about Ned and Emily and Tom Bascomb and the Dorsets. Tom Bascomb has become a kind of hero—and I don't mean a wartime hero—in her eyes, though of course not having grown up in Mero she has never seen him in her life. But she is a clever girl, and there are times when she will say to me, "Tell me about Mero. Tell me about the Dorsets." And I try to tell her. I tell her to remember that Mero looks upon itself as a rather old city. I tell her to remember that it was one of the first English-speaking settlements west of the Alleghenies and that by the end of the American Revolution, when veterans began pouring westward over the Wilderness Road or down the Ohio River, Mero was often referred to as a thriving village. Then she tells me that I am being dull, because it is hard for her to concentrate on any aspect of the story that doesn't center around Tom Bascomb and that night at the Dorsets'.

But I make her listen. Or at least one time I did. The Dorset family, I insisted on saying, was in Mero even in those earliest times right after the Revolution, but they had come here under somewhat different circumstances from those of the other early settlers. How could that really matter, Ned's wife asked, after a hundred and fifty years? How could distinctions between the first settlers matter after the Irish had come to Mero, after the Germans, after the Italians? Well, in West Vesey Place it could matter. It had to. If the distinction was false, it mattered all the more and it was all the more necessary to make it.

But let me interject here that Mero is located in a state about whose history most Mero citizens—not newcomers like Ned's wife, but old timers—have little interest and less knowledge. Most of us, for instance, are never even quite sure whether during the 1860's our state did secede or didn't secede. As for the city itself, some of us hold that it is geographically Northern and culturally Southern. Others say the reverse is true. We are all apt to want to feel misplaced in Mero, and so we are not content merely to say that it is a border city. How you stand on this important question is apt to depend entirely on whether your family is one of those with a good Southern name or one that had its origin in New England, because those are the two main categories of old society families in Mero.

But truly—I told Ned's wife—the Dorset family was never in either of those categories. The first Dorset had come, with his family and his possessions and even a little capital, direct from a city in the English Midlands to Mero. The Dorsets came not as pioneers but paying their way all the way. They had not bothered to stop for a generation or two to put down roots in Pennsylvania or Virginia or Massachusetts. And this was the distinction which some people wished always to make. Apparently those early Dorsets had cared no more for putting down roots in the soil of the New World than they had cared for whatever they had left behind in the Old. They were an obscure mercantile family who came to invest in a new western city. Within two generations the business—no, the industry!—which they established made them rich beyond any dreams they could have had in the beginning. For half a century they were looked upon, if any family ever was, as our first family.

And then the Dorsets left Mero—practically all of them except the one old bachelor and the one old maid—left it just as they had come, not caring much about what they were leaving or where they were going. They were city people, and they were Americans. They knew that what they had in Mero they could buy more of in other places. For them Mero was an investment that had paid off. They went to live in Santa Barbara and Laguna Beach, in Newport and on Long Island. And the truth which it was so hard for the rest of us to admit was that, despite our family memories of Massachusetts and Virginia, we were all more like the Dorsets—those Dorsets who left Mero—than we were unlike them. Their spirit was just a little closer to being the very essence of Mero than ours was. The obvious difference was that we had to stay on here and pretend that our life had a meaning which it did not. And if it was only by a sort of chance that Miss Louisa and Mr. Alfred played the role of social arbiters among the young people for a number of years, still no one could honestly question their divine right to do so.

"It may have been their right," Ned's wife said at this point, "but just think what might have happened."

"It's not a matter of what might have happened," I said. "It is a matter of what did happen. Otherwise, what have you and I been talking about?"

"Otherwise," she said with an irrepressible shudder, "I would not be forever getting you off in a corner at these parties to talk about my husband and my husband's sister and how it is they care so little for each other's company nowadays."

And I could think of nothing to say to that except that probably we had now pretty well exhausted our subject.

Ruth Suckow

MIDWESTERN PRIMITIVE

This familiar picture of Middle Western family life is a fine
illustration of one aspect of Americana in the farm belt. The
setting is an Iowa farmhouse, one that offers "country-style"
dinners to tourists. Here some urban sophisticates come,
happily, upon a purer example of the true Midwestern primitive
than they could ever have expected to find.

Bert went flying over to get May Douglas to come and look at
her table. It was all ready now, and she had to show it to someone.
There was nobody at home who knew or cared about such things.
Everything that she did there was done against indifference or opposition.

"May! Busy? Want to come and see the table now I've got it fixed?"
"Oh, yes!"

May was delighted. She left her ironing where it was and followed
Bert with eager excitement. She was one of the people in Shell Spring
who stuck up for Bert Statzer. She thought that Bert was a wonder.

"We'll go right through the kitchen. Smells kind of good, don't it?
There! Do you like it?"

"Bert!"

May was fairly speechless. She gazed at the table with fervent, faded
eyes. It seemed to her the most beautiful thing she had even seen. She
didn't see how Bert managed it!—how she ever thought of such things
and how she learned to do them. Bert was just a genius, that was all.

"You really think it looks nice?"

Bert drank in May's admiration thirstily. She knew it didn't amount
to much, that May would admire anything she did; but she had to get
appreciation from somewhere.

"I think it's just too beautiful for words. You little marvel!" She
hugged Bert's thin, tense little form in fond worship. "I just don't see
how you do it!" She sighed.

"Well, I'm glad you think it looks nice." Bert relaxed, with a long
gratified sigh; but stiffened again to say to Maynard, who had tagged
them into the dining room, "Be careful, Maynard! If you move one of
those things—!"

May was looking at everything: the little fringed napkins of pink crepe, the tinted glass goblets that Bert had sent away for, the spray of sweet peas at every place, one pink and then the next one lavender, made of tissue paper—such a pretty idea! She had never seen any napkins like those. Bert went on talking excitedly.

"Well, if it's good enough for these folks, it'll be good enough for anyone. I'll think that I've arrived, May!"

"I don't see how it can help—"

"Oh, but they're real big bugs. I've never had anyone from Des Moines before. It scares me. This looks nice to us, but those people have all seen things—oh, my! Then, you know, they're going to have that famous writer with them. That's what I'm so excited about. If he likes it, then I thought maybe I could use his name. You know that'll help to get me known—if I can get his recommendation. Like those cold cream ads and everything—they're all doing that. Oh, I'm so excited, May! Feel my hands? Aren't they cold?"

"Why, you poor child!" May took Bert's tense, thin little hands and rubbed and fondled them. "You don't need to feel that way. I don't see how anybody could ask for anything nicer. If *this* isn't good enough for them—"

"Oh, I know, but people like that who have been places and seen things—! Well, I don't care, I've done the best I could. Maynard, look *out!*"

Bert's face was still gratified but screwed with worry. She knew how she really wanted things to look. She wanted flowered curtains instead of these old ones, and little painted tables instead of this big old thing. . . . Of course, here was this stuck-in-the-mud little burg always holding her back, and her mother, and Arlie. . . . Well, *she* didn't intend to be stuck in the mud, anyway! She had put up her sign where people could see it. "Hillside Inn." It made people in town laugh. They wanted to know where the "hillside" was. But she'd made a go of it so far, all the same.

She burst out: "The only trouble is mother!" And that was true. She couldn't do a thing with mother. Arlie would stay out—he didn't want folks like that to see him in his old working clothes—but mother thought she had to go in and entertain them, just the way she did with anyone who came to the house. "I was so ashamed when those people from Cedar Rapids were here. The way mother came in! Now, of course, May, I know mother's good as gold and means it the best in the world, but what do folks like that think of her? I can't get her to fix herself up or anything. She doesn't understand. 'Ach, well, if they don't like the way I look, then they can look at something they do like.' That's the way she is. She doesn't *see* things. She doesn't know one person from another—doesn't see why these people are any different from any others." May kept making little distressed murmurs. She did know how Mrs. Hohenschuh was. "Now, May, I went and bought a nice up-to-date dress for her, like people are wearing, when I was in Dubuque last. She'd look awfully nice in it if she'd wear it. But do you think she will? No, sir. Won't so much as put it on. 'Ach, I never wore anything like that. I'll stick to what I been wearing.' You don't know, May—" Bert's voice tightened into bitterness—"nobody does, they all talk about how good-hearted mother is, and everything like that, they don't know how stubborn she is. Honestly, if mother didn't want to move, I don't believe a motor-cycle running into her could budge her one inch! She's just hopeless."

"Oh, well, Bert, it'll come out," May said soothingly.

"I suppose. But she gives these people who come here the wrong idea. I don't want them to think we're all like she is."

"Oh, well, I guess they won't think that about you!"

Bert felt encouraged after May's visit. It was nice to have somebody appreciate what she was trying to do, anyway! She was excited, flying around the kitchen, doing the last few things, watching out for Maynard so that he would keep his little suit clean. Where was mother?—she thought in exasperation. Oh, there!—out in the garden—*digging!* Why didn't she come in and get ready? Bert had no time now to run out after her. Bert snatched a look at the clock. Almost time for them to get here! Oh dear, but she did want everything just right. What was mother thinking of? Did she want to get caught looking like that? She was hopeless. "Maynard, if you don't keep away from that table—!" Bert thought she would go crazy.

Then mother came serenely waddling in.

"Want I should help?"

"Not at this late date!"

That was all Bert was going to say. But she couldn't hold in, even if it was more of a triumph to be simply cold and cutting and bitter; she had to let it all out.

"Here I am working, trying to get everything nice, with everything all fixed, and you don't care, you just go on with your old digging out there in the garden, and don't see or care!"

Mrs. Hohenschuh looked abashed. "Ach, well," she began; then she retorted: "Well, I ain't wanted around here. You wouldn't be satisfied anyway with things the way I'd do them. Ach, all this fuss! What are you making all this fuss about? All this business!"

She finished with an angry mutter, and went waddling off to the door. Bert didn't know whether she was going to change her clothes or not. Well, if she wanted them to catch her looking that way, if she didn't care, didn't know any better . . . Bert was left weak and trembling with anger. She flew about the kitchen, put a few more nuts on each plate of salad, with shaking fingers changed her apron for the bright green smock she was going to wear to do the serving . . . it was what they were wearing; it was like the one she'd seen in the photograph of "Betty Lee's Tearoom" in the cooking magazine. . . .

She went into the dining room. The shining glasses twinkled up at her, the sweet peas were rosy and stiff, the dishes looked so nice, the little napkins were so pretty . . . was everything right? She had got ideas wherever she could, but was she sure? It had to be right! Everything was so lovely. Her anger and fear changed into a shining glory. The whole table dazzled before her eyes. She caught hold of Maynard who was tagging her. "Look, Maynard!" she cried. "Isn't our table pretty?" She snatched a kiss from him in her trembling happiness.

Then she heard a car outside on the road. The people were coming!

A large green car rolled up to the cement block that still stayed in the thick grass beside the road as a relic of horse and buggy days. Bert in her green smock stood waiting, a tense dynamic little person with her thin face and shining black eyes and short black hair threaded with early white. It seemed to her that it took the people a long time to get out of the car. She had time to wonder and to agonize over the place —the old frame house . . . she wished they could have it stuccoed . . . what would these people think? Then the people were out and coming up the walk, and she had just a confused, eager sight of two men and three women. . . .

One man was in advance. A large man with a rosy face and shell-rimmed glasses, smooth blackish-gray hair—he came toward her smiling. That must be the one who had ordered the dinner, the Des Moines man, Mr. Drayton.

"Mrs. Statzer?" Yes, that was who he was. "We heard you gave such good meals here that we thought we'd have to stop and try one of them."

Bert was so pleased and flattered that she scarcely heard his introductions—forgot the names just as soon as he mentioned them. She had been trying from the first to pick out the writer. It was that tall man, then, with the thick gray hair. She hadn't expected him to look like that, somehow. She wanted to show him that she knew who he was, even if most of the people here in town didn't. They hadn't known whom she had meant when she said Harry Whetstone was coming here. She held out her hands, alert and eager.

"Oh, this is the writer, is it? I certainly was honored when I heard we were going to entertain you. I haven't read any of your works yet, but I intend to—I don't get much time for reading. . . ."

"No hurry, no hurry," the writer said with affable nonchalance.

She was looking, too, at the women. She hadn't got the relationships between the women and men figured out yet. One looked older, one wore that smart little green dress and hat, and then there was that one who might be any age—where did *she* come in? They were looking around. "Isn't this lovely!" one of them was saying. What did they mean? Bert's brilliant eyes were watching them. She wondered what they thought of her sign. People in town made such fun of that sign. They were pointing to that terrible old brown tile in which mother had some geraniums planted. "Look, Harry! Isn't that lovely?" They couldn't really think it was *lovely*. Lovely had a different, suspicious meaning as these women used it. Bert's eyes were devouring the details of their clothes. She led them into the house. She was burning with anxiety, sensitiveness, eagerness. She knew how many things were wrong.

"I suppose you people would like to wash a little after your drive. We haven't any bathroom, I'm sorry to say, we want to have one, but this town is so slow, they've never piped the water out this far. . . . But if you don't mind just washing in the old-fashioned washbowls—"

She hated that so. But they were nice about it. She was relieved.

"You know you're out in the country," she said with a nervous laugh, "and you have to take us the way you find us."

She ushered the women into her best bedroom, the guest room off the parlor. This was the one room in the house in which she could take some pride. She didn't mind showing them this room. She had fixed it up with furniture she had enameled herself, and white curtains with green ruffles, and she had put the stencil on the walls—all after the plan of the Model Bedroom she had seen in the household magazine for which she had taken subscriptions last winter.

"Now, if you'll just take off your hats and put them wherever you find a place—" She was eager and flustered. "I'm afraid I'll have to take you gentlemen upstairs."

"Well, now, can't we go out and give our hands a little shower bath under the pump?" Mr. Drayton asked genially.

Bert was horrified. He meant it for a joke, though. She was ashamed to take them up to her old room, full of horrid old dark furniture . . . was afraid, too, as she sped up the steep stairs ahead of them, although she knew it was all right, she had been up at four o'clock cleaning and getting the house ready. She banged the door of her mother's room shut as she went past. "Now I think you'll find everything—" She ran down.

The women were murmuring in the bedroom. She heard a soft laugh. She lingered in the front room, sensitive and alert, but she couldn't hear. The smartness of their clothes actually hurt her, showed her all sorts of unsuspected deficiencies in herself—although it pleased and gratified her too.

But when she went into the dining room and saw the table, she was exultant again. "If you'll excuse me," she called, "I'm afraid I'll have to be in the kitchen." They answered: "Oh, certainly!" She was in a flush of happiness. They were nice! Oh, dear. She had forgotten to ask the author to write in her visitors' book. Well, she would! And yet she was obscurely hurt and smarting. She wasn't sure they weren't laughing.

In the kitchen, she hustled about. Arlie had come in and was washing his hands at the wooden sink. "Well, are they here?" he asked. He didn't exactly like their coming, or to have Bert always fussing around with things like this—he didn't see why she wanted to do it—but then, he was all right, he kept out of the way. Bert was getting the roast chicken out of the oven. Roasted, not fried. She thought that was what these people were used to. "People in the East never think of *frying* chicken." She remembered hearing Mrs. Elliott say that when she came home from the East. Bert wanted these people to be able to say they had eaten as good a meal here in the Hillside Inn as ever they had got in any city restaurant. She had taken recipes out of cooking magazines. She was so excited now that the ordeal was on that she felt herself working in a kind of tense calm. She could manage everything, nothing could upset her. She gave Arlie his dinner in the back kitchen. These people, with this famous author, were even a notch above those wealthy people from Dubuque whom she had served, and who had told Mr. Drayton about the place. If she could make *them* satisfied—!

"You can come in to dinner now."

There was a moment of quiet and formality as she seated them. They didn't exclaim like those Dubuque people. "Well, well, I didn't know we were going to find a first-class hotel here in Shell Spring!" the Dubuque man had cried. But then, these were a different kind of people. She served them, wondering if she oughtn't to have got in Donna Peterson to help her—but then, Donna wouldn't "know," and she wanted things right. She didn't talk as she was serving. She tried to remember what things should go to the right and what to the left. When she went out into the kitchen, she ordered Maynard to keep back. She was going to bring him in after the meal, all dressed up in his new little suit, and just introduce him. "This is my little boy Maynard." She had read somewhere that that was the way people did other places.

Through her preoccupation with the food and the serving—wondering if everything tasted just right—she heard snatches of the conversation. It was low-toned. The people seemed a little tired, maybe from that long drive. "Well, this is familiar." What did they mean by that? Did they like the little napkins or were they laughing at them? But those napkins were exactly the kind that were used in all the tearooms now! They must be right. "Standardization, I tell you. It gets into all corners." That meant nothing to Bert. They certainly must like these salads that May Douglas had said were simply too beautiful to be eaten. Nice salads were things people here in town didn't want to fuss with— "all those do-dads," mother said. The people were all affable and talking among themselves, and yet Bert could sense that the dinner didn't seem to be going just exactly as it should, and she couldn't see why. Her thin cheeks were flushed. In the kitchen, it was as if she were working in a vacuum, not in that shining flush of triumph she knew and craved. How fast everything was going—how soon this great dinner would be over!

Mrs. Hohenschuh had come into the kitchen from the back way. "Mother, you went and put on that old percale dress of yours, and I had that new one all laid out for you ready!" That seemed the crowning catastrophe. Bert suddenly began to tremble with anger. When she came into the kitchen the next time, she whispered furiously. "You aren't going to let those people see you in that! Since you had to go put it on, just to be stubborn, you can stay out of sight." How could she ever get anywhere with all this family to pull up after her? Mother looked like an old farm woman. Bert felt trembly and ready to cry and could scarcely bear to hear the quiet sound of the voices in the dining room.

The coffee cups were all set out on the little old sewing table that she was using for a serving table. She was going to serve her coffee with dessert, the right way. "Ach, let 'em have their coffee!" Mrs. Hohenschuh pleaded. She thought it was terrible to deprive people of coffee all through a meal. She didn't much mind Bert's reproaches, either. "Ach, Bert, she always gets so cross when she's got anything to do, I don't know." The old lady made off into the garden. But Bert knew how mother was. It would be a miracle if she let any people get away without talking to them—and probably telling them the whole family history!

Bert took in the fragrant coffee and the homemade ice cream. They *must* like that. They did, too. They were much more complimentary. The woman in the cute green dress (she didn't seem to be the author's wife, after all; that was the one that didn't look nearly so much like "somebody"—it surprised Bert) said very flatteringly: "What delicious ice cream! Did you make it yourself?" The older woman—that was Mrs. Drayton—smiled up at Bert. They all praised the ice cream. The talk was freer now. The author seemed to be saying the least of any of them, though. That seemed funny to Bert. Mr. Drayton was lots more talkative and full of fun—peppier. She bet he could write awfully good stories, better than the other one, if he just wanted to.

She was almost happy, when she happened to look out of the window and saw mother climbing up from the cellarway outside, lugging something—a bottle! Oh, for . . . Before she got any chance to get out to the kitchen, the old lady came shy but beaming into the room, with a great big bottle of that dandelion wine. Bert was in torment. As if these people cared for anything like that!

But there mother stood and there was nothing to do but introduce her. Bert suffered agony. It was all the worse, somehow, that they were being so polite and nice. "This is my mother." Mother began to beam at that. She loved to entertain people . . . that was all right, of course, but then she had never learned that people didn't do things the way she used to any more.

And mother was starting right in.

"Well, I thought it was mean you folks had to go all that time without your coffee, so I just brought you something else to drink." That awful old dandelion wine—mother was so proud of it! Bert hated it. "If you ain't afraid somebody's going to get after you—ach, it's all so funny these days—maybe you'll take a little drink of this wine. It's dandelion. I made it."

Bert couldn't stand it. She made for the kitchen. She sat down there, clenched her fists, and felt that she would actually fly to pieces.

The voices were louder in the dining room. She heard delighted laughter. Yes, now mother had some folks there, she had an audience, and she was just laying herself out for them—Bert knew how! She burned with humiliation. The whole thing was spoiled. How could anybody in this town try to do things the way they ought to be done?

Her mother came smiling out to the kitchen.

"Where are them little glasses gone?"

"Mother, why did you have to go in there with that stuff?" .

"Ach, what are you fussing about? They like it."

After a while, Bert got up and began feverishly to get the messy plates cleaned off and stacked together. She couldn't eat a thing herself, not even good little crisp bits of chicken that were left. A lump in her throat was choking her. Mother had hold of them now. She heard them leave the dining room, and then the whole party trailed past the kitchen windows. Mother was waddling in the lead. She was going to take the whole bunch out and show them her flower beds.

Maynard was whining. "Are you going to take me in and introduce me, mother?"

Bert looked at him, cold and remote.

"No, I'm not going to introduce *any*-body."

They were all out in the garden. Mrs. Hohenschuh always thought it her duty as a hostess to take her guests out and show them everything she had. Here where she felt that she "had things nice," too—this place in town which she and Mr. Hohenschuh had bought when they moved

in from the country—she could take real enjoyment with visitors . . .
even if Bert did go on about the place and say how behind the times it
was now. But it was a long time since she had got hold of any people as
appreciative as these. Most folks came to see Bert. They only pretended
to like the kind of things she had in her garden. These people were really
enjoying it. Mrs. Hohenschuh expanded.

"Well, I don't know as there's anything you folks'll care much about
looking at—" (she didn't mean that; she said it in a rich, comfortable
tone)—"I only got the same old kind of flowers I've always had, they
ain't any of these new-fangled kinds with fancy names here—"

"Oh, we adore seeing them!" the woman in the green dress cried
enthusiastically.

Mrs. Hohenschuh beamed. "Well, I think they're pretty nice, they
suit me, but there's lots of folks nowadays wants different things, I
guess. Ja. Anyway, that don't worry me. I let 'em talk. I go on doing
things the way I want to."

The people all laughed, and she was gratified.

"Well, here's what I got! I put in all these things myself. Bert, she
don't want to bother. She's got too many irons in the fire all the time."

"This is lovely!"

Mrs. Hohenschuh stood fat and beaming while they looked and wandered about. She thought her garden was pretty nice—ja, you bet she
did! And these folks all seemed to think so too. Why, they was awful
nice folks! Why had Bert got so fussed up over having them here for
dinner? Why, they was real nice and common! That one in the green
dress (she was older than she wanted to let on, too, Mrs. Hohenschuh
shrewdly judged) did the most running around and palavering! But
those other two, that husband and wife, enjoyed things just as much.
The man in the glasses was *real* nice. Well, so was his wife, although
she didn't have so much to say. But those other two, she kind of liked
the best of the bunch. The woman was real sensible, the things she said
and the questions she asked! and the man kind of trailed around after
the others, and looked at things on his own account, the way Mrs.
Hohenschuh liked to have folks do. That showed he wasn't putting it
on, he was really enjoying himself.

Along with her answers and her explanations, Mrs. Hohenschuh
managed to get in a good part of the family history. Bert had a fit when
she told things like that; but Mrs. Hohenschuh never felt right until she'd
. . . well, kind of given folks the facts and the right idea about the
family. They'd hear it all anyway, so she might as well tell it herself.

"Have you had your garden long, Mrs. Hohenschuh?"

"Ja, ever since we moved into town. That's—how long is it a'ready?
—ach, it's twenty years, I guess! Bert, she was only just in high school,
then. That was partly why we come. The boys, they didn't get to finish,

but Pa he said Bert was to get her diploma, he was going to see to it, she was always the smartest, anyway. Ja, how old was Bert then? She was seventeen, I guess. She's thirty-seven now. Ja, she's such a thin little sliver, I don't know, women seems to want to be that way now, but she's thirty-seven! Her and Arlie's been married twelve years a'ready —and then this here little fellow's all they've got! Ach, I don't know!"

As she talked, all in her deep comfortable voice rich with chuckles and drolleries of German inflection, she waddled about among the flower beds, pointing out this kind and that. "These? Moss roses, I call 'em. I guess that ain't the right name, some folks say not, but they grow just the same—ain't that so? Ja, the old lady Douglas over there, when she was living, she had to have the right names for all her plants, but I told her mine grew better'n hers did if I did call 'em wrong! Ach, these names I know 'em by, them are the ones I like to call 'em!" The moss roses in their flat matted bed on the hot earth were gay spots of scarlet and crimson and yellow and cerise and white. They made one of the women think of the colors in old-fashioned patchwork quilts, she said.

"She's got the real old honest-to-God peppermint! I haven't smelled any of that for years. Come here, Mary!"

"Peppermint? Ja! That I always have. That I like too."

The woman in the green dress came running and clutched the other younger woman. "Come here, Jean! I want to show you. The pump! Isn't that just right? And see here—all these little flower pots set out and slips started in them . . . just see, this foliage stuff, this old red and green funny leaf stuff, my grandmother used to have that. And look back there! One of those great big green wire flower stands that I suppose used to stand in the bay window. Didn't you just yearn to take your dolls promenading on that, and they wouldn't let you, because you might spoil the plants? Isn't this per-fect!" Mrs. Hohenschuh had told them, "Ja, sure, you look around anywhere you want to, what's the use of hiding what you got?" Charlie Drayton was enjoying the old lady's naïve revelations, but the other man lounged about poking into the woodshed where the light fell dim and dusty through a little square window high up in the wall, and into a tool shed where pans of seeds were set about in the midst of a clutter of ancient furniture. It was like going back thirty years.

There was a little apple orchard at the side, grown up to tall grass now; and there, on one of his silent excursions, he discovered a two-foot china troll planted down in a tiny hollow with grass grown about his base as it binds in ancient tombstones, and a little casual offering of fallen apples about his chipped feet. He stood looking at it. The woman in the green dress saw him and came running over.

"What have you found, Harry? Oh! Oh, isn't that marvelous? Oh.

Mrs. Hohenschuh, we've found something simply wonderful, won't you tell us what that is?"

Mrs. Hohenschuh wandered over. "That? Ach, is that old thing still out there? Ja, it's funny, but then, I don't know . . . Pa, he was the one that got that thing."

"It's German, isn't it?"

"Ja, it's German, all right. Pa, he come from the old country, he come over here when he was only eighteen years old, he had just twenty dollars when he landed in this country. Ja, it's German, is what it is. Pa, he always wanted to fix up the back yard like the places he'd seen in the old country—that was why he got this funny fellow, that was one reason we moved into town when we did, because Pa wanted to fix up a place . . . ja, and then we hadn't lived here but a year or two when Pa got killed. He got run over, he was thinking of things the way he always done, and didn't hear the train coming . . . ja, that's the way of it!" But after a moment, while they all stood about her soberly, she roused herself and went on. "Bert, she always had a fit over that fellow. She was the one to put him out of the front yard and lugged him out here. But I don't know—" Mrs. Hohenschuh chuckled—"I always kind of liked the little fellow. Maybe because Pa thought so much of him. Well, I guess he's where she ain't likely to find him. She's too busy inside there to fool around out here much. I'm the one does that."

Slowly, Mrs. Hohenschuh in the lead, they trailed away from the orchard. The troll, with his colors faded to dim faint tints and curls chipped off his beard, stood smiling a one-sided but jovial smile at the rotting apples about his broken feet that had almost grown into the orchard ground.

Mrs. Hohenschuh picked some of each kind of flowers for every person. "Hold on, now! You ain't got any of the pansies yet." A circle of sticks set upright—little thin sticks with flaking bark—enclosed the massed, butterfly colors of the pansies. The tiger lilies grew in a straggling bunch tied with twine. "Pick yourself some if you like 'em. Go ahead!" What else were the flowers here for? "Here's a color you ain't got if you like them zinnies, Mrs. . . . well, you'll have to excuse me. I can't remember all you folkses' names." The sun shone down brightly on the garden, bringing out the hot colors of the moss roses, throwing clear antique shadows from the grape arbor, glinting and losing itself in coolness in the thick wet grass around the pump through which silent little streams of water soaked slowly. They all had a drink before they went into the house. The sides of the glass were frosted with wet. The family story was twined with their wanderings among the little paths of the garden, tangled with the bright colors of the flowers, and brightened over with sunshine.

The house seemed cool when they went inside.

"Oh, you don't want to go yet! Come in and set awhile and let's finish our visit."

Mrs. Hohenschuh led them into the parlor.

"There's lots of things you ain't seen yet."

Mrs. Drayton was tired, even Mr. Drayton—although still genial—was ready to stop; but the other three seemed insatiable. Bert had heard her mother's invitation and burned with helpless shame. What else was mother going to show? And it was hopeless to try to head her off now. Bert followed the others into the front room.

"I'll show you Pa's picture, Mr. . . . ach, that name's gone again! Well, I guess you know I mean you, don't you? Sure! That's right."

She got down that old faded purple plush album that held all the family pictures—Bert and the boys when they were youngsters, Mr. Hohenschuh when he first came to this country, wedding pictures of hired men. The two younger women sat eagerly close to her, the writer looked at all the pictures with a gravity that Bert couldn't fathom, Mr. Drayton laughed and made funny remarks about the clothes that pleased mother, and Mrs. Drayton looked at the pictures last with a pleased but tired smile; she wasn't quite in all the things the others were, Bert thought. "Ja, look at that one now! Ain't he funny-looking though? He was a cousin of mine. Ja, now they all look funny." Bert sat and suffered. Maynard sidled in. He couldn't give up the promise of being introduced. They were all nice to him. The author showed him a funny pin he had, carved by the Indians, and the women all smiled at him. But they went on making that fuss over mother.

When she had showed them the photographs, she had to let them see her other things: the shells and the "curios" that she prized so, and that she kept on a shelf in the bookcase. "Look here! Did you ever see anything like this before?" How could they act so pleased, unless they were just false and putting it on to get mother to make a fool of herself? Bert could have cried. That shell! Of course they'd seen shells. They'd been everywhere. Those old feathers from the tail of the peacock they used to have out on the farm, the cocoanut husk, that big long German pipe, the glass paper-weight with the snowfall inside. What else could she find to show them? They were asking about fancy work. Did she ever make the real old knitted lace? Ja, not so much knit' as crochet', though—wait, she'd show them! It would be just like her to ask them to all go up to her room with her and look through those terrible drawers —and if she did that! Bert was ready to kill herself. That room of mother's (and it wasn't any use talking to her about it, Bert couldn't make her do a *thing*) with dresses hanging on nails, and quilts piled up in the corner, drawers filled with junk—a perfect museum!

Well, they weren't paying any attention to her and Maynard anyway, so Bert went back to the dining room. She might as well finish with the table. . . . At least they were staying a long time and seemed to be enjoying themselves. In that way, she supposed the dinner was a success. But she couldn't understand them. It was she to whom they ought to be paying attention—she who appreciated them, and knew how different they were, and wanted to be like them; they couldn't really mean it when they made such a fuss over mother. Why should they? They must be laughing at her. What on earth could they see in all this old junk? It was so perverse and contrary and cruel that she wanted to cry. All the very awfullest things in the house—things *no*body had any more! What kind of an idea of the town would they get? She looked into the parlor, and there was mother getting out all her old fancy work —that terrible piece, that huge table spread, with horses and dogs and cows and roosters crocheted into it . . . and they were saying "lovely"! She heard them.

"That dress. Isn't it perfect? The real thing."

"Oh, she's a jewel!"

"Lovely!"

They were going at last. They were very nice to Bert then. The women sought her out in the dining room. "Such a wonderful dinner you gave us!"

"Well, I'm glad you liked it. I didn't know . . ."

She followed them into the parlor, feeling appeased and excited again, even though she seemed to scent a tactful patronage. But they were all complimenting her now, and she drank in the praise, eagerly, but afraid to believe they meant it.

Mr. Drayton had taken her aside. "And what do we owe you for this fine meal you gave us?" he asked her in a low, genial tone.

"Well . . . a dollar apiece." Bert said firmly. She blushed, but held her ground. She had heard that all the city tearooms charged a dollar and a quarter now. Of course, she couldn't ask quite as much as a city tearoom, that had everything just up to snuff; but her dinner was good and she knew it, and she was going to stick to business. He didn't seem to think that she was charging them too much, however. He counted out some bills and handed them right over to her. But when she came to look at them, there were too many—a five and an extra one!

"Oh, I can't—why, you've given me—"

He tapped her shoulder. "That's all right. Don't notice it. Doesn't begin to pay for the entertainment we've had here."

She still protested, flushed and happy, but he wouldn't listen to her; so she guessed there was nothing else for her to do. . . .

She hadn't forgotten about the visitors' book. She got it out now. All the tearooms in the East had those, Mrs. Elliott had said. She had seen several famous names in one place where she had eaten. It advertised the place; and then it was an honor, too, to think such people had eaten there. Bert was a little bashful but determined.

"I hope you don't mind before you go." She laid the new visitors' book, a notebook with black covers that she had bought at the drugstore, before the author. "I'd like to have you put your name in my book so other folks can see you've been here."

He didn't seem very much flattered about it, she thought, but anyway he wasn't going to refuse. How funny! She would have thought it would please folks to be asked to do things like that. The others teased him a little. "You can't escape 'em, Harry!" They seemed to think it was sort of a joke. Bert stood flushed, waiting and determined. She was satisfied when she saw, at the very beginning of her book, the small firm signature: "Harry Whetstone."

"How little you write!" she cried in amazement. It was funny for a man to write so small as that. "Now I want all the rest of you folks' names."

They protested.

"Yes I do. You're all along with him."

"Well, go on, girls. Sign yourselves," Mr. Drayton commanded.

They all signed. Mrs. Drayton blushed when she did it.

Bert wasn't through with the author yet. Before she let him go, she was going to get all she'd meant to get out of him.

"I wondered if you'd let me use your name, Mr. Whetstone."

He still had that funny, kind of bored way. His wife was really nicer.

"Say he ate with a large appetite, even mightier than usual," Mrs. Whetstone said.

But it seemed to Bert they were all amused.

She wanted to talk to the writer about his books. "You know I never met an author before," she said. "I've always been wanting to, because—" she flushed—"well, I've always wanted to write myself. I always thought I could if I just had the time to do it."

"Oh, don't," he assured her solemnly. But he wasn't as impressed as she had thought he would be. "It's much better to cook biscuits like those we devoured this noon. Infinitely better to make dandelion wine like your mother."

He was joking, of course. But Bert didn't quite like it. She had meant what she said, seriously. It was something she'd thought about all her life. He didn't seem to her a bit like an author.

Mrs. Hohenschuh came into the house, waddling and breathless.

"Dandelion wine!" she cried. "Ja, if you liked that, then you come back here and you'll get some of the wild grape I'm going to make this fall. You come and let *me* get you up a dinner. I'll give you some real genuine fried chicken and you won't have to wait all meal for your coffee."

They all laughed. They seemed to think that was *funny*.

She had been out in the garden again. She had dug up some plants, and wrapped them in newspapers and brought some slips for the women to take along and set out.

"You take these along with you. Oh sure, you go ahead!"

She parceled them out right and left and gave directions. The people went out to the car swamped with packages. They were thanking Mrs. Hohenschuh profusely, and promising to do just what she told them, laughing delightedly at everything she said. She went right up to the car with them, as she always did with people who were leaving. Bert stood back with the bills wadded up in her hot hand, and with Maynard beside her. They had complimented her on the dinner, and said nice things to her, done all that she had asked them: but she stood hungering for just the one thing they hadn't said to her.

"Good-by, Mrs. Hohenschuh. We certainly have enjoyed this."

"You come again. All of you. You just drop in any time you feel like it."

"Good-by, Mrs. Statzer! . . . And Maynard!"

But they had to remember to say that.

Mr. Drayton took the wheel, the big engine started humming, the car rolled ahead. They waved—they were going. . . .

"Well!" Mrs. Hohenschuh said gratified, climbing back onto the walk. "They was real folks! I don't see why you made such a fuss over having them."

"Look at your hands, mother!" Bert said bitterly.

"Ja, I know. I dug up them plants. Well, it don't matter now, they're gone anyway."

She waddled serenely to the house.

Bert stood looking after the car. She didn't know just what she had expected this dinner to mean to her. Anyway, she hadn't thought that everything would be just as it was before, that mother would be the one they got on with (mother, who hadn't really lifted her hand!), that she would just go back into the house with a lot of dirty dishes to wash. She didn't yet see what their idea was.

THE BEDQUILT

Mrs. Fisher once had occasion to give an account of how this
story came to be written. The result was a revealing commentary
on the writer's art of transposing actual events and characters
from fact to fiction. In the first part of his essay on
"Catharsis" Professor Frederick Pottle makes excellent use of
this commentary. It is an essay which will be of unusual
interest to the student, before or after reading "The Bedquilt."

For the express purpose of supplementing both these
selections, Mrs. Fisher wrote an additional note to the editor
giving some of the details of the personal experience that
formed the background of her story. She very generously
suggested that we include as much of her note as we might find
useful for the purposes of this book. It is a great privilege
to include the note in its entirety just as it was written.

Of all the Elwell family Aunt Mehetabel was certainly the most
unimportant member. It was in the New England days, when an un-
married woman was an old maid at twenty, at forty was everyone's
servant, and at sixty had gone through so much discipline that she could
need no more in the next world. Aunt Mehetabel was sixty-eight.

She had never for a moment known the pleasure of being important
to anyone. Not that she was useless in her brother's family; she was expected, as a matter of course, to take upon herself the most tedious and
uninteresting part of the household labors. On Mondays she accepted
as her share the washing of the men's shirts, heavy with sweat and stiff
with dirt from the fields and from their own hard-working bodies. Tues-
days she never dreamed of being allowed to iron anything pretty or
even interesting, like the baby's white dresses or the fancy aprons of her
young lady nieces. She stood all day pressing out a tiresome monotonous
succession of dish-cloths and towels and sheets.

In preserving-time she was allowed to have none of the pleasant
responsibility of deciding when the fruit had cooked long enough, nor
did she share in the little excitement of pouring the sweet-smelling stuff
into the stone jars. She sat in a corner with the children and stoned
cherries incessantly, or hulled strawberries until her fingers were dyed
red to the bone.

The Elwells were not consciously unkind to their aunt, they were even in a vague way fond of her; but she was so utterly insignificant a figure in their lives that they bestowed no thought whatever on her. Aunt Mehetabel did not resent this treatment; she took it quite as unconsciously as they gave it. It was to be expected when one was an old-maid dependent in a busy family. She gathered what crumbs of comfort she could from their occasional careless kindnesses and tried to hide the hurt which even yet pierced her at her brother's rough joking. In the winter when they all sat before the big hearth, roasted apples, drank mulled cider, and teased the girls about their beaux and the boys about their sweethearts, she shrank into a dusky corner with her knitting, happy if the evening passed without her brother saying, with a crude sarcasm, "Ask your Aunt Mehetabel about the beaux that used to come a-sparkin' her!" or, "Mehetabel, how was't when you was in love with Abel Cummings." As a matter of fact, she had been the same at twenty as at sixty, a quiet, mouse-like little creature, too timid and shy for anyone to notice, or to raise her eyes for a moment and wish for a life of her own.

Her sister-in-law, a big hearty housewife, who ruled indoors with as autocratic a sway as did her husband on the farm, was rather kind in an absent, offhand way to the shrunken little old woman, and it was through her that Mehetabel was able to enjoy the one pleasure of her life. Even as a girl she had been clever with her needle in the way of patching bedquilts. More than that she could never learn to do. The garments which she made for herself were the most lamentable affairs, and she was humbly grateful for any help in the bewildering business of putting them together. But in patchwork she enjoyed a tepid importance. She could really do that as well as anyone else. During years of devotion to this one art she had accumulated a considerable store of quilting patterns. Sometimes the neighbors would send over and ask "Miss Mehetabel" for such and such a design. It was with an agreeable flutter at being able to help someone that she went to the dresser, in her bare little room under the eaves, and extracted from her crowded portfolio the pattern desired.

She never knew how her great idea came to her. Sometimes she thought she must have dreamed it, sometimes she even wondered reverently, in the phraseology of the weekly prayer-meeting, if it had not been "sent" to her. She never admitted to herself that she could have thought of it without other help; it was too great, too ambitious, too lofty a project for her humble mind to have conceived. Even when she finished drawing the design with her own fingers, she gazed at it incredulously, not daring to believe that it could indeed be her handiwork. At first it seemed to her only like a lovely but quite unreal dream. She did not think of putting it into execution—so elaborate, so complicated, so beautifully difficult a pattern could be only for the angels in heaven to quilt. But so curiously does familiarity accustom us even to very wonderful things, that as she lived with this astonishing creation of her mind, the longing grew stronger and stronger to give it material life with her nimble old fingers.

She gasped at her daring when this idea first swept over her and put it away as one does a sinfully selfish notion, but she kept coming back to it again and again. Finally she said compromisingly to herself that she would make one "square," just one part of her design, to see how it would look. Accustomed to the most complete dependence on her brother and his wife, she dared not do even this without asking Sophia's permission. With a heart full of hope and fear thumping furiously against her old ribs, she approached the mistress of the house on churning-day, knowing with the innocent guile of a child that the country woman was apt to be in a good temper while working over the fragrant butter in the cool cellar.

Sophia listened absently to her sister-in-law's halting, hesitating petition. "Why, yes, Mehetabel," she said, leaning far down into the huge churn for the last golden morsels—"why, yes, start another quilt if you want to. I've got a lot of pieces from the spring sewing that will work in real good." Mehetabel tried honestly to make her see that this would be no common quilt, but her limited vocabulary and her emotion stood between her and expression. At last Sophia said, with a kindly impatience: "Oh, there! Don't bother me. I never could keep track of your quiltin' patterns, anyhow. I don't care what pattern you go by."

With this overwhelmingly, although unconsciously, generous permission, Mehetabel rushed back up the steep attic stairs to her room, and in a joyful agitation began preparations for the work of her life. It was even better than she hoped. By some heaven-sent inspiration she had invented a pattern beyond which no patchwork quilt could go.

She had but little time from her incessant round of household drudgery for this new and absorbing occupation, and she did not dare sit up late at night lest she burn too much candle. It was weeks before the little square began to take on a finished look, to show the pattern. Then Mehetabel was in a fever of impatience to bring it to completion. She was too conscientious to shirk even the smallest part of her share of the work of the house, but she rushed through it with a speed which left her panting as she climbed to the little room. This seemed like a radiant spot to her as she bent over the innumerable scraps of cloth which already in her imagination ranged themselves in the infinitely diverse pattern of her masterpiece. Finally she could wait no longer, and one evening ventured to bring her work down beside the fire where the family sat, hoping that some good fortune would give her a place near the tallow candles on the mantelpiece. She was on the last corner of the square, and her needle flew in and out with inconceivable rapidity. No one noticed her, a fact which filled her with relief, and by bedtime she had but a few more stitches to add.

As she stood up with the others, the square fluttered out of her trembling old hands and fell on the table. Sophia glanced at it carelessly. "Is that the new quilt you're beginning on?" she asked with a yawn. "It looks like a real pretty pattern. Let's see it." Up to that moment Mehetabel had labored in the purest spirit of disinterested devotion to an ideal, but as Sophia held her work toward the candle to examine it, and exclaimed in amazement and admiration, she felt an astonished joy to know that her creation would stand the test of publicity.

"Land sakes!" ejaculated her sister-in-law, looking at the many-colored square. "Why, Mehetabel Elwell, where'd you git that pattern?"

"I made it up," said Mehetabel quietly, but with unutterable pride.

"No!" exclaimed Sophia incredulously. "*Did* you! Why, I never see such a pattern in my life. Girls, come here and see what your Aunt Mehetabel is doing."

The three tall daughters turned back reluctantly from the stairs. "I don't seem to take much interest in patchwork," said one listlessly.

"No, nor I neither!" answered Sophia; "but a stone image would take an interest in this pattern. Honest, Mehetabel, did you think of it yourself? And how under the sun and stars did you ever git your courage up to start in a-making it? Land! Look at all those tiny squinchy little seams! Why the wrong side ain't a thing *but* seams!"

The girls echoed their mother's exclamations, and Mr. Elwell himself came over to see what they were discussing. "Well, I declare!" he said, looking at his sister with eyes more approving than she could ever remember. "That beats old Mis' Wightman's quilt that got the blue ribbons so many times at the county fair."

Mehetabel's heart swelled within her, and tears of joy moistened her old eyes as she lay that night in her narrow, hard bed, too proud and excited to sleep. The next day her sister-in-law amazed her by taking the huge pan of potatoes out of her lap and setting one of the younger children to peeling them. "Don't you want to go on with that quiltin' pattern?" she said; "I'd kind o' like to see how you're goin' to make the grape-vine design come out on the corner."

By the end of the summer the family interest had risen so high that Mehetabel was given a little stand in the sitting room where she could keep her pieces, and work in odd minutes. She almost wept over such kindness, and resolved firmly not to take advantage of it by neglecting her work, which she performed with a fierce thoroughness. But the whole atmosphere of her world was changed. Things had a meaning now. Through the longest task of washing milk pans there rose the rainbow of promise of her variegated work. She took her place by the little table and put the thimble on her knotted, hard finger with the solemnity of a priestess performing a sacred rite.

She was even able to bear with some degree of dignity the extreme honor of having the minister and the minister's wife comment admiringly on her great project. The family felt quite proud of Aunt Mehetabel as Minister Bowman had said it was work as fine as any he had ever seen, "and he didn't know but finer!" The remark was repeated verbatim to the neighbors in the following weeks when they dropped in and examined in a perverse silence some astonishingly difficult *tour de force* which Mehetabel had just finished.

The family especially plumed themselves on the slow progress of the quilt. "Mehetabel has been to work on that corner for six weeks, come Tuesday, and she ain't half done yet," they explained to visitors. They fell out of the way of always expecting her to be the one to run on errands, even for the children. "Don't bother your Aunt Mehetabel," Sophia would call. "Can't you see she's got to a ticklish place on the quilt?"

The old woman sat up straighter and looked the world in the face. She was a part of it at last. She joined in the conversation and her remarks were listened to. The children were even told to mind her when she asked them to do some service for her, although this she did but seldom, the habit of self-effacement being too strong.

One day some strangers from the next town drove up and asked if they could inspect the wonderful quilt which they had heard of, even down in their end of the valley. After that such visitations were not uncommon, making the Elwells' house a notable object. Mehetabel's quilt came to be one of the town sights, and no one was allowed to leave the town without having paid tribute to its worth. The Elwells saw to it that their aunt was better dressed than she had ever been before, and one of the girls made her a pretty little cap to wear on her thin white hair.

A year went by and a quarter of the quilt was finished; a second year passed and half was done. The third year Mehetabel had pneumonia and lay ill for weeks and weeks, overcome with terror lest she die before her work was completed. A fourth year and one could really see the grandeur of the whole design; and in September of the fifth year, the entire family watching her with eager and admiring eyes, Mehetabel quilted the last stitches in her creation. The girls held it up by the four corners, and they all looked at it in a solemn silence. Then Mr. Elwell smote one horny hand within the other and exclaimed: "By ginger! That's goin' to the county fair!" Mehetabel blushed a deep red at this. It was a thought which had occurred to her in a bold moment, but she had not dared to entertain it. The family acclaimed the idea, and one of the boys was forthwith dispatched to the house of the neighbor who was chairman of the committee for their village. He returned with radiant face. "Of course he'll take it. Like's not it may git a prize, so he says; but he's got to have it right off, because all the things are goin' to-morrow morning."

Even in her swelling pride Mehetabel felt a pang of separation as the bulky package was carried out of the house. As the days went on she felt absolutely lost without her work. For years it had been her one preoccupation, and she could not bear even to look at the little stand, now quite bare of the litter of scraps which had lain on it so long. One of the neighbors, who took the long journey to the fair, reported that the quilt was hung in a place of honor in a glass case in "Agricultural Hall." But that meant little to Mehetabel's utter ignorance of all that lay outside of her brother's home. The family noticed the old woman's depression, and one day Sophia said kindly, "You feel sort o' lost without the quilt, don't you, Mehetabel?"

"They took it away so quick!" she said wistfully; "I hadn't hardly had one real good look at it myself."

Mr. Elwell made no comment, but a day or two later he asked his sister how early she could get up in the morning.

"I dun'no'. Why?" she asked.

"Well, Thomas Ralston has got to drive clear to West Oldton to see a lawyer there, and that is four miles beyond the fair. He says if you can git up so's to leave here at four in the morning he'll drive you over to the fair, leave you there for the day, and bring you back again at night."

Mehetabel looked at him with incredulity. It was as though someone had offered her a ride in a golden chariot up to the gates of heaven. "Why, you can't *mean* it!" she cried, paling with the intensity of her emotion. Her brother laughed a little uneasily. Even to his careless indifference this joy was a revelation of the narrowness of her life in his home. "Oh, 'tain't so much to go to the fair. Yes, I mean it. Go git your things ready, for he wants to start to-morrow morning."

All that night a trembling, excited old woman lay and stared at the rafters. She, who had never been more than six miles from home in her life, was going to drive thirty miles away—it was like going to another world. She who had never seen anything more exciting than a church supper was to see the county fair. To Mehetabel it was like making the tour of the world. She had never dreamed of doing it. She could not at all imagine what it would be like.

Nor did the exhortations of the family, as they bade good-by to her, throw any light on her confusion. They had all been at least once to the scene of gayety she was to visit, and as she tried to eat her breakfast they called out conflicting advice to her till her head whirled. Sophia told her to be sure and see the display of preserves. Her brother said not to miss inspecting the stock, her nieces said the fancywork was the only thing worth looking at, and her nephews said she must bring them home an account of the races. The buggy drove up to the door, she was helped in, and her wraps tucked about her. They all stood together and waved good-by to her as she drove out of the yard. She waved back, but she scarcely saw them. On her return home that evening she was very pale, and so tired and stiff that her brother had to lift her out bodily, but her lips were set in a blissful smile. They crowded around her with thronging questions, until Sophia pushed them all aside, telling them Aunt Mehetabel was too tired to speak until she had had her supper. This was eaten in an enforced silence on the part of the children, and then the old woman was helped into an easy-chair before the fire. They gathered about her, eager for news of the great world, and Sophia said, "Now, come, Mehetabel, tell us all about it!"

Mehetabel drew a long breath. "It was just perfect!" she said; "finer even than I thought. They've got it hanging up in the very middle of a sort o' closet made of glass, and one of the lower corners is ripped and turned back so's to show the seams on the wrong side."

"What?" asked Sophia, a little blankly.

"Why, the quilt!" said Mehetabel in surprise. "There are a whole lot of other ones in that room, but not one that can hold a candle to it, if I do say it who shouldn't. I heard lots of people say the same thing. You ought to have heard what the women said about that corner, Sophia. They said—well, I'd be ashamed to *tell* you what they said. I declare if I wouldn't!"

Mr. Elwell asked, "What did you think of that big ox we've heard so much about?"

"I didn't look at the stock," returned his sister indifferently. "That set of pieces you gave me, Maria, from your red waist, come out just lovely!" she assured one of her nieces. "I heard one woman say you could 'most smell the red silk roses."

"Did any of the horses in our town race?" asked young Thomas.

"I didn't see the races."

"How about the preserves?" asked Sophia.

"I didn't see the preserves," said Mehetabel calmly. "You see, I went right to the room where the quilt was, and then I didn't want to leave it. It had been so long since I'd seen it. I had to look at it first real good myself, and then I looked at the others to see if there was any that could come up to it. And then the people begun comin' in and I got so interested in hearin' what they had to say I couldn't think of goin' any-wheres else. I ate my lunch right there too, and I'm as glad as can be I did, too; for what do you think?"—she gazed about her with kindling eyes—"while I stood there with a sandwich in one hand didn't the head of the hull concern come in and open the glass door and pin 'First Prize' right in the middle of the quilt!"

There was a stir of congratulation and proud exclamation. Then Sophia returned again to the attack. "Didn't you go to see anything else?" she queried.

"Why, no," said Mehetabel. "Only the quilt. Why should I?"

She fell into a reverie where she saw again the glorious creation of her hand and brain hanging before all the world with the mark of highest approval on it. She longed to make her listeners see the splendid vision with her. She struggled for words; she reached blindly after unknown superlatives. "I tell you it looked like—" she said, and paused, hesitating. Vague recollections of hymn-book phraseology came into her mind, the only form of literary expression she knew; but they were dismissed as being sacrilegious, and also not sufficiently forcible. Finally, "I tell you it looked real *well!*" she assured them, and sat staring into the fire, on her tired old face the supreme content of an artist who has realized his ideal.

An essay, related to Mrs. Fisher's story,
by Frederick A. Pottle

CATHARSIS

The really interesting part of this essay—a report of an unpublished lecture which I heard a good many years ago—belongs to Dorothy Canfield Fisher. Mrs. Fisher's lecture was a model of what artists ought more often to try to do. Instead of reading a paper dealing with abstract theories of art, she told us fully, frankly, and humbly just where and how she got the raw material for writing one of her own stories, and recounted the processes by which it was transformed in her mind into the stuff of fiction.

I had arrived at the lecture with a problem in the back of my mind. It was this: Why do some stories and plays of distressingly painful incident produce in us not pain and uneasiness but a feeling of exhilaration and relief?

I shall be told that Aristotle settled all that. I wish he had. What we can get from his surviving writings (beyond a statement of the observed fact) is no more than an analysis of the structure of the kind of fiction which he, and others since him, have found to provide this sense of relief and exhilaration most effectively. It is a masterly analysis, the type of all formal criticism, but it does not attempt to explain *why* this kind of fiction works as it does.

Tragedy, he says, "through pity and fear effects the purgation [catharsis] of these emotions." That can only be a metaphor, and there seems now to be general agreement that it is just the simple and direct kind of metaphor that we should infer from our own medical term "cathartic." We must, of course, understand the metaphor in terms of his medicine, not ours; must remember that in the Hippocratic system, where health was thought to consist of a proper blending and balance of the body liquids or humors, catharsis was a term of much wider application than it is today. It covered the expulsion of unwanted elements from any of the natural outlets of the body, and it meant (or at least could mean) not so much the getting rid of intrinsically bad substances as the restoring of the healthy balance of the humors by expelling superfluous quantities. The substances expelled were bad only because they were present in excessive amounts; they were regulated by catharsis but not entirely removed. And finally, there was in Hippocratic medicine, if only in an empirical sort of way, the notion of homeopathy: that you can alleviate morbid symptoms by a treatment which would produce similar symptoms in a healthy body.

Yet "catharsis," in spite of all annotations, seems a rather quaint metaphor for the operation of literary works, one that might perhaps occur to a naturalist who was the son of a physician, but hardly to anyone else. It is at best an unpleasant metaphor and emphasizes the practical function of art in a way repugnant to much modern critical theory. But it has stood up better than any other definition in the whole history of criticism; and it has undoubtedly been able to do so because, by its insistence on particular function, it has succeeded in limiting the area of discussion to the observed facts.

The weakness of all the substitute theories is that they include too much, that they have no real grounds for distinguishing the special relief provided by tragedy from the pleasure we feel in art generally, especially from the pleasure we feel in that kind of art which distresses without relieving us. Aristotle enables us to differentiate the "Oedipus Rex" from "Tess of the D'Urbervilles." He does not maintain that all kinds of fictions dealing with painful incident produce the catharsis; quite the contrary. And he accepts the task of writing the prescription for the kind that does. A good tragedy as he defines it is one based on concepts of cosmic order and moral responsibility. The cosmic order is stern but it is accepted as just; and the moral responsibility covers blindness of heart as well as deliberate wickedness, but it is felt to be real. Tragedy, to return to his famous metaphor, is not merely homeopathic medicine, it is a *specific* medicine.

Aristotle, then, analyzes carefully what (to extend his own figure) might be called the chemical composition of tragedy. But he does not go on to analyze the mechanical or chemical effect of the medicine upon the body of the patient. In one of his other works he promised to explain catharsis, and the "Poetics" as we have it is evidently incomplete; the original treatise (or lecture) probably contained a corresponding analysis of the human mind showing why tragedy affects us as it does.

Since we are (I think) wholly without aid from Aristotle, we are thrown back on our own experience and its psychological analysis. I suspect that we have tended too much to look for the secret in either the finished work of art or in our own experience of the finished work of art. Those two approaches would seem, indeed, to be the obvious ones. But the finished work of art by its very nature cannot tell us how it operates: it has been rigorously contrived to perform a function, not to explain it. Every work of art must operate somehow upon the conscious and unconscious memories of our own, the receivers', experiences; must elicit recollections and use these fragments of ourselves to build up its structure in our minds. If we were conscious of the sources and intrinsic nature of this material as it comes streaming and pushing up to clothe the bare symbols (which are all the artist in the nature of things can transmit), we might be able to tell why the work of art affects us as it does. Actually we can account for very little of it, either during or after the experience, and no amount of unaided introspection will help us to do so.

But the artist is sometimes vividly aware of a body of personal material that imperiously demands artistic handling; is aware at the same time that as mere autobiography or private fantasy it is not "right" or "what he wants to say"; is aware of a moment when he "gets it right" and the work of art emerges. Here, with luck, we may have an opportunity to compare the "before" with the "after," to see in what direction the personal matter was changed and at least to make a guess as to why it was changed.

I found, as I believe, an understanding of the working of catharsis outside of tragedy, in the fine piece of literary self-analysis provided by Mrs. Fisher. I concluded, and am asking you to assume, that a purging which operated in the mind of an artist as she transmuted the stuff of personal pity and fear into a fiction is the same sort of thing as the purging which operates in the mind of a reader when someone, by a fiction, rouses up his personal pity and fear and then allays it.

The demonstration would unquestionably be more persuasive if the matter of personal anguish that I have to recount were of a kind to furnish material for a "good" Aristotelian tragedy, and if the story into which it was transformed were more starkly tragic in tone. But Aristotle did not confine the catharsis to his ideal type of tragedy: a *kind* of catharsis, he tells us, is effected by music, and also (he seems to say) by epic poetry. His method being comparative, he might well have granted that evidence gained from a knowledge of the genesis of one of the lower forms would illuminate the operation of the higher. I should be glad to think so, but if the Master announced that I was outside the limits of orthodoxy in deserting the sharp division into genres, I should declare myself a heretic and proceed.

First, Mrs. Fisher read the story to us. It was "The Bedquilt," one of the short narratives in the book called "Hillsboro People." She had chosen it, she said, not because it was her best, but because she was sure of telling the truth if she talked about that one. At the time she was putting it on paper, she knew that she had to give a talk on the writing of short stories to a college class, and had taken pains to jot down some notes while everything was fresh in her mind.

"The Bedquilt" is about a maiden aunt in a New England family, an elderly, drab, rather stupid maiden aunt who did most of the hard and dirty work about the house and was hardly noticed by anyone. Her relatives did not in the least mean to be unkind to her; it just never occurred to them that there was any reason why they should pay any attention to Aunt Mehetabel. There was only one thing in the world which she did in such a way as to make people look twice at her. She made good patchwork quilts. One day, all by herself, she invented a new pattern so incredibly intricate and difficult that nobody could help noticing it. Her relatives were struck by it, and Aunt Mehetabel became an object of interest and solicitude. The pattern took so much time to piece that it was years before she could finish the squares. Her relatives made her work easier, urged her to sit and sew most of the time, tended her carefully when she was ill. She became the most talked-of member of the family.

Finally the quilt was done and was at once sent off to the county fair as an exhibit. Aunt Mehetabel was miserable. It had not been out of her thoughts or her sight for years: it was her whole life. The family suggested that as a supreme treat she drive over to the fair with a neighbor. It was the longest journey she had ever made. She went and returned in a trance of happiness. They asked her if she had seen the cattle, and the races, and the preserves. No, none of them. Arrived at the fair, she had gone directly to the place in the hall where her quilt hung, had hunted up a chair, and had sat all day looking at it.

The plot of the story, Mrs. Fisher said, grew out of three entirely unconnected incidents. That which suggested Aunt Mehetabel's spending the whole day in rapt contemplation of her own quilt, I shall not go into here, because it is of no importance for my special purpose. I am concerned with the character of Aunt Mehetabel herself and the part of the plot based on her making the wonderful quilt.

Aunt Mehetabel had her origin, Mrs. Fisher told us, in an elderly relative of her own, whom she would refer to as "Cousin Margaret." Cousin Margaret was an old woman, but her mind had never developed. She was really only a child, and had to be looked after. Her relatives took care of her by turns. She was a burden, of course, but it was the family duty to see that she was made comfortable. Plans were always made to provide for the comings and goings of Cousin Margaret, but sometimes she arrived at what seemed to be the most inopportune moments.

On one occasion, when Mrs. Fisher was still a little girl, her parents unexpectedly received word that Cousin Margaret was on her way to visit them. Something unforeseen had happened—a sudden illness, perhaps, in the family where she had been staying—and she was coming on ahead of time. The Canfields were that day giving a dinner party, in the very middle of which Cousin Margaret's train was due to arrive. Mrs. Canfield did the best that a harassed woman could do under the circumstances. She arranged for a cab to meet Cousin Margaret at the station, and got Dorothy to meet her at the door and conduct her up the back stairs to her room.

The cab drew up. Dorothy, a brisk, competent little girl, skipped down the walk to meet Cousin Margaret. Cousin Margaret was not beautiful. She was old, and she couldn't dress herself properly, and her face was tired and streaked with dirt. She had expected a relative to meet her at the station, and was still somewhat confused and upset. "Hello, Cousin Margaret," said Dorothy. "Mother and Father are busy, but they asked me to meet you and take you up to your room." Cousin Margaret sat still and looked at her. At the time the look made no particular impression on the child at all.

Years afterward, Mrs. Fisher was in Norway, spending the summer with a Norwegian family. In this family there were two daughters. The younger was pretty, was married, and had a fine baby; the older was lame and ugly and would never be married. Like Aunt Mehetabel in the story, she did most of the hard work about the house, wore plain clothes while her sister wore pretty ones, and was never noticed by anybody.

One day Mrs. Fisher went out to pick currants in the garden. It was, she said, a day when she was more keenly aware of things than usual, the kind of day that all people have, whether they are artists or not, when they see that a sunset is beautiful, or become indignant over a newspaper account of some injustice that would ordinarily leave them indifferent, or are frantically irritated by the squeaking of a door or someone rocking in a chair—small sounds that they would usually not observe.

Kneeling there between the rows of currant bushes, she could watch unobserved the older sister, who besides doing the housework that morning had also been taking care of her sister's baby. She had soothed him when he was fretful, had bathed and fed him, and now, having dressed him in a clean dress, had sat down with him a moment on the grass. Almost at once the younger sister, cool and pretty and unfatigued by housework or caring for her child, came, caught up the baby, and bore him off to be admired. Over the older sister's face came a look of profound sadness. She did not cry out, nor did she shed tears; it was a feeling so common with her that she did not think of rebelling against it. It was the dumb, patient, but deeply hurt look of a human creature who knew that she was merely taken for granted.

In a flash there came back to Mrs. Fisher that look on Cousin Margaret's face years before. The recollection cut her like a knife, so that she began to cry with the sharpness of the pain. How could they have been so cruel? How could one go on living when the world was so unkind to people? What could she do to make up for the way they had treated Cousin Margaret? Cousin Margaret was long since in her grave. Yet Mrs. Fisher's mind beat about in a frenzy, trying one thing after another. What could they have done? It makes people happy to be admired. Perhaps they could have paid more attention to some activity of Cousin Margaret's. Had she been in the habit of doing something they might have praised? She had not been at all clever, but Mrs. Fisher could remember that she used to crochet. Her mind played with that, and a remarkable thing happened. Gradually, without noticing the transition, she moved away from the historically limited matter of Cousin Margaret and began to compose a fiction. Not elaborated yet, but clear enough, the plot of "The Bedquilt" came into her mind. "And from that moment," said Mrs. Fisher, "I stopped crying, because the thought of Cousin Margaret stopped hurting me." This, I take it, was what Aristotle called "purging," and for the present I shall continue that terminology.

The mental experience which began in pain and ended in its purging was complicated and was certainly not all conscious. It did not have to terminate as it did; in fact, in most cases it would not terminate in that way at all. Let us say that the first reaction would have been about the same in all sensitive persons whether articulate or not. Cousin Margaret was not torpid and apathetic, she had exquisitely sensitive nerves just like me; she suffered; I made her suffer. Such a realization is not a new discovery in the sense that a scientific discovery is new: sensitive people have been having such intuitions from the beginning of time. It would be new and unique as a personal realization, would now be felt for the first time in a state of heightened consciousness, of quality. But so far there would be nothing literary in the experience.

There would be no necessary issue from this painful intuition. But many nonpoetic persons would have felt the necessity of assimilating the experience into their intellectual and moral natures. What did it mean? Must I conclude that the world is inevitably and eternally a place of meaningless suffering? Were Cousin Margaret's sufferings anybody's fault? If history could be repeated, could I behave in such a way as to make the result significantly different? Could I, with my new vision of awareness, behave in the future so as to eliminate some of the suffering? Is there in the structure of things anything that really allows us to find meaning in life?

The answer obviously could have been either hopeful or pessimistic. It would be possible to conclude that the pain of the world is due to a malign or unconcerned deity who simply orders things that way. It would be possible to conclude that the universe is ruled by chance; that pain and good will have no ultimate meaning. Or it would be possible to arrive at a hopeful and dynamic ordering of the experience. The "order" discerned or postulated might be of any degree of theological or moral complexity, might be harsh or tender, melancholy or ecstatic, but it would have at least to envisage the possibility of right and wrong action, would have somehow to connect the fact of suffering with beneficent order. This stage, again, would have nothing literary about it. It could end in speculation, or it could issue in conduct. If a satisfactory speculative reconciliation or a satisfactory practical adjustment could be made, the pain would be resolved. But such purging is not the literary catharsis.

I suspect that when the person concerned is, like Mrs. Fisher, an artist, the mind does not proceed so far in abstraction and does not depend so much for its relief on practical adjustment. Specifically literary activity occurs when the mind moves more or less directly from the concrete, historical matter of suffering, not into a speculative position, and not necessarily into a course of action, but into a myth or fable in which the normal implications of the matter are felt to be adequately symbolized. The symbol may be either pessimistic or hopeful.

But catharsis results when, in the myth or symbol, suffering is no longer casual or the result of malign Providence but is related to a hopeful moral order. It is, of all ways of ridding us of mental pain, the most powerful and practically satisfactory. Vows of reform can never be quite confident, for we have too clear a recollection of our past lapses. Abstract speculative conclusions are difficult and painful to draw, and all moral and theological systems, no matter how much we believe in them, present an honest mind with perplexities when it tries to apply them to a particular situation. The purgative literary work carries us directly to the hopeful conclusions without argument or striving. It does not tell us about a world of positive moral order; it catches us up into one.

And that, I think, is about all that can be presented as a generally acceptable explanation of the famous doctrine of catharsis: it is the removal of the pain in our human experience by means of a fiction in which pain is fitted into a plot that gives it meaning. It is not, after all, the thought of pain and suffering that makes life at times seem unbearable; it is the overwhelming suspicion that all the pain in the world is without motive, meaning, or direction. We are afraid that at any moment all our assurances may be stripped off and we shall be forced to admit that the universe is meaningless. William James somewhere has a fine remark to the effect that Job did not complain because God had allowed him to be afflicted, but because he was unable to see God's purpose. If he could only be assured that God had a purpose, he would be content to suffer.

Religious creeds satisfy man's passion for order and meaning by asserting, with varying degrees of supernatural sanction, that there are moral absolutes; even that man's life here, so fragmentary, so full of promise and yet so futile, is only a moment in a life that stretches beyond time. One of them indeed asserts that the Maker of the universe Himself, in order to assure us that the ways of God are merciful as well as just, became a man and shared the pain of the world with us. If one held that faith constantly as a vital intuition, one could hardly be overwhelmed. But no one does; probably no one can. The firmest of believers spends much of his life in doubt; the particular occasion generally finds us unprepared. Our creed needs constantly to be embodied if it is to console us. The life of this world is all the life we know. We want assurance that it is worthwhile in itself, not a mere probation for felicity in the other world. We should like to see our secular life completed and made beautiful.

The arts are capable of doing it, and they do it not by abstract statement but simply by presenting the desired thing in a myth. The values of the myth may be traditional or the sheer personal choices of the artist; they may be explicitly religious or robustly secular. Or in both cases anything in between. Man cannot, by taking thought, add one cubit to his own stature, but he can imagine the kind of body he would like to have, and carve it in marble. Life itself may be harsh and discordant, but if man listens a little, he can discern unfinished harmonies, which, in the art of music, he can carry through to completion.

And so with poetry. Poetry is not bound to reproduce life in its ordinary aspect of casualness, though it may do so; if it chooses, it can interpret and complete it. When poetry deals with life in this way, it does not ignore unpleasant things, but puts meaning into them; and when unpleasant things have been given meaning, they generally cease to be unpleasant. Tragedy of the grand sort does not blink the facts of defeat and death, but it allies them with purpose.

The greatest evil of man is I repeat, the haunting fear that he will be forced to admit that the universe is meaningless. The pity and terror with which tragedy deals are both reflections of this fear. Tragedy must use the material of pity and terror unsparingly, for only so can it embody our central problem; but by imposing form on pity and terror, by giving them direction, it makes us feel, at least temporarily, that there is purpose in our own afflictions and distractions. By regarding patterned pity and terror we are purged for the time being of our everyday or random pity and terror. Art of the grand kind does not present life as it is perceived, but as it ought to be—Aristotle's own remark.

I do not wish to give the impression that I am supplying the lost book of Aristotle's "Poetics." Since his metaphor of catharsis is certainly one that I should never have thought of, his explanation of its operation might be equally surprising. I am not completing Aristotle but stating a view of my own which I hope some other people will find useful. I have continued Aristotle's terminology because it is inevitable. The relief obtained from tragedy is always going to be called catharsis even though everybody should abandon the metaphor implied in the term. (Language is full of technical terms that are emptied metaphors.) I rather suspect that my theory is basically different from Aristotle's: that in my view the relief that comes from tragedy is really not due to an elimination of mental factors that cause uneasiness because they are present in excessive amounts, but rather to a process through which they are rendered acceptable by being given an altered significance. For this I have no metaphor that leads to such admirable conciseness of terminology as does Aristotle's. Perhaps the very mild one of a frame of meaning into which our unorganized suffering can be fitted, may be useful; but I do not insist on it.

A footnote to "The Bedquilt" and to Frederick A. Pottle's essay "Catharsis" by Dorothy Canfield Fisher

. . . . there is one suggestion I'd like to make, one addition which I hope you'll find it possible to place in your book. Since the book is for students of writing, I think it would be well to put in a very brief statement which Professor Pottle says he leaves out because it doesn't concern his thesis in his paper. It may not concern that, but from my letters from would-be writers, I think it does concern all inexperienced writers. They are, evidently, from the many letters I get from such people, brought to a standstill often by their literal-mindedness in their use of their own life-experience. And I find it hard to make them believe that, while any writer hasn't any real and true source of material except his own life, there is no need to consider that it must be cast in exactly the same form that life passes it along to him.

The material which was the "source of the plot" for my story of the long-ago old maid and her bedquilt had nothing to do with old maids or bedquilts, but of the actions of a group of mechanics who had worked for a long time on the first locomotive manufactured in the United States and consequently quite an event in the age of our American life, "their locomotive." It was to be taken to the Centennial World Fair of 1875 (I think that was the date) in Philadelphia, and, as a great treat for the men who had worked so faithfully in his factory, the owner paid their expenses to go to Philadelphia to see the great international World Fair where their handiwork was put on display.

Now I know nothing whatever about mechanics and have known in Vermont many taken-for-granted old maids and many patchwork quilts. Hence, in that moment (which Professor Pottle describes with real eloquence) of my weeping in the garden there in Norway as my mind rushed to and fro in the search for some skill which might have made Aunt Mehetabel admired, my mind vagrantly caught up this story of the mechanics but dropped it at once because of my total ignorance of the mechanical world, which made it unsuitable material.

We have all known how painfully unreal and hollow the work of even the most conscientious writer of fiction appears when he "gets up his research," trying to become acquainted through books with some human activity which he has never known in life. At that point comes in a process which may be worth your while (although it wasn't to Professor Pottle's purpose) to put into an anthology for students who wish to write fiction themselves. This is a process very much like the change of key for the composer of music—the transmutation of known material out of an unfamiliar setting into one familiar and hence usable for the author. For what those mechanics in 1875 had done when they arrived at the Centennial Fair was not to utilize all their time in seeing the strange new things on show everywhere, but to stand spellbound before their handiwork, not yet emerged from the spell of their own creativeness, and gaze minutely at it and to listen eagerly to the comments of the spectators. Artists have their hearts so shaken by the act of creation that they can't emerge from it as the cuckoo emerges from a cuckoo clock when the hour strikes.

Part IV

Wartime: overseas and at home

James A. Michener

DRY ROT

Many excellent stories were written to capture the events of
1941–45, and much is still being written in retrospect. Most of the
stories included here were written by writers who were
very close to the incidents which they describe, and accordingly
they have in common the quality of immediacy. Because it
cannot be recaptured, this quality obviously has value in
the interpretation of historical events. The first two selections are
scenes from the war in the Pacific, and the third is from
well behind the lines in France. The fourth is an impressive
interpretation of a wartime incident on the home front in Japan.
The next three are scenes from the war as fought at home in the
United States. And finally (lest we forget), a post-war episode
from World War I—it is not dated—by Ernest Hemingway.

James A. Michener, the author of "Dry Rot," served in the
South Pacific. He opens his famous collection of tales with
these vivid sentences:

"I wish I could tell you about the South Pacific. The way it
actually was. The endless ocean. The infinite specks of
coral we called islands. Coconut palms nodding gracefully towards
the ocean. Reefs upon which waves broke into spray, and
inner lagoons, lovely beyond description. I wish I could tell you
about the sweating jungle, the full moon rising behind
the volcanoes, and the waiting. The waiting . . . our war was
waiting. You rotted on New Caledonia waiting for
Guadalcanal. Then you sweated twenty pounds away in Guadal
waiting for Bougainville. . . ."

"Dry Rot," one of many realistic accounts of the way it actually
was, is a document of rather special interest, for it provides a
revealing sidelight on those men who saw inaction in the Navy.

J oe had fought it out on the rock for sixteen months when two
important events occurred in his life. He got a new skipper, and a liberty ship carrying some SeaBees stopped at the island for engine repairs.
Joe's old skipper was sent home under some kind of a cloud. Either he
went to pieces mentally or he got into trouble over the accounts of the
officers' club. Joe never got the right of it.

The new skipper was a Navy type. He was a commander fifty-two years old. He would never go higher. He was a hard-drinking man who could not be relied upon. Yet he was an excellent fellow, and no one would prefer charges against him. So he dragged on and on, from one unimportant job to another. Many loved him but few respected him. Ambitious young men sought to leave his command at any opportunity, but they buttered him up while he was their superior. Some of them even bit their lips in silence when he made passes at their lovely wives. Before he was on the rock a week even Joe knew that he had been sent there as some kind of punishment. Something he had done in the States. Joe never got the right of it.

The Skipper, as he was known, started innovations at once. By God, he was the boss and things were going to be different. If he had to come to this god-forsaken island, he'd show them a thing or two. His first order was that each man must sleep under mosquito nets at all times. He almost had a mutiny on his hands, and the ringleader was Joe.

The huts in which enlisted men slept were foul things. Quonsets for eight men housed twenty-four. Men slept in double deckers, and even though there was a breeze at night, it could not penetrate the crowded quonsets. On some nights Joe lay in bed and sweated all night long. When the order came for mosquito netting, therefore, he rebelled. He tried it for two nights and found that he had what a doctor would have termed claustrophobia. He struggled with the net and almost strangled. In the hot, sweaty night he swore he'd not use a net again. He tore it off.

Next day he was before the new skipper. "I'm going to make an example of you," that red-faced man said.

When the words were spoken, Joe visibly trembled. For sixteen months he had kept out of trouble, and now he was in, up to his ears. "Get me out of this! Get me out of this!" he prayed. "I don't want no trouble!"

"What the hell do you think you're doing?" the Skipper shouted. "You think you can get away with murder around here?" He looked up at the frightened seaman. Joe licked his lips. The Skipper was about to throw the book at Joe when he remembered why it was he had been sent to the rock. "Got to start over!" he muttered to himself. "This time I'm starting over!" he promised under his breath.

"Young man," he said aloud, "don't you *like* the Navy?"

"Oh, sir!" Joe replied in the seaman's stock reply to the Skipper's stock question, "I *love* the Navy!"

"You'd better show it!" the Skipper said gruffly. "If I catch you in trouble again, I'll bounce you right out of the Navy." Then he added the crusher: "And you'll find yourself in the Army!"

Joe came to attention and left. After that he slept under a mosquito netting. It was strange, but out there in the middle of the Pacific, with an island almost to himself, Joe was cramped and stifled. He would wake up at night gasping for breath. He finally solved the problem by compounding his earlier felony. He stole a dynamotor and rigged up an electric fan. "If they ask me about it," he muttered to himself, "I'll say I got it from one of them wrecked planes." He scuffed the dynamotor up a bit to make it look like salvage. The fan was a wonder and helped him to breathe. Once he stuck his hand in it, and several times mosquito netting got caught in the blades. But it was worth it!

The SeaBees landed late one evening. Joe was on the rude dock when they came ashore. He was surprised to see how happy they were to be on land again, even a place like the rock. He guessed that everybody in the Navy wanted to be where he wasn't. He often thought of that night in later years. It was the time he met Luther Billis!

Joe had never seen anybody quite like Luther Billis. The SeaBee was big, fat, and brown. He wore a gold ring in his left ear and several bracelets. He was beautifully tattooed. Billis was accompanied by a young Jewish boy who trailed along behind him. He accosted Joe in a bright, breezy manner. "Hiya, Joe! Whaddaya know?"

"Hello!" Joe replied.

"Got a ship's store here?" Billis asked.

"Over there!" Joe pointed.

"Well, come along, Joe, and I'll set you up! Won a lot of money on this trip. Teaching the boys a few facts of life!" He whisked out a bundle of banknotes. "Come along, Hyman!" he shouted peremptorily at the Jewish boy.

When Billis had treated half a dozen men whom he had never seen before, he pointed admiringly at his Jewish friend. "I want to tell you," he said. "There's a genius. A college professor!" Billis smiled proudly and his friend grinned. "Professor Hyman Weinstein, but it could just as well be Einstein!" He laughed uproariously at his joke. "The Professor can speak five languages. Toss them a little Yiddish, Hyman." Weinstein, who found in Billis both a champion and a wonderful friend, spoke a few words of the Old Testament in Yiddish.

"He ain't kidding, either!" a boy on the sidelines whispered. "The Psalms."

"German, Hyman!" Billis ordered like a ringmaster displaying the tricks of a prize lion. The Professor rattled off some German words.

"Wouldn't that kill Hitler!" Billis shouted. "Professor, give them some Latin." Hyman obliged with some legal phrases, and Billis thereupon asked for French. When his friend had spoken several phrases in French, Billis demanded quiet. "This one will kill you, guys. Give them some Russian, Hyman."

As Hyman rattled off a long series of Russian words, Billis started singing, "Yo, heave ho!" to the tune of the *Volga Boatmen*. His listeners started to laugh. "Knock it off! Knock it off!" he shouted. "Them Bolsheviks ain't doin' so bad! Hitler ain't laughin'!" He threw his big hand around Hyman's shoulder and pulled the little Jew to the bench on which he and Joe were sitting.

The next three hours were the most wonderful Joe had spent on the rock. He didn't know that sailors could be such fine people. Billis wasn't afraid of anything, had been everywhere. And Weinstein could speak five languages. They talked about everything. Billis thought there was a God and that after the war there would be a big boom in aviation. Weinstein thought France would be a great country again. "What do you think, Joe?" Billis inquired. Joe was flabbergasted that a stranger would want to know what he thought. But, encouraged by their inquiry, he blurted out his philosophy.

"I think it's dumb to be on this rock when you guys are going out to do some fightin'. All I do is sit here day after day. Three times a week planes come in, and I gas them up. The rest of the time I try to keep out of trouble. It's a hell of a way to spend the war. I feel ashamed of myself!"

Billis was appalled at Joe's statement. "Whatsa matter?" he demanded. "You ain't thinkin' right at all, Joe! You make me very surprised! I thought you was a much sounder man than that!"

"What did I say wrong?" Joe inquired.

"About you not bein' of any use? If you wasn't here, who would be?" Billis asked contentiously. "You know damn well who would be here. The Japs! And supposin' the Japs was here when we broke down? Where would we go for repairs? We would be in a hell of a mess, wouldn't we?" He appeared to be furious at Joe for turning the island over to the Japs.

"I never thought of it that way," Joe replied.

"We all can't fight the Japs," Billis added sagely.

"That's right, Luther," Joe agreed. "Are you and Hyman goin' up to the front?"

They didn't know where they were going, but they had a lot of heavy machinery. Probably going to some island. Going to invade some island.

"What you goin' to do when peace comes?" Billis asked.

"Back to my shop in Columbus, Ohio. I'm a shoemaker."

"What you goin' to do if we all start wearin' plastic shoes?" Billis demanded. "Won't have to have them mended?" The thought shocked Joe. He had never thought of such a thing before. He had no answer. People would always have to have their shoes fixed. But Luther Billis' agile mind was on to new problems. "You got a girl?" he asked.

"No," Joe replied. "I ain't."

"You ain't got a girl?" Billis shouted. "What the hell kind of a sailor are you?"

"I never went with girls very much," Joe explained.

"I tell you what I do," Billis said with his hand about Joe's shoulder. "I'm gonna get you a girl. I like you. You're a real Joe, ain't he, Hyman?" Hyman agreed.

"Look at the moon over the water!" Weinstein said. Billis turned to study the rare sight of moonlight upon tropic waters with palm trees along the shore and a ship at the dock.

"God, that's beautiful!" he said. "You ought to come down here lots, Joe. You ought to look at that. Like Hyman just done."

The three men sat there in silence and watched the moonlight wax and wane along the waves. Never before in sixteen months had Joe seen that strange and lovely thing. He suddenly wanted to go with Billis and the Professor. He wanted to be with men that talked happily and saw new things. He wanted . . .

But at midnight the boat pulled out. The SeaBees were gone. Joe followed the ship as long as it rode in the moonlight. He had never before felt so strange. Great inchoate thoughts welled up within him. He could not sleep, and so he walked along the edge of the island. The airstrip shone in the moonlight. "It's beautiful," he said. "And look at the water bouncin' on them cliffs. It's beautiful."

The world was beautiful that night. It was beautiful as only a tropic night on some distant island can be beautiful. A million men in the South Seas would deny it to one another, would ridicule it in their letters home. But it was beautiful. Perhaps some of the million would deny the beauty because, like Joe, they had never seen it.

Something like this was going through Joe's mind when he became aware that men were behind him. He started to walk along the edge of the cliff when a light flashed in his eyes. "No you don't!" a voice shouted. Quickly two men ran up and grabbed him.

"Here's another one of them," the voice with the light cried. Joe was hauled off to a jeep.

"Bunch of damned bootleggers!" a gruff voice said as he was thrust into a small truck. He looked at the other prisoners. He knew none of them.

"He ain't one of us!" the apparent leader of the gang said.

"Keep your mouth shut!" the gruff voice ordered.

"But he ain't one of us!"

"Shut up!"

"On your way, big time!" the leader of the gang grunted in surly tones.

That night Joe slept in the brig. He found himself among a group of six enlisted men who had been running a still in a cave along the cliffs. They had finally been caught. They were making pure alcohol from canned corn and sugar. They had a market for all they could make. Each man had been clearing two hundred dollars a month

Joe studied them. They were guys just like him. He wondered why they got mixed up in such a racket. He wondered if Luther Billis was like them. Luther had lots of money. But somehow he felt that Luther was different. These men were in trouble.

"I'm gonna spill the whole story!" a little machinist's mate said. He had built the still. "If they try to pin a rap on me, I'll spill the whole story!"

"You do," the leader whispered hoarsely, "and I'll kill you. That's a promise!"

But next morning the little machinist's mate did spill the whole story. Joe was shocked. The revelation came shortly after the Skipper had ordered Joe to stand aside. Obviously Joe wasn't implicated. So there he stood by the window, while the machinist's mate told how a lieutenant had sold them canned corn by the case and sugar by the barrel. He had taken one-fourth of the profits. Made four hundred bucks a month.

That was one time the Skipper didn't bellow. "Get him right away," he said in a very low voice. No one spoke until the lieutenant appeared. He was a young man. He took one look at the six culprits, grew faint, and sat down. "Have you anything to say?" the Skipper asked.

"No, sir!" the lieutenant replied.

"You are confined to your quarters!" the Skipper said briefly. "Take the rest of these men to the brig." Joe felt all funny inside. He knew his turn was next.

"Well," the Skipper said. "So it's you again! Always in trouble!"

"Oh, no, sir!"

"How did you happen to be down at the cliffs? One of their watchers?"

"Oh, no, sir! I never had anything to do with these men. Never."

"What were you doing at the cliff?"

Joe swallowed hard. At first the words wouldn't come. "I was watching the ship go, sir!"

In a flash, the Skipper saw himself, once on Haiti. A ship was leaving the bay. He was an ensign then, and sure that he would be an admiral one day. He could understand why young men look at ships. "You better stay out of trouble, young feller," he said. That was all.

It would not be fair to say that Joe had forgotten Billis. But he had ceased thinking constantly about the strange fellow when a letter came to the rock. It was for Joe and came from Miss Essie Schultz, Perkasie, Pennsylvania. Joe read the letter avidly:

Dear Joe,

Please excuse me for writing when we haven't been introduced, but my good friend Mr. Luther Billis told me that you didn't have any girl to write to. I write letters to seventeen sailors and one soldeir. I think you boys are

423

the bravest men in America. I would never be brave enough to fight against the Japs. I am glad we have boys like you to fight for us. I wish I had a good looking photograph to send you, but you know how it is these days. One or two prints is all you can get. So I am sending you this one. The one in the middle is me. Skinny, eh? I work in a pants factory. At present we are making sailors pants, so if yours don't fit, blame me. (Ha!) I like to dance and like Benny Goodman and Louie Prima the best. I listen to the radio a good deal and read some books every year. Mr. Billis said you were a very swell guy and that I would like you. I believe I would. Won't you please write and tell me all about yourself? I promise to answer right away.

Yours (?)

ESSIE SCHULTZ.

P.S. Send me a picture.

The letter simply bowled Joe over! It passed his comprehension that Luther Billis would have taken the trouble to do such a thing. But that Essie should have written to him . . . That was a true miracle! He read the letter eight or ten times. It was so nicely written, in straight lines. And it smelled good. And there was Essie in front of a building. And there was snow on the ground! He looked and looked. Essie wasn't the worst looking, either. Not by a long shot!

He got seven more letters from Essie, sweet, cheerful letters. He showed her picture to several of his friends. You couldn't see much of her face, but what there was looked mighty neat and clean. Joe felt fine. Then one day he got a brief letter. "I am going to marry the soldeir," Essie said. "He thinks I ought to stop writing to the rest of you boys. I tell him he's jealous of the Navy. (Ha!)"

Joe was glum for several days. He tore up Essie's picture. "Don't want no picture of no married woman," he said to himself. "I wanta stay out of trouble."

But he was miserable. Essie's letters had been . . . Well, he couldn't say it in words. All he knew was that weeks were a lot longer now. What if she had been writing to seventeen other fellows? She had also written to him, and that was what mattered. Joe tried four times to send her congratulations, but couldn't find the words. Then one day he was at the airstrip when some enlisted men flew in from Noumea. One of them had a grass skirt, a lovely thing of yellow and red.

"How much you want for that, buddy?" Joe asked.

"Fifteen dollars," the seaman replied.

"That's a lot of money," Joe answered.

"That's right," the seaman replied. "You can get 'em cheaper in Noumea, but you ain't in Noumea."

Still, the skirt seemed such a wonderful present for a girl that Joe bought it. He wrapped it carefully, addressed the package to Essie Schultz, Perkasie, Pennsylvania, and had it censored. After the officer had finished looking at the skirt, Joe slipped in the little piece of paper: "All happiness, Joe."

It wasn't that he didn't see girls on the rock. Every three or four months some plane would come in with a USO vaudeville troupe aboard. If they had time, the girls always danced or sang in the Red Cross hut. But that wasn't like having a girl . . . Well, a special girl.

Some time later Joe received a letter direct from Billis. It was brief. "A girl named Alice Baker from Corvallis is going to write to you pretty soon. I know her big sister and her brother. He is a dogface. (Ha!) She is a fine girl. Her sister thinks I am an officer dont tell her different. Your best buddy, L. Billis."

Joe was delighted with news from Luther. He wondered if Luther had worn an officer's uniform when he was in Corvallis. That was dangerous stuff. They really threw the book at you if they caught you.

While Joe waited for news from Alice Baker, a strange thing happened. One night at eleven-thirty he was routed out of bed by the guard. "You're wanted at the Skipper's shack!" he was told. In the darkness he went along coral paths to where the Skipper had had a mansion built for himself. It cost, men figured, about $9,000. The Skipper said that by God, if he was going to live on this rock, he'd live like a gentleman. He had quarters that many an admiral would envy.

"Joe!" he said, "when I was walking across the floor tonight, I felt a splinter over there. There's a sander in the closet. Rub the thing down, will you?"

Joe broke out the sander and went to work. As he did so, the Skipper slid his bare feet from one board to another. "Give this a touch, will you?" "Sand that joint down a little." Joe worked till one-thirty. "Better take the day off tomorrow," the Skipper said.

Joe told nobody of what had happened. A few nights later he was called out again. This time the linoleum in the bathroom was loose. Joe fixed it. In the middle of his work the Skipper interrupted. "Joe," he said, "in that cabinet there's a bottle of very fine whiskey. I'm going to walk along the beach for twenty minutes. If I catch you drinking it when I get back, I'll raise hell with you. What time have you?" The two men synchronized their watches at exactly 0119. "Mind you," the Skipper said, "I'll be back in twenty minutes."

Joe worked on, keeping his mind off the cabinet. He liked whiskey, but he didn't want no trouble with nobody. At 0139 the Skipper returned singing gently. He went archly to the cabinet and peeked in. Then he snorted and pulled out the whiskey bottle.

"I didn't touch it, sir!" Joe protested.

"Goddamned squarehead!" the Skipper shouted. "I told you I was going to be gone twenty minutes."

"I didn't touch it!" Joe insisted.

"I know you didn't, Joe," the Skipper said in a tired voice. "But I meant you to. You're a good boy. You work hard. I'll go out again. If you want a nip, help yourself. But if I ever see you doing it, I'll throw you in the clink!" He went out again, singing. After that Joe spent a good deal of his time fixing up the Skipper's shack. But he never told a soul. He wanted no trouble.

At mail call one day Joe got a letter from Corvallis. It was from Alice Baker. She was eighteen and a senior in Corvallis High School. She had no boy friend, and her brother was a soldier in England. Ensign Billis had told her sister about Joe and her sister had asked her to write. She felt silly, but she guessed it was all right. She concluded, "Ensign Billis said you were slow, but I like slow boys. Some of the boys in Corvallis are so fast they think if they look at a girl, why she falls in love with them. This picture of me is pretty much the way I look. Sincerely, Alice Baker."

Joe could not believe that any girl as lovely as Alice Baker's picture would write to him. He looked at the picture eight or ten times a day, but would show it to no one. He was afraid they wouldn't believe him. After two days he decided that he must reply to her sweet letter. He labored over his answer a long time. It came out like this:

Dear Alice,
I nearly fell out of my chair when they gave me that letter from you. It was the nicest letter I have ever got from anyone. I have read it twenty four times so far and I will keep right on reading till another comes. I don't believe you when you say you have no boy friends. A girl as pretty as you could have a hundred. I am afraid to show your picture to the men in my hut. They would all want to write to you. It is your picture, isn't it, Alice? I suppose Ensign Billis told you all about me. I am a shoemaker in Columbus Ohio and right now I am riding nineteen months on this rock. I am not good looking and I like whiskey but I never get drunk. I hope you will write to me. I would like to send you a picture, Alice, but we can't get none made on this rock. It is no good trying. My uncle has a picture of me took a long time ago. I will ask him to send it to you. I am fatter now. Please anser this letter, Alice, as I think you are one fine girl.

Yours truly,
JOE.

The correspondence went on from there. Finally Alice was writing to Joe three times a week. And finally Joe got up nerve enough to show his friends her picture. In Navy fashion they went mad about her. Half of them called her "that bag" and the other half wanted to know who the movie star was. Joe stood by in rapt pleasure. They kidded him a lot, and that evening an older man who knew a thing or two about sailors came by and asked if he could see the picture again. Joe practically fell over himself to think that anyone had remembered her.

They sat on the quonset steps and studied Alice Baker's picture. "A fine girl," the older man said.

One day a letter from Alice arrived soaked with salt water. Joe could barely read the writing. He took it down to the postoffice to find what had happened. "A plane went into the drink somewhere up the line."

"Anybody hurt?" Joe inquired.

"Ten dead. They got the mail bags, though. A diver went down for them."

Joe handled the letter gingerly. It was a terrible thing. A letter from the girl you loved, passed on by the hands of dead men. Joe had seen little of death, but it frightened him vastly. It was like getting into trouble. It ruined everything. One of the officers had said, when the lieutenant's court-martial was read for selling government property to the bootleggers, "I'd commit suicide!" But the lieutenant, who was sentenced to jail for three years, didn't commit suicide. He lived on, and so did the bootleggers. They went to jail and lived. Joe was also one of the men who live on, no matter what happens.

He assured himself of that the night they found the yeoman hanging in the palm grove. Nobody ever understood exactly why he did it just then. His wife had a baby after he was overseas sixteen months, but he agreed to the divorce and she married the other man. The yeoman took it OK. Joe knew him well, and then seven months after it was all over he strung himself up.

Two other incidents reminded Joe of death on his hot, lonely, barren, sticky rock. One was a letter from Luther Billis. It made Joe shudder with apprehension for his buddy. "The Navy took this pitcher of me," he wrote. "Youd a thought it would of busted the camera. You see I aint got the ring in my ear. They made me take it out but now I got it back in. The pitcher is for the Navy when they give me my medal. What I did they should of had a hero do. Anyway I got two Jap swords out of it and they are beauties. I am sending one to my mom and the other I give to my skipper, Commander Hoag, who was the best guy that ever lived, even if he was an officer. I hope you have heard from Alice Baker. She is a fine girl I tried to kiss her once and she slapped my face. Your best buddy, L. Billis."

The second incident occurred on June 7. They had a ball game that afternoon, and as they came in from the game they heard a lot of shouting. "We invaded France!" everybody was yelling. There was some shooting to celebrate, and the Skipper ordered a whistle to blow. "Any goddamned whistle, but blow it!" They used the fire truck's, and it sounded fine. Then the chaplain suggested they have a prayer meeting. The Skipper stood beside him on the platform. "Our prayers go out tonight," the chaplain intoned, "for all the brave men who are fighting the enemy. Wherever brave men are fighting and dying, O Lord, protect them." They sang two hymns and the Skipper asked if anyone could sing the Marseillaise. A former schoolteacher could, and the rest hummed.

These events deepened Joe's perceptions. If a fine man like Luther Billis could risk his life, why was he, Joe, sitting the war out on this rock? If Alice Baker's brother could land in France what was Joe doing on a coral reef? Up to this time Joe had never thought about the men back home. But on the evening of June 7, 1944, he thought about them a great deal. Some men died in France. Some men like Luther Billis fought against the Japs. Some men like the yeoman lost everything they had and committed suicide. Some men like the bootleggers got heebie-jeebies on the rock. Some men worked in airplane factories or helped keep the country running. And some men did nothing.

But before his thoughts ran away with him, Joe stopped. "It's the same on this rock," he mused. "Look how little some guys have! And look what I got! Alice Baker, an electric fan, a shot of the Skipper's whiskey now and then, and a best buddy who is already a hero!"

Thoughts of death, however, persisted. One night he sat bolt upright in bed. He was sweating all over. Phantasms of horror assailed him! Luther Billis was dead! On an island teeming with Japs Luther lay beside a coconut log. Joe wiped the sweat from his face and tried to go back to sleep. But all night, in the hot quonset, he could see Luther Billis and the coconut log. It was not until he received a short letter from Billis that his mind gained rest. The SeaBee was fine and was teaching Professor Weinstein Beche-le-Mer so he would be able to speak six languages!

His worry about Luther decided him upon one thing, however. He wanted Alice and Luther to have pictures of him, just in case. He would have his picture taken after all! That was a solemn decision on the rock. First of all you had to find somebody who had stolen film and photographic paper. Then you had to arrange the sitting surreptitiously. And finally you had to get the photograph through the mail. So Joe, who never wanted any trouble with anybody, set out in search of a bootlegging photographer. He found one on the other end of the island. He was a thin, round-shouldered man. Where he got his equipment no one knew. He had a big deal of some kind on the fire. They all knew that.

"It'll be ten dollars," the photographer growled. "You get two prints and the negative."

Joe whistled. The photographer snapped at him. "You ain't bein' forced into this, buddy. I'm the guy that's takin' the chances. You saw what them bootleggers got. The price is ten bucks."

Joe took out his wallet and gave the man two fives. It was a lot to pay, but if your girl was in Corvallis, had never seen you, had no picture of you but that skinny one your uncle sent, well . . . what better you got to spend ten bucks on?

The photographer made ready with a cheap box camera. "Don't look so stiff!" he told Joe, but Joe was no dummy. If he was playing ten bucks for one photograph, it would be the best. So, like a ramrod, his hair smoothed back, he glanced stonily at the expensive birdie. The photographer shrugged his pale shoulders and went ahead. "Come back in three days. Remember, you get two prints and the negative. I don't want no beefing. I'm the guy that takes the risks."

Three days later Joe got his two pictures. They were pretty good. Mostly you saw his uniform and pronounced jaw. But he looked like a clean, quiet sailor. Just like eight hundred other guys on the rock. Only the others didn't look quite so sure of themselves when they'd been on the rock as long as Joe. He grinned at the pictures and all the way back to camp kept stealing furtive glances at himself.

When he arrived at the camp the chaplain was waiting for him. The padre was a Catholic and Joe a Methodist, but they were friends. The chaplain's business was brief. Alice Baker had been killed. An auto accident. Her sister sent the news.

The padre had never heard of Alice Baker. All he knew was that a human being of greater or less importance to some other human being was dead. No message could transcend that. He cast about for words, which never seemed to be available for such emergencies. The day was hot. Sweat ran down Joe's face until it looked like tears. "Brave people are dying throughout the world," the chaplain said. "And brave people live after them." There was nothing more to say. Joe sat looking at the priest for a few minutes and then left.

He went into the brilliant sunlight. Glare from the airstrip was intense. Even the ocean was hot. Joe looked at the waves whose beauty Luther Billis had discovered. They came rippling toward the rock in overwhelming monotony. Joe counted them. One, two, three! They were the months he had been on the rock. Fourteen, fifteen, sixteen. That was when he met Luther Billis. Seventeen, eighteen. The yeoman had committed suicide. Nineteen, twenty, twenty-one. Alice Baker had become his girl. Twenty-five, twenty-six, twenty-seven. They were all the same, one after the other, like the dreary months.

Joe dropped his head in his hands. A girl he had never seen. A funny town he had never visited. "I want to get out of here," he muttered to himself. "I got to get out of here!"

BINKY'S VOICE

Elsewhere in the South Pacific theater of war we hear Binky's
voice, over the radio, at an air base in New Guinea.
Binky was a member of a fighter squadron "operating from
'Brimstone,' which was a muddy little airstrip hacked out of a
green, stagnant strip of jungle." To the north "the great steaming
mountains tumble up on the horizon, and there, too,
was the fighting." So the author tells us at the beginning of this
remarkable story, one of the strangest incidents to find
its way into the literature of our war in the air.

I'm sorry this story has to be about the war. Some of us ordinary people who were in it got such a concentrated dose of living that
we have had trouble digesting all of it. This story about Binky has been
sitting heavily upon me for the past three years. I'm going to tell it now,
and try to get rid of it, once and for all.

I was an Intelligence Officer in New Guinea, assigned to one of General Kenney's Fighter Squadrons. If you ever saw that British picture
Target for Tonight, you'll remember that the Intelligence Officer was
the man who briefed the air crews before their missions and interrogated them after they landed. Of course, in New Guinea our pilots didn't
need much briefing, and they never saw anything but jungle and mountains to be interrogated about, so my job boiled down to being a friend
and guide to them.

I tried to keep them interested in the job, even when there were
weeks of milk runs with never any real action. I had to keep telling them
that they were important to the Grand Strategy of the war, even when
they were flying P-40s that creaked with age and weariness and which
had no hope of being replaced. I helped them write letters to their girls,
and listened to their troubles, and got beaten by them at poker. It was
all part of my job.

Binky was one of our pilots.

He had been with us about four months, which was long enough for
a new man to shake down, and Binky was really very much like any of

the others. He was an Easterner and had a university degree; and, as you might expect, he was a bit reserved and standoffish when he first joined the family. But it's pretty hard to stay that way when you are working with thirty-five other young men like you, and being interdependent with them, the way fighter pilots are. His reticence was all in his favor, for we were suspicious of a new man who made too much noise, and we respected Binky for his hard work in the air.

He was a handsome boy—lean and dark, and built like an athlete. When he stepped up on the wing of his Kittyhawk, with his goggles pushed up on his helmet and his oxygen mask flapping under his chin, he looked like one of those magazine advertisements—"In the Air Forces, it's Camels every time!" or whatever it was in those days.

It's unusual for such a good-looking man to be popular, but Binky was. He would have made a good Commanding Officer.

One morning, early in 1943, the squadron was alerted for a strike on the Jap base at Pandau. We were operating from "Brimstone," which was a muddy little airstrip hacked out of a green, stagnant sea of jungle. Only to the north was this shimmering ocean of giant trees and black swamps broken. There, the great steaming mountains tumble up on the horizon, and there, too, was the fighting.

Our pilots knew the tortuous valleys in those mountains as they knew the lines in their own hands; and they also knew the weather—the way the clouds built up into a towering wall, faster than our tired old planes could climb over them. We flew most of our missions up there, in those days, escorting the transports that brought supplies and reinforcements to the Australian Infantry at "Outhouse."

That's a funny name, I suppose, but to us it was deadly serious. Outhouse was a little gold-mining settlement in the mountains. The Nip wanted it, and for three months he had his foot on the threshold. But those Australians held him, and finally began to push him slowly back, back through the misty valleys, to his advance base at Pandau, thirty miles away. Our squadron was overhead all through that show.

II

Well, we were alerted for a combined bomber-fighter strike on Pandau, and we were also detailed to send two ships off at first light of dawn for a weather recco. That meant simply flying up to the target, checking the weather, and reporting it in code on the way home. The weather was so treacherous over the mountains that you could judge it only about ten minutes in advance.

A Flight Commander named Shaw was posted to make this weather hop, and since Binky usually flew Shaw's wing, he was picked as the second man. When we drove down to the strip in the jeeps that morning, the night was still black and the air was cool. We passed the revetments where our ships were parked, and there was the roar of their engines, and the blue flashes of their exhausts, as the crew chiefs pre-flighted them.

Shaw and Binky got ready right away, carrying their parachutes and Mae Wests out to their ships and strapping on their guns and jungle knives. I never thought of briefing them. A weather hop was so simple! I've often wondered since if I should have.

As soon as they could see the strip, they taxied to the end, checked their mags, and off they went. I didn't stand beside them and stick my thumb up, the way they do in the movies. I didn't even know they were gone, until I heard the snarl of their engines as they climbed up into the morning.

The sun came up, and the day's heat started to set in. The pilots lay around in the cool of the alert shack, playing bridge or solitaire, or just dozing. Davis, the CO, got the flight leaders together to figure out spacing and positions in the air, and that sort of thing. Davis was a stickler for tactics.

Little by little, there was a certain tightening of the atmosphere in-side that grass-roofed shack. The time for the strike to take off came nearer and nearer, and the boys were quieter as their wrist watches ticked away the seconds.

I got some new intelligence reports out of my safe-box, and was passing them around, when there was the whine of an Allison engine, and we glanced out in time to see a P-40 slip around the traffic pattern and land. One P-40. No one thought much about there being only one. It just meant that either Shaw or Binky had found some sort of trouble and had been forced to return early. The boys lit cigarettes, and mur-mured over their bridge games, and turned the pages of their dog-eared magazines.

Shaw walked in. His face was streaked with dust, except where his goggles had been, and his shirt was dark with sweat under his shoulder holster. He lit a soggy cigarette and looked up at me as I came over to get his report.

"Binky went on alone," he said. "I told him to come back with me, but he wasn't receiving me."

"What was the trouble?" I asked.

"Damned carburetor. . . . I couldn't get over the hump."

"How was the weather?"

"Not too hot. Binky should be reporting it by now."

We had a receiving set on my desk. Davis nodded to me, and I went over and switched it on. I found fighter frequency, but there was noth-ing but the scratch of static and, occasionally, a ground station asking Brimstone control for a radio check. Shaw took off his holster and unbuttoned his shirt, and flopped down on one of the cots. His bare chest glistened in the heat. Davis sat beside me as I listened to the hoarse breath of the radio. The shack was quiet except for the flutter of cards being shuffled and the sound of someone softly whistling to himself. I turned the volume up, and the static rattled so viciously that I turned it down again.

Someone said, "Two no trump," and just then Davis and I both heard a faint voice over the ether. It was unintelligible, but Davis said, "That sounds like him."

The control station boomed out, very loud in comparison. "Station calling Brimstone, repeat your call, repeat your call. Go ahead."

We waited, and listened, but there was nothing but static. It was bad that day. Davis looked at his watch. "He isn't receiving them, either," he said. "He should be back in about half an hour."

He started to get up, and just then we heard the voice again, and could distinguish a few faint, blurred words: ". . . not receiving . . . Pittsburg Mary, Pittsburg Mary, New York . . ."

"Hah!" Davis grinned at me. *"Mary* means lousy weather. Hey, Shaw!" he called. "What's *Pittsburg?"*

Shaw rolled off the cot onto his feet and came over to the desk. *"Pittsburg's* the target," he said. "Did you hear him?"

"Yeah. He said something about *New York.* What's that?"

"That's the mountains. They'll probably be *Mary* too."

"Here he is again," I said.

Binky's voice swelled in, this time, loud and clear: ". . . Brimstone from Daisy Special, I am not receiving. Pittsburg Mary, New York Mary. Pittsburg Mary, New York Mary . . ."

The pilots had forgotten their cards and their magazines and were looking towards us expectantly. Davis glanced up at them.

"No mission today, boys," he said.

I could feel the atmosphere snap, like a stretched elastic band that has been cut. The alert shack that had been so quiet before was suddenly full of voices and laughter. We were a veteran squadron. Our pilots weren't very eager any more.

I pushed back my canvas chair and got up to turn the radio off. As I bent towards it, I became conscious that Binky's voice was speaking again. I remember that as I heard it I was glad that Binky was well out of that bad weather—safely on the way home. Then I became aware of his words, and I looked up and shouted, "Quiet!"

There must have been urgency in my shout, for every voice was suddenly still. Except one—Binky's.

". . . from Daisy Special. I am still circling at Pittsburg, angels four, cannot get above overcast. Everything is Mary . . ."

"Jesus!" Shaw said, softly. "He's right in the middle of it!"

We were all packed around the radio, but there was nothing but our breathing.

Davis cleared his throat. "He's only got four thousand feet. He must be down in a valley."

I looked at the big typographical map that was pinned to the table beside my desk. Every peak around Pandau and Outhouse went to at least six thousand. Binky was caught in a box, and the clouds formed the lid.

"Do you think he could get to Outhouse?" I asked Davis.

"Depends on how lost he is," Davis muttered. "Shh!"

That lonely, tired voice wavered again through the crackle of static: ". . . will attempt to visit Outhouse. Brimstone from Daisy Special, will attempt to visit Outhouse. Please inform them to expect me." The formal wording was too much for Binky, and we could feel his exasperation as he broke away from it: "Tell Outhouse I'm coming, and I can't hear a damn thing!"

A drop of sweat rolled down the length of my nose and splashed on the desk. There was a hot press of bodies as we crowded together, listening.

A new voice came in—Australian. That could only be Outhouse.

"Brimstone from Outhouse, we understand situation. We are standing by for Daisy Special. Over."

Our controller answered with relief in his voice. "Roger, Outhouse. Thank you."

We all felt better. It was good to know that Binky had friends expecting him—if he could make it.

We waited and listened—to the continuous mutter of static, and to Brimstone occasionally snapping at some ground station to "clear the air." I looked at the faces of my friends around me and realized that at moments like these, I could never hope to be really close to them. Each man was living every second with Binky. Each was intent, peering through a rain-swept canopy as he plunged through foggy valleys at two hundred miles an hour. Each man was probing the blurred earth for a sight of a tiny, rutted runway that meant a chance for life.

Outhouse didn't have enough of a strip to take care of a fighter. Binky would have to crash-land there, but at least he would be safe.

A new pilot voiced a thought that had been in my mind. "Why doesn't he bail out?" he asked Davis.

Davis pointed to the map. "All the terrain here is over three thousand feet high. He's only showing four thousand on his dial. There's only a few spots where he has room for his chute to open. Anyway, those valleys are crawling with Nips."

We were all very quiet after that.

I was thinking about the enemy at Pandau. I could picture some Jap Intelligence Officer listening to his radio, just as we were, and making notes that a Yankee Kittyhawk was lost, almost over his head. It would be quite a thrill for him, I guessed. But he would be like me in one way. He wouldn't really be able to picture it. We were both just ground officers, after all.

When the voice came in again, we all jumped. There was a lull in the static, and Binky was very clear. He sounded tired as hell, but there was a sharp quality to his voice that was eloquent of fear and, at the same time, hope.

"Outhouse from Daisy Special. Believe I am north of you. Will vector one eighty, angels zero. Give me a flare if . . ." It faded right out.

"He's right down on the deck!" someone said.

I tried to think of Binky sweeping over the treetops in a valley I had never seen.

Brimstone boomed in, very loud and formal: "Outhouse from Brimstone, did you receive Daisy Special's last message? Go ahead."

"Brimstone from Outhouse, we are firing flares and standing by. Over."

"This is Brimstone. Roger."

The static rasped again in my ears. We held our breaths, and the air in the alert shack was as heavy as a blanket.

Tediously, the seconds ticked past on our watches. Somewhere at the other end of the airstrip, a B-25 was running up its engine. The distant growl floated to our ears through the still, hot air. We waited by the radio, without moving. Only, sometimes, a man would swallow.

Then, wavering through the miles of ether, so small a sound that it might have been voiced inside our own heads, we heard one word— one lone monosyllable—from Binky. It had a whole world of relief pent up in its utterance: "Thanks!"

Shaw looked up from the radio. "He's made it!" he whispered.

Davis scratched his nose and grinned vacantly. We stirred, and breathed, and my heart pounded in my ears as we waited for the confirmation that he was safe on the ground. The radio hummed softly, waiting. Even the static had let up momentarily.

Then the Brimstone controller spoke. His voice was impersonal and disciplined, but there was a current of excitement as he said: "Outhouse from Brimstone, is Daisy Special with you? Go ahead."

The Australian voice at Outhouse came back in deliberate words, with no attempt at coding: "Brimstone from Outhouse, Daisy Special is not here. There is no aircraft in our vicinity. Sorry."

There was a long pause, and then Brimstone said, "Roger," and the implacable static hummed again. You see, there was only one other place where Binky could have landed.

We went quietly out into the sun. It felt cool after being cooped up over that radio for so long.

IV

For the week that followed, the squadron's morale was in bad shape. As a ground officer, and consequently an outsider, I could sense the change in the pilots better than they could themselves. I could see that their bargain-counter, life-and-death religion had been shattered, and I could feel all about me the heartbreaking bewilderment of youth towards injustice.

Their greatest defense had been their belief that if they followed the rules of the game, they would come through. If a man "bought it," there was always a reason—a rule he had broken.

The trouble was, Binky had followed the rules. He had been trapped unavoidably in bad weather, in an old crate that couldn't take the buffeting of a tropical storm and was useless for instrument flight. He had been too low to bail out, so he had made a valiant attempt to land at Outhouse. And the Nips, hearing his request for a flare, had obliged him and brought him safely down on their own strip at Pandau.

It simply wasn't fair.

Of course it was a death sentence for Binky. That particular crowd of jungle-isolated Japs wasn't taking prisoners. They were half-starved, anyway, and they couldn't spare transport to get people back to their prison cages. I knew all this through my reports, better than the pilots did. Some of them held out hope for Binky, but I knew.

I was glad when, the next week, everyone was alerted for the same strike on Pandau and our squadron once more was ordered to provide two planes for a weather hop. I felt that the boys needed to face that job again, and I think Davis felt the same way. He asked Shaw to make the flight, and picked Collins, who had been Binky's tentmate, to fly wing.

That black early morning was so precisely like the other in every detail that, as the two pilots were getting their equipment ready, I found myself looking twice at Collins to make sure he wasn't Binky after all. They set their parachutes on the hood of a jeep and drove the fifty yards to their revetments, where the warmed-up planes were waiting. Abruptly, as it happens in the tropics, the darkness melted away, and in the twilight I heard their engines cough into life. A moment later they were taxiing out to the strip, and then there was the beating roar of their take-off.

I had a funny feeling that morning, almost as though I were about to take off on a combat mission myself. It was the same gnawing in my gut that I'd had when I debated at college—the feeling I used to get during the speech before mine. I went over to my desk and fiddled with some reports, and then I switched on the radio and tuned it to fighter frequency. As it warmed up, Collins's voice faded in, giving Shaw a radio check.

". . . from Peacock Special Two, you are loud and clear. Can you hear me? Go ahead." Our squadron code name had been changed since last week.

Shaw's voice answered, "Roger." At least they were making sure of their communications, this time.

I lit a cigarette and settled myself for a long vigil. I knew those two pilots were just starting on a long mission, during which they would keep radio silence to a great extent, but I couldn't help that feeling of wanting to be on hand. I couldn't get over that curious stage fright.

It *was* a long vigil. Many of the pilots moved their cots closer to the radio so that they could hear any message that might come through. Davis sat down beside me after a while, because he didn't want to miss anything. We talked quietly together while the radio buzzed and the card players murmured and the heat pressed heavier upon us.

"They must have been listening all the time—just like this," Davis said. I knew what he meant. He was thinking of last week, of the Nips at Pandau squatting around a radio receiver in some moldy dugout.

There was a pause, and then he said, "I wrote his mother last night."

I looked up at him. "What did you tell her?"

"Missing."

Of course. There was nothing else he could have said. Just "Missing," and hope that after a while she wouldn't expect him home any more.

Davis drummed on the desk with his fingers. He looked tired and thin, and yellow. He looked as though he needed about six months' leave. Finally he spoke again. "He doesn't have a prayer, does he?"

I shook my head. "No."

He swore, vulgarly, tersely, and wearily. I flipped him a cigarette and we lit up again. We smoked too much in those days.

"What are you going to do after the war?" he asked.

"Probably sell apples," I said.

He twitched his mouth in a smile. "Make room for me at your corner."

A little dusty breeze sprang up, and whispered through the alert shack. I undid my shirt and held it open.

"You were at college before, weren't you?" I asked.

"Technical school, yeah," he said. "I got in two years."

"Whereabouts?"

I never did find out where Davis went to school. Just as I asked that question, we heard a faint voice on the radio.

V

I've read novels which describe people's hair standing on end. It's one of those things you read so often that it ceases to mean anything. You see it in the book, and just go on reading. But at that moment, when I heard that tiny voice reaching out through the layers of static, I felt a twitching in my scalp—a sensation of something changing its position. I think I have sufficient license to say that my hair stood on end. The voice we heard was distant, and weary, and compelling, and so hideously familiar that for a moment I thought my mind must have snapped. *It was Binky's voice!*

"Brimstone from Daisy Special, will attempt to visit Outhouse. Please inform them to expect me. Tell Outhouse I'm coming, and I can't hear a damn thing!"

I guess we all went white. I was looking at Davis, and I know he turned sickly pale as he half stood up. There was a curtain of silence inside the shack as the other pilots sat up and stared at us. The radio was utterly still. Someone got up and walked over towards us, then stopped for a moment, as if to consider, and then stepped up beside us. That started the others, and there was a sudden stirring as everyone moved closer to the radio. Still, there was not a word from anyone. The radio seemed dead, except for that slight, monotonous power tone. We started when there was a snap of sound, and then a new tone on a different pitch. A voice spoke, slowly and carefully, in all the formality of radio procedure: "Peacock Special Leader from Special Two, did you hear a message just then?"

Shaw's voice was expressionless. "Yes."

There was no answer. The radio tone snapped back to normal pitch, and everything else was still. I stared at the ugly grillwork of the loud-speaker, and the thought entered my head that I should turn it off. I almost reached out my hand for the switch, but I didn't. I just sat and stared at it.

Binky's voice kept echoing in my ears. I could recapture every syllable, every intonation of that speech—the same words that he had spoken near the end of that last flight. It had been real. It had come out of that very loud-speaker, in the English language, in the radio idiom of the Air Forces, in an Eastern American accent.

Binky's voice had just spoken to us, and Binky had landed, one week ago, on the Jap strip at Pandau, where the enemy had a policy of coolly murdering every prisoner.

The radio tone broke into that carrier pitch again, and we stiffened in our seats. It was Shaw, this time. "Brimstone from Peacock Special, everything is Jane, everything is Jane. Go ahead."

Jane was code for clear weather, and that meant the mission was to take off as scheduled.

Brimstone acknowledged, and Davis, beside me, seemed to wake up from a sleep. He straightened, and looked at the faces around us, and cleared his throat. He looked at his watch. "Take off in ten minutes," he said. His voice was husky.

No one moved. Everyone's attention was welded to that radio, as if to capture and inspect each insignificant rill of static. We waited because we knew something more would happen.

We were right!

There was a click, and a prolonged burst of static. Then that faint, horrifying voice, searching, appealing, desperate; and yet, most dreadful of all to us, *it sounded hopeful!*

"Outhouse from Daisy Special. Believe I am north of you. Will vector one eighty, angels zero. Give me a flare if I am clear to land."

There was a second of breathlessness before a little sigh went through all of us. Then the radio chattered with high-strung, barely audible words.

"That was him! Let's go back!"

Shaw's voice answered firmly. "Stay with me, Collins. Stay in position!"

We tensed over the loud-speaker, breathless, while the seconds ticked by. A paralysis of bewilderment seemed to have gripped us.

It was shattered by Davis, who jumped to his feet, startling us so that we all looked at him. For the first time we saw him crimson with anger.

"Son of a bitch!" he roared. "Get the hell out to those ships and stand by for take-off! On the double!"

That hotheaded bellow was the saving of our squadron. What we needed was a burst of clean, hot temper to disperse the stench of fear that had settled upon us. I could see the color come back into each pilot's face as he strapped on his equipment and ran for his plane. I stood outside the hut and listened to the increasing roar as one engine after another broke into life. The smell of high-octane exhaust filled my nostrils, and the dirty brown dust from sixteen propellers swirled around me, and I felt strong again, and confident.

The rest is a story which you can read in any official log of operations. I can't describe it, because I wasn't in it. When Shaw and Collins landed, ashen white and trembling, I took them to the radio, and the three of us listened to the few curt orders and remarks which constituted the conversation of a squadron in action: "Stay in close, Four!" and "Take the left, Blue Flight!" and "Peacock, four o'clock high!" and "Don't drop your tanks yet!" We had to be contented with that much until the boys landed and told us their story—how they cleared the sky above the low-level Mitchells; how they were intercepted by five scared Nips and downed three of them within ten seconds; how the Mitchells plowed up the strip with their bombs, and then our boys followed in a strafe, viciously attacking everything they could find, until their ammo was nearly gone.

Pandau never recovered from the devastation of that raid. Three weeks later the first Australian patrols, ragged and bearded, slipped around the perimeter of the base. In two days, after a short, bitter fight, a brawny Australian Brigadier stretched out for a much needed nap, on a captured Jap hammock, in the bullet-scarred Jap headquarters. Pandau had fallen.

Among the trophies that the Aussies found at Pandau were two which came to the attention of the Intelligence Section, and subsequently into my possession. One was a class ring from one of our Eastern universities. It was found on a dead Jap officer, along with a photograph he had taken of a recent execution ceremony. None of us wanted the photograph. I gave the ring to Davis, and he enclosed it in the second letter he wrote to Binky's mother.

The other souvenir is simply a broken record—an unmarked eight-inch disk, cracked down the center. It was found in the wreckage of what had once been a recording machine. The enemy used them occasionally to pick up our radio talk and play it back at his leisure. This disk is facing me, on my desk. Although the crack makes it difficult, it is possible to play it on any phonograph. It's not very interesting—just some dull Army radio messages, one of them from a lost flyer who is trying to land at a place called "Outhouse."

Now that I've finished this story, I think I'll take that record outside and smash it to bits.

ACT OF FAITH

The setting is an army post in France, and in the beginning the
all-important question is where the money is to come from
to finance three GI's on a well-deserved leave. "You might as
well be dead," they argue, convincingly enough, "as be in
Paris broke." The conflict is resolved not by a loan from the
captain, who has recently lost eleven hundred francs in
a poker game, but by a truly inspiring sacrifice on the part of
Norman Seeger, one of the three.

Although the war is over, Norman Seeger continues to be
disturbed about the tragic fate of the Jewish people in
Europe and, ironically, about the aftermath of the war at home
in Ohio. He has just had a letter from home. When Seeger
finishes his father's letter, the reader will appreciate Seeger's
anxiety and the full extent of his act of faith.

P resent it to him in a pitiful light," Olson was saying as they
picked their way through the almost frozen mud toward the orderly-room
tent. "Three combat-scarred veterans, who fought their way from
Omaha Beach to . . . What was the name of the town we fought our
way to?"

"Königstein," Seeger said.

"Königstein." Olson lifted his right foot heavily out of a puddle and
stared admiringly at the three pounds of mud clinging to his overshoe.
"The backbone of the Army. The noncommissioned officer. We deserve
better of our country. Mention our decorations, in passing."

"What decorations should I mention?" Seeger asked. "The Marks-
man's Medal?"

"Never quite made it," Olson said. "I had a cross-eyed scorer at
the butts. Mention the Bronze Star, the Silver Star, the Croix de Guerre
with palms, the Unit Citation, the Congressional Medal of Honor."

"I'll mention them all." Seeger grinned. "You don't think the C.O.'ll
notice that we haven't won most of them, do you?"

441

"Gad, sir," Olson said with dignity, "do you think that one Southern military gentleman will dare doubt the word of another Southern military gentleman in the hour of victory?"

"I come from Ohio," Seeger said.

"Welch comes from Kansas," Olson said, coolly staring down a second lieutenant who was passing. The lieutenant made a nervous little jerk with his hand, as though he expected a salute, then kept it rigid, as a slight, superior smile of scorn twisted at the corner of Olson's mouth. The lieutenant dropped his eyes and splashed on through the mud. "You've heard of Kansas," Olson said. "Magnolia-scented Kansas."

"Of course," said Seeger. "I'm no fool."

"Do your duty by your men, Sergeant." Olson stopped to wipe the cold rain off his face and lectured him. "Highest-ranking noncom present took the initiative and saved his comrades, at great personal risk, above and beyond the call of you-know-what, in the best traditions of the American Army."

"I will throw myself in the breach," Seeger said.

"Welch and I can't ask more," said Olson.

They walked heavily through the mud on the streets between the rows of tents. The camp stretched drearily over the Reims plain, with the rain beating on the sagging tents. The division had been there over three weeks, waiting to be shipped home, and all the meagre diversions of the neighborhood had been sampled and exhausted, and there was an air of watchful suspicion and impatience with the military life hanging over the camp now, and there was even reputed to be a staff sergeant in C Company who was laying odds they would not get back to America before July 4th.

"I'm redeployable," Olson sang. "It's so enjoyable." It was a jingle he had composed, to no recognizable melody, in the early days after the victory in Europe, when he had added up his points and found they came to only sixty-three, but he persisted in singing it. He was a short, round boy who had been flunked out of air cadets' school and transferred to the infantry but whose spirits had not been damaged in the process. He had a high, childish voice and a pretty, baby face. He was very good-natured, and had a girl waiting for him at the University of California, where he intended to finish his course at government expense when he got out of the Army, and he was just the type who is killed off early and predictably and sadly in moving pictures about the war, but he had gone through four campaigns and six major battles without a scratch.

Seeger was a large, lanky boy, with a big nose, who had been wounded at St.-Lô but had come back to his outfit in the Siegfried Line quite unchanged. He was cheerful and dependable and he knew his business. He had broken in five or six second lieutenants, who had later been killed or wounded, and the C.O. had tried to get him commissioned in the field, but the war had ended while the paperwork was being fumbled over at headquarters.

They reached the door of the orderly tent and stopped. "Be brave, Sergeant," Olson said. "Welch and I are depending on you."

"O.K.," Seeger said, and went in.

The tent had the dank, Army-canvas smell that had been so much a part of Seeger's life in the past three years. The company clerk was reading an October, 1945, issue of the Buffalo *Courier-Express,* which had just reached him, and Captain Taney, the company C.O., was seated at a sawbuck table which he used as a desk, writing a letter to his wife, his lips pursed with effort. He was a small, fussy man, with sandy hair that was falling out. While the fighting had been going on, he had been lean and tense and his small voice had been cold and full of authority. But now he had relaxed, and a little pot belly was creeping up under his belt and he kept the top button of his trousers open when he could do it without too public loss of dignity. During the war, Seeger had thought of him as a natural soldier—tireless, fanatic about detail, aggressive, severely anxious to kill Germans. But in the last few months, Seeger had seen him relapsing gradually and pleasantly into the small-town hardware merchant he had been before the war, sedentary and a little shy, and, as he had once told Seeger, worried, here in the bleak champagne fields of France, about his daughter, who had just turned twelve and had a tendency to go after the boys and had been caught by her mother kissing a fifteen-year-old neighbor in the hammock after school.

"Hello, Seeger," he said, returning the salute with a mild, offhand gesture. "What's on your mind?"

"Am I disturbing you, sir?"

"Oh, no. Just writing a letter to my wife. You married, Seeger?" He peered at the tall boy standing before him.

"No, sir."

"It's very difficult," Taney sighed, pushing dissatisfiedly at the letter before him. "My wife complains I don't tell her I love her often enough. Been married fifteen years. You'd think she'd know by now." He smiled at Seeger. "I thought you were going to Paris," he said. "I signed the passes yesterday."

"That's what I came to see you about, sir."

"I suppose something's wrong with the passes." Taney spoke resignedly, like a man who has never quite got the hang of Army regulations and has had requisitions, furloughs, and requests for courts-martial returned for correction in a baffling flood.

"No, sir," Seeger said. "The passes're fine. They start tomorrow.

Well, it's just—" He looked around at the company clerk, who was on the sports page.

"This confidential?" Taney asked.

"If you don't mind, sir."

"Johnny," Taney said to the clerk, "go stand in the rain someplace."

"Yes, sir," the clerk said, and slowly got up and walked out.

Taney looked shrewdly at Seeger and spoke in a secret whisper. "You pick up anything?" he asked.

Seeger grinned. "No, sir, haven't had my hands on a girl since Strasbourg."

"Ah, that's good." Taney leaned back, relieved, happy that he didn't have to cope with the disapproval of the Medical Corps.

"It's—well," said Seeger, embarrassed, "It's hard to say—but it's money."

Taney shook his head sadly. "I know."

"We haven't been paid for three months, sir, and—"

"Damn it!" Taney stood up and shouted furiously. "I would like to take every bloody, chair-warming old lady in the Finance Department and wring their necks."

The clerk stuck his head into the tent. "Anything wrong? You call for me, sir?"

"No!" Taney shouted. "Get out of here!"

The clerk ducked out.

Taney sat down again. "I suppose," he said, in a more normal voice, "they have their problems. Outfits being broken up, being moved all over the place. But it's rugged."

"It wouldn't be so bad," Seeger said, "but we're going to Paris tomorrow. Olson, Welch, and myself. And you need money in Paris."

"Don't I know it?" Taney wagged his head. "Do you know what I paid for a bottle of champagne on the Place Pigalle in September?" He paused significantly. "I won't tell you. You wouldn't have any respect for me the rest of your life."

Seeger laughed. "Hanging is too good for the guy who thought up the rate of exchange," he said.

"I don't care if I never see another franc as long as I live." Taney waved his letter in the air, although it had been dry for a long time.

There was silence in the tent, and Seeger swallowed a little embarrassedly. "Sir," he said, "the truth is, I've come to borrow some money for Welch, Olson, and myself. We'll pay it back out of the first pay we get, and that can't be too long from now. If you don't want to give it to us, just tell me and I'll understand and get the hell out of here. We don't like to ask, but you might just as well be dead as be in Paris broke."

Taney stopped waving his letter and put it down thoughtfully. He peered at it, wrinkling his brow, looking like an aged bookkeeper in the single, gloomy light that hung in the middle of the tent.

"Just say the word, Captain," Seeger said, "and I'll blow."

"Stay where you are, son," said Taney. He dug in his shirt pocket and took out a worn, sweat-stained wallet. He looked at it for a moment. "Alligator," he said, with automatic, absent pride. "My wife sent it to me when we were in England. Pounds don't fit in it. However . . ." He opened it and took out all the contents. There was a small pile of francs on the table in front of him when he finished. He counted them. "Four hundred francs," he said. "Eight bucks."

"Excuse me," Seeger said humbly. "I shouldn't've asked."

"Delighted," Taney said vigorously. "Absolutely delighted." He started dividing the francs into two piles. "Truth is, Seeger, most of my money goes home in allotments. And the truth is, I lost eleven hundred francs in a poker game three nights ago, and I ought to be ashamed of myself. Here." He shoved one pile toward Seeger. "Two hundred francs."

Seeger looked down at the frayed, meretricious paper, which always seemed to him like stage money anyway. "No, sir," he said. "I can't take it."

"Take it," Taney said. "That's a direct order."

Seeger slowly picked up the money, not looking at Taney. "Sometime, sir," he said, "after we get out, you have to come over to my house, and you and my father and my brother and I'll go on a real drunk."

"I regard that," Taney said gravely, "as a solemn commitment."

They smiled at each other, and Seeger started out.

"Have a drink for me," said Taney, "at the Café de la Paix. A small drink." He was sitting down to tell his wife he loved her when Seeger went out of the tent.

Olson fell into step with Seeger and they walked silently through the mud between the tents.

"Well, *mon vieux?*" Olson said finally.

"Two hundred francs," said Seeger.

Olson groaned. "Two hundred francs! We won't be able to pinch a whore's behind on the Boulevard des Capucines for two hundred francs. That miserable, penny-loving Yankee!"

"He only had four hundred," Seeger said.

"I revise my opinion," said Olson.

They walked disconsolately and heavily back toward their tent.

Olson spoke only once before they got there. "These raincoats," he said, patting his. "Most ingenious invention of the war. Highest saturation point of any modern fabric. Collect more water per square inch, and hold it, than any material known to man. All hail the quartermaster!"

Welch was waiting at the entrance of their tent. He was standing there peering excitedly and shortsightedly out at the rain through his glasses, looking angry and tough, like a big-city hack driver, individual and incorruptible even in the ten-million colored uniform. Every time Seeger came upon Welch unexpectedly, he couldn't help smiling at the belligerent stance, the harsh stare through the steel-rimmed G.I. glasses, which had nothing at all to do with the way Welch really was. "It's a family inheritance," Welch had once explained. "My whole family stands as though we were getting ready to rap a drunk with a beer glass. Even my old lady." Welch had six brothers, all devout, according to Welch, and Seeger from time to time idly pictured them standing in a row, on Sunday mornings in church, seemingly on the verge of general violence, amid the hushed Latin and the Sabbath millinery.

"How much?" Welch asked loudly.

"Don't make us laugh," Olson said, pushing past him into the tent.

"What do you think I could get from the French for my combat jacket?" Seeger said. He went into the tent and lay down on his cot.

Welch followed them in and stood between the two of them. "Boys," he said, "on a man's errand."

"I can just see us now," Olson murmured, lying on his cot with his hands clasped behind his head, "painting Montmartre red. Please bring on the naked dancing girls. Four bucks' worth."

"I am not worried," Welch announced.

"Get out of here." Olson turned over on his stomach.

"I know where we can put our hands on sixty-five bucks." Welch looked triumphantly first at Olson, then at Seeger.

Olson turned over slowly and sat up. "I'll kill you," he said, "if you're kidding."

"While you guys are wasting your time fooling around with the infantry," Welch said, "I used my head. I went into Reems and used my head."

"Rance," Olson said automatically. He had had two years of French in college and he felt, now that the war was over, that he had to introduce his friends to some of his culture.

"I got to talking to a captain in the Air Force," Welch said eagerly. "A little, fat old paddle-footed captain that never got higher off the ground than the second floor of Com Z headquarters, and he told me that what he would admire to do more than anything else is take home a nice shiny German Luger pistol with him to show to the boys back in Pacific Grove, California."

Silence fell on the tent, and Welch and Olson looked at Seeger.

"Sixty-five bucks for a Luger, these days," Olson said, "is a very good figure."

"They've been sellin' for as low as thirty-five," said Welch hesitantly. "I'll bet," he said to Seeger, "you could sell yours now and buy another one back when you got some dough, and make a clear twenty-five on the deal."

Seeger didn't say anything. He had killed the owner of the Luger, an enormous S.S. major, in Coblenz, behind some bales of paper in a warehouse, and the major had fired at Seeger three times with it, once nicking his helmet, before Seeger hit him in the face at twenty feet. Seeger had kept the Luger, a heavy, well-balanced gun, lugging it with him, hiding it at the bottom of his bedroll, oiling it three times a week, avoiding all opportunities of selling it, although he had once been offered a hundred dollars for it and several times eighty and ninety, while the war was still on, before German weapons became a glut on the market.

"Well," said Welch, "there's no hurry. I told the captain I'd see him tonight around eight o'clock in front of the Lion d'Or Hotel. You got five hours to make up your mind. Plenty of time."

"Me," said Olson, after a pause, "I won't say anything."

Seeger looked reflectively at his feet, and the two other men avoided looking at him.

Welch dug in his pocket. "I forgot," he said. "I picked up a letter for you." He handed it to Seeger.

"Thanks," Seeger said. He opened it absently, thinking about the Luger.

"Me," said Olson, "I won't say a bloody word. I'm just going to lie here and think about that nice, fat Air Force captain."

Seeger grinned a little at him and went to the tent opening to read the letter in the light. The letter was from his father, and even from one glance at the handwriting, scrawly and hurried and spotted, so different from his father's usual steady, handsome, professorial script, he knew that something was wrong.

"Dear Norman," it read, "sometime in the future, you must forgive me for writing this letter. But I have been holding this in so long, and there is no one here I can talk to, and because of your brother's condition I must pretend to be cheerful and optimistic all the time at home, both with him and your mother, who has never been the same since Leonard was killed. You're the oldest now, and although I know we've never talked very seriously about anything before, you have been through a great deal by now, and I imagine you must have matured considerably, and you've seen so many different places and people. Norman, I need help. While the war was on and you were fighting, I kept this to myself. It wouldn't have been fair to burden you with this. But now the war is over, and I no longer feel I can stand up under this alone. And you will have to face it sometime when you get home, if you haven't faced it already, and perhaps we can help each other by facing it together."

"I'm redeployable. It's so enjoyable," Olson was singing softly, on his cot. He fell silent after his burst of song.

Seeger blinked his eyes in the gray, wintry, rainy light, and went on reading his father's letter, on the stiff white stationery with the university letterhead in polite engraving at the top of each page.

"I've been feeling this coming on for a long time," the letter continued, "but it wasn't until last Sunday morning that something happened to make me feel it in its full force. I don't know how much you've guessed about the reason for Jacob's discharge from the Army. It's true he was pretty badly wounded in the leg at Metz, but I've asked around, and I know that men with worse wounds were returned to duty after hospitalization. Jacob got a medical discharge, but I don't think it was for the shrapnel wound in his thigh. He is suffering now from what I suppose you call combat fatigue, and he is subject to fits of depression and hallucinations. Your mother and I thought that as time went by and the war and the Army receded, he would grow better. Instead, he is growing worse. Last Sunday morning when I came down into the living room from upstairs he was crouched in his old uniform, next to the window, peering out."

"What the hell," Olson was saying. "If we don't get the sixty-five bucks we can always go to the Louvre. I understand the Mona Lisa is back."

"I asked Jacob what he was doing," the letter went on. "He didn't turn around. 'I'm observing,' he said. 'V-1s and V-2s. Buzz bombs and rockets. They're coming in by the hundred.' I tried to reason with him and he told me to crouch and save myself from flying glass. To humor him I got down on the floor beside him and tried to tell him the war was over, that we were in Ohio, 4,000 miles away from the nearest spot where bombs had fallen, that America had never been touched. He wouldn't listen. 'These're the new rocket bombs,' he said, 'for the Jews.' "

"Did you ever hear of the Panthéon?" Olson asked loudly.

"No," said Welch.

"It's free."

"I'll go," said Welch.

Seeger shook his head a little and blinked his eyes before he went back to the letter.

"After that," his father went on, "Jacob seemed to forget about the bombs from time to time, but he kept saying that the mobs were coming up the street armed with bazookas and Browning automatic rifles. He mumbled incoherently a good deal of the time and kept walking back and forth saying, 'What's the situation? Do you know what the situation is?' And once he told me he wasn't worried about himself, he was a soldier and he expected to be killed, but he was worried about Mother and myself and Leonard and you. He seemed to forget that Leonard was dead. I tried to calm him and get him back to bed before your mother came down, but he refused and wanted to set out immediately to rejoin his division. It was all terribly disjointed, and at one time he took the ribbon he got for winning the Bronze Star and threw it in the fireplace, then he got down on his hands and knees and picked it out of the ashes and made me pin it on him again, and he kept repeating, 'This is when they are coming for the Jews.' "

"The next war I'm in," said Olson, "they don't get me under the rank of colonel."

It had stopped raining by now, and Seeger folded the unfinished letter and went outside. He walked slowly down to the end of the company street, and, facing out across the empty, soaked French fields, scarred and neglected by various armies, he stopped and opened the letter again.

"I don't know what Jacob went through in the Army," his father wrote, "that has done this to him. He never talks to me about the war and he refuses to go to a psychoanalyst, and from time to time he is his own bouncing, cheerful self, playing handball in the afternoons and going around with a large group of girls. But he has devoured all the concentration-camp reports, and I found him weeping when the newspapers reported that a hundred Jews were killed in Tripoli some time ago.

"The terrible thing is, Norman, that I find myself coming to believe that it is not neurotic for a Jew to behave like this today. Perhaps Jacob is the normal one, and I, going about my business, teaching economics in a quiet classroom, pretending to understand that the world is comprehensible and orderly, am really the mad one. I ask you once more to forgive me for writing you a letter like this, so different from any letter or any conversation I've ever had with you. But it is crowding me, too. I do not see rockets and bombs, but I see other things.

"Wherever you go these days—restaurants, hotels, clubs, trains— you seem to hear talk about the Jews, mean, hateful, murderous talk. Whatever page you turn to in the newspapers, you seem to find an article about Jews being killed somewhere on the face of the globe. And there are large, influential newspapers and well-known columnists who each day are growing more and more outspoken and more popular. The day that Roosevelt died I heard a drunken man yelling outside a bar, 'Finally they got the Jew out of the White House.' And some of the people who heard him merely laughed, and nobody stopped him. And on V-J Day, in celebration, hoodlums in Los Angeles savagely beat a Jewish writer. It's difficult to know what to do, whom to fight, where to look for allies.

"Three months ago, for example, I stopped my Thursday-night poker game, after playing with the same men for over ten years. John Reilly happened to say that the Jews got rich out of the war, and when I demanded an apology, he refused, and when I looked around at the faces of the men who had been my friends for so long, I could see they were not with me. And when I left the house, no one said good night to me. I know the poison was spreading from Germany before the war and during it, but I had not realized it had come so close.

"And in my economics class, I find myself idiotically hedging in my lectures. I discover that I am loath to praise any liberal writer or any liberal act, and find myself somehow annoyed and frightened to see an article of criticism of existing abuses signed by a Jewish name. And I hate to see Jewish names on important committees, and hate to read of Jews fighting for the poor, the oppressed, the cheated and hungry. Somehow, even in a country where my family has lived a hundred years, the enemy has won this subtle victory over me—he has made me disfranchise myself from honest causes by calling them foreign, Communist, using Jewish names connected with them as ammunition against them.

"Most hateful of all, I found myself looking for Jewish names in the casualty lists and secretly being glad when I saw them there, to prove that there, at least, among the dead and wounded, we belonged. Three times, thanks to you and your brothers, I found our name there, and, may God forgive me, at the expense of your blood and your brother's life, through my tears, I felt that same twitch of satisfaction.

"When I read the newspapers and see another story that Jews are still being killed in Poland, or Jews are requesting that they be given back their homes in France or that they be allowed to enter some country where they will not be murdered, I am annoyed with them. I feel that they are boring the rest of the world with their problems, that they are making demands upon the rest of the world by being killed, that they are disturbing everyone by being hungry and asking for the return of their property. If we could all fall in through the crust of the earth and vanish in one hour, with our heroes and poets and prophets and martyrs, perhaps we would be doing the memory of the Jewish race a service.

"This is how I feel today, son. I need some help. You've been to the war, you've fought and killed men, you've seen the people of other countries. Maybe you understand things that I don't understand. Maybe you see some hope somewhere. Help me. Your loving Father."

Seeger folded the letter slowly, not seeing what he was doing, because the tears were burning his eyes. He walked slowly and aimlessly across the dead, sodden grass of the empty field, away from the camp. He tried to wipe away his tears, because, with his eyes full and dark, he kept seeing his father and brother crouched in the old-fashioned liv ing room in Ohio, and hearing his brother, dressed in the old, discarded uniform, saying, "These're the new rocket bombs. For the Jews."

He sighed, looking out over the bleak, wasted land. Now, he thought, now I have to think about it. He felt a slight, unreasonable twinge of anger at his father for presenting him with the necessity of thinking about it. The Army was good about serious problems. While you were fighting, you were too busy and frightened and weary to think about anything, and at other times you were relaxing, putting your brain on a shelf, postponing everything to that impossible time of clarity and beauty after the war. Well, now, here was the impossible, clear, beautiful time, and here was his father, demanding that he think. There are all sorts of Jews, he thought: there are the sort whose every waking moment is ridden by the knowledge of Jewishness; who see signs against the Jew in every smile on a streetcar, every whisper; who see pogroms in every newspaper article, threats in every change of the weather, scorn in every handshake, death behind each closed door. He had not been like that. He was young, he was big and healthy and easygoing, and people of all kinds had liked him all his life, in the Army and out. In America, especially, what was going on in Europe had been remote, unreal, unrelated to him. The chanting, bearded old men burning in the Nazi furnaces, and the dark-eyed women screaming prayers in Polish and Russian and German as they were pushed naked into the gas chambers, had seemed as shadowy and almost as unrelated to him, as he trotted out onto the stadium field for a football game, as they must have been to the men named O'Dwyer and Wickersham and Poole who played in the line beside him.

These tortured people had seemed more related to him in Europe. Again and again, in the towns that had been taken back from the Germans, gaunt, gray-faced men had stopped him humbly, looking searchingly at him, and had asked, peering at his long, lined, grimy face under the anonymous helmet, "Are you a Jew?" Sometimes they asked it in English, sometimes French, sometimes Yiddish. He didn't know French or Yiddish, but he learned to recognize that question. He had never understood exactly why they asked the question, since they never demanded anything of him, rarely even could speak to him. Then, one day in Strasbourg, a little, bent old man and a small, shapeless woman had stopped him and asked, in English, if he was Jewish. "Yes," he'd said, smiling at them. The two old people had smiled widely, like children. "Look," the old man had said to his wife. "A young American soldier. A Jew. And so large and strong." He had touched Seeger's arm reverently with the tips of his fingers, then had touched the Garand Seeger was carrying. "And such a beautiful rifle."

And there, for a moment, although he was not particularly sensitive, Seeger had got an inkling of why he had been stopped and questioned by so many before. Here, to these bent, exhausted old people, ravaged of their families, familiar with flight and death for so many years, was a symbol of continuing life. A large young man in the uniform of the liberator, blood, as they thought, of their blood, but not in hiding, not quivering in fear and helplessness, but striding secure and victorious down the street, armed and capable of inflicting terrible destruction on his enemies.

Seeger had kissed the old lady on the cheek and she had wept, and the old man had scolded her for it while shaking Seeger's hand fervently and thankfully before saying good-bye.

Thinking back on it, he knew that it was silly to pretend that, even before his father's letter, he had been like any other American soldier going through the war. When he had stood over the huge, dead S.S. major with the face blown in by his bullets in the warehouse in Coblenz, and taken the pistol from the dead hand, he had tasted a strange little extra flavor of triumph. How many Jews, he'd thought, has this man killed? How fitting it is that I've killed him. Neither Olson nor Welch, who were like his brothers, would have felt that in picking up the Luger, its barrel still hot from the last shots its owner had fired before dying. And he had resolved that he was going to make sure to take this gun back with him to America, and plug it and keep it on his desk at home, as a kind of vague, half-understood sign to himself that justice had once been done and he had been its instrument.

Maybe, he thought, maybe I'd better take it back with me, but not as a memento. Not plugged, but loaded. America by now was a strange country for him. He had been away a long time and he wasn't sure what was waiting for him when he got home. If the mobs were coming down the street toward his house, he was not going to die singing and praying.

When he had been taking basic training, he'd heard a scrawny, clerkish soldier from Boston talking at the other end of the PX bar, over the watered beer. "The boys at the office," the scratchy voice was saying, "gave me a party before I left. And they told me one thing. 'Charlie,' they said, 'hold onto your bayonet. We're going to be able to use it when you get back. On the Yids.' "

He hadn't said anything then, because he'd felt it was neither possible nor desirable to fight against every random overheard voice raised against the Jews from one end of the world to the other. But again and again, at odd moments, lying on a barracks cot, or stretched out trying to sleep on the floor of a ruined French farmhouse, he had heard that voice, harsh, satisfied, heavy with hate and ignorance, saying above the beery grumble of apprentice soldiers at the bar, "Hold onto your bayonet."

And the other stories. Jews collected stories of hatred and injustice and inklings of doom like a special, lunatic kind of miser. The story of the Navy officer, commander of a small vessel off the Aleutians, who in the officers' wardroom had complained that he hated the Jews because it was the Jews who had demanded that the Germans be beaten first, and the forces in the Pacific had been starved in consequence. And when one of his junior officers, who had just come aboard, had objected and told the commander that he was a Jew, the commander had risen from the table and said, "Mister, the Constitution of the United States says I have to serve in the same Navy with Jews, but it doesn't say I have to eat at the same table with them." In the fogs and the cold, swelling Arctic seas off the Aleutians, in a small boat, subject to sudden, mortal attack at any moment. . . . And the million other stories. Jews, even the most normal and best adjusted, became living treasuries of them, scraps of malice and bloodthirstiness, clever and confusing and cunningly twisted so that every act by every Jew became suspect and blameworthy and hateful. Seeger had heard the stories and had made an almost conscious effort to forget them. Now, holding his father's letter in his hand, he remembered them all.

He stared unseeingly out in front of him. Maybe, he thought, maybe it would've been better to have been killed in the war, like Leonard. Simpler. Leonard would never have to face a crowd coming for his mother and father. Leonard would not have to listen and collect these hideous, fascinating little stories that made of every Jew a stranger in any town, on any field, on the face of the earth. He had come so close to being killed so many times; it would have been so easy, so neat and final. Seeger shook his head. It was ridiculous to feel like that, and he was ashamed of himself for the weak moment. At the age of twenty-one, death was not an answer.

"Seeger!" It was Olson's voice. He and Welch had sloshed silently up behind Seeger, standing in the open field. "Seeger, *mon vieux,* what're you doing—grazing?"

Seeger turned slowly to them. "I wanted to read my letter," he said.

Olson looked closely at him. They had been together so long, through so many things, that flickers and hints of expression on each other's faces were recognized and acted upon. "Anything wrong?" Olson asked.

"No," said Seeger. "Nothing much."

"Norman," Welch said, his voice young and solemn. "Norman, we've been talking, Olson and me. We decided—you're pretty attached to that Luger, and maybe, if you—well—"

"What he's trying to say," said Olson, "is we withdraw the request. If you want to sell it, O.K. If you don't, don't do it for our sake. Honest."

453

Seeger looked at them standing there, disreputable and tough and familiar. "I haven't made up my mind yet," he said.

"Anything you decide," Welch said oratorically, "is perfectly all right with us. Perfectly."

The three of them walked aimlessly and silently across the field, away from camp. As they walked, their shoes making a wet, sliding sound in the damp, dead grass, Seeger thought of the time Olson had covered him in the little town outside Cherbourg, when Seeger had been caught, going down the side of a street, by four Germans with a machine gun in the second story of a house on the corner and Olson had had to stand out in the middle of the street with no cover at all for more than a minute, firing continuously, so that Seeger could get away alive. And he thought of the time outside St.-Lô when he had been wounded and had lain in a minefield for three hours and Welch and Captain Taney had come looking for him in the darkness and had found him and picked him up and run for it, all of them expecting to get blown up any second. And he thought of all the drinks they'd had together, and the long marches and the cold winter together, and all the girls they'd gone out with together, and he thought of his father and brother crouching behind the window in Ohio waiting for the rockets and the crowds armed with Browning automatic rifles.

"Say." He stopped and stood facing them. "Say, what do you guys think of the Jews?"

Welch and Olson looked at each other, and Olson glanced down at the letter in Seeger's hand.

"Jews?" Olson said finally. "What're they? Welch, you ever hear of the Jews?"

Welch looked thoughtfully at the gray sky. "No," he said. "But remember, I'm an uneducated fellow."

"Sorry, bud," Olson said, turning to Seeger. "We can't help you. Ask us another question. Maybe we'll do better."

Seeger peered at the faces of his friends. He would have to rely upon them, later on, out of uniform, on their native streets, more than he had ever relied on them on the bullet-swept street and in the dark minefield in France. Welch and Olson stared back at him, troubled, their faces candid and tough and dependable.

"What time," Seeger asked, "did you tell that captain you'd meet him?"

"Eight o'clock," Welch said. "But we don't have to go. If you have any feeling about that gun—"

"We'll meet him," Seeger said. "We can use that sixty-five bucks."

"Listen," Olson said, "I know how much you like that gun, and I'll feel like a heel if you sell it."

"Forget it," Seeger said, starting to walk again. "What could I use it for in America?"

Pearl S. Buck

THE ENEMY

This story may help to develop an awareness of our need to understand "the enemy." Pearl Buck, who has done so much to create a sympathetic and intelligent understanding of the Chinese—as in her Pulitzer-prize-winning novel *The Good Earth*—here turns her attention to the Japanese. The story was published in 1942, a time when feeling against the Japanese people, as well as their military leaders, was running high. The ambivalence of Dr. Sadao Hoki's feelings is an example of what we need to try to understand. The whole story is an important contribution to the literature of international understanding, but its concluding paragraphs are especially revealing.

The fortunes of war have placed Dr. Hoki, with his American medical training and first-hand knowledge of *his* enemy, in a distressing dilemma, a dilemma deepened by the ethics of his profession. Mrs. Buck's dramatization of the Japanese mind in action reveals a mental conflict between funda- mental human values and the imperatives of war, for the doctor (like ourselves) has not entirely escaped the pressures of racial and national prejudice.

D r. Sadao Hoki's house was built on a spot of the Japanese coast where as a little boy he had often played. The low square stone house was set upon rocks well above a narrow beach that was outlined with bent pines. As a boy Sadao had climbed the pines, supporting him- self on his bare feet, as he had seen men do in the South Seas when they climbed for coconuts. His father had taken him often to the islands of those seas, and never had he failed to say to the little grave boy at his side, "Those islands yonder, they are the stepping stones to the future for Japan."

"Where shall we step from them?" Sadao had asked seriously.

"Who knows?" his father had answered. "Who can limit our future? It depends on what we make it."

Sadao had taken this into his mind as he did everything his father said, his father who never joked or played with him but who spent infinite pains upon him who was his only son. Sadao knew that his education was his father's chief concern. For this reason he had been sent at twenty-two to America to learn all that could be learned of surgery and medicine. He had come back at thirty and before his father died he had seen Sadao become famous not only as a surgeon but as a scientist. Because he was now perfecting a discovery which would render wounds entirely clean he had not been sent abroad with the troops. Also, he knew, there was some slight danger that the old General might need an operation for a condition for which he was now being treated medically, and for this possibility Sadao was being kept in Japan.

Clouds were rising from the ocean now. The unexpected warmth of the past few days had at night drawn heavy fog from the cold waves. Sadao watched mists hide outlines of a little island near the shore and then come creeping up the beach below the house, wreathing around the pines. In a few minutes fog would be wrapped about the house too. Then he would go into the room where Hana, his wife, would be waiting for him with the two children.

But at this moment the door opened and she looked out, a dark-blue woolen *haori* over her kimono. She came to him affectionately and put her arm through his as he stood, smiled and said nothing. He had met Hana in America, but he had waited to fall in love with her until he was sure she was Japanese. His father would never have received her unless she had been pure in her race. He wondered often whom he would have married if he had not met Hana, and by what luck he had found her in the most casual way, by chance literally, at an American professor's house. The professor and his wife had been kind people, anxious to do something for their few foreign students, and the students, though bored, had accepted this kindness. Sadao had often told Hana how nearly he had not gone to Professor Harley's house that night— the rooms were so small, the food so bad, the professor's wife so voluble. But he had gone and there he had found Hana, a new student, and had felt he would love her if it were at all possible.

Now he felt her hand on his arm and was aware of the pleasure it gave him, even though they had been married years enough to have the two children. For they had not married heedlessly in America. They had finished their work at school and had come home to Japan, and when his father had seen her the marriage had been arranged in the old Japanese way, although Sadao and Hana had talked everything over beforehand. They were perfectly happy. She laid her cheek against his arm.

It was at this moment that both of them saw something black come out of the mists. It was a man. He was flung up out of the ocean—

flung, it seemed, to his feet by a breaker. He staggered a few steps, his body outlined against the mist, his arms above his head. Then the curled mists hid him again.

"Who is that?" Hana cried. She dropped Sadao's arm and they both leaned over the railing of the veranda. Now they saw him again. The man was on his hands and knees crawling. Then they saw him fall on his face and lie there.

"A fisherman perhaps," Sadao said, "washed from his boat." He ran quickly down the steps and behind him Hana came, her wide sleeves flying. A mile or two away on either side there were fishing villages, but here was only the bare and lonely coast, dangerous with rocks. The surf beyond the beach was spiked with rocks. Somehow the man had managed to come through them—he must be badly torn.

They saw when they came toward him that indeed it was so. The sand on one side of him had already a stain of red soaking through.

"He is wounded," Sadao exclaimed. He made haste to the man, who lay motionless, his face in the sand. An old cap stuck to his head soaked with sea water. He was in wet rags of garments. Sadao stooped, Hana at his side, and turned the man's head. They saw the face.

"A white man!" Hana whispered.

Yes, it was a white man. The wet cap fell away and there was his wet yellow hair, long, as though for many weeks it had not been cut, and upon his young and tortured face was a rough yellow beard. He was unconscious and knew nothing that they did to him.

Now Sadao remembered the wound, and with his expert fingers he began to search for it. Blood flowed freshly at his touch. On the right side of his lower back Sadao saw that a gun wound had been reopened. The flesh was blackened with powder. Sometime, not many days ago, the man had been shot and had not been tended. It was bad chance that the rock had struck the wound.

"Oh, how he is bleeding!" Hana whispered again in a solemn voice. The mists screened them now completely, and at this time of day no one came by. The fishermen had gone home and even the chance beachcombers would have considered the day at an end.

"What shall we do with this man?" Sadao muttered. But his trained hands seemed of their own will to be doing what they could to stanch the fearful bleeding. He packed the wound with the sea moss that strewed the beach. The man moaned with pain in his stupor but he did not awaken.

"The best thing that we could do would be to put him back in the sea," Sadao said, answering himself.

Now that the bleeding was stopped for the moment he stood up and dusted the sand from his hands.

"Yes, undoubtedly that would be best," Hana said steadily. But she continued to stare down at the motionless man.

"If we sheltered a white man in our house we should be arrested and if we turned him over as a prisoner, he would certainly die," Sadao said.

"The kindest thing would be to put him back into the sea," Hana said. But neither of them moved. They were staring with a curious repulsion upon the inert figure.

"What is he?" Hana whispered.

"There is something about him that looks American," Sadao said. He took up the battered cap. Yes, there, almost gone, was the faint lettering. "A sailor," he said, "from an American warship." He spelled it out: "U.S. Navy." The man was a prisoner of war!

"He has escaped," Hana cried softly, "and that is why he is wounded."

"In the back," Sadao agreed.

They hesitated, looking at each other. Then Hana said with resolution:

"Come, are we able to put him back into the sea?"

"If I am able, are you?" Sadao asked.

"No," Hana said. "But if you can do it alone . . ."

Sadao hesitated again. "The strange thing is," he said, "that if the man were whole I could turn him over to the police without difficulty. I care nothing for him. He is my enemy. All Americans are my enemy. And he is only a common fellow. You see how foolish his face is. But since he is wounded . . ."

"You also cannot throw him back to the sea," Hana said. "Then there is only one thing to do. We must carry him into the house."

"But the servants?" Sadao inquired.

"We must simply tell them that we intend to give him to the police—as indeed we must, Sadao. We must think of the children and your position. It would endanger all of us if we did not give this man over as a prisoner of war."

"Certainly," Sadao agreed. "I would not think of doing anything else."

Thus agreed, together they lifted the man. He was very light, like a fowl that has been half-starved for a long time until it is only feathers and skeleton. So, his arms hanging, they carried him up the steps and into the side door of the house. This door opened into a passage and down the passage they carried the man toward an empty bedroom. It had been the bedroom of Sadao's father and since his death it had not been used. They laid the man on the deeply matted floor. Everything here had been Japanese to please the old man, who would never in his own home sit on a chair or sleep in a foreign bed. Hana went to the wall cupboards and slid back a door and took out a soft quilt. She hesitated. The quilt was covered with flowered silk and the lining was pure white silk.

"He is so dirty," she murmured in distress.

"Yes, he had better be washed," Sadao agreed. "If you will fetch hot water I will wash him."

"I cannot bear for you to touch him," she said. "We shall have to tell the servants he is here. I will tell Yumi now. She can leave the children for a few minutes and she can wash him."

Sadao considered a moment. "Let it be so," he agreed. "You tell Yumi and I will tell the others."

But the utter pallor of the man's unconscious face moved him first to stoop and feel his pulse. It was faint but it was there. He put his hand against the man's cold breast. The heart too was yet alive.

"He will die unless he is operated on," Sadao said, considering. "The question is whether he will not die anyway."

Hana cried out in fear. "Don't try to save him! What if he should live?"

"What if he should die?" Sadao replied. He stood gazing down on the motionless man. This man must have extraordinary vitality or he would have been dead by now. But then he was very young—perhaps not yet twenty-five.

"You mean die from the operation?" Hana asked.

"Yes," Sadao said.

Hana considered this doubtfully, and when she did not answer Sadao turned away. "At any rate something must be done with him," he said, "and first he must be washed." He went quickly out of the room and Hana came behind him. She did not wish to be left alone with the white man. He was the first she had seen since she left America and now he seemed to have nothing to do with those whom she had known there. Here he was her enemy, a menace, living or dead.

She turned to the nursery and called, "Yumi!"

But the children heard her voice and she had to go in for a moment and smile at them and play with the baby boy, now nearly three months old.

Over the baby's soft black hair she motioned with her mouth, "Yumi —come with me!"

"I will put the baby to bed," Yumi replied. "He is ready."

She went with Yumi into the bedroom next to the nursery and stood with the boy in her arms while Yumi spread the sleeping quilts on the floor and laid the baby between them.

Then Hana led the way quickly and softly to the kitchen. The two servants were frightened at what their master had just told them. The old gardener who was also a house servant pulled the few hairs on his upper lip.

"The master ought not to heal the wound of this white man," he said bluntly to Hana. "The white man ought to die. First he was shot. Then the sea caught him and wounded him with her rocks. If the master heals what the gun did and what the sea did they will take revenge on us."

"I will tell him what you say," Hana replied courteously. But she herself was also frightened, although she was not superstitious as the old man was. Could it ever be well to help an enemy? Nevertheless she told Yumi to fetch the hot water and bring it to the room where the white man was.

She went ahead and slid back the partitions. Sadao was not yet there. Yumi, following, put down her wooden bucket. Then she went over to the white man. When she saw him her thick lips folded themselves into stubbornness. "I have never washed a white man," she said, "and I will not wash so dirty a one now."

Hana cried at her severely, "You will do what your master commands you!"

"My master ought not to command me to wash the enemy," Yumi said stubbornly.

There was so fierce a look of resistance upon Yumi's round dull face that Hana felt unreasonably afraid. After all, if the servants should report something that was not as it happened?

"Very well," she said with dignity. "You understand we only want to bring him to his senses so that we can turn him over as a prisoner?"

"I will have nothing to do with it," Yumi said. "I am a poor person and it is not my business."

"Then please," Hana said gently, "return to your own work."

At once Yumi left the room. But this left Hana with the white man alone. She might have been too afraid to stay had not her anger at Yumi's stubbornness now sustained her.

"Stupid Yumi," she muttered fiercely. "Is this anything but a man? And a wounded helpless man!"

In the conviction of her own superiority she bent impulsively and untied the knotted rags that kept the white man covered. When she had his breast bare she dipped the small clean towel that Yumi had brought into the steaming hot water and washed his face carefully. The man's skin, though rough with exposure, was of a fine texture and must have been very blond when he was a child.

While she was thinking these thoughts, though not really liking the man better now that he was no longer a child, she kept on washing him until his upper body was quite clean. But she dared not turn him over.

Where was Sadao? Now her anger was ebbing and she was anxious again and she rose, wiping her hands on the wrung towel. Then lest the man be chilled she put the quilt over him.

"Sadao!" she called softly.

He had been about to come in when she called. His hand had been on the door and now he opened it. She saw that he had brought his surgeon's emergency bag and that he wore his surgeon's coat.

"You have decided to operate!" she cried.

"Yes," he said shortly. He turned his back to her and unfolded a sterilized towel upon the floor of the *takonoma* alcove, and put his instruments out upon it.

"Fetch towels," he said.

She went obediently, but how anxious now, to the linen shelves and took out the towels. There ought also to be old pieces of matting so that the blood would not ruin the fine floor covering. She went out to the back veranda where the gardener kept strips of matting with which to protect delicate shrubs on cold nights and took an armful of them.

But when she went back into the room, she saw this was useless. The blood had already soaked through the packing in the man's wound and had ruined the mat under him.

"Oh, the mat!" she cried.

"Yes, it is ruined," Sadao replied, as though he did not care. "Help me to turn him," he commanded her.

She obeyed him without a word, and he began to wash the man's back carefully.

"Yumi would not wash him," she said.

"Did you wash him then?" Sadao asked, not stopping for a moment his swift concise movements.

"Yes," she said.

He did not seem to hear her. But she was used to his absorption when he was at work. She wondered for a moment if it mattered to him what was the body upon which he worked so long as it was for the work he did so excellently.

"You will have to give the anesthetic if he needs it," he said.

"I?" she repeated blankly. "But never have I!"

"It is easy enough," he said impatiently.

He was taking out the packing now and the blood began to flow more quickly. He peered into the wound with the bright surgeon's light fastened on his forehead. "The bullet is still there," he said with cool interest. "Now I wonder how deep this rock wound is. If it is not too deep it may be that I can get the bullet. But the bleeding is not superficial. He has lost much blood."

At this moment Hana choked. He looked up and saw her face the color of sulphur.

"Don't faint," he said sharply. He did not put down his exploring instrument. "If I stop now the man will surely die." She clapped her hands to her mouth and leaped up and ran out of the room. Outside in the garden he heard her retching. But he went on with his work.

"It will be better for her to empty her stomach," he thought. He had forgotten that of course she had never seen an operation. But her distress and his inability to go to her at once made him impatient and irritable with this man who lay like dead under his knife.

"This man," he thought, "there is no reason under heaven why he should live."

Unconsciously this thought made him ruthless and he proceeded swiftly. In his dream the man moaned but Sadao paid no heed except to mutter at him.

"Groan," he muttered, "groan if you like. I am not doing this for my own pleasure. In fact, I do not know why I am doing it."

The door opened and there was Hana again. She had not stopped even to smooth back her hair.

"Where is the anesthetic?" she asked in a clear voice.

Sadao motioned with his chin. "It is as well that you came back," he said. "This fellow is beginning to stir."

She had the bottle and some cotton in her hand.

"But how shall I do it?" she asked.

"Simply saturate the cotton and hold it near his nostrils," Sadao replied without delaying for one moment the intricate detail of his work. "When he breathes badly move it away a little."

She crouched close to the sleeping face of the young American. It was a piteously thin face, she thought, and the lips were twisted. The man was suffering whether he knew it or not. Watching him, she wondered if the stories they heard sometimes of the sufferings of prisoners were true. They came like flickers of rumor, told by word of mouth and always contradicted. In the newspapers the reports were always that wherever the Japanese armies went the people received them gladly, with cries of joy at their liberation. But sometimes she remembered such men as General Takima, who at home beat his wife cruelly, though no one mentioned it now that he had fought so victorious a battle in Manchuria. If a man like that could be so cruel to a woman in his power, would he not be cruel to one like this for instance?

She hoped anxiously that this young man had not been tortured. It was at this moment that she observed deep red scars on his neck, just under the ear. "Those scars," she murmured, lifting her eyes to Sadao.

But he did not answer. At this moment he felt the tip of his instrument strike against something hard, dangerously near the kidney. All thought left him. He felt only the purest pleasure. He probed with his fingers, delicately, familiar with every atom of this human body. His old American professor of anatomy had seen to that knowledge. "Ignorance of the human body is the surgeon's cardinal sin, sirs!" he had thundered at his classes year after year. "To operate without as complete knowledge of the body as if you had made it—anything less than that is murder."

"It is not quite at the kidney, my friend," Sadao murmured. It was his habit to murmur to the patient when he forgot himself in an operation."My friend," he always called his patients and so now he did, forgetting that this was his enemy.

Then quickly, with the cleanest and most precise of incisions, the bullet was out. The man quivered but he was still unconscious. Nevertheless he muttered a few English words.

"Guts," he muttered, choking. "They got . . . my guts . . ."

"Sadao!" Hana cried sharply.

"Hush," Sadao said.

The man sank again into silence so profound that Sadao took up his wrist, hating the touch of it. Yes, there was still a pulse so faint, so feeble, but enough, if he wanted the man to live, to give hope. ·

"But certainly I do not want this man to live," he thought.

"No more anesthetic," he told Hana.

He turned as swiftly as though he had never paused and from his medicines he chose a small vial and from it filled a hypodermic and thrust it into the patient's left arm. Then, putting down the needle, he took the man's wrist again. The pulse under his fingers fluttered once or twice and then grew stronger.

"This man will live in spite of all," he said to Hana and sighed.

The young man woke, so weak, his blue eyes so terrified when he perceived where he was, that Hana felt compelled to apology. She served him herself, for none of the servants would enter the room.

When she came in the first time she saw him summon his strength to be prepared for some fearful thing.

"Don't be afraid," she begged him softly.

"How come . . . you speak English . . ." he gasped.

"I was a long time in America," she replied.

She saw that he wanted to reply to that but he could not, and so she knelt and fed him gently from the porcelain spoon. He ate unwillingly, but still he ate.

"Now you will soon be strong," she said, not liking him and yet moved to comfort him.

He did not answer.

When Sadao came in the third day after the operation he found the young man sitting up, his face bloodless with the effort.

"Lie down," Sadao cried. "Do you want to die?"

He forced the man down gently and strongly and examined the wound. "You may kill yourself if you do this sort of thing," he scolded.

"What are you going to do with me?" the boy muttered. He looked just now barely seventeen. "Are you going to hand me over?"

For a moment Sadao did not answer. He finished his examination and then pulled the silk quilt over the man.

"I do not know myself what I shall do with you," he said. "I ought of course to give you to the police. You are a prisoner of war—no, do not tell me anything." He put up his hand as he saw the young man about to speak. "Do not even tell me your name unless I ask it."

They looked at each other for a moment, and then the young man closed his eyes and turned his face to the wall.

"Okay," he whispered, his mouth a bitter line.

Outside the door Hana was waiting for Sadao. He saw at once that she was in trouble.

"Sadao, Yumi tells me the servants feel they cannot stay if we hide this man here any more," she said. "She tells me that they are saying that you and I were so long in America that we have forgotten to think of our own country first. They think we like Americans."

"It is not true," Sadao said harshly, "Americans are our enemies. But I have been trained not to let a man die if I can help it."

"The servants cannot understand that," she said anxiously.

"No," he agreed.

Neither seemed able to say more, and somehow the household dragged on. The servants grew daily more watchful. Their courtesy was as careful as ever, but their eyes were cold upon the pair to whom they were hired.

"It is clear what our master ought to do," the old gardener said one morning. He had worked with flowers all his life, and had been a specialist too in moss. For Sadao's father he had made one of the finest moss gardens in Japan, sweeping the bright green carpet constantly so that not a leaf or a pine needle marred the velvet of its surface. "My old master's son knows very well what he ought to do," he now said, pinching a bud from a bush as he spoke. "When the man was so near death why did he not let him bleed?"

"That young master is so proud of his skill to save life that he saves any life," the cook said contemptuously. She split a fowl's neck skilfully and held the fluttering bird and let its blood flow into the roots of a wistaria vine. Blood is the best of fertilizers, and the old gardener would not let her waste a drop of it.

"It is the children of whom we must think," Yumi said sadly. "What will be their fate if their father is condemned as a traitor?"

They did not try to hide what they said from the ears of Hana as she stood arranging the day's flowers in the veranda or a lily and also knew they spoke on purpose that she might hear. That they were right she knew too in most of her being. But there was another part of her which she herself could not understand. It was not sentimental liking of the prisoner. She had come to think of him as a prisoner. She had not liked him even yesterday when he had said in his impulsive way, "Anyway, let me tell you that my name is Tom." She had only bowed her little distant bow. She saw hurt in his eyes but she did not wish to assuage it. Indeed, he was a great trouble in this house.

As for Sadao, every day he examined the wound carefully. The last stitches had been pulled out this morning, and the young man would in a fortnight be nearly as well as ever. Sadao went back to his office and carefully typed a letter to the chief of police reporting the whole matter. "On the twenty-first day of February an escaped prisoner was washed up on the shore in front of my house." So far he typed and then he opened a secret drawer of his desk and put the unfinished report into it.

On the seventh day after that two things happened. In the morning the servants left together, their belongings tied in large square cotton kerchiefs. When Hana got up in the morning nothing was done, the house not cleaned and the food not prepared, and she knew what it meant. She was dismayed and even terrified, but her pride as a mistress would not allow her to show it. Instead, she inclined her head gracefully when they appeared before her in the kitchen, and she paid them off and thanked them for all that they had done for her. They were crying, but she did not cry. The cook and the gardener had served Sadao since he was a little boy in his father's house, and Yumi cried because of the children. She was so grieving that after she had gone she ran back to Hana.

"If the baby misses me too much tonight send for me. I am going to my own house and you know where it is."

"Thank you," Hana said smiling. But she told herself she would not send for Yumi however the baby cried.

She made the breakfast and Sadao helped with the children. Neither of them spoke of the servants beyond the fact that they were gone. But after Hana had taken morning food to the prisoner she came back to Sadao.

"Why is it we cannot see clearly what we ought to do?" she asked him. "Even the servants see more clearly than we do. Why are we different from other Japanese?"

Sadao did not answer. But a little later he went into the room where the prisoner was and said brusquely, "Today you may get up on your feet. I want you to stay up only five minutes at a time. Tomorrow you may try it twice as long. It would be well that you get back your strength as quickly as possible."

He saw the flicker of terror on the young face that was still very pale.

"Okay," the boy murmured. Evidently he was determined to say more. "I feel I ought to thank you, doctor, for having saved my life."

"Don't thank me too early," Sadao said coldly. He saw the flicker of terror again in the boy's eyes—terror as unmistakable as an animal's. The scars on his neck were crimson for a moment. Those scars! What were they? Sadao did not ask.

In the afternoon the second thing happened. Hana, working hard on unaccustomed labor, saw a messenger come to the door in official uniform. Her hands went weak and she could not draw her breath. The servants must have told already. She ran to Sadao, gasping, unable to utter a word. But by then the messenger had simply followed her through the garden and there he stood. She pointed at him helplessly.

Sadao looked up from his book. He was in his office, the outer partition of which was thrown open to the garden for the southern sunshine.

"What is it?" he asked the messenger and then he rose, seeing the man's uniform.

"You are to come to the palace," the man said, "the old General is in pain again."

"Oh," Hana breathed, "is that all?"

"All?" the messenger exclaimed. "Is it not enough?"

"Indeed it is," she replied. "I am very sorry."

When Sadao came to say good-by she was in the kitchen, but doing nothing. The children were asleep and she sat merely resting for a moment, more exhausted from her fright than from work.

"I thought they had come to arrest you," she said.

He gazed down into her anxious eyes. "I must get rid of this man for your sake," he said in distress. "Somehow I must get rid of him."

"Of course," the General said weakly, "I understand fully. But that is because I once took a degree in Princeton. So few Japanese have."

"I care nothing for the man, Excellency," Sadao said, "but having operated on him with such success . . ."

"Yes, yes," the General said. "It only makes me feel you more indispensable to me. Evidently you can save anyone—you are so skilled. You say you think I can stand one more such attack as I have had today?"

"Not more than one," Sadao said.

"Then certainly I can allow nothing to happen to you," the General said with anxiety. His long pale Japanese face became expressionless, which meant that he was in deep thought. "You cannot be arrested," the General said, closing his eyes. "Suppose you were condemned to death and the next day I had to have my operation?"

"There are other surgeons, Excellency," Sadao suggested.

"None I trust," the General replied. "The best ones have been trained by Germans and would consider the operation successful even if I died. I do not care for their point of view." He sighed. "It seems a pity that we cannot better combine the German ruthlessness with the American sentimentality. Then you could turn your prisoner over to execution and yet I could be sure you would not murder me while I was unconscious." The General laughed. He had an unusual sense of humor. "As a Japanese, could you not combine these two foreign elements?" he asked.

Sadao smiled. "I am not quite sure," he said, "but for your sake I would be willing to try, Excellency."

The General shook his head. "I had rather not be the test case," he said. He felt suddenly weak and overwhelmed with the cares of his life as an official in times such as these when repeated victory brought great responsibilities all over the south Pacific. "It is very unfortunate that this man should have washed up on your doorstep," he said irritably.

"I feel it so myself," Sadao said gently.

"It would be best if he could be quietly killed," the General said. "Not by you, but by someone who does not know him. I have my own private assassins. Suppose I send two of them to your house tonight— or better, any night. You need know nothing about it. It is now warm— what would be more natural than that you should leave the outer partition of the white man's room open to the garden while he sleeps?"

"Certainly it would be very natural," Sadao agreed. "In fact, it is so left open every night."

"Good," the General said, yawning. "They are very capable assassins—they make no noise and they know the trick of inward bleeding. If you like I can even have them remove the body."

Sadao considered. "That perhaps would be best, Excellency," he agreed, thinking of Hana.

He left the General's presence then and went home, thinking over the plan. In this way the whole thing would be taken out of his hands. He would tell Hana nothing, since she would be timid at the idea of assassins in the house, and yet certainly such persons were essential in an absolute state such as Japan was. How else could rulers deal with those who opposed them?

He refused to allow anything but reason to be the atmosphere of his mind as he went into the room where the American was in bed. But as he opened the door, to his surprise he found the young man out of bed, and preparing to go into the garden.

"What is this!" he exclaimed. "Who gave you permission to leave your room?"

"I'm not used to waiting for permission," Tom said gaily. "Gosh, I

feel pretty good again! But will the muscles on this side always feel stiff?"

"Is it so?" Sadao inquired surprised. He forgot all else. "Now I thought I had provided against that," he murmured. He lifted the edge of the man's shirt and gazed at the healing scar. "Massage may do it," he said, "if exercise does not."

"It won't bother me much," the young man said. His young face was gaunt under the stubbly blond beard. "Say, doctor, I've got something I want to say to you. If I hadn't met a Jap like you—well, I wouldn't be alive today. I know that."

Sadao bowed but he could not speak.

"Sure, I know that," Tom went on warmly. His big thin hands gripping a chair were white at the knuckles. "I guess if all the Japs were like you there wouldn't have been a war."

"Perhaps," Sadao said with difficulty. "And now I think you had better go back to bed."

He helped the boy back into bed and then bowed. "Good night," he said.

Sadao slept badly that night. Time and time again he woke, thinking he heard the rustling of footsteps, the sound of a twig broken or a stone displaced in the garden—a noise such as men might make who carried a burden.

The next morning he made the excuse to go first into the guest room. If the American were gone he then could simply tell Hana that so the General had directed. But when he opened the door he saw at once that it was not last night. There on the pillow was the shaggy blond head. He could hear the peaceful breathing of sleep and he closed the door again quietly.

"He is asleep," he told Hana. "He is almost well to sleep like that."

"What shall we do with him?" Hana whispered her old refrain.

Sadao shook his head. "I must decide in a day or two," he promised.

But certainly, he thought, the second night must be the night. There rose a wind that night, and he listened to the sounds of bending boughs and whistling partitions.

Hana woke too. "Ought we not to go and close the sick man's partition?" she asked.

"No," Sadao said. "He is able now to do it for himself."

But the next morning the American was still there.

Then the third night of course must be the night. The wind changed to quiet rain and the garden was full of the sound of dripping eaves and running springs. Sadao slept a little better, but he woke at the sound of a crash and leaped to his feet.

"What was that?" Hana cried. The baby woke at her voice and began to wail. "I must go and see."

But he held her and would not let her move.

"Sadao," she cried, "what is the matter with you?"

"Don't go," he muttered, "don't go!"

His terror infected her and she stood breathless, waiting. There was only silence. Together they crept back into the bed, the baby between them.

Yet when he opened the door of the guest room in the morning there was the young man. He was very gay and had already washed and was now on his feet. He had asked for a razor yesterday and had shaved himself and today there was a faint color in his cheeks.

"I am well," he said joyously.

Sadao drew his kimono round his weary body. He could not, he decided suddenly, go through another night. It was not that he cared for this young man's life. No, simply it was not worth the strain.

"You are well," Sadao agreed. He lowered his voice. "You are so well that I think if I put my boat on the shore tonight, with food and extra clothing in it, you might be able to row to that little island not far from the coast. It is so near the coast that it has not been worth fortifying. Nobody lives on it because in storm it is submerged. But this is not the season of storm. You could live there until you saw a Korean fishing boat pass by. They pass quite near the island because the water is many fathoms deep there."

The young man stared at him, slowly comprehending. "Do I have to?" he asked.

"I think so," Sadao said gently. "You understand—it is not hidden that you are here."

The young man nodded in perfect comprehension. "Okay," he said simply.

Sadao did not see him again until evening. As soon as it was dark he had dragged the stout boat down to the shore and in it he put food and bottled water that he had bought secretly during the day, as well as two quilts he had bought at a pawnshop. The boat he tied to a post in the water, for the tide was high. There was no moon and he worked without a flashlight.

When he came to the house he entered as though he were just back from his work, and so Hana knew nothing. "Yumi was here today," she said as she served his supper. Though she was so modern, still she did not eat with him. "Yumi cried over the baby," she went on with a sigh. "She misses him so."

"The servants will come back as soon as the foreigner is gone," Sadao said.

He went into the guest room that night before he went to bed and himself checked carefully the American's temperature, the state of the wound, and his heart and pulse. The pulse was irregular but that was perhaps because of excitement. The young man's pale lips were pressed together and his eyes burned. Only the scars on his neck were red.

"I realize you are saving my life again," he told Sadao.

"Not at all," Sadao said. "It is only inconvenient to have you here any longer."

He had hesitated a good deal about giving the man a flashlight. But he had decided to give it to him after all. It was a small one, his own, which he used at night when he was called.

"If your food runs out before you catch a boat," he said, "signal me two flashes at the same instant the sun drops over the horizon. Do not signal in darkness, for it will be seen. If you are all right but still there, signal me once. You will find fish easy to catch but you must eat them raw. A fire would be seen."

"Okay," the young man breathed.

He was dressed now in the Japanese clothes which Sadao had given him, and at the last moment Sadao wrapped a black cloth about his blond head.

"Now," Sadao said.

The young American without a word shook Sadao's hand warmly, and then walked quite well across the floor and down the step into the darkness of the garden. Once—twice—Sadao saw his light flash to find his way. But that would not be suspected. He waited until from the shore there was one more flash. Then he closed the partition. That night he slept.

"You say the man escaped?" the General asked faintly. He had been operated upon a week before, an emergency operation to which Sadao had been called in the night. For twelve hours Sadao had not been sure the General would live. The gall bladder was much involved. Then the old man had begun to breathe deeply again and to demand food. Sadao had not been able to ask about the assassins. So far as he knew they had never come. The servants had returned and Yumi had cleaned the guest room thoroughly and had burned sulphur in it to get the white man's smell out of it. Nobody said anything. Only the gardener was cross because he had got behind with his chrysanthemums.

But after a week Sadao felt the General was well enough to be spoken to about the prisoner.

"Yes, Excellency, he escaped," Sadao now said. He coughed, signifying that he had not said all he might have said, but was unwilling to disturb the General farther. But the old man opened his eyes suddenly,

"That prisoner," he said with some energy, "did I not promise you I would kill him for you?"

"You did, Excellency," Sadao said.

"Well, well!" the old man said in a tone of amazement, "so I did! But you see, I was suffering a good deal. The truth is, I thought of nothing but myself. In short, I forgot my promise to you."

"I wondered, Your Excellency," Sadao murmured.

"It was certainly very careless of me," the General said. "But you understand it was not lack of patriotism or dereliction of duty." He looked anxiously at his doctor. "If the matter should come out you would understand that, wouldn't you?"

"Certainly, Your Excellency," Sadao said. He suddenly comprehended that the General was in the palm of his hand and that as a consequence he himself was perfectly safe. "I can swear to your loyalty, Excellency," he said to the old General, "and to your zeal against the enemy."

"You are a good man," the General murmured and closed his eyes. "You will be rewarded."

But Sadao, searching the spot of black in the twilighted sea that night, had his reward. There was no prick of light in the dusk. No one was on the island. His prisoner was gone—safe, doubtless, for he had warned him to wait only for a Korean fishing boat.

He stood for a moment on the veranda, gazing out to the sea from whence the young man had come that other night. And into his mind, although without reason, there came other white faces he had known —the professor at whose house he had met Hana, a dull man, and his wife had been a silly talkative woman, in spite of her wish to be kind. He remembered his old teacher of anatomy, who had been so insistent on mercy with the knife, and then he remembered the face of his fat and slatternly landlady. He had had great difficulty in finding a place to live in America because he was a Japanese. The Americans were full of prejudice and it had been bitter to live in it, knowing himself their superior. How he had despised the ignorant and dirty old woman who had at last consented to house him in her miserable home! He had once tried to be grateful to her because she had in his last year nursed him through influenza, but it was difficult, for she was no less repulsive to him in her kindness. But then, white people were repulsive of course. It was a relief to be openly at war with them at last. Now he remembered the youthful, haggard face of his prisoner—white and repulsive.

"Strange," he thought, "I wonder why I could not kill him?"

PAGE FROM AN UNFINISHED-WAR NOVEL

There were many men in Calvin Sallow's condition and desperate
state of mind when World War II overtook them in 1941.
His story—an incident of which is briefly told here—
would have no special significance otherwise. Calvin Sallow was,
no doubt, unduly conscious of his age. For him, as for many
others like him, the first World War had been a reality.
Like most of his boyhood friends with brothers who were just a
few years older, he had been fired with enthusiasm to join
up and go overseas with the A.E.F. But though he had
belonged to a volunteer R.O.T.C. outfit and had drilled with a
wooden gun, he had been a little too young for the draft
and had looked too young to enlist. And now, in 1942, his
enthusiasm somewhat dampened by the nature of the war
service for which he would be eligible, he was actually too old to
enlist in anything that called for a uniform. About all he
could hope for was a desk job on the sixth floor of the National
Bank Building—in the local headquarters of the Red Cross.
Calvin Sallow was a professor, and professors were believed to be
good at paper work. There were many to chose from in
this college town, home of the State University.

He had about decided to help win the war here, punching a
typewriter, when, unexpectedly, things changed. The
Air Force sent a detachment to the campus, and all of a sudden
the University classrooms were filled with men in uniform.

But we should let Professor Sallow tell his story, or at least one
page from it. What follows is an episode from the novel
that Professor Sallow has been for many years engaged in writing
—with the actual name of its hero, and of its author, not
yet revealed for publication. A war novel, it is about the people
who stayed at home. The war was unfinished in 1942,
and so was the novel when its author was last heard from.

After his Saturday morning class Professor Sallow picked up his
brief case, dusted the chalk from his sleeve, and walked out of new Old
North Hall (not to be confused by the alumni with old Old North) into

the sunlight. He wanted to get downtown before the bank closed, and of course he couldn't take his car—on account of the gas situation.

Everybody said the gas shortage was getting pretty bad. Walking to class, rain or shine, was supposed to make him feel virtuous anyway. And Marcia said that stopping on the way home to pick up the marketing, and not forgetting the ration book, was another thing he was doing to help win the war. Marcia was his wife. She talked to the woman next door about the Emergency. They were agreed that the Home Front situation was awful tough any more, but that we must all keep a stiff upper lip. Marcia was always talking about ration points and saying how hard it was to plan meals. Take butter now. . . . As he walked along he knew he was indulging in petty thoughts, as he had been doing much too often of late. He was in a rut, he supposed. There was a big war going on, and he had no part of it—except a lot of students who soon would be in it. He wasn't on the beam, in campus parlance, or in the groove. He was in a rut . . .

"G'morning, Dr. Sallow!" a voice interrupted him. A boy in a private's uniform had overtaken him; then he slowed down for a moment, turned and grinned. A little yellow ribbon over his heart looked very new and bright in the sunlight. (Asiatic-Pacific theater of operations . . .) Embarrassed, perhaps, at having spoken out unexpectedly, he lengthened his stride and walked on. It was Lew Gorgas, home on furlough. "Gorgeous" the co-eds had called Lew just a year ago— Lew with his short, shoe-brush hair—and they had always giggled when, in class, he had said "unprepared"—as he usually was then, in freshman English class. . . . Where would Lew Gorgas be a year from now?

His own theater of operations, he reflected, would continue to be new Old North.

Every time he walked across the campus and down East College Street and saw young men in uniform, he became aware of a spiritual unrest which he found hard to put into words. Now, he said to himself, was the winter of his discontent. Being middle-aged wouldn't ordinarily get him down, but these days it was painful to realize what it signified to belong in the neither-old-nor-young middle forties, the generation that had flourished between wars. It was the generation of baldheaded and paunchy kibitzers at a football game, the impotent and futile fringe on the sidelines. . . . Today he was actually on the sidelines not of a game but of an overwhelming struggle which was being fought to a finish with weapons that only the inmates of an insane asylum would select. His own generation in its incredible stupidity had acquiesced in the development of these mad forces of totalitarianism now loose in the world, and such forces could be checked only by the younger generation, who had had no part in the creation of their inescapable tragedy. This was the idea he had developed in a recent commencement speech to a local high school. Yes, it was the men of his age who should have been thrown into the struggle first. The statesmen and the politicians should have been called upon to lead their contemporaries into the fires, to burn (as their own sons were in fact burning, in the Pacific and in Italy) as punishment for their political failure in the years between wars. . . . Here was the root of the sickness of his spirit: what *could* he do, what could anyone of his age do, that was comparable to what the younger men *had* to do? No action or sacrifice, other than brave talk accompanied by futile gestures, seemed possible in modern war, waged as it was with the diabolical weapons his generation had devised for these same young to use now in their desperate effort to recapture the conditions of peace, the conditions that should never have been relinquished in the years between. . . .

There were details that the historians of the future, painting the picture on the big canvas, would not include, in their desire to give the proper shade and color to the Major Issues of World War II. Right now, those details were all that he could see in the troubled eye of his mind . . . the homesick draftee, the kid in the upper berth, bound for God knew where—with no return-trip in his pocket . . . figures in the mist, creeping through the green New Guinea forests with Japs like murderous monkeys in the trees, fixing their gun sights . . . bodies on a rubber raft, floating silent on the oily surface of the grey ocean. . . .

Professor Sallow had reached the National Bank Building. On the steps he was greeted by a bright-eyed little man wearing a battered grey felt hat and a skimpy drab overcoat, one of his colleagues, holding his salary check aloft. "They've got us again," he said grimly. "It's this new way of paying for the war out of our salary. I tell you, we in the middle-income bracket are sure taking it on the chin these days!" He looked at Professor Sallow and drew his lips into a thin line as he folded the check into his billfold. Professor Sallow, his hand on the heavy handle of the door, had already turned to enter the bank.

As he stepped inside, there was that War Bond poster again, the one with the soldier wearing a blood-stained bandage around his head, the soldier who gave you a sidelong look with narrowed eyes. And the caption: DOING ALL YOU CAN . . . ?

Ten years from now, he wondered, would he be asking himself a similar question, "What were you waiting for, brother?"

OUT OF LINE

Those of us—like Calvin Sallow in the previous story—who
fought the war with ration books and put up with shortages, and
occasionally felt put out by such inconveniences, were
quite used to standing in line. Everybody stood in line, waiting
for buses, buying cigarettes, mailing packages for overseas
—like the author of this story. We recall the etiquette, or the
ethics, pertaining to this activity. But revealed in Mr. Beck's
experience is more than simply a breach of the unwritten code.
Character is put to strange tests, to be sure, but this
incident has deeper implications than a selfish affront to wartime
esprit de corps. The reader will understand the author's thoughtful
self-appraisal in the light of his own immediate reaction
to the incident and will also wonder "whose blood is on whose
head." The author (this "middle-aged party," this
"medium-fat guy with glasses" at the sub-postal station) is faced
with a problem of far-reaching importance.

She bustled into the crowded little sub-postal station, a dark-
haired, stoutly stylish woman in silver fox fur over conspicuously expensive clothes. Her large black eyes looked around sharply. Their expression roused him out of the boredom of delay. Such a demanding glance
suggested that the prominent nose might actually and audibly sniff for
an advantage. And when she shifted her large purse, her only burden,
from one hand to another, it was as if she readied her grip on a weapon.
He grew surer of her intention to make these passively waiting people
give ground and stand aside.

They were ranged, about a dozen men and women, in an irregular
but orderly arc from the postal counter past the tobacco cases and
around along the racked magazines on the other wall. Some held letters to stamp, but most had parcels, apparently for posting. Packages
for the boys in training camps, on ships, and overseas—that was what
had boomed business at the sub-postal station. He, too, had a parcel
—hard candy for his son—with an A.P.O. address.

While he had waited at the confectionery to have the box properly
wrapped, he had thought back over the years since he had bought any

kind of candy for his boy. Twelve or thirteen years at least, because his son was twenty-five now, and bringing home a roll of mints or a cellophane bag of gumdrops was a bit of that demonstrativeness—like laying his hand in passing on the boy's head—from which he had gradually desisted as he realized the child was growing up. Now, however, he bought his son hard candy again, sent him chocolate, and whatever cigarettes he could get, and pipe tobacco, talcum powder, potted meats, razor blades, fruit cakes—anything exportable that might be of some use or momentary pleasure to the man of the family who had been a soldier at the front. A first lieutenant, not only too far away, but too tall to have his head patted—anyhow, not without an awkward gesture on his old man's part, his civilian, stay-at-home, and slightly dumpy old man.

He had noticed that the round-shouldered woman in the shabby coat just ahead of him in line also held a package, addressed to an A.P.O., San Francisco. It seemed a flimsy box to make the endless journey across the Pacific and to some island army post. The woman shifted and sighed as if with aching feet. He wondered what was her present conception of her boy's distance from her. She would feel it, yes —as the thousands, millions of mothers like her had felt it, whose sons had been whisked away, as if by sorcery, beyond home's four walls and the known turnings of parochial streets. Only gradually, though, with the slow reply to letters, could housekeeping mothers realize the separation in space. After that they could wonder, not only whether the pre-war shoebox stuffed with cookies would stand the rigors of a six weeks' or two months' journey but whether the boy would receive and enjoy it.

The mother in the worn coat certainly had no idea, either, that the fashionable woman who had come in last was maneuvering to squeeze into the line ahead of turn. That was just what she was going to try, though, he bet with himself. It seemed as obvious as the flaunting perfume that already dominated the small space. Her pretense of examining the racked magazines at long range was so hasty that it showed she thought these people wouldn't be hard to get by. Such casual craftiness was, he felt, an insult worse than the imposition she intended against them. Another glance or two at the magazines and she would begin to edge in. He looked over at her again. Big as her purse was, he doubted that she had a package in it. Probably she wanted one stamp.

Now she turned her eyes, glittering black, directly towards him, catching his stare. She made the slight movement, the unmistakable feminine gesture of imperious dependency to which a gentleman, of course, would be expected to respond. She was actually soliciting him to abet her and thus to shield her from the others' possible protest. He should make his slight motion in return, just perceptibly drop back, to show her it would be all right for her to slip in ahead of him. As if there weren't four women behind him, rightfully in line, and one of them gray-haired and plainly weary. He looked straight at the searching dark eyes and moved a bit, but forward, almost closing up the inches between him and the person ahead; and then he turned sidewards in the line, so that he also narrowed the space behind him, and confronted the threatened intrusion.

The bold stare flinched and fell aside. But the woman did not turn and take a place at the end of the line. She shifted from one foot to another and stood her neutral ground, with an undirected look of distaste that he knew was for him, and was intended for him to see. Then she opened her handbag and began a hen-like pantomime of flurried scratching in its contents. He supposed she was waiting for him to get out of her way. So he decided not to get out of her way—he'd stick around.

When he had got his package mailed, he moved back into the other corner of the crowded room. He picked up a magazine off the rack and glanced at the table of contents on its cover. The woman twitched her silver fox and at the same time took a couple of sidling steps towards the postal counter. The gesture with her hand was, he judged, a kind of feint, to draw attention away from the movement of her feet. Or was it habitual—maybe under her fingers that costly fur seemed an amulet. Anyhow, now she was closer, so close that she could make an inconspicuous turn and put herself almost elbow to elbow with the second person in the line. She adjusted the fur again and raised her chin slightly, with a blank settled look on her face, as if she had been right there for hours, a well-groomed figure of patience.

Damn her, she was pulling it off, he thought. Damn her! Then he wondered why he was hanging around, watching, and taking it so hard. He felt certain that there wasn't an ounce of race prejudice in his attitude. He never made distinctions on that basis; he simply didn't. He would never use that mealymouthed phrase, "Some of my best friends—" with its oily smirk, its tone of preening broad-mindedness which fell just short of the real thing. He never sank to such an affected show of tolerance, like a cheaply bought poppy on the lapel. And one of his best reasons for never saying "Some of my best friends" was that some were friends of his indeed, real friends, with no holds barred and no condescension or self-consciousness on either side. He was, he admitted, critical enough of people, especially in these latter years when so much human malevolence had run wild, abroad and at home, until it had to be fought; but he didn't condemn by mean standards, he hoped. He wasn't perfect himself, not by a hell of a lot, and didn't claim to be, but he trusted that in his resentments he was on the side of the angels now and then. As, for instance, here and now. This woman had absolutely no right to muscle in, that was all there was to it. Her complexion and features had nothing whatever to do with his antipathy. Or with his resistance, he hoped.

Now she was at the postal counter, still side by side with the woman to whom she had silently joined herself. What next, he wondered, watching openly, the magazine dropping forward in his hands. The dark-eyed woman waited while the other bought her stamps. Wily, he thought. She must have reckoned very nearly what she could and could not get away with. The truism that they were close calculators sprang into his mind, and he rejected it, for its damnable word "they." He had warred against that sneaking bogy. Whenever he heard anyone grumble and sneer about something one of "them" had got away with, or had only tried, he would counter-charge. He would cite comparable offenses by fellows who would be termed white men—simply because they had straight noses or turned-up ones, and maintained vaguely respectable connections with the Trinity through their check books and perhaps their wives, and came of stock that had remained barbaric for the first several hundred years of our Lord. His broadening the discussion thus to take in any sharp dealings as such always irked the grumbling demonologists, the great racers after scapegoats, and seldom wrung any immediate concession from them, but he persisted in his open rebuttals. For one thing, he always hoped it would have a softening effect in the long run, even on some of the fanatics, and certainly on some of the cooler-headed bystanders. For another thing, its very difficulty and unpleasantness had made the duty of speaking up seem all the more imperative, ever since his son had gone to war.

So he was not prejudiced, he trusted. He was not judging them, but only this woman. He was not mistaken about her, either. Plainly this woman would push, up to the limit. But not enough further to get herself actually slapped down. Not, at least, by any of the people waiting in this slow line. Now the other woman had picked up her stamps. The intruder snatched the chance, timing her movement exactly. She dropped some coins with a clatter upon the metal counter.

"All I want is ten eight-cent air-mail stamps," she said distinctly, "and here's the correct change."

The old newsdealer, tobacconist, and part-time postal clerk raised faded blue eyes, briefly, with a chill look in them, and then glanced down and flipped pages of the book which stored the stamps. The line stood still and silent.

The magazine held for ambush trembled in his hands. Furiously he thrust it back into the rack. He stepped quickly to the door. Turning with uncontrollable impulse, he spoke in a clear voice that sounded as strange to him as it it must have been to them.

"You folks oughtn't to let anybody get away with a thing like that," he said.

The men and women waiting in line all looked over at him, with an almost uniform turning of heads, just as if he were a tennis tournament, he thought wildly. They surveyed him with a passive bovine wonder, but without evident approval or aversion. Then they looked away again, one at a time. The tournament, it seemed, was over. Nobody said anything. It was so quiet he could hear the old clerk tearing the ten air-mail stamps from the perforated sheet. The woman herself was watching that as if it were a feat of great skill, her whole concern for the moment.

He stepped out and let the door slam behind him. He lit a cigarette. He stood there, waiting. He had started something and he would finish it. He would tell her the rest of it, straight, and if the lady had any last words, okay. Looking back through the glass door, he saw that she had moved slightly aside, allowing the line to come up, now that she had got her stamps. These she was tucking carefully into her purse, and she didn't seem to be in any hurry now. In fact, it looked as if she was stalling for time. Several of the men and women in line were watching her now, too. After a moment she snapped the purse shut, gave her furs another quick jerk, and came towards the door. He took his cigarette out of his mouth and waited. She looked down at the latch with a pointedly careful air as she opened the door. Then she started past him with eyes averted.

"Wait a minute," he said.

She stopped and turned just her head to look askance at him, with a sneer that seemed about to be a snarl.

"Don't you know better than to act like that?" he demanded. "Can't you understand you're laying up grief for others who are completely innocent and well-behaved? You're asking for trouble for your relatives and friends, can't you see that? If anything happens here the way it happened in Germany to your people, some of their blood will be on your head. Your children's blood, maybe, on your own head."

Slowly her face turned further towards him now, as if drawn by a power not her own. Her mouth gaped, in astonishment. Gaped and twitched slightly—in utter fear, he realized, seeing the rouge and lipstick stand out on her blanching skin. Then she turned suddenly away, starting off down the sidewalk on her precarious heels with quick stilted steps. He stood there watching her go. His cigarette began to burn his fingers, and he dropped it without looking down. Once she glanced back over her shoulder, as if in dread of an actual pursuit. Then hurrying on still faster, she disappeared among the pedestrians further down the street.

What had he done, he asked himself ruefully, to have brought that look of awful panic into her face? Had he pierced too deeply through her years of habitual arrogance that was a shell, a shield—thrust into sorrows and terrors inherited from bygone generations? Standing there still to question himself, he took out another cigarette and lit it. And even though he had only tried to warn her reasonably against stirring up more prejudice, had he really protested without prejudice? Suppose she had been a blonde and had acted that way. No, that wasn't a fair question. If she had been a pure damned pork-fed Nordic, her acting like that would have been just as intolerably rude, and he'd have despised and resisted it just as much; but it wouldn't have been so serious, really —not so dangerous in its possible repercussions. Except as anything hateful makes other people readier to hate. But that's just where what this woman had done was worse. What he had told her about its special badness was exactly true. Perhaps she was more deeply and pitifully conditioned to such a brazen act than those in that room whom she offended, but she should feel, too, the special burden now laid upon her, to avoid adding fuel to an always smoldering fire, that had been smoking pretty hard of late.

He could imagine how others in that waiting line would react. Though they had stood quiet and unprotesting while it had happened, they would talk about it later. They would tell their spouses about it at supper, tell their friends about it at card parties and in bars. He imagined the whispers, the exchanged talk. Her crowding in that way was just like them, they would say. There would be noddings in agreement; there would be other anecdotes about them, perhaps including distasteful reference to the badge; and the established conclusion would be voiced that, now the war is over, we're going to have to do something about them.

A man and a woman who had been well behind him in the line came out in quick succession and glanced at him curiously as they went by. He turned and started slowly down the street. One more thing, too, the talk would probably include, he reflected. That guy sure told her off, they'd say—the medium fat guy with glasses, he sure told her where to head in. Everybody heard him; everybody was so surprised you could have heard a pin drop. And what's more, he waited outside for her— yeh, that's what he did, and you could see him telling her a lot more. She looked plenty scared, too. That's what they need, he now imagined the talkers saying—as he had often heard it said—in bars, on trains, in offices, at dinner parties, on the streets, over card tables, in movie queues. They need to have the pants scared off of them, that's what they need. Now that the war is over, we're going to have to do something. Right here at home. About them. But this middle-aged party, he didn't wait; he told her off right there. That, he supposed, was what the talkers would be saying, having forgotten almost at once that it was the men and women standing in line, the non-resisters countenancing unfairness, whom he had first reproached.

An emerging certainty that those waiting people would think he had protested on racial grounds agitated him. What a hideous thing, all the worse for having been unintended. Why he had spoken out he really didn't know, now, except that he suddenly felt he had to. But should he feel so uneasy about it now? It was true, what he had said, that folks shouldn't let anybody get away with a thing like that. It was fair play for all that he had stood up for, and standing in line in turn wasn't too much to expect, even from perfumed women in furs.

Furthermore, he went on to himself, wasn't it better to come right out with it in a particular case, with plain reference to an action and not a prejudice, as he had done, rather than to accept injury without protest and then whisper about it afterward and work it up into an indiscriminate, cruel, horribly dangerous emotional feud? As between himself and the army of whisperers, he tried to feel justified. But these problems, he thought, were getting too damned complicated, in crowded little rooms and in the world at large. Under present confusions it was hard enough to be just; but besides that a man must worry, too, about whether a good motive might be mistaken for a bad one, so that even a right act might have an evil influence. But maybe the folks in line would have whispered just as much, having witnessed her behavior, even if he had not objected publicly. And, just possibly, he might have influenced the woman. If she behaved better hereafter, it would be a net gain, however small. But damn it, he could have told her that outside without sounding off in front of those others at all.

Walking along slowly, his unseeing eyes fixed on the sidewalk, he almost collided with a brisk young blonde. "Careful, Pop," she said, smiling, and was past him before he could get out an apology. He went on, trying to be a bit more alert. Careful, Pop. He couldn't help thinking that not all the people who had been waiting in line would talk about it later. Some of them, he felt certain now, would simply let it ride, both at the time and afterward. They'd forgive her for what she'd done. And forgive him, too, for yelling about it. Though the word "forgive" was maybe a bit strong. Perhaps they weren't even that assertive. They'd just let it ride and forget it, the way they had grown accustomed to do with so many things. So much was let ride, with so many forms of the same fatalism: that's life for you, it's the Lord's will, it's human nature, you can't have everything, forget it.

Some of the men and women out of that line would be like that, certainly; so many people were like that. So what did that make them, the salt of the earth? Or dopes? Staring and never speaking a word or raising a hand. Never. Until finally, the people who tried to muscle in and the people who tried to speak up for principle, between them—

481

selves, whipped up another big fight, maybe. And then the salt of the earth, the poor dopes, could send off their sons to foreign shores and fields, and send after them, as a supreme gesture, home-baked cookies in packages that would get mashed on the way. Or at best like himself, he thought miserably, be able to send nothing more, no matter how well boxed and wrapped, than some pieces of hard candy.

A little hard candy, then, from the middle-aged party in bifocals who tried to be on the side of the angels by making remarks pretty likely to increase the world's total stores of inflammable hatreds. So whose blood was on whose head, anyhow? he mused, as he walked along. So should he be sorry for what he had done? But that way pacifism lies, he told himself, and it's plain now where pacifism helped to get us, or rather our sons. Right into the necessity of letting a lot of blood, including quantities of their own. So first people stand by and say nothing against the beginnings of a wrong, and then soon they're standing in line to mail fruit cakes to their boys abroad. So then, even among the "blessed" meek, who let things ride, whose blood is on whose head?

He drew out of his side pocket the bit of paper with which his fingers had been fidgeting irritably. It was the sales slip for his recent purchase —item, merchandise—item, packing charge—and total, an infallible addition, machine-stamped, untouched by human hands. Or by human passions, whether for a place at the head of the line, or the last word, or peace at any price. Just total. Not total war or totalitarianism or total depravity or total abstinence—merely total, complete with dollar sign. Here now was something certain, logical, and just—the true, the beautiful, and the good carried out to two decimal places. Which is about as far as we go, he thought, as he curved over towards the sidewalk's edge and dropped the slip of paper into a trash container. At least, his son would like the candy, he hoped.

MISS LAURIE WILL BE LATE TONIGHT

The setting for this story is a garage in the city, just down the
street and around the corner. You can store your car
here, in the winter, overnight. This is a good garage; they'll wash
the old car for you, and when your generator's off they'll
give your battery a quick charge. It's a well-run place,
considering that there's a war on—in 1943.
Tuck, the night man, is dependable, friendly, and sensitive too.
When the story begins, Tuck is somewhat sobered by the
sentimental feeling a person often has when he realizes he is
about to go through an old familiar routine for the last
time. And this night will be Tuck's last—for the duration—because, of course, he too is in the Army now. He leaves
for Fort Devens in the morning. He has a number of good-byes
to say tonight when the customers come in to leave
their cars. . . .

It was about nine that evening in winter when the tall pilot from
Westover Field came to my garage to pick up his car. Now, like always
when I saw the pilot walking toward me, everything got keener. This
pilot did something to you. His eyes were set deep in his head, and they
made you think about distance and horizons. He had spent nine thousand hours in the sky. Maybe from looking so long at clouds and stars
he had got hold of some kind of knowledge that you couldn't find on
earth.

I lifted the elevating door, drove his car out, and gave it a last touch
with the cleaning cloth.

"There you are, Captain," I said. "She's all set."

"Will she take me out to the Coast?"

"The Coast?" I was surprised.

"Yes," he said. "I've been transferred. I'm leaving right now."

You'd have thought he was just going down to Springfield to see the
Ice Carnival instead of starting on a three-thousand mile trip. He was
sure pretty casual about it, but I felt sorry when I realized that if I ever

saw him again it would be a lucky accident. There were sure being some big changes made these days. I had one coming to myself, and the thought of it made me feel closer to the pilot than before.

I tapped the hood of his car with my knuckles and said: "She'll take you to the Coast easy. That's my last ring-and-valve job, so I made it the best."

"Your last one?" asked the pilot.

"That's right." I looked at his uniform and grinned. "I passed my physical like a breeze," I told him. "I'm going to Fort Devens tomorrow. I'm in it, too."

"You enlisted?"

"Sure I did."

"What about your garage?"

"Closing it up—except for my live-storage customers. Old Man Burke'll take care of them. Only a few left, anyway. People are saving tires and repairs."

The pilot nodded. He came over near me, and we stood together in the open doorway looking into the garage. My push broom leaned against the wall near a pile of dirt I'd gathered to throw out. Beyond, to the left, were the two hydraulic lifts, the fast battery charger, and the greasing set-up—all in swell shape. In the back room you could see lights reflecting from the polished windshields and fenders of cars in dead storage. For the hundredth time I noticed the blown bulb in the center line of overhead lights, and for the hundredth time in as many nights I told myself I'd put in a new one, but didn't.

I could feel the pilot's eyes on me. He seemed kind of quiet and thoughtful, like when people say good-bye for the last time. He said: "It's been nice doing business with you. You've run a good place. How long have you owned it?"

"Seven years."

"Seven years," said the pilot, "and this is your last night on duty." His voice was so low you could hardly hear him. "How will it seem to you?"

The pilot had something extra, all right. He saw into your mind. He asked you the very question you hadn't quite dared to ask yourself, as if he had guessed the secret thing you would miss most—and for me, that secret was Miss Laurie, who had stored her car in my place for more than a year.

There were a lot of things I'd remember in the months or years ahead of me, but I wouldn't miss them. I'd remember the white gleam of enamel on the casings of the motor analyzers; the thoughts that always crowded into me when I swept the dead flower petals from the undertaker's hearse; and the hiss of the valves operating the greasing lifts.

Sure! All these and more—but they were nothing compared to Miss Laurie.

I had been trying not to think about Miss Laurie, but I couldn't help it now. Today, about four, when I had brought her car to her door, she had said: "Why, Tuck! You look so solemn. What's the matter?"

Nothing was the matter, except that I wanted to remember all of her forever. I wanted to get the sound of her voice fastened in my ears and the look of her high-boned face written in my eyes. I wanted to tell her this, but it wasn't in the cards, so I said: "Everything's okay, Miss Laurie."

While we were driving back to the garage, where she was to drop me off, she kept looking at my hands holding the wheel, and I worried about how they looked, with cracks in the knuckles, and my nails thick and broken from fussing around inside of engines. But at the garage she said, "Thanks, Tuck," as if I had done her a favor, when all the time she was doing me one just by being alive.

No one knew how I felt about her, least of all Miss Laurie. She was studying at the college for some kind of a degree, Master of Arts, I think. So it was plenty good enough for me just to sit beside her on the seat of her coupé, and see the copper lights in her hair, and exchange a few sentences with her that didn't mean anything, except to me.

Once when she was sick I sent her some roses, but didn't enclose a card for fear she'd think I was out of place. Next time I saw her she was wearing one of the roses in her hair. It looked red as fire against the whiteness of her forehead. I was so excited and surprised I could hardly talk.

"That's pretty, Miss Laurie," I managed to say. "That flower in your hair, I mean."

Her fingers touched my arm for a second, like a bird lighting on a limb. She took them away, but I could still feel them there. She looked down at my hands so long I wanted to hide them, and then she said: "Oh, thanks, Tuck. Someone sent me a whole dozen roses. I don't know who it was. I've been wondering."

"I wouldn't know."

"I must have a secret admirer."

"I guess you must have."

"It's all very mysterious and romantic."

"Yes, it sure is."

All of a sudden she turned her eyes up to mine, took the rose from her hair, and tossed it to me. I stood there after she had gone, holding the rose, feeling weak and strong by turns, and my heart big.

Right now I tried to tear my thoughts away from Miss Laurie. I didn't want the pilot to see that deep into me. But the memories began to jump out of the shadows. I could see Miss Laurie's face framed in the dark fur collar of her coat; her gloves lying on the seat of her car, holding the shape of her fingers; and the times I'd picked up the gloves and held them as if her hands were still inside.

She seemed so near, and yet so far. We lived in the same town, but in different worlds. Did she notice the little extra things I did for her? Did she have the faintest idea I did them because I loved her? Sometimes I thought she knew. But I was mostly afraid she would find out, and at the same time afraid she wouldn't.

I hadn't answered the pilot's question yet. He had asked how it would seem to go through the night routine for the last time. I really didn't know, so I just said: "Well, it's like this: tonight will be the same as any other night."

"No," he answered in that low, thinking voice. "Last nights are always different, even when you do the same old things."

He wrote out a check for the work I'd done for him, shook hands with me, and got into his car. As he drove down the cement apron to the street, he looked back at me and raised his hand in a slow-motion salute. "So-long, Tuck. I'll be thinking of you," he called, and was gone, and I never saw him again.

I dropped the elevating door and walked into the shop office through the small door. It was like the pilot had cast a spell over the place and over me. All my nerves seemed to rise up on tiptoe. He sure must have left a lot of places for the last time. He knew what it did to a man, all right. Things were the same—only different—even to the familiar night-sounds like the humming of the air compressor, the ventilator creaking in the wind, and the ticking of the time-clock.

I cut the switches on the four gas pumps and through the shop office window watched the four globes go dark. How many thousands of gallons had I fed from those pumps? How many miles did they represent and in what directions? I could hear the echoes of a thousand travelers' voices: "Fill her up. Check the oil. Twenty-eight pounds all around."

Before, I never thought twice about those words; but now they seemed to mean the destination of a race of restless people. It made me feel like singing. No matter where you were tomorrow, you couldn't be lonely with your memory full of ballast like that.

Without realizing it, I began to look around for more ballast. I lifted the memo pad from its hook by the cash register and glanced at the day's notations written by Old Man Burke, who had gone off duty at six. Old Man Burke called each car by its owner's name, and that way made his notes into wisecracks.

486 *Ware*

1. Wash Mr. Foss.
2. Mrs. Johnson won't start.
3. Dent in Mrs. Bemis. Not responsible.
4. Karowski's clutch slipping. The life he leads.
5. Give the Reverend Ward two quarts of alcohol. Ought to hold him for a spell.

I smiled, thinking of the fun Old Man Burke got out of being disrespectful. But when I turned the page and read the next and last note, I could feel the smile changing to a different kind. My heart skipped like an engine with a stuck valve. Was the tall pilot some kind of prophet? No, that couldn't be. But he had made me feel that something big was going to happen to me, and this was it. The note was the promise of a perfect ending to my life of yesterday, and a perfect beginning to the new way of tomorrow. I read the words aloud, and I loved the sound and the meaning of them:

Miss Laurie will be late tonight.

Unless my live-storage customers notified the garage to the contrary, it was understood that I wouldn't stay open for them after midnight. Tonight, my last night, Miss Laurie was the only one who had notified. Old Man Burke must have taken the message while I was out buying parts for the pilot's car. I wanted to thank someone or something. I wanted to thank Miss Laurie, because my last duty would be to drive her home. How would it be in that little minute that always went so fast while she gathered up her purse and books from the seat? What would she say?

"Good night, Tuck. Thanks ever so much for staying open."

"That's all right, Miss Laurie."

She'd hesitate a second and look over at my hands on the wheel. Then: "Will you bring my car tomorrow about four?"

"Well, no. Old Man Burke'll bring it. I'm in the Army."

I couldn't make it any better than that, even in my imagination. It wouldn't go any farther. I'd watch her go up the steps to her apartment. She'd open the door, and it would close behind her. She'd disappear into her world, and I'd be left alone in mine. I'd drive her car back to the garage and store it on the Number One lift, forward near the door. I'd lock up for the last time and walk home along the empty, hollow-sounding street. My last memory would be of her. I couldn't have dreamed of a better break than that.

Now, because of tomorrow, and the spell of the pilot, but mostly because of Miss Laurie, all the routine night-jobs seemed exciting to me, little jobs like fixing the furnace fire, wiping off the bulk oil pumps, and disconnecting the two air hoses.

While I was outside coiling the hoses, I noticed a man standing in front of the tavern next door. It was pretty dark in the street, but I recognized the man. He was Doc Bennett, and he was swaying a little, like always. In the days before he began hitting the stuff hard, Doc Bennett stored his two custom-built jobs in my place and gave me all his repair business. There wasn't much left of him now, only dignity. But a lot of people in our town owed their lives and their children's lives to Doc.

I put the two coiled hoses inside and walked out to where he was standing on the curb, trying to get his bearings.

"Hello, Doc," I said. "It's a cold night."

He turned to me and bowed, and his old, pale eyes recognized me in the darkness. "Good evening, Tuck. Yes, it's very cold."

My beach wagon that I used for odd jobs stood in the alley between the garage and the tavern. "Jump in, Doc," I said. "I'll give you a ride home."

He lived in a rooming house six blocks from the garage. I helped him up the icy steps, and he grabbed my hand and held it. "You don't forget your friends, do you?" he said.

"I try not to, Doc."

Someone had told him I was leaving for Fort Devens. "I shall miss you," he said. "I want to wish you God-speed."

"Sure, Doc. Thanks. You were swell to me when you had it."

He grabbed my hand again and hung on tight. "When I had it," he said, like an echo. "Well, in a way, I'm still helping your business. I brought some of your customers into the world. Did you know that?"

I'd never realized it, but I saw how it was likely. "You did, Doc? Who?"

"Let me think: there's that young Amherst student, Charles Atwood; and Ed Johnson's wife—Blanchard, her name was. And then that lovely Miss Laurie. Louise Laurie."

"Miss Laurie?" I said, gripping his hand hard. "Honest, Doc? Miss Laurie, that's studying for a degree at the college?"

"Yes."

I wanted to stay there a long time with Doc Bennett asking him questions about Miss Laurie and her family, things I could never find out by myself. It seemed wonderful, and strange, and somehow sad that this old, burnt-out man had brought Miss Laurie into the world. He was so old and tired, and she was so young, and beautiful, and full of life.

"Look, Doc," I said. "Any time you feel like a ride home, you just step into the garage and tell Old Man Burke. He'll see you don't walk. I'll leave a standing order—for the duration."

"The duration," he said. "It won't be long," and he swayed in through the door.

On the way back to the garage I realized that he didn't mean the war so much as himself. He didn't want to live any more. I parked the beach wagon in the alley and walked across the apron by the gas pumps. I saw the blue light shining like a dead eye through the stained-glass window of the funeral home next door. We used to laugh about the garage being centrally located between a saloon and a mortician's, but it didn't seem funny tonight. I remembered a time when Doc Bennett had said he wanted nothing but a colon engraved on his tombstone. He said a colon was a punctuation mark indicating that a lot had been left unsaid, unthought, and undone. I guess Doc knew a lot about death to make a statement like that. But he knew a lot about life, too. He had saved lives and made lives. He had made my life when he brought Miss Laurie into the world.

I went into the shop and looked over the check list of the cars out and in. Old Man Burke had it fixed accurately. The red tabs indicated cars out, and there were only three—Mr. Ayer, the County Treasurer; Professor Hartley, who taught English Literature at the college; and Miss Laurie.

It was dim and quiet in the garage. There weren't any sounds but the singing in my ears, my footsteps on the cement floor, and the ticking of the time-clock that no one punched any more. I looked up and noticed the blown bulb in the center line of lights again, and I said to myself once more: I ought to put in a new one. But I didn't. I just let it go, like a hundred other times.

Every now and then between jobs I'd go into the office, take the memo pad from its hook, and read the last note all over again just to make sure. The words were there, all right. *Miss Laurie will be late tonight.*

Will it be any different this last time, I asked myself? What will I say, and what will she answer? Why is she late tonight? Is she out with some guy from up at the college? What right have I got to wonder, even to my own self? It's just that I want to talk to her about the thoughts I've been having and the questions I've been asking myself about yesterday and tomorrow. I want to leave her some kind of souvenir of myself and take away with me a souvenir of her.

I was standing there by the cash register holding the memo pad when Mr. Ayer drove up outside and honked his horn. I dropped the pad and felt in my unionall's pocket to make sure my key was there. I sprang the lock on the shop office door as I went out. The elevating door was locked from the inside.

"Hello, Tuck," Mr. Ayer said. "Do you mind driving tonight? I'm tired."

"Sure," I said. "Okay."

He moved over, and I climbed in behind the wheel. We drove up Main Street and turned left on South where he lived. He began to explain why he was tired, and his voice sounded blue.

"I've been up at the Court House organizing the report center for air-raid alarms. Been there since eight o'clock this morning."

"You're sure doing plenty," I said. "And your own job on top of that."

He was quiet for a time before he answered: "I've got to do something to feel worthwhile. The Army doesn't want me."

"But in this war everyone's in the Army, and no fooling."

That seemed to cheer him up. He sat straighter in the seat, and his voice brightened. "It would do your heart good to see them coöperating," he said. "The ones that work hardest at their regular jobs are most willing to take the tough tricks at the signal lights at night. Take Louise Laurie, for instance; works all day long studying for her Master's degree, and—"

"Did you say Miss Laurie? Louise Laurie?"

"Yes."

"Is she on duty at the report center?"

"Yes."

"So that's why she'll be late tonight."

"She'll be late, all right," Mr. Ayer said. "She's on four hours—ten till two. You're not staying open for her, are you?"

"Oh, I don't mind hanging around."

We had stopped in front of his house. The motor was idling, and I could feel him looking at me. After a while he said: "Well, Tuck—you're going to Fort Devens."

"Sure. Tomorrow morning."

He was feeling blue again. He got out of his car and stood with one foot on the running board. He was a swell, quiet guy. He had tried half a dozen times to enlist, but every time they turned him down because of his heart.

"I'll miss you," he said. "It won't be the same. We'll all miss you."

He took his foot off the running board, then reached in and shook hands with me. "So-long," he said, and turned away up the walk to his house.

On the way back to the garage I felt proud and kind of lonely to know that Mr. Ayer would miss me. Doc Bennett had said he would miss me, too. Would Miss Laurie? I didn't know, but somehow I wanted her to. I thought of all the good people who came to the garage, and how most of them seemed to have a place in Miss Laurie's world. Doc Bennett knew her family and all about her since she'd been born. Mr. Ayer worked with her at the report center. What was her world like, anyway? What did people talk about in places where she felt at home? I never figured I'd get even a glimpse of Miss Laurie's world, but I did, and it changed everything.

Professor Hartley's car was waiting on the apron when I drove up. I saw the twin tail-lights, and the headlights focused sharp on the elevating door. His motor was running, and the cold white vapor foaming out of the exhaust. I pulled up alongside and jumped out of Mr. Ayer's car.

"Sorry to keep you waiting, Professor," I said.

He had a thin, wonderful face. He was wearing a fur cap like teamsters used to wear and a wool scarf around his neck. He seemed happy and eager about something.

"I forgot to notify you I'd be a bit late," he said. "I've been out on the bridge spotting airplanes—ten to midnight shift."

"That's all right, Professor. There's one more car to come in, anyway. Was it cold out there?"

I parked Mr. Ayer's car in the garage near the wash-stand, then came out and got into Professor Hartley's car to drive him home. We started, and he told me he had heard a big plane going over high. He had reported it over the phone in the bridge pylon to Army Flash. You could feel the pride in his voice. He was an old man, but he was in there doing his stuff like the rest.

"The plane was doubtless from Westover Field," he said, "but we are instructed to report everything."

When I drew up in front of the professor's house, he reached over with his long, bony hand and switched off the ignition. "This is a special night, Tuck. You're leaving us. Come in a minute. We'll have a glass of sherry—a ceremonial."

I started to say no, but he was already out of the car and backing up the porch steps, moving his arms as if to draw me after him. It was the first time I had ever been inside the professor's living-room. It sort of got to me, and for a second I couldn't figure out why. It was a gentle kind of room, and you knew there had been a lot of thinking and conversation in it. You could smell pipe smoke, and a leather smell from the bindings of books. There was a fireplace with logs smouldering, and a pine table covered with books and papers. I looked down and read the title of one of the books: *English Literature in the Eighteenth Century*. Was Miss Laurie's subject literature? Did she read books like this?

The professor took off his fur cap, scarf, and overcoat. He motioned toward an easy chair, and said: "Sit down, Tuck. I'll pour some sherry."

I only half heard him. The dim light in the room was like a mist, and things seemed to move toward me from the mist. I only half saw the professor as he opened a cabinet and got out glasses and a decanter. He must have thought I was in a trance, but I wasn't. I was in Miss Laurie's world for the first time, and I could feel it folding around me.

"Here you are, Tuck," the professor said.

I took the filled glass and said "Thanks"—but in my mind I was saying: This is her world. I'm a little way in. I just stepped through the door into a place where she would belong. I can see her and feel her all around me here.

"Here's to you, Tuck," the professor said, raising his glass. "Here's to the day of your return. We all look forward to that day."

"Thanks," I said. "And—thanks for asking me in here."

"Ah! You like this room?"

"Yes, sir. I do. I love it!"

I had never felt so near Miss Laurie. I saw her in the room, her lips apart as she concentrated on a book. I saw the clean, white curve of her throat, and her hand going up slowly to touch her hair. Her voice came whispering to me from the mistiness of the room. What was she saying? She wanted something, and I didn't know what it was. There was a longing and a curiosity in her eyes. She came over close to me and looked down at the backs of my hands. . . .

Suddenly I wanted to go back quick to the garage and wait for her there alone. I wanted to be alone with my thoughts of her and of her world. It seemed wrong that anyone should be looking at me when I was thinking of her—even this kind old professor who had the shadows of wisdom in his sunken eyes.

"Tuck! You're not going so soon!"

"Yes, sir. I must go back now. There's one more car out. And thank you again for asking me in, sir. It's another good thing to remember."

He followed me half-way down the porch steps, then shook hands with me, and he was still waving when I turned the corner at the end of his street.

It was quarter of one when I got to the garage and backed the professor's car in beside Mr. Ayer's. I drove the beach wagon into a space by the far wall, and that left room for Miss Laurie's car on the Number One lift, forward.

I had never known it to be so still in the garage. The wind had died, and the ventilator didn't creak at all. You could just hear the time-clock, and then, when the motor in the professor's car began to cool and contract, you could hear the sudden snap of a loose baffle-plate in the muffler.

I tried to find things to do to make the time go faster. I soaked up chamois cloths that were already good and moist and tested the valves on the air compressor that I knew were already closed tight. Twice I saw headlights fan bright across the walls, and both times I rushed out —but it was only some night-owl turning around on the apron.

I went to the sink and washed my hands, dried them on a clean towel, and rubbed salve on the cracked places. Then I went to the shop office and took down the memo pad. I tore off a blank sheet and wrote a note to Old Man Burke: "Give Doc Bennett a ride home any time he wants it for as long as he wants it." But after doing all these things, the minute hand on the time-clock had moved only ten or twelve jumps.

I don't know what it was that made me remember a test they had given us years ago in high school. It just popped into my head as a good way to make the time pass. It was one of those psychological tests where they give you a word and ask you to write down other words it suggests. Supposing the key word was night. You'd write down dark, or black, or stars, or fear, or ghosts, or whatever.

I dreamed I was sitting at my old desk back in school, but it was really my desk in the shop office, and the key word was Louise Laurie. I closed my eyes tight and wrote whatever came—feeling my way along the paper with Old Man Burke's stub of a pencil.

So I didn't even see the lights of Miss Laurie's car. And I didn't hear a sound. I just opened my eyes and looked straight into hers. She was staring at me through the office window, her face close to the glass, and one gloved hand resting against the sash. She couldn't possibly have seen what I had written, but she knew it was about her. She knew from my eyes and from the way my hand went down to cover the paper—and in her expression I saw some kind of longing that half troubled me, and made me still.

I stuffed the sheet of paper in my unionall pocket and opened the shop door. "Hello, Miss Laurie."

"Hello, Tuck. You were kind to stay open so late for me."

She stepped to one side to let me pass, and I could feel her eyes following me. I got behind the wheel of her car, and she waited while I slid the seat back to make room for my legs. Then she got in beside me, and we started.

"I thought you were asleep when I looked in the window," she said. "But then I saw you writing, with your eyes closed. What did you write?"

"Nothing."

I drove a block, and another block, and all my thoughts and feelings seemed dammed up inside me, and there was no way of breaking the dam. There was frost on the windshield, and the soft hum of the heater fan, and the scent of her hair filled the car and flowed into my nostrils. This was our last ride together, and I hadn't said anything, and in five minutes we would be at her door. I felt choked with things I didn't dare say, and no time to say them.

"Tuck, aren't your hands cold without any gloves?"

"No."

Another block, and another, and I stopped the car beside her house. Here was the last minute that always went so fast—only this time she didn't gather up her things, but sat looking at me. I held the wheel tight, waiting.

"I guess I shouldn't have asked you to stay open tonight," she said. "It's your last night, isn't it?"

"Yes."

"I'm awfully sorry I was late."

"That's all right."

"But you're angry, Tuck—aren't you?"

"No."

"Then why are you so quiet?"

I tightened my hands still harder on the wheel, turned my head half toward her, and said: "I've been wondering about that myself. I guess I'm quiet because there's so much I want to say."

The heater fan hummed for a long time. She was looking straight into my eyes, then down at my hands. "What do you want to say, Tuck?"

"I'm glad you were late, tonight, Miss Laurie."

"Glad? Why are you glad?"

It was now or never. I had to tell her, even if she laughed at me, even if she hated me. I couldn't look at her when I said it. I made myself think of Professor Hartley's living-room. It kind of pulled me back a little way into her world and gave me the courage to tell her. "I'm glad you were late because you'll be the last one I'll remember. But maybe you would be, anyway."

I saw her eyes grow dark and wide. Her gloved hand moved a little toward me on the seat. The panel light gleamed white on her throat and showed me the strange, haunting expression on her face. She looked as if she had discovered something and didn't know whether it was true.

"You wanted me to be late?" she said. "You want me to be in your memory?"

"Yes."

"Why, Tuck?"

"Because it makes a perfect ending to yesterday and a perfect beginning for tomorrow."

Her hand moved a little closer on the seat, and the doubting, puzzled look came over her face again. "You—you really care that much for me, Tuck?"

"Yes."

"How long have you felt this way about me?"

"Over a year. Sometimes I thought I couldn't hide it. Sometimes I thought you could see it in my eyes. When you left your gloves in the car, I'd pick them up and hold them, as if your hands were inside."

"Did you? Did you really?"

"Yes."

I was all braced for her to laugh, or to say something cool and far away. But she didn't. She seemed happy because of what I had told her

—happy, and quiet, and wondering. She put her fingers up slowly and touched my sleeve, and said: "My hand's inside, now."

I reached down and held her hand in mine. She drew her hand away, and took off her glove, and I kissed the tips of her fingers, one by one. I thought maybe I was dreaming. I thought it couldn't be true and that there was a trick somewhere. Then her voice came again:

"Did you send me those roses when I was sick last fall?"

"Yes."

"Why didn't you enclose a card?"

"I was afraid you'd think I was out of line."

"Why, Tuck? Why did you think that?"

"Because I run a garage, and you're a scholar."

She looked past me through the window and out into the cold, still starlight. "Tuck," she said, "is there any difference?"

There was a difference, but now, for a little while, it was either gone, or it didn't matter. We were just two people, close to each other in the night, and I didn't dare look beyond that.

She turned toward me, moving closer to me on the seat. She took both my hands and held them in hers, looking down at them, smiling in some strange secret way, her lips moving as if she were whispering to herself. I didn't understand how she could be so kind, so gentle, and so natural. I kept waiting for it to turn the wrong way and drop me flat, back where I had started.

"I want to tell you something," she said, all the while staring at my hands. "I want to tell you something good that you have done for me. I love your hands, and when they touch me I am real. When you talk to me and tell me what I mean to you, I am real. I am not in a library any more, reading words that were written two hundred years ago. I'm real, Tuck—I am a person, and I am needed. Do you know what I am saying?"

"No, I don't think I do, Miss Laurie—not quite. Only it makes me happy when you talk like that."

"Will you do something for me?"

"Yes. Anything."

She pressed her shoulder against me, tipped her head back, her eyes half closed, and said: "Put your arms around me and hold me."

I did, and her face looked happy, like a child's face when the child is asleep and dreaming of being always safe. I kissed her, and she pressed herself closer to me, then opened her eyes—and I saw the doubt again and the uncertain curiosity.

"Tuck, do you really feel that way about me? Will this, will tonight, will I, mean something in your tomorrow?"

"Yes."

"Tell me again."

I thought suddenly of the sheet of note-paper in my unionall pocket. I reached around with my left hand and fished it out and gave it to her. "There. That's what I was writing when you came to the garage. It's just a few words and things that came into my head when I thought about you with my eyes closed, and let the pencil go along on its own."

She took the paper, leaned forward, and held it under the dash-light. With her head bowed, her hair swung forward, half hiding her face. After she had read, she put her hands up to her eyes, and I saw her shoulders shaking, and I figured the trick had been sprung on me at last.

"Go ahead," I said. "Go ahead and have a good laugh."

Her shoulders kept right on shaking, and I thinned myself away from her on the seat. "So it's funny, is it?" I said. "I ought to have known."

She brought her head up fast, looking at me as if I had struck her. "No! No! It isn't funny. It's beautiful," she said. She wasn't laughing. She was crying.

She hugged the paper against her, then spread it out under the light and read it again, and I read it again over her shoulder:

Louise Laurie: sweet, sunlight, alone, love, hidden in me to take away, hope, peace, my darling, forever, the last time with her, to remember, to carry, to think, to dream about wherever I am.

I still felt hollow and frightened from the feeling that she had been laughing at me. I had to make sure, just the way she had to make sure that I loved her.

"So you weren't really laughing," I said. "It didn't seem funny to you, after all."

"No. It's serious, and it's beautiful."

"Why are you crying?"

"Oh, I don't know, Tuck. I guess because I had been feeling helpless and useless, not meaning anything to anyone. And then, tonight, you come along—someone that does things, and you give me your love. You think your love isn't good enough for me, don't you?"

"Yes."

She nodded, smiling as if she thought I didn't understand what I was saying. She reached up her long, strong arms, and pulled my head down to hers, and whispered: "It's too good, Tuck. It's perfect. It's unselfish. And any woman who wouldn't be proud of it, to have and to hold, is shallow and cruel."

I held my face against her hair, and said: "Even if there's no future in it?"

"Even if there's no future in it, and who knows about that?"

Her arms loosened and slid down slowly to her lap, and I knew it was good-bye. She drew a long, tired breath and gathered up her purse and her books, and put the sheet of note-paper in her coat pocket. "That's mine, Tuck," she said.

"It sure is."

She lifted her head back, kissed me once more, and said: "Good-bye, my darling."

The words rose up in my throat and caught, and I had to tear them loose for her: "Good-bye, my darling."

She got out of the car, walked to her front door, and stood there in the darkness, waiting for me to go. I put the car in gear, and let in the clutch. I never looked back, but I know she stood there till I was out of sight. I didn't have to look back. I could see the pale shape of her face in the night, written in my eyes for good. . . .

I parked Miss Laurie's car on the Number One lift and stood there for a while, looking at it. I wondered who would ride beside her on the seat. "Who will listen to her laughter?" I asked myself. "Who will feel the warmth of her lips and the pressure of her shoulder? Who will wake up in the night, remembering her eyes and touch of her hands? Why, I will!" I said it aloud in the empty, reëchoing garage. "I will, Tuck Roberts!"

I stood there looking around the garage, my heart singing and happy. I never felt so strong, or so happy, or so sure. I heard myself laughing, and it sounded pretty swell. I walked all around the place looking at things and touching them with my hands that Miss Laurie loved. Some hands, I thought! Some wonderful hands! Do something with 'em, Tuck! Quick!

So I went to the supply closet, got out a new bulb, and screwed it in the place of the blown one that I'd never got around to changing. The base of the bulb made contact in the socket, and it lighted bright in my eyes. "There," I said. "There—I'll just make everything perfect tonight, just the way Miss Laurie made everything perfect for me."

I turned off all the lights, tested both doors to see if they were locked, and went out into the street. Walking home that last time was like no other time. Miss Laurie was with me! Louise Laurie! I was thinking how you could lose a ring, a locket, or a picture. But I couldn't lose the memory of Miss Laurie. I would carry it with me wherever I went, because it was inside me, in my mind and heart, and I could never, never lose it—even if I died.

Ernest Hemingway

SOLDIER'S HOME

The return of Harold Krebs after World War I brings with it the
soldier's problem of adjusting himself to the old surroundings
and to family life at home. Though the word *maladjustment* was
not so freely or so loosely used then as it is today in
conversation about the veterans and their problems, it may
certainly be applied to Krebs and many others like him.
For one thing, they felt betrayed into a sense of spiritual apart-
ness that no one at home could be expected to understand.
This feeling came as a result of realizing that they were
no longer an integral part of something like the A.E.F. which
was big and important and had a mission to perform.
Krebs, we are told, "did not want to leave Germany. He did not
want to come home. Still he had come home."
The same story might well have been written in 1946.

Krebs went to the war from a Methodist college in Kansas.
There is a picture which shows him among his fraternity brothers, all of
them wearing exactly the same height and style collar. He enlisted in
the Marines in 1917 and did not return to the United States until the
second division returned from the Rhine in the summer of 1919.

There is a picture which shows him on the Rhine with two German
girls and another corporal. Krebs and the corporal look too big for their
uniforms. The German girls are not beautiful. The Rhine does not show
in the picture.

By the time Krebs returned to his home town in Oklahoma the greeting of heroes was over. He came back much too late. The men from
the town who had been drafted had all been welcomed elaborately on
their return. There had been a great deal of hysteria. Now the reaction
had set in. People seemed to think it was rather ridiculous for Krebs to
be getting back so late, years after the war was over.

At first Krebs, who had been at Belleau Wood, Soissons, the Champagne, St. Mihiel and in the Argonne, did not want to talk about the war
at all. Later he felt the need to talk but no one wanted to hear about it.
His town had heard too many atrocity stories to be thrilled by actualities. Krebs found that to be listened to at all he had to lie, and after

he had done this twice he, too, had a reaction against the war and against talking about it. A distaste for everything that had happened to him in the war set in because of the lies he had told. All of the times that had been able to make him feel cool and clear inside himself when he thought of them; the times so long back when he had done the one thing, the only thing for a man to do, easily and naturally, when he might have done something else, now lost their cool, valuable quality and then were lost themselves.

His lies were quite unimportant lies and consisted in attributing to himself things other men had seen, done or heard of, and stating as facts certain apocryphal incidents familiar to all soldiers. Even his lies were not sensational at the pool room. His acquaintances, who had heard detailed accounts of German women found chained to machine guns in the Argonne forest and who could not comprehend, or were barred by their patriotism from interest in, any German machine gunners who were not chained, were not thrilled by his stories.

Krebs acquired the nausea in regard to experience that is the result of untruth or exaggeration, and when he occasionally met another man who had really been a soldier and they talked a few minutes in the dressing room at a dance he fell into the easy pose of the old soldier among other soldiers: that he had been badly, sickeningly frightened all the time. In this way he lost everything.

During this time, it was late summer, he was sleeping late in bed, getting up to walk down town to the library to get a book, eating lunch at home, reading on the front porch until he became bored and then walking down through the town to spend the hottest hours of the day in the cool dark of the pool room. He loved to play pool.

In the evening he practised on his clarinet, strolled down town, read and went to bed. He was still a hero to his two young sisters. His mother would have given him breakfast in bed if he had wanted it. She often came in when he was in bed and asked him to tell her about the war, but her attention always wandered. His father was non-committal.

Before Krebs went away to the war he had never been allowed to drive the family motor car. His father was in the real estate business and always wanted the car to be at his command when he required it to take clients out into the country to show them a piece of farm property. The car always stood outside the First National Bank building where his father had an office on the second floor. Now, after the war, it was still the same car.

Nothing was changed in the town except that the young girls had grown up. But they lived in such a complicated world of already defined alliances and shifting feuds that Krebs did not feel the energy or the courage to break into it. He liked to look at them, though. There were so many good-looking young girls. Most of them had their hair cut short.

When he went away only little girls wore their hair like that or girls that were fast. They all wore sweaters and shirt waists with round Dutch collars. It was a pattern. He liked to look at them from the front porch as they walked on the other side of the street. He liked to watch them walking under the shade of the trees. He liked the round Dutch collars above their sweaters. He liked their silk stockings and flat shoes. He liked their bobbed hair and the way they walked.

When he was in town their appeal to him was not very strong. He did not like them when he saw them in the Greek's ice cream parlor. He did not want them themselves really. They were too complicated. There was something else. Vaguely he wanted a girl but he did not want to have to work to get her. He would have liked to have a girl but he did not want to have to spend a long time getting her. He did not want to get into the intrigue and the politics. He did not want to have to do any courting. He did not want to tell any more lies. It wasn't worth it.

He did not want any consequences. He did not want any consequences ever again. He wanted to live along without consequences. Besides he did not really need a girl. The army had taught him that. It was all right to pose as though you had to have a girl. Nearly everybody did that. But it wasn't true. You did not need a girl. That was the funny thing. First a fellow boasted how girls mean nothing to him, that he never thought of them, that they could not touch him. Then a fellow boasted that he could not get along without girls, that he had to have them all the time, that he could not go to sleep without them.

That was all a lie. It was all a lie both ways. You did not need a girl unless you thought about them. He learned that in the army. Then sooner or later you always got one. When you were really ripe for a girl you always got one. You did not have to think about it. Sooner or later it would come. He had learned that in the army.

Now he would have liked a girl if she had come to him and not wanted to talk. But here at home it was all too complicated. He knew he could never get through it all again. It was not worth the trouble. That was the thing about French girls and German girls. There was not all this talking. You couldn't talk much and you did not need to talk. It was simple and you were friends. He thought about France and then he began to think about Germany. On the whole he had liked Germany better. He did not want to leave Germany. He did not want to come home. Still, he had come home. He sat on the front porch.

He liked the girls that were walking along the other side of the street. He liked the look of them much better than the French girls or the German girls. But the world they were in was not the world he was in. He would like to have one of them. But it was not worth it. They were such a nice pattern. He liked the pattern. It was exciting. But he would not go through all the talking. He did not want one badly enough. He liked to look at them all, though. It was not worth it. Not now when things were getting good again.

He sat there on the porch reading a book on the war. It was a history and he was reading about all the engagements he had been in. It was the most interesting reading he had ever done. He wished there were more maps. He looked forward with a good feeling to reading all the really good histories when they would come out with good detail maps. Now he was really learning about the war. He had been a good soldier. That made a difference.

One morning after he had been home about a month his mother came into his bedroom and sat on the bed. She smoothed her apron.

"I had a talk with your father last night, Harold," she said, "and he is willing for you to take the car out in the evenings."

"Yeah?" said Krebs, who was not fully awake. "Take the car out? Yeah?"

"Yes. Your father has felt for some time that you should be able to take the car out in the evenings whenever you wished but we only talked it over last night."

"I'll bet you made him," Krebs said.

"No. It was your father's suggestion that we talk the matter over."

"Yeah. I'll bet you made him." Krebs sat up in bed.

"Will you come down to breakfast, Harold?" his mother said.

"As soon as I get my clothes on," Krebs said.

His mother went out of the room and he could hear her frying something downstairs while he washed, shaved and dressed to go down into the dining-room for breakfast. While he was eating breakfast his sister brought in the mail.

"Well, Hare," she said. "You old sleepy-head. What do you ever get up for?"

Krebs looked at her. He liked her. She was his best sister.

"Have you got the paper?" he asked.

She handed him *The Kansas City Star* and he shucked off its brown wrapper and opened it to the sporting page. He folded *The Star* open and propped it against the water pitcher with his cereal dish to steady it, so he could read while he ate.

"Harold," his mother stood in the kitchen doorway, "Harold, please don't muss up the paper. Your father can't read his *Star* if it's been mussed."

"I won't muss it," Krebs said.

His sister sat down at the table and watched him while he read.

"We're playing indoor over at school this afternoon," she said. "I'm going to pitch."

"Good," said Krebs. "How's the old wing?"

"I can pitch better than lots of the boys. I tell them all you taught me. The other girls aren't much good."

"Yeah?" said Krebs.

"I tell them all you're my beau. Aren't you my beau, Hare?"

"You bet."

"Couldn't your brother really be your beau just because he's your brother?"

"I don't know."

"Sure you know. Couldn't you be my beau, Hare, if I was old enough and if you wanted to?"

"Sure. You're my girl now."

"Am I really your girl?"

"Sure."

"Do you love me?"

"Uh, huh."

"Will you love me always?"

"Sure."

"Will you come over and watch me play indoor?"

"Maybe."

"Aw, Hare, you don't love me. If you loved me, you'd want to come over and watch me play indoor."

Kreb's mother came into the dining-room from the kitchen. She carried a plate with two fried eggs and some crisp bacon on it and a plate of buckwheat cakes.

"You run along, Helen," she said. "I want to talk to Harold."

She put the eggs and bacon down in front of him and brought in a jug of maple syrup for the buckwheat cakes. Then she sat down across the table from Krebs.

"I wish you'd put down the paper a minute, Harold," she said.

Krebs took down the paper and folded it.

"Have you decided what you are going to do yet, Harold?" his mother said, taking off her glasses.

"No," said Krebs.

"Don't you think it's about time?" His mother did not say this in a mean way. She seemed worried.

"I hadn't thought about it," Krebs said.

"God has some work for every one to do," his mother said. "There can be no idle hands in His Kingdom."

"I'm not in His Kingdom," Krebs said.

"We are all of us in His Kingdom."

Krebs felt embarrassed and resentful as always.

"I've worried about you so much, Harold," his mother went on. "I know the temptations you must have been exposed to. I know how weak men are. I know what your own dear grandfather, my own father, told us about the Civil War and I have prayed for you. I pray for you all day long, Harold."

Krebs looked at the bacon fat hardening on his plate.

"Your father is worried, too," his mother went on. "He thinks you have lost your ambition, that you haven't got a definite aim in life. Charley Simmons, who is just your age, has a good job and is going to be married. The boys are all settling down; they're all determined to get somewhere; you can see that boys like Charley Simmons are on their way to being really a credit to the community."

Krebs said nothing.

"Don't look that way, Harold," his mother said. "You know we love you and I want to tell you for your own good how matters stand. Your father does not want to hamper your freedom. He thinks you should be allowed to drive the car. If you want to take some of the nice girls out riding with you, we are only too pleased. We want you to enjoy yourself. But you are going to have to settle down to work, Harold. Your father doesn't care what you start in at. All work is honorable as he says. But you've got to make a start at something. He asked me to speak to you this morning and then you can stop in and see him at his office."

"Is that all?" Krebs said.

"Yes. Don't you love your mother, dear boy?"

"No," Krebs said.

His mother looked at him across the table. Her eyes were shiny. She started crying.

"I don't love anybody," Krebs said.

It wasn't any good. He couldn't tell her, he couldn't make her see it. It was silly to have said it. He had only hurt her. He went over and took hold of her arm. She was crying with her head in her hands.

"I didn't mean it," he said. "I was just angry at something. I didn't mean I didn't love you."

His mother went on crying. Krebs put his arm on her shoulder.

"Can't you believe me, mother?"

His mother shook her head.

"Please, please, mother. Please believe me."

"All right," his mother said chokily. She looked up at him. "I believe you, Harold."

Krebs kissed her hair. She put her face up to him.

"I'm your mother," she said. "I held you next to my heart when you were a tiny baby."

Krebs felt sick and vaguely nauseated.

"I know, Mummy," he said. "I'll try and be a good boy for you."

"Would you kneel and pray with me, Harold?" his mother asked.

They knelt down beside the dining-room table and Krebs's mother prayed.

"Now, you pray, Harold," she said.

"I can't," Krebs said.

"Try, Harold."

"I can't."

"Do you want me to pray for you?"

"Yes."

So his mother prayed for him and then they stood up and Krebs kissed his mother and went out of the house. He had tried so to keep his life from being complicated. Still, none of it had touched him. He had felt sorry for his mother and she had made him lie. He would go to Kansas City and get a job and she would feel all right about it. There would be one more scene maybe before he got away. He would not go down to his father's office. He would miss that one. He wanted his life to go smoothly. It had just gotten going that way. Well, that was all over now, anyway. He would go over to the schoolyard and watch Helen play indoor baseball.

A variety in theme and form

A few words should be said about the contents of Part V, "A Variety." It has been convenient to arrange all of the stories in the book thus far in groups designated by headings which are more or less appropriate; for, although the stories brought together in each group are vastly different in mood, style, and subject matter, they have at least a common theme. But such is not the case in this final part. Here there is no suggestion of a common theme. And, as has been characteristic of the contents of this whole anthology, the stories differ widely in subject matter and style. They illustrate the wide range of the short story as a literary form. Here is variety indeed, from "Theft" by Katherine Anne Porter to "The Tree of Knowledge" by Henry James; from a light anecdote briefly told by Peter De Vries to what is almost a novelette, the long, tensely dramatic study of the dark well of human character by John Galsworthy.

The first three stories in Part V are distinctive in one important respect: in form they are "short shorts," and as such they reveal certain characteristics which set them apart from what might otherwise be called simply shorter stories. The "short short" (as the term is interpreted here) is basically an anecdote, and this can be a little work of art.

Somerset Maugham, one of the established masters of the storyteller's art, speaks highly of the anecdote, noting that many have written well in this form—and, incidentally, "no one more admirably than Maupassant." One thing you will notice about this type of story, Maugham observes, is that you can tell it "over the dinner table or in a ship's smoking room and hold the attention of your listeners. . . . When you

have read it to find out what happens you can read it
again for the cleverness of the telling." [1] It is the sort of story
that Mr. Maugham likes best and is furthermore the sort
that he himself writes well. Many of the other stories
in this anthology are basically anecdotes—notably "Jeeves and
the Song of Songs"—as the reader can easily discover for
himself, for their length is determined mainly by the
amount of exposition and description with which their authors
have chosen to adorn them. But in its pure form, stripped
of all nonessentials, the anecdote simply tells of an incident that
is "curious, striking, and original."

James Thurber

THE TOPAZ CUFFLINKS MYSTERY

A collection would seem somehow incomplete without a story—
even a very short one—by Thurber. Who but Thurber
would lead off with just this sort of disarming matter-of-fact
sentence: ". . . the man was on his knees in the long
grass beside the road, barking like a dog"? Who but a Thurber
character would get himself into such a situation as is set
forth here? The reader may have to read this mystery a second
time to find out exactly what does actually happen here.
When the motorcycle cop waves his hand and roars away, *he*
may be satisfied. He has proved something to the lady's
husband, has even settled a pretty important controversy—so
he thinks. But the lady is not convinced, and neither is
the reader, who (if he wants to make a similar bet and really
wants to settle it) must undertake the same experiment
for himself some night.

W hen the motorcycle cop came roaring up, unexpectedly,
out of Never-Never Land (the way motorcycle cops do), the man was
on his hands and knees in the long grass beside the road, barking like
a dog. The woman was driving slowly along in a car that stopped about
eighty feet away; its headlights shone on the man: middle-aged, bewildered, sedentary. He got to his feet.

---

[1] *Tellers of Tales,* Selected and with an Introduction by W. Somerset Maugham (New
York: Doubleday, Doran, 1939), p. xviii.

"What's goin' on here?" asked the cop. The woman giggled. "Cock-eyed," thought the cop. He did not glance at her.

"I guess it's gone," said the man. "I—ah—could not find it."

"What was it?"

"What I lost?" The man squinted unhappily. "Some—some cuff-links; topazes set in gold." He hesitated: the cop didn't seem to believe him. "They were the color of a fine Moselle," said the man. He put on a pair of spectacles which he had been holding in his hand. The woman giggled.

"Hunt things better with ya glasses off?" asked the cop. He pulled his motorcycle to the side of the road to let a car pass. "Better pull over off the concrete, lady," he said. She drove the car off the roadway.

"I'm nearsighted," said the man. "I can hunt things at a distance with my glasses on, but I do better with them off if I am close to some-thing." The cop kicked his heavy boots through the grass where the man had been crouching.

"He was barking," ventured the lady in the car, "so that I could see where he was." The cop pulled his machine up on its stand-ard; he and the man walked over to the automobile.

"What I don't get," said the officer, "is how you lose ya cufflinks a hundred feet in front of where ya car is; a person usually stops his car *past* the place he loses somethin', not a hundred feet before he gits *to* the place."

The lady laughed again; her husband got slowly into the car, as if he were afraid the officer would stop him any moment. The officer studied them.

"Been to a party?" he asked. It was after midnight.

"We're not drunk, if that's what you mean," said the woman, smiling. The cop tapped his fingers on the door of the car.

"You people didn't lose no topazes," he said.

"Is it against the law for a man to be down on all fours beside a road, barking in a perfectly civil manner?" demanded the lady.

"No, ma'm," said the cop. He made no move to get on his motor-cycle, however, and go on about his business. There was just the quiet chugging of the cycle engine and auto engine, for a time.

"I'll tell you how it was, Officer," said the man, in a crisp new tone. "We were settling a bet, O.K.?"

"O.K.," said the cop. "Who win?" There was another pulsing silence.

"The lady bet," said her husband, with dignity, as though he were explaining some important phase of industry to a newly hired clerk, "the lady bet that my eyes would shine like a cat's do at night, if she came upon me suddenly close to the ground alongside the road. We had passed a cat, whose eyes gleamed. We had passed several persons, whose eyes did *not* gleam—"

"Simply because they were above the light and not under it," said the lady. "A man's eyes would gleam like a cat's if people were ordinarily caught by headlights at the same angle as cats are." The cop walked over to where he had left his motorcycle, picked it up, kicked the standard out, and wheeled it back.

"A cat's eyes," he said, "are different than yours and mine. Dogs, cats, skunks, it's all the same. They can see in a dark room."

"Not in a totally dark room," said the lady.

"Yes, they can," said the cop.

"No, they can't; not if there is no light at all in the room, not if it's absolutely *black,*" said the lady. "The question came up the other night; there was a professor there and he said there must be at least a ray of light, no matter how faint."

"That may be," said the cop, after a solemn pause, pulling at his gloves. "But people's eyes don't shine—I go along these roads every night an' pass hunderds of cats and hunderds of people."

"The people are never close to the ground," said the lady.

"*I* was close to the ground," said her husband.

"Look at it this way," said the cop. "I've seen wildcats in *trees* at night and *their* eyes shine."

"There you are!" said the lady's husband. "That proves it."

"I don't see how," said the lady. There was another silence.

"Because a wildcat in a tree's eyes are higher than the level of a man's," said her husband. The cop may possibly have followed this, the lady obviously did not; neither one said anything. The cop got on his machine, raced his engine, seemed to be thinking about something, and throttled down. He turned to the man.

"Took ya glasses off so the headlights wouldn't make ya glasses shine, huh?" he asked.

"That's right," said the man. The cop waved his hand triumphantly, and roared away. "Smart guy," said the man to his wife, irritably.

"I still don't see where the wildcat proves anything," said his wife. He drove off slowly.

"Look," he said. "You claim that the whole thing depends on how *low* a *cat's* eyes are; I—"

"I didn't say that; I said it all depends on how *high* a *man's* eyes . . ."

CATCH AS CATCH CAN

When Peter De Vries tries to find out what Mickey's full name is, he does so without realizing that he will have to reckon with Irma. This is one of those embarrassing-moment situations that are much funnier to tell about than to experience. This anecdote would be equally good if it were told by Irma, and from her point of view. It would probably lose nothing in the telling!

Not catching the name may be even more disastrous socially than Emily Post and other authorities say, judging from an experience I had recently. Some time ago, I was introduced to a girl by an old friend of mine named Ed Salzburg. I ran into Ed and the girl on the street one day, he presented her without my catching the name, and I went on and forgot about her. Then, one evening a few weeks later, he phoned and dropped in, bringing her along.

Luckily, I had heard him call her by what was apparently her nickname, during our encounter on the street, so I was able to introduce her after a fashion to my wife. "And this is Mickey," I said, beaming, a hand on Ed's shoulder, for he and Mickey were even then conspicuously in love. So everything was all right for that evening. But when Ed bade us good night he asked us to have dinner the next week with him and Mickey, and we eventually returned the invitation, and so on, till, one thing leading to another, I found I had begun to see Ed Salzburg regularly again and had struck up a friendship with a woman whose name I hadn't the slightest idea of. I eat and drink with her (I was presently telling myself), I dance with her and go with her to the theatre, and I don't know who the woman is.

"How can we find out?" I asked my wife, when the whole affair began to have a tincture of unreality. It was long past the time when I could have asked Ed or Mickey what her name was without bringing everything down in a ridiculous heap. She is a sensitive sort anyhow, and I didn't want to risk embarrassment. I tried various methods of extracting the information deviously. One evening, for instance, I proposed a parlor game in which everybody writes down his name in full on a large sheet of paper. But that fell through; nobody wanted to play. I found out where Mickey lived by dropping her and Ed off at her apartment house on our way home from Carnegia Hall in a cab one night, and the next day made a special trip there to read the mailboxes, but the entry wall was a solid mass of names, rendering the effort hopeless. "I wish he'd get rid of that woman," I would say to my wife, and, laughing like a lout, to Ed, "Why don't you two get married?" The reckoning I knew was inevitable lay in wait for me at a cocktail party we gave.

I was in the living room dropping olives into Martini glasses, preparatory to the party, with that queasy expectation that for me precedes all large-scale entertaining when I suddenly remembered. "My God!" I called to my wife in the kitchen. "Ed and Mickey. Will they know everybody?"

"Don't bother me with that now," she called back.

I dropped a few more olives into glasses, thinking. Obviously I couldn't go around saying "And this is Mickey" to everybody. Presently, I had an inspiration. "I think I've got it," I said, going to the kitchen door. "One of us says to her casually, 'By the way, Mickey, we were just talking about you, wondering how you spelled your name. How do you spell it?' How's that?"

"Fine," my wife said. "Especially if it's Barnes."

I was giving thought to how I might get out of this trap, when I heard a loud "bong" from the front-door chime. The first guests turned out to be Ed and Mickey themselves, and I saw them into the living room, where Mickey went right to the canapés, remarking apologetically that she hadn't had any lunch. The bell rang again almost immediately and I started to answer it, but before I reached the door an impulse spun me around, like a rat revolving in a corner. "Oh, say, Mick," I said, "we were just talking about you, wondering how you spelled your name. How do you?" I ground my teeth and hung on.

She finished eating what she had in her mouth and wiped her fingers on a napkin. "With an 'i,' " she said. "Lots of people spell it with a 'y,' of course, but our family never have."

Ball one. By this time, my wife had gone to answer the door, and I ran and hid in the kitchen, where the maid from the caterers was preparing a pan of cheese puffs for the oven. "I'll give you a hand with these," I said, pitching in. With my ears keyed for the sound of any new developments, I could hear bits of Ed's and Mickey's chitchat, which appeared to be about a letter Mickey had written but forgotten to mail. "Remind me to mail it when we leave," I heard her say, and then there was a spate of chatter from the newcomers, who turned out to be Harry and Irma Welch, closely followed by three other couples. I was straining to place all the voices, calculating swiftly who knew Mickey and who didn't, when suddenly what I'd heard her say popped back into my mind: "Remind me to mail it when we leave." That meant

Mickey had the letter with her, possibly in the pocket of her coat, which this minute was lying on the bed where the guests were leaving their wraps. If so, what was to prevent me from sneaking a look at it, just in case there was a return name and address on the envelope?

I slipped into the bedroom and was burrowing among the coats when I heard the approach of female laughter, and, leaving the bed dishevelled, I scurried for a large mahogany wardrobe that serves us for a closet. From inside it, I heard several women enter the bedroom and, a few minutes later, heard my wife querulously calling my name, complaining that the guests were piling up. When at last the coast seemed clear, I crept out and stole back to the bed. Mickey's coat, which I knew was a gray tweed I had always liked her in, was at the bottom of the growing pile, and I pulled it out. I was frisking the pockets when I heard a noise behind me, and turned to see Irma Welch watching me from the doorway. I giggled nervously and dropped the coat. "I don't know Mickey's name," I said.

Irma walked to the bed, glancing at me oddly, picked up her own coat, and took a fresh pack of cigarettes and a book of matches from one of the pockets. She opened the cigarettes.

"Her last name," I said, moving around the foot of the bed. "I didn't catch it the first time, which was—oh, three or four months ago—and I've felt too embarrassed to ask. It's one of those things"—I laughed—"and you know how they are."

Irma, a very beautiful woman, lit a cigarette and then paused to comb out the ends of her hair and draw a stocking up, regarding me in the mirror. I went around the bed a step farther. "Well, so as they were coming in a while ago, I thought I heard Mick say something about a letter she had to mail, and I was looking for her name on it, or, rather, looking for the letter in her coat," I jabbered in a brisk falsetto. "By the way, Irma, what *is* her name? Do you know?"

Irma turned with a kind of smile and opened her mouth to say something, but just then my wife came in, and Irma went out. "Where in God's name have you been?" my wife asked.

"Trying to find out Mickey's name," I said in a vexed whisper, looking after Irma.

"It's Striker. Mary Ann Striker," my wife said. "Now I wish you'd get in there and start taking care of people."

"How did you find out?" I inquired resentfully.

"I asked somebody," she said.

So that was how we found out Mickey's name. I went on into the living room and began circulating among my guests, grinning like a stuffed weasel every time I got near Irma. What made me especially wretched was not knowing what she had been going to say when I asked her what Mickey's name was. It still harasses me. I keep thinking it may have been something arch and cynical, because Irma is a girl who tends to be arch and cynical. Still, I don't know. I just know that I feel peculiar every time I see Irma. Maybe she believes me; then, again, maybe she retains something of what must have been her first suspicion: that I'm a kleptomaniac or have some other obscure quirk, a shabby Raffles who invites people to his house and then rifles their belongings for pocket money. Anyhow, the whole experience has tidied up at least one aspect of my deportment. I may forget a face now and again, but I damn well never miss a name.

THE MAN IN THE MIDDLE

A story that can surely be read again for the "cleverness of the
telling"—after the reader has found out what happens
—is this one, told by Alexander Woollcott, supreme raconteur,
writing for the young *New Yorker*'s "talk of the town."
Here the Woollcott personality, the Woollcott style, established
itself early, just as later the artistry of his narrative skill
was to impress itself memorably on the thousands of listeners
who tuned their radios regularly to the familiar voice of
the "Town Crier." Here is the type of anecdote that must not
give itself away until the very last word has been written.

T hen there is the story of the home-bound girl and the three
thugs in the subway. For the past year or so it has been a rumor in the
air, a part of the very murmur of the town. I dare say every city-editor
in New York has had to throw it in his scrap-basket at least once a
week—the same yawning scrap-basket into which his predecessor
used to pitch the hot weekly tip that Oscar Wilde was not buried beneath the morose Epstein monument in Père-Lachaise at all, but was
alive, in a quiet way, and lodged incognito behind a brownstone front
in our unconscious midst.

As it first reached me, the story had its setting in a subway local
plodding toward Fort Hamilton Parkway at an hour long past one in the
morning. The girl, a stenographer who lived out that way with her folks,
had been to a theatre and supper party in Manhattan. One of the men
at the supper had made what it would be effusive to call a half-hearted
offer to see her home, but she had rewarded that heroic gesture by an
amiable refusal. Accustomed to pushing competently about in the
crowds downtown, the thought of an untimely jaunt into darkest
Brooklyn seemed dreary but not alarming.

Her first disquiet came shortly after there got into the almost deserted train at the first stop beyond Myrtle Avenue three forbidding ruffians. The man in the middle seemed so drunk that his companions were practically carrying him, and his insouciant legs had the curious detachment of a scarecrow's. Our heroine was eyeing these wastrels with distaste when she realized that the man in the middle had fixed one bleary eye upon her, and, nervously following the direction of his gaze, she saw that there on her wrist, defiantly visible, was her bracelet watch with its chain of diamonds. She hastily drew her sleeve down over it, made a slight pretense of looking up and down the car, and then, out of the corner of her eye, reconnoitered. It was true. Slouched down between his friends, he *was* looking at her, and out of the corners of their eyes, as furtive and as wary as herself, his two companions were looking at her too.

Her heart sank. Two more stops and she would be at her own station. Suppose they followed her? Suppose there was no one on the echoing platform at that chilly hour, no one in the change booth? In her imagination she was already trying to make her legs walk up the stairway to the street, sick with the knowledge that the monstrous three were following silently at her heels. Her knees turned to water. Panic possessed her. She had an impulse to tear her foolish watch from her wrist and pitch it across the aisle. She glanced up and down the car. By this time its only other occupants were a benign, bespectacled old gentleman and his wife, a serene, white-haired couple who would not be of much help if she should absurdly scream out to them that the mute triumvirate across the car were plotting assault and robbery, when, as some remnant of her reason told her, they were probably doing nothing of the kind. Besides, the old couple were getting up to leave at the next station. They were passing her on their way to the door. She had a numbing sense that all law and order was then and there taking its departure when, without looking at her and without moving his lips, the old gentleman said something.

"Follow us off this train."

It took her a second to realize that this was meant for her. In another, she found herself on the station platform, the door closing behind them. In still another, the train grunted, pulled itself together and lurched off into the tunnel, carrying the dreadful three with it. She wanted to laugh hysterically at her own relief. Now the old gentleman was speaking to her.

"My dear," he said, "I apologize for issuing orders to you, but there was no time for ceremony. Did you notice those men who sat across from you?"

It seemed she had.

"Well," he went on, "I didn't like to leave you in the train with them. I am a doctor, my dear, and I could not help noticing an odd thing about that little group. Did you observe anything peculiar about that man in the middle?"

"He was very drunk," the girl said.

The doctor shook his head.

"Perhaps he had been," he admitted, "but not when they carried him into the train. When they carried him into the train, the man in the middle was dead."

JEEVES AND THE SONG OF SONGS

The story that is at heart an anecdote is, of course, not always told as a "short short." Somerset Maugham's comment about this type of story certainly applies to "Jeeves and the Song of Songs," as it would to many delightful anecdotes told by the incomparable Wodehouse. Once you have read the account of an exploit carried out by Jeeves—that supreme example of the gentleman's gentleman—you will want to read it again to appreciate the technical artistry of the author. Jeeves in this instance proves equal to the task of saving his master's friend, Mr. Glossop, from a marriage to one woman, thus preserving him for another. And we are not surprised, for Jeeves is endowed with a keen insight into character, an inside knowledge of the frothy social set graced by his master, and a comprehension of woman's ways. The bride-to-have-been is an incipient opera singer, and Jeeves contrives to let her beat herself at her own game, singing. Didn't Aunt Dahlia say in the first place, "Put the thing squarely up to Jeeves and let Nature take its course"?

Another day dawned all hot and fresh and, in pursuance of my unswerving policy at that time, I was singing "Sonny Boy" in my bath, when Jeeves's voice filtered through the woodwork.

"I beg your pardon, sir."

I had just got to that bit about the angels being lonely, where you need every ounce of concentration in order to make the spectacular finish, but I signed off courteously.

"Yes, Jeeves? Say on."

"Mr. Glossop, sir."

"What about him?"

"He is in the sitting room, sir."

"Young Tuppy Glossop?"

"Yes, sir," Jeeves answered in his monosyllabic way.

"You say that he is in the sitting room?" I asked.

"Yes, sir."

"Desiring speech with me?"

"Yes, sir."

"H'm!"

"Sir?"

"I only said 'H'm.' "

And I'll tell you why I said "H'm." It was because the man's story had interested me strangely. And I'll tell you why the man's story had interested me strangely. Owing to a certain episode that had occurred one night at the Drones' Club, there had sprung up recently a coolness, as you might describe it, between this Glossop and myself. The news, therefore, that he was visiting me at my flat, especially at an hour when he must have known that I would be in my bath and consequently in a strong strategic position to heave a wet sponge at him, surprised me considerably.

I hopped out with some briskness and, slipping a couple of towels about the torso, made for the sitting room. I found young Tuppy at the piano, playing "Sonny Boy" with one finger.

"What ho!" I said, not without hauteur.

"Oh, hullo, Bertie," said Tuppy. "I say, Bertie, I want to see you about something important."

It seemed to me that the bloke was embarrassed. He had moved to the mantelpiece, and now he broke a vase in a constrained way.

"The fact is, Bertie, I'm engaged."

"Engaged?"

"Engaged," said young Tuppy, coyly dropping a photograph frame upon the fender. "Practically, that is."

"Practically?"

"Yes. You'll like her, Bertie. Her name is Cora Bellinger. She's studying for opera. Wonderful voice she has. Also dark, flashing eyes and a great soul."

"How do you mean, 'practically'?"

"Well, it's this way. Before ordering the trousseau there is one little point she wants cleared up. You see, what with her great soul and all that, she has a rather serious outlook on life, and the one thing she absolutely bars is anything in the shape of hearty humour. You know, practical joking and so forth.

"She said if she thought I was a practical joker she would never speak to me again. And unfortunately she appears to have heard about that little affair at the Drones'. . . . I expect you have forgotten all about that, Bertie?"

"I have not!"

"No, no, not forgotten exactly. What I mean is, nobody laughs more heartily at the recollection than you. And what I want you to do, old man, is to seize an early opportunity of taking Cora aside and categorically denying that there is any truth in the story. My happiness, Bertie, is in your hands, if you know what I mean."

Well, of course, if he put it like that, what could I do? We Woosters have our code.

"Oh, all right," I said, but far from brightly.

"Splendid fellow!"

"When do I meet this blighted female?" I asked.

"Don't call her 'this blighted female,' Bertie, old man. I have planned all that out. I will bring her around here to-day for a spot of lunch."

"What!"

"At one-thirty. Right. Good. Fine. Thanks. I knew I could rely on you."

He pushed off, and I turned to Jeeves, who had shimmered in with the morning meal.

"Lunch for three to-day, Jeeves," I said.

"Very good, sir."

"You know, Jeeves, it's a bit thick. You remember my telling you about what Mr. Glossop did to me that night at the Drones'?"

"Yes, sir."

"For months I have been cherishing dreams of a hideous vengeance. And now, so far from crushing him into the dust, I've got to fill him and fiancée with rich food, and generally rally round and be the good angel."

"Life is like that, sir."

"True, Jeeves. What have we here?" I asked, inspecting the tray.

"Kippered herrings, sir."

"And I shouldn't wonder," I said, for I was in thoughtful mood, "if even herrings haven't troubles of their own."

"Quite possibly, sir."

"I mean, apart from getting kippered."

"Yes, sir."

"And so it goes on, Jeeves, so it goes on."

I can't say I saw exactly eye to eye with young Tuppy in his admiration for the Bellinger female. Delivered on the mat at one-twenty-five, she proved to be an upstanding light-heavyweight of some thirty summers with a commanding eye and a square chin which I, personally, would have steered clear of.

She seemed to me a good deal like what Cleopatra would have been after going in too freely for the starches and cereals. I don't know why it is, but women who have anything to do with opera, even if they're only studying for it, always appear to run to surplus poundage.

Tuppy, however, was obviously all for her. His whole demeanour, both before and during luncheon, was that of one striving to be worthy

of a noble soul. When Jeeves offered him a cocktail he practically recoiled as from a serpent. It was terrible to see the change which love
had effected in the man. The spectacle put me off my food.

At half-past two the Bellinger left to go to a singing lesson. Tuppy
trotted after her to the door, bleating and frisking a goodish bit, and
then came back and looked at me in a marked manner.

"Well, Bertie?"

"Well, what?"

"I mean, isn't she?"

"Oh, rather," I said, humouring the poor fish.

"Wonderful eyes?"

"Oh, rather."

"Wonderful figure?"

"Oh, quite."

"Wonderful voice?"

Here I was able to intone the response with a little more heartiness.
The Bellinger, at Tuppy's request, had sung us a few songs before digging in at the trough, and nobody could have denied that her pipes
were in great shape. The plaster was still falling from the ceiling.

"Terrific," I said.

Tuppy sighed, and, having helped himself to about four inches of
whisky and one of soda, took a deep, refreshing draft.

"Ah!" he said. "I needed that."

"Why didn't you have it at lunch?"

"Well, it's this way," said Tuppy. "I have not actually ascertained
what Cora's opinions are on the subject of the taking of slight snorts
from time to time, but I thought it more prudent to lay off. The view I
took was that laying off would seem to indicate the serious mind. It is
touch and go, as you might say, at the moment, and the smallest thing
may turn the scale."

"What beats me is how on earth you expect to make her think you've
got a mind at all—let alone a serious one."

"Well, I have my own methods, Bertie, old man."

"I bet they're rotten, Tuppy."

"You do, do you?" said Tuppy warmly. "Well, let me tell you, my
lad, that that's exactly what they're anything but. I am handling this
affair with consummate generalship. Do you remember Beefy Bingham
who was at Oxford with us?"

"I ran into him only the other day. He's a parson now."

"Yes. Down in the East End. Well, he runs a lads' club for the local
toughs—you know the sort of thing—cocoa and backgammon in the
reading room and occasional clean, bright entertainments in the Oddfellows' Hall; and I've been helping him. I don't suppose I've passed an
evening away from the backgammon board for weeks.

"Cora is extremely pleased. I've got her to promise to sing on Tuesday at Beefy's next clean, bright entertainment."

"You have?"

"I absolutely have. And now mark my devilish ingenuity, Bertie. I'm going to sing, too."

"Why do you suppose that's going to get you anywhere?"

"Because the way I intend to sing the song I intend to sing will prove to her that there are great deeps in my nature, whose existence she has not suspected. She will see that rough, unlettered audience wiping the tears out of its bally eyes and she will say to herself, 'What ho! The old egg really has a soul!'

"For it is not one of your mouldy comic songs, Bertie. No low buffoonery of that sort for me. It is all about angels being lonely and what not."

I uttered a sharp cry. "You can't mean you're going to sing 'Sonny Boy'?"

"I jolly well do."

I was shocked. Yes, dash it, I was shocked. You see, I held strong views on "Sonny Boy." I considered it a song only to be attempted by a few of the elect in the privacy of the bathroom. And the thought of its being murdered in open Oddfellows' Hall by a bloke who could treat a pal as young Tuppy had treated me that night at the Drones' sickened me. Yes, sickened me.

I hadn't time, however, to express my horror and disgust, for at this juncture Jeeves came in.

"Mrs. Travers has just rung up on the telephone, sir. She desired me to say that she will be calling to see you in a few minutes."

"Contents noted, Jeeves," I said. "Now listen, Tuppy—" I began.

I stopped. The fellow wasn't there.

"Mr. Glossop has left, sir."

"Left? How can he have left? He was sitting there."

"That is the front door closing now, sir."

"But what made him shoot off like that?"

"Possibly Mr. Glossop did not wish to meet Mrs. Travers, sir."

"Why not?"

"I could not say, sir. But undoubtedly at the mention of Mrs. Travers's name he rose very swiftly."

"Strange, Jeeves."

"Yes, sir."

I turned to a subject of more moment.

"Jeeves," I said, "Mr. Glossop proposes to sing 'Sonny Boy' at an entertainment down in the East End next Tuesday before an audience consisting mainly of costermongers, with a sprinkling of whelk-stall owners, purveyors of blood oranges, and minor pugilists."

"Indeed, sir?"

"Make a note to remind me to be there. He will infallibly get the bird, and I want to witness his downfall."

"Very good, sir."

"And when Mrs. Travers arrives I shall be in the sitting room."

Those who know Bertram Wooster best are aware that in his journey through life he is impeded and generally snookered by about as scaly a collection of aunts as was ever assembled. But there is one exception to the general ghastliness—viz. my aunt Dahlia. She married old Tom Travers the year Bluebottle won the Cambridgeshire, and is one of the best. It is always a pleasure to me to chat with her, and it was with a courtly geniality that I rose to receive her as she sailed over the threshold at about two-fifty-five.

She seemed somewhat perturbed, and plunged into the agenda without delay. Aunt Dahlia is one of those big, hearty women. She used to go in a lot for hunting, and she generally speaks as if she had just sighted a fox on a hillside half a mile away.

"Bertie," she cried, in the manner of one encouraging a platoon of hounds to renewed efforts, "I want your help."

"And you shall have it, Aunt Dahlia," I replied suavely. "I can honestly say that there is no one to whom I would more readily do a good turn, no one to whom I am more delighted to be—"

"Less of it," she begged; "less of it. You know that friend of yours, young Glossop?"

"He's just been lunching here."

"He has, has he? Well, I wish you'd poisoned his soup."

"We didn't have soup. And when you describe him as a 'friend of mine,' I wouldn't quite say the term absolutely squared with the facts. Some time ago, one night when we had been dining together at the Drones'—"

At this point Aunt Dahlia—a little brusquely, it seemed to me—said that she would rather wait for the story of my life till she could get it in book form. I could see now that she was definitely not her usual sunny self, so I shelved my personal grievances and asked what was biting her.

"It's that young hound Glossop," she said.

"What's he been doing?"

"Breaking Angela's heart."

(Angela. Daughter of above. My cousin. Quite a good egg.)

"What!"

"I say he's—breaking—Angela's—*heart!*"

"You say he's breaking Angela's heart?"

She begged me to suspend the vaudeville cross-talk stuff.

"How's he doing that?" I asked.

"With his neglect. With his low, callous, double-crossing duplicity."

" 'Duplicity' is the word, Aunt Dahlia," I said. "In treating of young Tuppy Glossop, it springs naturally to the lips. Let me tell you what he did to me one night at the Drones'. We had finished dinner—"

"Ever since the beginning of the season, up to about three weeks ago, he was all over Angela. The sort of thing which, when I was a girl, we should have described as courting."

"Or wooing?"

"Wooing or courting, whichever you like."

"Whichever *you* like, Aunt Dahlia," I said courteously.

"Well, anyway, he haunted the house, lapped up daily lunches, took her out dancing half the night, and so on, till naturally the poor kid, who's quite off her oats about him, took it for granted that it was only a question of time before he suggested that they should feed for life out of the same crib. And now he's gone and dropped her like a hot brick, and I hear he's infatuated with some girl he met at a Chelsea tea party —a girl named—now, what was it?"

"Cora Bellinger."

"How do you know?"

"She was lunching here to-day."

"He brought her?"

"Yes."

"What's she like?"

"Pretty massive. In shape, a bit on the lines of the Albert Hall."

"Did he seem very fond of her?"

"Couldn't take his eyes off the chassis."

"The modern young man," said Aunt Dahlia, "is a pot of poison and wants a nurse to lead him by the hand and some strong attendant to kick him regularly at intervals of a quarter of an hour."

I tried to point out the silver lining.

"If you ask me, Aunt Dahlia," I said, "I think Angela is well out of it. This Glossop is a tough baby. One of London's toughest. I was trying to tell you just now what he did to me one night at the Drones'.

"First, having got me in sporting mood with a bottle of the ripest, he bet me that I wouldn't swing myself across the swimming pool by the ropes and rings. I knew I could do it on my head, so I took him on, exulting in the fun, so to speak. And when I'd done half the trip, and was going strong, I found he had looped the last rope back against the rail, leaving me no alternative but to drop into the depths and swim ashore in correct evening costume."

"He did?"

"He certainly did. It was months ago, and I haven't got really dry yet. You wouldn't want your daughter to marry a man capable of a thing like that!"

"On the contrary, you restore my faith in the young hound. I see that there must be lots of good in him, after all. And I want this Bellinger business broken up, Bertie."

"How?"

"I don't care how. Any way you please."

"But what can I do?"

"Do? Why, put the whole thing before your man Jeeves. Jeeves will find a way. One of the most capable fellers I ever met. Put the thing squarely up to Jeeves and let Nature take its course."

"There may be something in what you say, Aunt Dahlia," I said thoughtfully.

"Of course there is," said Aunt Dahlia. "A little thing like this will be child's play to Jeeves. Get him working on it right away, and I'll look in to-morrow to hear the result."

With which, she biffed off, and I summoned Jeeves to the presence.

"Jeeves," I said, "you have heard all?"

"Yes, sir."

"I thought you would. Aunt Dahlia has what you might call a carrying voice. Has it ever occurred to you that, if all other sources of income failed, she could make a good living calling the cattle home across the sands of Dee?"

"I had not considered the point, sir, but no doubt you are right."

"Well, how do we go? What is your reaction? I think we should do our best to help and assist."

"Yes, sir."

"I am fond of Aunt Dahlia, and I am fond of Angela. Fond of them both, if you get my drift. What the misguided girl finds to attract her in young Tuppy, I cannot say, Jeeves, and you cannot say. But apparently she loves the man—which shows it can be done, a thing I wouldn't have believed myself—and is pining away like—"

"Patience on a monument, sir."

"Like Patience, as you very shrewdly remark, on a monument. So we must cluster round. Bend your brain to the problem, Jeeves. It is one that will tax you to the uttermost."

Aunt Dahlia blew in on the morrow, and I rang the bell for Jeeves. He appeared, looking brainier than one could have believed possible—sheer intellect shining from every feature—and I could see at once that the engine had been turning over.

"Speak, Jeeves," I said.

"Very good, sir."

"You have brooded?"

"Yes, sir."

"With what success?"

"I have a plan, sir, which I fancy may produce satisfactory results."

"Let's have it," said Aunt Dahlia.

"In affairs of this description, madam, the first essential is to study the psychology of the individual."

"The what?"

"The psychology, madam."

"He means the psychology," I said.

"Oh, ah," said Aunt Dahlia.

"And by psychology, Jeeves," I went on, to help the thing along, "you imply—?"

"The natures and dispositions of the principals in the matter, sir."

"You mean, what they're like?"

"Precisely, sir."

"Does he talk like this when you're alone, Bertie?" asked Aunt Dahlia.

"Sometimes. Occasionally. And on the other hand, sometimes not. Proceed, Jeeves."

"Well, sir, if I may say so, the thing that struck me most forcibly about Miss Bellinger when she was under my observation was that hers was a somewhat imperious nature. I could envisage Miss Bellinger applauding success. I could not so easily see her pitying and sympathizing with failure.

"Possibly you will recall, sir, her attitude when Mr. Glossop endeavored to light her cigarette with his automatic lighter? I thought I detected a certain impatience at his inability to produce the necessary flame."

"True, Jeeves. She ticked him off."

"Precisely, sir."

"Let me get this straight," said Aunt Dahlia. "You think if he goes on trying to light her cigarette with his automatic lighter long enough, she will eventually get fed up and hand him the mitten?"

"I merely mentioned the episode, madam, as an indication of Miss Bellinger's somewhat ruthless nature."

"Ruthless," I said, "is right. The Bellinger is hard-boiled. Those eyes. That chin. I could read them. A vicious specimen, if ever there was one."

"Precisely, sir. I think, therefore, that, should Miss Bellinger be a witness of Mr. Glossop's appearing to disadvantage in public, she would cease to entertain affection for him. In the event, for instance, of his failing to entertain the audience on Tuesday with his singing—"

I saw daylight.

"By Jove, Jeeves! You mean if he gets the bird all will be off?"

"I shall be greatly surprised if such is not the case, sir."

I shook my head

"We cannot leave this thing to chance, Jeeves. Young Tuppy singing 'Sonny Boy' is the likeliest prospect for the bird that I can think of—but no . . . You see for yourself that we must do more than simply trust to luck."

"We need not trust to luck, sir. I would suggest that you approach your friend Mr. Bingham and volunteer your services at his forthcoming entertainment. It could readily be arranged to have you sing immediately before Mr. Glossop. I fancy, sir, that if Mr. Glossop were to sing 'Sonny Boy' directly after you had sung 'Sonny Boy' the audience would respond satisfactorily. By the time Mr. Glossop began to sing they would have lost their taste for that particular song and would express their feelings warmly."

"Jeeves," said Aunt Dahlia, "you're a marvel!"

"Thank you, madam."

"Jeeves," I said, "you're an ass!"

"What do you mean, he's an 'ass'?" said Aunt Dahlia hotly. "I think it's the greatest scheme I ever heard."

"Me sing 'Sonny Boy' at Beefy Bingham's clean, bright entertainment? I can see myself!"

"You sing it daily in your bath, sir. Mr. Wooster," said Jeeves, turning to Aunt Dahlia, "has a pleasant, light barytone."

"I bet he has," said Aunt Dahlia.

I checked the man with one of my looks.

"Between singing 'Sonny Boy' in one's bath, Jeeves, and singing it before a hall full of assorted blood-orange merchants and their young, there is a substantial difference."

"Bertie," said Aunt Dahlia, "you'll sing, and like it!"

"I will not."

"Bertie!"

"Nothing will induce—"

"Bertie," said Aunt Dahlia firmly, "you will sing 'Sonny Boy' on Tuesday, the third *prox.,* or may an aunt's curse—"

"I won't!"

"Think of Angela!"

"Dash Angela!"

"Bertie!"

"No, I mean, hang it all!"

"You won't?"

"No, I won't."

"That is your last word, is it?"

"It is. Once and for all, Aunt Dahlia, nothing will induce me to let out so much as a single note."

And so that afternoon I sent a prepaid wire to Beefy Bingham, offering my services in the cause, and by nightfall the thing was fixed up.

I was billed to perform next but one after the intermission. Following me, came Tuppy. And immediately after him, Miss Cora Bellinger, the well-known operatic soprano.

How these things happen, I couldn't say. The chivalry of the Woosters, I suppose.

"Jeeves," I said that evening, and I said it coldly, "I shall be glad if you will pop round to the nearest music shop and procure me a copy of 'Sonny Boy.' It will now be necessary for me to learn both verse and refrain. Of the trouble and nervous strain which this will involve, I say nothing."

"Very good, sir."

"But this I do say—"

"I had better be starting immediately, sir, or the shop will be closed."

"Ha!" I said.

And I meant it to sting.

Although I had steeled myself to the ordeal before me and had set out full of the calm, quiet courage which makes men do desperate deeds with proud, set faces, I must admit that there was a moment, just after I had entered the Oddfellows' Hall at Bermondsey East and run an eye over the assembled pleasure seekers, when it needed all the bulldog pluck of the Woosters to keep me from calling it a day and taking a cab back to civilization.

The clean, bright entertainment was in full swing when I arrived, and somebody who looked as if he might be the local undertaker was reciting "Gunga Din." And the audience, though not actually chiyiking in the full technical sense of the term, had a grim look which I didn't like at all.

As I scanned the multitude it seemed to me that they were for the nonce suspending judgment. Did you ever tap on the door of one of those New York speakeasy places and see the grille snap back and a Face appear? There is one long, silent moment when its eyes are fixed on yours and all your past life seems to rise up before you. Then you say that you are a friend of Mr. Zinzinheimer and he told you they would treat you right if you mentioned his name, and the strain relaxes.

Well, these costermongers and whelk stallers appeared to me to be looking just like that Face. Start something, they seemed to say, and they would know what to do about it. And I couldn't help feeling that my singing "Sonny Boy" would come, in their opinion, under the head of Starting Something.

"A nice, full house, sir," said a voice at my elbow.

It was Jeeves, watching the proceedings with an indulgent eye.

"You here, Jeeves?" I said coldly.

"Yes, sir. I have been present since the commencement."

"Oh?" I said. "Any casualties yet?"

"Sir?"

"You know what I mean, Jeeves," I said sternly, "and don't pretend you don't. Anybody got the bird yet?"

"Oh, no, sir."

"I shall be the first, you think?"

"No, sir, I see no reason to expect such a misfortune. I anticipate that you will be well received."

A sudden thought struck me. "And you think everything will go according to plan?"

"Yes, sir."

"Well, I don't," I said. "I've spotted a flaw in your beastly scheme."

"A flaw, sir?"

"Yes. Do you suppose for a moment that when Mr. Glossop hears me singing that dashed song he'll come calmly on a minute after me and sing it, too? Use your intelligence, Jeeves. He will perceive the chasm in his path and pause in time. He will back out and refuse to go on at all."

"Mr. Glossop will not hear you sing, sir. At my advice he has stepped across the road to the Jug and Bottle, an establishment immediately opposite the hall, and he intends to remain there until it is time for him to appear on the platform."

"Oh!" I said.

"If I might suggest it, sir, there is another house named the Goat and Grapes only a short distance down the street. I think it might be a judicious move—"

"If I were to put a bit of custom in their way?"

"It would ease the nervous strain of waiting, sir."

I had not been feeling any too pleased with the man for having let me in for this ghastly binge, but at these words I'm bound to say my austerity softened a trifle. He was undoubtedly right.

He had studied the psychology of the individual, if you see what I mean, and it had not led him astray. A quiet ten minutes at the Goat and Grapes was exactly what my system required. To buzz off there and inhale a couple of swift whisky-and-sodas was with Bertram Wooster the work of a moment.

The treatment worked like magic. What they had put into the stuff, besides vitriol, I could not have said; but it completely altered my outlook on life. That curious, gulpy feeling passed. I was no longer conscious of the sagging sensation at the knees. The limbs ceased to quiver gently, the tongue became loosened in its socket, and the backbone stiffened.

Pausing merely to order and swallow another of the same, I bade the barmaid a cheery good-night, nodded affably to one or two fellows in the bar whose faces I liked, and came prancing back to the hall, ready for anything.

And shortly afterward I was on the platform with about a million bulging eyes goggling up at me. There was a rummy sort of buzzing in my ears, and then through the buzzing I heard the sound of a piano starting to tinkle; and, commending my soul to God, I took a good long breath and charged in.

Well, it was a close thing. If ever my grandchildren cluster about my knee and want to know what I did in the Great War, I shall say, "Never mind about the Great War. Ask me about the time I sang 'Sonny Boy' at the Oddfellows' Hall at Bermondsey East."

The whole incident is a bit blurred, but I seem to recollect a kind of murmur as I hit the refrain. I thought at the time it was an attempt on the part of the many-headed to join in the chorus, and at the moment it rather encouraged me.

I passed the thing over the larynx with all the vim at my disposal, hit the high note, and went off gracefully into the wings. I didn't come on again to take a bow. I just receded and oiled round to where Jeeves awaited me among the standees at the back.

"Well, Jeeves," I said, anchoring myself at his side and brushing the honest perspiration from the brow. "They didn't rush the platform."

"No, sir."

"But you can spread it about that that's the last time I perform outside my bath. My 'swan song,' Jeeves. Anybody who wants to hear me in future must present himself at the bathroom door and shove his ear against the keyhole. I may be wrong, but it seemed to me that toward the end they were hotting up a trifle. The bird was hovering in the air. I could hear the beating of its wings."

"I did detect a certain restlessness, sir, in the audience. I fancy they had lost their taste for that particular melody. I should have informed you earlier, sir, that the song had already been sung twice before you arrived."

"What!"

"Yes, sir. Once by a lady and once by a gentleman. It is a very popular song, sir."

I gaped at the man. That, with this knowledge, he could calmly have allowed the young master to step straight into the jaws of death, so to speak, paralyzed me. It seemed to show that the old feudal spirit had passed away altogether. I was about to give him my views on the matter in no uncertain fashion, when I was stopped by the spectacle of young Tuppy lurching onto the platform.

Young Tuppy had the unmistakable air of a man who has recently been round to the Jug and Bottle. A few cheery cries of welcome, presumably from some of his backgammon-playing pals who felt that blood was thicker than water, had the effect of causing the genial smile on his face to widen till it nearly met at the back.

He was plainly feeling about as good as a man can feel and still remain on his feet. He waved a kindly hand to his supporters and bowed in a regal sort of manner, rather like an Eastern monarch acknowledging the plaudits of the mob.

Then the female at the piano struck up the opening bars of "Sonny Boy," and Tuppy swelled like a balloon, clasped his hands together, rolled his eyes up at the ceiling in a manner denoting Soul, and began.

I think the populace was too stunned for the moment to take immediate steps. It may seem incredible, but I give you my word that young Tuppy got right through the verse without so much as a murmur. Then they seemed to pull themselves together.

A costermonger roused is a terrible thing. I have never seen the proletariat really stirred before, and I'm bound to say it rather awed me. I mean, it gave you some idea of what it must have been like during the French Revolution.

From every corner of the hall there proceeded simultaneously the sort of noise you hear at one of those East End boxing places when the referee disqualifies the popular favourite and makes the quick dash for life. And then they passed beyond mere words and began to introduce the vegetable motif.

I don't know why, but somehow I had got it into my head that the first thing thrown at Tuppy would be a potato. One gets these fancies. It was, however, as a matter of fact, a banana, and I saw in an instant that the choice had been made by wiser heads than mine. These blokes who have grown up from childhood in the knowledge of how to treat a dramatic entertainment that doesn't please them are aware by a sort of instinct just what is best to do, and the moment I saw that banana splash on Tuppy's shirt front I realized how infinitely more effective and artistic it was than any potato could have been.

Not that the potato school of thought had not also its supporters. As the proceedings warmed up I noticed several intelligent-looking fellows who threw nothing else.

The effect on young Tuppy was rather remarkable. His eyes bulged and his hair seemed to stand up, and yet his mouth went on opening and shutting, and you could see that in a dazed, automatic way he was still singing "Sonny Boy."

Then, coming out of his trance, he began to pull for the shore with some rapidity. The last seen of him, he was beating a tomato to the exit by a short head.

Presently the tumult and the shouting died. I turned to Jeeves.

"Painful, Jeeves," I said. "But what would you?"

"Yes, sir."

"The surgeon's knife, what?"

"Precisely, sir."

"Well, with this happening beneath her eyes, I think that we may definitely consider the Glossop-Bellinger romance off."

"Yes, sir."

At this point old Beefy Bingham came out upon the platform.

I supposed that he was about to rebuke his flock for the recent expression of feeling. But such was not the case. No doubt he was accustomed by now to the wholesome give-and-take of these clean, bright entertainments and had ceased to think it worth while to make any comment when there was a certain liveliness.

"Ladies and gentlemen," said old Beefy. "The next item on the program was to have been songs by Miss Cora Bellinger, the well-known operatic soprano. I have just received a telephone message from Miss Bellinger, saying that her car has broken down. She is, however, on her way here in a cab and will arrive shortly. Meanwhile, our friend Mr. Enoch Simpson will recite 'The Charge of the Light Brigade.' "

I clutched at Jeeves. "Jeeves! You heard?"

"Yes, sir."

"She wasn't here!"

"No, sir."

"She saw nothing of Tuppy's Waterloo."

"No, sir."

"The whole bally scheme has blown a fuse."

"Yes, sir."

"Come, Jeeves," I said, and those standing by wondered, no doubt, what had caused that clean-cut face to grow so pale and set. "I have been subjected to a nervous strain unparalleled since the days of the early martyrs. I have lost pounds in weight and permanently injured my entire system. I have gone through an ordeal which will make me wake up screaming in the night for months to come. And all for nothing. Let us go."

"If you have no objection, sir, I would like to witness the remainder of the entertainment."

"Suit yourself, Jeeves," I said moodily. "Personally, my heart is dead and I am going to look in at the Goat and Grapes for another of their cyanide specials and then home."

It must have been about half-past ten, and I was in the old sitting room sombrely sucking down a more or less final restorative, when the front doorbell rang, and there on the mat was young Tuppy. He looked like a man who has passed through some great experience and stood face to face with his soul. He had the beginnings of a black eye.

"Oh, hullo, Bertie," said young Tuppy

He came in and hovered about the mantelpiece, as if he were looking for things to fiddle with and break.

"I've just been singing at Beefy Bingham's entertainment," he said after a pause. "You weren't there, by any chance?"

"Oh, no," I said. "How did you go?"

"Like a breeze," said young Tuppy. "Held them spellbound."

"Knocked 'em, eh?"

"Cold," said young Tuppy. "Not a dry eye."

And this, mark you, a man who had had a good upbringing and had, no doubt, spent years at his mother's knee being taught to tell the truth.

"I suppose Miss Bellinger is pleased?" I said.

"Oh, yes. Delighted."

"So now everything's all right?"

"Oh, quite." Tuppy paused. "On the other hand, Bertie—"

"Yes?"

"Well, I've been thinking things over. Somehow, I don't believe Miss Bellinger is the mate for me, after all."

"What!"

"No, I don't."

"What makes you think that?"

"Oh, I don't know. These things sort of flash on you. I respect Miss Bellinger, Bertie. I admire her. But—er—well, I can't help feeling now that a sweet, gentle girl—er—like your cousin Angela, Bertie—would —er—in fact— Well, what I came round for was to ask if you would phone Angela and find out how she reacts to the idea of coming out with me to-night to the Berkeley for a bit of supper and a spot of dancing."

"Go ahead. There's the phone."

"No; I'd rather you asked her, Bertie. What with one thing and another, if you paved the way— You see, there's just a chance that she may be—I mean, you know how misunderstandings occur—and— Well, what I'm driving at, Bertie, old man, is that I'd rather you surged round and did a bit of paving, if you don't mind."

I went to the phone and called up Angela.

"She says come right round," I said.

"Tell her," said Tuppy, in a devout sort of voice, "that I will be with her in something under a couple of ticks."

He had barely biffed when I heard a click in the keyhole and a soft padding in the passage without.

"Jeeves," I called.

"Sir," said Jeeves, manifesting himself.

"Jeeves, a remarkably rummy thing has happened. Mr. Glossop has just been here. He tells me all is off between him and Miss Bellinger."

"Yes, sir."

"You don't seem surprised."

"No, sir. I confess I had anticipated some such eventuality."

"Eh? What gave you that idea?"

"It came to me, sir, when I observed Miss Bellinger strike Mr. Glossop in the eye."

"Strike him!"

"Yes, sir."

"In the eye?"

"The right eye, sir."

I clutched the brow. "What on earth made her do that?"

"I fancy she was a little upset, sir, at the reception accorded her singing."

"Great Scott! Don't tell me she got the bird, too?"

"Yes, sir."

"But why? She's got a red-hot voice."

"Yes, sir. But I think the audience resented her choice of a song."

"Jeeves!" Reason was beginning to do a bit of tottering on its throne. "You aren't going to stand there and tell me that Miss Bellinger sang 'Sonny Boy,' too!"

"Yes, sir. And—mistakenly, in my opinion—brought a large doll onto the platform to sing it to. The audience affected to mistake it for a ventriloquist's dummy, and there was some little disturbance."

"But Jeeves, what a coincidence!"

"Not altogether, sir. I ventured to take the liberty of accosting Miss Bellinger on her arrival at the hall and recalling myself to her recollection. I then said that Mr. Glossop had asked me to request her that as a particular favour to him—the song being a favourite of his—she would sing 'Sonny Boy.'

"And when she found that you and Mr. Glossop had also sung the song immediately before her, I rather fancy that she supposed that she had been made a victim of a practical pleasantry by Mr. Glossop. Will there be anything further, sir?"

"No, thanks."

"Good-night, sir."

"Good-night, Jeeves," I said reverently.

Thomas Beer

BIOGRAPHY

Research is one of the great indoor sports of our time, in and out
of the library. And biography, the science of digging up the
past coupled with the art of recreating it on the printed
page, is to many modern readers the most fascinating form of
contemporary literature. They, like Dr. Johnson, love it
best. In this entirely credible story, the author (who was a practicing biographer himself) shows what happens when a
biographer finds that the object of his research is a sophisticated,
clever woman: how clever, he will never know!

Mrs. Damfort resented her second son, Gordon, most keenly
whenever she had to ask him questions. He got toplofty at once as he
smacked open the double doors of the long living room and slung his
hat into a chair. She knew that he would say, "Well, now!" in his curiously raw barytone and she cut him short by drawling, "Ah! So your
office located you, sonny?" Gordon did not like to be called "sonny,"
of course. But this kept him from saying, "Well, now!" He said nothing
at all. He looked at her. Mrs. Damfort straightened her legs on the couch
and smiled.

"New dress, mother?"

"Quite," she said.

"Tea party?"

She drawled as slowly as she could, "No. Just this Mr. Newton Wood.
It's why I 'phoned your office, Gordon. You know him. Heard you
speak of him. Is he at all presentable?"

Gordon howled, "Newton Wood!"

Mrs. Damfort crossed her ankles. White satin slushed round her as
she shifted on the yellow couch. She said, "Gordon, please don't begin
to tell me that Mr. Wood is a famous writer. I know he's a celebrity. I
merely asked you if he was a presentable person. If he's anything like
the other writers—or the writers you bring here, sonny!—I must manage
to get rid of him before six. Admiral Coles is dropping in for a glass of
sherry. And that reminds me. Where should I send your friend Miss
Ravel a bill for repairing the bathroom? I've no intention of overlooking
a broken mirror and a dislocated faucet. Please don't tell me that the

silly creature was drunk. I quite know that. She drank a whole bottle of sherry. Leave me a note of her address. And now let's get back to Mr. Wood. Is he presentable?"

Her son rallied. "He's perfectly presentable, mother. Goes to dances and all that. He's I think—from Baltimore. But what the hell's he coming here for?"

"To talk to me about Michael Majendie. It seemed," said Mrs. Damfort, "to be a matter of duty. I happened to notice that he's writing a biography of Mr. Majendie. I knew Mr. Majendie, and—"

"You knew Michael Majendie?"

"Gordon, you're twenty-seven years old. Must you howl?"

He picked up *Memories of Two Embassies* from the Italian table. "I've never heard you say a word about Majendie, mother! I— You're funny! Whenever you get reminiscent it's always about meetin' King Edward or socialites or—"

"Socialites! Gordon, what fun does your generation get out of being quite so vulgar?"

"Oh," he said, "I suppose we are. Yes, we are. Had lunch with Gummy Ravel. She was building a house with all the sugar lumps when we were having coffee. The waiter hated her! But you are funny, mother. How did you come to know a tough hero like Majendie? He got killed over a woman out in San Francisco, you know? Shot in a restaurant. Her husb—"

"I naturally know that, Gordon. I remember what happened in 1905 —still!"

"But, you're funny! You lie round here, looking like Manet's 'Olympia,' and never—"

"Like what?"

He spun his aunt's memoirs on his palm. "It's a famous nude by Manet, mother. A woman on a couch. You don't look anything like her, really. I . . . Dad was a big surgeon. You must have known reams of interestin' people. Gosh," he said, flopping the book down, "what a bore this stuff of Aunt Selene's is! And—and I'm rather sore about it. Dad was her doctor besides bein' her brother-in-law. And she doesn't even mention that he was a surgeon who got her through her peritonitis in '20. Realize she doesn't mention you by name in the damn' book at all? You're 'my twin sister' in the first part, there. She doesn't—"

"Candidly," Mrs. Damfort drawled, "I haven't been able to read the thing, Gordon. Don't they call them ghost writers? The experts who write books for people? Selene should have had one. No, I can't read it."

"You're handsomer than she is," he said. "I mean that. But where in hell did you bump into Majendie? He was an anarchist, y'know. Old Karl Winter was talking about him other night at the Copes'. Says he was the handsomest dark man he ever saw. Where'd you meet him?"

"At a dinner party at your uncle Bill's. Please remember that Bill was an architect. He was studying in Paris when Mr. Majendie was studying painting. I met Michael," she said, "at a St. Valentine's Day dinner Bill gave in 1899. There's a note on the desk, there."

Her son murmured, "Michael!" and paced to the desk between the windows. He read the yellow note aloud. " 'Dear Blake, my wife says the peach at my left at your dinner is your sister, Mrs. Damfort. I apologize. I told her about you assaulting that *vache* in Paris, that time' . . . Wow! Imagine Uncle Bill having a fight with a cop!"

Mrs. Damfort was glad to know what *vache* meant. Oh, yes, she could get through with it. Yes, yes, yes. And now she knew that Michael Majendie was dark. That had not been plain in the one photograph at the Public Library yesterday. She ordered, "Careful of that, please. It's the only letter of Michael's I have left. The others were all burned when the house on Long Island went up."

Gordon said, scowling at her, "You—you knew this fellow well enough to call him Michael?"

"Certainly."

"Mother, I apologize! Always thought you were the complete *bourgeoise*—didn't know anybody that wasn't correct."

"Really?" she said. "Run along, please. I've no intention of discussing Michael's unhappy married life with Mr. Wood in front of you. You'd tell Miss Gummy Ravel and Mr. Rex Israel and the Kelly youth all about it."

"Newton Wood's from Philadelphia," said Gordon. "Just remembered. His father's a High Church parson. Yes, he's presentable, mother."

"So glad. Run along, please."

But she was frightened, now, listening to Gordon as he trotted upstairs. It would have been easier if Newton Wood were not the son of a High Church pastor in Philadelphia. He might know things. She wished that the celebrated person was something like little Kelly or the Israel boy who had asked her if her family had "much social position back in the '90s." She was suddenly cold on the yellow couch. She drew out a long slip of print from under the pillow and read, "Mr. Majendie was born in 1869 at Jerusalem, Pa. He was the son of a paperhanger. In 1887 he entered Princeton but was dropped after two months. He worked in the office of a Philadelphia newspaper for some months and got together enough money for a ticket to Paris where he lived precariously for three years, studying painting and supporting himself by illustrations for the comic papers. In 1891 he came to New York, where he worked as an illustrator. Tall, handsome, and cheerful, he became a well-known figure in Bohemian restaurants. He was a Socialist. In 1895 some of his paintings were displayed at the Dietrich gallery on Fifth Avenue and members of a religious organization took objection to a nude study, *Girl on Grass,* which suggests the influence of Manet. In 1897, returning from a trip to Paris, Mr. Majendie met Miss Beatrice Ripley, daughter of General Thomas Ripley, of Columbus, Ohio. They were married without the consent of the bride's family, on September 17, 1897, and lived in Englewood, N.J., until 1903 when Mrs. Majendie left him. She died of pneumonia at Columbus last year. No reason for the separation was given to the press. In January, 1904, Mr. Majendie went on a trip to Japan with Mr. Karl Winter, the well-known writer. It is said that Mr. Majendie met the heroine of yesterday's tragedy at Honolulu, on the return trip. Mr. Majendie settled in San Francisco last April. Reports from San Francisco so far indicate that Captain Hilliker was incensed by some letters from Mr. Majendie to his wife, found in a drawer of her desk, and that yesterday's tragedy . . ." The paper squashed in her hand. She drawled to a shadow, "Yes?"

The butler said, "Mr. Wood, ma'am."

"Please see that we're not disturbed, Ford."

"Yes, ma'am."

The world was a frozen globe, spinning under her couch. She could not get up. She would never get through it, never, never. It was worse than knowing that the man in a silver bracelet beside her on the cliff really was King Edward and that she had to speak. Mr. Newton Wood wore a white flower in his morning coat and the coat fitted. His face was square.

"This is awfully good of you, Mrs. Damfort. Oh, d'you mind gardenias? The scent, I mean."

"N-not at all," she said, tearing the obituary. "Rather like it."

"I've been at a wedding. Usher."

"The Trowbridge girl's?"

He said, "Yes. Known the happy bridegroom all my life. Kind of third cousin. But your note startled me. Can't imagine Majendie having known anybody in the—the ranks of conservatism. Saw a gorgeous photograph of you, the other day, Mrs. Damfort. 1902. Mrs. Joel Damfort as Artemis. *Tableaux vivants* for a charity."

The frozen globe spun faster. Cousin of the Trowbridge girl's husband! Mrs. Damfort drawled, "Those *tableaux!* Heavens, I'd forgotten that. Yes, Artemis. Got in such a row about it, too. No stockings. The man who posed us . . . Was it Stanford White? Anyhow, he insisted on no stockings for me. Old Mrs. Vail Abercrombie lectured me so. Had convulsions. Dear old dragon!" she said. "Do you mind if I lie here? I'm beastly tired. Shopping all day. My oldest granddaughter comes out next week. Joel's wife died. I've rather had to look after young Frederica. She's named for me. And I'm sixty-two."

He smiled. And the world did not spin. Let him look at her, in fresh white satin, with her hair freshly waved. Let him look at her. Let him think that Mrs. Vail Abercrombie had scolded her in 1902 for not wearing stockings in those *tableaux*. She crossed her ankles.

"Would you mind telling me what color your hair was, Mrs. Damfort?"

"Mr. Sargent got it exactly," she said, and pointed to the rosy picture above the fireplace. "I hope you don't mind being asked to look at a Sargent? My son's literary friends suggest that I should burn it."

He said, "How kind of them!" and moved off to the hearth. Frederica Damfort looked across his smooth head at the painting. Well, what was wrong with it? She stiffened to defend it. Her husband had called it "soapsuds" in 1901. Why shouldn't Mr. Sargent have made the scarf blow from her shoulders in those nice curves? It was a lovely picture. Everybody knew it was a Sargent as soon as they saw it.

"I call it pretty good," said Mr. Wood. "We undervalue him a bit, I think. Yes, we undervalue him. Did acres of awful things, of course. So your hair was chestnut?"

Mrs. Damfort drawled, "Sweet of you not to say red. Read that note on the desk, please. I met Michael at a St. Valentine dinner my brother gave in '99. He was William Clandon Blake, the architect. Died in '24."

The lean man stopped midway between the hearth and the yellow couch. She knew that "Michael" had stopped him. Then he walked on to the Spanish desk. She watched him reading. Oh, such luck not to have thrown the thing away when she was going over Bill's papers with his secretary! She had remembered, in '24, that Michael Majendie was somebody. She did not know who he was. But people began to talk about him. Somebody gave a show of his paintings, somewhere, last year.

"Mr. Majendie ever see that Sargent, Mrs. Damfort?"

"Michael called it soapsuds—of course."

"Of course! But I think he was rather too scornful of the portrait painters, Mrs. Damfort. I mean—calling them a lot of leeches on the plutocracy—that sort of thing. Did he ever sketch you?"

"Yes. On my horse in Central Park."

"He'd have liked that," said Mr. Wood. "His horse mania! Where is it?"

"Nowhere. I had the sketch—and a lovely sketch he did of my oldest boy, Joel, and all his letters in a box, down at our house on Long Island. They all went up in 1914. Bad insulation. The whole house went," she said. "My father's Civil War diaries, a mass of Dr. Damfort's papers and the only decent family portrait we owned." She felt the complete ease of truth. The painting of Grandmamma Blake was nice. "My sister mentions it in her memoirs. You probably haven't read them. She's Mrs. Austin Terhune."

Mr. Newton Wood laughed. "I . . . It's one reason your note startled me. I reviewed *Memories of Two Embassies*. I was rather pleasantly—surprised that you were willing to see me. This indicates that you didn't read my review."

"I hope it was savage," said Mrs. Damfort. "I . . . Well, Selene's a darling, but—I think she should have turned over her material to some expert. Too bad. Because really she's had a most interesting life. No. I didn't read your review, Mr. Wood. I read the book and then didn't want to read the reviews. Well, you have no time to waste and I've such a dear old bore coming in at six for a drop of sherry. His wife's one of the dullest women alive. He—he comes round here for a breath of air." She sat up. "I met Michael at this dinner my brother gave. I— Bill asked me to look after Michael a bit. It was a big dinner. For some Frenchman. Nasty little man. Had a title. I forget what. It was—was rather a tremendous dinner."

"Wealth and fashion, you mean?"

"Precisely," said Mrs. Damfort. "The Vail Abercrombies and old Lucius Kent. That kind of thing."

"Do tell me," Mr. Wood asked, "how old Kent got himself taken so seriously up here? My mother's always so amused about him. He was a vet's son from Germantown, you know."

Mrs. Damfort shuddered. She said, "I'm not old enough to tell you, young man. But he did get himself taken seriously. One wonders why, now. He was handsome of course. Slim and tall. Had an agreeable voice too. He bored me." She shrugged her shoulders. "The things we did take seriously! Well, I met Michael at this dinner. I do want you to understand that Michael may have been a socialist or an anarchist or anything you please, but he had charming manners and he got along with—with people of means perfectly. Too bad Mrs. Charlie Brace is gone! She liked him. They weren't—weren't dear friends. But Maud did like him."

"The banker's wife, you mean?"

"Yes. Maud met him here and she had him at luncheon two or three times—at least."

A notebook had come out. Mr. Wood leaned on the Spanish desk. "That's what's so maddening about biography—and writers," he said. "I sit around with Karl Winter and old Corley and hear that dear old Mike wouldn't have crossed the street to shake hands with a man who had ten thousand a year. It's comic! One-track minds . . . Oh, well!"

"I'm so sorry my husband's dead. Michael sometimes—not often, though!—did talk politics to him. He could have told you things. Dr. Damfort was very liberal. He saw a great deal in some of the socialist theories."

"I see. So Majendie took to coming here?"

"A good deal. In the afternoon generally. There—there was some ferry or train he always had to catch. He lived in Englewood, you know."

"And had to be home for dinner at six-thirty or get hell," said Newton Wood. "Yes."

"I didn't want to say that, Mr. Wood. But that was so very much it, you see. Yes, she had to have dinner at six-thirty," Mrs. Damfort drawled.

"Ever meet her?"

Frederica Damfort crumpled her handkerchief and nodded. Yes, that was what he wanted. He wanted to know about Mrs. Michael Majendie, out in Englewood, New Jersey. She said, "Yes. My impressions would not be valuable. I only met her once. She'd come to town to shop. I met her on Fifth Avenue somewhere."

"Do be frank!"

Mrs. Damfort opened her hand with the handkerchief. "Oh, a complete *bourgeoise*. Awfully Middle Western. Asked where I got my gloves and—and that sort of thing. I—I barely met her. Don't quote me, please."

"Never saw her again?"

"I asked her to lunch. Wrote. Got back an icy little note. Didn't bother again."

Mr. Wood grinned. "Resented you on sight?"

"I didn't say that, young man!"

"It's what happened to Mrs. Karl Winter. She was awfully handsome. Mrs. Majendie resented her on sight. You're just filling in a frame, Mrs. Damfort. Happened three or four times."

Mrs. Damfort was sorry for Michael Majendie's wife. Poor thing, stuck out in Englewood, scared about pretty women in New York! He was handsome. She sighed. Mr. Wood wrote something. A log broke in the fireplace with a little sound, like another sigh.

"Funny business," said Newton Wood. "Because she was so lovely. And she had a certain amount of sense. Couple of her notes to him are rather witty. His sister has those. By gum! Of course! You're 'my friend in Sixty-Eighth Street'! His sister's forgotten so much. That's it. In 1902. Says he's been lunching with his friend in Sixty-Eighth Street. He wrote you occasionally?"

The world spun, cold, for a moment. Frederica Damfort said, "I—there were about a hundred notes. I couldn't have let you print any of them. But it's such a shame to lose the sketches. He scribbled sketches on them. Little things he thought would amuse me. Such a good one from Honolulu—a native diving. Such a shame. Dr. Damfort said, 'Freddie, you ought to have those photographed. People will want to see them, some day.' And I did think of it. No use now."

That log rolled and sighed again in the fireplace. This silvery room with its black furniture was crushed full of a silence. Newton Wood stared at her. Let him stare. Let him stare. This silence packed the long room.

"You couldn't have let me print any of them?"

"Very few," she said.

"You mean—just what do you mean, Mrs. Damfort?"

"I wish to be perfectly frank. Michael wrote me absolutely nothing he shouldn't have. He never mentioned his wife—directly. Oh, yes! One of them did begin, 'Life is awful, this morning.' Something like that. I don't think it was worse than that. But he took to calling me Olympia, and—"

"Olympia?"

"That Manet picture. The woman on the couch."

"This is one of my dumb days. The Olympia, of course." He wrote. "Please go on, Mrs. Damfort."

"Oh, that's all about it. He did write things that would look—look odd in print. I had very pretty feet. He used to write, My compliments to your adorable feet. Things of that kind. I . . . there was a wonderful sketch of a Japanese temple. Shame that's gone."

The lean man was not writing. Yes, she would be in his book. He said, "Funny to be talking to you. So many photographs of you in society rags back then." He paused. He was thinking in the silence. "Hope this isn't offensive. Did Majendie write to you after he came back from Japan? He met this Mrs. Hilliker in Honolulu. She was on an army transport. They were coming from the Philippines. Did he mention her?"

"Not directly—no."

"Indirectly?"

Mrs. Damfort let there be a pause. "Please smoke. I forgot to tell you to."

"I don't smoke, thanks."

"Amazing young man!"

"I'm thirty-six, and discreet. I've a theory about Mrs. Hilliker. Did Majendie ever mention her to you?"

She let there be another pause. "What is your theory?"

"That he wasn't much in love with her. They let me read her statement to the police, in San Francisco. Only parts of it were printed."

"I don't think he was much in love," said Frederica Damfort. "About a month before he was killed . . . Oh, first! Michael was handsome, you know? I used to tease him about it. Well, about a month before the —the end, he wrote me, 'My fatal beauty has got me into a tiresome mess, out here.' I—it worried me. It was such a funny note, Mr. Wood. Tired and *distrait*. Dr. Damfort said, 'That's a woman, Freddie.' But you haven't any right, have you, to say he—he really didn't care about her much? You've no proof."

"A biographer has a right to state his theory, Mrs. Damfort. And you've confirmed it. Oh, he liked her. Handsome and someone to sit around in a restaurant with. Like the Albin girl in Paris—Thérèse Albin."

"I never heard of her."

Mr. Wood said, "Naturally."

Mrs. Damfort was glad she had never known Michael Majendie except at that dinner. She was going to be in a book about him, but it was nice not to have known him. Must have been all wrong. One of the Americans you saw in Paris, sitting with cheap girls in bad restaurants. Oh, she would be in this book though! People would talk to her about it at Southampton. It would not be a book like Selene's memories of being an ambassadress. People would buy a book by Newton Wood, four or five printings. But thank God, she had never known Majendie!

Then the room packed with silence again. Mr. Wood put away his notebook. The room was very silent. Newton Wood's gardenia turned brown at the edges and the scent flowed. He was going to ask her something. In a minute. After a little more silence. Yes. In a second. He stirred.

"I'll have to risk being ordered out of your house, Mrs. Damfort. Did Majendie ever make love to you?"

If she could flush. If she could just flush a little now. And then she was flushing. And it would be right to roll the handkerchief in her hand. So she rolled the handkerchief in her hand. "Mr. Wood, any intelligent woman can avoid being made love to," she said. "That's all—I am sorry I haven't a good memory of conversation. I can't remember phrases well. I'm not being much help to you, am I? And, of course, he never discussed painting technically with me."

"I'm sorry to have been offensive, Mrs. Dam—"

"No. You had a perfect right to ask the question. Michael admired my appearance, I know. But—we simply stayed very good friends. He liked my husband tremendously and Dr. Damfort liked him. Please leave it at that."

"Of course," said Newton Wood.

He paced off to the fireplace, once more. Oh, yes, she was going to be in the biography of Michael Majendie, this brilliant man who had been killed over a woman. It would be better than having been an ambassadress. Nobody cared about *Memories of Two Embassies*. But they would care about a book by a man whose novels sold sixty thousand copies.

"Can I have this photographed, Mrs. Damfort?" he asked. "The Sargent."

"Why?"

"As an illustration."

"An illustration in your book? But that's making me too important, Mr. Wood!"

"Are you sure you weren't pretty important?"

Mrs. Damfort stared at the floor. She would be important in this book, with "Sargent" in fine print under the photograph. She would be there. Selene had said in *Memories of Two Embassies,* "our father's Civil War diaries were destroyed when my twin sister's house on Long Island burned in 1920 . . ." and that was all there was about Mrs. Joel Damfort in the long book. Mrs. Damfort remembered Grandfather Blake cackling, "Freddie always gets the best of it!" in the garden at Nyack when she got the rake away from Selene. Yes. She would be in a book about a man killed over a woman, about a brilliant artist who was shot about his woman. People would read the whisper of her importance to him. Whisper and whisper.

"I must think. When does the book come out, Mr. Wood?"

"In May. Please?"

"Oh, yes. Oh, perhaps I was of some importance to him, Mr. Wood. A little!"

"You're a brick," he said.

When he was gone she strolled down the room for a cigarette. It had been so right not to smoke. It had been so right to be the beautiful Mrs. Joel Damfort in white satin on the yellow Empire couch for him, whitehaired but still slim and still beautiful. Selene was distinctly thick now. Her white skirt whispered on the maroon rug. Whisper and whisper. The book would be out in time for summer. People would read it at Southampton. Young men would ask to be brought to tea. Whisper and whisper. A famous man had loved her a little, they would whisper. More than a little. You should have seen her when she was young. That's Mrs. Damfort. You should have seen her in 1900. He was insane about her. Whisper and whisper.

"How'd you get on with Wood, mother?"

"Very nicely, Gordon. He seems very agreeable. Tactful, too."

"Tactful about what?"

She touched his nose with the cigarette. "About not asking awkward questions, sonny."

" 'Bout what?"

"You'll see it all," she said, "in the biography."

E. M. Forster

MR. AND MRS. ABBEY'S
DIFFICULTIES

In this exquisitely written narrative one of England's most
distinguished novelists turns biographer, offering biography as
short story (if short story this can be termed at all). For
readers who do not at once recognize the principal characters—
and what long-neglected subjects they have been, hitherto
overlooked by the literary biographers of their time and ours—
this appraisal of the Abbeys and their problems will take
on a new significance.

Mr. and Mrs. Abbey's problems were indeed many and hard
to put up with, in view of the characters of the four children
for whom they had been called upon to act as guardians.
Managing the money in trust for these restless young wards was
actually the least of Mr. Abbey's difficulties. John, the
oldest, for example—in love with his landlady's daughter and
not really getting anywhere in his medical career—was also,
it appeared, a victim of the tuberculosis that
proved fatal to the youngest boy, Tom. And there was
George, next to John in age and equally irresponsible, who
"decamped" with the seventeen-year-old daughter of a sea
captain to America, of all places. Fanny, the youngest of all and
the only one of the four who actually lived with the
Abbeys, was not properly appreciative of the care bestowed
upon her by her guardians. She was far too noticeably
under the influence of her brother John. And John, who wrote
nonsense verses from time to time to his little sister, was
not only disrespectful but openly subversive in his letters.

No wonder Mr. and Mrs. Abbey considered themselves, like
so many upright people in this world, unappreciated. They
did not live to see the day when a biographer would come along,
at long last, to set their case properly before readers of a
literary disposition. If he had known, Mr. Abbey would have
agreed that there would be a measure of poetic justice in
such belated recognition. On John's tomb, in Rome—the city
where the oldest and most troublesome of his wards had
gone, after having withdrawn himself from the Abbeys' control
forever—the following text had been inscribed: "Here lies
one whose name was writ in water," a text, we are told, which
rather pleased Mr. Abbey, "despite its fanciful wording."

It was an appropriate inscription, he felt, not only for John, who had had a habit of writing verses, but for the three others as well.

The death of Mrs. Rawlings, followed four years afterwards by that of Mrs. Jennings, her respectable parent, involved Mr. and Mrs. Abbey in appreciable difficulties finally. They did not at first realize the possible consequences of becoming guardian to the four children—John, George, Tom, and Fanny—the offspring of Mrs. Rawlings by a previous union; indeed Mr. Abbey acted with unusual precipitancy, and, without troubling Mr. Sandall, his co-executor under Mrs. Jennings' will, undertook sole charge even in the grandmother's lifetime. The sum of £8,000—and £8,000 was a substantial sum a hundred years ago—passed into his control, and he proceeded to administer it for the benefit of the young people as only a business man can.

The connection of the two deceased ladies had been with the livery trade. They had kept the stables attached to the Swan and Hoop, Finsbury Pavement, and the first husband of Mrs. Rawlings had actually been killed by falling off one of his own horses on a dark night not far from Southgate. Mr. Abbey's own position was more secure. A broker in tea, and in coffee also, although scarcely in coffee to an equal extent, he had added to his office in Pancras Lane a residence at Walthamstow, and to the latter a conservatory, and to everything that he undertook the conviction of some ultimate issue. It was at Walthamstow that he made provision for the child Fanny, who was aged but seven years only when she came under his charge. He arranged that she should live with Mrs. and Miss Abbey, she should attend a young ladies' school where she might acquire such education as her sex necessitated. The education of her brother John was already complete, for he had attained his sixteenth year, and Mr. Abbey was prompt to remove him from his studies and to apprentice him to a surgeon. George (aged thirteen) and Tom (eleven) were received as clerks into his own office. Thus suitable provision for all concerned was rapidly and adequately made.

Unfortunately the children were restless—a defect inherited from their father, who had been of rustic origin. John would not stick to his gallipots, nor George and Tom to their stools; and Fanny wished to learn the flageolet. They were always asking for money to satisfy their whims, and since Mr. Abbey had in view their ultimate good alone and had reinvested the £8,000 to that end, he negatived all such demands. What they wasted on letter-paper alone was deplorable, for, as the three boys grew up, they were in constant correspondence with one another and with their sister. Mr. and Mrs. Abbey valued a united family highly none higher; but saw no advantage in Tom communicating with George that it was raining in Devonshire, or in John informing Fanny that he had counted the buns and tarts in a pastry-cook's window, and "was just beginning with the jellies." Mrs. Abbey, in particular, felt that family affection was used as a cloak for something else: that they communicated, as she expressed it, "behind my back," and were not so much devoted to each other, which is all very proper and well, as interested in what each other thought. An unfortunate discovery gave her some pain. Fanny left her letters lying about, as young girls will, and Mrs. Abbey's eye was caught by the strange appearance of one of them. It was written in short lines, certainly just nonsense, yet she did not relish it, the more so since it was in John's handwriting, and he a notorious makegame.

> Two or three Posies
> With two or three simples—
> Two or three Noses
> With two or three pimples—
> Two or three sandies
> And two or three tabbies—
> Two or three dandies
> And two Mrs. —— mum!

Who might "Mrs. —— mum!" be? Mrs. Abbey reread the paragraph and then saw that it was a crambo or forfeit, the last line of which concealed her own name. She was affronted, the more so since the name must be in the plural gender. "Two Mrs. Abbeys," she repeated to herself. "And why two?" She inquired of her husband next time he came down from Pancras Lane, of Miss Caley, the headmistress of Fanny's school, of Miss Tucker, the headmistress of the school to which she was subsequently transferred. They all agreed that an unkindness was intended. She kept a lookout for John's letters in the future, and discovered in another that she was to be sent up to the London office "to count coffee-berries," while the grass plot was used for dancing. Elsewhere Fanny was to "pay no attention to Mrs. Abbey's unfeeling and ignorant gabble. You can't stop an old woman's crying any more than you can a child's. The old woman is the greatest nuisance, because she is too old for the rod. Many people live opposite a blacksmith's till they cannot hear the hammer." Here all was too plain, except, indeed, the blacksmith, whose forge was at the further extremity of the village; and Mrs. Abbey was obliged to take up a different line with Fanny. She would not allow the girl to go up to see her brother in town, and she discouraged his visiting Walthamstow.

How necessary her strictness was, the following anecdote will evince. While the children were deficient in character and breeding on the one side, they had inherited from their mother, Mrs. Rawlings, on the other, a tendency to consumption, and Tom was the first to sicken. Fanny professed to be heartbroken, and permission for a visit to his bedside could not well be withheld. She went up to Hampstead, and saw him, thus paying lip service to truth, but afterwards proceeded to act the fine lady, and made a round of calls with her brother John. She returned to Walthamstow in an unseemly state, could give Mrs. Abbey no interesting details as to the progress of Tom's malady, nothing but chatter about Mr. So-and-so and Miss T'other, what they said and ate and wore and contributed to the newspapers, and might she buy a magazine once a month, even if it meant giving up her spaniel, and she did not think Miss Tucker would object, for newspapers opened the world as Mr. Dilke had remarked, and Mrs. Dilke was at Brighton. She was easily silenced, but the Abbeys realized how susceptible she was to bad influences, and how sternly they must guard her against them. Letters like the following could not be indefinitely allowed to arrive:

My dear Fanny—

I called on Mr. Abbey in the beginning of last week, when he seemed averse to letting you come again from having heard that you had been to other places besides Well Walk. I do not mean to say you did wrongly in speaking of it, for there should rightly be no objection to such things: but you know with what People we are obliged in the course of Childhood to associate, whose conduct forces us into duplicity and falsehood to them. . . . Perhaps I am talking too deeply for you: if you do not know, you will understand what I mean in the course of a few years. I think poor Tom is a little Better, he sends his love to you. I shall call on Mr. Abbey tomorrow: when I hope to settle when to see you again. Mrs. Dilke is expected home in a day or two. She will be pleased, I am sure, with your present. I will try for permission for you to remain all Night should Mrs. D. return in time.

Your affectionate brother

John.

Permission was refused. The Dilkes and their set were no companions for a growing girl of fourteen, and Fanny remained under discipline at the time of Tom's death. The discipline had even to be increased, as the following letter, dated four months later, indicates; it had proved impossible to keep her in a healthy and modest frame of mind without almost entirely forbidding any intercourse between her and the rest of her family; it had also proved desirable to remove her from Miss Tucker's, owing to the expense:

My dear Fanny—

Your letter to me at Bedhampton hurt me very much. What objection can there be to your receiving a letter from me? At Bedhampton I was unwell and did not go out of the Garden Gate but twice or thrice during the fortnight I was there— Since I came back I have been taking care of myself— I have been obliged to do so, and am now in hopes that by this care I shall get rid of a sore throat which has haunted me at intervals nearly a twelve-month. I always had a presentiment of not being able to succeed in persuading Mr. Abbey to let you remain longer at School—I am very sorry that he will not consent. I recommend you to keep up all that you know and to learn more by yourself, however little. The time will come when you will be more pleased with Life—look forward to that time, and though it may be a trifle be careful not to let the idle and retired Life you lead fix any awkward habit or behaviour on you—whether you sit or walk endeavour to let it be in a seemly and, if possible, a graceful manner. We have been very little together: but you have not the less been with me in thought. You have no one in the world besides me who would sacrifice anything for you—I feel myself the only Protector you have. In all your little troubles think of me with the thought that there is at least one person in England who, if he could, would help you out of them—I live in hopes of being able to make you happy—I should not perhaps write in this manner if it were not for the fear of not being able to see you often or long together. I am in hopes that Mr. Abbey will not object any more to your receiving a letter now and then from me. How unreasonable! . . .

Your affectionate brother

JOHN.

Though less coarse in tone than its predecessors, this letter was even more calculated to undermine authority. Oh, mark the impudence of calling life at Walthamstow "idle"—he who had never done a stroke of real work for years, had weakened his constitution by dissipation and drift, falling in love with his landlady's daughter, and had vainly tried, when it was too late, to continue his medical career and obtain a post as surgeon upon an East Indiaman! The "sore-throat" of which he complained was the precursor of the usual hereditary trouble, its later developments proving fatal. Kindly Mr. and Mrs. Abbey were distressed, and, Fanny herself falling ill, called in the family practitioner to attend her. Yet they could not but feel that sickness had all along been used to claim illicit privileges and to undermine their authority as guardians, and that just as in the case of Tom so in the case of John there had been duplicity. In view of his departure abroad, John was permitted to write his sister as often as he wished, and almost his last letter to her contained the venomous sentence, "In case my strength returns, I will do all in my power to extricate you from the Abbies." He could not even spell.

Blessed with excellent health himself, Mr. Abbey left illness to doctors. But in money matters he felt himself on firmer ground, and, a man of business through and through, brooked no interference in his own domain. When the three boys had abandoned the professions assigned to them, he could not prevent them, but he could cut off their supplies whenever fit without giving a reason. There was so much that boys could not understand. In the first place, the reinvestment of the £8,000 had, he owned frankly to himself, not been a success. In the second place, old Mr. Jennings, the original stableman, had left a confused will. He had died worth £13,160 19s. 5d., £9,343 2s. of which had gone to his widow and thence in more compact form to the grandchildren as £8,000; but he had also left his grandchildren £1,000 direct and £50 a year besides in reversion after their mother's death.

Mr. Abbey was aware of these additional legacies, but they were not often in his mind, for, like all city men, he had much to think about, and he deemed it fitter to leave them alone; they would do no harm, the interest would accumulate in Chancery, and when documents came about them it was his habit to clear his throat and drop everything together into a safe. And as years went on and the children failed to mention the legacies to him, he ceased mentioning them to himself. He had so much to think about. After the first excitement of guardianship, he had done what nine men out of ten of substance would do in his place: nothing; so he said nothing. When John and George called with troubled faces at Pancras Lane and asked exactly how poor they were, he rightly replied, "This is no ordinary question," and silenced them by some reference to their own inexperience. Or, "Ask your Aunt Midgely," he would say. They knew not what he meant, nor did he, for Mrs. Midgely Jennings was unlikely to afford information, since she was herself dissatisfied with her income, and periodically threatened to bring suits, against whom or for what Mr. Abbey was not quite cognisant.

He was not clear either about the great Chancery suit, Rawlings v. Jennings, which the mother and grandmother had initiated by mutual consent in their lifetimes in order to clear up in an amicable spirit the obscurities of Mr. Jennings's will. Not one to interfere with another man's job, Mr. Abbey left law to the lawyers, and thanks to his attitude the Chancery suit lasted twenty years. Ah, he did not know much, but he always knew a little more than his wards; he performed that duty, and Tom and John remained ignorant until the day of their death, while Fanny believed for many years that she was a pauper and owed Mrs. Abbey for her board and lodging. Much extravagance was averted by this timely reticence, many loans to undesirable friends, and tours both in England and on the Continent, which could have led to no useful purposes. "Ever let the fancy roam, pleasure never is at home," wrote John to George openly in one of his letters; atrocious advice as coming from an elder brother to a younger, and alluding to the fact that George had decamped with the daughter of a sea-captain to America. All this Mr. Abbey realized, deprecated, and strove to check, and it was not his fault when Fanny terminated her connection with Walthamstow in the arms of a Spaniard.

The last years of the stewardship were very painful. Being small and sickly, and two of her brothers dead and the third abroad, Fanny seemed inclined to settle down. She spoke little, she dressed plainly, and never tossed her head when Mrs. Abbey repeated that she resembled her father, who had fallen off the horse, and that nought but idleness had ever been found on that side of the family. But, unfortunately, George came from America on a visit. Fanny was upset again, and all the careful accumulations of so many years came tumbling down. George was more robust than his brothers, had married, and had acquired a hard effrontery which passed for business ability among the Yankees, though it was not so estimated by Mr. Abbey. Retrenchment and deliberation were to Mr. Abbey the twin pillars of commercial achievement, he never hurried others and he did not expect to be hurried. He greeted the prodigal in measured tones, and received in reply a point-blank demand that the trust should be wound up. "Ask your Aunt Midgely," he said; but retorting that he knew whom to ask, George prepared to take the case into court. He insisted on the safe being opened, he discovered that the two additional legacies, ever Mr. Abbey's weak point, had been invested twenty years previously in Consols by order of the court, £1,550 7s. 10d. of Consols in the one case and £1,666 13s. 4d. in the other, and that the interest had been accumulating ever since his mother's death. He dragged every detail, including what had been paid as lawyers' fees, to the light, and before Mr. Abbey could collect himself had returned to America with £1,147 5s. 1d. in his pocket.

Worse was to follow; when Fanny came of age, which she did two years after George's visit, she claimed her share also. Mr. Abbey might have ceded it without protest, had she not claimed in addition the shares of her two dead brothers. Such rapacity was childish, and Mr. Abbey was quick to reply that the arrangement would be unfair to George. Fanny retorted, "No, George's own wish!" and she applied to Mr. Dilke, who produced the necessary documents. Fanny annexed the balance, no less than £3,375 5s. 7d., and quitted Walthamstow. Her Spanish adventurer married her soon afterwards, but Mr. and Mrs. Abbey could never feel it retribution sufficient. Although the money was not theirs to spend, they had come to feel that it was theirs to keep, and they would have liked it to accumulate at compound interest for ever. Bitter words had passed, Fanny insolently hinting that if Tom and John had been given their proper dues, the additional procurable comfort might have prolonged their lives.

Of course it would not have, and in any case what is the use of such people, Mr. Abbey could not help thinking as he sat at Walthamstow in the evening of his own life. Now that the worrying and badgering was over and the trust that he had so faithfully administered was filched from him, now that Rawlings v. Jennings was wound up, and idle verses about his wife no longer fell through the letter-box, he could not feel that his four wards had ever existed in the sense in which he, in which

Mrs. Abbey, in which Miss Abbey and the conservatory existed. Already were they forgotten—George in America, Fanny in Spain, Tom in the graveyard of St. Stephen's, Coleman Street, John at Rome. On the tomb of the last-mentioned had been placed a text which rather pleased the old gentleman, despite its fanciful wording. He found it appropriate to the whole family. "Here lies one whose name was writ in water," it said. He had written in water himself once with the point of a wet umbrella, and he remembered that almost before the servant arrived to open the door, his signature had evaporated. He himself has expressed the same truth in sounder English in the one letter of his that has been preserved, a business letter addressed to Messrs. Taylor and Hessey, publishers, Waterloo Place; he has summed up once for all the world's judgment upon inefficiency:

Pancras Lane,
Cheapside.
April 18, 1821.

Sir—

I beg pardon for not replying to your favour of the 30th ult. respecting the late Mr. Jno. Keats.

I am obliged by your note, but he having withdrawn himself from my controul, and acted contrary to my advice, I cannot interfere with his affairs.

I am, Sir,
Yr. mo. Hble. St.
RICHARD ABBEY.

Samuel Yellen

THE PASSIONATE SHEPHERD

This unusual story about a professor in search of his identity will,
no doubt, raise some questions regarding the manner of his
search. From one point of view, certainly, as he himself pointed
out, he created a "problem in public relations"! Many
readers (and not only those who are also professors), recognizing
the nature of Professor Gray's predicament, will realize the
significance of the remembered sentence from the letters
of Charles Lamb: "He seems to have run the whole scenery of
life, and now rests as the precisian of non-existence." Cyrus
Gray, who counted himself among "the quiet ones, the
unobtrusive ones," was a tragic figure. "Credo, ergo sum" had
lost its meaning. His story will seem less tragic, of course,
to student readers than to their professors. That point must be
conceded at the outset, but the impact of this man's
experience will make its impression, possibly a lasting one,
upon some students—despite the professor's unhappy suggestion
to the contrary: "Those young egotists at the most egotistical
hour of life hardly conceded existence to their teachers."

Have you ever stopped in the middle of a sentence to see if
the person you were talking to was paying any attention? I don't recommend it, unless you brace yourself beforehand for a jolt. That is precisely what I did at a cocktail party last October, seven months ago.
I was engaged in conversation with a good-looking young brunette,
Rose Matthews, whose husband had just joined our faculty. I even remember (as if I could forget) what I was saying at the time, though I
hesitate to repeat it here. It was the sort of thing my friends the psy-
chologists would call verbalizing, a piece of cocktail party prattle which
I had lifted from Marlowe: "Come live with me, and be my love, and
we will all the pleasures prove. And I assure you this passionate shepherd will—" Some sudden caprice which I still cannot account for made
me break off at that point. To my chagrin, the Passionate Shepherd discovered that his love was simply not listening and Marlowe's poesy was
wasted on the smoke-laden air. Her ears, her eyes, her whole being
were bent elsewhere. What stood there before me was only the empty

shell. And even though the shell itself was, as we say, not at all bad, being endowed, for example, with full and firm breasts, I must confess that Professor Cyrus Richard Gray suffered a sharp pain near the heart. Yes, it was a veritable stab of pain, and I am sure that I grew pale. At that moment, while a needle caught in a groove of my brain kept playing *pleasures prove pleasures prove pleasures prove pleasures prove,* I had my first intimation that I did not exist.

It was the usual faculty cocktail party held in the usual faculty home during the Saturday twilight after a football game. The furniture was all straight lines and angles in chromium plate and blond wood. On the walls hung the ubiquitous Sunflowers of Van Gogh, two studies of ballet girls by Degas, and a number of Cubist abstractions tardily executed in water colors by our hostess. Seen through the pall of cigarette smoke, the fifty men and women standing jammed in the small living room and adjoining dining room were shades clamoring in the mists for a sip of the life-giving blood. Except that *these* shades were drinking Martinis and Manhattans. Perhaps my parallel is too lurid, and the illustrator should be not Doré, but Hogarth or Daumier. However, the scene was pathetic, almost tragic, rather than comic. The climate was one of desperation. But not the *quiet* desperation Thoreau speaks of. Far from it. Shrieks, screams, and squeals rebounded from wall and ceiling. Everyone seemed intent on a most frantic search for *something,* something without substance, without form, without name. Wives in their forties and fifties ogled, winked, grimaced, flirted with a frenzied gaiety, as if to give the lie to wrinkle, crow's foot, wattle, and hairy mole. Husbands with dewlap and sagging paunch embraced waists, only to recoil at flaccid breast or inflexibly ribbed girdle. Our host was busy saving on his liquor bill by going heavy on the vermouth. Our hostess, her face stamped with a bright fixed smile, was worrying about cigarette butts and spilled drinks, and wishing the party were over and done with. It was a motley assemblage, the kind you get when the hostess is wiping out her accumulation of social obligations in order to begin the new season with a clean sheet. Otherwise, how account for the presence of E. Feverell Dobson, Professor of Salesmanship (pause for raucous laughter) in our School of Commerce?

I realize that I must sound the petty academic snob indigenous to our large state universities. But that was not it at all. No, my attitude does not derive from the traditional respectability of my position as Professor of History (actually I took my doctorate at Harvard in American Civilization). Dobson *qua* Dobson is without significance in my story. True, he was hollow brass, undoubtedly an ignoramus, a hail fellow well met given to off-color limericks and guffaws. Likewise true, his title to local fame lay in a great collection of gaudy shirts and Countess Mara ties. Nevertheless, all of that was only his manner of saying to the world, *Regardez! I exist!* Others of my colleagues took other ways of making the same assertion. Some grew beards, some drove around in flashy yellow or crimson convertibles, some issued statements to the press, some dressed in tartan jackets, some cultivated eccentricities, some were constantly and ostentatiously off to Washington on mysterious topdrawer business, some never wore the same suit twice in a month, some never wore anything but the same suit month after month. And even *my* own unobtrusive behavior and dress, invariably, like my name, a neutral gray which rendered me almost invisible against the academic foliage, may have been, after all, nothing more than the reverse side of the medal. Without getting hopelessly lost in the maze of the ego, who can be sure that Dobson was not right? At least, his brassy loudness was a sign of his *presence*. It indicated *his* existence. And certainly at this party he was the gorgeous prismatic cock around whom the silly hens fluttered.

Let me hasten to add that any bitterness expressed above was really a symptom of inner discontent and pain. In part, I suppose, it was pique at the fact that Rose Matthews was not even conscious of disregarding me. Perhaps mine was the occupational sensitivity of the professor. But I think not. It was something else. When Rose Matthews stood before me, all attention fixed, as if by a tropism, on E. Feverell Dobson, I suddenly was simply not there. She had wiped me out of existence. It happened to be a time when I was particularly vulnerable. I had just turned fifty-six. I was raw, without integument to shield me. No longer could I delude myself that the sixties, hemorrhages of the brain, palsy, and *finis* were not breathing hard down my neck. Of course, the handwriting had always been up there on the wall, but now, myopic as I might be, I had come close enough to read it. Moreover, the season of the year vibrated sympathetically, and each leaf falling desiccated and crumpled to the earth echoed my dismal thoughts. Standing there with the Matthews woman, I was stricken with panic. I looked across the room and observed my wife shrilling to some blurred figure who had an arm around her. During the rest of the party, I moved along, an automaton somehow making the expected response to the anticipated stimulus.

As we were driving home that evening, my wife said, "That Rose Matthews is an extremely attractive woman, don't you think?"

Before answering, I waited a minute as though to consider. "Yes, I suppose some would think she is."

I foresaw not only what Helen would say next, but the valiantly matter-of-fact tone she would employ. "Well, I noticed that the men seemed to be taken with her."

Why we skirmished thus I don't understand. I am sure that she could predict my reply and the inflection of my voice as accurately as I could predict hers. Nevertheless, I pursed my lips and said, "She's a bit flamboyant for *my* taste, but *de gustibus*—" I shrugged my shoulders.

Helen should have known that the problem was not Rose Matthews, nor any of the other women whose sting she tried to neutralize by such epithets as "attractive" or "charming" or "beautiful." And yet, perhaps she did know well enough, and she was herself helpless before the compulsion to beat ineffectually against the ruins of time.

In the quiet streets, the lights of the car caught the leaves drifting down. There was no end to them, falling, falling, falling; and what they whispered as they fluttered in the air and their clatter as they dropped to the ground seemed, for the moment, to drown out the purr of the motor. In alarm I glanced quickly at Helen. She was staring ahead, her sharp chin lifted high to undo the half-a-century folds in her throat, her thin straight hair drawn close to the skull into a tight little knot at the back of her neck. My heart suddenly ached with pity. That face, which once launched a thousand ships each time I looked at it, now would no longer launch a single small vessel. And I remembered the fragrance of her young body when she first undressed for me, shy and yet in her pride wanting me to behold the flower which had bloomed in secret. Even that beauty had fallen victim to physiology and chemical equations. Maybe each commonplace reassurance I gave her helped temper the icy wind of truth. We had reached, I felt, a moment of high silent communion. But perversely that was the very moment Helen chose to turn eagerly to me. "Cy, I heard something interesting this afternoon. Guess who's going to get a divorce." I was not the sentient being, Cyrus Richard Gray. I was merely a patient and capacious ear to pour her post-party gossip into. Again I had the sensation that I did not exist.

That night at home I was unable to fall asleep. I lay in our bed as still as possible in order not to awaken Helen. The bed was spacious and obese, the kind without footboard called, I believe, a "Hollywood bed," which Helen had seen in *House Beautiful*. Had I not known her deficiency in the sense of humor, I might have thought she had got this voluptuous couch meant for an unmatrimonial orgy of fleshy passions as a piece of mockery for the decorous conjugality we had declined into. Getting up finally, I slipped out and closed the door carefully behind me. I tiptoed past the bedrooms of Joan and Ned, down the stairs, and into my study. There I sat for a time in a cocoon of silence trying to analyze the disturbing sensation which had come on me. But the longer I pondered the more elusive became my identity. At last I went into the bathroom and got a sleeping pill to give myself the relief of temporary oblivion. As I was shutting the medicine cabinet, there in the mirror was my image. I studied it closely. Each separate item in the physiognomy was itself familiar enough—the rumpled and ragged slate-colored hair streaked with gray, the regularity of chin and nose, the pale gray eyes, the liverish skin. (Indeed, so ordinary were the items that I wished for a moment I might have some Dickensian grotesquerie of feature to serve as a handle for my identity, so that I might think of myself as the Man with the Red Bulbous Nose or the Man with the Black Beetling Brow.) And yet the total image was that of a stranger. There was about it a suggestion of distortion, as if the parts had been jarred slightly after being assembled, or as if the mirror had some minute flaws. I could not be sure whether the image represented reality or phantom. But I felt that I was on the verge of discovering the real person. Within that gray outwardness I seemed to remember a younger face and a boyish head. Underneath that cracked and peeling surface I thought I could almost see brighter and fresher colors. With a little more effort—no, it was no use. I kept slipping away from myself. And I could not persuade myself to believe that the stranger in the mirror existed. "Well," I said to him, *"gnothi seauton,* Passionate Shepherd, know thyself! That great Thespian, Cyrus Richard Gray, will now enact a little morality quaintly entitled *Passion Redivivus, or the Shepherd in Search of Himself."*

During the following days, while burning leaves spiced the air, a strange unrest took hold of me. My hands often trembled violently as they lifted a cup of coffee, a semaphore ticked unceasingly in my left eyelid, and fever patches blazed through the liverish skin over my cheekbones. I could not rid myself of the conviction that I had somehow, somewhere lost my inner self, that I was nothing but an empty container moving mechanically on fixed tracks. In my desperation, I crept back into the deepest recesses of the shell which had given me shelter in the past during fits of fluttering uncertainty. Like a neurotic straightening books, pictures, dishes, furniture in an effort to padlock his indefinable anxiety, I sought refuge in the formula of routine. Twenty-four years of treading the same invariable paths had rendered my motions automatic. In the morning I met my freshman class in the Introduction to Western Civilization, my advanced class in The Experimental Society in America, or my graduate seminar in The Brook Farm Group, obediently opening and shutting my mouth to the tintinnabulation of bells. The rest of the morning was taken up with correspondence, reading blue books and term papers, conferring with students, and filling out the official forms that streamed from the robots over in Administration. At noon I lunched in the Faculty Club. After lunch I glanced at the *New York Times* or played a hand of bridge. Then came the period of the day, from one-thirty to four o'clock, which twenty years before I had dedicated to research. The small basement room in the Library where I spent those two and a half hours had become my second home. There every afternoon without fail I added the grain of sand to the slowly but steadily growing mound out of which had already come five monographs and nineteen shorter articles. The hour from four to five was given over to faculty meetings and committees. Dinner at home was followed by an evening concert, a lecture, a movie, a visit, or reading the *Saturday Evening Post* serial.

For how many thousands of days this not unpleasant routine had fitted me comfortably! Yet now I sank unaccountably into absent states, from which I would come to with the blood thundering to my head as after a faint. Fortunately (praise be to William James for Habit!) I always found myself performing the proper task at the customary time and place. Nevertheless, these spells worried me, and presently I realized that the Matthews woman was haunting my thoughts. Not, mind you, in the role of femme fatale, but rather as if she had stolen something I needed desperately to get back. It was this necessity, I suppose, which compelled me now and again to walk slowly past her house in one of the side streets off the campus. To my irrational temper, it seemed that the sight of her might restore whatever it was I had lost, might furnish me with the precious clue. At any moment during the day (even in the period sacrosanct to research), like a somnambulist, I would be driven to take my foolish peripatetic exercise. Of course, I never caught so much as a glimpse of Rose Matthews.

In my increasing agitation, there was no one I could turn to for help. Helen did look anxiously at me for a while. But I easily threw her off the scent by allowing myself to be caught in the kitchen furtively mixing myself a bicarbonate of soda, and my malady was, I am sure, soon diagnosed and dismissed as a bout of indigestion. How long this state of affairs might have gone on I can only guess. For it came to an abrupt end one afternoon as I was seated in my basement cell at the Library (such is the treachery of the familiar) reading the letters of Charles Lamb. Unless my memory fails me, it was a letter to Coleridge. *Unless my memory fails me*—now there's an expression! Vestigium of exquisite academic dishonesty! Not only does my memory not fail me, but the very date of the letter—May 20, 1803—is engraved in red upon my private calendar. The fatal words sprang forward from the page to meet my eye: "He seems to have run the whole scenery of life, and now rests as the formal precisian of non-existence."

Even now, so ingrained are the accustomed academic gestures, I find myself obliged to explain why I was reading Lamb, what I was doing, as we like to say, outside my field. (As though it still matters that one of my colleagues might think I was spreading myself thin.) I must first make clear that my specialty is (or was) early Utopian experiments in America. Indeed, two of my monographs, those on New Harmony and Brook Farm, are, with all due modesty, not entirely unknown to the world of scholarship. At the time, I was following up some leads on the pantisocracy which Coleridge, Southey, and Lovell had planned to establish on the banks of the Susquehanna. Since many of Lamb's letters were written to Coleridge and Southey, I inevitably encountered the passage that was to open my eyes. For a minute, I recall, I took *precisian* to be a misspelling, until I realized that it was the noun not for the quality, but for the person. On the instant, I recognized that I had been brought unto Lamb to see what he would call me, and I had been named. I, *I*, Cyrus Richard Gray, was the formal precisian of nonexistence. I was the vacant outline, with the Roman numerals, capital letters, Arabic numerals, and lower case letters all correctly indented and set forth. The *content* had faded out of the realm of being. I felt stagnant, lusterless, inert. My heart began to quiver. But that, I told myself, was only because the creature of habit was fearful at the threat to his smug routine. *Creature* of habit? No, I was simply the habit itself. I was that old coat which William James describes as falling into its habitual folds and wrinkles. And no one was inside.

As I sat with the volume of Lamb's letters open on the table before me, I looked around at the old familiar face of my cloister. *There* was the whole scenery of my life. The walls were painted a dull rough gray, and the surface bulged and billowed to the ridges and whorls of the plaster underneath. My long table, strewn with books, pamphlets, note cards, and pads of paper, stood in the center of the worn pine floor. The two large rickety bookcases were loaded with dusty books, piles of off-prints sent me by colleagues, and thirty or so of those mottled black-and-gray cardboard boxes, each neatly labeled, in which the industrious scholar files his note cards. Ah, those boxes! Those boxes! In them reposed what thousands upon thousands of cards, each one covered with my small precise backward-slanting hand. Cards of two sizes, two colors— three-by-five for bibliographical data, four-by-six for notes on my reading, white for the factual or objective, yellow for my own comments and suggestions. Over the years it had been my sustaining faith that each card contributed its mite to the sum total of human knowledge. What a silly farce—written, staged, played, and directed by Vanity! No, each card was the measure of a certain number of pulse beats lost and never to be recaptured. In those mottled black-and-gray caskets were interred the bones of my youth and enthusiasm. There came to my mind the story of the Harvard professor who, on his death, left hundreds of boxes and baskets of notes, choking his shelves and even suspended by pulleys from the ceiling. For his university they were an embarrassment, and not of riches. They were the indecent remains of a corpse which finally had to be disposed of hugger-mugger. I could imagine how, after my departure from this vale of tears, *my* boxes would perplex the university. What to do with them? Whom to entrust them to? Certainly my colleagues would want nothing to do with them: each one was diligently storing up his own boxes of note cards.

I went over to the window, whose sill was level with the ground, and looked through the ancient fly specks and grime. The cold November sun painted the skeleton trees upon the earth, with pen-and-ink punctilio for the filigree of twig. A host of shriveled brown leaves scuttled like chipmunks before the wind. Some students came along the campus walk outside the Library, the bare legs of the coeds smooth, strong, and shapely. I could almost hear the crunch of the dead leaves being trodden down by those merciless feet. No one is more aware than the college professor of the hungry generations. No one can have a keener sense of how quickly and impatiently youth discards age. When it came my turn to go, who would there be to know the difference? Assuredly not my students. Those young egotists at the most egotistical hour of life hardly conceded existence to their teachers. Some of the more fatuous among my colleagues talked fervidly about *reaching* their students. I could not help remembering the student who had sat through an entire semester of my course under the impression that I was Professor *Thompson!* No, I could not flatter myself that I so much as cracked the glaze of those young egotists. And yet, distant as I was from my students, I was in many ways closer to them than to my own children. Joan and Ned no longer needed me. To them, I was an old stick of furniture that got in the way around the house. The language they spoke might as well have been one of those African tongues, all clicks and grunts. Joan, a senior at the university, was engaged to an accounting major, and already knew that callow brash stranger much better than she had ever known me. As for Ned, he was a sophomore wrapped up in his fraternity's hell week, pajama parties, and other such foolishness. Whenever I tried to enter their world, they merely waited with ill-concealed patience for me to make a more or less graceful exit.

Standing there at the window feeling a twinge of pity for old Shepherd Gray, I realized that I was whistling a tune under my breath while my fingers drummed a rhythm on the sill. The tune was very familiar, and yet I could not place it. Yes, a thing might be too familiar to be in focus. Surely, if anyone knew me, it was Helen. And yet I could go through a crisis like this without her being aware of it. While the tune teased me with its elusive familiarity, I let my thoughts play about Helen. She had been, in her way, a good wife and would, no doubt, notice my absence from the scene. But how soon she would get over it, and go on with her household concerns, her clubs, her teas, bridges, and luncheons. I watched the leaves scamper along outside. That tune nagged at me in a most distracting way. I recalled the cases of colleagues who had suddenly and inexplicably thrown overboard family, friends, position in the community, hard-earned academic security and reputation. Of Dewhirst, who had deserted a wife and three children to run off to Mexico with a coed. Of the professor of Latin whose name I had forgotten, who had joined an African safari and never returned. Of Templeton, who had gone berserk and shot two of his colleagues. Of Baker, who had simply disappeared into the ether and left no trace. Somehow they were never the E. Feverell Dobsons, but always the quiet ones, the unobtrusive ones. About each one, the rest of us would shake our heads and ask over a cocktail glass, "What*ever* got into him?" Well, now I knew. Just then, I identified the nagging tune, and at the same moment I realized that the semaphore had stopped ticking in my left eyelid. It was a gay tune, the patter song from *The Mikado.* "He never would be missed," I sang aloud. "I'm sure he'd not be missed."

It is not at all difficult to disappear. Indeed, I believe that I could now write a successful handbook for weary academics on *How to Vanish and Leave Not a Rack Behind.* Of course, having time and place which I did not have to account for was of great help. No one ever questioned what I was doing each afternoon between one-thirty and four, and so seldom did anyone else, even the janitor, enter my basement room at the Library that I could have safely kept a chorus girl there. My preparations took only a few days and carried me into the first week of December. I had never realized that Professor Gray had it in him to be such a man of action. I withdrew five hundred dollars from the bank, knowing that Helen would not miss the money until the beginning of the next month. Then down on the levee (a row of secondhand stores, saloons, greasy-spoon restaurants, and disreputable hotels facing the railroad tracks) I bought an old brown suit, a battered brown hat, two woolen work shirts, a heavy sweater, a worn pair of brown shoes, and a cheap black cardboard suitcase, spreading my purchases over three stores. The chief risk I ran was getting these things into the Library. However, luck accommodated me. A little-used side door leads directly to the basement, and no one happened to see me enter that afternoon. My briefcase served to bring over some underwear, socks, and handkerchiefs, a few pieces each day.

On the appointed morning, as I said goodby to Joan and Ned and kissed Helen, I savored to the full the irony of being as perfunctory as usual. In fact, everything was as usual as usual, even the beating of my heart. I met my classes, answered some letters at the office, had lunch at the Faculty Club, played a hand of bridge, and strolled over to my secluded cloister. There I set about transforming myself. Most of my predecessors in the fine art of fading away into thin air had, I decided, tried too hard to disguise themselves and, since nothing is so unoriginal as efforts at originality, had used the very ham-actor stencils foreseen by

559

the police. My commonplace face and figure, my undistinguished dress and manner, the absence of any oddity of feature were in my favor. I did not resort to artificial scars, dark glasses, moustache, or limp. All I did was to remove my glasses and comb my hair in a pompadour instead of parting it as I ordinarily did. Then I changed to the woolen work shirt and brown suit and hat, and put the clothes I had been wearing into the suitcase. A study of my reflection in the grimy window showed me that the metamorphosis was adequate. I was still unobtrusive enough to be completely overlooked. Nevertheless, I must confess that my heart was thumping when I left the Library by the side door, carrying the suitcase. However, on the walk outside the door one of my colleagues passed by me without so much as a second glance. That restored my confidence.

Of course, I had already picked out my destination, and without hesitating I caught the bus which crosses the railroad tracks over into the West Side. During the 1880's and 1890's, that had been the fashionable section of town, and my interest in nineteenth-century domestic architecture had taken me there on occasional walks to view the dozen or so homes in the General Grant style still standing, though now converted into funeral parlors or rooming houses. One of the latter, need I say, was my *immediate* destination. Again luck was obliging to me, for I found a room at the first house I tried. I gave my name as George Brown and paid a week's rent in advance. The room, up in the square central tower which marks the General Grant house, was shabbily furnished, but clean enough, large, and well-lighted. For two weeks I holed up there, going out to the levee for my meals. Actually I did not stay close to my room, nor otherwise behave furtively. I took long walks through the streets of the West Side, over to the gas works, the cemetery, the furniture factory, or the slaughter house. I felt as if I were a tourist in a foreign town. And in a sense I was. For even a city of only sixty-three thousand is really a cluster of quite separate towns, each with its own economy, culture, social strata, flora and fauna.

My chief occupation was studying the local paper to keep track of my *alter idem*. It did not surprise me that my disappearance was not announced until the third day. I could surmise the quiet and discreet efforts of Helen and the university officials to locate me before deciding that they could no longer put off calling the police in. After the news broke, I read and reread the accounts avidly. I enjoyed observing the skill of our publicity director, who always succeeded in balancing the disgrace to the university of having one of its professors turn into an irresponsible missing person by some reference to the "important" research done by the "noted authority" on early Utopian experiments. I had become a problem in public relations. I also enjoyed following the activities of the police, who broadcast descriptions of me and bustled around the university interviewing my colleagues. And the embarrassment of the officers who "found" me in Chicago, New Orleans, and St. Louis furnished me with a perverse amusement.

However, the irony soon doubled back on me. It was something of a shock, yes, a blow to my self-esteem, to see how quickly all the fuss died down. In four days I passed from the front page to a spot among the advertisements for trusses and rheumatism remedies. In another three days I slipped from the news altogether, except for an occasional brief notice that police had begun to suspect foul play and were about to ask the FBI for assistance. Sometimes, with an understandable reluctance to vanish completely from the scene, I tried to chat about the *affaire Gray* with my landlady or with the waitress at the restaurant, but it was amazing how little interest the aborigines of the West Side had in the university and the mysterious disappearance of one of its distinguished professors. I could guess that the crescendo of chatter at the cocktail parties had passed its peak. Sitting for hours at a time in my room, I found that I thought seldom about Helen, and even less about the children. Joan and Ned were well on the way to taking care of themselves. As for Helen, she would have security enough. The house was paid for, our savings were considerable, and in due time she would draw benefits from our insurance policies and the ample pension fund which I had accumulated. I knew, moreover, that the university always found some clerical or secretarial job for its widows and abandoned wives. No, if anything, my desertion might prove a good thing for her. Occasionally I considered my own destiny, what I would do with myself and how I would go about making a living. But most often, I thought despairingly of my lost identity. Where and when would I recover myself? How many other formal precisians of non-existence had engaged in the same frantic search in that very room? While a phantom troop of forlorn figures paced the threadbare flowered carpet, sat brooding in the horsehair chairs, or lay despondently upon the tarnished brass bed, Descartes' first postulate, slightly altered, twanged in my head: *Credo ergo sum. If* I could believe, I would be.

During recent years I had often wondered how an underground was able to flourish in the very teeth of enemy occupation. Now I could see that it might be managed. Even with the police, so to speak, hot on my trail, establishing myself as an approved member of society took but a few minutes. I applied for a job in one of the limestone quarries south of town, saying that I had come from a farm in the hills of Tennessee near Murfreesboro. Without much ado, I was given a social security card and number, as well as a membership card in the stone workers' union. By signing my name half-a-dozen times, I became George Edward Brown. What surprised me was the ease with which I adapted myself. From the first I got along well with the men, who were soon calling me

Tennessee. Somewhere Emerson says that the truck driver and the college professor give themselves away by their speech. The Sage of Concord was mistaken. The secret is not to try to speak unlike yourself. The men I worked with accepted me at face value, and whatever formality there was in my speech or manner they attributed to my supposed Southern origin. The work itself was hard in the beginning. But I liked it, and relished the sense of physical exhaustion each night. I slept soundly, and without benefit of pills. Although the pay was low (I *was* inexperienced labor and at what is called an advanced age), it was sufficient for my simple needs. All in all, the life was good. And I well remember the thrill I felt one morning when, clinging shakily to the iron cables, I took my first ride on a huge block of limestone swung high in the air by the derrick. All around me the sheer limestone walls dazzled my eyes with a brilliant display of color. I had not known that there could be so many tints of brown and yellow and orange and purple in such a variety of stippling and shading. Far below was the engine, crowned with a coiling plume of smoke. And (as though to provide the fitting touch for the Passionate Shepherd), on a nearby hillside, in the cold pastoral landscape surrounding the quarry, huddled a flock of sheep.

January and February brought snow, frost, and ice. My hands and face put forth a leathery weatherbeaten skin, and I became quite tough physically. My days were little else than work and sleep. Sometimes after the whistle blew at four o'clock, I accompanied some of the men to a cafe in the vicinity of the quarries for a glass of beer and a game of checkers or dominoes. Since I was tired at the end of the day and went to bed early, the evening passed quickly and I had little time for speculation. Aside from the *Post* and the local paper, I read almost nothing. Now and then I managed to get hold of the campus newspaper, and through it I kept an eye on my family and my deserted track at the university. Frequently I had heard people say that they would like to visit the earth after their death to see whether they were missed and how they were spoken of. That was the position I was in, a ghost haunting the scenes of his former life. And I can testify that I needed all the comfort I could suck from ironic detachment. For a while, it was entertaining to see who would be put into my slot. From various items in the campus paper, I learned that young Bob Hendricks had taken over my advanced course and graduate seminar, and also my seat on three or four special committees. Except that he had already launched himself in early railroad history, I suppose that he might even have been willing to inherit my thirty caskets of note cards. I had a picture of him, gradually taking on my manner, my dress, my neutral gray coloration. Indeed, I began to feel that it would be no more than proper for him to move in with Helen and take my place in that Hollywood bed.

There was undeniably an element of hurt in seeing how soon my shoes were filled. Nevertheless, watching young Hendricks pour, like raw molten metal, into the channels and molds so long occupied by Professor Gray was to have, in the long run, a wholesome effect upon me. I no longer had a carapace to crawl back into. Young Hendricks had cut off my retreat. George Edward Brown was now absolutely on his own. This realization first struck me just a couple of weeks ago, as the calendar wheeled away from Winter. March came in with a roar of wind and a flurry of soggy snow that soaked into the frozen earth. I could almost hear the iron bonds cracking and falling apart. These presentiments of Spring persuaded me to buy a bright red plaid mackinaw and the kind of scarlet cap worn by deer hunters. And it was only last Saturday that, impelled by some unnamed yearning, instead of having a beer and a game of checkers, I donned my new outfit and loitered on the courthouse square, not the fashionable east side with its expensive shops like Mademoiselle, but the west side where were the five-and-tens, the hardware stores, and the loan sharks. This plebeian side swarmed with farmers and laborers on Saturday afternoon, and I felt safely camouflaged as I lounged against a store front. The yearning which had seized me was, I admitted to myself, for someone to take cognizance of *me,* to fill my void with a sense of being. Had Helen come by then, I might even have revealed myself to her. But that futility was avoided. The thread by which fate hung held firm. It was rare for Helen to come to that side of the square. However, two of my former colleagues *did* pass by and fail to recognize me. And then suddenly my heart began to pound furiously. There, coming along my side of the street, was Rose Matthews. Her figure, I now noticed, was even more abundant, riper, than I had remembered. As she passed, without thinking I gave a low whistle. She halted.

"Pleasures prove," I said. "Pleasures prove."

She turned back uncertainly and looked at me. Then I saw that she was not Rose Matthews at all, but another woman I had never seen before. Without glasses, my eyes had played me a trick. The woman was not even a brunette, but a decided blonde.

"What was that you said?" she demanded.

There was a roughness to her voice which I found exciting. For a full minute we looked at each other, hardly conscious of the crowds passing by. Unlike Rose Matthews at the cocktail party, this woman really knew I was there. Not *credo ergo sum,* I suddenly understood, but *credis ergo sum. You* believe, therefore I am. In that moment the distressing conviction of non-existence dropped away from me like a sloughed skin. I felt alive, as you do on shipboard with a new companion to whom nothing about you is old shoe. I studied the woman's face before replying. It was round and lush, with the blood about to flood into the fair skin. Her nose was a saucy pug, and her full chin was pertly dimpled. A little hat perched on her honey-colored hair, and her blue eyes were examining me with a mixture of interest and puzzlement. No doubt, the bright red mackinaw and the cap were doing their work. I gave her body a bold up-and-down glance. I said, "Treasure trove, treasure trove."

She hesitated for an instant, and then smiled. "Now, Daddy," she said with mock reproach. "Behave yourself, Daddy." She gave my arm a pat and walked on, flipping her tail provocatively. I was sure that I would see her again.

Katherine Anne Porter

THEFT

In this story of a characteristic evening in a young lady's life,
together with the epilogue of the following morning, we can see
clearly enough how accurate she is in reading the significance
of what has taken place, not only on this occasion but
on similar occasions in the past. The walk in the rain, the ride in
the cab, the talk and drink with her fellow writer, the
encounter with the janitress—not to mention the letter she burns
—all these tell the story. But do they tell the whole story?
The thoughtful reader may not entirely agree with the young
lady's analysis of the tragic flaw in her own character.

She had the purse in her hand when she came in. Standing in
the middle of the floor, holding her bathrobe around her and trailing a
damp towel in one hand, she surveyed the immediate past and remembered everything clearly. Yes, she had opened the flap and spread it out
on the bench after she had dried the purse with her handkerchief.

She had intended to take the Elevated, and naturally she looked in
her purse to make certain she had the fare, and was pleased to find
forty cents in the coin envelope. She was going to pay her own fare, too,
even if Camilo did have the habit of seeing her up the steps and dropping a nickel in the machine before he gave the turnstile a little push
and sent her through it with a bow. Camilo by a series of compromises
had managed to make effective a fairly complete set of smaller courte-
sies, ignoring the larger and more troublesome ones. She had walked
with him to the station in a pouring rain, because she knew he was almost as poor as she was, and when he insisted on a taxi, she was firm
and said, "You know it simply will not do." He was wearing a new hat
of a pretty biscuit shade, for it never occurred to him to buy anything
of a practical color; he had put it on for the first time and the rain was
spoiling it. She kept thinking, "But this is dreadful, where will he get
another?" She compared it with Eddie's hats that always seemed to be
precisely seven years old and as if they had been quite purposely left
out in the rain, and yet they sat with a careless and incidental rightness
on Eddie. But Camilo was far different; if he wore a shabby hat it would
be merely shabby on him, and he would lose his spirits over it. If she

565

had not feared Camilo would take it badly, for he insisted on the practice of his little ceremonies up to the point he had fixed for them, she
would have said to him as they left Thora's house, "Do go home. I can
surely reach the station by myself."

"It is written that we must be rained upon tonight," said Camilo,
"so let it be together."

At the foot of the platform stairway she staggered slightly—they
were both nicely set up on Thora's cocktails—and said: "At least,
Camilo, do me the favor not to climb these stairs in your present state,
since for you it is only a matter of coming down again at once, and you'll
certainly break your neck."

He made three quick bows, he was Spanish, and leaped off through
the rainy darkness. She stood watching him, for he was a very graceful
young man, thinking that tomorrow morning he would gaze soberly at
his spoiled hat and soggy shoes and possibly associate her with his
misery. As she watched, he stopped at the far corner and took off his
hat and hid it under his overcoat. She felt she had betrayed him by
seeing, because he would have been humiliated if he thought she even
suspected him of trying to save his hat.

Roger's voice sounded over her shoulder above the clang of the rain
falling on the stairway shed, wanting to know what she was doing out
in the rain at this time of night, and did she take herself for a duck?
His long, imperturbable face was streaming with water, and he tapped
a bulging spot on the breast of his buttoned-up overcoat: "Hat," he
said. "Come on, let's take a taxi."

She settled back against Roger's arm which he laid around her shoulders, and with the gesture they exchanged a glance full of long amiable
associations, then she looked through the window at the rain changing
the shapes of everything, and the colors. The taxi dodged in and out
between the pillars of the Elevated, skidding slightly on every curve,
and she said: "The more it skids the calmer I feel, so I really must be
drunk."

"You must be," said Roger. "This bird is a homicidal maniac, and I
could do with a cocktail myself this minute."

They waited on the traffic at Fortieth Street and Sixth Avenue, and
three boys walked before the nose of the taxi. Under the globes of light
they were cheerful scarecrows, all very thin and all wearing very seedy
snappy-cut suits and gay neckties. They were not very sober either, and
they stood for a moment wobbling in front of the car, and there was an
argument going on among them. They leaned toward each other as if
they were getting ready to sing, and the first one said: "When I get
married it won't be jus' for getting married, I'm gonna marry for *love*,
see?" and the second one said, "Aw, gwan and tell that stuff to her, why
n't yuh?" and the third one gave a kind of hoot, and said, "Hell, dis guy?

Wot the hell's he got?" and the first one said: "Aaah, shurrup yuh mush, I got plenty." Then they all squealed and scrambled across the street beating the first one on the back and pushing him around.

"Nuts," commented Roger, "pure nuts."

Two girls went skittering by in short transparent raincoats, one green, one red, their heads tucked against the drive of the rain. One of them was saying to the other, "Yes, I know all about *that*. But what about me? You're always so sorry for *him* . . ." and they ran on with their little pelican legs flashing back and forth.

The taxi backed up suddenly and leaped forward again, and after a while Roger said: "I had a letter from Stella today, and she'll be home on the twenty-sixth, so I suppose she's made up her mind and it's all settled."

"I had a sort of letter today too," she said, "making up my mind for me. I think it is time for you and Stella to do something definite."

When the taxi stopped on the corner of West Fifty-third Street, Roger said, "I've just enough if you'll add ten cents," so she opened her purse and gave him a dime, and he said, "That's beautiful, that purse."

"It's a birthday present," she told him, "and I like it. How's your show coming?"

"Oh, still hanging on, I guess. I don't go near the place. Nothing sold yet. I mean to keep right on the way I'm going and they can take it or leave it. I'm through with the argument."

"It's absolutely a matter of holding out, isn't it?"

"Holding out's the tough part."

"Good night, Roger."

"Good night, you should take aspirin and push yourself into a tub of hot water, you look as though you're catching cold."

"I will."

With the purse under her arm she went upstairs, and on the first landing Bill heard her step and poked his head out with his hair tumbled and his eyes red, and he said: "For Christ's sake, come in and have a drink with me. I've had some bad news."

"You're perfectly sopping," said Bill, looking at her drenched feet. They had two drinks, while Bill told how the director had thrown his play out after the cast had been picked over twice, and had gone through three rehearsals. "I said to him, 'I didn't say it was a masterpiece, I said it would make a good show.' And he said, 'It just doesn't *play,* do you see? It needs a doctor.' So I'm stuck, absolutely stuck," said Bill, on the edge of weeping again. "I've been crying," he told her, "in my cups." And he went on to ask her if she realized his wife was ruining him with her extravagance. "I send her ten dollars every week of my unhappy life, and I don't really have to. She threatens to jail me if I don't, but she can't do it. God, let her try it after the way she treated me! She's no right to alimony and she knows it. She keeps on saying she's got to have it for the baby and I keep on sending it because I can't bear to see anybody suffer. So I'm way behind on the piano and the victrola, both—"

"Well, this is a pretty rug, anyhow," she said.

Bill stared at it and blew his nose. "I got it at Ricci's for ninety-five dollars," he said. "Ricci told me it once belonged to Marie Dressler, and cost fifteen hundred dollars, but there's a burnt place on it, under the divan. Can you beat that?"

"No," she said. She was thinking about her empty purse and that she could not possibly expect a check for her latest review for another three days, and her arrangement with the basement restaurant could not last much longer if she did not pay something on account. "It's no time to speak of it," she said, "but I've been hoping you would have by now that fifty dollars you promised for my scene in the third act. Even if it doesn't play. You were to pay me for the work anyhow out of your advance."

"Weeping Jesus," said Bill, "you, too?" He gave a loud sob, or hiccough, in his moist handkerchief. "Your stuff was no better than mine, after all. Think of that."

"But you got something for it," she said. "Seven hundred dollars."

Bill said, "Do me a favor, will you? Have another drink and forget about it. I can't, you know I can't, I would if I could, but you know the fix I'm in."

"Let it go, then," she found herself saying almost in spite of herself. She had meant to be quite firm about it. They drank again without speaking, and she went to her apartment on the floor above.

There, she now remembered distinctly, she had taken the letter out of the purse before she spread the purse out to dry.

She had sat down and read the letter over again: but there were phrases that insisted on being read many times, they had a life of their own separate from the others, and when she tried to read past and around them, they moved with the movement of her eyes, and she could not escape them . . . "thinking about you more than I mean to . . . yes, I even talk about you . . . why were you so anxious to destroy . . . even if I could see you now I would not . . . not worth all this abominable . . . the end . . ."

Carefully she tore the letter into narrow strips and touched a lighted match to them in the coal grate.

Early the next morning she was in the bathtub when the janitress knocked and then came in, calling out that she wished to examine the radiators before she started the furnace going for the winter. After moving about the room for a few minutes, the janitress went out, closing the door very sharply.

She came out of the bathroom to get a cigarette from the package in the purse. The purse was gone. She dressed and made coffee, and sat by the window while she drank it. Certainly the janitress had taken the purse, and certainly it would be impossible to get it back without a great deal of ridiculous excitement. Then let it go. With this decision of her mind, there rose coincidentally in her blood a deep almost murderous anger. She set the cup carefully in the center of the table, and walked steadily downstairs, three long flights and a short hall and a steep short flight into the basement, where the janitress, her face streaked with coal dust, was shaking up the furnace. "Will you please give me back my purse? There isn't any money in it. It was a present, and I don't want to lose it."

The janitress turned without straightening up and peered at her with hot flickering eyes, a red light from the furnace reflected in them. "What do you mean, your purse?"

"The gold cloth purse you took from the wooden bench in my room," she said. "I must have it back."

"Before God I never laid eyes on your purse, and that's the holy truth," said the janitress.

"Oh, well then, keep it," she said, but in a very bitter voice; "keep it if you want it so much." And she walked away.

She remembered how she had never locked a door in her life, on some principle of rejection in her that made her uncomfortable in the ownership of things, and her paradoxical boast before the warnings of her friends, that she had never lost a penny by theft; and she had been pleased with the bleak humility of this concrete example designed to illustrate and justify a certain fixed, otherwise baseless and general faith which ordered the movements of her life without regard to her will in the matter.

In this moment she felt that she had been robbed of an enormous number of valuable things, whether material or intangible: things lost or broken by her own fault, things she had forgotten and left in houses when she moved: books borrowed from her and not returned, journeys she had planned and had not made, words she had waited to hear spoken to her and had not heard, and the words she had meant to answer with; bitter alternatives and intolerable substitutes worse than nothing, and yet inescapable: the long patient suffering of dying friendships and the dark inexplicable death of love—all that she had had, and all that she had missed, were lost together, and were twice lost in this landslide of remembered losses.

The janitress was following her upstairs with the purse in her hand and the same deep red fire flickering in her eyes. The janitress thrust the purse towards her while they were still a half dozen steps apart, and said: "Don't never tell on me. I musta been crazy. I get crazy in the head sometimes, I swear I do. My son can tell you."

She took the purse after a moment, and the janitress went on: "I got a niece who is going on seventeen, and she's a nice girl and I thought I'd give it to her. She needs a pretty purse. I musta been crazy; I thought maybe you wouldn't mind, you leave things around and don't seem to notice much."

She said: "I missed this because it was a present to me from someone . . .."

The janitress said: "He'd get you another if you lost this one. My niece is young and needs pretty things, we oughta give the young ones a chance. She's got young men after her maybe will want to marry her. She oughta have nice things. She needs them bad right now. You're a grown woman, you've had your chance, you ought to know how it is!"

. She held the purse out to the janitress saying: "You don't know what you're talking about. Here, take it, I've changed my mind. I really don't want it."

The janitress looked up at her with hatred and said: "I don't want it either now. My niece is young and pretty, she don't need fixin' up to be pretty, she's young and pretty anyhow! I guess you need it worse than she does!"

"It wasn't really yours in the first place," she said, turning away. "You mustn't talk as if I had stolen it from you."

"It's not from me, it's from her you're stealing it," said the janitress, and went back downstairs.

She laid the purse on the table and sat down with the cup of chilled coffee, and thought: I was right not to be afraid of any thief but myself, who will end by leaving me nothing.

A QUEER HEART

Mrs. Cadman is in many ways one of the most delightfully
human characters to be found in this book. But unfortunately,
like many delightful and well-meaning people, Hilda Cadman
is misunderstood. It too often happens that the world
misjudges people from a misreading of the very motives and
tendencies that, properly regarded, are their most enduring and
endearing qualities. The symbolism of the concluding
scene is scarcely needed to underscore the nature of Hilda's
conflict with Rosa and Lucille. But it is not altogether
this temperamental conflict that engages the interest and the
sympathy of the reader; it is Hilda Cadman herself.

Rosa should have had that fairy doll. Hilda could have got
along cheerfully enough without it, just as now, after she
has lost Rosa, she will continue to get along.

M rs. Cadman got out of the bus backwards. No amount of
practice ever made her more agile; the trouble she had with her big
bulk amused everyone, and herself. Gripping the handles each side
of the bus door so tightly that the seams of her gloves cracked, she
lowered herself cautiously, like a climber, while her feet, overlapping
her smart shoes, uneasily scrabbled at each step. One or two people
asked why the bus made, for one passenger, such a long, dead stop. But
on the whole she was famous on this line, for she was constantly in and
out of town. The conductor waited behind her, smiling, holding her
basket, arms wide to catch her if she should slip.

Having got safe to the ground, Mrs. Cadman shook herself like a
satisfied bird. She took back her shopping basket from the conductor
and gave him a smile instead. The big kind scarlet bus once more ground
into movement, off up the main road hill: it made a fading blur in the
premature autumn dusk. Mrs. Cadman almost waved after it, for with it
went the happy part of her day. She turned down the side road that
led to her gate.

A wet wind of autumn, smelling of sodden gardens, blew in her face
and tilted her hat. Leaves whirled along it, and one lime leaf, as though
imploring shelter, lodged in her fur collar. Every gust did more to sadden

the poor trees. This was one of those roads outside growing provincial cities that still keep their rural mystery. They seem to lead into something still not known. Traffic roars past one end, but the other end is in silence: you see a wood, a spire, a haughty manor gate, or your view ends with the turn of an old wall. Here some new raw-looking villas stood with spaces between them; in the spaces were orchards and market-gardens. A glasshouse roof reflected the wet grey light; there was a shut chapel farther along. And, each standing back in half an acre of ground, there were two or three stucco houses with dark windows, sombre but at the same time ornate, built years ago in this then retired spot. Dead lime leaves showered over their grass plots and evergreens. Mrs. Cadman's house, Granville, was one of these: its name was engraved in scrolls over the porch. The solid house was not large, and Mrs. Cadman's daughter, Lucille, could look after it with a daily help.

The widow and her daughter lived here in the state of cheerless meekness Lucille considered suitable for them now. *Mr.* Cadman had liked to have everything done in style. But twelve years ago he had died, travelling on business, in a hotel up in the North. Always the gentleman, he had been glad to spare them this upset at home. He had been brought back to the Midlands for his impressive funeral, whose size showed him a popular man. How unlike Mr. Cadman was Rosa proving herself. One can be most unfriendly on one's way of dying. Ah, well, one chooses one's husband; one's sister is dealt out to one by fate.

Mrs. Cadman, thumb on the latch of her own gate, looked for a minute longer up and down the road—deeply, deeply unwilling to go in. She looked back at the corner where the bus had vanished, and an immense sigh heaved up her coat lapels and made a cotton carnation, pinned to the fur, brush a fold of her chin. Laced, hooked, buttoned so tightly into her clothes, she seemed to need to deflate herself by these sudden sighs, by yawns or by those explosions of laughter that often vexed Lucille. Through her face—embedded in fat but still very lively, as exposed, as ingenuous as a little girl's—you could see some emotional fermentation always at work in her. Her smiles were frequent, hopeful and quick. Her pitching walk was due to her tight shoes.

When she did go in, she went in with a sort of rush. She let the door bang back on the hall wall, so that the chain rattled and an outraged clatter came from the letterbox. Immediately she knew she had done wrong. Lucille, appalled, looked out of the dining-room. *"Shissssssh! How can you, mother!"* she said.

"Ever so sorry, dear," said Mrs. Cadman, cast down.

"She'd just dropped off," said Lucille. "After her bad night and everything. It really does seem hard."

Mrs. Cadman quite saw that it did. She glanced nervously up the stairs, then edged into the dining-room. It was not cheerful in here: a monkey puzzle, too close to the window, drank the last of the light up; the room still smelt of dinner; the fire smouldered resentfully, starved for coal. The big mahogany furniture lowered, with no shine. Mrs. Cadman, putting her basket down on the table, sent an uncertain smile across at Lucille, whose glasses blankly gleamed high up on her long face. She often asked herself where Lucille could have come from. *Could this be the baby daughter she had borne, and tied pink bows on, and christened a pretty name?* In the sun in this very bow window she had gurgled into the sweet-smelling creases of Lucille's neck—one summer lost in time.

"You *have* been an age," Lucille said.

"Well, the shops were quite busy. I never *saw,*" she said with irrepressible pleasure, "I never *saw* so many people in town!"

Lucille, lips tighter than ever shut, was routing about, unpacking the shopping basket, handling the packages. Chemist's and grocer's parcels. Mrs. Cadman watched her with apprehension. Then Lucille pounced; she held up a small soft parcel in frivolous wrappings. "Oho," she said. "So you've been in at Babbington's?"

"Well, I missed one bus, so I had to wait for the next. So I just popped in there a minute out of the cold. And, you see, I've been wanting a little scarf—"

"Little scarf!" said Lucille. "I don't know what to make of you, mother. I don't really. How *could* you, at such a time? How you ever could have the heart!" Lucille, standing the other side of the table, leaned across it, her thin weight on her knuckles. This brought her face near her mother's. "Can't you understand?" she said. "Can't you take *anything* in? The next little scarf *you'll* need to buy will be black!"

"What a thing to say!" exclaimed Mrs. Cadman, profoundly offended. "With that poor thing upstairs now, waiting to have her tea."

"Tea? She can't take her tea. Why, since this morning she can't keep a thing down."

Mrs. Cadman blenched and began unbuttoning her coat. Lucille seemed to feel that her own prestige and Aunt Rosa's entirely hung on Aunt Rosa's approaching death. You could feel that she and her aunt had thought up this plan together. These last days had been the climax of their complicity. And there was Mrs. Cadman—as ever, as usual—put in the wrong, frowned upon, out of things. Whenever Rosa arrived to stay Mrs. Cadman had no fun in her home, and now Rosa was leaving for ever it seemed worse. A perverse kick of the heart, a flicker of naughtiness, made Mrs. Cadman say: "Oh, well, while there's life there's hope."

Lucille said: "If you won't face it, you won't. But I just say it does fall heavy on me. . . . We had the vicar round here this afternoon. He was up with Aunt for a bit, then he looked in and said he did feel I needed a prayer too. He said he thought I was wonderful. He asked where you were, and he seemed to wonder you find the heart to stay out so long. I thought from his manner he wondered a good deal."

Mrs. Cadman, with an irrepressible titter, said: "Give him something to think about! Why if I'd ha' shown up that vicar'd have popped out as fast as he popped in. Thinks I'd make a mouthful of him! Why, I've made him bolt down the street. Well, well. He's not *my* idea of a vicar. When your father and I first came here we had a rural dean. Oh, he was as pleasant as anything."

Lucille, with the air of praying for Christian patience, folded her lips. Jabbing her fingers down the inside of her waistbelt, she more tightly tucked in her tight blouse. She liked looking like Mrs. Noah—no, *Miss* Noah. "The doctor's not been again. We're to let him know of any change."

"Well, let's do the best we can," said Mrs. Cadman. "But don't keep on *talking*. You don't make things any better, keeping on going on. My opinion is one should keep bright to the last. When my time comes, oh, I would like a cheery face."

"It's well for you . . ." began Lucille. She bit the remark off and, gathering up the parcels, stalked scornfully out of the dining-room. Without comment she left exposed on the table a small carton of goodies Mrs. Cadman had bought to cheer herself up with and had concealed in the toe of the shopping bag. Soon, from the kitchen came the carefully muffled noises of Lucille putting away provisions and tearing the wrappings off the chemist's things. Mrs. Cadman, reaching out for the carton, put a peppermint into each cheek. She, oh so badly, wanted a cup of tea but dared not follow Lucille into the kitchen in order to put the kettle on.

Though, after all, Granville *was* her house. . . .

You would not think it was her house—not when Rosa was there. While Lucille and her mother were *tête à tête* Lucille's disapproval was at least fairly tacit. But as soon as Rosa arrived on one of these yearly autumn visits—always choosing the season when Mrs. Cadman felt in her least good form, the fall of the leaf—the aunt and niece got together and found everything wrong. Their two cold natures ran together. They found Mrs. Cadman lacking; they forbade the affection she would have offered them. They censured her the whole time. Mrs. Cadman could date her real alienation from Lucille from the year when Rosa's visits began. During Mr. Cadman's lifetime Rosa had never come for more than an afternoon. Mr. Cadman had been his wife's defence from her sister —a great red kind of rumbustious fortification. He had been a man who kept every chill wind out. Rosa, during those stilted afternoon visits, had adequately succeeded in conveying that she found marriage *low*. She might just have suffered a pious marriage; she openly deprecated this high living, this state of fleshly bliss. In order not to witness it too closely she lived on in lodgings in her native town. . . . But once widowhood left her sister exposed, Rosa started flapping round Granville like a doomed bird. She instituted these yearly visits, which, she made plain at the same time, gave her not much pleasure. The journey was tedious, and by breaking her habits, leaving her lodgings, Rosa was, out of duty, putting herself about. Her joyless and intimidating visits had, therefore, only one object—to protect the interests of Lucille.

Mrs. Cadman had suspected for some time that Rosa had something the matter with her. No one looks as yellow as that for nothing. But she was not sufficiently intimate with her sister to get down to the cosy subjects of insides. This time, Rosa arrived looking worse than ever, and three days afterwards had collapsed. Lucille said now she had known her aunt was poorly. Lucille said now she had always known. "But of course you wouldn't notice, mother," she said.

Mrs. Cadman sat down by the fire and, gratefully, kicked off her tight shoes. In the warmth her plump feet uncurled, relaxed, expanded like sea-anemones. She stretched her legs out, propped her heels on the fender and wiggled her toes voluptuously. They went on wiggling of their own accord: they seemed to have an independent existence. Here, in her home, where she felt so "put wrong" and chilly, they were like ten stout confidential friends. She said, out loud: "Well, *I* don't know what I've done."

The fact was: Lucille and Rosa resented her. (She'd feel better when she had had her tea.) She should *not* have talked as she had about the vicar. But it seemed so silly, Lucille having just him. She did wish Lucille had a better time. No young man so much as paused at the gate. Lucille's aunt had wrapped her own dank virginity round her, like someone sharing a mackintosh.

Mrs. Cadman had had a good time. A really good time always lasts: you have it with all your nature and all your nature stays living with it. She had been a pretty child with long, blonde hair that her sister Rosa, who was her elder sister, used to tweak when they were alone in their room. She had grown used, in that childish attic bedroom, to Rosa's malevolent silences. Then one had grown up, full of great uppish curves. Hilda Cadman could sing. She had sung at parties and sung at charity concerts, too. She had been invited from town to town, much fêted in business society. She had sung in a dress cut low at the bosom, with a rose or carnation tucked into her hair. She had drunk port wine in great red rooms blazing with chandeliers. Mr. Cadman had whisked her away from her other gentlemen friends, and not for a moment had she regretted it. Nothing had been too good for her; she had gone on singing. She had felt warm air on her bare shoulders; she still saw the kind, flushed faces crowding round. Mr. Cadman and she belonged to the jolly set. They all thought the world of her, and she thought the world of them.

Mrs. Cadman, picking up the poker, jabbed the fire into a spurt of light. It does not do any good to sit and think in the dark.

The town was not the same now. They had all died, or lost their money, or gone. But you kept on loving the town for its dear old sake. She sometimes thought: Why not move and live at the seaside, where there would be a promenade and a band? But she knew her nature clung to the old scenes; where you had lived, you lived—your nature clung like a cat. While there was *something* to look at she was not one to repine. It kept you going to keep out and about. Things went, but then new things came in their place. You can't cure yourself of the habit of loving life. So she drank up the new pleasures—the big cafés, the barging buses, the cinemas, the shops dripping with colour, almost all built of glass. She could be perfectly happy all alone in a café, digging into a cream bun with a fork, the band playing, smiling faces all round. The old faces had not gone: they had dissolved, diluted into the ruddy blur through which she saw everything.

Meanwhile, Lucille was hard put to it, living her mother down. Mother looked ridiculous, always round town like that.

Mrs. Cadman heard Lucille come out of the kitchen and go upstairs with something rattling on a tray. She waited a minute more, then sidled into the kitchen, where she cautiously started to make tea. The gas-ring, as though it were a spy of Lucille's, popped loudly when she applied the match.

"Mother, she's asking for you."

"Oh, dear—do you mean she's—?"

"She's much more herself this evening," Lucille said implacably.

Mrs. Cadman, at the kitchen table, had been stirring sugar into her third cup. She pushed her chair back, brushed crumbs from her bosom and followed Lucille like a big unhappy lamb. The light was on in the hall, but the stairs led up into shadow: she had one more start of reluctance at their foot. Autumn draughts ran about in the top story: up there the powers of darkness all seemed to mobilize. Mrs. Cadman put her hand on the banister knob. "Are you sure she *does* want to see me? Oughtn't she to stay quiet?"

"You should go when she's asking. You never know. . . ."

Breathless, breathing unevenly on the top landing, Mrs. Cadman pushed open the spare-room—that was the sick-room—door. In there —in here—the air was dead, and at first it seemed very dark. On the ceiling an oil-stove printed its flower-pattern; a hooded lamp, low down, was turned away from the bed. On that dark side of the lamp she could just distinguish Rosa, propped up, with the sheet drawn to her chin.

"Rosa?"

"Oh, it's you?"

"Yes; it's me, dear. Feeling better this evening?"

"Seemed funny, you not coming near me."

"They said for you to keep quiet."

"My own sister. . . . You never liked sickness, did you? Well, I'm going. I shan't trouble you long."

"Oh, don't talk like that!"

"I'm glad to be going. Keeping on lying here. . . . We all come to it. Oh, give over crying, Hilda. Doesn't do any good."

Mrs. Cadman sat down, to steady herself. She fumbled in her lap with her handkerchief, perpetually, clumsily knocking her elbows against the arms of the wicker chair. "It's such a shame," she said. "It's such a pity. You and me, after all . . ."

"Well, it's late for all that now. Each took our own ways." Rosa's voice went up in a sort of ghostly sharpness. "There were things that couldn't be otherwise. I've tried to do right by Lucille. Lucille's a good girl, Hilda. You should ask yourself if you've done right by her."

"Oh, for shame, Rosa," said Mrs. Cadman, turning her face through the dark towards that disembodied voice. "For shame, Rosa, even if you *are* going. You know best what's come between her and me. It's been you and her, you and her. I don't know where to turn sometimes—"

Rosa said: "You've got such a shallow heart."

"How should you know? Why, you've kept at a distance from me ever since we were tots. Oh, I know I'm a great silly, always after my fun, but I never took what was yours; I never did harm to you. I don't see what call we have got to judge each other. You didn't want my life that I've had."

Rosa's chin moved: she was lying looking up at her sister's big rippling shadow, splodged up there by the light of the low lamp. It is frightening, having your shadow watched. Mrs. Cadman said: "But what did I do to you?"

"I *could* have had a wicked heart," said Rosa. "A vain, silly heart like yours. I could have fretted, seeing you take everything. One thing, then another. But I was shown. God taught me to pity you. God taught me my lesson. . . . You wouldn't even remember that Christmas tree."

"What Christmas tree?"

"No, you wouldn't even remember. Oh, I thought it was lovely. I could have cried when they pulled the curtains open, and there it was, all blazing away with candles and silver and everything—"

"Well, isn't that funny. I—"

"No; you've had all that pleasure since. All of us older children couldn't take it in, hardly, for quite a minute or two. It didn't look real. Then I looked up, and there was a fairy doll fixed on the top, right on

577

the top spike, fixed on to a star. I set my heart on her. She had wings and long fair hair, and she was shining away. I couldn't take my eyes off her. They cut the presents down; but she wasn't for anyone. In my childish blindness I kept praying to God. If I am not to have her, I prayed, let her stay there."

"And what did God do?" Hilda said eagerly.

"Oh, He taught me and saved me. You were a little thing in a blue sash; you piped up and asked might you have the doll."

"Fancy me! Aren't children awful!" said Mrs. Cadman. "Asking like that."

"They said: 'Make her sing for it.' They were taken with you. So you piped up again, singing. You got her, all right. I went off where they kept the coats. I've thanked God ever since for what I had to go through! I turned my face from vanity that very night. I had been shown."

"Oh, what a shame!" said Hilda. "Oh, I think it was cruel; you poor little mite."

"No; I used to see that doll all draggled about the house till no one could bear the sight of it. I said to myself: that's how those things end. Why, I'd learnt more in one evening than you've ever learnt in your life. Oh, yes, I've watched you, Hilda. Yes, and I've pitied you."

"Well, you showed me no pity."

"You asked for no pity—all vain and set up."

"No wonder you've been against me. Fancy me not knowing. I didn't *mean* any harm—why, I was quite a little thing. I don't even remember."

"Well, you'll remember one day. When you lie as I'm lying you'll find that everything comes back. And you'll see what it adds up to."

"Well, if I do?" said Hilda. "I haven't been such a baby; I've seen things out in my own way; I've had my ups and downs. It hasn't been all jam." She got herself out of the arm-chair and came and stood uncertainly by the foot of the bed. She had a great wish to reach out and turn the hooded lamp round, so that its light could fall on her sister's face. She felt she should *see* her sister, perhaps for the first time. Inside the flat, still form did implacable disappointment, then, stay locked? She wished she could give Rosa some little present. Too late to give Rosa anything pretty now: she looked back—it had always, then, been too late? She thought: you poor queer heart; you queer heart, eating yourself out, thanking God for the pain. She thought: I did that to her; then what have I done to Lucille?

She said: "You're ever so like me, Rosa, really, aren't you? Setting our hearts on things. When you've got them you don't notice. No wonder you wanted Lucille. . . . You did ought to have had that fairy doll."

Henry James

THE TREE OF KNOWLEDGE

In this story it is the initial situation that the reader must
understand to appreciate the ramifications of the plot that
follows from it. A Henry James story is not likely to be simple in
its development, but the situation set forth in the opening
pages, at least, may be explained in a few sentences. Morgan
Mallow is a sculptor and the central character. The plot is
centered upon various persons' true estimate of Mallow's ability
as an artist, an estimate not always in keeping with his own
favorable but mistaken view of himself as a sculptor of the first
rank, albeit unrecognized by the public. ("Morgan," wè are
told, "had at all events everything of the sculptor but the spirit of
Phidias . . .") The relationships of the people close to
Morgan Mallow provide the human interest, and the complexity,
of the story. The continuing interest is in these characters
—in their reactions to the central situation and in what James
refers to as the "noble duplicity" that they feel called upon
to display in their dealings with one another.

It was one of the secret opinions, such as we all have, of Peter
Brench that his main success in life would have consisted in his never
having committed himself about the work, as it was called, of his
friend Morgan Mallow. This was a subject on which it was, to the best
of his belief, impossible with veracity to quote him, and it was nowhere
on record that he had, in the connexion, on any occasion and in any embarrassment, either lied or spoken the truth. Such a triumph had its
honour even for a man of other triumphs—a man who had reached
fifty, who had escaped marriage, who had lived within his means, who
had been in love with Mrs. Mallow for years without breathing it, and
who, last not least, had judged himself once for all. He had so judged
himself in fact that he felt an extreme and general humility to be his
proper portion; yet there was nothing that made him think so well of his
parts as the course he had steered so often through the shallows just
mentioned. It became thus a real wonder that the friends in whom he
had most confidence were just those with whom he had most reserves.
He couldn't tell Mrs. Mallow—or at least he supposed, excellent man,

579

he couldn't—that she was the one beautiful reason he had never married; any more than he could tell her husband that the sight of the multiplied marbles in that gentleman's studio was an affliction of which even time had never blunted the edge. His victory, however, as I have intimated, in regard to these productions, was not simply in his not having let it out that he deplored them; it was, remarkably, in his not having kept it in by anything else.

The whole situation, among these good people, was verily a marvel, and there was probably not such another for a long way from the spot that engages us—the point at which the soft declivity of Hampstead began at that time to confess in broken accents to Saint John's Wood. He despised Mallow's statues and adored Mallow's wife, and yet was distinctly fond of Mallow, to whom, in turn, he was equally dear. Mrs. Mallow rejoiced in the statues—though she preferred, when pressed, the busts; and if she was visibly attached to Peter Brench it was because of his affection for Morgan. Each loved the other moreover for the love borne in each case to Lancelot, whom the Mallows respectively cherished as their only child and whom the friend of their fireside identified as the third—but decidedly the handsomest—of his godsons. Already in the old years it had come to that—that no one, for such a relation, could possibly have occurred to any of them, even to the baby itself, but Peter. There was luckily a certain independence, of the pecuniary sort, all round: the Master could never otherwise have spent his solemn *Wanderjahre* in Florence and Rome, and continued by the Thames as well as by the Arno and the Tiber to add unpurchased group to group and model, for what was too apt to prove in the event mere love, fancy-heads of celebrities either too busy or too buried—too much of the age or too little of it—to sit. Neither could Peter, lounging in almost daily, have found time to keep the whole complicated tradition so alive by his presence. He was massive but mild, the depositary of these mysteries—large and loose and ruddy and curly, with deep tones, deep eyes, deep pockets, to say nothing of the habit of long pipes, soft hats and brownish greyish weather-faded clothes, apparently always the same.

He had "written," it was known, but had never spoken, never spoken in particular of that; and he had the air (since, as was believed, he continued to write) of keeping it up in order to have something more—as if he hadn't at the worst enough—to be silent about. Whatever his air, at any rate, Peter's occasional unmentioned prose and verse were quite truly the result of an impulse to maintain the purity of his taste by establishing still more firmly the right relation of fame to feebleness. The little green door of his domain was in a garden-wall on which the discoloured stucco made patches, and in the small detached villa behind it everything was old, the furniture, the servants, the books, the prints, the immemorial habits and the new improvements. The Mallows, at Carrara Lodge, were within ten minutes, and the studio there was on their little land, to which they had added, in their happy faith, for building it. This was the good fortune, if it was not the ill, of her having brought him in marriage a portion that put them in a manner at their ease and enabled them thus, on their side, to keep it up. And they did keep it up—they always had—the infatuated sculptor and his wife, for whom nature had refined on the impossible by relieving them of the sense of the difficult. Morgan had at all events everything of the sculptor but the spirit of Phidias—the brown velvet, the becoming *beretto,* the "plastic" presence, the fine fingers, the beautiful accent in Italian and the old Italian factotum. He seemed to make up for everything when he addressed Egidio with the "tu" and waved him to turn one of the rotary pedestals of which the place was full. They were tremendous Italians at Carrara Lodge, and the secret of the part played by this fact in Peter's life was in a large degree that it gave him, sturdy Briton as he was, just the amount of "going abroad" he could bear. The Mallows were all his Italy, but it was in a measure for Italy he liked them. His one worry was that Lance—to which they had shortened his godson—was, in spite of a public school, perhaps a shade too Italian. Morgan meanwhile looked like somebody's flattering idea of somebody's own person as expressed in the great room provided at the Uffizzi Museum for the general illustration of that idea by eminent hands. The Master's sole regret that he hadn't been born rather to the brush than to the chisel sprang from his wish that he might have contributed to that collection.

It appeared with time at any rate to be to the brush that Lance had been born; for Mrs. Mallow, one day when the boy was turning twenty, broke it to their friend, who shared, to the last delicate morsel, their problems and pains, that it seemed as if nothing would really do but that he should embrace the career. It had been impossible longer to remain blind to the fact that he was gaining no glory at Cambridge, where Brench's own college had for a year tempered its tone to him as for Brench's own sake. Therefore why renew the vain form of preparing him for the impossible? The impossible—it had become clear—was that he should be anything but an artist.

"Oh dear, .dear!" said poor Peter.

"Don't you believe in it?" asked Mrs. Mallow, who still, at more than forty, had her violet velvet eyes, her creamy satin skin and her silken chestnut hair.

"Believe in what?"

"Why in Lance's passion."

"I don't know what you mean by 'believing in it.' I've never been unaware, certainly, of his disposition, from his earliest time, to daub and draw; but I confess I've hoped it would burn out."

"But why should it," she sweetly smiled, "with his wonderful heredity? Passion is passion—though of course indeed *you,* dear Peter, know nothing of that. Has the Master's ever burned out?"

Peter looked off a little and, in his familiar formless way, kept up for a moment, a sound between a smothered whistle and a subdued hum. "Do you think he's going to be another Master?"

She seemed scarce prepared to go that length, yet she had on the whole a marvellous trust. "I know what you mean by that. Will it be a career to incur the jealousies and provoke the machinations that have been at times almost too much for his father? Well—say it may be, since nothing but clap-trap, in these dreadful days, *can,* it would seem, make its way, and since, with the curse of refinement and distinction, one may easily find one's self begging one's bread. Put it at the worst—say he *has* the misfortune to wing his flight further than the vulgar taste of his stupid countrymen can follow. Think, all the same, of the happiness—the same the Master has had. He'll *know.*"

Peter looked rueful. "Ah but *what* will he know?"

"Quiet joy!" cried Mrs. Mallow, quite impatient and turning away.

II

He had of course before long to meet the boy himself on it and to hear that practically everything was settled. Lance was not to go up again, but to go instead to Paris where, since the die was cast, he would find the best advantages. Peter had always felt he must be taken as he was, but had never perhaps found him so much of that pattern as on this occasion. "You chuck Cambridge then altogether? Doesn't that seem rather a pity?"

Lance would have been like his father, to his friend's sense, had he had less humour, and like his mother had he had more beauty. Yet it was a good middle way for Peter that, in the modern manner, he was, to the eye, rather the young stockbroker than the young artist. The youth reasoned that it was a question of time—there was such a mill to go through, such an awful lot to learn. He had talked with fellows and had judged. "One has got, today," he said, "don't you see? to know."

His interlocutor, at this, gave a groan. "Oh hang it, *don't* know!"

Lance wondered. " 'Don't'? Then what's the use—?"

"The use of what?"

"Why of anything. Don't you think I've talent?"

Peter smoked away for a little in silence; then went on: "It isn't knowledge, it's ignorance that—as we've been beautifully told—is bliss."

"Don't you think I've talent?" Lance repeated.

Peter, with his trick of queer kind demonstrations, passed his arm round his godson and held him a moment. "How do I know?"

"Oh," said the boy, "if it's your own ignorance you're defending—!"

Again, for a pause, on the sofa, his godfather smoked. "It isn't. I've the misfortune to be omniscient."

"Oh well," Lance laughed again, "if you know *too* much—!"

"That's what I do, and it's why I'm so wretched."

Lance's gaiety grew. "Wretched? Come, I say!"

"But I forgot," his companion went on—"you're not to know about that. It would indeed for you too make the too much. Only I'll tell you what I'll do." And Peter got up from the sofa. "If you'll go up again I'll pay your way at Cambridge."

Lance stared, a little rueful in spite of being still more amused. "Oh Peter! You disapprove so of Paris?"

"Well, I'm afraid of it."

"Ah I see!"

"No, you don't see—yet. But you will—that is you would. And you mustn't."

The young man thought more gravely. "But one's innocence, already—!"

"Is considerably damaged? Ah that won't matter," Peter persisted—"we'll patch it up here."

"Here? Then you want me to stay at home?"

Peter almost confessed to it. "Well, we're so right—we four together —just as we are. We're so safe. Come, don't spoil it."

The boy, who had turned to gravity, turned from this, on the real pressure in his friend's tone, to consternation. "Then what's a fellow to be?"

"My particular care. Come, old man"—and Peter now fairly pleaded —"*I'll* look out for you."

Lance, who had remained on the sofa with his legs out and his hands in his pockets, watched him with eyes that showed suspicion. Then he got up. "You think there's something the matter with me—that I can't make a success."

"Well, what do you call a success?"

Lance thought again. "Why the best sort, I suppose, is to please one's self. Isn't that the sort that, in spite of cabals and things, is—in his own peculiar line—the Master's?"

There were so much too many things in this question to be answered at once that they practically checked the discussion, which became particularly difficult in the light of such renewed proof that, though the young man's innocence might, in the course of his studies, as he contended, somewhat have shrunken, the finer essence of it still remained. That was indeed exactly what Peter had assumed and what above all he desired; yet perversely enough it gave him a chill. The boy believed in the cabals and things, believed in the peculiar line, believed, to be brief, in the Master. What happened a month or two later wasn't that he went up again at the expense of his godfather, but that a fortnight after he had got settled in Paris this personage sent him fifty pounds.

He had meanwhile at home, this personage, made up his mind to the worst; and what that might be had never yet grown quite so vivid to him as when, on his presenting himself one Sunday night, as he never failed to do, for supper, the mistress of Carrara Lodge met him with an appeal as to—of all things in the world—the wealth of the Canadians. She was earnest, she was even excited. "Are many of them *really* rich?"

He had to confess he knew nothing about them, but he often thought afterwards of that evening. The room in which they sat was adorned with sundry specimens of the Master's genius, which had the merit of being, as Mrs. Mallow herself frequently suggested, of an unusually convenient size. They were indeed of dimensions not customary in the products of the chisel, and they had the singularity that, if the objects and features intended to be small looked too large, the objects and features intended to be large looked too small. The Master's idea, either in respect to this matter or to any other, had in almost any case, even after years, remained undiscoverable to Peter Brench. The creations that so failed to reveal it stood about on pedestals and brackets, on tables and shelves, a little staring white population, heroic, idyllic, allegoric, mythic, symbolic, in which "scale" had so strayed and lost itself that the public square and the chimney-piece seemed to have changed places, the monumental being all diminutive and the diminutive all monumental; branches at any rate, markedly, of a family in which stature was rather oddly irrespective of function, age and sex. They formed, like the Mallows themselves, poor Brench's own family—having at least to such a degree the note of familiarity. The occasion was one of those he had long ago learnt to know and to name—short flickers of the faint flame, soft gusts of a kinder air. Twice a year regularly the Master believed in his fortune, in addition to believing all the year round in his genius. This time it was to be made by a bereaved couple from Toronto, who had given him the handsomest order for a tomb to three lost children, each of whom they desired to see, in the composition, emblematically and characteristically represented.

Such was naturally the moral of Mrs. Mallow's question: if their wealth was to be assumed, it was clear, from the nature of their admiration, as well as from mysterious hints thrown out (they were a little odd!) as to other possibilities of the same mortuary sort, that their further patronage might be; and not less evident that should the Master become at all known in those climes nothing would be more inevitable than a run of Canadian custom. Peter had been present before at runs of custom, colonial and domestic—present at each of those of which the aggregation had left so few gaps in the marble company round him; but it was his habit never at these junctures to prick the bubble in advance. The fond illusion, while it lasted, eased the wound of elections never won, the long ache of medals and diplomas carried off, on every chance, by every one but the Master; it moreover lighted the lamp that would glimmer through the next eclipse. They lived, however, after all—as it was always beautiful to see—at a height scarce susceptible of ups and downs. They strained a point at times charmingly, strained it to admit that the public was here and there not too bad to buy; but they would have been nowhere without their attitude that the Master was always too good to sell. They were at all events deliciously formed, Peter often said to himself, for their fate; the Master had a vanity, his wife had a loyalty, of which success, depriving these things of innocence, would have diminished the merit and the grace. Any one could be charming under a charm, and as he looked about him at a world of prosperity more void of proportion even than the Master's museum he wondered if he knew another pair that so completely escaped vulgarity.

"What a pity Lance isn't with us to rejoice!" Mrs. Mallow on this occasion sighed at supper.

"We'll drink to the health of the absent," her husband replied, filling his friend's glass and his own and giving a drop to their companion; "but we must hope he's preparing himself for a happiness much less like this of ours this evening—excusable as I grant it to be!—than like the comfort we have always (whatever has happened or has not happened) been able to trust ourselves to enjoy. The comfort," the Master explained, leaning back in the pleasant lamplight and firelight, holding up his glass and looking round at his marble family, quartered more or less, a monstrous brood, in every room—"the comfort of art in itself!"

Peter looked a little shyly at his wine. "Well—I don't care what you may call it when a fellow doesn't—but Lance must learn to *sell,* you know. I drink to his acquisition of the secret of a base popularity!"

"Oh yes, *he* must sell," the boy's mother, who was still more, however, this seemed to give out, the Master's wife, rather artlessly allowed.

"Ah," the sculptor after a moment confidently pronounced, "Lance *will.* Don't be afraid. He'll have learnt."

"Which is exactly what Peter," Mrs. Mallow gaily returned—"why in the world were you so perverse, Peter?—wouldn't when he told him hear of."

Peter, when this lady looked at him with accusatory affection—a grace on her part not infrequent—could never find a word; but the Master, who was always all amenity and tact, helped him out now as he had often helped him before. "That's his old idea, you know—on which we've so often differed: his theory that the artist should be all impulse and instinct. *I* go in of course for a certain amount of school. Not too much—but a due proportion. There's where his protest came in," he continued to explain to his wife, "as against what *might,* don't you see? be in question for Lance."

"Ah well"—and Mrs. Mallow turned the violet eyes across the table at the subject of this discourse—"he's sure to have meant of course nothing but good. Only that wouldn't have prevented him, if Lance *had* taken his advice, from being in effect horribly cruel."

They had a sociable way of talking of him to his face as if he had been in the clay or—at most—in the plaster, and the Master was unfailingly generous. He might have been waving Egidio to make him revolve. "Ah but poor Peter wasn't so wrong as to what it may after all come to that he *will* learn."

"Oh but nothing artistically bad," she urged—still, for poor Peter, arch and dewy.

"Why just the little French tricks," said the Master: on which their friend had to pretend to admit, when pressed by Mrs. Mallow, that these aesthetic vices had been the objects of his dread.

III

"I know now," Lance said to him the next year, "why you were so much against it." He had come back supposedly for a mere interval and was looking about him at Carrara Lodge, where indeed he had already on two or three occasions since his expatriation briefly reappeared. This had the air of a longer holiday. "Something rather awful has happened to me. It *isn't* so very good to know."

"I'm bound to say high spirits don't show in your face," Peter was rather ruefully forced to confess. "Still, are you very sure you do know?"

"Well, I at least know about as much as I can bear." These remarks were exchanged in Peter's den, and the young man, smoking cigarettes, stood before the fire with his back against the mantel. Something of his bloom seemed really to have left him.

Poor Peter wondered. "You're clear then as to what in particular I wanted you not to go for?"

"In particular?" Lance thought. "It seems to me that in particular there can have been only one thing."

They stood for a little sounding each other. "Are you quite sure?"

"Quite sure I'm a beastly duffer? Quite—by this time."

"Oh!"—and Peter turned away as if almost with relief.

"It's *that* that isn't pleasant to find out."

"Oh I don't care for 'that,'" said Peter, presently coming round again. "I mean I personally don't."

"Yet I hope you can understand a little that I myself should!"

"Well, what do you mean by it?" Peter sceptically asked.

And on this Lance had to explain—how the upshot of his studies in Paris had inexorably proved a mere deep doubt of his means. These studies had so waked him up that a new light was in his eyes; but what the new light did was really to show him too much. "Do you know what's the matter with me? I'm too horribly intelligent. Paris was really the last place for me. I've learnt what I can't do."

Poor Peter stared—it was a staggerer; but even after they had had, on the subject, a longish talk in which the boy brought out to the full the hard truth of his lesson, his friend betrayed less pleasure than usually breaks into a face to the happy tune of "I told you so!" Poor Peter himself made now indeed so little a point of having told him so that Lance broke ground in a different place a day or two after. "What was it then that—before I went—you were afraid I should find out?" This, however, Peter refused to tell him—on the ground that if he hadn't yet guessed perhaps he never would, and that in any case nothing at all for either of them was to be gained by giving the thing a name. Lance eyed him on this an instant with the bold curiosity of youth—with the air indeed of having in his mind two or three names, of which one or other would be right. Peter nevertheless, turning his back again, offered no encouragement, and when they parted afresh it was with some show of impatience on the side of the boy. Accordingly on their next encounter Peter saw at a glance that he had now, in the interval, divined and that, to sound his note, he was only waiting till they should find themselves alone. This he had soon arranged and he then broke straight out. "Do you know your conundrum has been keeping me awake? But in the watches of the night the answer came over me—so that, upon my honour, I quite laughed out. Had you been supposing I had to go to Paris to learn *that?*" Even now, to see him still so sublimely on his guard, Peter's young friend had to laugh afresh. "You won't give a sign till you're sure? Beautiful old Peter!" But Lance at last produced it. "Why, hang it, the truth about the Master."

It made between them for some minutes a lively passage, full of wonder for each at the wonder of the other. "Then how long have you understood—"

"The true value of his work? I understood it," Lance recalled, "as soon as I began to understand anything. But I didn't begin fully to do that, I admit, till I got *là-bas.*"

"Dear, dear!"—Peter gasped with retrospective dread.

"But for what have you taken me? I'm a hopeless muff—that I *had* to have rubbed in. But I'm not such a muff as the Master!" Lance declared.

"Then why did you never tell me—?"

"That I hadn't, after all"—the boy took him up—"remained such an

587

idiot? Just because I never dreamed *you* knew. But I beg your pardon. I only wanted to spare you. And what I don't now understand is how the deuce then for so long you've managed to keep bottled."

Peter produced his explanation, but only after some delay and with a gravity not void of embarrassment. "It was for your mother."

"Oh!" said Lance.

"And that's the great thing now—since the murder *is* out. I want a promise from you. I mean"—and Peter almost feverishly followed it up—"a vow from you, solemn and such as you owe me here on the spot, that you'll sacrifice anything rather than let her ever guess—"

"That *I've* guessed?"—Lance took it in. "I see." He evidently after a moment had taken in much. "But what is it you've in mind that I may have a chance to sacrifice?"

"Oh one has always something."

Lance looked at him hard. "Do you mean that *you've* had—?" The look he received back, however, so put the question by that he found soon enough another. "Are you really sure my mother doesn't know?"

Peter, after renewed reflexion, was really sure. "If she does she's too wonderful."

"But aren't we all too wonderful?"

"Yes," Peter granted—"but in different ways. The thing's so desperately important because your father's little public consists only, as you know then," Peter developed—"well, of how many?"

"First of all," the Master's son risked, "of himself. And last of all too. I don't quite see of whom else."

Peter had an approach to impatience. "Of your mother, I say—*always.*"

Lance cast it all up. "You absolutely feel that?"

"Absolutely."

"Well then with yourself that makes three."

"Oh *me!*"—and Peter, with a wag of his kind old head, modestly excused himself. "The number's at any rate small enough for any individual dropping out to be too dreadfully missed. Therefore, to put it in a nutshell, take care, my boy—that's all—that *you're* not!"

"I've got to keep on humbugging?" Lance wailed.

"It's just to warn you of the danger of your failing of that that I've seized this opportunity."

"And what do you regard in particular," the young man asked, "as the danger?"

"Why this certainty: that the moment your mother, who feels so strongly, should suspect your secret—well," said Peter desperately, "the fat would be on the fire."

Lance for a moment seemed to stare at the blaze. "She'd throw me over?"

"She'd throw *him* over."

"And come round to us?"

Peter, before he answered, turned away. "Come round to *you*." But he had said enough to indicate—and, as he evidently trusted, to avert—the horrid contingency.

IV

Within six months again, none the less, his fear was on more occasions than one all before him. Lance had returnèd to Paris for another trial; then had reappeared at home and had had, with his father, for the first time in his life, one of the scenes that strike sparks. He described it with much expression to Peter, touching whom (since they had never done so before) it was the sign of a new reserve on the part of the pair at Carrara Lodge that they at present failed, on a matter of intimate interest, to open themselves—if not in joy then in sorrow—to their good friend. This produced perhaps practically between the parties a shade of alienation and a slight intermission of commerce—marked mainly indeed by the fact that to talk at his ease with his old playmate Lance had in general to come to see him. The closest if not quite the gayest relation they had yet known together was thus ushered in. The difficulty for poor Lance was a tension at home—begotten by the fact that his father wished him to be at least the sort of success he himself had been. He hadn't "chucked" Paris—though nothing appeared more vivid to him than that Paris had chucked. him: he would go back again because of the fascination in trying, in seeing, in sounding the depths—in learning one's lesson, briefly, even if the lesson were simply that of one's impotence in the presence of one's larger vision. But what did the Master, all aloft in his senseless fluency, know of impotence, and what vision—to be called such—had he in all his blind life ever had? Lance, heated and indignant, frankly appealed to his godparent on this score.

His father, it appeared, had come down on him for having, after so long, nothing to show, and hoped that on his next return this deficiency would be repaired. *The* thing, the Master complacently set forth was—for any artist, however inferior to himself—at least to "do" something. "What can you do? That's all I ask!" *He* had certainly done enough, and there was no mistake about what he had to show. Lance had tears in his eyes when it came thus to letting his old friend know how great the strain might be on the "sacrifice" asked of him. It wasn't so easy to continue humbugging—as from son to parent—after feeling one's self despised for not grovelling in mediocrity. Yet a noble duplicity was what, as they intimately faced the situation, Peter went on requiring; and it was still for a time what his young friend, bitter and sore, managed loyally to comfort him with. Fifty pounds more than once again, it was true, rewarded both in London and in Paris the young friend's loyalty; none the less sensibly, doubtless, at the moment, that the money was a direct advance on a decent sum for which Peter had long since privately prearranged an ultimate function. Whether by these arts or others, at all events, Lance's just resentment was kept for a season—but only for a season—at bay. The day arrived when he warned his companion that he could hold out—or hold in—no longer. Carrara Lodge had had to listen to another lecture delivered from a great height —an infliction really heavier at last than, without striking back or in some way letting the Master have the truth, flesh and blood could bear.

"And what I don't see is," Lance observed with a certain irritated eye for what was after all, if it came to that, owing to himself too; "what I don't see is, upon my honour, how *you*, as things are going, can keep the game up."

"Oh the game for me is only to hold my tongue," said placid Peter. "And I have my reason."

"Still my mother?"

Peter showed a queer face as he had often shown it before—that is by turning it straight away. "What will you have? I haven't ceased to like her."

"She's beautiful—she's a dear of course," Lance allowed; "but what is she to you, after all, and what is it to you that, as to anything whatever, she should or she shouldn't?"

Peter, who had turned red, hung fire a little. "Well—it's all simply what I make of it."

There was now, however, in his young friend a strange, an adopted insistence. "What are you after all to *her*?"

"Oh nothing. But that's another matter."

"She cares only for my father," said Lance the Parisian.

"Naturally—and that's just why."

"Why you've wished to spare her?"

"Because she cares so tremendously much."

Lance took a turn about the room, but with his eyes still on his host. "How awfully—always—you must have liked her!"

"Awfully. Always," said Peter Brench.

The young man continued for a moment to muse—then stopped again in front of him. "Do you know how much she cares?" Their eyes met on it, but Peter, as if his own found something new in Lance's, appeared to hesitate, for the first time in an age, to say he did know. "*I've* only just found out," said Lance. "She came to my room last night, after being present, in silence and only with her eyes on me, at what I had had to take from him: she came—and she was with me an extraordinary hour."

He had paused again and they had again for a while sounded each other. Then something—and it made him suddenly turn pale—came to Peter. "She *does* know?"

"She does know. She let it all out to me—so as to demand of me no more than 'that,' as she said, of which she herself had been capable. She has always, always known," said Lance without pity.

Peter was silent a long time; during which his companion might have heard him gently breathe, and on touching him might have felt within him the vibration of a long low sound suppressed. By the time he spoke at last he had taken everything in. "Then I do see how tremendously much."

"Isn't it wonderful?" Lance asked.

"Wonderful," Peter mused.

"So that if your original effort to keep me from Paris was to keep me from knowledge—!" Lance exclaimed as if with a sufficient indication of this futility.

It might have been at the futility Peter appeared for a little to gaze. "I think it must have been—without my quite at the time knowing it—to keep *me!*" he replied at last as he turned away.

Edith Wharton

THE HOUSE OF THE DEAD HAND

For young Wyant, an Englishman sojourning in Siena, the
opportunity to view Dr. Lombard's Old Master, a rare and
practically unknown painting by Leonardo da Vinci, leads to his
involvement in a strange and unexpectedly romantic situation.
Edith Wharton's description of Wyant's contemplation of the
famous painting under the watchful eye of Dr. Lombard is
skillfully done, and in a manner that is more than a little
reminiscent of Henry James. (Certainly in the cultivated society
that Henry James found congenial, Wyant would have found
himself entirely at home.) Not until the last words have been
spoken do we realize, with Wyant, the full significance of his part
in the destiny of at least two of the characters.

A bove all," the letter ended, "don't leave Siena without seeing
Doctor Lombard's Leonardo. Lombard is a queer old Englishman, a
mystic or a madman (if the two are not synonymous), and a devout student of the Italian Renaissance. He has lived for years in Italy, exploring its remotest corners, and has lately picked up an undoubted Leonardo, which came to light in a farmhouse near Bergamo. It is believed
to be one of the missing pictures mentioned by Vasari, and is at any
rate, according to the most competent authorities, a genuine and almost
untouched example of the best period.

"Lombard is a queer stick, and jealous of showing his treasures; but
we struck up a friendship when I was working on the Sodomas in Siena
three years ago, and if you will give him the enclosed line you may
get a peep at the Leonardo. Probably not more than a peep, though, for
I hear he refuses to have it reproduced. I want badly to use it in my
monograph on the Windsor drawings, so please see what you can do
for me, and if you can't persuade him to let you take a photograph or
make a sketch, at least jot down a detailed description of the picture
and get from him all the facts you can. I hear that the French and
Italian governments have offered him a large advance on his purchase, but that he refuses to sell at any price, though he certainly can't
afford such luxuries; in fact, I don't see where he got enough money to
buy the picture. He lives in the Via Papa Giulio."

Wyant sat at the table d'hôte of his hotel, re-reading his friend's letter over a late luncheon. He had been five days in Siena without having found time to call on Doctor Lombard; not from any indifference to the opportunity presented, but because it was his first visit to the strange red city and he was still under the spell of its more conspicuous wonders—the brick palaces flinging out their wrought-iron torch-holders with a gesture of arrogant suzerainty; the great council-chamber emblazoned with civic allegories; the pageant of Pope Julius on the Library walls; the Sodomas smiling balefully through the dusk of mouldering chapels —and it was only when his first hunger was appeased that he remembered that one course in the banquet was still untasted.

He put the letter in his pocket and turned to leave the room, with a nod to its only other occupant, an olive-skinned young man with lustrous eyes and a low collar, who sat on the other side of the table, perusing the *Fanfulla di Domenica*. This gentleman, his daily vis-à-vis, returned the nod with a Latin eloquence of gesture, and Wyant passed on to the ante-chamber, where he paused to light a cigarette. He was just restoring the case to his pocket when he heard a hurried step behind him, and the lustrous-eyed young man advanced through the glass doors of the dining-room.

"Pardon me, sir," he said in measured English, and with an intonation of exquisite politeness; "you have let this letter fall."

Wyant, recognizing his friend's note of introduction to Doctor Lombard, took it with a word of thanks, and was about to turn away when he perceived that the eyes of his fellow diner remained fixed on him with a gaze of melancholy interrogation.

"Again pardon me," the young man at length ventured, "but are you by chance the friend of the illustrious Doctor Lombard?"

"No," returned Wyant, with the instinctive Anglo-Saxon distrust of foreign advances. Then, fearing to appear rude, he said with a guarded politeness: "Perhaps, by the way, you can tell me the number of his house. I see it is not given here."

The young man brightened perceptibly. "The number of the house is thirteen; but any one can indicate it to you—it is well known in Siena. It is called," he continued after a moment, "the House of the Dead Hand."

Wyant stared. "What a queer name!" he said.

"The name comes from an antique hand of marble which for many hundred years has been above the door."

Wyant was turning away with a gesture of thanks, when the other added: "If you would have the kindness to ring twice."

"To ring twice?"

"At the doctor's." The young man smiled. "It is the custom."

It was a dazzling March afternoon, with a shower of sun from the

593

mid-blue, and a marshalling of slaty clouds behind the umber-colored hills. For nearly an hour Wyant loitered on the Lizza, watching the shadows race across the naked landscape and the thunder blacken in the west; then he decided to set out for the House of the Dead Hand. The map in his guidebook showed him that the Via Papa Giulio was one of the streets which radiate from the Piazza, and thither he bent his course, pausing at every other step to fill his eye with some fresh image of weather-beaten beauty. The clouds had rolled upward, obscuring the sunshine and hanging like a funereal baldachin above the projecting cornices of Doctor Lombard's street, and Wyant walked for some distance in the shade of the beetling palace fronts before his eye fell on a doorway surmounted by a sallow marble hand. He stood for a moment staring up at the strange emblem. The hand was a woman's—a dead drooping hand, which hung there convulsed and helpless, as though it had been thrust forth in denunciation of some evil mystery within the house, and had sunk struggling into death.

A girl who was drawing water from the well in the court said that the English doctor lived on the first floor, and Wyant, passing through a glazed door, mounted the damp degrees of a vaulted stairway with a plaster Æsculapius mouldering in a niche on the landing. Facing the Æsculapius was another door, and as Wyant put his hand on the bell-rope he remembered his unknown friend's injunction, and rang twice.

His ring was answered by a peasant woman with a low forehead and small close-set eyes, who, after a prolonged scrutiny of himself, his card, and his letter of introduction, left him standing in a high, cold ante-chamber floored with brick. He heard her wooden pattens click down an interminable corridor, and after some delay she returned and told him to follow her.

They passed through a long saloon, bare as the ante-chamber, but loftily vaulted, and frescoed with a seventeenth-century Triumph of Scipio or Alexander—martial figures following Wyant with the filmed melancholy gaze of shades in limbo. At the end of this apartment he was admitted to a smaller room, with the same atmosphere of mortal cold, but showing more obvious signs of occupancy. The walls were covered with tapestry which had faded to the gray-brown tints of decaying vegetation, so that the young man felt as though he were entering a sunless autumn wood. Against these hangings stood a few tall cabinets on heavy gilt feet, and at a table in the window three persons were seated: an elderly lady who was warming her hands over a brazier, a girl bent above a strip of needle-work, and an old man.

As the latter advanced toward Wyant, the young man was conscious of staring with unseemingly intentness at his small round-backed figure, dressed with shabby disorder and surmounted by a wonderful head, lean, vulpine, eagle-beaked as that of some art-loving despot of the

Renaissance: a head combining the venerable hair and large prominent eyes of the humanist with the greedy profile of the adventurer. Wyant, in musing on the Italian portrait-medals of the fifteenth century, had often fancied that only in that period of fierce individualism could types so paradoxical have been produced; yet the subtle craftsmen who committed them to the bronze had never drawn a face more strangely stamped with contradictory passions than that of Doctor Lombard.

"I am glad to see you," he said to Wyant, extending a hand which seemed a mere framework held together by knotted veins. "We lead a quiet life here and receive few visitors, but any friend of Professor Clyde's is welcome." Then, with a gesture which included the two women, he added dryly: "My wife and daughter often talk of Professor Clyde."

"Oh yes—he used to make me such nice toast; they don't understand toast in Italy," said Mrs. Lombard in a high plaintive voice.

It would have been difficult, from Doctor Lombard's manner and appearance, to guess his nationality; but his wife was so inconsciently and ineradicably English that even the silhouette of her cap seemed a protest against Continental laxities. She was a stout fair woman, with pale cheeks netted with red lines. A brooch with a miniature portrait sustained a bogwood watch-chain upon her bosom, and at her elbow lay a heap of knitting and an old copy of *The Queen*.

The young girl, who had remained standing, was a slim replica of her mother, with an apple-cheeked face and opaque blue eyes. Her small head was prodigally laden with braids of dull fair hair, and she might have had a kind of transient prettiness but for the sullen droop of her round mouth. It was hard to say whether her expression implied ill-temper or apathy; but Wyant was struck by the contrast between the fierce vitality of the doctor's age and the inanimateness of his daughter's youth.

Seating himself in the chair which his host advanced, the young man tried to open the conversation by addressing to Mrs. Lombard some random remark on the beauties of Siena. The lady murmured a resigned assent, and Doctor Lombard interposed with a smile: "My dear sir, my wife considers Siena a most salubrious spot, and is favorably impressed by the cheapness of the marketing; but she deplores the total absence of muffins and cannel coal, and cannot resign herself to the Italian method of dusting furniture."

"But they don't, you know—they don't dust it!" Mrs. Lombard protested, without showing any resentment of her husband's manner.

"Precisely—they don't dust it. Since we have lived in Siena we have not once seen the cobwebs removed from the battlements of the Mangia. Can you conceive of such housekeeping? My wife has never yet dared to write it home to her aunts at Bonchurch."

Mrs. Lombard accepted in silence this remarkable statement of her views, and her husband, with a malicious smile at Wyant's embarrassment, planted himself suddenly before the young man.

"And now," said he, "do you want to see my Leonardo?"

"Do I?" cried Wyant, on his feet in a flash.

The doctor chuckled. "Ah," he said, with a kind of crooning deliberation, "that's the way they all behave—that's what they all come for." He turned to his daughter with another variation of mockery in his smile. "Don't fancy it's for your *beaux yeux*, my dear; or for the mature charms of Mrs. Lombard," he added, glaring suddenly at his wife, who had taken up her knitting and was softly murmuring over the number of her stitches.

Neither lady appeared to notice his pleasantries, and he continued, addressing himself to Wyant: "They all come—they all come; but many are called and few are chosen." His voice sank to solemnity. "While I live," he said, "no unworthy eye shall desecrate that picture. But I will not do my friend Clyde the injustice to suppose that he would send an unworthy representative. He tells me he wishes a description of the picture for his book; and you shall describe it to him—if you can."

Wyant hesitated, not knowing whether it was a propitious moment to put in his appeal for a photograph.

"Well, sir," he said, "you know Clyde wants me to take away all I can of it."

Doctor Lombard eyed him sardonically. "You're welcome to take away all you can carry," he replied; adding, as he turned to his daughter: "That is, if he has your permission, Sybilla."

The girl rose without a word, and laying aside her work, took a key from a secret drawer in one of the cabinets, while the doctor continued in the same note of grim jocularity: "For you must know that the picture is not mine—it is my daughter's."

He followed with evident amusement the surprised glance which Wyant turned on the young girl's impassive figure.

"Sybilla," he pursued, "is a votary of the arts; she has inherited her fond father's passion for the unattainable. Luckily, however, she also recently inherited a tidy legacy from her grandmother; and having seen the Leonardo, on which its discoverer had placed a price far beyond my reach, she took a step which deserves to go down to history: she invested her whole inheritance in the purchase of the picture, thus enabling me to spend my closing years in communion with one of the world's masterpieces. My dear sir, could Antigone do more?"

The object of this strange eulogy had meanwhile drawn aside one of the tapestry hangings, and fitted her key into a concealed door.

"Come," said Doctor Lombard, "let us go before the light fails us."

Wyant glanced at Mrs. Lombard, who continued to knit impassively.

"No, no," said his host, "my wife will not come with us. You might not suspect it from her conversation, but my wife has no feeling for art —Italian art, that is; for no one is fonder of our early Victorian school." "Frith's *Railway Station,* you know," said Mrs. Lombard, smiling. "I like an animated picture."

Miss Lombard, who had unlocked the door, held back the tapestry to let her father and Wyant pass out; then she followed them down a narrow stone passage with another door at its end. This door was iron-barred, and Wyant noticed that it had a complicated patent lock. The girl fitted another key into the lock, and Doctor Lombard led the way into a small room. The dark panelling of this apartment was irradiated by streams of yellow light slanting through the disbanded thunder clouds, and in the central brightness hung a picture concealed by a curtain of faded velvet.

"A little too bright, Sybilla," said Doctor Lombard. His face had grown solemn, and his mouth twitched nervously as his daughter drew a linen drapery across the upper part of the window. "That will do—that will do." He turned impressively to Wyant. "Do you see the pomegranate bud in this rug? Place yourself there—keep your left foot on it, please. And now, Sybilla, draw the cord."

Miss Lombard advanced and placed her hand on a cord hidden behind the velvet curtain.

"Ah," said the doctor, "one moment: I should like you, while looking at the picture, to have in mind a few lines of verse. Sybilla—"

Without the slightest change of countenance, and with a promptness which proved her to be prepared for the request, Miss Lombard began to recite, in a full round voice like her mother's, St. Bernard's invocation to the Virgin, in the thirty-third canto of the *Paradise.*

"Thank you, my dear," said her father, drawing a deep breath as she ended. "That unapproachable combination of vowel sounds prepares one better than anything I know for the contemplation of the picture."

As he spoke the folds of velvet slowly parted, and the Leonardo appeared in its frame of tarnished gold.

From the nature of Miss Lombard's recitation Wyant had expected a sacred subject, and his surprise was therefore great as the composition was gradually revealed by the widening division of the curtain.

In the background a steel-colored river wound through a pale calcareous landscape; while to the left, on a lonely peak, a crucified Christ hung livid against indigo clouds. The central figure of the foreground, however, was that of a woman seated in an antique chair of marble with bas-reliefs of dancing mænads. Her feet rested on a meadow sprinkled with minute wild-flowers, and her attitude of smiling majesty recalled that of Dosso Dossi's Circe. She wore a red robe, flowing in closely fluted lines from under a fancifully embroidered cloak. Above her high forehead the crinkled golden hair flowed sideways beneath a veil; one hand drooped on the arm of her chair; the other held up an inverted human skull, into which a young Dionysus, smooth, brown and sidelong as the St. John of the Louvre, poured a stream of wine from a high-poised flagon. At the lady's feet lay the symbols of art and luxury: a flute and a roll of music, a platter heaped with grapes and roses, the torso of a Greek statuette, and a bowl overflowing with coins and jewels; behind her, on the chalky hilltop, hung the crucified Christ. A scroll in a corner of the foreground bore the legend: *Lux Mundi.*

Wyant, emerging from the first plunge of wonder, turned inquiringly toward his companions. Neither had moved. Miss Lombard stood with her hand on the cord, her lids lowered, her mouth drooping; the doctor, his strange Thoth-like profile turned toward his guest, was still lost in rapt contemplation of his treasure.

Wyant addressed the young girl.

"You are fortunate," he said, "to be the possessor of anything so perfect."

"It is considered very beautiful," she said coldly.

"Beautiful—*beautiful!*" the doctor burst out. "Ah, the poor, worn out, overworked word! There are no adjectives in the language fresh enough to describe such pristine brilliancy: all their brightness has been worn off by misuse. Think of the things that have been called beautiful, and then look at *that!*"

"It is worthy of a new vocabulary," Wyant agreed.

"Yes," Doctor Lombard continued, "my daughter is indeed fortunate. She has chosen what Catholics call the higher life—the counsel of perfection. What other private person enjoys the same opportunity of understanding the master? Who else lives under the same roof with an untouched masterpiece of Leonardo's? Think of the happiness of being always under the influence of such a creation; of living *into* it; of partaking of it in daily and hourly communion! This room is a chapel; the sight of that picture is a sacrament. What an atmosphere for a young life to unfold in itself in! My daughter is singularly blessed. Sybilla, point out some of the details to Mr. Wyant: I see that he will appreciate them."

The girl turned her dense blue eyes toward Wyant; then, glancing away from him, she pointed to the canvas.

"Notice the modelling of the left hand," she began in a monotonous voice; "it recalls the hand of the Mona Lisa. The head of the naked genius will remind you of that of the St. John of the Louvre, but it is more purely pagan and is turned a little less to the right. The embroidery on the cloak is symbolic: you will see that the roots of this plant have burst through the vase. This recalls the famous definition of Hamlet's character in *Wilhelm Meister.* Here are the mystic rose, the flame, and the serpent, emblem of eternity. Some of the other symbols we have not yet been able to decipher."

Wyant watched her curiously: she seemed to be reciting a lesson

"And the picture itself?" he said. "How do you explain that? *Lux Mundi*—what a curious device to connect with such a subject! What can it mean?"

Miss Lombard dropped her eyes: the answer was evidently not included in her lesson.

"What, indeed?" the doctor interposed. "What does life mean? As one may define it in a hundred different ways, so one may find a hundred different meanings in this picture. Its symbolism is as many-faceted as a well-cut diamond. Who, for instance, is that divine lady? Is it she who is the true *Lux Mundi*—the light reflected from jewels and young eyes, from polished marble and clear waters and statues of bronze? Or is that the Light of the World, extinguished on yonder stormy hill, and is this lady the Pride of Life, feasting blindly on the wine of iniquity, with her back turned to the light which has shone for her in vain? Something of both these meanings may be traced in the picture; but to me it symbolizes rather the central truth of existence: that all that is raised in incorruption is sown in corruption; art, beauty, love, religion; that all our wine is drunk out of skulls, and poured for us by the mysterious genius of a remote and cruel past."

The doctor's face blazed: his bent figure seemed to straighten itself and become taller.

"Ah," he cried, growing more dithyrambic, "how lightly you ask what it means! How confidently you expect an answer! Yet here am I who have given my life to the study of the Renaissance; who have violated its tomb, laid open its dead body, and traced the course of every muscle, bone and artery; who have sucked its very soul from the pages of poets and humanists; who have wept and believed with Joachim of Flora, smiled and doubted with Æneas Sylvius Piccolomini; who have patiently followed to its source the least inspiration of the masters, and groped in neolithic caverns and Babylonian ruins for the first unfolding tendrils of the arabesques of Mantegna and Crivelli; and I tell you that I stand abashed and ignorant before the mystery of this picture. It means nothing—it means all things. It may represent the period which saw its creation; it may represent all ages past and to come. There are volumes of meaning in the tiniest emblem on the lady's cloak; the blossoms of its border are rooted in the deepest soil of myth and tradition. Don't ask what it means, young man, but bow your head in thankfulness for having seen it!"

Miss Lombard laid her hand on his arm.

"Don't excite yourself, father," she said in the detached tone of a professional nurse.

He answered with a despairing gesture. "Ah, it's easy for you to talk. You have years and years to spend with it; I am an old man, and every moment counts!"

"It's bad for you," she repeated with gentle obstinacy.

The doctor's sacred fury had in fact burnt itself out. He dropped into a seat with dull eyes and slackening lips, and his daughter drew the curtain across the picture.

Wyant turned away reluctantly. He felt that his opportunity was slipping from him, yet he dared not refer to Clyde's wish for a photograph. He now understood the meaning of the laugh with which Doctor Lombard had given him leave to carry away all the details he could remember. The picture was so dazzling, so unexpected, so crossed with elusive and contradictory suggestions, that the most alert observer, when placed suddenly before it, must lose his coördinating faculty in a sense of confused wonder. Yet how valuable to Clyde the record of such a work would be! In some ways it seemed to be the summing up of the master's thought, the key to his enigmatic philosophy.

The doctor had risen and was walking slowly toward the door. His daughter unlocked it, and Wyant followed them back in silence to the room in which they had left Mrs. Lombard. That lady was no longer there, and he could think of no excuse for lingering.

He thanked the doctor, and turned to Miss Lombard, who stood in the middle of the room as though awaiting further orders.

"It is very good of you," he said, "to allow one even a glimpse of such a treasure."

She looked at him with her odd directness. "You will come again?" she said quickly; and turning to her father she added: "You know what Professor Clyde asked. This gentleman cannot give him any account of the picture without seeing it again."

Doctor Lombard glanced at her vaguely; he was still like a person in a trance.

"Eh?" he said, rousing himself with an effort.

"I said, father, that Mr. Wyant must see the picture again if he is to tell Professor Clyde about it," Miss Lombard repeated with extraordinary precision of tone.

Wyant was silent. He had the puzzled sense that his wishes were being divined and gratified for reasons with which he was in no way connected.

"Well, well," the doctor muttered, "I don't say no—I don't say no. I know what Clyde wants—I don't refuse to help him." He turned to Wyant. "You may come again—you may make notes," he added with a sudden effort. "Jot down what occurs to you. I'm willing to concede that."

Wyant again caught the girl's eye, but its emphatic message perplexed him.

"You're very good," he said tentatively, "but the fact is the picture is so mysterious—so full of complicated detail—that I'm afraid no notes I could make would serve Clyde's purpose as well as—as a photograph, say. If you would allow me—"

Miss Lombard's brow darkened, and her father raised his head furiously.

"A photograph? A photograph, did you say? Good God, man, not ten people have been allowed to set foot in that room! A *photograph?*"

Wyant saw his mistake, but saw also that he had gone too far to retreat.

"I know, sir, from what Clyde has told me, that you object to having any reproduction of the picture published; but he hoped you might let me take a photograph for his personal use—not to be reproduced in his book, but simply to give him something to work by. I should take the photograph myself, and the negative would of course be yours. If you wished it, only one impression would be struck off, and that one Clyde could return to you when he had done with it."

Doctor Lombard interrupted him with a snarl. "When he had done with it? Just so: I thank thee for that word! When it had been rephotographed, drawn, traced, autotyped, passed about from hand to hand, defiled by every ignorant eye in England, vulgarized by the blundering praise of every art-scribbler in Europe! Pah! I'd as soon give you the picture itself: why don't you ask for that?"

"Well, sir," said Wyant calmly, "if you will trust me with it, I'll engage to take it safely to England and back, and to let no eye but Clyde's see it while it is out of your keeping."

The doctor received this remarkable proposal in silence; then he burst into a laugh.

"Upon my soul!" he said with sardonic good humor.

It was Miss Lombard's turn to look perplexedly at Wyant. His last words and her father's unexpected reply had evidently carried her beyond her depth.

"Well, sir, am I to take the picture?" Wyant smilingly pursued.

"No, young man; nor a photograph of it. Nor a sketch, either; mind that,—nothing that can be reproduced. Sybilla," he cried with sudden passion, "swear to me that the picture shall never be reproduced! No photograph, no sketch—now or afterward. Do you hear me?"

"Yes, father," said the girl quietly.

"The vandals," he muttered, "the desecrators of beauty; if I thought it would ever get into their hands I'd burn it first, by God!" He turned to Wyant, speaking more quietly. "I said you might come back—I never retract what I say. But you must give me your word that no one but Clyde shall see the notes you make."

Wyant was growing warm.

"If you won't trust me with a photograph I wonder you trust me not to show my notes!" he exclaimed.

The doctor looked at him with a malicious smile.

"Humph!" he said; "would they be of much use to anybody?"

Wyant saw that he was losing ground and controlled his impatience.

"To Clyde, I hope, at any rate," he answered, holding out his hand. The doctor shook it without a trace of resentment, and Wyant added: "When shall I come, sir?"

"To-morrow—to-morrow morning," cried Miss Lombard, speaking suddenly.

She looked fixedly at her father, and he shrugged his shoulders. "The picture is hers," he said to Wyant.

In the ante-chamber the young man was met by the woman who had admitted him. She handed him his hat and stick, and turned to unbar the door. As the bolt slipped back he felt a touch on his arm.

"You have a letter?" she said in a low tone.

"A letter?" He stared. "What letter?"

She shrugged her shoulders, and drew back to let him pass.

II

As Wyant emerged from the house he paused once more to glance up at its scarred brick façade. The marble hand drooped tragically above the entrance: in the waning light it seemed to have relaxed into the passiveness of despair, and Wyant stood musing on its hidden meaning. But the Dead Hand was not the only mysterious thing about Doctor Lombard's house. What were the relations between Miss Lombard and her father? Above all, between Miss Lombard and her picture? She did not look like a person capable of a disinterested passion for the arts; and there had been moments when it struck Wyant that she hated the picture.

The sky at the end of the street was flooded with turbulent yellow light, and the young man turned his steps toward the church of San Domenico, in the hope of catching the lingering brightness on Sodoma's St. Catherine.

The great bare aisles were almost dark when he entered, and he had to grope his way to the chapel steps. Under the momentary evocation of the sunset, the saint's figure emerged pale and swooning from the dusk, and the warm light gave a sensual tinge to her ecstasy. The flesh seemed to glow and heave, the eyelids to tremble; Wyant stood fascinated by the accidental collaboration of light and color.

Suddenly he noticed that something white had fluttered to the ground at his feet. He stooped and picked up a small thin sheet of note-paper, folded and sealed like an old-fashioned letter, and bearing the super-scription:—

To the Count Ottaviano Celsi.

Wyant stared at this mysterious document. Where had it come from? He was distinctly conscious of having seen it fall through the air, close to his feet. He glanced up at the dark ceiling of the chapel; then he turned and looked about the church. There was only one figure in it, that of a man who knelt near the high altar.

Suddenly Wyant recalled the question of Doctor Lombard's maid-servant. Was this the letter she had asked for? Had he been uncon-sciously carrying it about with him all the afternoon? Who was Count Ottaviano Celsi, and how came Wyant to have been chosen to act as that nobleman's ambulant letter-box?

Wyant laid his hat and stick on the chapel steps and began to ex-plore his pockets, in the irrational hope of finding there some clue to the mystery; but they held nothing which he had not himself put there, and he was reduced to wondering how the letter, supposing some un-known hand to have bestowed it on him, had happened to fall out while he stood motionless before the picture.

At this point he was disturbed by a step on the floor of the aisle, and turning, he saw his lustrous-eyed neighbor of the table d'hôte.

The young man bowed and waved an apologetic hand.

"I do not intrude?" he inquired suavely.

Without waiting for a reply, he mounted the steps of the chapel, glancing about him with the affable air of an afternoon caller.

"I see," he remarked with a smile, "that you know the hour at which our saint should be visited."

Wyant agreed that the hour was indeed felicitous.

The stranger stood beamingly before the picture.

"What grace! What poetry!" he murmured, apostrophizing the St. Catherine, but letting his glance slip rapidly about the chapel as he spoke.

Wyant, detecting the manœuvre, murmured a brief assent.

"But it is cold here—mortally cold; you do not find it so?" The in-truder put on his hat. "It is permitted at this hour—when the church is empty. And you, my dear sir—do you not feel the dampness? You are an artist, are you not? And to artists it is permitted to cover the head when they are engaged in the study of the paintings."

He darted suddenly toward the steps and bent over Wyant's hat.

"Permit me—cover yourself!" he said a moment later, holding out the hat with an ingratiating gesture.

A light flashed on Wyant.

"Perhaps," he said, looking straight at the young man, "you will tell me your name. My own is Wyant."

The stranger, surprised, but not disconcerted, drew forth a coroneted card, which he offered with a low bow. On the card was engraved:—

Il Conte Ottaviano Celsi.

"I am much obliged to you," said Wyant; "and I may as well tell you that the letter which you apparently expected to find in the lining of my hat is not there, but in my pocket."

He drew it out and handed it to its owner, who had grown very pale.

"And now," Wyant continued, "you will perhaps be good enough to tell me what all this means."

There was no mistaking the effect produced on Count Ottaviano by this request. His lips moved, but he achieved only an ineffectual smile.

"I suppose you know," Wyant went on, his anger rising at the sight of the other's discomfiture, "that you have taken an unwarrantable liberty. I don't yet understand what part I have been made to play, but it's evident that you have made use of me to serve some purpose of your own, and I propose to know the reason why."

Count Ottaviano advanced with an imploring gesture.

"Sir," he pleaded, "you permit me to speak?"

"I expect you to," cried Wyant. "But not here," he added, hearing the clank of the verger's keys. "It is growing dark, and we shall be turned out in a few minutes."

He walked across the church, and Count Ottaviano followed him out into the deserted square.

"Now," said Wyant, pausing on the steps.

The Count, who had regained some measure of self-possession, began to speak in a high key, with an accompaniment of conciliatory gesture.

"My dear sir—my dear Mr. Wyant—you find me in an abominable position—that, as a man of honor, I immediately confess. I have taken advantage of you—yes! I have counted on your amiability, your chivalry—too far, perhaps? I confess it! But what could I do? It was to oblige a lady"—he laid a hand on his heart—"a lady whom I would die to serve!" He went on with increasing volubility, his deliberate English swept away by a torrent of Italian, through which Wyant, with some difficulty, struggled to a comprehension of the case.

Count Ottaviano, according to his own statement, had come to Siena some months previously, on business connected with his mother's property; the paternal estate being near Orvieto, of which ancient city his father was syndic. Soon after his arrival in Siena the young Count had met the incomparable daughter of Doctor Lombard, and falling deeply in love with her, had prevailed on his parents to ask her hand in marriage. Doctor Lombard had not opposed his suit, but when the question of settlements arose it became known that Miss Lombard, who was possessed of a small property in her own right, had a short time before invested the whole amount in the purchase of the Bergamo Leonardo. Thereupon Count Ottaviano's parents had politely suggested that she should sell the picture and thus recover her independence; and this proposal being met by a curt refusal from Doctor Lombard, they had withdrawn their consent to their son's marriage. The young lady's attitude had hitherto been one of passive submission; she was horribly afraid of her father, and would never venture openly to oppose him; but she had made known to Ottaviano her intention of not giving him up, of waiting patiently till events should take a more favorable turn. She seemed hardly aware, the Count said with a sigh, that the means of escape lay in her own hands; that she was of age, and had a right to sell the picture, and to marry without asking her father's consent. Meanwhile her suitor spared no pains to keep himself before her, to remind her that he, too, was waiting and would never give her up.

Doctor Lombard, who suspected the young man of trying to persuade Sybilla to sell the picture, had forbidden the lovers to meet or to correspond; they were thus driven to clandestine communication, and had several times, the Count ingenuously avowed, made use of the doctor's visitors as a means of exchanging letters.

"And you told the visitors to ring twice?" Wyant interposed.

The young man extended his hands in a deprecating gesture. Could Mr. Wyant blame him? He was young, he was ardent, he was enamored! The young lady had done him the supreme honor of avowing her attachment, of pledging her unalterable fidelity; should he suffer his devotion to be outdone? But his purpose in writing to her, he admitted, was not merely to reiterate his fidelity; he was trying by every means in his power to induce her to sell the picture. He had organized a plan of action; every detail was complete; if she would but have the courage to carry out his instructions he would answer for the result. His idea was that she should secretly retire to a convent of which his aunt was the Mother Superior, and from that stronghold should transact the sale of the Leonardo. He had a purchaser ready, who was willing to pay a large sum; a sum, Count Ottaviano whispered, considerably in excess of the young lady's original inheritance; once the picture sold, it could, if necessary, be removed by force from Doctor Lombard's house, and his daughter, being safely in the convent, would be spared the painful scenes incidental to the removal. Finally, if Doctor Lombard were vindictive enough to refuse his consent to her marriage, she had only to make a *sommation respectueuse,* and at the end of the prescribed delay no power on earth could prevent her becoming the wife of Count Ottaviano.

Wyant's anger had fallen at the recital of this simple romance. It was absurd to be angry with a young man who confided his secrets to the first stranger he met in the streets, and placed his hand on his heart whenever he mentioned the name of his betrothed. The easiest way out of the business was to take it as a joke. Wyant had played the wall to this new Pyramus and Thisbe, and was philosophic enough to laugh at the part he had unwittingly performed.

He held out his hand with a smile to Count Ottaviano.

"I won't deprive you any longer," he said, "of the pleasure of reading your letter."

"Oh, sir, a thousand thanks! And when you return to the casa Lombard, you will take a message from me—the letter she expected this afternoon?"

"The letter she expected?" Wyant paused. "No, thank you. I thought you understood that where I come from we don't do that kind of thing —knowingly."

"But, sir, to serve a young lady!"

"I'm sorry for the young lady, if what you tell me is true"—the Count's expressive hands resented the doubt—"but remember that if I am under obligations to any one in this matter, it is to her father, who has admitted me to his house and has allowed me to see his picture."

"*His* picture? Hers!"

"Well, the house is his, at all events."

"Unhappily—since to her it is a dungeon!"

"Why doesn't she leave it, then?" exclaimed Wyant impatiently.

The Count clasped his hands. "Ah, how you say that—with what force, with what virility! If you would but say it to *her* in that tone—you, her countryman! She has no one to advise her; the mother is an idiot; the father is terrible; she is in his power; it is my belief that he would kill her if she resisted him. Mr. Wyant, I tremble for her life while she remains in that house!"

"Oh, come," said Wyant lightly, "they seem to understand each other well enough. But in any case, you must see that I can't interfere—at least you would if you were an Englishman," he added with an escape of contempt.

III

Wyant's affiliations in Siena being restricted to an acquaintance with his landlady, he was forced to apply to her for the verification of Count Ottaviano's story.

The young nobleman had, it appeared, given a perfectly correct account of his situation. His father, Count Celsi-Mongirone, was a man of distinguished family and some wealth. He was syndic of Orvieto, and lived either in that town or on his neighboring estate of Mongirone. His wife owned a large property near Siena, and Count Ottaviano, who was the second son, came there from time to time to look into its management. The eldest son was in the army, the youngest in the Church; and an aunt of Count Ottaviano's was Mother Superior of the Visitandine convent in Siena. At one time it had been said that Count Ottaviano, who was a most amiable and accomplished young man, was to marry the daughter of the strange Englishman, Doctor Lombard, but difficulties having arisen as to the adjustment of the young lady's dower, Count Celsi-Mongirone had very properly broken off the match. It was sad for the young man, however, who was said to be deeply in love, and to find frequent excuses for coming to Siena to inspect his mother's estate.

Viewed in the light of Count Ottaviano's personality the story had a tinge of opera bouffe; but the next morning, as Wyant mounted the stairs of the House of the Dead Hand, the situation insensibly assumed another aspect. It was impossible to take Doctor Lombard lightly; and there was a suggestion of fatality in the appearance of his gaunt dwelling. Who could tell amid what tragic records of domestic tyranny and fluttering broken purposes the little drama of Miss Lombard's fate was being played out? Might not the accumulated influences of such a house modify the lives within it in a manner unguessed by the inmates of a suburban villa with sanitary plumbing and a telephone?

One person, at least, remained unperturbed by such fanciful problems; and that was Mrs. Lombard, who, at Wyant's entrance, raised a placidly wrinkled brow from her knitting. The morning was mild, and her chair had been wheeled into a bar of sunshine near the window, so that she made a cheerful spot of prose in the poetic gloom of her surroundings.

"What a nice morning!" she said; "it must be delightful weather at Bonchurch."

Her dull blue glance wandered across the narrow street with its threatening house fronts, and fluttered back baffled, like a bird with clipped wings. It was evident, poor lady, that she had never seen beyond the opposite houses.

Wyant was not sorry to find her alone. Seeing that she was surprised at his reappearance he said at once: "I have come back to study Miss Lombard's picture."

"Oh, the picture—" Mrs. Lombard's face expressed a gentle disappointment, which might have been boredom in a person of acuter sensibilities. "It's an original Leonardo, you know," she said mechanically.

"And Miss Lombard is very proud of it, I suppose? She seems to have inherited her father's love for art."

Mrs. Lombard counted her stitches, and he went on: "It's unusual in so young a girl. Such tastes generally develop later."

Mrs. Lombard looked up eagerly. "That's what I say! I was quite different at her age, you know. I liked dancing, and doing a pretty bit of fancy-work. Not that I couldn't sketch, too; I had a master down from London. My aunts have some of my crayons hung up in their drawing-room now—I did a view of Kenilworth which was thought pleasing. But I liked a picnic, too, or a pretty walk through the woods with young people of my own age. I say it's more natural, Mr. Wyant; one may have a feeling for art, and do crayons that are worth framing, and yet not give up everything else. I was taught that there were other things."

Wyant, half-ashamed of provoking these innocent confidences, could not resist another question. "And Miss Lombard cares for nothing else?"

Her mother looked troubled.

"Sybilla is so clever—she says I don't understand. You know how self-confident young people are! My husband never said that of me, now —he knows I had an excellent education. My aunts were very particular; I was brought up to have opinions, and my husband has always respected them. He says himself that he wouldn't for the world miss hearing my opinion on any subject; you may have noticed that he often refers to my tastes. He has always respected my preference for living in England; he likes to hear me give my reasons for it. He is so much interested in my ideas that he often says he knows just what I am going to say before I speak. But Sybilla does not care for what I think—"

At this point Doctor Lombard entered. He glanced sharply at Wyant. "The servant is a fool; she didn't tell me you were here." His eye turned to his wife. "Well, my dear, what have you been telling Mr. Wyant? About the aunts at Bonchurch, I'll be bound!"

Mrs. Lombard looked triumphantly at Wyant, and her husband rubbed his hooked fingers, with a smile.

"Mrs. Lombard's aunts are very superior women. They subscribe to the circulating library, and borrow *Good Words* and the *Monthly Packet* from the curate's wife across the way. They have the rector to tea twice a year, and keep a page-boy, and are visited by two baronets' wives. They devoted themselves to the education of their orphan niece, and I think I may say without boasting that Mrs. Lombard's conversation shows marked traces of the advantages she enjoyed."

Mrs. Lombard colored with pleasure.

"I was telling Mr. Wyant that my aunts were very particular."

"Quite so, my dear; and did you mention that they never sleep in anything but linen, and that Miss Sophia puts away the furs and blankets every spring with her own hands? Both those facts are interesting to the student of human nature." Doctor Lombard glanced at his watch. "But we are missing an incomparable moment; the light is perfect at this hour."

Wyant rose, and the doctor led him through the tapestried door and down the passageway.

The light was, in fact, perfect, and the picture shone with an inner radiancy, as though a lamp burned behind the soft screen of the lady's flesh. Every detail of the foreground detached itself with jewel-like precision. Wyant noticed a dozen accessories which had escaped him on the previous day.

He drew out his notebook, and the doctor, who had dropped his sardonic grin for a look of devout contemplation, pushed a chair forward, and seated himself on a carved settle against the wall.

"Now, then," he said, "tell Clyde what you can; but the letter killeth."

He sank down, his hands hanging on the arm of the settle like the claws of a dead bird, his eyes fixed on Wyant's notebook with the obvious intention of detecting any attempt at a surreptitious sketch.

Wyant, nettled at this surveillance, and disturbed by the speculations which Doctor Lombard's strange household excited, sat motionless for a few minutes, staring first at the picture and then at the blank pages of the notebook. The thought that Doctor Lombard was enjoying his discomfiture at length roused him, and he began to write.

He was interrupted by a knock on the iron door. Doctor Lombard rose to unlock it, and his daughter entered.

She bowed hurriedly to Wyant, without looking at him.

"Father, had you forgotten that the man from Monte Amiato was to come back this morning with an answer about the bas-relief? He is here now; he says he can't wait."

"The devil!" cried her father impatiently. "Didn't you tell him——"

"Yes; but he says he can't come back. If you want to see him you must come now."

"Then you think there's a chance?——"

She nodded.

He turned and looked at Wyant, who was writing assiduously.

"You will stay here, Sybilla; I shall be back in a moment."

He hurried out, locking the door behind him.

Wyant had looked up, wondering if Miss Lombard would show any surprise at being locked in with him; but it was his turn to be surprised, for hardly had they heard the key withdrawn when she moved close to him, her small face pale and tumultuous.

"I arranged it—I must speak to you," she gasped. "He'll be back in five minutes."

Her courage seemed to fail, and she looked at him helplessly.

Wyant had a sense of stepping among explosives. He glanced about him at the dusky vaulted room, at the haunting smile of the strange picture overhead, and at the pink-and-white girl whispering of conspiracies in a voice meant to exchange platitudes with a curate.

"How can I help you?" he said with a rush of compassion.

"Oh, if you would! I never have a chance to speak to any one; it's so difficult—he watches me—he'll be back immediately."

"Try to tell me what I can do."

"I don't dare; I feel as if he were behind me." She turned away, fixing her eyes on the picture. A sound startled her. "There he comes, and I haven't spoken! It was my only chance; but it bewilders me so to be hurried."

"I don't hear any one," said Wyant, listening. "Try to tell me."

"How can I make you understand? It would take so long to explain." She drew a deep breath, and then with a plunge—"Will you come here again this afternoon—at about five?" she whispered.

"Come here again?"

"Yes—you can ask to see the picture,—make some excuse. He will come with you, of course; I will open the door for you—and—and lock you both in"—she gasped.

"Lock us in?"

"You see? You understand? It's the only way for me to leave the house—if I am ever to do it"—She drew another difficult breath. "The key will be returned—by a safe person—in half an hour—perhaps sooner—"

She trembled so much that she was obliged to lean against the settle for support.

Wyant looked at her steadily; he was very sorry for her.

"I can't, Miss Lombard," he said at length.

"You can't?"

"I'm sorry; I must seem cruel; but consider—"

He was stopped by the futility of the word: as well ask a hunted rabbit to pause in its dash for a hole!

Wyant took her hand; it was cold and nerveless.

"I will serve you in any way I can; but you must see that this way is impossible. Can't I talk to you again? Perhaps—"

"Oh," she cried, starting up, "there he comes!"

Doctor Lombard's step sounded in the passage.

Wyant held her fast. "Tell me one thing: he won't let you sell the picture?"

"No—hush!"

"Make no pledges for the future, then; promise me that."

"The future?"

"In case he should die: your father is an old man. You haven't promised?"

She shook her head.

"Don't, then; remember that."

She made no answer, and the key turned in the lock.

As he passed out of the house, its scowling cornice and façade of ravaged brick looked down on him with the startlingness of a strange face, seen momentarily in a crowd, and impressing itself on the brain as part of an inevitable future. Above the doorway, the marble hand reached out like the cry of an imprisoned anguish.

Wyant turned away impatiently.

"Rubbish!" he said to himself. "*She* isn't walled in; she can get out if she wants to."

IV

Wyant had any number of plans for coming to Miss Lombard's aid: he was elaborating the twentieth when, on the same afternoon, he stepped into the express train for Florence. By the time the train reached Certaldo he was convinced that, in thus hastening his departure, he had followed the only reasonable course; at Empoli, he began to reflect that the priest and the Levite had probably justified themselves in much the same manner.

A month later, after his return to England, he was unexpectedly relieved from these alternatives of extenuation and approval. A paragraph in the morning paper announced the sudden death of Doctor Lombard, the distinguished English dilettante who had long resided in Siena. Wyant's justification was complete. Our blindest impulses become evidence of perspicacity when they fall in with the course of events.

Wyant could now comfortably speculate on the particular complications from which his foresight had probably saved him. The climax was unexpectedly dramatic. Miss Lombard, on the brink of a step which, whatever its issue, would have burdened her with retrospective compunction, had been set free before her suitor's ardor could have had time to cool, and was now doubtless planning a life of domestic felicity on the proceeds of the Leonardo. One thing, however, struck Wyant as odd—he saw no mention of the sale of the picture. He had scanned the papers for an immediate announcement of its transfer to one of the great museums; but presently concluding that Miss Lombard, out of filial piety, had wished to avoid an appearance of unseemly haste in the disposal of her treasure, he dismissed the matter from his mind. Other affairs happened to engage him; the months slipped by, and gradually the lady and the picture dwelt less vividly in his mind.

It was not till five or six years later, when chance took him again to Siena, that the recollection started from some inner fold of memory. He found himself, as it happened, at the head of Doctor Lombard's street, and glancing down that grim thoroughfare, caught an oblique glimpse of the doctor's house front, with the Dead Hand projecting above its threshold.

The sight revived his interest, and that evening, over an admirable *frittata,* he questioned his landlady about Miss Lombard's marriage.

"The daughter of the English doctor? But she has never married, signore."

"Never married? What, then, became of Count Ottaviano?"

"For a long time he waited; but last year he married a noble lady of the Maremma."

"But what happened—why was the marriage broken?"

The landlady enacted a pantomime of baffled interrogation.

"And Miss Lombard still lives in her father's house?"

"Yes, signore; she is still there."

"And the Leonardo—"

"The Leonardo, also, is still there."

The next day, as Wyant entered the House of the Dead Hand, he remembered Count Ottaviano's injunction to ring twice, and smiled mournfully to think that so much sublety had been vain. But what could have prevented the marriage? If Doctor Lombard's death had been long delayed, time might have acted as a dissolvent, or the young lady's resolve have failed; but it seemed impossible that the white heat of ardor in which Wyant had left the lovers should have cooled in a few short weeks.

As he ascended the vaulted stairway the atmosphere of the place seemed a reply to his conjectures. The same numbing air fell on him, like an emanation from some persistent will-power, a something fierce and imminent which might reduce to impotence every impulse within its range. Wyant could almost fancy a hand on his shoulder, guiding him upward with the ironical intent of confronting him with the evidence of its work.

A strange servant opened the door, and he was presently introduced to the tapestried room, where, from their usual seats in the window, Mrs. Lombard and her daughter advanced to welcome him with faint ejaculations of surprise.

Both had grown oddly old, but in a dry, smooth way, as fruits might shrivel on a shelf instead of ripening on the tree. Mrs. Lombard was still knitting, and pausing now and then to warm her swollen hands above the brazier; and Miss Lombard, in rising, had laid aside a strip of needlework which might have been the same on which Wyant had first seen her engaged.

Their visitor inquired discreetly how they had fared in the interval, and learned that they had thought of returning to England, but had somehow never done so.

"I am sorry not to see my aunts again," Mrs. Lombard said resignedly; "but Sybilla thinks it best that we should not go this year."

"Next year, perhaps," murmured Miss Lombard, in a voice which seemed to suggest that they had a great waste of time to fill.

She had returned to her seat, and sat bending over her work. Her hair enveloped her head in the same thick braids, but the rose color of her cheeks had turned to blotches of dull red, like some pigment which has darkened in drying.

"And Professor Clyde—is he well?" Mrs. Lombard asked affably; continuing, as her daughter raised a startled eye: "Surely, Sybilla, Mr. Wyant was the gentleman who was sent by Professor Clyde to see the Leonardo?"

Miss Lombard was silent, but Wyant hastened to assure the elder lady of his friend's well-being.

"Ah—perhaps, then, he will come back some day to Siena," she said, sighing. Wyant declared that it was more than likely; and there ensued a pause, which he presently broke by saying to Miss Lombard: "And you still have the picture?"

She raised her eyes and looked at him. "Should you like to see it?" she asked.

On his assenting, she rose, and extracting the same key from the same secret drawer, unlocked the door beneath the tapestry. They walked down the passage in silence, and she stood aside with a grave gesture, making Wyant pass before her into the room. Then she crossed over and drew the curtain back from the picture.

The light of the early afternoon poured full on it: its surface appeared to ripple and heave with a fluid splendor. The colors had lost none of their warmth, the outlines none of their pure precision; it seemed to Wyant like some magical flower which had burst suddenly from the mould of darkness and oblivion.

He turned to Miss Lombard with a movement of comprehension. "Ah, I understand—you couldn't part with it, after all!" he cried.

"No—I couldn't part with it," she answered.

"It's too beautiful,—too beautiful,"—he assented.

"Too beautiful?" She turned on him with a curious stare. "I have never thought it beautiful, you know."

He gave back the stare. "You have never—"

She shook her head. "It's not that. I hate it; I've always hated it. But he wouldn't let me—he will never let me now."

Wyant was startled by her use of the present tense. Her look surprised him, too: there was a strange fixity of resentment in her innocuous eye. Was it possible that she was laboring under some delusion? Or did the pronoun not refer to her father?

"You mean that Doctor Lombard did not wish you to part with the picture?"

"No—he prevented me; he will always prevent me."

There was another pause. "You promised him, then, before his death—"

"No; I promised nothing. He died too suddenly to make me." Her voice sank to a whisper. "I was free—perfectly free—or I thought I was till I tried."

"Till you tried?"

"To disobey him—to sell the picture. Then I found it was impossible. I tried again and again; but he was always in the room with me."

She glanced over her shoulder as though she had heard a step; and to Wyant, too, for a moment, the room seemed full of a third presence.

"And you can't"—he faltered, unconsciously dropping his voice to the pitch of hers.

She shook her head, gazing at him mystically. "I can't lock him out; I can never lock him out now. I told you I should never have another chance."

Wyant felt the chill of her words like a cold breath in his hair.

"Oh"—he groaned; but she cut him off with a grave gesture.

"It is too late," she said; "but you ought to have helped me that day."

THE OUTSTATION

Although this story derives its immediate interest from the setting, which is a government post in the Borneo jungle, where at first the government representative—the resident—is the only white man in the area and the other characters are Malays, the reader's interest is focused not mainly on the setting or even on the plot (which becomes tense enough before the end), but rather on the character of the resident himself, Mr. Warburton. He is a full-blown, old-fashioned snob; he is the prototype of the old-school English gentleman in government service who, though stationed alone in the tropics, far from civilization, always dresses for dinner—"in a boiled shirt and a high collar, silk socks and patent-leather shoes"—for he believes that thus he can best retain not only his own self-respect but also the respect of the natives. A conflict develops upon the arrival of the only other white man, his new subordinate, with whom, as the exigencies of his position demand, he must associate.

The story indicates—by positive and negative example—one of the secrets of effective administration by the British in the heyday of empire-building. This is, of course, a prewar story, but our own government officials, working for the United Nations or representing the United States in the underprivileged areas of the world, can learn something from Mr. Warburton.

The new assistant arrived in the afternoon. When the Resident, Mr. Warburton, was told that the prahu was in sight he put on his solar topee and went down to the landing-stage. The guard, eight little Dyak soldiers, stood to attention as he passed. He noted with satisfaction that their bearing was martial, their uniforms neat and clean, and their guns shining. They were a credit to him. From the landing-stage he watched the bend of the river round which in a moment the boat would sweep. He looked very smart in his spotless ducks and white shoes. He held under his arm a gold-headed Malacca cane which had been given him by the Sultan of Perak. He awaited the newcomer with mingled feelings. There was more work in the district than one man could properly do, and during his periodical tours of the country under his charge it had been inconvenient to leave the station in the hands of a native clerk, but he had been so long the only white man there that he could not face the arrival of another without misgiving. He was accustomed to loneliness. During the war he had not seen an English face for three years; and once when he was instructed to put up an afforestation officer he was seized with panic, so that when the stranger was due to arrive, having arranged everything for his reception, he wrote a note telling him he was obliged to go up-river, and fled; he remained away till he was informed by a messenger that his guest had left.

Now the prahu appeared in the broad reach. It was manned by prisoners, Dyaks under various sentences, and a couple of warders were waiting on the landing-stage to take them back to jail. They were sturdy fellows, used to the river, and they rowed with a powerful stroke. As the boat reached the side a man got out from under the attap awning and stepped on shore. The guard presented arms.

"Here we are at last. By God, I'm as cramped as the devil. I've brought you your mail."

He spoke with exuberant joviality. Mr. Warburton politely held out his hand.

"Mr. Cooper, I presume?"

"That's right. Were you expecting any one else?"

The question had a facetious intent, but the Resident did not smile.

"My name is Warburton. I'll show you your quarters. They'll bring your kit along."

He preceded Cooper along the narrow pathway and they entered a compound in which stood a small bungalow.

"I've had it made as habitable as I could, but of course no one has lived in it for a good many years."

It was built on piles. It consisted of a long living-room which opened on to a broad verandah, and behind, on each side of a passage, were two bedrooms.

"This'll do me all right," said Cooper.

"I daresay you want to have a bath and a change. I shall be very much pleased if you'll dine with me tonight. Will eight o'clock suit you?"

"Any old time will do for me."

The Resident gave a polite, but slightly disconcerted, smile and withdrew. He returned to the Fort where his own residence was. The impression which Allen Cooper had given him was not very favorable, but he was a fair man, and he knew that it was unjust to form an opinion on so brief a glimpse. Cooper seemed to be about thirty. He was a tall, thin fellow, with a sallow face in which there was not a spot of color. It was a face all in one tone. He had a large, hooked nose and blue eyes. When, entering the bungalow, he had taken off his topee and flung it to a waiting boy, Mr. Warburton noticed that his large skull, covered with short, brown hair, contrasted somewhat oddly with a weak, small chin. He was dressed in khaki shorts and a khaki shirt, but they were shabby and soiled; and his battered topee had not been cleaned for days. Mr. Warburton reflected that the young man had spent a week on a coasting steamer and had passed the last forty-eight hours lying in the bottom of a prahu.

"We'll see what he looks like when he comes in to dinner."

He went into his room where his things were as neatly laid out as if he had an English valet, undressed, and, walking down the stairs to the bathhouse, sluiced himself with cool water. The only concession he made to the climate was to wear a white dinner-jacket; but otherwise, in a boiled shirt and a high collar, silk socks and patent-leather shoes, he dressed as formally as though he were dining at his club in Pall Mall. A careful host, he went into the dining-room to see that the table was properly laid. It was gay with orchids and the silver shone brightly. The napkins were folded into elaborate shapes. Shaded candles in silver candlesticks shed a soft light. Mr. Warburton smiled his approval and returned to the sitting-room to await his guest. Presently he appeared. Cooper was wearing the khaki shorts, the khaki shirt, and the ragged jacket in which he had landed. Mr. Warburton's smile of greeting froze on his face.

"Hulloa, you're all dressed up," said Cooper. "I didn't know you were going to do that. I very nearly put on a sarong."

"It doesn't matter at all. I daresay your boys were busy."

"You needn't have bothered to dress on my account, you know."

"I didn't. I always dress for dinner."

"Even when you're alone?"

"Especially when I'm alone," replied Mr. Warburton, with a frigid stare.

He saw a twinkle of amusement in Cooper's eyes, and he flushed an angry red. Mr. Warburton was a hot-tempered man; you might have guessed that from his red face with its pugnacious features and from his red hair, now growing white; his blue eyes, cold as a rule and observing, could flush with sudden wrath; but he was a man of the world and he hoped a just one. He must do his best to get on with this fellow.

"When I lived in London I moved in circles in which it would have been just as eccentric not to dress for dinner every night as not to have a bath every morning. When I came to Borneo I saw no reason to discontinue so good a habit. For three years, during the war, I never saw a white man. I never omitted to dress on a single occasion on which I was well enough to come in to dinner. You have not been very long in this country; believe me, there is no better way to maintain the proper pride which you should have in yourself. When a white man surrenders in the slightest degree to the influences that surround him he very soon loses his self-respect, and when he loses his self-respect you may be quite sure that the natives will soon cease to respect him."

"Well, if you expect me to put on a boiled shirt and a stiff collar in this heat I'm afraid you'll be disappointed."

"When you are dining in your own bungalow you will, of course, dress as you think fit, but when you do me the pleasure of dining with me, perhaps you will come to the conclusion that it is only polite to wear the costume usual in civilized society."

Two Malay boys, in sarongs and songkoks, with smart white coats and brass buttons, came in, one bearing gin pahits, and the other a tray on which were olives and anchovies. Then they went in to dinner. Mr. Warburton flattered himself that he had the best cook, a Chinese, in Borneo, and he took great trouble to have as good food as in the difficult circumstances was possible. He exercised much ingenuity in making the best of his materials.

"Would you care to look at the menu?" he said, handing it to Cooper.

It was written in French and the dishes had resounding names. They were waited on by the two boys. In opposite corners of the room two more waved immense fans, and so gave movement to the sultry air. The fare was sumptuous and the champagne excellent.

"Do you do yourself like this every day?" said Cooper.

Mr. Warburton gave the menu a careless glance.

"I have not noticed that the dinner is any different from usual," he said. "I eat very little myself, but I make a point of having a proper dinner served to me every night. It keeps the cook in practice and it's good discipline for the boys."

The conversation proceeded with effort. Mr. Warburton was elaborately courteous, and it may be that he found a slightly malicious amusement in the embarrassment which he thereby occasioned in his companion. Cooper had not been more than a few months in Sembulu, and Mr. Warburton's inquiries about friends of his in Kuala Solor were soon exhausted.

"By the way," he said presently, "did you meet a lad called Hennerley? He's come out recently, I believe."

"Oh, yes, he's in the police. A rotten bounder."

"I should hardly have expected him to be that. His uncle is my friend Lord Barraclough. I had a letter from Lady Barraclough only the other day asking me to look out for him."

"I heard he was related to somebody or other. I suppose that's how he got the job. He's been to Eton and Oxford and he doesn't forget to let you know it."

"You surprise me," said Mr. Warburton. "All his family have been at Eton and Oxford for a couple of hundred years. I should have expected him to take it as a matter of course."

"I thought him a damned prig."

"To what school did you go?"

"I was born in Barbados. I was educated there."

"Oh, I see."

Mr. Warburton managed to put so much offensiveness into his brief reply that Cooper flushed. For a moment he was silent.

"I've had two or three letters from Kuala Solor," continued Mr. Warburton, "and my impression was that young Hennerley was a great success. They say he's a first-rate sportsman."

"Oh, yes, he's very popular. He's just the sort of fellow they would like in K.S. I haven't got much use for the first-rate sportsman myself. What does it amount to in the long run that a man can play golf and tennis better than other people? And who cares if he can make a break of seventy-five at billiards? They attach a damned sight too much importance to that sort of thing in England."

"Do you think so? I was under the impression that the first-rate sportsman had come out of the war certainly no worse than any one else."

"Oh, if you're going to talk of the war then I do know what I'm talking about. I was in the same regiment as Hennerley and I can tell you that the men couldn't stick him at any price."

"How do you know?"

"Because I was one of the men."

"Oh, you hadn't got a commission."

"A fat chance I had of getting a commission. I was what was called a Colonial. I hadn't been to a public school and I had no influence. I was in the ranks the whole damned time."

Cooper frowned. He seemed to have difficulty in preventing himself from breaking into violent invective. Mr. Warburton watched him, his little blue eyes narrowed, watched him and formed his opinion. Changing the conversation, he began to speak to Cooper about the work that would be required of him, and as the clock struck ten he rose.

"Well, I won't keep you any more. I daresay you're tired by your journey."

They shook hands.

"Oh, I say, look here," said Cooper, "I wonder if you can find me a boy. The boy I had before never turned up when I was starting from K.S. He took my kit on board and all that and then disappeared. I didn't know he wasn't there till we were out of the river."

"I'll ask my head-boy. I have no doubt he can find you some one."

"All right. Just tell him to send the boy along and if I like the look of him I'll take him."

There was a moon, so that no lantern was needed. Cooper walked across from the Fort to his bungalow.

"I wonder why on earth they've sent me a fellow like that?" reflected Mr. Warburton. "If that's the kind of man they're going to get out now I don't think much of it."

He strolled down his garden. The Fort was built on the top of a little hill and the garden ran down to the river's edge; on the bank was an arbor, and hither it was his habit to come after dinner to smoke a cheroot. And often from the river that flowed below him a voice was heard, the voice of some Malay too timorous to venture into the light of day, and a complaint or an accusation was softly wafted to his ears, a piece of information was whispered to him or a useful hint, which otherwise would never have come into his official ken. He threw himself heavily into a long rattan chair. Cooper! An envious, ill-bred fellow, bumptious, self-assertive and vain. But Mr. Warburton's irritation could not withstand the silent beauty of the night. The air was scented with the sweet-smelling flowers of a tree that grew at the entrance to the arbor, and the fireflies, sparkling dimly, flew with their slow and silvery flight. The moon made a pathway on the broad river for the light feet of Siva's bride, and on the further bank a row of palm trees was delicately silhouetted against the sky. Peace stole into the soul of Mr. Warburton.

He was a queer creature and he had had a singular career. At the age of twenty-one he had inherited a considerable fortune, a hundred thousand pounds, and when he left Oxford he threw himself into the gay life which in those days (now Mr. Warburton was a man of four and fifty) offered itself to the young man of good family. He had his flat in Mount Street, his private hansom, and his hunting-box in Warwickshire. He went to all the places where the fashionable congregate. He was handsome, amusing and generous. He was a figure in the society of London in the early nineties, and society then had not lost its exclusiveness nor its brilliance. The Boer War which shook it was unthought of; the Great War which destroyed it was prophesied only by the pessimists. It was no unpleasant thing to be a rich young man in those days, and Mr. Warburton's chimney-piece during the season was packed with cards for one great function after another. Mr. Warburton displayed them with complacency. For Mr. Warburton was a snob. He was not a timid snob, a little ashamed of being impressed by his betters, nor a snob who sought the intimacy of persons who had acquired celebrity in politics or notoriety in the arts, nor the snob who was dazzled by riches; he was the naked, unadulterated common snob who dearly loved a lord. He was touchy and quick-tempered, but he would much rather have been snubbed by a person of quality than flattered by a commoner. His name figured insignificantly in *Burke's Peerage,* and it was marvelous to watch the ingenuity he used to mention his distant relationship to the noble family he belonged to; but never a word did he say of the honest Liverpool manufacturer from whom, through his mother, a Miss Cub bins, he had come by his fortune. It was the terror of his fashionable life that at Cowes, maybe, or at Ascot, when he was with a duchess or even with a prince of the blood, one of these relatives would claim acquaintance with him.

His failing was too obvious not soon to become notorious, but its extravagance saved it from being merely despicable. The great whom he adored laughed at him, but in their hearts felt his adoration not unnatural. Poor Warburton was a dreadful snob, of course, but after all he was a good fellow. He was always ready to back a bill for an impecunious nobleman, and if you were in a tight corner you could safely count on him for a hundred pounds. He gave good dinners. He played whist badly, but never minded how much he lost if the company was select. He happened to be a gambler, an unlucky one, but he was a good loser, and it was impossible not to admire the coolness with which he lost five hundred pounds at a sitting. His passion for cards, almost as strong as his passion for titles, was the cause of his undoing. The life he led was expensive and his gambling losses were formidable. He began to plunge more heavily, first on horses, and then on the Stock Exchange. He had a certain simplicity of character and the unscrupulous found him an ingenuous prey. I do not know if he ever realized that his smart friends laughed at him behind his back, but I think he had an obscure instinct that he could not afford to appear other than careless of his money. He got into the hands of money-lenders. At the age of thirty-four he was ruined.

He was too much imbued with the spirit of his class to hesitate in the choice of his next step. When a man in his set had run through his money he went out to the colonies. No one heard Mr. Warburton repine. He made no complaint because a noble friend had advised a disastrous speculation, he pressed nobody to whom he had lent money to repay it, he paid his debts (if he had only known it, the despised blood of the Liverpool manufacturer came out in him there), sought help from no one, and, never having done a stroke of work in his life, looked for a means of livelihood. He remained cheerful, unconcerned and full of humor. He had no wish to make any one with whom he happened to be uncomfortable by the recital of his misfortune. Mr. Warburton was a snob, but he was also a gentleman.

The only favor he asked of any of the great friends in whose daily company he had lived for years was a recommendation. The able man who was at that time Sultan of Sembulu took him into his service. The night before he sailed he dined for the last time at his club.

"I hear you're going away, Warburton," the old Duke of Hereford said to him.

"Yes, I'm going to Borneo."

"Good God, what are you going there for?"

"Oh, I'm broke."

"Are you? I'm sorry. Well, let us know when you come back. I hope you have a good time."

"Oh, yes. Lots of shooting, you know."

The Duke nodded and passed on. A few hours later Mr. Warburton watched the coast of England recede into the mist, and he left behind everything which to him made life worth living.

Twenty years had passed since then. He kept up a busy correspondence with various great ladies and his letters were amusing and chatty. He never lost his love for titled persons and paid careful attention to the announcements in *The Times* (which reached him six weeks after publication) of their comings and goings. He perused the column which records births, deaths, and marriages, and he was always ready with his letter of congratulation or condolence. The illustrated papers told him how people looked and on his periodical visits to England, able to take up the threads as though they had never been broken, he knew all about any new person who might have appeared on the social surface. His interest in the world of fashion was as vivid as when himself had been a figure in it. It still seemed to him the only thing that mattered.

But insensibly another interest had entered into his life. The position he found himself in flattered his vanity; he was no longer the sycophant craving the smiles of the great, he was the master whose word was law. He was gratified by the guard of Dyak soldiers who presented arms as he passed. He liked to sit in judgment on his fellow men. It pleased him to compose quarrels between rival chiefs. When the head-hunters were troublesome in the old days he set out to chastise them with a thrill of pride in his own behavior. He was too vain not to be of dauntless courage, and a pretty story was told of his coolness in adventuring single-handed into a stockaded village and demanding the surrender of a blood-thirsty pirate. He became a skilful administrator. He was strict, just and honest.

And little by little he conceived a deep love for the Malays. He interested himself in their habits and customs. He was never tired of listening to their talk. He admired their virtues, and with a smile and a shrug of the shoulders condoned their vices.

"In my day," he would say, "I have been on intimate terms with some of the greatest gentlemen in England, but I have never known finer gentlemen than some well-born Malays whom I am proud to call my friends."

He liked their courtesy and their distinguished manners, their gentleness and their sudden passions. He knew by instinct exactly how to treat them. He had a genuine tenderness for them. But he never forgot that he was an English gentleman and he had no patience with the white men who yielded to native customs. He made no surrenders. And he did not imitate so many of the white men in taking a native woman to wife, for an intrigue of this nature, however sanctified by custom, seemed to him not only shocking but undignified. A man who had been called George by Albert Edward, Prince of Wales, could hardly be expected to have any connection with a native. And when he returned to Borneo from his visits to England it was now with something like relief. His friends, like himself, were no longer young, and there was a new generation which looked upon him as a tiresome old man. It seemed to him that the England of today had lost a good deal of what he had loved in the England of his youth. But Borneo remained the same. It was home to him now. He meant to remain in the service as long as was possible, and the hope in his heart was that he would die before at last he was forced to retire. He had stated in his will that wherever he died he wished his body to be brought back to Sembulu and buried among the people he loved within sound of the softly flowing river.

But these emotions he kept hidden from the eyes of men; and no one, seeing this spruce, stout, well-set-up man, with his clean-shaven strong face and his whitening hair, would have dreamed that he cherished so profound a sentiment.

He knew how the work of the station should be done, and during the next few days he kept a suspicious eye on his assistant. He saw very soon that he was painstaking and competent. The only fault he had to find with him was that he was brusque with the natives.

"The Malays are shy and very sensitive," he said to him. "I think you will find that you will get much better results if you take care always to be polite, patient and kindly."

Cooper gave a short, grating laugh.

"I was born in Barbadoes and I was in Africa in the war. I don't think there's much about niggers that I don't know."

"I know nothing," said Mr. Warburton acidly. "But we were not talking of them. We were talking of Malays."

"Aren't they niggers?"

"You are very ignorant," replied Mr. Warburton.

He said no more.

On the first Sunday after Cooper's arrival he asked him to dinner. He did everything ceremoniously, and though they had met on the previous day in the office and later, on the Fort Verandah where they drank a gin and bitters together at six o'clock, he sent a polite note across to the bungalow by a boy. Cooper, however unwillingly, came in evening dress and Mr. Warburton, though gratified that his wish was respected, noticed with disdain that the young man's clothes were badly cut and his shirt ill-fitting. But Mr. Warburton was in a good temper that evening.

"By the way," he said to him, as he shook hands, "I've talked to my head-boy about finding you some one and he recommends his nephew. I've seen him and he seems a bright and willing lad. Would you like to see him?"

"I don't mind."

"He's waiting now."

Mr. Warburton called his boy and told him to send for his nephew. In a moment a tall, slender youth of twenty appeared. He had large dark eyes and a good profile. He was very neat in his sarong, a little white coat, and a fez, without a tassel, of plum-colored velvet. He answered to the name of Abas. Mr. Warburton looked on him with approval, and his manner insensibly softened as he spoke to him in fluent and idiomatic Malay. He was inclined to be sarcastic with white people, but with the Malays he had a happy mixture of condescension and kindliness. He stood in the place of the Sultan. He knew perfectly how to preserve his own dignity, and at the same time put a native at his ease.

"Will he do?" said Mr. Warburton, turning to Cooper.

"Yes, I daresay he's no more of a scoundrel than any of the rest of them."

Mr. Warburton informed the boy that he was engaged and dismissed him.

"You're very lucky to get a boy like that," he told Cooper. "He belongs to a very good family. They came over from Malacca nearly a hundred years ago."

"I don't much mind if the boy who cleans my shoes and brings me a drink when I want it has blue blood in his veins or not. All I ask is that he should do what I tell him and look sharp about it."

Mr. Warburton pursed his lips, but made no reply.

They went in to dinner. It was excellent, and the wine was good. Its influence presently had its effect on them and they talked not only without acrimony, but even with friendliness. Mr. Warburton liked to do himself well, and on Sunday night he made it a habit to do himself even a little better than usual. He began to think he was unfair to Cooper. Of course he was not a gentleman, but that was not his fault, and when you got to know him it might be that he would turn out a very good fellow. His faults, perhaps, were faults of manner. And he was certainly good at his work, quick, conscientious and thorough. When they reached the dessert Mr. Warburton was feeling kindly disposed towards all mankind.

"This is your first Sunday and I'm going to give you a very special glass of port. I've only got about two dozen of it left and I keep it for special occasions."

He gave his boy instructions and presently the bottle was brought. Mr. Warburton watched the boy open it

"I got this port from my old friend Charles Hollington. He'd had it for forty years and I've had it for a good many. He was well known to have the best cellar in England."

"Is he a wine merchant?"

"Not exactly," smiled Mr. Warburton. "I was speaking of Lord Hollington of Castle Reagh. He's one of the richest peers in England. A very old friend of mine. I was at Eton with his brother."

This was an opportunity that Mr. Warburton could never resist and he told a little anecdote of which the only point seemed to be that he knew an earl. The port was certainly very good; he drank a glass and then a second. He lost all caution. He had not talked to a white man for months. He began to tell stories. He showed himself in the company of the great. Hearing him you would have thought that at one time ministries were formed and policies decided on his suggestion whispered into the ear of a duchess or thrown over the dinner-table to be gratefully acted on by the confidential adviser of the sovereign. The old days at Ascot, Goodwood and Cowes lived again for him. Another glass of port. There were the great house-parties in Yorkshire and in Scotland to which he went every year.

"I had a man called Foreman then, the best valet I ever had, and why do you think he gave me notice? You know in the Housekeeper's Room the ladies' maids and the gentlemen's gentlemen sit according to to the precedence of their masters. He told me he was sick of going to party after party at which I was the only commoner. It meant that he always had to sit at the bottom of the table and all the best bits were taken before a dish reached him. I told the story to the old Duke of Hereford and he roared. 'By God, sir,' he said, 'if I were King of England I'd make you a viscount just to give your man a chance.' 'Take him yourself, Duke,' I said. 'He's the best valet I've ever had.' 'Well, Warburton,' he said, 'if he's good enough for you he's good enough for me. Send him along.' "

Then there was Monte Carlo where Mr. Warburton and the Grand Duke Fyodor, playing in partnership, had broken the bank one evening; and there was Marienbad. At Marienbad Mr. Warburton had played baccarat with Edward VII.

"He was only Prince of Wales then, of course. I remember him saying to me, 'George, if you draw on a five you'll lose your shirt.' He was right; I don't think he ever said a truer word in his life. He was a wonderful man. I always said he was the greatest diplomatist in Europe. But I was a young fool in those days, I hadn't the sense to take his advice. If I had, if I'd never drawn on a five, I daresay I shouldn't be here today."

Cooper was watching him. His brown eyes, deep in their sockets, were hard and supercilious, and on his lips was a mocking smile. He had heard a good deal about Mr. Warburton in Kuala Solor. Not a bad sort, and he ran his district like clockwork, they said, but by heaven, what a snob! They laughed at him good-naturedly, for it was impossible to dislike a man who was so generous and so kindly, and Cooper had already heard the story of the Prince of Wales and the game of baccarat. But Cooper listened without indulgence. From the beginning he had resented the Resident's manner. He was very sensitive and he writhed under Mr. Warburton's polite sarcasms. Mr. Warburton had a knack of receiving a remark of which he disapproved with a devastating silence. Cooper had lived little in England and he had a peculiar dislike of the English. He resented especially the public-school boy since he always feared that he was going to patronize him. He was so much afraid of others putting on airs with him that, in order as it were to get in first, he put on such airs as to make every one think him insufferably conceited.

"Well, at all events the war has done one good thing for us," he said at last. "It's smashed up the power of the aristocracy. The Boer War started it, and 1914 put the lid on."

"The great families of England are doomed," said Mr. Warburton with the complacent melancholy of an *émigré* who remembered the court of Louis XV. "They cannot afford any longer to live in their splendid palaces and their princely hospitality will soon be nothing but a memory."

"And a damned good job too in my opinion."

"My poor Cooper, what can you know of the glory that was Greece and the grandeur that was Rome?"

Mr. Warburton made an ample gesture. His eyes for an instant grew dreamy with a vision of the past.

"Well, believe me, we're fed up with all that rot. What we want is a business government by business men. I was born in a Crown Colony and I've lived practically all my life in the colonies. I don't give a row of pins for a lord. What's wrong with England is snobbishness. And if there's anything that gets my goat it's a snob."

A snob! Mr. Warburton's face grew purple and his eyes blazed with anger. That was a word that had pursued him all his life. The great ladies whose society he had enjoyed in his youth were not inclined to look upon his appreciation of themselves as unworthy, but even great ladies are sometimes out of temper and more than once Mr. Warburton had had the dreadful word flung in his teeth. He knew, he could not help knowing, that there were odious people who called him a snob. How unfair it was! Why, there was no vice he found so detestable as snobbishness. After all, he liked to mix with people of his own class, he was only at home in their company, and how in heaven's name could any one say that was snobbish? Birds of a feather.

"I quite agree with you," he answered. "A snob is a man who admires or despises another because he is of a higher social rank than his own. It is the most vulgar failing of our English middle class."

He saw a flicker of amusement in Cooper's eyes. Cooper put up his hand to hide the broad smile that rose to his lips, and so made it more noticeable. Mr. Warburton's hands trembled a little.

Probably Cooper never knew how greatly he had offended his chief. A sensitive man himself, he was strangely insensitive to the feelings of others.

Their work forced them to see one another for a few minutes now and then during the day, and they met at six to have a drink on Mr. Warburton's verandah. This was an old-established custom of the country which Mr. Warburton would not for the world have broken. But they ate their meals separately, Cooper in his bungalow and Mr. Warburton at the Fort. After the office work was over they walked till dusk fell, but they walked apart. There were but few paths in this country, where the jungle pressed close upon the plantations of the village, and when Mr. Warburton caught sight of his assistant passing along with his loose stride, he would make a circuit in order to avoid him. Cooper, with his bad manners, his conceit in his own judgment and his intolerance, had already got on his nerves; but it was not till Cooper had been on the station for a couple of months that an incident happened which turned the Resident's dislike into bitter hatred.

Mr. Warburton was obliged to go up-country on a tour of inspection, and he left the station in Cooper's charge with more confidence, since he had definitely come to the conclusion that he was a capable fellow. The only thing he did not like was that he had no indulgence. He was honest, just and painstaking, but he had no sympathy for the natives. It bitterly amused Mr. Warburton to observe that this man, who looked upon himself as every man's equal, should look upon so many men as his own inferiors. He was hard, he had no patience with the native mind, and he was a bully. Mr. Warburton very quickly realized that the Malays disliked and feared him. He was not altogether displeased. He would not have liked it very much if his assistant had enjoyed a popularity which might rival his own. Mr. Warburton made his elaborate preparations, set out on his expedition, and in three weeks returned. Meanwhile the mail had arrived. The first thing that struck his eyes when he entered his sitting-room was a great pile of open newspapers. Cooper had met him, and they went into the room together. Mr. Warburton turned to one of the servants who had been left behind and sternly asked him what was the meaning of those open papers. Cooper hastened to explain.

"I wanted to read all about the Wolverhampton murder and so I borrowed your *Times*. I brought them back again. I knew you wouldn't mind."

Mr. Warburton turned on him, white with anger.

"But I do mind. I mind very much."

"I'm sorry," said Cooper, with composure. "The fact is, I simply couldn't wait till you came back."

"I wonder you didn't open my letters as well."

Cooper, unmoved, smiled at his chief's exasperation.

"Oh, that's not quite the same thing. After all, I couldn't imagine you'd mind my looking at your newspapers. There's nothing private in them."

"I very much object to any one reading my paper before me." He went up to the pile. There were nearly thirty numbers there. "I think it extremely impertinent of you. They're all mixed up."

"We can easily put them in order," said Cooper, joining him at the table.

"Don't touch them," cried Mr. Warburton.

"I say, it's childish to make a scene about a little thing like that."

"How dare you speak to me like that?"

"Oh, go to hell," said Cooper, and he flung out of the room.

Mr. Warburton, trembling with passion, was left contemplating his papers. His greatest pleasure in life had been destroyed by those callous, brutal hands. Most people living in out-of-the-way places when the mail comes tear open impatiently their papers and taking the last ones first glance at the latest news from home. Not so Mr. Warburton. His newsagent had instructions to write on the outside of the wrapper the date of each paper he despatched and when the great bundle arrived Mr. Warburton looked at these dates and with his blue pencil numbered them. His head-boy's orders were to place one on the table every morning in the verandah with the early cup of tea, and it was Mr. Warburton's especial delight to break the wrapper as he sipped his tea, and read the morning paper. It gave him the illusion of living at home. Every Monday morning he read the Monday *Times* of six weeks back and so went through the week. On Sunday he read *The Observer*. Like his habit of dressing for dinner it was a tie to civilization. And it was his pride that no matter how exciting the news was he had never yielded to the temptation of opening a paper before its allotted time. During the war the suspense sometimes had been intolerable, and when he read one day that a push was begun he had undergone agonies of suspense which he might have saved himself by the simple expedient of opening a later paper which lay waiting for him on a shelf. It had been the severest trial to which he had ever exposed himself, but he victoriously surmounted it. And that clumsy fool had broken open those neat tight packages because he wanted to know whether some horrid woman had murdered her odious husband.

Mr. Warburton sent for his boy and told him to bring wrappers. He folded up the papers as neatly as he could, placed a wrapper round each and numbered it. But it was a melancholy task.

"I shall never forgive him," he said. "Never."

Of course his boy had been with him on his expedition; he never traveled without him, for his boy knew exactly how he liked things, and Mr. Warburton was not the kind of jungle traveler who was prepared to dispense with his comforts; but in the interval since their arrival he had been gossiping in the servants' quarters. He had learnt that Cooper had had trouble with his boys. All but the youth Abas had left him. Abas had desired to go too, but his uncle had placed him there on the instructions of the Resident, and he was afraid to leave without his uncle's permission.

"I told him he had done well, Tuan," said the boy. "But he is unhappy. He says it is not a good house and he wishes to know if he may go as the others have gone."

"No, he must stay. The tuan must have servants. Have those who went been replaced?"

"No, Tuan, no one will go."

Mr. Warburton frowned. Cooper was an insolent fool, but he had an official position and must be suitably provided with servants. It was not seemly that his house should be improperly conducted.

"Where are the boys who ran away?"

"They are in the kampong, Tuan."

"Go and see them tonight and tell them that I expect them to be back in Tuan Cooper's house at dawn tomorrow."

"They say they will not go, Tuan."

"On my order?"

The boy had been with Mr. Warburton for fifteen years, and he knew every intonation of his master's voice. He was not afraid of him, they had gone through too much together, once in the jungle the Resident had saved his life and once, upset in some rapids, but for him the Resident would have been drowned; but he knew when the Resident must be obeyed without question.

"I will go to the kampong," he said.

Mr. Warburton expected that his subordinate would take the first opportunity to apologize for his rudeness, but Cooper had the ill-bred man's inability to express regret; and when they met next morning in the office he ignored the incident. Since Mr. Warburton had been away for three weeks it was necessary for them to have a somewhat prolonged interview. At the end of it Mr. Warburton dismissed him.

"I don't think there's anything else, thank you." Cooper turned to go, but Mr. Warburton stopped him. "I understand you've been having some trouble with your boys."

Cooper gave a harsh laugh.

"They tried to blackmail me. They had the damned cheek to run away, all except that incompetent fellow Abas—he knew when he was well off—but I just sat tight. They've all come to heel again."

"What do you mean by that?"

"This morning they were all back on their jobs, the Chinese cook and all. There they were, as cool as cucumbers; you would have thought they owned the place. I suppose they'd come to the conclusion that I wasn't such a fool as I looked."

"By no means. They came back on my express order."

Cooper flushed slightly.

"I should be obliged if you wouldn't interfere with my private concerns."

"They're not your private concerns. When your servants run away it makes you ridiculous. You are perfectly free to make a fool of yourself, but I cannot allow you to be made a fool of. It is unseemly that your house should not be properly staffed. As soon as I heard that your boys had left you, I had them told to be back in their places at dawn. That'll do."

Mr. Warburton nodded to signify that the interview was at an end. Cooper took no notice.

"Shall I tell you what I did? I called them and gave the whole bally lot the sack. I gave them ten minutes to get out of the compound."

Mr. Warburton shrugged his shoulders.

"What makes you think you can get others?"

"I've told my own clerk to see about it."

Mr. Warburton reflected for a moment.

"I think you behaved very foolishly. You will do well to remember in future that good masters make good servants."

"Is there anything else you want to teach me?"

"I should like to teach you manners, but it would be an arduous task, and I have not the time to waste. I will see that you get boys."

"Please don't put yourself to any trouble on my account. I'm quite capable of getting them for myself."

Mr. Warburton smiled acidly. He had an inkling that Cooper disliked him as much as he disliked Cooper, and he knew that nothing is more galling than to be forced to accept the favors of a man you detest.

"Allow me to tell you that you have no more chance of getting Malay or Chinese servants here now than you have of getting an English butler or a French chef. No one will come to you except on an order from me. Would you like me to give it?"

"No."

"As you please. Good morning."

Mr. Warburton watched the development of the situation with acrid humor. Cooper's clerk was unable to persuade Malay, Dyak or Chinese to enter the house of such a master. Abas, the boy who remained faithful' to him, knew how to cook only native food, and Cooper, a coarse feeder, found his gorge rise against the everlasting rice. There was no water-carrier, and in that great heat he needed several baths a day. He cursed Abas, but Abas opposed him with sullen resistance and would not do more than he chose. It was galling to know that the lad stayed with him only because the Resident insisted. This went on for a fortnight and then, one morning, he found in his house the very servants whom he had previously dismissed. He fell into a violent rage, but he had learnt a little sense, and this time, without a word, he let them stay. He swallowed his humiliation, but the impatient contempt he had felt for Mr. Warburton's idiosyncrasies changed into a sullen hatred; the Resident with this malicious stroke had made him the laughing-stock of all the natives.

The two men now held no communication with one another. They broke the time-honored custom of sharing, notwithstanding personal dislike, a drink at six o'clock with any white man who happened to be at the station. Each lived in his own house as though the other did not exist. Now that Cooper had fallen into the work, it was necessary for them to have little to do with one another in the office. Mr. Warburton used his orderly to send any message he had to give his assistant, and his instructions he sent by formal letter. They saw one another constantly, that was inevitable, but did not exchange half a dozen words in a week. The fact that they could not avoid catching sight of one another got on their nerves. They brooded over their antagonism and Mr. Warburton, taking his daily walk, could think of nothing but how much he detested his assistant.

And the dreadful thing was that in all probability they would remain thus, facing each other in deadly enmity, till Mr. Warburton went on leave. It might be three years. He had no reason to send in a complaint to headquarters: Cooper did his work very well, and at that time men were hard to get. True, vague complaints reached him and hints that the natives found Cooper harsh. There was certainly a feeling of dissatisfaction among them. But when Mr. Warburton looked into specific cases, all he could say was that Cooper had shown severity where mildness would not have been misplaced and had been unfeeling when himself would have been sympathetic. He had done nothing for which he could be taken to task. But Mr. Warburton watched him. Hatred will often make a man clear-sighted, and he had a suspicion that Cooper was using the natives without consideration, yet keeping within the law, because he felt that thus he could exasperate his chief. One day perhaps he would go too far. None knew better than Mr. Warburton how irritable the incessant heat could make a man and how difficult it was to keep one's self-control after a sleepless night. He smiled softly to himself. Sooner or later Cooper would deliver himself into his hand.

When at last the opportunity came Mr. Warburton laughed aloud. Cooper had charge of the prisoners; they made roads, built sheds, rowed when it was necessary to send the prahu up- or down-stream, kept the town clean and otherwise usefully employed themselves. If well-behaved they even on occasion served as house-boys. Cooper kept them hard at it. He liked to see them work. He took pleasure in devising tasks for them; and seeing quickly enough that they were being made to do useless things the prisoners worked badly. He punished them by lengthening their hours. This was contrary to the regulations, and as soon as it was brought to the attention of Mr. Warburton, without referring the matter back to his subordinate, he gave instructions that the old hours should be kept; Cooper, going out for his walk, was astounded to see the prisoners strolling back to the jail; he had given instructions that they were not to knock off till dusk. When he asked the warder in charge why they had left off work he was told that it was the Resident's bidding.

White with rage he strode to the Fort. Mr. Warburton, in his spotless white ducks and his neat topee, with a walking-stick in his hand, followed by his dogs, was on the point of starting out on his afternoon stroll. He had watched Cooper go and knew that he had taken the road by the river. Cooper jumped up the steps and went straight up to the Resident.

"I want to know what the hell you mean by countermanding my order that the prisoners were to work till six," he burst out, beside himself with fury.

Mr. Warburton opened his cold blue eyes very wide and assumed an expression of great surprise.

"Are you out of your mind? Are you so ignorant that you do not know that that is not the way to speak to your official superior?"

"Oh, go to hell. The prisoners are my pidgin and you've got no right to interfere. You mind your business and I'll mind mine. I want to know what the devil you mean by making a damned fool of me. Every one in the place will know that you've countermanded my order."

Mr. Warburton kept very cool.

"You had no power to give the order you did. I countermanded it because it was harsh and tyrannical. Believe me, I have not made half such a damned fool of you as you have made of yourself."

"You disliked me from the first moment I came here. You've done everything you could to make the place impossible for me because I wouldn't lick your boots for you. You got your knife into me because I wouldn't flatter you."

Cooper, spluttering with rage, was nearing dangerous ground, and Mr. Warburton's eyes grew on a sudden colder and more piercing.

"You are wrong. I thought you were a cad, but I was perfectly satisfied with the way you did your work."

"You snob. You damned snob. You thought me a cad because I hadn't been to Eton. Oh, they told me in K.S. what to expect. Why, don't you know that you're the laughing-stock of the whole country? I could hardly help bursting into a roar of laughter when you told your celebrated story about the Prince of Wales. My God, how they shouted at the club when they told it. By God, I'd rather be the cad I am than the snob you are."

He got Mr. Warburton on the raw.

"If you don't get out of my house this minute I shall knock you down," he cried.

The other came a little closer to him and put his face in his.

"Touch me, touch me," he said. "By God, I'd like to see you hit me. Do you want me to say it again? Snob. Snob."

Cooper was three inches taller than Mr. Warburton, a strong, muscular young man. Mr. Warburton was fat and fifty-four. His clenched fist shot out. Cooper caught him by the arm and pushed him back.

"Don't be a damned fool. Remember I'm not a gentleman. I know how to use my hands."

He gave a sort of hoot, and, grinning all over his pale, sharp face, jumped down the verandah steps. Mr. Warburton, his heart in his anger pounding against his ribs, sank exhausted into a chair. His body tingled as though he had prickly heat. For one horrible moment he thought he was going to cry. But suddenly he was conscious that his head-boy was on the verandah and instinctively regained control of himself. The boy came forward and filled him a glass of whisky and soda. Without a word Mr. Warburton took it and drank it to the dregs.

"What do you want to say to me?" asked Mr. Warburton, trying to force a smile on to his strained lips.

"Tuan, the assistant tuan is a bad man. Abas wishes again to leave him."

"Let him wait a little. I shall write to Kuala Solor and ask that Tuan Cooper should go elsewhere."

"Tuan Cooper is not good with the Malays."

"Leave me."

The boy silently withdrew. Mr. Warburton was left alone with his thoughts. He saw the club at Kuala Solor, the men sitting round the table in the window in their flannels, when the night had driven them in from golf and tennis, drinking whiskies and gin pahits and laughing when they told the celebrated story of the Prince of Wales and himself at Marienbad. He was hot with shame and misery. A snob! They all thought him a snob. And he had always thought them very good fellows, he had always been gentleman enough to let it make no difference to him that they were of very second-rate position. He hated them now. But his hatred for them was nothing compared with his hatred for Cooper. And if it had come to blows Cooper could have thrashed him. Tears of mortification ran down his red, fat face. He sat there for a couple of hours smoking cigarette after cigarette, and he wished he were dead.

At last the boy came back and asked him if he would dress for dinner. Of course! He always dressed for dinner. He rose wearily from his chair and put on his stiff shirt and the high collar. He sat down at the prettily decorated table and was waited on as usual by the two boys while two others waved their great fans. Over there in the bungalow, two hundred yards away, Cooper was eating a filthy meal clad only in a sarong and a baju. His feet were bare and while he ate he probably read a detective story. After dinner Mr. Warburton sat down to write a letter. The Sultan was away, but he wrote, privately and confidentially, to his representative. Cooper did his work very well, he said, but the fact was that he couldn't get on with him. They were getting dreadfully on each other's nerves and he would look upon it as a very great favor if Cooper could be transferred to another post.

He despatched the letter next morning by special messenger. The answer came a fortnight later with the month's mail. It was a private note and ran as follows:

MY DEAR WARBURTON:

I do not want to answer your letter officially and so I am writing you a few lines myself. Of course if you insist I will put the matter up to the Sultan, but I think you would be much wiser to drop it. I know Cooper is a rough diamond, but he is capable, and he had a pretty thin time in the war, and I think he should be given every chance. I think you are a little too much inclined to attach importance to a man's social position. You must remember that times have changed. Of course it's a very good thing for a man to be a gentleman, but it's better that he should be competent and hard-working. I think if you'll exercise a little tolerance you'll get on very well with Cooper.

Yours very sincerely,

RICHARD TEMPLE.

The letter dropped from Mr. Warburton's hand. It was easy to read between the lines. Dick Temple, whom he had known for twenty years, Dick Temple, who came from quite a good county family, thought him a snob and for that reason had no patience with his request. Mr. Warburton felt on a sudden discouraged with life. The world of which he was a part had passed away, and the future belonged to a meaner generation. Cooper represented it and Cooper he hated with all his heart.

He stretched out his hand to fill his glass and at the gesture his head-boy stepped forward.

"I didn't know you were there."

The boy picked up the official letter. Ah, that was why he was waiting.

"Does Tuan Cooper go, Tuan?"

"No."

"There will be a misfortune."

For a moment the words conveyed nothing to his lassitude. But only for a moment. He sat up in his chair and looked at the boy. He was all attention.

"What do you mean by that?"

"Tuan Cooper is not behaving rightly with Abas."

Mr. Warburton shrugged his shoulders. How should a man like Cooper know how to treat servants? Mr. Warburton knew the type: he would be grossly familiar with them at one moment and rude and inconsiderate the next.

"Let Abas go back to his family."

"Tuan Cooper holds back his wages so that he may not run away. He has paid him nothing for three months. I tell him to be patient. But he is angry, he will not listen to reason. If the tuan continues to use him ill there will be a misfortune."

"You were right to tell me."

The fool! Did he know so little of the Malays as to think he could safely injure them? It would serve him damned well right if he got a kris in his back. A kris. Mr. Warburton's heart seemed on a sudden to miss a beat. He had only to let things take their course and one fine day he would be rid of Cooper. He smiled faintly as the phrase, a masterly inactivity, crossed his mind. And now his heart beat a little quicker, for he saw the man he hated lying on his face in a pathway of the jungle with a knife in his back. A fit end for the cad and the bully. Mr. Warburton sighed. It was his duty to warn him and of course he must do it. He wrote a brief and formal note to Cooper asking him to come to the Fort at once.

In ten minutes Cooper stood before him. They had not spoken to one another since the day when Mr. Warburton had nearly struck him. He did not now ask him to sit down.

"Did you wish to see me?" Cooper asked.

He was untidy and none too clean. His face and hands were covered with little red blotches where mosquitoes had bitten him and he had scratched himself till the blood came. His long, thin face bore a sullen look.

"I understand that you are again having trouble with your servants. Abas, my head-boy's nephew, complains that you have held back his wages for three months. I consider it a most arbitrary proceeding. The lad wishes to leave you, and I certainly do not blame him. I must insist on your paying what is due to him."

"I don't choose that he should leave me. I am holding back his wages as a pledge of his good behaviour."

"You do not know the Malay character. The Malays are very sensitive to injury and ridicule. They are passionate and revengeful. It is my duty to warn you that if you drive this boy beyond a certain point you run a great risk."

Cooper gave a contemptuous chuckle.

"What do you think he'll do?"

"I think he'll kill you."

"Why should you mind?"

"Oh, I wouldn't," replied Mr. Warburton, with a faint laugh. "I should bear it with the utmost fortitude. But I feel the official obligation to give you a proper warning."

"Do you think I'm afraid of a damned nigger?"

"It's a matter of entire indifference to me."

"Well, let me tell you this, I know how to take care of myself; that boy Abas is a dirty, thieving rascal, and if he tries any monkey tricks on me, by God, I'll wring his bloody neck."

"That was all I wished to say to you," said Mr. Warburton. "Good evening."

Mr. Warburton gave him a little nod of dismissal. Cooper flushed, did not for a moment know what to say or do, turned on his heel and stumbled out of the room. Mr. Warburton watched him go with an icy smile on his lips. He had done his duty. But what would he have thought had he known that when Cooper got back to his bungalow, so silent and cheerless, he threw himself down on his bed and in his bitter loneliness on a sudden lost all control of himself? Painful sobs tore his chest and heavy tears rolled down his thin cheeks.

After this Mr. Warburton seldom saw Cooper, and never spoke to him. He read his *Times* every morning, did his work at the office, took his exercise, dressed for dinner, dined and sat by the river smoking his cheroot. If by chance he ran across Cooper he cut him dead. Each, though never for a moment unconscious of the propinquity, acted as though the other did not exist. Time did nothing to assuage their animosity. They watched one another's actions and each knew what the other did. Though Mr. Warburton had been a keen shot in his youth, with age he had acquired a distaste for killing the wild things of the jungle, but on Sundays and holidays Cooper went out with his gun: if he got something it was a triumph over Mr. Warburton; if not, Mr. Warburton shrugged his shoulders and chuckled. These counter-jumpers trying to be sportsmen! Christmas was a bad time for both of them; they ate their dinners alone, each in his own quarters, and they got deliberately drunk. They were the only white men within two hundred miles and they lived within shouting distance of each other. At the beginning of the year Cooper went down with fever, and when Mr. Warburton caught sight of him again he was surprised to see how thin he had grown. He looked ill and worn. The solitude, so much more unnatural because it was due to no necessity, was getting on his nerves. It was getting on Mr. Warburton's too, and often he could not sleep at night. He lay awake brooding. Cooper was drinking heavily and surely the breaking point was near; but in his dealings with the natives he took care to do nothing that might expose him to his chief's rebuke. They fought a grim and silent battle with one another. It was a test of endurance. The months passed, and neither gave sign of weakening. They were like men dwelling in regions of eternal night, and their souls were oppressed with the knowledge that never would the day dawn for them. It looked as though their lives would continue for ever in this dull and hideous monotony of hatred.

And when at last the inevitable happened it came upon Mr. Warburton with all the shock of the unexpected. Cooper accused the boy Abas of stealing some of his clothes, and when the boy denied the theft took him by the scruff of the neck and kicked him down the steps of the bungalow. The boy demanded his wages, and Cooper flung at his head every word of abuse he knew. If he saw him in the compound in an hour he would hand him over to the police. Next morning the boy waylaid him outside the Fort when he was walking over to his office, and again demanded his wages. Cooper struck him in the face with his clenched fist. The boy fell to the ground and got up with blood streaming from his nose.

Cooper walked on and set about his work. But he could not attend to it. The blow had calmed his irritation, and he knew that he had gone too far. He was worried. He felt ill, miserable and discouraged. In the adjoining office sat Mr. Warburton, and his impulse was to go and tell him what he had done; he made a movement in his chair, but he knew with what icy scorn he would listen to the story. He could see his patronizing smile. For a moment he had an uneasy fear of what Abas might do. Warburton had warned him all right. He sighed. What a fool he had been! But he shrugged his shoulders impatiently. He did not care; a fat lot he had to live for. It was all Warburton's fault; if he hadn't put his back up nothing like this would have happened. Warburton had made life a hell for him from the start. The snob. But they were all like that: it was because he was a Colonial. It was a damned shame that he had never got his commission in the war; he was as good as any one else. They were a lot of dirty snobs. He was damned if he was going to knuckle under now. Of course Warburton would hear of what had happened; the old devil knew everything. He wasn't afraid. He wasn't afraid of any Malay in Borneo, and Warburton could go to blazes.

He was right in thinking that Mr. Warburton would know what had happened. His head-boy told him when he went in to tiffin.

"Where is your nephew now?"

"I do not know, Tuan. He has gone."

Mr. Warburton remained silent. After luncheon as a rule he slept a little, but today he found himself very wide awake. His eyes involuntarily sought the bungalow where Cooper was now resting.

The idiot! Hesitation for a little was in Mr. Warburton's mind. Did the man know in what peril he was? He supposed he ought to send for him. But each time he had tried to reason with Cooper, Cooper had insulted him. Anger, furious anger welled up suddenly in Mr. Warburton's heart, so that the veins on his temples stood out and he clenched his fists. The cad had had his warning. Now let him take what was coming to him. It was no business of his and if anything happened it was not his fault. But perhaps they would wish in Kuala Solor that they had taken his advice and transferred Cooper to another station.

He was strangely restless that night. After dinner he walked up and down the verandah. When the boy went away to his own quarters, Mr. Warburton asked him whether anything had been seen of Abas.

"No, Tuan, I think maybe he has gone to the village of his mother's brother."

Mr. Warburton gave him a sharp glance, but the boy was looking down and their eyes did not meet. Mr. Warburton went down to the river and sat in his arbor. But peace was denied him. The river flowed ominously silent. It was like a great serpent gliding with sluggish movement towards the sea. And the trees of the jungle over the water were heavy with a breathless menace. No bird sang. No breeze ruffled the leaves of the cassias. All around him it seemed as though something waited.

He walked across the garden to the road. He had Cooper's bungalow in full view from there. There was a light in his sitting-room and across the road floated the sound of rag-time. Cooper was playing his gramophone. Mr. Warburton shuddered; he had never got over his instinctive dislike of that instrument. But for that he would have gone over and spoken to Cooper. He turned and went back to his own house. He read late into the night, and at last he slept. But he did not sleep very long, he had terrible dreams, and he seemed to be awakened by a cry. Of course that was a dream too, for no cry—from the bungalow for instance —could be heard in his room. He lay awake till dawn. Then he heard hurried steps and the sound of voices, his head-boy burst suddenly into the room without his fez, and Mr. Warburton's heart stood still.

"Tuan, Tuan."

Mr. Warburton jumped out of bed.

"I'll come at once."

He put on his slippers, and in his sarong and pyjama-jacket walked across his compound and into Cooper's. Cooper was lying in bed, with his mouth open, and a kris sticking in his heart. He had been killed in his sleep. Mr. Warburton started, but not because he had not expected to see just such a sight, he started because he felt in himself a sudden glow of exultation. A great burden had been lifted from his shoulders.

Cooper was quite cold. Mr. Warburton took the kris out of the wound, it had been thrust in with such force that he had to use an effort to get it out, and looked at it. He recognized it. It was a kris that a dealer had offered him some weeks before and which he knew Cooper had bought.

"Where is Abas?" he asked sternly.

"Abas is at the village of his mother's brother."

The sergeant of the native police was standing at the foot of the bed.

"Take two men and go to the village and arrest him."

Mr. Warburton did what was immediately necessary. With set face he gave orders. His words were short and peremptory. Then he went back to the Fort. He shaved and had his bath, dressed and went into the dining-room. By the side of his plate *The Times* in its wrapper lay waiting for him. He helped himself to some fruit. The head-boy poured out his tea while the second handed him a dish of eggs. Mr. Warburton ate with a good appetite. The head-boy waited.

"What is it?" asked Mr. Warburton.

"Tuan, Abas, my nephew, was in the house of his mother's brother all night. It can be proved. His uncle will swear that he did not leave the kampong."

Mr. Warburton turned upon him with a frown.

"Tuan Cooper was killed by Abas. You know it as well as I know it. Justice must be done."

"Tuan, you would not hang him?"

Mr. Warburton hesitated an instant, and though his voice remained set and stern a change came into his eyes. It was a flicker which the Malay was quick to notice and across his own eyes flashed an answering look of understanding.

"The provocation was very great. Abas will be sentenced to a term of imprisonment." There was a pause while Mr. Warburton helped himself to marmalade. "When he has served a part of his sentence in prison I will take him into this house as a boy. You can train him in his duties. I have no doubt that in the house of Tuan Cooper he got into bad habits."

"Shall Abas give himself up, Tuan?"

"It would be wise of him."

The boy withdrew. Mr. Warburton took his *Times* and neatly slit the wrapper. He loved to unfold the heavy, rustling pages. The morning, so fresh and cool, was delicious and for a moment his eyes wandered out over his garden with a friendly glance. A great weight had been lifted from his mind. He turned to the columns in which were announced the births, deaths, and marriages. That was what he always looked at first. A name he knew caught his attention. Lady Ormskirk had had a son at last. By George, how pleased the old dowager must be! He would write her a note of congratulation by the next mail.

Abas would make a very good house-boy.

That fool Cooper!

THE BLUE CROSS

The detective story, of all the varieties included in this book,
probably stands least in need of an introduction. If anything, it
needs an apology. No one these days—or nights—must *read*
this sort of thing; the television screen is heavily charged
with mystery, and the detection of crime is everybody's business.
But still—there's Chesterton. When we began to search for
something really exceptional in crime and mystery and related
thrills, we turned at once to "The Blue Cross," a classic of
its kind, notable for its style and even for its philosophical
overtones, a rare combination. Written by a master of the
paradox, the story is full of surprises. Two of the main
characters are "Valentin himself, the head of the Paris police
and the most famous investigator of the world . . . coming
from Brussels to London to make the greatest arrest of
the century"; and his quarry, that "colossus of crime," Flambeau,
who was "in his best days (I mean, of course, his worst) . . .
a figure as statuesque and international as the Kaiser." There is,
to be sure, a third character, but we resist the temptation to
say anything about him here, for in doing so we might spoil the
reader's delight in meeting for the first time—the little priest.

Between the silver ribbon of morning and the green glittering
ribbon of sea, the boat touched Harwich and let loose a swarm of folk
like flies, among whom the man we must follow was by no means conspicuous—nor wished to be. There was nothing notable about him, except a slight contrast between the holiday gayety of his clothes and the
official gravity of his face. His clothes included a slight, pale gray
jacket, a white waistcoat, and a silver straw hat with a gray-blue ribbon.
His lean face was dark by contrast, and ended in a curt black beard that
looked Spanish and suggested an Elizabethan ruff. He was smoking a
cigarette with the seriousness of an idler. There was nothing about him
to indicate the fact that the gray jacket covered a loaded revolver, that
the white waistcoat covered a police card, or that the straw hat covered

one of the most powerful intellects in Europe. For this was Valentin himself, the head of the Paris police and the most famous investigator of the world; and he was coming from Brussels to London to make the greatest arrest of the century.

Flambeau was in England. The police of three countries had tracked the great criminal at last from Ghent to Brussels, from Brussels to the Hook of Holland; and it was conjectured that he would take some advantage of the unfamiliarity and confusion of the Eucharistic Congress, then taking place in London. Probably he would travel as some minor clerk or secretary connected with it; but, of course, Valentin could not be certain; nobody could be certain about Flambeau.

It is many years now since this colossus of crime suddenly ceased keeping the world in a turmoil; and when he ceased, as they said after the death of Roland, there was a great quiet upon the earth. But in his best days (I mean, of course, his worst) Flambeau was a figure as statuesque and international as the Kaiser. Almost every morning the daily paper announced that he had escaped the consequences of one extraordinary crime by committing another. He was a Gascon of gigantic stature and bodily daring; and the wildest tales were told of his outburst of athletic humor; how he turned the *juge d'instruction* upside down and stood him on his head, "to clear his mind"; how he ran down the Rue de Rivoli with a policeman under each arm. It is due to him to say that his fantastic physical strength was generally employed in such bloodless though undignified scenes; his real crimes were chiefly those of ingenious and wholesale robbery. But each of his thefts was almost a new sin, and would make a story by itself. It was he who ran the great Tyrolean Dairy Company in London, with no dairies, no cows, no carts, no milk, but with some thousand subscribers. These he served by the simple operation of moving the little milk cans outside people's doors to the doors of his own customers. It was he who had kept up an unaccountable and close correspondence with a young lady whose whole letter-bag was intercepted, by the extraordinary trick of photographing his messages infinitesimally small upon the slides of a microscope. A sweeping simplicity, however, marked many of his experiments. It is said that he once repainted all the numbers in a street in the dead of night merely to divert one traveler into a trap. It is quite certain that he invented a portable pillar-box, which he put up at corners in quiet suburbs on the chance of strangers dropping postal orders into it. Lastly, he was known to be a startling acrobat; despite his huge figure, he could leap like a grasshopper and melt into the tree-tops like a monkey. Hence the great Valentin, when he set out to find Flambeau, was perfectly aware that his adventures would not end when he had found him.

But how was he to find him? On this the great Valentin's ideas were still in process of settlement.

There was one thing which Flambeau, with all his dexterity of disguise, could not cover, and that was his singular height. If Valentin's quick eye had caught a tall apple-woman, a tall grenadier, or even a tolerably tall duchess, he might have arrested them on the spot. But all along his train there was nobody that could be a disguised Flambeau, any more than a cat could be a disguised giraffe. About the people on the boat he had already satisfied himself; and the people picked up at Harwich or on the journey limited themselves with certainty to six. There was a short railway official traveling up to the terminus, three fairly short market gardeners picked up two stations afterwards, one very short widow lady going up from a small Essex town, and a very short Roman Catholic priest going up from a small Essex village. When it came to the last case, Valentin gave it up and almost laughed. The little priest was so much the essence of those Eastern flats; he had a face as round and dull as a Norfolk dumpling; he had eyes as empty as the North Sea; he had several brown paper parcels, which he was quite incapable of collecting. The Eucharistic Congress had doubtless sucked out of their local stagnation many such creatures, blind and helpless, like moles disinterred. Valentin was a skeptic in the severe style of France, and could have no love for priests. But he could have pity for them, and this one might have provoked pity in anybody. He had a large, shabby umbrella, which constantly fell on the floor. He did not seem to know which was the right end of his return ticket. He explained with a moon-calf simplicity to everybody in the carriage that he had to be careful, because he had something made of real silver "with blue stones" in one of his brown-paper parcels. His quaint blending of Essex flatness with saintly simplicity continuously amused the Frenchman till the priest arrived (somehow) at Tottenham with all his parcels, and came back for his umbrella. When he did the last, Valentin even had the good nature to warn him not to take care of the silver by telling everybody about it. But to whomever he talked, Valentin kept his eye open for some one else; he looked out steadily for any one, rich or poor, male or female, who was well up to six feet; for Flambeau was four inches above it.

He alighted at Liverpool Street, however, quite conscientiously secure that he had not missed the criminal so far. He then went to Scotland Yard to regularize his position and arrange for help in case of need; he then lit another cigarette and went for a long stroll in the streets of London. As he was walking in the streets and squares beyond Victoria, he paused suddenly and stood. It was a quaint, quiet square, very typical of London, full of an accidental stillness. The tall, flat houses round looked at once prosperous and uninhabited; the square of shrubbery in the center looked as deserted as a green Pacific islet. One of the four sides was much higher than the rest, like a dais; and the line of this side was broken by one of London's admirable accidents—a restaurant that looked as if it had strayed from Soho. It was an unreasonably attractive object, with dwarf plants in pots and long, striped blinds of lemon yellow and white. It stood specially high above the street, and in the usual patchwork way of London, a flight of steps from the street ran up to meet the front door almost as a fire-escape might run up to a first-floor window. Valentin stood and smoked in front of the yellow-white blinds and considered them long.

The most incredible thing about miracles is that they happen. A few clouds in heaven do come together into the staring shape of one human eye. A tree does stand up in the landscape of a doubtful journey in the exact and elaborate shape of a note of interrogation. I have seen both these things myself within the last few days. Nelson does die in the instant of victory; and a man named Williams does quite accidentally murder a man named Williamson; it sounds like a sort of infanticide. In short, there is in life an element of elfin coincidence which people reckoning on the prosaic may perpetually miss. As it has been well expressed in the paradox of Poe, wisdom should reckon on the unforeseen.

Aristide Valentin was unfathomably French; and the French intelligence is intelligence specially and solely. He was not "a thinking machine"; for that is a brainless phrase of modern fatalism and materialism. A machine only *is* a machine because it cannot think. But he was a thinking man, and a plain man at the same time. All his wonderful successes, that looked like conjuring, had been gained by plodding logic, by clear and commonplace French thought. The French electrify the world not by starting any paradox, they electrify it by carrying out a truism. They carry a truism so far—as in the French Revolution. But exactly because Valentin understood reason, he understood the limits of reason. Only a man who knows nothing of motors talks of motoring without petrol; only a man who knows nothing of reason talks of reasoning without strong, undisputed first principles. Here he had no strong first principles. Flambeau had been missed at Harwich; and if he was in London at all, he might be anything from a tall tramp on Wimbledon Common to a tall toastmaster at the Hôtel Métropole. In such a naked state of nescience, Valentin had a view and a method of his own.

In such cases he reckoned on the unforeseen. In such cases, when he could not follow the train of the reasonable, he coldly and carefully followed the train of the unreasonable. Instead of going to the right places—banks, police stations, rendezvous—he systematically went to the wrong places; knocked at every empty house, turned down every *cul de sac,* went up every lane blocked with rubbish, went round every crescent that led him uselessly out of the way. He defended this crazy course quite logically. He said that if one had a clue this was the worst way; but if one had no clue at all it was the best, because there was just the chance that any oddity that caught the eye of the pursuer might be the same that had caught the eye of the pursued. Somewhere a man must begin, and it had better be just where another man might stop. Something about that flight of steps up to the shop, something about the quietude and quaintness of the restaurant, roused all the detective's rare romantic fancy and made him resolve to strike at random. He went up the steps, and sitting down at a table by the window, asked for a cup of black coffee.

It was half-way through the morning, and he had not breakfasted; the slight litter of other breakfasts stood about on the table to remind him of his hunger; and adding a poached egg to his order, he proceeded musingly to shake some white sugar into his coffee, thinking all the time about Flambeau. He remembered how Flambeau had escaped, once by a pair of nail scissors, and once by a house on fire; once by having to pay for an unstamped letter, and once by getting people to look through a telescope at a comet that might destroy the world. He thought his detective brain as good as the criminal's, which was true. But he fully realized the disadvantage. "The criminal is the creative artist; the detective only the critic," he said with a sour smile, and lifted his coffee cup to his lips slowly, and put it down very quickly. He had put salt in it.

He looked at the vessel from which the silvery powder had come; it was certainly a sugar-basin; as unmistakably meant for sugar as a champagne bottle for champagne. He wondered why they should keep salt in it. He looked to see if there were any more orthodox vessels. Yes; there were two salt-cellars quite full. Perhaps there was some specialty in the condiment in the salt-cellars. He tasted it; it was sugar. Then he looked round at the restaurant with a refreshed air of interest, to see if there were any other traces of that singular artistic taste which puts the sugar in the salt-cellars and the salt in the sugar-basin. Except for an odd splash of some dark fluid on one of the white-papered walls, the whole place appeared neat, cheerful and ordinary. He rang the bell for the waiter.

When that official hurried up, fuzzy-haired and somewhat blear-eyed at that early hour, the detective (who was not without an appreciation of the simpler forms of humor) asked him to taste the sugar and see if it was up to the high reputation of the hotel. The result was that the waiter yawned suddenly and woke up.

"Do you play this delicate joke on your customers every morning?" inquired Valentin. "Does changing the salt and sugar never pall on you as a jest?"

The waiter, when this irony grew clearer, stammeringly assured him that the establishment had certainly no such intention; it must be a most curious mistake. He picked up the sugar-basin and looked at it; he picked up the salt-cellar and looked at that, his face growing more and more bewildered. At last he abruptly excused himself, and hurrying away, returned in a few seconds with the proprietor. The proprietor also examined the sugar-basin and then the salt-cellar; the proprietor also looked bewildered.

Suddenly the waiter seemed to grow inarticulate with a rush of words. "I zink," he stuttered eagerly, "I zink it is those two clergymen."

"What two clergymen?"

"The two clergymen," said the waiter, "that threw soup at the wall."

"Threw soup at the wall?" repeated Valentin, feeling sure this must be some singular Italian metaphor.

"Yes, yes," said the attendant excitedly, and pointing at the dark splash on the white paper; "threw it over there on the wall."

Valentin looked his query at the proprietor, who came to his rescue with fuller reports.

"Yes, sir," he said, "it's quite true, though I don't suppose it has anything to do with the sugar and salt. Two clergymen came in and drank soup here very early, as soon as the shutters were taken down. They were both very quiet, respectable people; one of them paid the bill and went out; the other, who seemed a slower coach altogether, was some minutes longer getting his things together. But he went at last. Only, the instant before he stepped into the street he deliberately picked up his cup, which he had only half emptied, and threw the soup slap on the wall. I was in the back room myself, and so was the waiter; so I could only rush out in time to find the wall splashed and the shop empty. It don't do any particular damage, but it was confounded cheek; and I tried to catch the men in the street. They were too far off though; I only noticed they went round the next corner into Carstairs Street."

The detective was on his feet, hat settled and stick in his hand. He had already decided that in the universal darkness of his mind he could only follow the first odd finger that pointed; and this finger was odd enough. Paying his bill and clashing the glass doors behind him, he was soon swinging round into the other street.

It was fortunate that even in such fevered moments his eye was cool and quick. Something in a shop-front went by him like a mere flash; yet he went back to look at it. The shop was a popular greengrocer and fruiterer's, an array of goods set out in the open air and plainly ticketed with their names and prices. In the two most prominent compartments were two heaps, of oranges and of nuts respectively. On the heap of nuts lay a scrap of cardboard, on which was written in bold, blue chalk, "Best tangerine oranges, two a penny." On the oranges was the equally clear and exact description, "Finest Brazil nuts, 4d. a lb." M. Valentin looked at these two placards and fancied he had met this highly subtle form of humor before, and that somewhat recently. He drew the attention of the red-faced fruiterer, who was looking rather sullenly up and down the street, to this inaccuracy in his advertisements. The fruiterer said nothing, but sharply put each card into its proper place. The detective, leaning elegantly on his walking-cane, continued to scrutinize the shop. At last he said, "Pray excuse my apparent irrelevance, my good sir, but I should like to ask you a question in experimental psychology and the association of ideas."

The red-faced shopman regarded him with an eye of menace; but he continued gayly, swinging his cane. "Why," he pursued, "why are two tickets wrongly placed in a greengrocer's shop like a shovel hat that has come to London for a holiday? Or, in case I do not make myself clear, what is the mystical association which connects the idea of nuts marked as oranges with the idea of two clergymen, one tall and the other short?"

The eyes of the tradesman stood out of his head like a snail's; he really seemed for an instant likely to fling himself upon the stranger. At last he stammered angrily: "I don't know what you 'ave to do with it, but if you're one of their friends, you can tell 'em from me that I'll knock their silly 'eads off, parsons or no parsons, if they upset my apples again."

"Indeed," asked the detective, with great sympathy. "Did they upset your apples?"

"One of 'em did," said the heated shopman; "rolled 'em all over the street. I'd 'ave caught the fool but for havin' to pick 'em up."

"Which way did these parsons go?" asked Valentin.

"Up that second road on the left-hand side, and then across the square," said the other promptly.

"Thanks," replied Valentin, and vanished like a fairy. On the other side of the second square he found a policeman, and said: "This is urgent, constable; have you seen two clergymen in shovel hats?" ·

The policeman began to chuckle heavily. "I 'ave, sir; and if you arst me, one of 'em was drunk. He stood in the middle of the road that bewildered that—"

"Which way did they go?" snapped Valentin.

"They took one of them yellow buses over there," answered the man; "them that go to Hampstead."

Valentin produced his official card and said very rapidly: "Call up two of your men to come with me in pursuit," and crossed the road with such contagious energy that the ponderous policeman was moved to almost agile obedience. In a minute and a half the French detective was joined on the opposite pavement by an inspector and a man in plain clothes.

"Well, sir," began the former, with smiling importance, "and what may—?"

Valentin pointed suddenly with his cane. "I'll tell you on the top of that omnibus," he said, and was darting and dodging across the tangle of the traffic. When all three sank panting on the top seats of the yellow vehicle, the inspector said: "We could go four times as quick in a taxi."

"Quite true," replied their leader placidly, "if we only had an idea of where we were going."

"Well, where *are* you going?" asked the other, staring.

Valentin smoked frowningly for a few seconds; then, removing his cigarette, he said: "If you *know* what a man's doing, get in front of him; but if you want to guess what he's doing, keep behind him. Stray when he strays; stop when he stops; travel as slowly as he. Then you may see what he saw and may act as he acted. All we can do is to keep our eyes skinned for a queer thing."

"What sort of queer thing do you mean?" asked the inspector.

"Any sort of queer thing," answered Valentin, and relapsed into obstinate silence.

The yellow omnibus crawled up the northern roads for what seemed like hours on end; the great detective would not explain further, and perhaps his assistants felt a silent and growing doubt of his errand. Perhaps, also, they felt a silent and growing desire for lunch, for the hours crept long past the normal luncheon hour, and the long roads of the North London suburbs seemed to shoot out into length after length like an infernal telescope. It was one of those journeys on which a man perpetually feels that now at last he must have come to the end of the universe, and then finds he has only come to the beginning of Tufnell Park. London died away in draggled taverns and dreary scrubs, and then was unaccountably born again in blazing high streets and blatant hotels. It was like passing through thirteen separate vulgar cities all just touching each other. But though the winter twilight was already threatening the road ahead of them, the Parisian detective still sat silent and watchful, eyeing the frontage of the streets that slid by on either side. By the time they had left Camden Town behind, the policemen were nearly asleep; at least, they gave something like a jump as Valentin leaped erect, struck a hand on each man's shoulder, and shouted to the driver to stop.

They tumbled down the steps into the road without realizing why they had been disolodged; when they looked round for enlightenment they found Valentin triumphantly pointing his finger towards a window on the left side of the road. It was a large window, forming part of the long façade of a gilt and palatial public-house; it was the part reserved for respectable dining, and labeled "Restaurant." This window, like all the rest along the frontage of the hotel, was of frosted and figured glass; but in the middle of it was a big, black smash, like a star in the ice.

"Our cue at last," cried Valentin, waving his stick: "the place with the broken window."

"What window? What cue?" asked his principal assistant. "Why, what proof is there that this has anything to do with them?"

Valentin almost broke his bamboo stick with rage.

"Proof!" he cried. "Good God! the man is looking for proof! Why, of course, the chances are twenty to one that it has *nothing* to do with them. But what else can we do? Don't you see we must either follow one wild possibility or else go home to bed?" He banged his way into the restaurant, followed by his companions, and they were soon seated at a late luncheon at a little table, and looking at the star of smashed glass from the inside. Not that it was very informative to them even then.

"Got your window broken, I see," said Valentin to the waiter as he paid the bill.

"Yes, sir," answered the attendant, bending busily over the change, to which Valentin silently added an enormous tip. The waiter straightened himself with mild but unmistakable animation.

"Ah, yes, sir," he said. "Very odd thing, that, sir."

"Indeed? Tell us about it," said the detective with careless curiosity.

"Well, two gents in black came in," said the waiter; "two of those foreign parsons that are running about. They had a cheap and quiet little lunch, and one of them paid for it and went out. The other was just going out to join him when I looked at my change again and found he'd paid me more than three times too much. 'Here,' I says to the chap who was nearly out of the door, 'you've paid too much.' 'Oh,' he says, very cool, 'have we?' 'Yes,' I says, and picks up the bill to show him. Well, that was a knockout."

"What do you mean?" asked his interlocutor.

"Well, I'd have sworn on seven Bibles that I'd put 4s. on that bill. But now I saw I'd put 14s., as plain as paint."

"Well?" cried Valentin, moving slowly, but with burning eyes, "and then?"

"The parson at the door he says all serene, 'Sorry to confuse your accounts, but it'll pay for the window.' 'What window?' I says. 'The one I'm going to break,' he says, and smashed that blessed pane with his umbrella."

All three inquirers made an exclamation; and the inspector said under his breath, "Are we after escaped lunatics?" The waiter went on with some relish for the ridiculous story:

"I was so knocked silly for a second, I couldn't do anything. The man marched out of the place and joined his friend just round the corner. Then they went so quick up Bullock Street that I couldn't catch them, though I ran round the bars to do it."

"Bullock Street," said the detective, and shot up that thoroughfare as quickly as the strange couple he pursued.

649

Their journey now took them through bare brick ways like tunnels; streets with few lights and even with few windows; streets that seemed built out of the blank backs of everything and everywhere. Dusk was deepening, and it was not easy even for the London policemen to guess in what exact direction they were treading. The inspector, however, was pretty certain that they would eventually strike some part of Hampstead Heath. Abruptly one bulging gas-lit window broke the blue twilight like a bull's-eye lantern; and Valentin stopped an instant before a little garish sweetstuff shop. After an instant's hesitation he went in; he stood amid the gaudy colors of the confectionery with entire gravity and bought thirteen chocolate cigars with a certain care. He was clearly preparing an opening, but he did not need one.

An angular, elderly young woman in the shop had regarded his elegant appearance with a merely automatic inquiry; but when she saw the door behind him blocked with the blue uniform of the inspector, her eyes seemed to wake up.

"Oh," she said, "if you've come about that parcel, I've sent it off already."

"Parcel!" repeated Valentin; and it was his turn to look inquiring.

"I mean the parcel the gentleman left—the clergyman gentleman."

"For goodness' sake," said Valentin, leaning forward with his first real confession of eagerness, "for Heaven's sake tell us what happened exactly."

"Well," said the woman a little doubtfully, "the clergymen came in about half an hour ago and bought some peppermints and talked a bit, and then went off towards the Heath. But a second after, one of them runs back into the shop and says, 'Have I left a parcel?' Well, I looked everywhere and couldn't see one; so he says, 'Never mind; but if it should turn up, please post it to this address,' and he left me the address and a shilling for my trouble. And sure enough, though I thought I'd looked everywhere, I found he'd left a brown paper parcel, so I posted it to the place he said. I can't remember the address now; it was somewhere in Westminster. But as the thing seemed so important, I thought perhaps the police had come about it."

"So they have," said Valentin shortly. "Is Hampstead Heath near here?"

"Straight on for fifteen minutes," said the woman, "and you'll come right out on the open." Valentin sprang out of the shop and began to run. The other detectives followed him at a reluctant trot.

The street they threaded was so narrow and shut in by shadows that when they came out unexpectedly into the void common and vast sky they were startled to find the evening still so light and clear. A perfect dome of peacock-green sank into gold amid the blackening trees and the dark violet distances. The glowing green tint was just deep enough to pick out in points of crystal one or two stars. All that was left of the day-light lay in a golden glitter across the edge of Hampstead and that popular hollow which is called the Vale of Health. The holiday makers who roam this region had not wholly dispersed; a few couples sat shapelessly on benches; and here and there a distant girl still shrieked in one of the swings. The glory of heaven deepened and darkened around the sublime vulgarity of man; and standing on the slope and looking across the valley, Valentin beheld the thing which he sought.

Among the black and breaking groups in that distance was one especially black which did not break—a group of two figures clerically clad. Though they seemed as small as insects, Valentin could see that one of them was much smaller than the other. Though the other had a student's stoop and an inconspicuous manner, he could see that the man was well over six feet high. He shut his teeth and went forward, whirling his stick impatiently. By the time he had substantially diminished the distance and magnified the two black figures as in a vast microscope, he had perceived something else; something which startled him, and yet which he had somehow expected. Whoever was the tall priest, there could be no doubt about the identity of the short one. It was his friend of the Harwich train, the stumpy little *curé* of Essex whom he had warned about his brown paper parcels.

Now, so far as this went, everything fitted in finally and rationally enough. Valentin had learned by his inquiries that morning that a Father Brown from Essex was bringing up a silver cross with sapphires, a relic of considerable value, to show some of the foreign priests at the congress. This undoubtedly was the "silver with blue stones"; and Father Brown undoubtedly was the little greenhorn in the train. Now there was nothing wonderful about the fact that what Valentin had found out Flambeau had also found out; Flambeau found out everything. Also there was nothing wonderful in the fact that when Flambeau heard of a sapphire cross he should try to steal it; that was the most natural thing in all natural history. And most certainly there was nothing wonderful about the fact that Flambeau should have it all his own way with such a silly sheep as the man with the umbrella and the parcels. He was the sort of man whom anybody could lead on a string to the North Pole; it was not surprising that an actor like Flambeau, dressed as another priest, could lead him to Hampstead Heath. So far the crime seemed clear enough; and while the detective pitied the priest for his helplessness, he almost despised Flambeau for condescending to so gullible a victim. But when Valentin thought of all that had happened in between, of all that had led him to his triumph, he racked his brains for the smallest rhyme or reason in it. What had the stealing of a blue-and-silver cross from a priest from Essex to do with chucking soup at wall paper? What had it to do with calling nuts oranges, or with paying for windows first and breaking them afterwards? He had come to the end of his chase; yet somehow he had missed the middle of it. When he failed (which was seldom), he had usually grasped the clue, but nevertheless missed the criminal. Here he had grasped the criminal, but still he could not grasp the clue.

The two figures that they followed were crawling like black flies across the huge green contour of a hill. They were evidently sunk in conversation, and perhaps did not notice where they were going; but they were certainly going to the wilder and more silent heights of the Heath. As their pursuers gained on them, the latter had to use the undignified attitudes of the deer-stalker, to crouch behind clumps of trees and even to crawl prostrate in deep grass. By these ungainly ingenuities the hunters even came close enough to the quarry to hear the murmur of the discussion, but no word could be distinguished except the word "reason" recurring frequently in a high and almost childish voice. Once over an abrupt dip of land and a dense tangle of thickets, the detectives actually lost the two figures they were following. They did not find the trail again for an agonizing ten minutes, and then it led round the brow of a great dome of hill overlooking an amphitheater of rich and desolate sunset scenery. Under a tree in this commanding yet neglected spot was an old ramshackle wooden seat. On this seat sat the two priests still in serious speech together. The gorgeous green and gold still clung to the darkening horizon; but the dome above was turning slowly from peacock-green to peacock-blue, and the stars detached themselves more and more like solid jewels. Mutely motioning to his followers, Valentin contrived to creep up behind the big branching tree, and, standing there in deathly silence, heard the words of the strange priests for the first time.

After he had listened for a minute and a half, he was gripped by a devilish doubt. Perhaps he had dragged the two English policemen to the wastes of a nocturnal heath on an errand no saner than seeking figs on its thistles. For the two priests were talking exactly like priests, piously, with learning and leisure, about the most aerial enigmas of theology. The little Essex priest spoke the more simply, with his round face turned to the strengthening stars; the other talked with his head bowed, as if he were not even worthy to look at them. But no more innocently clerical conversation could have been heard in any white Italian cloister or black Spanish cathedral.

The first he heard was the tail of one of Father Brown's sentences, which ended: ". . . what they really meant in the Middle Ages by the heavens being incorruptible."

The taller priest nodded his bowed head and said:

"Ah, yes, these modern infidels appeal to their reason; but who can look at those millions of worlds and not feel that there may well be wonderful universes above us where reason is utterly unreasonable?"

"No," said the other priest: "reason is always reasonable, even in the last limbo, in the lost borderland of things. I know that people charge the Church with lowering reason, but it is just the other way. Alone on earth, the Church makes reason really supreme. Alone on earth, the Church affirms that God himself is bound by reason."

The other priest raised his austere face to the spangled sky and said: "Yet who knows if in that infinite universe—?"

"Only infinite physically," said the little priest, turning sharply in his seat, "not infinite in the sense of escaping from the laws of truth."

Valentin behind his tree was tearing his finger-nails with silent fury. He seemed almost to hear the sniggers of the English detectives whom he had brought so far on a fantastic guess only to listen to the metaphysical gossip of two mild old parsons. In his impatience he lost the equally elaborate answer of the tall cleric, and when he listened again it was Father Brown who was speaking:

"Reason and justice grip the remotest and loneliest star. Look at those stars. Don't they look as if they were single diamonds and sapphires? Well, you can imagine any mad botany or geology you please. Think of forests of adamant with leaves of brilliants. Think the moon is a blue moon, a single elephantine sapphire. But don't fancy that all that frantic astronomy would make the smallest difference to the reason and justice of conduct. On plains of opal, under cliffs cut out of pearl, you would still find a notice-board, 'Thou shalt not steal.' "

Valentin was just in the act of rising from his rigid and crouching attitude and creeping away as softly as might be, felled by the one great folly of his life. But something in the very silence of the tall priest made him stop until the latter spoke. When at last he did speak, he said simply, his head bowed and his hands on his knees:

"Well, I still think that other worlds may perhaps rise higher than our reason. The mystery of heaven is unfathomable, and I for one can only bow my head."

Then, with brow yet bent and without changing by the faintest shade his attitude or voice, he added:

"Just hand over that sapphire cross of yours, will you? We're all alone here, and I could pull you to pieces like a straw doll."

The utterly unaltered voice and attitude added a strange violence to that shocking change of speech. But the guarder of the relic only seemed to turn his head by the smallest section of the compass. He seemed still to have a somewhat foolish face turned to the stars. Perhaps he had not understood. Or, perhaps, he had understood and sat rigid with terror.

"Yes," said the tall priest, in the same low voice and in the same still posture, "yes, I am Flambeau."

Then, after a pause, he said:

"Come, will you give me that cross?"

"No," said the other, and the monosyllable had an odd sound.

Flambeau suddenly flung off all his pontifical pretensions. The great robber leaned back in his seat and laughed low but long.

"No," he cried, "you won't give it me, you proud prelate. You won't give it me, you little celibate simpleton. Shall I tell you why you won't give it me? Because I've got it already in my own breast-pocket."

The small man from Essex turned what seemed to be a dazed face in the dusk, and said, with the timid eagerness of "The Private Secretary":

"Are—are you sure?"

Flambeau yelled with delight.

"Really, you're as good as a three-act farce," he cried. "Yes, you turnip, I am quite sure. I had the sense to make a duplicate of the right parcel, and now, my friend, you've got the duplicate and I've got the jewels. An old dodge, Father Brown—a very old dodge."

"Yes," said Father Brown, and passed his hand through his hair with the same strange vagueness of manner. "Yes, I've heard of it before."

The colossus of crime leaned over to the little rustic priest with a sort of sudden interest.

"*You* have heard of it?" he asked. "Where have *you* heard of it?"

"Well, I mustn't tell you his name, of course," said the little man simply. "He was a penitent, you know. He had lived prosperously for about twenty years entirely on duplicate brown paper parcels. And so, you see, when I began to suspect you, I thought of this poor chap's way of doing it at once."

"Began to suspect me?" repeated the outlaw with increased intensity. "Did you really have the gumption to suspect me just because I brought you up to this bare part of the heath?"

"No, no," said Father Brown with an air of apology. "You see, I suspected you when we first met. It's that little bulge up the sleeve where you people have the spiked bracelet."

"How in Tartarus," cried Flambeau, "did you ever hear of the spiked bracelet?"

"Oh, one's little flock, you know!" said Father Brown, arching his eyebrows rather blankly. "When I was a curate in Hartlepool, there were three of them with spiked bracelets. So, as I suspected you from the first, don't you see, I made sure that the cross should go safe, anyhow. I'm afraid I watched you, you know. So at last I saw you change the parcels. Then, don't you see, I changed them back again. And then I left the right one behind."

"Left it behind?" repeated Flambeau, and for the first time there was another note in his voice beside his triumph.

"Well, it was like this," said the little priest, speaking in the same unaffected way. "I went back to that sweet-shop and asked if I'd left a parcel, and gave them a particular address if it turned up. Well, I knew I hadn't; but when I went away again I did. So, instead of running after me with that valuable parcel, they have sent it flying to a friend of mine in Westminster." Then he added rather sadly: "I learnt that, too, from a poor fellow in Hartlepool. He used to do it with handbags he stole at railway stations, but he's in a monastery now. Oh, one gets to know, you know," he added, rubbing his head again with the same sort of desperate apology. "We can't help it being priests. People come and tell us these things."

Flambeau tore a brown paper parcel out of his inner pocket and rent it in pieces. There was nothing but paper and sticks of lead inside it. He sprang to his feet with a gigantic gesture, and cried:

"I don't believe you. I don't believe a bumpkin like you could manage all that. I believe you've still got the stuff on you, and if you don't give it up—why, we're all alone, and I'll take it by force!"

"No," said Father Brown simply, and stood up also, "you won't take it by force. First, because I really haven't still got it. And, second, because we are not alone."

Flambeau stopped in his stride forward.

"Behind that tree," said Father Brown, pointing, "are two strong policemen and the greatest detective alive. How did they come here, do you ask? Why, I brought them, of course! How did I do it? Why, I'll tell you if you like! Lord bless you, we have to know twenty such things when we work among the criminal classes! Well, I wasn't sure you were a thief, and it would never do to make a scandal against one of our own clergy. So I just tested you to see if anything would make you show yourself. A man generally makes a small scene if he finds salt in his coffee; if he doesn't, he has some reason for keeping quiet. I changed the salt and sugar, and *you* kept quiet. A man generally objects if his bill is three times too big. If he pays it, he has some motive for passing unnoticed. I altered your bill, and *you* paid it."

The world seemed waiting for Flambeau to leap like a tiger. But he was held back as by a spell; he was stunned with the utmost curiosity.

"Well," went on Father Brown, with lumbering lucidity, "as you wouldn't leave any tracks for the police, of course somebody had to. At every place we went to, I took care to do something that would get us talked about for the rest of the day. I didn't do much harm—a splashed wall, spilt apples, a broken window; but I saved the cross, as the cross will always be saved. It is at Westminster by now. I rather wonder you didn't stop it with the Donkey's Whistle."

"With the what?" asked Flambeau.

"I'm glad you've never heard of it," said the priest, making a face.

"It's a foul thing. I'm sure you're too good a man for a Whistler. I couldn't have countered it even with the Spots myself; I'm not strong enough in the legs."

"What on earth are you talking about?" asked the other.

"Well, I did think you'd know the Spots," said Father Brown, agreeably surprised. "Oh, you can't have gone so very wrong yet!"

"How in blazes do you know all these horrors?" cried Flambeau.

The shadow of a smile crossed the round, simple face of his clerical opponent.

"Oh, by being a celibate simpleton, I suppose," he said. "Has it never struck you that a man who does next to nothing but hear men's real sins is not likely to be wholly unaware of human evil? But, as a matter of fact, another part of my trade, too, made me sure you weren't a priest."

"What?" asked the thief, almost gaping.

"You attacked reason," said Father Brown. "It's bad theology."

And even as he turned away to collect his property, the three policemen came out from under the twilight trees. Flambeau was an artist and a sportsman. He stepped back and swept Valentin a great bow.

"Do not bow to me, *mon ami,*" said Valentin with silver clearness. "Let us both bow to our master."

And they both stood an instant uncovered while the little Essex priest blinked about for his umbrella.

John Galsworthy

THE FIRST AND THE LAST

"The First and the Last," the longest story in this book and a
masterpiece of dramatic narrative, offers to the reader a
splendid opportunity to study the short story as a literary form.
Its theme is established by a searching treatment of character
and a well-managed plot. Though there is no mystery here,
the plot effectively keeps the abiding question, "How will it end?"
constantly before the reader. The setting, too, is vividly
drawn to create and sustain the atmosphere of Galsworthy's
London—from the quiet elegance of the exclusive West End
club and the richly appointed lodgings on the Thames
Embankment to the mean streets, dark alleys, and murky
dwellings of Soho. Altogether, for the student who reads this
story for its technique alone, attentive to the unobtrusive
rightness of its dialogue and closely observant of the perfection
of its narrative and descriptive detail, there are few examples
of modern fiction more rewarding.

A Biblical quotation heads this story and provides a
commentary on its theme: "So the first shall be last, and the last
first." The protagonists of the drama—one can easily imagine
it as taking place on the stage—are two brothers. Keith
Darrant is a prominent lawyer, a King's Counsel "well on
towards a judgeship," and first in the eyes of that London
society in which he is a respected leader. His ne'er-do-well
brother Larry would be last in the eyes of that same society if
the fact of his existence were so much as mentioned to the
people who make up Keith's circle of distinguished friends and
professional associates. On the fateful evening when the story
begins, Keith has been thinking: "His brother Laurence—
wasted—all through women—atrophy of will power! A man on
the edge of things; living from hand to mouth; his gifts all
down at heel! . . . Curious that their mother's blood should
have worked so differently in her two sons." Curious indeed, for,
as the events of the drama move towards the moment of
decision, it proves to be Larry's character (which his brother
fails to comprehend) as much as Keith's that must resolve the
conflict.

"So the last shall be first, and the first last."—HOLY WRIT.

It was a dark room at that hour of six in the evening, when just the single oil reading-lamp under its green shade let fall a dapple of light over the Turkey carpet; over the covers of books taken out of the bookshelves, and the open pages of the one selected; over the deep blue and gold of the coffee service on the little old stool with its Oriental embroidery. Very dark in the winter, with drawn curtains, many rows of leather-bound volumes, oak-paneled walls and ceiling. So large, too, that the lighted spot before the fire where he sat was just an oasis. But that was what Keith Darrant liked, after his day's work—the hard early morning study of his "cases," the fret and strain of the day in court; it was his rest, these two hours before dinner, with books, coffee, a pipe, and sometimes a nap. In red Turkish slippers and his old brown velvet coat, he was well suited to that framing of glow and darkness. A painter would have seized avidly on his clear-cut, yellowish face, with its black eyebrows twisting up over eyes—gray or brown, one could hardly tell, and its dark grizzling hair still plentiful, in spite of those daily hours of wig. He seldom thought of his work while he sat there, throwing off with practiced ease the strain of that long attention to the multiple threads of argument and evidence to be disentangled—work profoundly interesting, as a rule, to his clear intellect, trained to almost instinctive rejection of all but the essential, to selection of what was legally vital out of the mass of confused tactical and human detail presented to his scrutiny; yet sometimes tedious and wearing. As for instance today, when he had suspected his client of perjury, and was almost convinced that he must throw up his brief. He had disliked the weak-looking, white-faced fellow from the first, and his nervous, shifty answers, his prominent startled eyes—a type too common in these days of canting tolerations and weak humanitarianism; no good, no good!

Of the three books he had taken down, a volume of Voltaire—curious fascination that Frenchman had, for all his destructive irony!—a volume of Burton's travels, and Stevenson's *New Arabian Nights,* he had pitched upon the last. He felt, that evening, the want of something sedative, a desire to rest from thought of any kind. The court had been crowded, stuffy; the air, as he walked home, soft, sou'-westerly, charged with coming moisture, no quality of vigor in it; he felt relaxed, tired, even nervy, and for once the loneliness of his house seemed strange and comfortless.

Lowering the lamp, he turned his face towards the fire. Perhaps he would get a sleep before that boring dinner at the Tellassons'. He wished it were vacation, and Maisie back from school. A widower for many years, he had lost the habit of a woman about him; yet tonight he had a positive yearning for the society of his young daughter, with her quick ways, and bright, dark eyes. Curious what perpetual need of a woman some men had! His brother Laurence—wasted—all through women—atrophy of will power! A man on the edge of things; living from hand to mouth; his gifts all down at heel! One would have thought the Scottish strain might have saved him; and yet, when a Scotsman did begin to go downhill, who could go faster? Curious that their mother's blood should have worked so differently in her two sons. He himself had always felt he owed all his success to it.

His thoughts went off at a tangent to a certain issue troubling his legal conscience. He had not wavered in the usual assumption of omniscience, but he was by no means sure that he had given right advice. Well! without that power to decide and hold to decision in spite of misgiving, one would never have been fit for one's position at the Bar, never have been fit for anything. The longer he lived, the more certain he became of the prime necessity of virile and decisive action in all the affairs of life. A word and a blow—and the blow first! Doubts, hesitation, sentiment—the muling and puking of this twilight age—! And there welled up on his handsome face a smile that was almost devilish—the tricks of firelight are so many! It faded again in sheer drowsiness; he slept. . . .

He woke with a start, having a feeling of something out beyond the light, and without turning his head said: "What's that?" There came a sound as if somebody had caught his breath. He turned up the lamp.

"Who's there?"

A voice over by the door answered:

"Only I—Larry."

Something in the tone, or perhaps just being startled out of sleep like this, made him shiver. He said:

"I was asleep. Come in!"

It was noticeable that he did not get up, or even turn his head, now that he knew who it was, but waited, his half-closed eyes fixed on the fire, for his brother to come forward. A visit from Laurence was not an unmixed blessing. He could hear him breathing, and became conscious of a scent of whisky. Why could not the fellow at least abstain when he was coming here! It was so childish, so lacking in any sense of proportion or of decency! And he said sharply:

"Well, Larry, what is it?"

It was always something. He often wondered at the strength of that sense of trusteeship, which kept him still tolerant of the troubles, amenable to the petitions of this brother of his; or was it just "blood" feeling, a Highland sense of loyalty to kith and kin; an old-time quality which judgment and half his instincts told him was weakness, but which, in spite of all, bound him to the distressful fellow? Was he drunk now, that he kept lurking out there by the door? And he said less sharply: "Why don't you come and sit down?"

He was coming now, avoiding the light, skirting along the walls just beyond the radiance of the lamp, his feet and legs to the waist brightly lighted, but his face disintegrated in shadow, like the face of a dark ghost.

"Are you ill, man?"

Still no answer, save a shake of that head, and the passing up of a hand, out of the light, to the ghostly forehead under the disheveled hair. The scent of whisky was stronger now; and Keith thought: "He really is drunk. Nice thing for the new butler to see! If he can't behave—"

The figure against the wall heaved a sigh—so truly from an over-burdened heart that Keith was conscious with a certain dismay of not having yet fathomed the cause of this uncanny silence. He got up, and, back to the fire, said with a brutality born of nerves rather than design:

"What is it, man? Have you committed a murder, that you stand there dumb as a fish?"

For a second no answer at all, not even of breathing; then, just the whisper:

"Yes."

The sense of unreality which so helps one at moments of disaster enabled Keith to say vigorously:

"By Jove! You *have* been drinking!"

But it passed at once into deadly apprehension.

"What do you mean? Come here, where I can see you. What's the matter with you, Larry?"

With a sudden lurch and dive, his brother left the shelter of the shadow, and sank into a chair in the circle of light. And another long, broken sigh escaped him.

"There's nothing the matter with me, Keith! It's true!"

Keith stepped quickly forward, and stared down into his brother's face; and instantly he saw that it *was* true. No one could have simulated the look in those eyes—of horrified wonder, as if they would never again get on terms with the face to which they belonged. To see them squeezed the heart—only real misery could look like that. Then that sudden pity became angry bewilderment.

"What in God's name is this nonsense?"

But it was significant that he lowered his voice; went over to the door, too, to see if it were shut. Laurence had drawn his chair forward, huddling over the fire—a thin figure, a worn, high-cheek-boned face with deep-sunk blue eyes, and wavy hair all ruffled, a face that still had a certain beauty. Putting a hand on that lean shoulder, Keith said:

"Come, Larry! Pull yourself together, and drop imagination."

"It's true, I tell you; I've killed a man."

The noisy violence of that outburst acted like a douche. What was the fellow about—shouting out such words! But suddenly Laurence lifted his hands and wrung them. The gesture was so utterly painful that it drew a quiver from Keith's face.

"Why did you come here," he said, "and tell *me* this?"

Larry's face was really unearthly sometimes, such strange gleams passed up on to it!

"Whom else should I tell? I came to know what I'm to do, Keith. Give myself up, or what?"

At that sudden introduction of the practical, Keith felt his heart twitch. Was it then as real as all that? But he said, very quietly:

"Just tell me— How did it come about, this—affair?"

That question linked the dark, gruesome, fantastic nightmare on to actuality.

"When did it happen?"

"Last night."

In Larry's face there was—there had always been—something childishly truthful. He would never stand a chance in court! And Keith said:

"How? Where? You'd better tell me quietly from the beginning. Drink this coffee; it'll clear your head."

Laurence took the little blue cup and drained it.

"Yes," he said. "It's like this, Keith. There's a girl I've known for some months now—"

Women! And Keith said between his teeth: "Well?"

"Her father was a Pole who died over here when she was sixteen, and left her all alone. A man called Walenn, a mongrel American, living in the same house, married her, or pretended to—she's very pretty, Keith—he left her with a baby six months old, and another coming. That one died, and she did nearly. Then she starved till another fellow took her on. She lived with him two years; then Walenn turned up again, and made her go back to him. The brute used to beat her black and blue, all for nothing. Then he left her again. When I met her she'd lost her elder child, too, and was taking anybody who came along."

He suddenly looked up into Keith's face.

"But I've never met a sweeter woman, nor a truer, that I swear. Woman! She's only twenty now! When I went to her last night that brute —that Walenn—had found her out again; and when he came for me, swaggering and bullying— Look!" he touched a dark mark on his forehead—"I took his throat in my hands, and when I let go—"

"Yes?"

"Dead. I never knew till afterwards that she was hanging on to him behind."

Again he made that gesture—wringing his hands.

In a hard voice Keith said:

"What did you do then?"

"We sat by it a long time. Then I carried it on my back down the street, round a corner to an archway."

"How far?"

"About fifty yards."

"Was any one—did any one see?"

"No."

"What time?"

"Three."

"And then?"

"Went back to her."

"Why—in Heaven's name?"

"She was lonely and afraid; so was I, Keith."

"Where is this place?"

"Forty-two, Borrow Street, Soho."

"And the archway?"

"Corner of Glove Lane."

"Good God! Why—I saw it in the paper!"

And seizing the journal that lay on his bureau, Keith read again that paragraph: "The body of a man was found this morning under an archway in Glove Lane, Soho. From marks about the throat suspicions of foul play are entertained. The body had apparently been robbed, and nothing was discovered leading to identification."

It was real earnest, then. Murder! His own brother! He faced round and said:

"You saw this in the paper, and dreamed it. Understand—you dreamed it!"

The wistful answer came:

"If only I had, Keith—if only I had!"

In his turn, Keith very nearly wrung his hands.

"Did you take anything from the—body?"

"This dropped while we were struggling."

It was an empty envelope with a South American postmark addressed: "Patrick Walenn, Simon's Hotel, Farrier Street, London." Again with that twitching in his heart, Keith said:

"Put it in the fire."

Then suddenly he stooped to pluck it out. By that command—he had—identified himself with this—this— But he did not pluck it out. It blackened, writhed, and vanished. And once more he said:

"What in God's name made you come here and tell *me?*"

"You know about these things. I didn't mean to kill him. I love the girl. What shall I do, Keith?"

Simple! How simple! To ask what he was to do! It was like Larry!
And he said:

"You were not seen, you think?"

"It's a dark street. There was no one about."

"When did you leave this girl the second time?"

"About seven o'clock."

"Where did you go?"

"To my rooms."

"In Fitzroy Street?"

"Yes."

"Did any one see you come in?"

"No."

"What have you done since?"

"Sat there."

"Not been out?"

"No."

"Not seen the girl?"

"No."

"You don't know, then, what she's done since?"

"No."

"Would she give you away?"

"Never."

"Would she give herself away—hysteria?"

"No."

"Who knows of your relations with her?"

"No one."

"No one?"

"I don't know who should, Keith."

"Did any one see you going in last night, when you first went to her?"

"No. She lives on the ground floor. I've got keys."

"Give them to me. What else have you that connects you with her?"

"Nothing."

"In your rooms?"

"No."

"No photographs? No letters?"

"No."

"Be careful."

"Nothing."

"No one saw you going back to her the second time?"

"No."

"No one saw you leave her in the morning?"

"No."

"You were fortunate. Sit down again, man. I must think."

Think! Think out this accursed thing—so beyond all thought, and all belief. But he could not think. Not a coherent thought would come. And he began again:

"Was it his first reappearance with her?"

"Yes."

"She told you so?"

"Yes."

"How did he find out where she was?"

"I don't know."

"How drunk were you?"

"I was not drunk."

"How much had you drunk?"

"About a bottle of claret—nothing."

"You say you didn't mean to kill him?"

"No—God knows!"

"That's something. What made you choose the arch?"

"It was the first dark place."

"Did his face look as if he had been strangled?"

"Don't!"

"Did it?"

"Yes."

"Very disfigured?"

"Yes."

"Did you look to see if his clothes were marked?"

"No."

"Why not?"

"Why not? My God! If you had done it—!"

"You say he was disfigured. Would he be recognizable?"

"I don't know."

"When she lived with him last—where was that?"

"I don't know for certain. Pimlico, I think."

"Not Soho?"

"No."

"How long has she been at the Soho place?"

"Nearly a year."

"Always the same rooms?"

"Yes."

"Is there any one living in that house or street who would be likely to know her as his wife?"

"I don't think so."

"What was he?"

"I should think he was a professional 'bully.' "

"I see. Spending most of his time abroad, then?"

"Yes."

"Do you know if he was known to the police?"

"I haven't heard of it."

"Now listen, Larry. When you leave here go straight home, and don't go out till I come to you, tomorrow morning. Promise that!"

"I promise."

"I've got a dinner engagement. I'll think this out. Don't drink. Don't talk! Pull yourself together."

"Don't keep me longer than you can help, Keith!"

That white face, those eyes, that shaking hand! With a twinge of pity in the midst of all the turbulence of his revolt, and fear, and disgust, Keith put his hand on his brother's shoulder, and said:

"Courage!"

And suddenly he thought: "My God! Courage! I shall want it all myself!"

II

Laurence Darrant, leaving his brother's house in the Adelphi, walked northwards, rapidly, slowly, rapidly again. For, if there are men who by force of will do one thing only at a time, there are men who from lack of will do now one thing, now another, with equal intensity. To such natures, to be gripped by the Nemesis which attends the lack of self-control is no reason for being more self-controlled. Rather does it foster their pet feeling: "What matter? Tomorrow we die!" The effort of will required to go to Keith had relieved, exhausted and exasperated him. In accordance with those three feelings was the progress of his walk. He started from the door with the fixed resolve to go home and stay there quietly till Keith came. He was in Keith's hands; Keith would know what was to be done. But he had not gone three hundred yards before he felt so utterly weary, body and soul, that if he had but had a pistol in his pocket he would have shot himself in the street. Not even the thought of the girl—this young unfortunate with her strange devotion, who had kept him straight these last five months, who had roused in him a depth of feeling he had never known before—would have availed against that sudden black dejection. Why go on—a waif at the mercy of his own nature, a straw blown here and there by every gust which rose in him? Why not have done with it for ever, and take it out in sleep?

He was approaching the fatal street, where he and the girl, that early morning, had spent the hours clutched together, trying in the refuge of love to forget for a moment their horror and fear. Should he go in? He had promised Keith not to. Why had he promised? He caught sight of himself in a chemist's lighted window. Miserable, shadowy brute! And he remembered suddenly a dog he had picked up once in the streets of Pera, a black-and-white creature—different from the other dogs, not one of their breed, a pariah of pariahs, who had strayed there somehow. He had taken it home to the house where he was staying, contrary to all

665

custom of the country; had got fond of it; had shot it himself, sooner than leave it behind again to the mercies of its own kind in the streets. Twelve years ago! And those sleeve-links made of little Turkish coins he had brought back for the girl at the hairdresser's in Chancery Lane where he used to get shaved—pretty creature, like a wild rose. He had asked of her a kiss for payment. What queer emotion when she put her face forward to his lips—a sort of passionate tenderness and shame, at the softness and warmth of that flushed cheek, at her beauty and trustful gratitude. She would soon have given herself to him—that one! He had never gone there again! And to this day he did not know why he had abstained; to this day he did not know whether he were glad or sorry not to have plucked that rose. He must surely have been very different then! Queer business, life—queer, queer business!—to go through it never knowing what you would do next. Ah! to be like Keith, steady, buttoned-up in success; a brass pot, a pillar of society! Once, as a boy, he had been within an ace of killing Keith, for sneering at him. Once in Southern Italy he had been near killing a driver who was flogging his horse. And now, that dark-faced, swinish bully who had ruined the girl he had grown to love—he had done it! Killed him! Killed a man!

He who did not want to hurt a fly. The chemist's window confronted him with the sudden thought that he had at home that which made him safe, in case they should arrest him. He would never again go out without some of those little white tablets sewn into the lining of his coat. Restful, even exhilarating thought! They said a man should not take his own life. Let *them* taste horror—those glib citizens! Let them live as that girl had lived, as millions lived all the world over, under their canting dogmas! A man might rather even take his life than watch their cursed inhumanities.

He went into the chemist's for a bromide; and, while the man was mixing it, stood resting one foot like a tired horse. The "life" he had squeezed out of that fellow! After all, a billion living creatures gave up life each day, had it squeezed out of them, mostly. And perhaps not one a day deserved death so much as that loathly fellow. Life! a breath —a flame! Nothing! Why, then, this icy clutching at his heart?

The chemist brought the draught.

"Not sleeping, sir?"

"No."

The man's eyes seemed to say: "Yes! Burning the candle at both ends—I know!" Odd life, a chemist's; pills and powders all day long, to hold the machinery of men together! Devilish odd trade!

In going out he caught the reflection of his face in a mirror; it seemed too good altogether for a man who had committed murder. There was a sort of brightness underneath, an amiability lurking about its shadows; how—how could it be the face of a man who had done what he had done? His head felt lighter now, his feet lighter; he walked rapidly again.

Curious feeling of relief and oppression all at once! Frightful—to long for company, for talk, for distraction; and—to be afraid of it! The girl—the girl and Keith were now the only persons who would not give him that feeling of dread. And, of those two—Keith was not—! Who could consort with one who was never wrong, a successful, righteous fellow; a chap built so that he knew nothing about himself, wanted to know nothing, a chap all solid actions? To be a quicksand swallowing up one's own resolutions was bad enough! But to be like Keith—all will power, marching along, treading down his own feelings and weaknesses!— No! One could not make a comrade of a man like Keith, even if he were one's brother. The only creature in all the world was the girl. She alone knew and felt what he was feeling; would put up with him and love him whatever he did, or was done to him. He stopped and took shelter in a doorway, to light a cigarette.

He had suddenly a fearful wish to pass the archway where he had placed the body; a fearful wish that had no sense, no end in view, no anything; just an insensate craving to see the dark place again. He crossed Borrow Street to the little lane. There was only one person visible, a man on the far side with his shoulders hunched against the wind; a short, dark figure which crossed and came towards him in the flickering lamplight. What a face! Yellow, ravaged, clothed almost to the eyes in a stubbly grayish growth of beard, with blackish teeth, and haunting bloodshot eyes. And what a figure of rags—one shoulder higher than the other, one leg a little lame, and thin! A surge of feeling came up in Laurence for this creature, more unfortunate than himself. There were lower depths than his!

"Well, brother," he said, "*you* don't look too prosperous!"

The smile which gleamed out on the man's face seemed as unlikely as a smile on a scarecrow.

"Prosperity doesn't come my way," he said in a rusty voice. "I'm a failure—always been a failure. And yet—you wouldn't think it, would you?—I was a minister of religion once."

Laurence held out a shilling. But the man shook his head.

"Keep your money," he said. "I've got more than you today, I daresay. But thank you for taking a little interest. That's worth more than money to a man that's down."

"You're right."

"Yes," the rusty voice went on; "I'd as soon die as go on living as I do. And now I've lost my self-respect. Often wondered how long a starving man could go without losing his self-respect. Not so very long. You take my word for that." And without the slightest change in the monotony of that creaking voice he added:

"Did you read of the murder? Just here. I've been looking at the place."

The words, "So have I!" leaped up to Laurence's lips; he choked them down with a sort of terror.

"I wish you better luck," he said. "Good night!" and hurried away. A sort of ghastly laughter was forcing its way up in his throat. Was every one talking of the murder he had committed? Even the very scarecrow?

III

There are some natures so constituted that, due to be hung at ten o'clock, they will play chess at eight. Such men invariably rise. They make especially good bishops, editors, judges, impresarios, Prime Ministers, moneylenders, and generals; in fact, fill with exceptional credit any position of power over their fellow-men. They have spiritual cold storage, in which are preserved their nervous systems. In such men there is little or none of that fluid sense and continuity of feeling known under those vague terms, speculation, poetry, philosophy. Men of facts and of decision switching imagination on and off at will, subordinating sentiment to reason . . . one does not think of them when watching wind ripple over cornfields, or swallows flying.

Keith Darrant had need for being of that breed during his dinner at the Tellassons'. It was just eleven when he issued from the big house in Portland Place and refrained from taking a cab. He wanted to walk that he might better think. What crude and wanton irony there was in his situation! To have been made father-confessor to a murderer, he—well on towards a judgeship! With his contempt for the kind of weakness which landed men in such abysses, he felt it all so sordid, so "impossible," that he could hardly bring his mind to bear on it at all. And yet he must, because of two powerful instincts—self-preservation and blood-loyalty.

The wind had still the sapping softness of the afternoon, but rain had held off so far. It was warm, and he unbuttoned his fur overcoat. The nature of his thoughts deepened the dark austerity of his face, whose thin, well-cut lips were always pressing together, as if, by meeting, to dispose of each thought as it came up. He moved along the crowded pavements glumly. That air of festive conspiracy, which drops with the darkness on to lighted streets, galled him. He turned off on a darker route.

This ghastly business! Convinced of its reality, he yet could not see it. The thing existed in his mind, not as a picture, but as a piece of irrefutable evidence. Larry had not meant to do it, of course. But it was murder, all the same. Men like Larry—weak, impulsive, sentimental, introspective creatures—did they ever mean what they did? This man, this Walenn, was, by all accounts, better dead than alive; no need to waste a thought on him! But, crime—the ugliness—Justice unsatisfied! Crime concealed—and his own share in the concealment! And yet—brother to brother! Surely no one could demand action from him! It was only a question of what he was going to advise Larry to do. To keep silent, and disappear? Had that a chance of success? Perhaps—if the answers to his questions had been correct. But this girl! Suppose the dead man's relationship to her were ferreted out, could she be relied on not to endanger Larry? These women were all the same, unstable as water, emotional, shiftless—pests of society. Then, too, a crime untracked, dogging all his brother's after life; a secret following him wherever he might vanish to; hanging over him, watching for some drunken moment to slip out of his lips. It was bad to think of. A clean breast of it? But his heart twitched within him. "Brother of Mr. Keith Darrant, the well-known King's Counsel"—visiting a woman of the town, strangling with his bare hands the woman's husband! No intention to murder, but—a dead man! A dead man carried out of the house, laid under a dark archway! Provocation! Recommended to mercy—penal servitude for life! Was that the advice he was going to give Larry tomorrow morning?

And he had a sudden vision of shaven men with clay-colored features, run, as it were, to seed, as he had seen them once in Pentonville, when he had gone there to visit a prisoner. Larry! whom, as a baby creature, he had watched straddling; whom, as a little fellow, he had fagged; whom he had seen through scrapes at college; to whom he had lent money time and again, and time and again admonished in his courses. Larry! Five years younger than himself; and committed to his charge by their mother when she died. To become for life one of those men with faces like diseased plants; with no hair but a bushy stubble; with arrows marked on their yellow clothes! Larry! One of those men herded like sheep; at the beck and call of common men! A gentleman, his own brother, to live that slave's life, to be ordered here and there, year after year, day in, day out. Something snapped within him. He could not give that advice. Impossible! But, if not, he must make sure of his ground, must verify, must know. This Glove Lane—this archway? It would not be far from where he was that very moment. He looked for some one of whom to make inquiry. A policeman was standing at the corner, his stolid face illumined by a lamp; capable and watchful—an excellent officer, no doubt; but, turning his head away, Keith passed him without a word. Strange to feel that cold, uneasy feeling in presence of the law! A grim little driving home of what it all meant! Then, suddenly, he saw that the turning to his left was Borrow Street itself. He walked up one side, crossed over, and returned. He passed Number Forty-two, a small house with business names printed on the lifeless windows of the first and second floors; with dark-curtained windows on the ground floor, or was there just a slink of light in one corner? Which way had Larry turned? Which way under that grisly burden? Fifty paces of this squalid street—narrow, and dark, and empty, thank heaven! Glove Lane! Here it was! A tiny runlet of a street. And here—! He had run right on to the arch, a brick bridge connecting two portions of a warehouse, and dark indeed.

"That's right, gov'nor! There's the place!" He needed all his self-control to turn leisurely to the speaker. " 'Ere's where they found the body —very spot—leanin' up 'ere. They ain't got 'im yet. Lytest—me lord!"

It was a ragged boy holding out a tattered yellowish journal. His lynx eyes peered up from under lanky wisps of hair, and his voice had the proprietary note of one making "a corner" in his news. Keith took the paper and gave him twopence. He even found a sort of comfort in the young ghoul's hanging about there; it meant that others besides himself had come morbidly to look. By the dim lamplight he read: "Glove Lane garrotting mystery. Nothing has yet been discovered of the murdered man's identity; from the cut of his clothes he is supposed to be a foreigner." The boy had vanished, and Keith saw the figure of a policeman coming slowly down this gutter of a street. A second's hesitation, and he stood firm. Nothing obviously could have brought him here save this "mystery," and he stayed quietly staring at the arch. The policeman moved up abreast. Keith saw that he was the one whom he had passed just now. He noted the cold offensive question die out of the man's eyes when they caught the gleam of white shirt-front under the open fur collar. And holding up the paper, he said:

"Is this where the man was found?"

"Yes, sir."

"Still a mystery, I see?"

"Well, we can't always go by the papers. But I don't fancy they do know much about it, yet."

"Dark spot. Do fellows sleep under here?"

The policeman nodded. "There's not an arch in London where we don't get 'em sometimes."

"Nothing found on him—I think I read?"

"Not a copper. Pockets inside out. There's some funny characters about this quarter. Greeks, Hitalians—all sorts."

Queer sensation this, of being glad of a policeman's confidential tone!

"Well, good-night!"

"Good-night, sir. Good-night!"

He looked back from Borrow Street. The policeman was still standing there holding up his lantern, so that its light fell into the archway, as if trying to read its secret.

Now that he had seen this dark, deserted spot, the chances seemed to him much better. "Pockets inside out!" Either Larry had had presence of mind to do a very clever thing, or some one had been at the body before the police found it. That was the more likely. A dead backwater of a place. At three o'clock—loneliest of all hours—Larry's five minutes' grim excursion to and fro might well have passed unseen! Now, it all depended on the girl; on whether Laurence had been seen coming to her or going away; on whether, if the man's relationship to her were discovered, she could be relied on to say nothing. There was not a soul in Borrow Street now; hardly even a lighted window; and he took one of those rather desperate decisions only possible to men daily accustomed to the instant taking of responsibility. He would go to her, and see for himself. He came to the door of Forty-two, obviously one of those which are only shut at night, and tried the larger key. It fitted, and he was in a gas-lighted passage, with an oil-clothed floor, and a single door to his left. He stood there undecided. She must be made to understand that he knew everything. She must not be told more than that he was a friend of Larry's. She must not be frightened, yet must be forced to give her very soul away. A hostile witness—not to be treated as hostile—a matter for delicate handling! But his knock was not answered.

Should he give up this nerve-racking, bizarre effort to come at a basis of judgment; go away, and just tell Laurence that he could not advise him? And then—what? Something *must* be done. He knocked again. Still no answer. And with that impatience of being thwarted, natural to him, and fostered to the full by the conditions of his life, he tried the other key. It worked, and he opened the door. Inside all was dark, but a voice from some way off, with a sort of breathless relief in its foreign tones, said:

"Oh! then it's you, Larry! Why did you knock? I was so frightened. Turn up the light, dear. Come in!"

Feeling by the door for a switch in the pitch blackness, he was conscious of arms round his neck, a warm thinly clad body pressed to his own; then withdrawn as quickly, with a gasp, and the most awful terror-stricken whisper:

"Oh! Who is it?"

With a glacial shiver down his own spine, Keith answered:

"A friend of Laurence. Don't be frightened!"

There was such silence that he could hear a clock ticking, and the sound of his own hand passing over the surface of the wall, trying to find the switch. He found it, and in the light which leaped up he saw, stiffened against a dark curtain evidently screening off a bedroom, a girl standing, holding a long black coat together at her throat, so that her face with its pale brown hair, short and square-cut and curling up underneath, had an uncanny look of being detached from any body. Her face was so alabaster pale that the staring, startled eyes, dark blue or brown, and the faint rose of the parted lips, were like color stainings on a white mask; and it had a strange delicacy, truth, and pathos, such as only suffering brings. Though not susceptible to aesthetic emotion, Keith was curiously affected. He said gently:

"You needn't be afraid. I haven't come to do you harm—quite the contrary. May I sit down and talk?" And, holding up the keys, he added: "Laurence wouldn't have given me these, would he, if he hadn't trusted me?"

Still she did not move, and he had the impression that he was looking at a spirit—a spirit startled out of its flesh. Nor at the moment did it seem in the least strange that he should conceive such an odd thought. He stared round the room—clean and tawdry, with its tarnished gilt mirror, marble-topped side-table, and plush-covered sofa. Twenty years and more since he had been in such a place. And he said:

"Won't you sit down? I'm sorry to have startled you."

But still she did not move, whispering:

"Who are you, please?"

And, moved suddenly beyond the realm of caution by the terror in that whisper, he answered:

"Larry's brother."

She uttered a little sigh of relief which went to Keith's heart, and, still holding the dark coat together at her throat, came forward and sat down on the sofa. He could see that her feet, thrust into slippers, were bare; with her short hair, and those candid startled eyes, she looked like a tall child. He drew up a chair and said:

"You must forgive me coming at such an hour; he's told me, you see."

He expected her to flinch and gasp; but she only clasped her hands together on her knees, and said:

"Yes?"

Then horror and discomfort rose up in him afresh.

"An awful business!"

Her whisper echoed him:

"Yes, oh! yes! Awful—it is awful!"

And suddenly realizing that the man must have fallen dead just where he was sitting, Keith became stock silent, staring at the floor.

"Yes," she whispered; "just there. I see him now always falling!"

How she said that! With what a strange gentle despair! In this girl of evil life, who had brought on them this tragedy, what was it which moved him to a sort of unwilling compassion?

"You look very young," he said.

"I am twenty."

"And you are fond of—my brother?"

"I would die for him."

Impossible to mistake the tone of her voice, or the look in her eyes, true deep Slav eyes; dark brown, not blue as he had thought at first. It was a very pretty face—either her life had not eaten into it yet, or the suffering of these last hours had purged away those marks; or perhaps this devotion of hers to Larry. He felt strangely at sea, sitting there with this child of twenty; he, over forty, a man of the world, professionally used to every side of human nature. But he said, stammering a little: "I—I have come to see how far you can save him. Listen, and just answer the questions I put to you."

She raised her hands, squeezed them together, and murmured: "Oh! I will answer anything."

"This man, then—your—your husband—was he a bad man?"

"A dreadful man."

"Before he came here last night, how long since you saw him?"

"Eighteen months."

"Where did you live when you saw him last?"

"In Pimlico."

"Does anybody about here know you as Mrs. Walenn?"

"No. When I came here, after my little girl died, I came to live a bad life. Nobody knows me at all. I am quite alone."

"If they discover who he was, they will look for his wife?"

"I do not know. He did not let people think I was married to him. I was very young; he treated many, I think, like me."

"Do you think he was known to the police?"

She shook her head. "He was very clever."

"What is your name now?"

"Wanda Livinska."

"Were you known by that name before you were married?"

"Wanda is my Christian name. Livinska—I just call myself."

"I see; since you came here."

"Yes."

"Did my brother ever see this man before last night?"

"Never."

"You had told him about his treatment of you?"

"Yes. And that man first went for him."

"I saw the mark. Do you think any one saw my brother come to you?"

"I do not know. He says not."

"Can you tell if any one saw him carrying the—the thing away?"

"No one in this street—I was looking."

"Nor coming back?"

"No one."

"Nor going out in the morning?"

"I do not think it."

"Have you a servant?"

"Only a woman who comes at nine in the morning for an hour."

"Does she know Larry?"

"No."

"Friends, acquaintances?"

"No; I am very quiet. And since I knew your brother, I see no one. Nobody comes here but him for a long time now."

"How long?"

"Five months."

"Have you been out today?"

"No."

"What have you been doing?"

"Crying."

It was said with a certain dreadful simplicity, and pressing her hands together she went on:

"He is in danger because of me. I am so afraid for him."

Holding up his hand to check that emotion, he said:

"Look at me!"

She fixed those dark eyes on him, and in her bare throat, from which the coat had fallen back, he could see her resolutely swallowing down her agitation.

"If the worst comes to the worst, and this man is traced to you, can you trust yourself not to give my brother away?"

Her eyes shone. She got up and went to the fireplace:

"Look! I have burned all the things he has given me—even his picture. Now I have nothing from him."

Keith, too, got up.

"Good! One more question: Do the police know you, because—because of your life?"

She shook her head, looking at him intently with those mournfully true eyes. And he felt a sort of shame.

"I was obliged to ask. Do you know where he lives?"

"Yes."

"You must not go there. And he must not come to you here."

Her lips quivered; but she bowed her head. Suddenly he found her quite close to him, speaking almost in a whisper:

"Please do not take him from me altogether. I will be so careful. I will not do anything to hurt him; but if I cannot see him sometimes I shall die. Please do not take him from me." And catching his hand between her own she pressed it desperately. It was several seconds before Keith said:

"Leave that to me. I will see him. I shall arrange. You must leave that to me."

"But you will be kind?"

He felt her lips kissing his hand. And the soft moist touch sent a queer feeling through him, protective, yet just a little brutal, having in it a shiver of sensuality. He withdrew his hand. And as if warned that she had been too pressing, she recoiled humbly. But suddenly she turned, and stood absolutely rigid; then almost inaudibly whispered: "Listen! Some one out—out there!" And darting past him she turned out the light.

Almost at once came a knock on the door. He could feel—actually feel the terror of this girl beside him in the dark. And he, too, felt terror. Who could it be? No one came but Larry, she had said. Who else then could it be? Again came the knock, louder! He felt the breath of her whisper on his cheek: "If it is Larry! I must open." He shrank back against the wall, heard her open the door and say faintly: "Yes. Please! Who?"

Light painted a thin moving line on the wall opposite, and a voice which Keith recognized answered:

"All right, miss. Your outer door's open here. You ought to keep it shut after dark."

God! That policeman! And it had been his own doing, not shutting the outer door behind when he came in. He heard her say timidly in her foreign voice: "Thank you, sir!" the policeman's retreating steps, the outer door being shut, and felt her close to him again. That something in her youth and strange prettiness had touched and kept him gentle, no longer blunted the edge of his exasperation, now that he could not see her. They were all the same, these women; could not speak the truth! And he said brusquely:

"You told me they didn't know you!"

Her voice answered like a sigh:

"I did not think they did, sir. It is so long I was not out in the town, not since I had Larry."

The repulsion which all the time seethed deep in Keith welled up at those words. His brother—son of *his* mother, a gentleman—the property of this girl, bound to her, body and soul, by this unspeakable event! But she had turned up the light. Had she some intuition that darkness was against her? Yes, she *was* pretty with that soft face, colorless save for its lips and dark eyes, with that face somehow so touching, so unaccountably good, and like a child's.

"I am going now," he said. "Remember! He mustn't come here; you mustn't go to him. I shall see him tomorrow. If you are as fond of him as you say—take care, take care!"

She sighed out, "Yes! oh, yes!" and Keith went to the door. She was standing with her back to the wall, and to follow him she only moved her head—that dove-like face with all its life in eyes which seemed saying: "Look into us; nothing we hide; all—all is there!"

And he went out.

In the passage he paused before opening the outer door. He did not want to meet that policeman again; the fellow's round should have taken him well out of the street by now, and, turning the handle cautiously, he looked out. No one in sight. He stood a moment, wondering if he should turn to right or left, then briskly crossed the street. A voice to his right hand said:

"Good-night, sir."

There in the shadow of a doorway the policeman was standing. The fellow must have seen him coming out! Utterly unable to restrain a start, and muttering "Good-night!" Keith walked on rapidly.

He went full quarter of a mile before he lost that startled and uneasy feeling in sardonic exasperation that he, Keith Darrant, had been taken for a frequenter of a lady of the town. The whole thing—the whole thing!—a vile and disgusting business! His very mind felt dirty and breathless; his spirit, drawn out of sheath, had slowly to slide back before he could at all focus and readjust his reasoning faculty. Certainly, he had got the knowledge he wanted. There was less danger than he thought. That girl's eyes! No mistaking her devotion. She would not give Larry away. Yes! Larry must clear out—South America—the East—it did not matter. But he felt no relief. The cheap, tawdry room had wrapped itself round his fancy with its atmosphere of murky love, with the feeling it inspired, of emotion caged within those yellowish walls and the red stuff of its furniture. That girl's face! Devotion; truth, too, and beauty, rare and moving, in its setting of darkness and horror, in that nest of vice and of disorder! . . . The dark archway; the street arab, with his gleeful: "They 'ain't got 'im yet!"; the feel of those bare arms round his neck; that whisper of horror in the darkness; above all, again, her child face looking into his, so truthful! And suddenly he stood quite still in the street. What in God's name was he about? What grotesque juggling amongst shadows, what strange and ghastly eccentricity was all this? The forces of order and routine, all the actualities of his daily life, marched on him at that moment and swept everything before them. It was a dream, a nightmare—not real! It was ridiculous! That he—*he* should thus be bound up with things so black and bizarre!

He had come by now to the Strand, that street down which every day he moved to the Law Courts, to his daily work; his work so dignified and regular, so irreproachable and solid. No! The thing was all a monstrous nightmare! It would go, if he fixed his mind on the familiar objects around, read the names on the shops, looked at the faces passing. Far down the thoroughfare he caught the outline of the old church, and beyond, the loom of the Law Courts themselves. The bell of a fire-engine sounded, and the horses came galloping by, with the shining metal, rattle of hoofs, and hoarse shouting. Here was a sensation, real and harmless, dignified and customary! A woman flaunting round the corner looked up at him and leered out: "Good-night!" Even that was customary, tolerable. Two policemen passed, supporting between them a man the worse for liquor, full of fight and expletives; the sight was soothing, an ordinary thing which brought passing annoyance, interest, disgust. It had begun to rain; he felt it on his face with pleasure—an actual thing, not eccentric, a thing which happened every day!

He began to cross the street. Cabs were going at furious speed now that the last omnibus had ceased to run; it distracted him to take this actual, ordinary risk run so often every day. During that crossing of the Strand, with the rain in his face and the cabs shooting past, he regained for the first time his assurance, shook off this unreal sense of being in the grip of something, and walked resolutely to the corner of his home turning. But passing into that darker stretch, he again stood still. A policeman had also turned into that street on the other side. Not—surely not—! Absurd! They were all alike to look at—those fellows! Absurd! He walked on sharply, and let himself into his house. But on his way upstairs he could not for the life of him help raising a corner of a curtain and looking from the staircase window. The policeman was marching solemnly, about twenty-five yards away, paying apparently no attention to anything whatever.

IV

Keith woke at five o'clock, his usual hour, without remembrance. But the grisly shadow started up when he entered his study, where the lamp burned, and the fire shone, and the coffee was set ready, just as when yesterday afternoon Larry had stood out there against the wall. For a moment he fought against realization; then, drinking off his coffee, sat down sullenly at the bureau to his customary three hours' study of the day's cases.

Not one word of his brief could he take in. It was all jumbled with murky images and apprehensions, and for full half an hour he suffered mental paralysis. Then the sheer necessity of knowing something of the case which he had to open at half-past ten that morning forced him to a concentration which never quite subdued the *malaise* at the bottom of his heart. Nevertheless, when he rose at half-past eight and went into the bathroom, he had earned his grim satisfaction in this victory of will power. By half-past nine he must be at Larry's. A boat left London for the Argentine tomorrow. If Larry was to get away at once, money must be arranged for. And then at breakfast he came on this paragraph in the paper:

SOHO MURDER

Inquiry late last night established the fact that the police have discovered the identity of the man found strangled yesterday morning under an archway in Glove Lane. An arrest has been made.

677

By good fortune he had finished eating, for the words made him feel physically sick. At this very minute Larry might be locked up, waiting to be charged—might even have been arrested before his own visit to the girl last night. If Larry were arrested she must be implicated. What, then, would be his own position? Idiot to go and look at that archway, to go and see the girl! Had that policeman really followed him home? Accessory after the fact! Keith Darrant, King's Counsel, man of mark! He forced himself by an effort, which had something of the heroic, to drop this panicky feeling. Panic never did good. He must face it and see. He refused even to hurry, calmly collected the papers wanted for the day, and attended to a letter or two before he set out in a taxi-cab to Fitzroy Street.

Waiting outside there in the gray morning for his ring to be answered, he looked the very picture of a man who knew his mind, a man of resolution. But it needed all his will power to ask without tremor: "Mr. Darrant in?" to hear without sign of any kind the answer: "He's not up yet, sir."

"Never mind; I'll go in and see him. Mr. Keith Darrant."

On his way to Laurence's bedroom, in the midst of utter relief, he had the self-possession to think: "This arrest is the best thing that could have happened. It'll keep their noses on a wrong scent till Larry's got away. The girl must be sent off too, but not with him." Panic had ended in quite hardening his resolution. He entered the bedroom with a feeling of disgust. The fellow was lying there, his bare arms crossed behind his tousled head, staring at the ceiling, and smoking one of many cigarettes whose ends littered a chair beside him, whose sickly reek tainted the air. That pale face, with its jutting cheekbones and chin, its hollow cheeks and blue eyes far sunk back—what a wreck of goodness!

He looked up at Keith through the haze of smoke and said quietly: "Well, brother, what's the sentence? 'Transportation for life, and then to be fined forty pounds'?"

The flippancy revolted Keith. It was Larry all over! Last night horrified and humble, this morning, "Don't care" and feather-headed. He said sourly:

"Oh! You can joke about it now?"

Laurence turned his face to the wall.

"Must!"

Fatalism! How detestable were natures like that!

"I've been to see her," he said.

"You?"

"Last night. She can be trusted."

Laurence laughed.

"That I told you."

"I had to see for myself. You must clear out at once, Larry. She can come out to you by the next boat; but you can't go together. Have you any money?"

"No."

"I can foot your expenses, and lend you a year's income in advance. But it must be a clean cut; after you get out there your whereabouts must only be known to me."

A long sigh answered him.

"You're very good to me, Keith; you've always been very good. I don't know why."

Keith answered drily:

"Nor I. There's a boat to the Argentine tomorrow. You're in luck; they've made an arrest. It's in the paper."

"What?"

The cigarette end dropped, the thin pyjama'd figure writhed up and stood clutching at the bedrail.

"What?"

The disturbing thought flitted through Keith's brain: "I was a fool. He takes it queerly; what now?"

Laurence passed his hand over his forehead and sat down on the bed.

"I hadn't thought of that," he said. "It does me!"

Keith stared. In his relief that the arrested man was not Laurence, this had not occurred to him. What folly!

"Why?" he said quickly. "An innocent man's in no danger. They always get the wrong man first. It's a piece of luck, that's all. It gives us time."

How often had he not seen that expression on Larry's face, wistful, questioning, as if trying to see the thing with his—Keith's—eyes, trying to submit to better judgment? And he said, almost gently:

"Now, look here, Larry; this is too serious to trifle with. Don't worry about that. Leave it to me. Just get ready to be off. I'll take your berth and make arrangements. Here's some money for kit. I can come round between five and six and let you know. Pull yourself together, man. As soon as the girl's joined you out there, you'd better get across to Chile, the further the better. You must simply lose yourself. I must go now, if I'm to get to the Bank before I go down to the courts." And looking very steadily at his brother, he added:

"Come! You've got to think of me in this matter as well as of yourself. No playing fast and loose with the arrangements. Understand?"

But still Larry gazed up at him with that wistful questioning, and not till he had repeated, "Understand?" did he receive "Yes" for answer.

Driving away, he thought: "Queer fellow! I don't know him, shall never know him!" and at once began to concentrate on the practical arrangements. At his bank he drew out £400; but waiting for the notes to be counted he suffered qualms. A clumsy way of doing things! If there had been more time! The thought "Accessory after the fact!" now infected everything. Notes were traceable. No other way of getting him away at once, though. One must take lesser risks to avoid greater. From the bank he drove to the office of the steamship line. He had told Larry he would book his passage. But that would not do! He must only ask anonymously if there were accommodations. Having discovered that there were vacant berths, he drove on to the Law Courts. If he could have taken a morning off, he would have gone down to the police court and seen them charge this man. But even that was not too safe, with a face so well known as his. What would come of this arrest? Nothing, surely! The police always took somebody up to keep the public quiet. Then, suddenly, he had again the feeling that it was all a nightmare; Larry had never done it; the police had got the right man! But instantly the memory of the girl's awe-stricken face, her figure huddling on the sofa, her words: "I see him always falling!" came back. God! What a business!

He felt he had never been more clear-headed and forcible than that morning in court. When he came out for lunch he bought the most sensational of the evening papers. But it was yet too early for news, and he had to go back into court no whit wiser concerning the arrest. When at last he threw off wig and gown, and had got through a conference and other necessary work, he went out to Chancery Lane, buying a paper on the way. Then he hailed a cab and drove once more to Fitzroy Street.

V

Laurence had remained sitting on his bed for many minutes. An innocent man in no danger! Keith had said it—the celebrated lawyer! Could he rely on that? Go out 8,000 miles, he and the girl, and leave a fellow-creature perhaps in mortal peril for an act committed by himself?

In the past night he had touched bottom, as he thought: become ready to face anything. When Keith came in he would without murmur have accepted the advice: "Give yourself up!" He was prepared to pitch away the end of his life as he pitched from him the fag-ends of his cigarettes. And the long sigh he had heaved, hearing of reprieve, had been only half relief. Then, with incredible swiftness there had rushed through him a feeling of unutterable joy and hope. Clean away— into a new country, a new life! The girl and he! Out there he wouldn't care, would rejoice even to have squashed the life out of such a noisome beetle of a man. Out there! Under a new sun, where blood ran thicker than in this foggy land, and people took justice into their own hands. For it had been justice on that brute even though he had not meant to kill him. And then to hear of this arrest! They would be charging the man today. He could go and see the poor creature accused of the murder he himself had committed! And he laughed. Go and see how likely it was that they might hang a fellow-man in place of himself? He dressed, but too shaky to shave himself, went out to a barber's shop. While there he read the news which Keith had seen. In this paper the name of the arrested man was given: "John Evan, no address." To be brought up on the charge at Bow Street. Yes! He must go. Once, twice, three times he walked past the entrance of the court before at last he entered and screwed himself away among the tag and bobtail.

The court was crowded; and from the murmurs round he could tell that it was his particular case which had brought so many there. In a dazed way he watched charge after charge disposed of with lightning quickness. But were they never going to reach his business? And then suddenly he saw the little scarecrow man of last night advancing to the dock between two policemen, more ragged and miserable than ever by light of day, like some shaggy, wan, gray animal surrounded by sleek hounds.

A sort of satisfied purr was rising all round; and with horror Laurence perceived that this—this was the man accused of what he himself had done—this queer, battered unfortunate to whom he had shown a passing friendliness. Then all feeling merged in the appalling interest of listening. The evidence was very short. Testimony of the hotel-keeper where Walenn had been staying, the identification of his body, and of a snake-shaped ring he had been wearing at dinner that evening. Testimony of a pawnbroker, that this same ring was pawned with him the first thing yesterday morning by the prisoner. Testimony of a policeman that he had noticed the man Evan several times in Glove Lane, and twice moved him on from sleeping under that arch. Testimony of another policeman that, when arrested at midnight, Evan had said: "Yes; I took the ring off his finger. I found him there dead. . . . I know I oughtn't to have done it. . . . I'm an educated man; it was stupid to pawn the ring. I found him with his pockets turned inside out."

Fascinating and terrible to sit staring at the man in whose place he should have been; to wonder when those small bright-gray bloodshot eyes would spy him out, and how he would meet that glance. Like a baited raccoon the little man stood, screwed back into a corner, mournful, cynical, fierce, with his ridged, obtuse yellow face, and his stubbly gray beard and hair, and his eyes wandering now and again amongst the crowd. But with all his might, Laurence kept his face unmoved. Then came the word, "Remanded"; and, more like a baited beast than ever, the man was led away.

Laurence sat on, a cold perspiration thick on his forehead. Some one else, then, had come on the body and turned the pockets inside out before John Evan took the ring. A man such as Walenn would not be out at night without money. Besides, if Evan had found money on the body he would never have run the risk of taking that ring. Yes, some one else had come on the body first. It was for that one to come forward and prove that the ring was still on the dead man's finger when he left him, and thus clear Evan. He clung to that thought; it seemed to make him less responsible for the little man's position; to remove him and his own deed one step further back. If they found the person who had taken the money, it would prove Evan's innocence. He came out of the court in a sort of trance. And a craving to get drunk attacked him. One could not go on like this without the relief of some oblivion. If he could only get drunk, keep drunk till this business was decided and he knew whether he must give himself up or no. He had now no fear at all of people suspecting him; only fear of himself—fear that he might go and give himself up. Now he could see the girl, the danger from that was as nothing compared with the danger from his own conscience. He had promised Keith not to see her. Keith had been decent and loyal to him—good old Keith! But he would never understand that this girl was now all he cared about in life; that he would rather be cut off from life itself than be cut off from her. Instead of becoming less and less, she was becoming more and more to him—experience strange and thrilling! Out of deep misery she had grown happy—through him; out of a sordid, shifting life recovered coherence and bloom, through devotion to him—*him,* of all people in the world! It was a miracle. She demanded nothing of him, adored him, as no other woman ever had—it was this which had anchored his drifting barque; this—and her truthful mild intelligence, and that burning warmth of a woman who, long treated by men as but a sack of sex, now loves at last.

And suddenly, mastering his craving to get drunk, he made towards Soho. He had been a fool to give those keys to Keith. She must have been frightened by his visit; and, perhaps, doubly miserable since, knowing nothing, imagining everything! Keith was sure to have terrified her. Poor little thing!

Down the street where he had stolen in the dark with the dead body on his back, he almost ran for the cover of her house. The door was opened to him before he knocked, her arms were round his neck, her lips pressed to his. The fire was out, as if she had been unable to remember to keep warm. A stool had been drawn to the window, and there she had evidently been sitting, like a bird in a cage, looking out into the gray street. Though she had been told that he was not to come, instinct had kept her there; or the pathetic, arching hope against hope which lovers never part with.

Now that he was there, her first thoughts were for his comfort. The fire was lighted. He must eat, drink, smoke. There was never in her doings any of the "I am doing this for you, but you ought to be doing that for me" which belongs to so many marriages and *liaisons.* She was like a devoted slave, so in love with the chains that she never knew she wore them. And to Laurence, who had so little sense of property, this only served to deepen tenderness, and the hold she had on him. He had resolved not to tell her of the new danger he ran from his own conscience. But resolutions with him were but the opposite of what was sure to come; and at last the words, "They've arrested some one," escaped him.

From her face he knew she had grasped the danger at once; had divined it, perhaps, before he spoke. But she only twined her arms round him and kissed his lips. And he knew that she was begging him to put his love for her above his conscience. Who would ever have thought that he could feel as he did to this girl who had been in the arms of so many! The stained and suffering past of a loved woman awakens in some men only chivalry; in others, more respectable, it rouses a tigerish itch, a rancorous jealousy of what in the past was given to others. Sometimes it will do both. When he had her in his arms he felt no remorse for killing the coarse, handsome brute who had ruined her. He savagely rejoiced in it. But when she laid her head in the hollow of his shoulder, turning to him her white face with the faint color-staining on the parted lips, the cheek, the eyelids; when her dark, wide-apart, brown eyes gazed up in the happiness of her abandonment—he felt only tenderness and protection.

He left her at five o'clock, and had not gone two streets' length before the memory of the little gray vagabond, screwed back in the far corner of the dock like a baited raccoon, of his dreary, creaking voice, took possession of him again; and a kind of savagery mounted in his brain against a world where one could be so tortured without having meant harm to any one.

At the door of his lodgings Keith was getting out of a cab. They went in together, but neither of them sat down; Keith standing with his back to the carefully shut door, Laurence with his back to the table, as if they knew there was a tug coming. And Keith said:

"There's room on that boat. Go down and book your berth before they shut. Here's the money!"

"I'm going to stick it, Keith."

Keith stepped forward and put a roll of notes on the table.

"Now look here, Larry. I've read the police-court proceedings. There's nothing in that. Out of prison, or in prison for a few weeks, it's all the same to a night-bird of that sort. Dismiss it from your mind—there's not nearly enough evidence to convict. This gives you your chance. Take it like a man, and make a new life for yourself."

Laurence smiled; but the smile had a touch of madness and a touch of malice. He took up the notes.

"Clear out, and save the honour of brother Keith. Put them back in your pocket, Keith, or I'll put them in the fire. Come, take them!" And, crossing to the fire, he held them to the bars. "Take them, or in they go!"

Keith took back the notes.

"I've still got some kind of honour, Keith; if I clear out I shall have none, not the rag of any, left. It may be worth more to me than that—I can't tell yet—I can't tell."

There was a long silence before Keith answered:

"I tell you you're mistaken; no jury will convict. If they did, a judge would never hang on it. A ghoul who can rob a dead body *ought* to be in prison. What he did is worse than what you did, if you come to that!"

Laurence lifted his face.

"Judge not, brother," he said; "the heart is a dark well."

Keith's yellowish face grew red and swollen, as though he were mastering the tickle of a bronchial cough.

"What are you going to do, then? I suppose I may ask you not to be entirely oblivious of our name; or is such a consideration unworthy of your honour?"

Laurence bent his head. The gesture said more clearly than words: "Don't kick a man when he's down!"

"I don't know what I'm going to do—nothing at present. I'm awfully sorry, Keith; awfully sorry."

Keith looked at him, and without another word went out.

VI

To any, save philosophers, reputation may be threatened almost as much by disgrace to name and family as by the disgrace of self. Keith's instinct was always to deal actively with danger. But this blow, whether it fell on him by discovery or by confession, could not be countered. As blight falls on a rose from who knows where, the scandalous murk would light on him. No repulse possible! Not even a wriggling from under! Brother of a murderer hung or sent to penal servitude! His daughter niece to a murderer! His dead mother—a murderer's mother! And to wait day after day, week after week, not knowing whether the blow would fall, was an extraordinary atrocious penance, the injustice of which, to a man of rectitude, seemed daily the more monstrous.

The remand had produced evidence that the murdered man had been drinking heavily on the night of his death, and further evidence of the accused's professional vagabondage and destitution; it was shown, too, that for some time the archway in Glove Lane had been his favorite night haunt. He had been committed for trial in January. This time, despite misgivings, Keith had attended the police court. To his great relief Larry was not there. But the policeman who had come up while he was looking at the archway, and given him afterwards that scare in the girl's rooms, was chief witness to the way the accused man haunted Glove Lane. Though Keith held his silk hat high, he still had the uncomfortable feeling that the man had recognized him.

His conscience suffered few, if any, twinges for letting this man rest under the shadow of the murder. He genuinely believed that there was not evidence enough to convict; nor was it in him to appreciate the tortures of a vagabond shut up. The scamp deserved what he had got for robbing a dead body; and in any case such a scarecrow was better off in prison than sleeping out under archways in December. Sentiment was foreign to Keith's character, and his justice that of those who subordinate the fates of the weak and shiftless to the needful paramountcy of the strong and well established.

His daughter came back from school for the Christmas holidays. It was hard to look up from her bright eyes and rosy cheeks and see this shadow hanging above his calm and ordered life, as in a glowing room one's eye may catch an impending patch of darkness drawn like a spider's web across a corner of the ceiling.

On the afternoon of Christmas Eve they went, by her desire, to a church in Soho, where the Christmas Oratorio was being given; and coming away passed, by chance of a wrong turning, down Borrow Street. Ugh! How that startled moment, when the girl had pressed herself against him in the dark, and her terror-stricken whisper: "Oh! Who is it?" leaped out before him! Always that business—that ghastly business! After the trial he would have another try to get them both away. And he thrust his arm within his young daughter's, hurrying her on, out of this street where shadows filled all the winter air.

But that evening when she had gone to bed he felt uncontrollably restless. He had not seen Larry for weeks. What was he about? What desperations were hatching in his disorderly brain? Was he very miserable; had he perhaps sunk into a stupor of debauchery? And the old feeling of protectiveness rose up in him; a warmth born of long-ago Christmas Eves, when they had stockings hung out in the night stuffed by a Santa Claus whose hand never failed to tuck them up, whose kiss was their nightly waft into sleep.

Stars were sparkling out there over the river; the sky frosty-clear, and black. Bells had not begun to ring as yet. And obeying an obscure, deep impulse, Keith wrapped himself once more into his fur coat, pulled a motoring cap over his eyes, and sallied forth.

In the Strand he took a cab to Fitzroy Street. There was no light in Larry's windows, and on a card he saw the words "To Let." Gone! Had he after all cleared out for good? But how—without money? And the girl? Bells were ringing now in the silent frostiness. Christmas Eve! And Keith thought: "If only this wretched business were off my mind! Monstrous that one should suffer for the faults of others!"

He took a route which led him past Borrow Street. Solitude brooded there, and he walked resolutely down on the far side, looking hard at the girl's window. There was a light. The curtains just failed to meet, so that a thin gleam shone through. He crossed; and after glancing swiftly up and down, deliberately peered in.

He only stood there perhaps twenty seconds, but visual records gleaned in a moment sometimes outlast the visions of hours and days. The electric light was not burning; but in the center of the room the girl was kneeling in her night-gown before a little table on which were four lighted candles. Her arms were crossed on her breast; the candlelight shone on her fair cropped hair, on the profile of cheek and chin, on her bowed white neck. For a moment he thought her alone; then behind her saw his brother in a sleeping suit, leaning against the wall, with arms crossed, watching. It was the expression on his face which burned the whole thing in, so that always afterwards he was able to see that little scene—such an expression as could never have been on the face of one even faintly conscious that he was watched by any living thing on earth. The whole of Larry's heart and feeling seemed to have come up out of him. Yearning, mockery, love, despair! The depth of his feeling for this girl, his stress of mind, fears, hopes; the flotsam good and evil of his soul, all transfigured there, exposed and unforgettable. The candle-light shone upward on to his face, twisted by the strangest smile; his eyes, darker and more wistful than mortal eyes should be, seemed to beseech and mock the white-clad girl, who, all unconscious, knelt without movement, like a carved figure of devotion. The words seemed coming from his lips: "Pray for us! Bravo! Yes! Pray for us!" And suddenly Keith saw her stretch out her arms and lift her face with a look of ecstasy, and Laurence starting forward. What had she seen beyond the candle flames? It is the unexpected which invests visions with poignancy. Nothing more strange could Keith have seen in this nest of the murky and illicit. But in sheer panic lest he might be caught thus spying he drew back and hurried on.

So Larry was living there with her! When the moment came he could still find him.

Before going in, he stood full five minutes leaning on the terrace parapet before his house, gazing at the star-frosted sky, and the river cut by the trees into black pools, oiled over by gleams from the Embankment lamps. And, deep down, behind his mere thoughts, he ached—somehow, somewhere ached. Beyond the cage of all that he saw and heard and thought, he had perceived something he could not reach. But the night was cold, the bells silent, for it had struck twelve. Entering his house, he stole upstairs.

VII

If for Keith those six weeks before the Glove Lane murder trial came on were fraught with uneasiness and gloom, they were for Laurence almost the happiest since his youth. From the moment when he left his rooms and went to the girl's to live, a kind of peace and exaltation took possession of him. Not by any effort of will did he throw off the nightmare hanging over him. Nor was he drugged by love. He was in a sort of spiritual catalepsy. In face of fate too powerful for his will, his turmoil, anxiety, and even restlessness had ceased; his life floated in the ether of "what must come, will." Out of this catalepsy, his spirit sometimes fell headlong into black waters. In one such whirlpool he was struggling on the night of Christmas Eve. When the girl rose from her knees he asked her:

"What did you see?"

Pressing close to him, she drew him down on to the floor before the fire; and they sat, knees drawn up, hands clasped, like two children trying to see over the edge of the world.

"It was the Virgin I saw. She stood against the wall and smiled. We shall be happy soon."

"When we die, Wanda," he said, suddenly, "let it be together. We shall keep each other warm out there."

Huddling to him she whispered: "Yes, oh, yes! If you die, I could not go on living."

It was this utter dependence on him, the feeling that he had rescued something, which gave him sense of anchorage. That, and his buried life in the retreat of these two rooms. Just for an hour in the morning, from nine to ten, the charwoman would come, but not another soul all day. They never went out together. He would stay in bed late, while Wanda bought what they needed for the day's meals; lying on his back, hands clasped behind his head, recalling her face, the movements of her slim, rounded, supple figure, robing itself before his gaze; feeling again the kiss she had left on his lips, the gleam of her soft eyes, so strangely dark in so fair a face. In a sort of trance he would lie still till she came back. Then get up to breakfast about noon of things she had cooked, drinking coffee. In the afternoon he would go out alone and walk for hours, anywhere, so long as it was east. To the east there was always suffering to be seen, always that which soothed him with the feeling that he and his troubles were only a tiny part of trouble; that while so many other sorrowing and shadowy creatures lived he was not cut off. To go west was to encourage dejection. In the west all was like Keith, successful, immaculate, ordered, resolute. He would come back tired out, and sit watching her cook their little dinner. The evenings were given up to love. Queer trance of an existence, which both were afraid to break. No sign from her of wanting those excitements which girls who have lived her life, even for a few months, are supposed to need. She never asked him to take her anywhere; never, in word, deed, look, seemed anything but almost rapturously content. And yet he knew, and she knew, that they were only waiting to see whether Fate would turn her thumb down on them. In these days he did not drink. Out of his quarter's money, when it came in, he had paid his debts—their expenses were very small. He never went to see Keith, never wrote to him, hardly thought of him. And from those dread apparitions—Walenn lying with the breath choked out of him, and the little gray, driven animal in the dock—he hid, as only a man can who must hide or be destroyed. But daily he bought a newspaper, and feverishly, furtively scanned its columns.

VIII

Coming out of the Law Courts on the afternoon of January 28, at the triumphant end of a desperately fought will case, Keith saw on a poster the words: "Glove Lane Murder: Trial and Verdict"; and with a rush of dismay he thought: "Good God! I never looked at the paper this morning!" The elation which had filled him a second before, the absorption he had felt for two days now in the case so hardly won, seemed suddenly quite sickeningly trivial. What on earth had he been doing to forget that horrible business even for an instant? He stood quite still on the crowded pavement, unable, really unable, to buy a paper. But his face was like a piece of iron when he did step forward and hold his penny out. There it was in the "Stop Press"! "Glove Lane Murder. The jury returned a verdict of Guilty. Sentence of death was passed."

His first sensation was simple irritation. How had they come to commit such an imbecility? Monstrous! The evidence—! Then the futility of even reading the report, of even considering how they had come to record such a verdict struck him with savage suddenness. There it was, and nothing he could do or say would alter it; no condemnation of this idiotic verdict would help reverse it. The situation was desperate, indeed! That five minutes' walk from the Law Courts to his chambers was the longest he had ever taken.

Men of decided character little know beforehand what they will do in certain contingencies. For the imaginations of decided people do not endow mere contingencies with sufficient actuality. Keith had never really settled what he was going to do if this man were condemned. Often in those past weeks he had said to himself: "Of course, if they bring him in guilty, that's another thing!" But, now that they had, he was beset by exactly the same old arguments and feelings, the same instincts of loyalty and protection towards Laurence and himself, intensified by the fearful imminence of the danger. And yet, here was this man about to be hung for a thing he had not done! Nothing could get over that! But then he was such a worthless vagabond, a ghoul who had robbed a dead body. If Larry were condemned in his stead, would there be any less miscarriage of justice? To strangle a brute who had struck you, by the accident of keeping your hand on his throat a few seconds too long, was there any more guilt in that—was there even as much as in deliberate theft from a dead man? Reverence for order, for justice, and established fact, will often march shoulder to shoulder with Jesuitry in natures to whom success is vital.

In the narrow stone passage leading to his staircase a friend called out: "Bravo, Darrant! That was a squeak! Congratulations!" And with a bitter little smile Keith thought: "Congratulations! I!"

At the first possible moment he hurried back to the Strand, and, hailing a cab, he told the man to put him down at a turning near to Borrow Street.

It was the girl who opened to his knock. Startled, clasping her hands, she looked strange to Keith in her black skirt and blouse of some soft velvety stuff the color of faded roses. Her round, rather long throat was bare; and Keith noticed fretfully that she wore gold earrings. Her eyes, so pitch dark against her white face, and the short fair hair which curled into her neck, seemed both to search and to plead.

"My brother?"

"He is not in, sir, yet."

"Do you know where he is?"

"No."

"He is living with you here now?"

"Yes."

"Are you still as fond of him as ever, then?"

With a movement, as though she despaired of words, she clasped her hands over her heart. And he said:

"I see."

He had the same strange feeling as on his first visit to her, and when through the chink in the curtains he had watched her kneeling—of pity mingled with some faint sexual emotion. And crossing to the fire he asked:

"May I wait for him?"

"Oh! Please! Will you sit down?"

But Keith shook his head. And with a catch in her breath she said:

"You will not take him from me. I should die."

He turned round on her sharply.

"*I* don't want him taken from you. I want to help you keep him. Are you ready to go away at any time?"

"Yes. Oh, yes!"

"And he?"

She answered almost in a whisper:

"Yes; but there is that poor man."

"That poor man is a graveyard thief; a hyena; a ghoul—not worth consideration." And the rasp in his own voice surprised him

"Ah!" she sighed. "But I am sorry for him. Perhaps he was hungry.

I have been hungry—you do things then that you would not. And perhaps he has no one to love; if you have no one to love you can be very bad. I think of him often—in prison."

Between his teeth Keith muttered: "And Laurence?"

"We do never speak of it; we are afraid."

"He's not told you, then, about the trial?"

Her eyes dilated.

"The trial! Oh! He was strange last night. This morning, too, he got up early. Is it—is it over?"

"Yes."

"What has come?"

"Guilty."

For a moment Keith thought she was going to faint. She had closed her eyes, and swayed so that he took a step and put his hands on her arms.

"Listen!" he said. "Help me, don't let Laurence out of your sight. We must have time. I must see what they intend to do. They can't be going to hang this man. I must have time, I tell you. You must prevent his giving himself up."

She stood, staring in his face, while he still held her arms, gripping into her soft flesh through the velvety sleeves.

"Do you understand?"

"Yes—but if he has already!"

Keith felt the shiver which ran through her. And the thought rushed into his mind: "My God! Suppose the police come round while I'm here!" If Larry had indeed gone to them! If that policeman who had seen him here the night after the murder should find him here again just after the verdict! He said almost fiercely:

"Can I trust you not to let Larry out of your sight? Quick! Answer!"

Clasping her hands to her breast, she answered humbly:

"I will try."

"If he hasn't already done this, watch him like a lynx! Don't let him go out without you. I'll come tomorrow morning early. You're a Catholic, aren't you? Swear to me that you won't let him do anything till he's seen me again."

She did not answer, looking past him at the door; and Keith heard a key in the latch. There was Laurence himself, holding in his hand a great bunch of pink lilies and white narcissi. His face was pale and haggard. He said quietly:

"Hallo, Keith!"

The girl's eyes were fastened on Larry's face; and Keith, looking from one to the other, knew that he had never had more need for wariness.

"Have you seen?" he said.

Laurence nodded. His expression, as a rule so tell-tale of his emotions, baffled Keith utterly.

"Well?"

"I've been expecting it."

"The thing can't stand—that's certain. But I must have time to look into the report. I must have time to see what I can do. D'you understand me, Larry?—I must have time." He knew he was talking at random. The only thing was to get them away at once out of reach of confession; but he dared not say so.

"Promise me that you'll do nothing, that you won't go out even till I've seen you tomorrow morning."

Again Laurence nodded. And Keith looked at the girl. Would she see that he did not break that promise? Her eyes were still fixed immovably on Larry's face. And with the feeling that he could get no further, Keith turned to go.

"Promise me," he said.

Laurence answered: "I promise."

He was smiling. Keith could make nothing of that smile, nor of the expression in the girl's eyes. And saying: "I have your promise, I rely on it!" he went.

IX

To keep from any woman who loves, knowledge of her lover's mood, is as hard as to keep music from moving the heart. But when that woman has lived in suffering, and for the first time knows the comfort of love, then let the lover try as he may to disguise his heart—no use! Yet by virtue of subtler abnegation she will often succeed in keeping it from him that she knows.

When Keith was gone the girl made no outcry, asked no questions, managed that Larry should not suspect her intuition; all that evening she acted as if she knew of nothing preparing within him, and through him, within herself.

His words, caresses, the very zest with which he helped her to prepare the feast, the flowers he had brought, the wine he made her drink, the avoidance of any word which could spoil their happiness, all—all told her. He was too inexorably gay and loving. Not for her—to whom every word and every kiss had uncannily the desperate value of a last word and kiss—not for her to deprive herself of these by any sign or gesture which might betray her prescience. She took all, and would have taken more, a hundredfold. She did not want to drink the wine he kept tilting into her glass, but, with the acceptance learned by women who have lived her life, she did not refuse. She had never refused him anything.

Laurence drank deeply. The wine gave an edge to these few hours of pleasure, an exaltation of energy. It dulled his sense of pity, too. It was pity he was afraid of for himself and for this girl. To make even this tawdry room look beautiful, with firelight and candlelight, dark amber wine in the glasses, tall pink lilies spilling their saffron, exuding their hot perfume—she and even himself must look their best. Not even music was lacking to their feast. Some one was playing a pianola across the street, and the sound, very faint, came stealing—swelling, sinking, festive, mournful; having a far-off life of its own, like the flickering fire-flames before which they lay embraced, or the lilies delicate between the candles. Listening to that music, tracing with his finger the tiny veins on her breast, he lay like one recovering from a swoon. No parting. None! But sleep, as the firelight sleeps when flames die; as music sleeps on its deserted strings!

And the girl watched him.

It was nearly ten when he bade her go to bed. And after she had gone obedient into the bedroom, he brought ink and paper down by the fire. The drifter, the unstable, the good-for-nothing—did not falter. He had thought, when it came to the point, he would fail himself; but a sort of rage bore him forward. If he lived on and confessed, they would shut him up, take from him the one thing he loved, cut him off from her; sand up his only well in the desert. Curse them! And he wrote by firelight which mellowed the white sheets of paper; while, against the dark curtain, the girl, in her nightgown, unconscious of the cold, stood watching.

A man, when he drowns, remembers his past. Like the lost poet he had "gone with the wind." Now it was for him to be true in his fashion. A man may falter for weeks and weeks, consciously, subconsciously, even in his dreams, till there comes that moment when the only thing impossible is to go on faltering. The black cap, the little driven gray man looking up at it with a sort of wonder—faltering had ceased!

He had finished now, and was but staring into the fire.

The fire, the candles, and the fire—no more the flame and flicker!

And, by the dark curtain, the girl watched.

X

Keith went, not home, but to his club; and in the room devoted to the reception of guests, empty at this hour, he sat down and read the report of the trial. The fools had made out a case that looked black enough. And for a long time, on the thick soft carpet which let out no sound of footfall, he paced up and down, thinking. He might see the defending counsel, might surely do that as an expert who thought there had been miscarriage of justice. They must appeal; a petition, too, might be started in the last event. The thing could—must be put right yet, if only Larry and that girl did nothing!

He had no appetite, but the custom of dining is too strong. And while he ate, he glanced with irritation at his fellow-members. They looked so at their ease. Unjust—that this black cloud should hang over one blameless as any of them! Friends, connoisseurs of such things—a judge among them—came specially to his table to express their admiration of his conduct of that will case. Tonight he had real excuse for pride, but he felt none. Yet, in this well-warmed quietly glowing room, filled with decorously eating, decorously talking men, he gained insensibly some comfort. This surely was reality; that shadowy business out there only the drear sound of a wind one must and did keep out—like the poverty and grime which had no real existence for the secure and prosperous. He drank champagne. It helped to fortify reality, to make shadows seem more shadowy. And down in the smoking-room he sat before the fire, in one of those chairs which embalm after-dinner dreams. He grew sleepy there, and at eleven o'clock rose to go home. But when he had once passed down the shallow marble steps, out through the revolving door which let in no draughts, he was visited by fear, as if he had drawn it in with the breath of the January wind. Larry's face; and the girl watching it! Why had she watched like that? Larry's smile; the flowers in his hand? Buying flowers at such a moment! The girl was his slave—whatever he told her, she would do. But she would never be able to stop him. At this very moment he might be rushing to give himself up!

His hand, thrust deep into the pocket of his fur coat, came in contact suddenly with something cold. The keys Larry had given him all that time ago. There they had lain forgotten ever since. The chance touch decided him. He turned off towards Borrow Street, walking at full speed. He could but go again and see. He would sleep better if he knew that he had left no stone unturned. At the corner of that dismal street he had to wait for solitude before he made for the house which he now loathed with a deadly loathing. He opened the outer door and shut it to behind him. He knocked, but no one came. Perhaps they had gone to bed. Again and again he knocked, then opened the door, stepped in, and closed it carefully. Candles lighted, the fire burning; cushions thrown on the floor in front of it and strewn with flowers! The table, too, covered with flowers and with the remnants of a meal. Through the half-drawn curtain he could see that the inner room was also lighted. Had they gone out, leaving everything like this? Gone out! His heart beat. Bottles! Larry had been drinking!

Had it really come? Must he go back home with this murk on him; knowing that his brother was a confessed and branded murderer? He went quickly to the half-drawn curtains and looked in. Against the wall he saw a bed, and those two in it. He recoiled in sheer amazement and relief. Asleep with curtains undrawn, lights left on? Asleep through all his knocking! They must both be drunk. The blood rushed up in his neck. Asleep! And rushing forward again, he called out: "Larry!" Then, with a gasp he went towards the bed. "Larry!" No answer! No movement! Seizing his brother's shoulder, he shook it violently. It felt cold. They were lying in each other's arms, breast to breast, lips to lips, their faces white in the light shining above the dressing-table. And such a shudder shook Keith that he had to grasp the brass rail above their heads. Then he bent down, and, wetting his finger, passed it close to their joined lips. No two could ever swoon so utterly as that; not even a drunken sleep could be so fast. His wet finger felt not the faintest stir of air, nor was there any movement in the pulses of their hands. No breath! No life! The eyes of the girl were closed. How strangely innocent she looked! Larry's open eyes seemed to be gazing at her shut eyes; but Keith saw that they were sightless. With a sort of sob he drew down the lids. Then, by an impulse that he could never have explained, he laid a hand on his brother's head, and a hand on the girl's fair hair. The clothes had fallen down a little from her bare shoulder; he pulled them up, as if to keep her warm, and caught the glint of metal; a tiny gilt crucifix no longer than a thumb-nail, on a thread of steel chain, had slipped down from her breast into the hollow of the arm which lay round Larry's neck. Keith buried it beneath the clothes and noticed an envelope pinned to the coverlet; bending down he read: "Please give this at once to the police.—LAURENCE DARRANT." He thrust it into his pocket. Like elastic stretched beyond its uttermost, his reason, will, faculties of calculation and resolve snapped to within him. He thought with incredible swiftness: "I must know nothing of this. I must go!" And, almost before he knew that he had moved, he was out again in the street.

He could never have told of what he thought while he was walking home. He did not really come to himself till he was in his study. There, with a trembling hand, he poured himself out whisky and drank it off! If he had not chanced to go there, the charwoman would have found them when she came in the morning, and given that envelope to the police! He took it out. He had a right—a right to know what was in it! He broke it open.

"I, Laurence Darrant, about to die by my own hand, declare that this is a solemn and true confession. I committed what is known as the Glove Lane Murder on the night of November the 27th last in the following way"—on and on to the last words—"We didn't want to die; but we could not bear separation, and I couldn't face letting an innocent man be hung for me. I do not see any other way. I beg that there may be no *post-mortem* on our bodies. The stuff we have taken is some of that which will be found on the dressing-table. Please bury us together.

LAURENCE DARRANT.

January the 28th, about ten o'clock P.M.

Full five minutes Keith stood with those sheets of paper in his hand while the clock ticked, the wind moaned a little in the trees outside, the flames licked the logs with the quiet click and ruffle of their intense far-away life down there on the hearth. Then he roused himself, and sat down to read the whole again.

There it was, just as Larry had told it to him—nothing left out, very clear; even to the addresses of people who could identify the girl as having once been Walenn's wife or mistress. It would convince. Yes! It would convince.

The sheets dropped from his hand. Very slowly he was grasping the appalling fact that on the floor beside his chair lay the life or death of yet another man; that by taking this confession he had taken into his own hands the fate of the vagabond lying under sentence of death; that he could not give him back his life without incurring the smirch of this disgrace, without even endangering himself. If he let this confession reach the authorities he could never escape the gravest suspicion that he had known of the whole affair during these two months. He would have to attend the inquest, be recognized by that policeman as having come to the archway to see where the body had lain, as having visited the girl the very evening after the murder. Who would believe in the mere coincidence of such visits on the part of the murderer's brother? But apart from that suspicion, the fearful scandal which so sensational an affair must make would mar his career, his life, his young daughter's life! Larry's suicide with this girl would make sensation enough as it was; but nothing to that other. Such a death had its romance; involved him in no way save as a mourner, could perhaps even be hushed up! The other—nothing could hush that up, nothing prevent its ringing to the house-tops. He got up from his chair, and for many minutes roamed the room unable to get his mind to bear on the issue. Images kept starting up before him. The face of the man who handed him wig and gown each morning, puffy and curious, with a leer on it he had never noticed before; his young daughter's lifted eyebrows, mouth drooping, eyes troubled; the tiny gilt crucifix glinting in the hollow of the dead girl's arm; the sightless look in Larry's unclosed eyes; even his own thumb and finger pulling the lids down. And then he saw a street and endless people passing, turning to stare at him. And, stopping in his tramp, he said aloud: "Let them go to hell! Seven days' wonder!" Was he not trustee to that confession! Trustee! After all he had done nothing to be ashamed of, even if he had kept knowledge dark. A brother! Who could blame him? And he picked up those sheets of paper. But, like a great murky hand, the scandal spread itself about him; its coarse malignant voice seemed shouting: "Paiper! . . . Paiper! . . . Glove Lane Murder! . . . Suicide and confession of brother of well-known K.C. . . . Well-known K.C.'s brother. . . . Murder and suicide. . . . Paiper!" Was he to let loose that flood of foulness? Was he, who had done nothing, to smirch his own little daughter's life; to smirch his dead brother, their dead mother—himself, his

695

own valuable, important future? And all for a sewer rat! Let him hang, let the fellow hang if he must! And that was not certain. Appeal! Petition! He might—he should be saved! To have got thus far and then, by his own action, topple himself down!

With a sudden darting movement he thrust the confession in among the burning coals. And a smile licked at the folds in his dark face, like those flames licking the sheets of paper, till they writhed and blackened. With the toe of his boot he dispersed their scorched and crumbling wafer. Stamp them in! Stamp in that man's life! Burnt! No more doubts, no more of this gnawing fear! Burnt? A man—an innocent—sewer rat! Recoiling from the fire he grasped his forehead. Burning hot.

Well, it was done! Only fools without will or purpose regretted. And suddenly he laughed. So Larry had died for nothing! He had no will, no purpose, and was dead! He and that girl might now have been living, loving each other in the warm night, away at the other end of the world, instead of lying dead in the cold night here! Fools and weaklings regretted, suffered from conscience and remorse. A man trod firmly, held to his purpose, no matter what came of it!

He went to the window and drew back the curtain. What was that? A gibbet in the air, a body hanging? Ah! Only the trees—the dark trees—the winter skeleton trees! Recoiling, he returned to his armchair and sat down before the fire. It had been shining like that, the lamp turned low, his chair drawn up, when Larry came in that afternoon two months ago. Bah! He had never come at all! It was a nightmare. He had been asleep. How his head burned! And leaping up, he looked at the calendar on his bureau. "January the 28th!" No dream! His face hardened and darkened. On! Not like Larry! On!

Biographies

WARREN BECK

Born in Richmond, Indiana, Warren Beck received his B.A. from Earlham College in 1921 and his M.A. from Columbia in 1926. At present he teaches at Lawrence College in Appleton, Wisconsin. His first novel, *Final Shore* (1944), was the winner of the 1945 Friends of American Writers Award. Two subsequent novels, *Pause Under the Sky* (1947) and *Into Thin Air* (1951), received considerable praise. Among other honors, Beck has been the recipient of a Rockefeller Foundation grant (1948–49) and a Ford Fellowship (1952–53). His short stories have appeared in the *Best American Short Stories*, and he has contributed articles and stories to *Story*, the *Virginia Quarterly*, and the *Yale Review*. Beck has also written a number of one-act plays. He has published three volumes of short stories: *The Blue Sash* (1941), *The First Fish* (1947), and *The Far Whistle* (1951).

THOMAS BEER, 1889–1940

Thomas Beer, biographer, novelist, and short-story writer, was born in Council Bluffs, Iowa, grew up in Ohio, and spent most of his life in New York City. He studied at Yale University (B.A., 1911) and at Columbia Law School. After returning from service in World War I, he decided to make writing his career. His first novel, *The Fair Rewards* (1922), was followed by *Stephen Crane: A Study in American Letters* (1923), which is now considered one of the standard biographies of Crane. His stories have appeared in the *O. Henry Award Stories* and *Best Short Stories*. His biography of Mark Hanna (1929) and his social history *The Mauve Decade* (1926) are two of his most successful works. He published one volume of stories, *The Egg and Other Barbarians* (1933).

STEPHEN VINCENT BENÉT, 1898–1943

Stephen Vincent Benét was born in Bethlehem, Pennsylvania, and attended schools in Georgia and California. He was the son of an Army officer and the younger brother of the poet William Rose Benét. His first interest was in verse-writing, and he had already published poems in *St. Nicholas* and other journals by the time he enrolled at Yale in 1915. In his senior year he edited the *Yale Literary Magazine* and saw his second volume of verse published.

Benét was a prolific writer of verse and stories all of his short life. His stories and poems were published in the *Saturday Evening Post*, *Collier's*, and the *Atlantic*, where they attracted many readers. Of his books of poetry, two long works based on American history—*John Brown's Body* (1928) and *Western Star* (1943)—were perhaps his most successful. One of his most popular stories, "The Devil and Daniel Webster," was made into an opera (with music by Douglas Moore) and a motion picture. Nearly all of his stories have been collected in *The Barefoot Saint* (1929), *The Devil and Daniel Webster* (1937), *Johnny Pye and the Fool Killer* (1938), and *Twenty-Five Short Stories* (1943).

ARNOLD BENNETT, 1867–1931

Enoch Arnold Bennett, English novelist—contemporary of John Galsworthy, H. G. Wells, and Joseph Conrad—was born and brought up in Hanley, North Staffordshire, one of the "five towns" in the pottery center of England which provide the setting for his best-known novels. He worked first in the office of his father, a solicitor, and then went to London. Here he attended the University and worked for a time in a law office.

He began his career as a writer about 1900, first as a reviewer of plays. His work from this time on included magazine articles, short stories, the many novels for which he is famous, and ultimately plays (of which the best known is *Milestones*, written in collaboration with Edward Knoblock). Bennett lived in France from 1900 to 1908, and it was during this period that he became interested in such realistic writers as Zola, Flaubert, and Dostoievsky. Influenced by them to some extent, Arnold Bennett was at his best as a novelist of the naturalistic school. For his work in a few novels—notably *The Old Wives' Tale*, *Riceyman Steps*, and *The Clayhanger Family*, a trilogy—from a list of perhaps twenty that were widely read in his day, he may be ranked with his distinguished contemporaries.

ELIZABETH BOWEN, 1899–

Elizabeth Bowen was born in Dublin and grew up in Ireland and England, where she studied at Darwin's former home, Downe House in Kent. She later traveled widely in Europe and America. During World War I she worked in a hospital in Ireland. In 1923 she married Alan Cameron, a teacher at Oxford; the same year saw the appearance of her first published work, a collection of stories, *Encounters*. Five years later *The Hotel*, the first of a series of distinguished novels, was published. During World War II she worked for the

Ministry of Information in London. In addition to her novels and stories, she writes criticism, book reviews, and scripts for the B.B.C., and in recent years has lectured extensively. *The Death of the Heart* (1938) and *The Heat of the Day* (1949) are two of her most highly-praised novels; among the more recent are *The Shelbourne Hotel* (1951) and *World of Love* (1955). Some of her most successful stories may be found in *The Cat Jumps* (1934) and *Ivy Gripped the Steps and Other Stories* (1946). *A Time in Rome* (1960) is representative of her nonfiction style.

CLIFFORD R. BRAGDON, 1905–

Born in St. Louis, Clifford Bragdon was graduated from Amherst in 1928. He received his M.A. from Western Reserve University in 1936 and his M.Ed. from Harvard in 1939. During part of this period he lived in Cleveland and taught English at the Hawken School. After teaching at Wheaton College for three years, he joined the faculty of Smith College in 1943 and is now professor of education there. During the war Mr. Bragdon served as operations analyst with the Second Air Force and was the author of "Guide to Better Flight Instruction," an Air Force publication. He has also written on educational subjects. Mr. Bragdon did research for the Harvard Committee on Education of Teachers and was later awarded a Sheldon fellowship. He has taught in summer sessions at Washington University, Johns Hopkins, and Harvard. In addition to his academic duties Mr. Bragdon has served on the Northampton Council of Social Agencies and has recently become a member of the board of the Clarke School of the Deaf.

Two of Mr. Bragdon's short stories, including this one, were chosen by Edward J. O'Brien for the *Best Short Stories*. Both were originally published in *The Midland*.

PEARL S. BUCK, 1892–

China has provided the settings and characters for nearly all of Pearl Buck's stories and novels. Although born in Hillsboro, West Virginia, she was raised in China, where her parents were Christian missionaries. She studied at Randolph-Macon College and at Cornell University, and later she taught English literature at the University of Nanking and at Southwestern University. Her first novel, *The Good Earth* (1931), was a popular and critical success and won the 1931 Pulitzer Prize. Several equally successful novels followed— *Sons* (1932), *The Mother* (1934), and *A House Divided* (1935). She was awarded the Nobel Prize for Literature in 1938, the third American writer to be so honored. She has published two volumes of short stories, *The First Wife* (1933) and *Far and Near* (1947). In recent years she has been on the editorial staff of the John Day Company, which has published, among her more recent works, *Peony* (1948), *Kinfolk* (1949), *Come, My Beloved* (1953), and *Command the Morning* (1959).

MORLEY CALLAGHAN, 1903–

Morley Callaghan, one of Canada's outstanding contemporary writers, was born in Toronto, Ontario, studied at St. Michael's College and the University of Toronto (A.B., 1925), and prepared for the practice of law at Osgoode Hall Law School. For a brief time he worked as a reporter for the Toronto *Daily Star*. The stories he had been writing in his spare time began to appear and attracted the interest of Ernest Hemingway. Shortly after the publication of his first novel, *Strange Fugitive* (1928), he went to Paris, where he joined Hemingway and the group of young expatriate American writers who made the Left Bank their headquarters. He now lives in Canada and divides his time between the practice of law and writing.

Two of Morley Callaghan's most recent novels are *The Varsity Story* (1948) and *The Loved and the Lost* (1951). His work frequently appears in the collection *Best Short Stories,* and many of his best stories have been collected in *A Native Argosy* (1929) and *Now That April's Here* (1936).

NANCY G. CHAIKIN, 1923–

Nancy G. Chaikin was brought up and educated in Brooklyn. She studied at the University of Michigan (B.A., 1945) with Alan Seager and won two Avery Hopwood awards for creative writing. After graduation from Michigan she wrote book reviews for the *Saturday Review* and also worked as a reader for the Book-of-the-Month Club in New York. She later studied creative writing under the direction of Martha Foley at Columbia. Since her marriage in 1946 to Marvin Chaikin, a communications engineer, she has made her home in Great Neck, Long Island. Her short stories and critical essays have been published in *Mademoiselle*, the *Saturday Review,* and the *University of Kansas City Review*—where the story "Bachelor of Arts" first appeared, before being chosen for the *Best American Short Stories, 1955*. "The Climate of the Family" is one of her better-known stories.

GILBERT KEITH CHESTERTON, 1874–1936

G. K. Chesterton, a versatile man of letters, was born and educated in London, where he attended St. Paul's and Stode (the art school of University College, London). A precocious and talented writer, he was a practicing journalist and a reviewer for *Bookman* before he reached the age of 21. His first novel, *The Napoleon of Notting Hill* (1904), met with considerable success, and in the following year he began writing a column in the *Illustrated London News* which he continued until 1930.

Chesterton wrote memorable novels, stories, essays, poetry, and criticism. *The Man Who Was Thursday* (1908) is one of his finest novels. Some of his most successful short stories have been published in *The Man Who Knew Too Much* (1922) and *The Secret of Father Brown* (1926). Perhaps his most popular writings are those novels and stories dealing with the amiable detective Father Brown.

During his life Chesterton traveled a great deal. He visited America twice, once in 1922 and again in 1930 when he lectured at Notre Dame.

JOSEPH CONRAD, 1857–1924

The irony so evident in Joseph Conrad's stories and novels played a prominent part in his own life. He was born and brought up in Russian Poland and educated at Cracow. In 1873 he signed on a French merchant ship as an ordinary seaman. Four years later he joined an English merchant ship and began to study the language of which he eventually became an acknowledged master. Conrad spent fifteen years at sea in English ships, most of the time as an officer. He became a British subject in 1886, and three years later he began the arduous task of writing a novel in his adopted language. Conrad left the sea in 1894 and devoted the remainder of his life to writing. *Almayer's Folly* appeared in 1895 and met with success; then came *An Outcast of the Islands* (1896) and *The Nigger of the Narcissus* (1898) in quick succession. Among his novels *Nostromo* (1904) and *Chance* (1913) are perhaps the most lucid expressions of his complex vision of life. "Youth," "Heart of Darkness," "Typhoon," and "The Secret Sharer" are some of Conrad's best-known short stories.

PETER DE VRIES, 1910–

Peter De Vries grew up in Chicago and studied at Calvin College in Grand Rapids, Michigan. In 1939, after several years of newspaper work and freelance writing, he became an editor of *Poetry* magazine in Chicago. His first novel *But Who Wakes the Bugler?* was published in 1940. A few years later James Thurber asked him to contribute to the *New Yorker,* and his work so impressed the editors that in 1944 he moved to New York and joined the staff of the magazine. A collection of his satirical stories, sketches, and literary parodies, *No, But I Saw the Movie,* appeared in 1952. Since then he has published four highly successful novels: *The Tunnel of Love* (1954), *Comfort Me With Apples* (1956), *The Mackerel Plaza* (1958), and *Tents of Wickedness* (1959).

WILLIAM FAULKNER, 1897–

William Faulkner has spent most of his adult life writing the "saga" of Yoknapatawpha County, the country which he alone created and populated and which exists only in his novels and stories and in his overmastering imagination. It is not unlike Lafayette County in northern Mississippi, where Faulkner was born.

During World War I Faulkner joined the Canadian Air Force and saw action in France. After the war he attended the University of Mississippi briefly, then lived for some time in New Orleans, where he met Sherwood Anderson, who was one of the most respected writers in America. Faulkner decided to try his hand at writing, and the result was *Soldier's Pay,* which Anderson sent to his publisher. The book was published in 1926 and received almost no popular or critical attention. After a visit to Europe in 1925 Faulkner returned to his home in Oxford, where he worked at a series of odd jobs and wrote in the evenings.

Sartoris (1929) was the first of the so-called Yoknapatawpha novels; it was followed by *The Sound and the Fury* (1929), one of his most highly-praised novels. During the next twenty years he produced a series of works that made him one of the most important writers in America. His only popular success was *Sanctuary* (1931). In 1950 Faulkner was awarded the Nobel Prize, however, and since then his writings have achieved a measure of popularity. *The Hamlet* (1940), *The Town* (1950), and *The Mansion* (1959), a trilogy, have made the name of his character Snopes almost as well known as his own. *A Fable* (1954) won both the National Book Award and the Pulitzer Prize. Nearly all of his short stories have been published in *Collected Stories* (1950).

DOROTHY CANFIELD FISHER, 1879–1958

Although born in Kansas, Dorothy Canfield Fisher came from a long line of New Englanders who had settled in Arlington, Vermont, in 1764. Her father was on the faculty of several universities in Kansas and Ohio and eventually became chief librarian of Columbia University. Mrs. Fisher's education began in Paris, where she was sent when she was ten, and continued wherever her father happened to be. She studied at Ohio State, the Sorbonne, and Columbia, where she took her Ph.D. in 1905. She traveled widely in Europe before finally settling down in her ancestral home in Arlington.

Among her works are novels, short stories, books on education, children's books, and translations. Mrs. Fisher's stories have been included in *Best American Short Stories, O. Henry Award Stories,* and *Best Short Stories.* She served on the editorial board of the Book-of-the-Month Club for twenty-five years. *The Bent Twig* (1915) and *The Deepening Stream* (1930) are two of her better-known novels. Her most successful and representative stories may be found in *Hillsboro People* (1915), *Basque People* (1931), and *Four-Square* (1949).

F. SCOTT FITZGERALD, 1896–1940

The romantic elements in the brief, blazing life of F. Scott Fitzgerald have attracted almost as much attention in our time as have his various stories and novels, and in his own way he is as much a symbol of the romantic agony as is Keats or Shelley. He grew up in St. Paul, Minnesota, where he attended the St. Paul Academy. After a short time at Princeton, where his interest in writing took a serious turn, he joined the A.E.F. as an officer. When World War I ended, he took a job in an advertising agency, writing in his spare time. His stories were first published in *The Smart Set.* His novel *This Side of Paradise* (1920) was a literary sensation and established the vogue of jazz-age fiction, with Fitzgerald its brightest star. Fitzgerald, handsome and brilliant, and his attractive, erratic wife, Zelda, quickly became famous public personalities, epitomizing in their lives all the beautiful and damned young men and women of the 1920's as they traveled from Paris to New York to Hollywood and back again.

Fitzgerald, however, was more than an international playboy, as the publication of *The Great Gatsby* (1925) proved. *All the Sad Young Men*

(1926) showed his mastery of the short story. Fitzgerald's star went into eclipse as the decade expired. One of his finest achievements, *Tender is the Night* (1934), received little attention. The title of a book of his stories, *Taps at Reveille* (1935), expressed the feeling of doom that had ambushed Fitzgerald. He died in 1940.

In the 1950's, a public preoccupation with all aspects of the 1920's was accompanied by a marked revival of interest in F. Scott Fitzgerald—not only in the novels but in the man as a novelist. Evidence of this interest is in two studies, both published in 1951 and both well received: *F. Scott Fitzgerald: The Man and His Work* by Alfred Kazin and *The Far Side of Paradise* by Arthur Mizener. There are also a novel by Budd Schulberg, *The Disenchanted* (based on the life of Fitzgerald), published in 1950, and a play by the same title and by the same author, in collaboration with Harvey Bright, produced on Broadway in 1959.

EDWARD MORGAN FORSTER, 1879–

One of England's most distinguished novelists, E. M. Forster is also highly regarded as a short-story writer and critic. He was educated at Tonbridge School and at King's College, Cambridge, where he has resided since 1946 as an Honorary Fellow. He was twenty-six when his first novel, *Where Angels Fear to Tread* (1905), was published. After spending some time in Italy, he returned to England in 1907 and lectured at the Working Man's College. During World War I he was engaged in civilian war work in Egypt. Returning to London after the war, he worked as a journalist and eventually became literary editor of the *Daily Herald*. In 1921 he made a second trip to India—the first had been in 1911—and the notes that he made of his impressions and experiences in that country he put to good use in the writing of his most celebrated novel, *A Passage to India* (1924). His study of the novel, *Aspects of the Novel* (1927), was based on the Clark Lectures given at King's College in 1927. He served as Rede lecturer at Cambridge in 1941 and as the W. P. Ker lecturer at Glasgow in 1944; in 1947 he lectured in the United States.

Forster's three other novels are *The Longest Journey* (1907), *A Room with a View* (1908), and *Howard's End* (1910). His stories have been collected in *The Celestial Omnibus* (1923) and *Collected Tales* (1947). Other shorter pieces, literary essays and sketches, have been collected in *Abinger Harvest* (1936). A most discerning and informative character sketch or "profile" of Mr. Forster by Mollie Panter-Downes was published in the *New Yorker* in September, 1959.

PAMELA FRANKAU, 1908–

Born in England, Pamela Frankau is the daughter of the novelist Gilbert Frankau. From her father she acquired, while still very young, an interest in writing. At eighteen she secured a position with the Amalgamated Press, and in the following year she published her first novel, *Marriage of Harlequin*

(1927). For a time she edited a woman's magazine, and later she worked in an advertising agency.

A volume of her stories, *Fifty-Fifty and Other Stories* (1936), was followed by *Appointment with Death* (1940), one of her best-known novels. Miss Frankau has lived intermittently in the United States; and her stories have appeared in *Collier's, Harper's,* and *Mademoiselle.* Her two most recent novels are *A Wreath for an Enemy* (1954) and *Ask Me No More* (1958).

JOHN GALSWORTHY, 1867–1933

John Galsworthy, one of the foremost novelists and playwrights of the first half of the twentieth century, was born into an upper-class family in Kingston, England. He studied at Bournemouth, Harrow, and New College, Oxford, where he was graduated in 1890 with honors in law. For some time afterward he traveled extensively. He began his career as a novelist writing under the pseudonym "John Sinjohn." In 1906 two events of importance in Galsworthy's career occurred, the publication of *The Man of Property* (destined to be the first of the celebrated *Forsyte Saga*) and the production of Galsworthy's first play, *The Silver Box.* He continued to write plays and novels, as well as essays and some poetry, throughout his life. Among his best-known plays are *Strife* (1909), *Justice* (1910), *Loyalties* (1922), and *Escape* (1926). Three volumes of his short stories were published during his lifetime: *The Little Man* (1915), *Five Tales* (1918), and *Caravan* (1925). John Galsworthy's most important work—one of the great novels of the present century—*The Forsyte Saga,* was published in 1922. Made up of three novels, *The Man of Property, In Chancery* (1919), and *To Let* (1920), together with two shorter, connecting narratives, "Indian Summer of a Forsyte" and "Awakening," it formed the first part of the chronicle of the Forsyte family, which was in fact a chronicle of "the ripeness, decline, and 'fall-off' " of the Victorian era itself. This was followed by two more trilogies, entitled *A Modern Comedy* (1929) and *End of the Chapter* (1935), the whole series thus rounding off (in the words of the Preface to the 1933 Memorial Edition) "the comprehensive and truly human chronicle of a group of English middle-class folk of Galsworthy's time, *i.e.,* from the eighteen-eighties to 1932." In 1929 Galsworthy received the Order of Merit and in 1931 the Nobel Prize for Literature.

EDMUND GILLIGAN, 1899–

Edmund Gilligan was born and brought up in Waltham, Massachusetts. During World War I he served on a submarine chaser in the North Atlantic with the U.S. Navy. Much of Gilligan's fiction is concerned with the sea and sailing. Gilligan graduated from Harvard in 1926. After being a reporter for the Boston *Post* and the New York *Sun,* and an associate editor of *Fortune,* he is now on the staff of the New York *Herald Tribune.*

Edmund Gilligan is the author of several highly acclaimed novels: *Our Lives to Tell the Tale* (1937), *White Sails Crowding* (1939), *The Gaunt*

Woman (1943), *I Name Thee Mara* (1946), *Storm at Sable Island* (1948), and *My Earth, My Sea* (1959). His stories and articles have appeared in *Esquire*, the *Atlantic Monthly*, and the *American Mercury*. "Sea Dog," "Too Many Ghosts," and "Hunter's Moon" are some of his most representative and successful short stories.

ELIZABETH HARDWICK, 1916–

Elizabeth Hardwick's stories have been included in the *Best American Short Stories* and in the *Prize Stories* of the *O. Henry Memorial Award* series several times. She was born in Lexington, Kentucky, and studied at the University of Kentucky and at Columbia. She lived abroad for several years. At present she resides in Boston with her husband, the poet Robert Lowell. She is the author of two novels, the autobiographical *The Ghostly Lover* (1945) and *The Simple Truth* (1955). Some of her best-known stories are "The People on the Roller Coaster," "What We Have Missed," and "The Mysteries of Eleusis." Miss Hardwick's articles and stories have appeared in the *Partisan Review*, the *Sewanee Review*, and the *New Yorker*.

ERNEST HEMINGWAY, 1899–

The son of a physician, Ernest Hemingway grew up and attended school in Oak Park, Illinois. After high school he worked briefly for the Kansas City *Star*, then volunteered for war service in an American ambulance unit bound for the Western Front. In France he transferred to the Italian army and was severely wounded in combat. After the war he became a roving correspondent for the Toronto *Star* and covered the Graeco-Turkish War. Determined to make himself into a writer, he settled in Paris, where he was encouraged and influenced by Sherwood Anderson and Gertrude Stein. His first book was a collection of stories called *In Our Time* (1924). With the publication of his novel *The Sun Also Rises* (1926) he achieved his first literary success. His reputation as a writer of genuine importance was confirmed when his next novel, *A Farewell to Arms* (1929), was published. Since then his novels have appeared at long intervals. One of his most widely-known novels, *For Whom the Bell Tolls* (1940), grew out of his experiences as a correspondent during the Spanish Civil War. His short novel *The Old Man and the Sea* was awarded the Pulitzer Prize in 1953, and in 1954 he won the Nobel Prize. Hemingway's reputation rests as much on his numerous short stories as it does on his novels. Nearly all of his stories have been collected in *The Short Stories of Ernest Hemingway* (1958).

CYRIL HUME, 1900–

When he was just out of college (Yale '22), Cyril Hume began a promising career with the publication of his novel *Wife of the Centaur* in 1923. The proceeds of this very successful first novel enabled the author and his wife to go to Italy and establish themselves in a villa in Florence. Here in 1925 he wrote his second novel, *Cruel Fellowship*, which is notable for its psychological study of a "modern ne'er-do-well." Some novels and some excellent short stories followed—collected in *Street of the Malcontents and Other Stories* (1927) and *Myself and the Young Bowman and Other Fantasies* (1932)—but Cyril Hume has not fulfilled the early promise of his impressive talent as a novelist.

Readers of the story included here will find "The Head" (*Harper's Magazine*, December, 1925) a noteworthy companion piece, written in the same manner.

ALDOUS HUXLEY, 1894–

Aldous Huxley is the bearer of an impressive heredity: his father, Leonard Huxley, was editor of the *Cornhill Magazine;* his grandfather was the famous biologist, T. H. Huxley; and on his mother's side his great-grandfather was Dr. Thomas Arnold of Rugby. Julian Huxley, the scientist, is his brother, Matthew Arnold was his great-uncle, and Mrs. Humphrey Ward, the popular novelist, was his aunt. One of Aldous Huxley's distinctive personal achievements, indeed, has been his success in avoiding being crushed under the weight of his pedigree.

Born in Godalming, England, he studied at Eton and Oxford, where the threat of blindness made him turn from a career in medicine to one in literature. As a young man he contributed poems, essays, and stories to the most important London literary magazines. His first novel, *Chrome Yellow* (1921), established his reputation as a brilliant, sophisticated satirist of modern society. The novels that followed confirmed this reputation: *Antic Hay* (1923), *Point Counter Point* (1928), *Brave New World* (1932), *Eyeless in Gaza* (1936), *After Many a Summer Dies the Swan* (1940), *Ape and Essence* (1948), and *The Genius and the Goddess* (1955).

Huxley has traveled over most of the world; for the last twenty-three years he has made his home in California. He is generally considered to be one of the outstanding men of letters in modern literature, having written brilliantly in a variety of literary forms. Some of his most penetrating short stories may be found in *Young Archimedes* (1924) and *Rotunda* (1932). His *Collected Short Stories* was published in 1958 and his *Collected Essays* in 1959.

HENRY JAMES, 1843–1916

Henry James and his brother William, the philosopher-scientist, were born into a family that lived at a pitch of intellectual intensity. Their father, Henry James, was interested in philosophy, religion, and all phases of art and culture, and his influence on his sons was pervasive. Henry was tutored privately in New York, where he was born, and received special schooling abroad between 1855 and 1860. He studied painting briefly, but in 1862 he entered Harvard Law School. Dissatisfied with law, he began to write stories which reflected his experiences in European society. From that time on, writing became the chief passion of his life. In 1875 his first volume of stories, *A Passionate Pilgrimage*, appeared, and the *Atlantic* serialized his first important novel, *Roderick Hudson*. He settled in London in 1876 and thereafter returned to the United States only for short visits. His impatience with American reluctance to become entangled in World War I led him to take up British citizenship in 1915.

The influence of James's novels, stories, and critical essays has been one of the animating forces in modern literature. The standard edition of James's works is *The Novels and Tales of Henry James* (26 volumes), 1907–1917, the so-called New York Edition. Many of his finest stories have been collected in *The Short Stories of Henry James* (1945), edited by Clifton Fadiman, and in *Stories of Writers and Artists* (1944), edited by F. O. Matthiessen. *The Portrait of a Lady* (1881), *What Maisie Knew* (1897), and *The Golden Bowl* (1904) are some of his outstanding novels.

JAMES JOYCE, 1882–1941

One of the most influential writers in modern literature, James Joyce was born in a suburb of Dublin and educated at several Jesuit schools before going on to University College. He received his B.A. degree there in 1902. In the same year he left Ireland for the Continent, where he spent most of the remainder of his life in self-imposed exile. He lived chiefly in Trieste, Zurich, and Paris, supporting himself and his family on his earnings as a tutor. For many years he had to contend with poverty and the threat of blindness.

Because of the controversial nature of his works he had great difficulty in securing their publication, but he was sustained by his absolute confidence in his own creative genius and the faith of a few admirers. Joyce produced several highly controversial novels, among them the autobiographical *A Portrait of the Artist as a Young Man* (1916), *Ulysses* (1922), and *Finnegan's Wake* (1939). *Ulysses* is considered to be one of the most important novels of the twentieth century. Although he produced only one volume of stories—*Dubliners* (1914)—his work has had considerable impact upon the form of the modern short story. Richard Ellmann's definitive biography, *James Joyce,* was published in 1959.

DAVID HERBERT LAWRENCE, 1885–1930

Short-story writer, travel writer, novelist, poet, painter, and prophet, D. H. Lawrence searched all his life for what he called "self-fulfillment." He was brought up in the English Midlands' coal-mining community of Eastwood, Nottinghamshire, which he used as the setting for some of his most successful novels. The strongest influence on his youth and young manhood was exerted by his mother, a possessive, domineering woman. *Sons and Lovers* (1913) is the story of their complex relationship. Lawrence studied at Nottingham high school, the British School at Eastwood, and, briefly, at University College, Nottingham. He taught biology until his first novel, *The White Peacock* (1911), was published. He then gave up teaching, eloped with the wife of one of his former teachers, and began a series of restless voyages about the world that ended only when he died in France at forty-five of the tuberculosis that had threatened him from boyhood.

Lawrence was possessed of a furious creative energy which he transmitted into some of the finest realistic and symbolic writings of our time. He was a master of the short story. Some of his finest work may be found in *The Prussian Officer and Other Stories* (1914), *The Woman Who Rode Away* (1928), and *The Tales of D. H. Lawrence* (1934). Among his best-known novels are *Sons and Lovers, The Rainbow* (1915), *Women in Love* (1920), and *Lady Chatterley's Lover* (1928, 1959).

VICTORIA LINCOLN, 1904–

A descendant of John Endicott, the early New England governor and founder of Salem, Victoria Endicott Lincoln was born in Fall River, Massachusetts. She attended Radcliffe and graduated in 1926. In 1934 she married Victor Lowe, now a professor of philosophy at Johns Hopkins. Her home now is Towson, Maryland. However, Miss Lincoln has lived in various parts of the United States—for a number of years in a suburb of Columbus, Ohio, while her husband was on the faculty of Ohio State—and she has spent some time in England and Germany. She is the mother of a son and two daughters —a fact worth noting in view of the marked success of her novel *Celia Amberley* (1949), which has been praised for its insight into the mind of a young girl. It is this novel from which "The Glass Wall" is taken.

Miss Lincoln's first novel was the notably successful *February Hill* (1934), which in 1939 was dramatized and produced as "The Primrose Path." It was also dramatized for radio, and in 1940 it was made into a successful movie. In 1944 she published a collection of short stories and verse under the title *Grandmother and the Comet,* and in 1951 another novel, *Out from Eden.* At present Miss Lincoln is engaged in writing another novel.

HANIEL LONG, 1888–1956

Haniel Clark Long was born in Rangoon, Burma, the son of American Methodist missionaries. His early years were spent in Pittsburgh, Pennsylvania, where his father was a minister. He attended Phillips Exeter Academy and Harvard, graduating in 1910, after which he worked briefly as a reporter in New York. His teaching career began at the Carnegie Institute of Technology in 1911, and here, as a professor of English, he was to become one of the truly great inspirational teachers of his day. In 1929 ill health forced him to retire, and he left Pittsburgh for Santa Fe, New Mexico, where he continued to write both prose and poetry.

One of his former students, Dorothy C. Mills (a talented and successful artist, now living in Los Angeles), contributes these notes on some of his better-known works, commenting first on the *Notes for a New Mythology* (1926): "Pittsburgh was a sleeping giant soon to rise like a Phoenix from its smoke and slag heaps by the snaking rivers; it brought forth 'The Professor of Dreams' and 'How Pittsburgh Returned to the Jungle.' . . . The Southwest was taken deeply to his heart and brought about the *Interlinear to*

Cabeza de Vaca and *Piñon Country* (in the American Folkways Series). His work will be republished and his stature felt—it reaches Thoreau, Emerson, and Whitman." He was the author of the well-received *Walt Whitman and the Springs of Courage,* published in 1938 by Writers' Editions, a cooperative publishing house established to foster the development of American literature by regional publishing—an enterprise of which Haniel Long was one the founders. His first novel, *Spring Returns,* was published posthumously.

Most of Haniel Long's manuscripts and journals are at present deposited in the libraries of Albuquerque, Santa Fe, the University of California at Los Angeles, and the University of New Mexico. The most readily accessible accounts of this important and too-little-known writer are by Harry Sylvester, "Cabeza de Vaca and Haniel Long," *Commonweal,* XXXVII (1943), 414–416, and by Lawrence C. Powell in the *Wilson Library Bulletin,* XXXII (September 1957), 56–57.

KATHERINE MANSFIELD, 1888–1923

Katherine Mansfield (Kathleen Beauchamp) was born in Wellington, New Zealand, where she spent her girlhood. Later she studied music at Queen's College, London. She early abandoned a career in music to devote her time to story writing. In 1909 she married George Bowden. Her first volume of stories, *In a German Pension,* appeared in 1911 but failed to attract much attention. Undismayed, she continued to develop her art, concentrating exclusively on the short-story form. Divorced from her first husband, she married the editor and critic John Middleton Murry in 1918. The true merit of her art went largely unrecognized until *Bliss and Other Stories* was published in 1920. Two more volumes of stories quickly followed—*The Garden Party* (1922) and *The Dove's Nest* (1923). She died in Paris at the peak of her fame in 1923. Most of her best stories may be found in *The Short Stories of Katherine Mansfield* (1937).

W. SOMERSET MAUGHAM, 1874–

W. Somerset Maugham was born in Paris, where his father was a solicitor attached to the British Embassy. He studied at King's School, Canterbury, and at Heidelberg, Germany. Returning to London, he studied medicine at St. Thomas's Medical School, Lambeth. Here he got the material for his first novel, *Liza of Lambeth* (1897). It was a success, and he turned from medicine to writing. His plays, however—notably *Lady Frederick* (1907)—were at first more successful than his novels, and his reputation as a playwright was securely established before he became well known as a writer of fiction. He had already written six novels, including *Mrs. Craddock* (1902), when in 1915 he published *Of Human Bondage,* widely regarded as his greatest work.

It has been often reprinted and is still one of the best-known novels of the twentieth century.

Mr. Maugham continued to produce novels, plays, short stories, and essays as he traveled around the world gathering material. His skill in the short story was revealed in *The Trembling of a Leaf* (1921) and in a number of collections that followed during the next twenty years. His *Collected Short Stories,* in three volumes, was published in 1952. Among his better-known novels are *The Moon and Sixpence* (1919), *Cakes and Ale* (1930), and *The Razor's Edge* (1944). Among his plays, *The Circle* (1921), *Our Betters* (1923), and *The Constant Wife* (1926) are most notable. Of literary interest are the autobiographical *The Summing Up* (1938), as well as *A Writer's Notebook* (1949), *Ten Novels and Their Authors* (1954), and *Points of View* (1959).

JAMES A. MICHENER, 1907–

James A. Michener grew up in Bucks County, Pennsylvania, attended Swarthmore, and graduated *summa cum laude.* A traveling fellowship gave him an opportunity to study in Europe. He then became a teacher, first of English and later of history. For a time he was a literary editor for Macmillan. After having served with the Navy in the Solomon Islands during World War II, he took on the duties of naval historian in the South Pacific. As a trouble shooter for the Air Force he had traveled widely, visiting most of the islands, and learned a great deal about the whole area. His knowledge served him well. Immediately out of his experience came the collection of stories, put together as a novel, which became one of the most widely read works of fiction written about the war. *Tales of the South Pacific* (1947) won the Pulitzer Prize in 1948 and, with music by Rodgers and Hammerstein, became one of the most successful musicals of the postwar period. Its scenes and characters are already a part of the literary heritage of World War II. Readers of this novel will also be interested in *Return to Paradise* (1951), *Sayonara* (1954), and, most recently, *Hawaii* (1959).

GEORGE MILBURN, 1906–

Born in Coweta, Oklahoma, George Milburn studied at the University of Tulsa (1923–24), Oklahoma A. and M. (1925), Commonwealth College in Arkansas (1927), and the University of Oklahoma (1928–30). In addition to working on the staffs of several newspapers as reporter and editor, he has written scripts for both radio and motion pictures. Mr. Milburn at present resides in New York City. Several of his stories have appeared in the collection *Best Short Stories,* and he has contributed essays and stories to such journals as the *New Yorker,* the *American Mercury,* the *Southern Review,* the *Yale Review,* and *Harper's.* He has produced two volumes of short stories —*Oklahoma Town* (1931) and *No More Trumpets* (1933)—and the novel *Flannigan's Folly* (1947). "The Apostate," "Cowboy Sang Soprano," "Yellow Paint," and "Pretty Little Stunt" are some of his better-known stories

FRANK O'CONNOR, 1903–

Although Frank O'Connor has lived in many parts of the world, at present in New York, in one sense he has never left the place of his birth—Cork, Ireland. Nearly all of his stories take place in Cork, and his characters speak its racy tongue. O'Connor started writing at an extremely early age, later became a professional librarian, and served a year in prison for his activities as a "gunman" during the Irish Revolution. He was an active figure in the Irish literary renaissance and was a director of the Abbey Theatre in its last days of glory.

O'Connor has taught at two universities in the United States, Northwestern and Harvard, written several plays and critical studies, and done many translations from the Gaelic. Many of his stories have been published in this country (particularly in the *New Yorker*) and widely reprinted in anthologies. O'Connor is a master of a muscular prose style close to the rhythms of speech. His stories have a deceptively amiable surface simplicity which only indirectly reveals O'Connor's tragic vision of life. His stories have been collected in *The Stories of Frank O'Connor* (1952) and *More Stories* (1954). His most recent collection, *Domestic Relations* (1957), contains some of his best work.

EDWARDS PARK

Edwards Park, a New Englander and a Yale graduate (1939), served for two years as a fighter pilot in New Guinea during World War II. He was there during the bad old days when Japanese air strength far outweighed American. He saw the tide turn the other way—even helped it a little. Park came out of the war with three things: an Australian wife, a niggling idea for a short story, and a whole skin. In a way, the story "Binky's Voice" is true. Every separate episode actually took place. Only with these episodes woven together as one is the story fiction. Park wrote it when he was living in Melbourne after the war—when he should have been doing advertising copy about breakfast cereal. He won an "Atlantic First" prize with it (1947), was fired from the ad agency, and became a newspaper man. Returning to the States, he worked on the Boston *Globe,* writing editorials and features, then joined the editorial staff of the *National Geographic,* in Washington, D.C., where he still cranes from his office window when the jets whistle by overhead. (For these vivid details we are indebted to Mr. Park.)

FRANCES GRAY PATTON, 1906–

Frances Gray was born in Raleigh and has spent most of her life in North Carolina. She attended Trinity College, now Duke University, and the University of North Carolina, where she was actively associated with the Carolina Playmakers. In 1927 she married Lewis Patton, who is now a professor of English at Duke.

Mrs. Patton did not take up the writing of fiction professionally until 1944. Her first published story appeared as one of two prize winners in the *Kenyon Review* and was reprinted in the *O. Henry Memorial Award* volume for 1945. This was a promising start. Over the years since then her work, of consistently high quality, has come out in various magazines—for the most part in the *New Yorker,* which has published more than twenty of her stories.

"Remold It Nearer," together with several other stories about the Potters, has been reprinted in the author's first collection, *The Finer Things of Life* (1951). Mrs. Patton's second book was her phenomenally successful novel, *Good Morning, Miss Dove* (1954), and her third was *A Piece of Luck* (1955), another collection of short stories.

KATHERINE ANNE PORTER, 1894–

Katherine Anne Porter has devoted her creative energies almost exclusively to the short-story form. She grew up in Indian Creek, Texas, and received her formal education at various private schools in the South. Her first stories appeared in the twenties in the little magazines. Her first collection of stories, *Flowering Judas* (1930), received considerable praise when it appeared. In 1931 and in 1938 she was the recipient of Guggenheim awards. In addition to writing, Miss Porter has done much teaching and lecturing both here and abroad; in 1949 she was a writer-in-residence at Stanford; she was guest lecturer at the University of Chicago in 1951; in 1953–54 she taught at the University of Michigan; she was a Fulbright Lecturer in Belgium in 1955. From time to time she has written for the movies. Several of her stories have appeared in *Best Short Stories* and the *O. Henry Prize Stories.* Many of her finest stories may be found in such collections of her work as: *Noon Wine* (1937), *Pale Horse, Pale Rider* (1939), and *The Leaning Tower* (1944).

FREDERICK A. POTTLE, 1897–

Frederick A. Pottle was born in Lovell, Maine, and educated at Colby College (B.A., 1917) and at Yale University (M.A., 1921; Ph.D., 1925). During World War I he served in the medical corps in France. This experience provided the background for his first work, *Stretchers, the Story of a Hospital on the Western Front* (1921).

Mr. Pottle taught in various high schools and colleges in New England before joining the English department at Yale in 1925. He is a widely-known literary scholar whose specialty is the eighteenth century in general and James Boswell in particular. At present he is chairman of the Boswell Papers editorial committee at Yale. In 1929 he published *The Literary Career of James Boswell* and, in 1941, *The Idiom of Poetry.* Since 1950, under the editorship of Mr. Pottle, the first six volumes of the Yale editions of *The Private Papers of James Boswell* have been published: *Boswell's London Journal, 1762–63* (1950), *Boswell in Holland, 1763–64* (1952), *Boswell on the Grand Tour, 1764* and *1765–66* (2 volumes, 1953 and 1955), *Boswell in Search of a Wife, 1766–69* (1956) —the two most recent volumes with Frank Brady as joint editor. The publication of this important series (to be supplemented by a complete and thoroughly documented "research" series) constitutes one of the most extensive and significant contributions to literary scholarship in our time.

CALVIN SALLOW

The reader is referred to the introduction to "Page from an Unfinished-War Novel" for the available biographical information about "Calvin Sallow." The secretary of his college class, meeting for its thirty-fifth reunion, makes a pertinent comment in the course of his report on the members and their achievements. It serves very well as a factual footnote to the page from the novel: "Owing to our age bracket, we have, in general, fallen between two wars. Not that we are less heroic than others—not a bit of it. We were just too young for World War I and too old for World War II. Surprisingly, four classmates were in the first war, two were in military service in the period between, and thirteen saw service in the second." One member, he adds, was in both. (Williams College, Class of 1924, 35th Reunion, June 5–6, 1959: *Report for Posterity*, p. 2.)

MARK SCHORER, 1908–

A scholar and literary critic, novelist, short-story writer, and teacher, Mark Schorer was born in Sauk City, Wisconsin. He studied at the University of Wisconsin (B.A., 1929, Ph.D., 1936) and at Harvard (M.A., 1930). Since 1945 he has taught at the University of California at Berkeley, having previously held positions at Dartmouth (1936–37) and Harvard (1937–40). He has received a Zona Gale Fellowship, a Mary L. Adams Fellowship, a Guggenheim, and a Fulbright. His scholarly work includes *William Blake: the Politics of Vision* (1946). Among his novels, *The Wars of Love* (1953) received much critical acclaim. His short stories have appeared in *Harper's,* the *Hudson Review,* the *Kenyon Review,* and the *New Yorker,* and they have been included in the *Best American Short Stories.* Some of the most notable of these stories are "Blockbuster," "Continued Humid," "Portrait of Ladies," and "In Populous City Pent." *The State of Mind,* a collection of thirty-two stories by Mark Schorer, was published in 1947.

IRWIN SHAW, 1913–

Irwin Shaw has had an active and varied life. Born in New York City, he received his B.A. degree from Brooklyn College in 1934. He began writing and publishing short stories while he was still in college, but his talents first gained wide recognition when his bitter antiwar play, *Bury the Dead* (1936), had a successful Broadway run. He was then only twenty-three. Shaw has played professional football and has written profitably for the movies and radio. During World War II he served with the army in Europe. Out of this experience he fashioned his much-praised novel *The Young Lions* (1948); and the well-known story included in this collection has its setting in a European army base.

Most of Irwin Shaw's work has been in the short-story form, and several of his stories have been included in the *Best American Short Stories*. Shaw is a skillful craftsman with a broad range of subject matter. Most of his best stories may be found in *Sailor off the Bremen* (1939), *Welcome to the City* (1942), and *Tip on a Dead Jockey* (1957).

WALLACE STEGNER, 1909–

A short-story writer, novelist, and teacher, Wallace Stegner was born in Lake Mills, Iowa. He attended the University of Utah (B.A., 1930) and the University of Iowa (M.A., 1932; Ph.D., 1935). In 1933 he began his teaching career at Augustana College in Illinois. He has taught at the University of Utah (1934–37), the University of Wisconsin (1937–39), and Harvard (1939–45). Since 1945 he has been the director of the Creative Writing Center at Stanford and editor of the *Stanford Short Story* series, a collection of stories by students in his creative-writing courses.

Several of Mr. Stegner's stories have been included in the *Best American Short Stories,* and he has published essays and stories in such journals as *Mademoiselle, Harper's,* the *Virginia Quarterly Review,* and the *Saturday Review.* His first novel, *Remembering Laughter* (1937), won the Little, Brown prize. It was followed by *On a Darkling Plain* (1940), *The Big Rock Candy Mountain* (1943), and *The Preacher and the Slave* (1950). Some of his most successful stories may be found in *The Women on the Wall* (1950) and *The City of the Living* (1956).

RUTH SUCKOW, 1892–1960

Ruth Suckow was born in Iowa and lived there for most of her life. She attended the University of Colorado, where she received her B.A. and M.A. degrees. In 1929 she was married to Ferner Nuhn, who is also a writer. Her first stories were published in *The Midland*—a fact that was in itself a claim to distinction in the 1920's—and in the *Smart Set,* then under the editorship of H. L. Mencken and George Jean Nathan, who were among the first to appreciate the quality of her work. She was one of the first and most gifted American regional writers. The story included here illustrates her characteristic interest in the German immigrant and her own Iowa background. Her best-known books include: *Country People* (1924), *The Odyssey of a Nice Girl* (1925), *Iowa Interiors* (1926), *Children and Older People* (1931), and *Some Others and Myself* (1952). The last three are collections of stories and sketches. Her most recent work was *The John Wood Case* (1959).

PETER TAYLOR, 1917–

Peter Hillsman Taylor grew up in Trenton, Tennessee, and studied at Southwestern and Vanderbilt universities before taking his B.A. degree in 1941 at Kenyon College. He spent four years in the army during World War II. Since then he has taught at the Woman's College of North Carolina, Indiana University, Kenyon, and, most recently, at Ohio State. His first book was *A Long Fourth* (1948), a collection of stories. In 1950 he held a Guggenheim Fellowship and published his only novel, *A Woman of Means*. His stories have been collected in *The Widows of Thornton* (1954) and *Happy Families Are All Alike* (1959). His work has appeared in the *New Yorker*, the *Sewanee Review*, the *Southern Review*, and the *Kenyon Review*. In addition to his novel and short stories, he has published a play, *Tennessee Day in St. Louis* (1957). Mr. Taylor has recently become a member of the editorial board of the *Kenyon Review*.

JAMES THURBER, 1894–

James Thurber, writer, cartoonist, and illustrator, grew up in Columbus, Ohio, and attended Ohio State University for three years. From 1918 to 1920 he was a code clerk in the State Department in Washington and Paris. He then returned to Columbus where he worked as a reporter on the Columbus *Dispatch*. He spent two years on the staff of the Chicago *Tribune* in Paris and then sailed for New York, where he worked for a time as a reporter for the New York *Evening Post*. With the help of his friend E. B. White, Thurber got a job on the staff of the newly-founded *New Yorker* magazine in 1925. He has been associated with that magazine in one capacity or another ever since.

Although now practically blind as the result of a childhood accident, Thurber still writes, first composing in his head and then dictating to his wife. Several of his stories have been published in the *O. Henry Prize Stories* and *Best American Short Stories*. *The Owl in the Attic* (1931), *The Middle-Aged Man on the Flying Trapeze* (1935), and *The Cream of Thurber* (1939) are collections of his stories and humorous sketches. *My Life and Hard Times* (1933) and *Thurber Country* (1953) contain much autobiographical information. Most recently, in the *Atlantic,* Thurber has written a series of reminiscent articles on Harold Ross and his editorship of the *New Yorker*. These articles contain an account of Thurber's own connection with the magazine and with many of its well-known contributors over the years since 1927. These reminiscences have been published (1959) as *The Years with Ross,* one of the author's most enlightening and entertaining books to date.

LIONEL TRILLING, 1905–

One of the most influential modern critics, Lionel Trilling grew up in New York City and received his education at Columbia University (B.A., 1925; M.A., 1926; Ph.D., 1938). Although he has been on the faculties of the

University of Wisconsin and Hunter College, his longest association has been with Columbia, where he is currently teaching. With John Crowe Ransom and F. O. Matthiessen he helped to organize the Kenyon School of Letters at Kenyon College.

Trilling has published several books of critical essays, as well as studies of E. M. Forster and Matthew Arnold. He is on the advisory boards of the *Kenyon Review* and the *Partisan Review*. His stories and articles have appeared in both of these, as well as in the *Nation* and the *New Republic*. His only novel, *The Middle of the Journey*, appeared in 1947. No collection of his stories has as yet been published. "The Other Margaret" and "The Lesson and the Secret" are two of his most representative stories.

EDMUND WARE, 1900–

Edmund Ware Smith—whose writing appears under the *nom de plume* of Edmund Ware—was born in Plantsville, Connecticut, and received his education at several eastern and midwestern schools. A journalist by profession, Mr. Ware has worked for various newspapers and magazines. He has been managing editor of sports magazines and, most recently, of the *Ford Times*. His articles and stories have been published in *Outdoor Life*, the *Atlantic*, *Better Homes and Gardens*, the *Saturday Evening Post*, and *Good Housekeeping*. His work has also appeared in the annual *Best Short Stories*. Some of his better-known stories are "So-Long Oldtimer," "An Underground Episode," "Jeff Raleigh's Piano Solo," "First Time Alone," and "The Courtship of Jeff Coongate." A collection of Ware's stories, *From Fact to Fiction*, a textbook for short-story writers, was published in 1946 under the joint editorship of Edmund Ware and Robeson Bailey.

EUDORA WELTY, 1909–

Eudora Welty was born in the South, in Jackson, Mississippi, and studied at Mississippi State College for Women, the University of Wisconsin (B.A., 1929), and Columbia University (1930–31). She makes her home in Mississippi, and the country of her fiction is the South. In 1949 Eudora Welty received the American Academy of Arts and Letters Award, and in 1955 she won the Howells Medal for her novel *The Ponder Heart*.

Her stories and articles have appeared in the *Sewanee Review*, the *Atlantic*, and the *New Yorker*. Several of her stories have been included in the annual *O. Henry Prize Stories* and *Best American Short Stories*. *The Robber Bridegroom* (1942), *Delta Wedding* (1946), and *The Ponder Heart* (1954) are examples of her skill in the novel. Her first collection of stories, *A Curtain of Green*, was published in 1941. Three more collections have appeared since then: *The Golden Apples* (1949), *Selected Stories* (1954), and *The Bride of Innisfallen* (1955).

EDITH WHARTON, 1862–1937

Born Edith Newbold Jones in New York City, Edith Wharton belonged to a distinguished and wealthy family. She was educated at home and on the Continent, and ever afterwards she felt at home in the capitals of the Western world. In 1880 she published some poems anonymously in the *Atlantic Monthly*. In 1885 she married the socially prominent Edward Wharton of Boston, and thereafter they made their home in New York, Rhode Island, and Massachusetts, visiting Europe frequently. They settled permanently in France in 1907. Her first collection of stories, *The Greater Inclination* (1899), revealed the poetic sensibility and ironic point of view that distinguishes all of her work. Such novels as *The House of Mirth* (1905) and *The Age of Innocence* (1920), which won the Pulitzer Prize, are some of her best satires of changing urban social structures. One of her best-known novels, *Ethan Frome* (1911), a grim domestic tragedy in a rural New England setting, is not characteristic. Mrs. Wharton's most accomplished stories may be found in *The Hermit and the Wild Woman* (1908) and *Xingu and Other Stories* (1916). In 1924 she published four novelettes under the title *Old New York*. Among her more recent works are *The Writing of Fiction* (1925), in which she discusses her method, and the novels *The Children* (1928) and *Hudson River Bracketed* (1929).

PELHAM GRENVILLE WODEHOUSE, 1881–

P. G. Wodehouse was born in Guildford, England, and studied at Dulwich College. His first job was as a clerk in a London bank, but before long he decided that writing was his true métier and he left the bank to write. After free-lancing for a time, he soon had his own column in the London *Globe*. His first novel, *The Pothunters* (1902), was published when he was only twenty-one; it won considerable popularity. Since then he has been one of the most popular and prolific writers on both sides of the Atlantic. He has written plays, stories, and more than sixty novels. His travels have been extensive; at present he lives on Long Island.

The Inevitable Jeeves (1924), *Blanding's Castle* (1935), and *Money in the Bank* (1942) are some of his most representative novels. Many of his stories have been collected in *Meet Mr. Mulliner* (1927), *Mr. Mulliner Speaking* (1929), and *Nothing Serious* (1951).

ALEXANDER WOOLLCOTT, 1887–1943

Alexander Woollcott was a landmark in the social and cultural landscape of New York City for thirty years. Woollcott was born in Phalanx, New Jersey. After studying at Hamilton College (Ph.B., 1909), he went to Columbia University for further study. In 1914 he became drama critic for the New York *Times*. World War I intervened, and he served in France with a hospital unit for a time until he joined the staff of *Stars and Stripes*. He resumed his position with the *Times* after the war, and in 1922 he moved to the New York *Herald*. A collection of his reviews and sketches, *Shouts and Murmurs*, appeared in 1923. During these years his reputation as critic and writer made him one of the best-known personalities in the city. In addition to his drama reviews, he contributed a celebrated column to the *New Yorker*, and, in 1929, he launched a weekly network radio program which made him even more widely known, *The Town Crier*. He acted in several plays, the most successful of which was *The Man Who Came to Dinner* (1939)—a satirical comedy by Kaufman and Hart, in which Woollcott portrayed a character not unlike himself. His essays and sketches have been collected in *Two Gentlemen and a Lady* (1928), *While Rome Burns* (1934), and *Long, Long Ago* (1943). Death overtook him while he was making a radio broadcast. His biography, *Alexander Woollcott, His Life and His World*, by Samuel Hopkins Adams, was published in 1945.

SAMUEL YELLEN, 1906–

Although born in Vilna, Russia, Samuel Yellen, poet and short-story writer, received most of his formal education in Ohio, taking his B.A. at Western Reserve University (1926) and his M.A. at Oberlin (1932). Since 1929 he has taught at Indiana University, where he edits the Indiana University Poetry Series. His stories have appeared in the *Best American Short Stories*, and he has contributed articles and stories to *Commentary*, the *Antioch Review*, the *University of Kansas City Review*, the *New Yorker*, and the *Saturday Evening Post*. Mr. Yellen has published a book of poems, *In the House and Out* (1952), and a collection of stories, *The Passionate Shepherd* (1957). "The Mystic Presences," "Stoneville Pike," and "There Are Things for Tears" are some of his most successful stories.

Index of authors

Victoria	Lincoln	27
Haniel	Long	174
Katherine	Mansfield	256
W. Somerset	Maugham	615
James A.	Michener	418
George	Milburn	157
Frank	O'Connor	223
Edwards	Park	430
Frances Gray	Patton	14
Katherine Anne	Porter	565
Frederick A.	Pottle	407
Calvin	Sallow	472
Mark	Schorer	193
Irwin	Shaw	441
Wallace	Stegner	287
Ruth	Suckow	385
Peter	Taylor	360
James	Thurber	506
Lionel	Trilling	111
Edmund	Ware	483
Eudora	Welty	348
Edith	Wharton	592
P. G.	Wodehouse	516
Alexander	Woollcott	513
Samuel	Yellen	551

DATE DUE